BLACKOUT

Connie Willis

GOLLANCZ

LONDON

The right of Connie Willis to be identified as the author
of this work has been asserted by her in accordance
with the Copyright, Designs and Patents Act 1988.

First published in Great Britain in 2011 by Gollancz
An imprint of the Orion Publishing Group
Orion House, 5 Upper St Martin's Lane, London WC2H 9EA
An Hachette UK Company

A CIP catalogue record for this book
is available from the British Library

ISBN 978 0 575 09926 5 (Cased)
ISBN 978 0 575 09927 2 (Trade Paperback)

3 5 7 9 10 8 6 4

Typeset by Deltatype Ltd, Birkenhead, Merseyside

Printed in Great Britain by Clays Ltd, St Ives plc

The Orion Publishing Group's policy is to use papers that are
natural, renewable and recyclable products and made from
wood grown in sustainable forests. The logging and manufacturing
processes are expected to conform to the environmental
regulations of the country of origin.

www.sftv.org/cw
www.orionbooks.co.uk

To Courtney and Cordelia,
who always do far more than their bit.

'History is now and England.'

T.S. Eliot, *Four Quartets*

'Come then: Let us to the task, to the battle, to the toil –
each to our part, each to our station, there is not a week,
nor a day, nor an hour to lose.'

WINSTON CHURCHILL, 1940

OXFORD – APRIL 2060

Colin tried the door, but it was locked. The porter, Mr Purdy, obviously hadn't known what he was talking about when he'd said Mr Dunworthy had gone to Research. *Blast it. I should have known he wasn't here*, Colin thought. Only historians prepping for assignments came to Research. Perhaps Mr Dunworthy'd told Mr Purdy he was going to do research, in which case he'd be in the Bodleian Library.

Colin went over to the Bodleian, but Mr Dunworthy wasn't there either. *I'll have to go ask his secretary*, Colin thought, loping back to Balliol. He wished Finch was still Mr Dunworthy's secretary instead of this new person Eddritch, who would probably ask a lot of questions. Finch wouldn't have asked any, and he'd have told him not only where Mr Dunworthy was, but what sort of mood he was in.

Colin ran up to Mr Dunworthy's rooms first, on the off chance Mr Purdy hadn't seen Mr Dunworthy come back in, but he wasn't there either. Then he ran across to Beard, up the stairs, and into the outer office. 'I need to see Mr Dunworthy,' he said. 'It's important. Can you tell me where—?'

Eddritch looked at him coldly. 'Did you have an appointment, Mr—?'

'Templer,' Colin said. 'No, I—'

'Are you an undergraduate here at Balliol?'

Colin debated saying yes, but Eddritch was the sort who would check to see if he was. 'No, I will be next year.'

'If you're applying to be a student at Oxford, you need the Provost's Office in Longwall Street.'

'I'm not applying to be a student. I'm a friend of Mr Dunworthy's—'

'Oh, Mr Dunworthy has told me about you.' He frowned. 'I thought you were at Eton.'

'We're on holiday,' Colin lied. 'It's vital that I see Mr Dunworthy. If you could tell me where he—'

'What did you wish to see him about?'

My future, Colin thought. *And it's none of your business*, but that obviously wouldn't get him anywhere. 'It's in regard to an historical assignment. It's urgent. If you could just tell me where he is, I—' he began, but Eddritch had already opened the appointment book. 'Mr Dunworthy can't see you until the end of next week.'

Which will be too late. Blast. I need to see him now, before Polly comes back.

'I can give you an appointment at one o'clock on the nineteenth,' Eddritch was saying. 'Or at half past nine on the twenty-eighth.'

What part of the word 'urgent' do you not understand? Colin thought. 'Never mind,' he said and went back downstairs and out to the gate to see if he could get any more information out of Mr Purdy. 'Are you certain Research was where he said he was going?' he asked the porter, and when he said yes, 'Did he say where he was going after that?'

'No. You might try the lab. He's been spending a good deal of time there these past few days. Or if he's not there, Mr Chaudhuri may know where he is.'

And if he's not there I can ask Badri when Polly's scheduled to come back. 'I'll try the lab,' Colin said, debating whether to ask him to tell Mr Dunworthy he was looking for him if he returned. No, better not. Forewarned was forearmed. He'd have a better chance if he sprang it on him suddenly. 'Thanks,' he said and ran down to the High and over to the lab.

Mr Dunworthy wasn't there. The only two people who were were Badri and a pretty tech who didn't look any older than the girls at school. They were both bent over the console. 'I need the coordinates for October fourth, 1950,' Badri said. 'And – what are you doing here, Colin? Aren't you supposed to be at school?'

Why was everyone acting like a truant officer?

'You haven't been sent down, have you?'

'No.' *Not if they don't catch me.* 'School holiday.'

'If you're here to talk me into letting you go to the Crusades, the answer is no.'

'The *Crusades*?' Colin said. 'That was *years* ago—'

'Does Mr Dunworthy know you're here?' Badri asked.

'Actually, I'm looking for him. The porter at Balliol told me he might be here.'

'He was,' the tech said. 'You only just missed him.'

'Do you know where he was going?'

'No. You might try Wardrobe.'

'*Wardrobe?*' First Research and now Wardrobe. Mr Dunworthy was obviously going somewhere. 'Where is he going? St Paul's?'

'Yes,' the tech said. 'He's researching—'

'Linna, I need those coordinates,' Badri said, glaring at her. The tech nodded and went over to the other side of the lab.

'He's going to St Paul's to rescue the treasures, isn't he?' Colin asked Badri.

'Mr Dunworthy's secretary should know where he is,' Badri said and walked back to the console. 'Why don't you go over to Balliol and ask him?'

'I did. He wouldn't tell me anything.'

And Badri clearly didn't want to either. 'Colin,' he said, 'we're very busy here.'

The tech, Linna, who'd come back with the coordinates, nodded. 'We have three retrievals and two drops to do this afternoon.'

'Is that what you're doing now?' Colin asked, walking over to look at the draped folds of the net. 'A drop?'

Badri immediately came over and blocked his way. 'Colin, if you're here to attempt to—'

'Attempt to what? You act as if I'm planning to sneak into the net or something.'

'It wouldn't be the first time.'

'And if I hadn't, Mr Dunworthy would have died, and so would Kivrin Engle.'

'That may be the case, but it doesn't mean you can make a habit of it.'

'I wasn't. All I wanted—'

'Was to know if Mr Dunworthy was here. He's not, and Linna and I are extremely busy,' Badri said. 'So if there's nothing else—'

'There is. I need to know when Polly Churchill's retrieval is scheduled for.'

'Polly Churchill?' Badri said, immediately suspicious. 'Why are you interested in Polly Churchill?'

'I've been helping her with her prep research. For the Blitz. I need to be here when she comes through to—' He began to say, 'to give it to her,' but Badri was likely to tell him to leave it instead and they'd give it to her.

'—to tell her what I've found,' he amended.

'We haven't scheduled her retrieval yet,' Badri said.

'Oh. Is she going straight to her Blitz assignment when she gets back?'

Linna shook her head. 'We still haven't found her a drop site—' she began, but Badri cut her off with another glare.

'It isn't going to be flash-time, too, is it?'

'No, real-time,' Badri said. 'Colin, we're extremely busy.'

'I know, I know. I'm going. If you see Mr Dunworthy, tell him I'm looking for him.'

'Linna, see Colin out,' Badri said, 'and then bring me the spatial-temporal coordinates for Pearl Harbor on December sixth, 1941.'

Linna nodded and escorted Colin to the door. 'Sorry. Badri's been in a foul mood this past fortnight,' she whispered. 'Polly Churchill's retrieval is scheduled for two o'clock Wednesday next.'

'Thanks,' Colin whispered back, grinned crookedly at her, and ducked out the door. Wednesday. He'd hoped it would be on the weekend so he wouldn't have to sneak away from school again, but at least it wasn't *this* Wednesday. He had over a week to talk Mr Dunworthy into letting him go somewhere. If Mr Dunworthy was going to rescue the treasures, Colin might be able to talk him into doing research in the past for him. If he was still at Wardrobe. He loped over to the Broad, down to Holywell, along the narrow street to Wardrobe, and up the stairs, hoping he hadn't missed him again.

He hadn't. Mr Dunworthy was standing in front of the mirror in a tweed blazer at least four sizes too large for him, and glaring at the cowering tech. 'But the only tweed jacket we had in your size has already been taken in to fit Gerald Phipps,' she was saying. 'He had to have a tweed jacket because he's going to—'

'I *know* where he's going,' Mr Dunworthy bellowed. He suddenly noticed Colin. 'What are you doing here?'

'Wearing clothes that fit a good deal better than that,' Colin said, grinning. 'Is that how you're planning to smuggle the treasures out of St Paul's – under your coat?'

Mr Dunworthy shrugged out of the jacket, said, 'Find me something in my size,' and half threw it at the tech, who scurried off with it.

'I think you should have kept it,' Colin said. 'You'd be able to fit *The Light of the World* and Newton's tomb under there.'

'Sir Isaac *Newton's* tomb is in Westminster Abbey. *Lord Nelson's* tomb is in St Paul's,' Mr Dunworthy said. 'Which you would know if you spent more time at school, where you are supposed to be at this very moment. Why aren't you?'

He would never buy the holiday story. 'A water main broke,' Colin said, 'and they had to cancel classes for the rest of the day, so I thought I'd take the opportunity to come and see what you were up to. And a good thing, too, since you're obviously haring off to St Paul's.'

'Water main,' Mr Dunworthy said dubiously.

'Yes. Flooded my house and half the quad. We nearly had to swim for it.'

'Odd your housemaster didn't mention it when Eddritch telephoned him.'

I knew I didn't like Eddritch, Colin thought.

'He did, however, mention your repeated absences. And the failing mark you got on your last essay.'

'That's because Beeson made me write it on this book, *The Impending Threat of Time Travel*, and it was total rubbish. It said time travel theory's rot, and historians *do* affect events, that they've been affecting them all along, but we haven't been able to see it yet because the space-time continuum's been able to cancel out the changes. But it won't be able to forever, so we need to stop sending historians to the past immediately and—'

'I am fully acquainted with Dr Ishiwaka's theories.'

'Then you know it's bollocks. All I did was say so in my essay, and Beeson gave me a failing mark! It's totally unfair. I mean, Ishiwaka says these ridiculous things, like slippage isn't to stop historians from going to times and places where they'll affect events at all. He says it's a symptom that something's wrong, like a fever in a patient with an infection, and that the amount of slippage will grow larger as the infection gets worse, but we won't be able to see that either, because it's exponential or something, so there's no proof of any of this, but we should

6

still stop sending historians because by the time we *do* have proof, it'll be too late and there won't be any time travel. It's total rubbish!'

Mr Dunworthy was frowning.

'Well, don't you think it is?'

Dunworthy didn't answer.

'Well, *don't* you?' Colin asked, and when he still stood there, 'You can't mean you believe his theory? Mr Dunworthy?'

'What? No. As you say, Dr Ishiwaka hasn't been able to produce convincing proof of his ideas. On the other hand, he raises some troubling questions that require investigation, *not* a dismissal as "total rubbish". But you obviously didn't come up here to debate time-travel theories with me. Or to, as you put it, see what I was up to.' He looked shrewdly at Colin. 'Why *did* you come?'

Here was where it got tricky. 'Because I'm wasting my time studying maths and Latin. I want to be studying history, and not dry-as-dust books – the real thing. I want to go on assignment. And don't say I'm too young. I was *twelve* when we went to the Black Death. And Jack Cargreaves was seventeen when he went to Mars.'

'And Lady Jane Grey was seventeen when she was beheaded,' Mr Dunworthy said, 'and being a historian is even more dangerous than being a pretender to the throne. There are all sorts of risks involved, which is why historians—'

'—have to be third-year students and at least twenty years old before they can go to the past,' Colin recited. 'I know all that. But I've already *been* to the past. To a ten. It can't get more dangerous than that. And there are all sorts of assignments where someone my age—'

Mr Dunworthy wasn't listening. He was staring at the tech, who'd come in carrying a black leather jacket covered with metallic slide fasteners. 'What exactly is that?' he demanded.

'A motorcycle jacket. You said something in your size,' she added defensively. 'It's from the correct historical era.'

'*Miss* Moss,' Mr Dunworthy said in the tone that always made Colin wince, 'the entire point of a historian's costume is that of camouflage – to keep from drawing attention to himself. To *blend in*. How do you expect me to do that,' he gestured at the leather jacket, 'dressed in *that*?'

'But we have photographs of a jacket like this from 1950 ...' the tech began and then thought better of it. 'I'll see what else I've got.' She retreated, wincing, into the workroom.

'In tweed,' Mr Dunworthy called after her.

'Blending in is exactly what I'm talking about,' Colin said. 'There are all sorts of historical events where a seventeen-year-old would blend in perfectly.'

'Like the Warsaw ghetto?' Mr Dunworthy said dryly. 'Or the Crusades?'

'I haven't wanted to go to the Crusades since I was *twelve*. That's exactly what I'm talking about. Both you and—' He caught himself. 'You and everyone at school still think of me as a child,' he said instead, 'but I'm not. I'm nearly eighteen. And there are all sorts of assignments I could be doing. Like al-Qaeda's second attack on New York.'

'New—?'

'Yes, there was a high school near the World Trade Center. I could pose as a student and see the entire thing.'

'I am *not* sending you to the World Trade Center.'

'Not to it. The school was four streets away, and none of the students got killed. No one was even injured, except for the toxins and asbestos they inhaled, and I could—'

'I am not sending you anywhere near the World Trade Center. It's far too dangerous. You could be killed—'

'Well, then send me somewhere that isn't dangerous. Send me to 1939, to the Phoney War. Or to the north of England to observe the evacuated children.'

'I am not sending you to World War II either.'

'You went to the Blitz, and you let Polly—'

'Polly?' Mr Dunworthy said alertly. 'Polly Churchill? What does she have to do with this?'

Bollocks. 'Nothing. Just that you let your historians go all sorts of dangerous places, and *you* go all sorts of dangerous places, and you won't even let me go to the north of England, which wouldn't be dangerous at all. The government evacuated the children there to be out of danger. I could pretend to be taking my younger brothers and sisters—'

'I already have a historian in 1940 observing the evacuated children.'

'But not in 1942 through 1945. I looked it up, and some of the children stayed in the country for the entire war. I could observe the effect that being separated from their parents that long had on them. And my missing school needn't be a problem. I could do it flash-time and—'

'Why are you so set on going to World War II? Is it because Polly Churchill's there?'

'I'm *not* set on going to World War II. I only suggested it because you didn't want me to go anywhere dangerous. And you're a fine one to talk about danger when you're going to St Paul's the night before the pinpoint bomb—'

Mr Dunworthy looked astonished. 'The night before the pinpoint bomb? What are you talking about?'

'You're rescuing the treasures.'

'Who told you I was rescuing St Paul's treasures?'

'No one, but it's obvious that's why you're going to St Paul's.'

'I am not—'

'Well, then, you're going to go and see what's there so you can rescue them later. I think you should take me with you. You need me. You'd have died if I hadn't gone with you to 1349. I can pose as a university student studying Nelson's tomb or something and make a list of all the treasures for you.'

'I don't know where you got this ridiculous idea, Colin. No one is going to St Paul's to rescue anything.'

'Then why *are* you going to St Paul's?'

'That doesn't concern you – what is *that*?' he said as the tech came in carrying a knee-length yellow satin coat embroidered with pink flowers.

'This?' she said. 'Oh, it's not for you. It's for Kevin Boyle. He's doing King Charles II's court. There's a telephone call from Research for you. Shall I tell them you're busy?'

'No, I'll take it.' He followed her into the workroom.

'Nothing on Paternoster Row? What about Ave Maria Lane? Or Amen Corner?' Colin heard him say, followed by a long pause, and then, 'What about the casualties lists? Were you able to find one for the seventeenth? No, that's what I was afraid of. Yes, well, let me know as soon as you do.' He came back out.

'Was that phone call about why you're going to St Paul's?' Colin said. 'Because if you need to find out something, I could go back to St Paul's and—'

'You are not going to St Paul's *or* World War II *or* the World Trade Center. You are going back to school. After you've passed your A-levels and been admitted to Oxford and the history programme, then we'll discuss your going to—'

'By then, it'll be too late,' Colin muttered.

'Too late?' Mr Dunworthy said sharply. 'What do you mean?'

'Nothing. I'm ready to go on assignment now, that's all.'

'Then why did you say "By then, it will be too late"?'

'Just that three years is ages, and by the time you let me go on assignment, all the best events will have been taken, and there won't be anything exciting left.'

'Like the evacuated children,' Mr Dunworthy said. 'Or the Phoney War. And that's why you cut class and came all the way up here to convince me to let you go on assignment now, because you were afraid someone else might take the Phoney—'

'What about this?' the tech said, coming in with a belted tweed shooting jacket and knee-length knickerbockers.

'What is *that* supposed to be?' Mr Dunworthy roared.

'A tweed jacket,' she said innocently. 'You said—'

'I *said* I wanted to blend in—'

'I must get back to school,' Colin said, and made his escape.

He shouldn't have said that about it being too late. Once Mr Dunworthy got hold of something, he was like a dog with a bone. He shouldn't have mentioned Polly either. *If he finds out why I want to go on assignment, he won't even consider it,* Colin thought, heading towards the Broad. Not that he was considering it now. Colin would have to think of some other argument to convince him. Or, failing that, some other way to get to the past. Perhaps if he could find out why Mr Dunworthy was going to St Paul's, he could convince him he needed to take him along. The tech had said something about the jacket's being from 1950. Why would Mr Dunworthy go to St Paul's in 1950?

Linna would know. He turned down Catte Street and ran down to the lab but it was locked.

They can't have closed, he thought. *They said they had two drops and three retrievals to do.* He knocked.

Linna opened the door a crack, looking distressed. 'I'm sorry. You can't come in,' she said.

'Why? Has something gone wrong? Nothing's happened to Polly, has it?'

'Polly?' she said, looking surprised. 'No, of course not.'

'Has something gone wrong with one of your retrievals?'

'No ... Colin, I'm not supposed to be talking to you.'

'I know you're busy, but I only need to ask you a few questions. Let me in and—'

'I can't,' she said and looked even more distressed. 'You're not allowed in the lab.'

'Not allowed? Did Badri—?'

'No. Mr Dunworthy rang us. He said we aren't to allow you anywhere near the net.'

'I said to the man who stood at the Gate of the Year, "Give me a light that I may tread safely into the unknown." And he replied, "Go out into the darkness, and put your hand into the Hand of God. That shall be to you better than light and safer than a known way."'

KING GEORGE VI, CHRISTMAS SPEECH, 1939

WARWICKSHIRE – DECEMBER 1939

When Eileen reached the station in Backbury, the train wasn't there. *Oh, don't let it have gone already*, Eileen thought, leaning over the edge of the platform to look down the tracks, but there was no sign of it in either direction.

'Where is it?' Theodore asked. 'I want to go home.'

I know you do, Eileen thought, turning to look at the little boy. *You've told me so every fifteen seconds since I arrived at the manor.* 'The train's not here yet.'

'When will it come?' Theodore asked.

'I don't know. Let's go and ask the stationmaster. He'll know.' She picked up Theodore's small pasteboard suitcase and gas-mask box and took his hand, and they walked down the platform to the tiny office where freight and luggage were stowed. 'Mr Tooley!' Eileen called, and knocked on the door.

No answer. She knocked again. 'Mr Tooley!'

She heard a grunt and then a shuffle, and Mr Tooley opened the door, blinking as though he'd been asleep, which was very likely the case.

'What's all this, then?' the old man growled.

'I want to go home,' Theodore said.

'The afternoon train to London hasn't already gone, has it?' Eileen asked.

Mr Tooley squinted at her. 'You're one of the maids up at the manor, an't ye?' He looked down at Theodore. 'This one of her ladyship's evacuees?'

'Yes, his mother sent for him. He's to take the train to London today. We haven't missed it, have we?'

'Sent for him, has she? I'll wager she said she missed her precious boy. Wants his ration book, more likely. Couldn't even be bothered to come and get him herself.'

'She works in an aircraft factory,' Eileen said defensively. 'She couldn't arrange time off from work.'

'Oh, they can manage it, all right, when they want to. Had two of 'em come in Wednesday on their way to Fitcham. "Taking our babies home so we can all be together for Christmas," they said. So they could sample the drink at Fitcham's pub, is more like it. And done a bit of drinking on the way up—'

You're a fine one to talk, Eileen thought. She could smell the alcohol on his breath from where she stood. 'Mr Tooley,' she said, trying to get him back to the matter at hand, 'when is the afternoon train for London due?'

'There's only the one at 11:19. They discontinued the other last week. The war, you know.'

Oh no, that meant they'd missed it, and she'd have to take Theodore all the way back to the manor.

'But it hasn't been through yet, and no tellin' when it will be. It's all these troop trains. They push the passenger trains onto a siding till they've gone past.'

'I want—' Theodore began.

'Bad as their mothers,' Mr Tooley said, glaring at him. 'No manners. And her ladyship working her fingers to the bone caring for the ungrateful tykes.'

Making her servants work their fingers to the bone, you

13

mean. Eileen only knew of two times Lady Caroline had had anything at all to do with the twenty-two children at the manor: once when they'd arrived – according to Mrs Bascombe, she'd wanted to ensure that she only got 'nice' ones, and had done so by going to the vicarage and choosing them herself like melons – and once when a reporter for the *Daily Herald* had come to do a piece on the 'wartime sacrifices of the nobility'. The rest of the time she confined her care to issuing orders to her servants and complaining about the children making too much noise, using too much hot water, and scuffing up her polished floors.

'It's wonderful the way her ladyship pitches in and does her bit for the war effort,' Mr Tooley said. 'I know some in her place wouldn't take in a stray kitten, let alone give a lot of slum brats a home.'

He shouldn't have said the word 'home'. Theodore immediately began tugging on Eileen's coat. 'How late do you think the train will be today, Mr Tooley?' she asked.

'No telling. Might be hours.'

Hours, and the afternoon was already drawing in. This time of year it began to grow dark by three and was pitch black by five. With the blackout …

'I don't want to wait hours,' Theodore said. 'I want to go home now.'

Mr Tooley snorted. 'Don't know when they're well off. Now Christmas is coming, they'll all want to go home.' Eileen hoped not. Evacuees had begun to trickle back to London as the months of the Phoney War went by, and by the time the Blitz began, seventy-five per cent had been back in London, but she hadn't thought it would happen so soon.

'You want to go home now, but when the bombing starts, you'll wish you were back here.' Mr Tooley shook his finger at Theodore. 'But it'll be too late then.' He stomped back to his office and slammed the door, but none of it had any effect on Theodore.

'I want to go home,' he repeated stolidly.

'The train will be here soon,' Eileen assured him.

'I'll wager it won't,' a little boy's voice said. 'It—' and was cut off by a fierce 'Shh.'

Eileen turned, but there was no one on the platform. She walked quickly over to the edge and looked down at the tracks. There was no one there either. 'Binnie! Alf!' she called. 'Come out from under there immediately,' and Binnie crawled out from underneath the platform, followed by her little brother, Alf. 'Come up off those tracks. It's dangerous. The train might come.'

'No, it won't,' Alf said, balancing on a rail.

'You don't know that. Come up here immediately.'

The two children climbed up onto the platform. They were both filthy. Alf's usual runny nose had produced a dirty smear, and his shirt was half out of his trousers. Eleven-year-old Binnie looked just as bedraggled, her stockings bunched, her hair ribbon untied and the ends hanging down. 'Wipe your nose, Alf,' Eileen said. 'What are you doing here? Why aren't you two in school?'

Alf wiped his nose on his sleeve and pointed at Theodore. ''E's not in school.'

'That's beside the point. What are you doing here?'

'We seen you goin' by,' Binnie said.

Alf nodded. 'We thought you was leavin'.'

'I didn't,' Binnie said. 'I thought she was going off to meet somebody. Like Una done.' She smiled slyly at Eileen.

'You ain't leavin', are you?' Alf asked, looking at Theodore's suitcase.

'We don't want you to. You're the only one wot's nice to us, you are. Mrs Bascombe and Una ain't.'

'Una sneaks off to meet a soldier,' Binnie said. 'In the woods.'

Alf nodded. 'We followed 'er on 'er half-day out.'

Binnie shot him such a deadly look that Eileen wondered if they'd been following her on her half-day as well. She'd have to make certain they were in school next week. If that were possible. The vicar, Mr Goode – a serious young man – had already been to the manor twice to discuss their repeated truancies. 'They seem to be having difficulty adapting to life here,' he'd said.

Eileen thought they'd adapted all too well. Within two days of their having been chosen by Lady Caroline (she had clearly failed to recognise the 'nice' ones in their case), they'd mastered apple-stealing, bull-teasing, vegetable garden trampling, and leaving open every gate in a ten-mile radius. 'It's too bad this evacuation scheme doesn't work both ways,' Mrs Bascombe had said. 'I'd evacuate them back to London with a luggage label round their necks in a minute. Little hooligans.'

'Mrs Bascombe says nice girls don't meet men in the woods,' Binnie was saying.

'Yes, well, nice girls don't spy on people either,' Eileen said. 'And they don't skip school.'

'Teacher sent us 'ome,' Binnie said. 'Alf took ill. 'Is 'ead's dreadful hot.'

Alf attempted to look ill. 'You ain't leavin', are you, Eileen?' he asked plaintively.

'No,' she said. *Unfortunately*. 'Theodore is.'

Mistake. Theodore immediately piped up, 'I want—'

'You will,' she said, 'as soon as the train comes.'

'It ain't comin',' Alf said. 'Anyway, yestiddy it didn't.'

'How do you know?' Eileen demanded, but she already knew the answer: They'd skipped school yesterday, too. She marched over to the office and hammered on the door. 'Is it true the passenger train sometimes doesn't come at all?' she said as soon as Mr Tooley opened the door.

'It— What are you two doin' here? If I catch you Hodbins again—' He raised his fist threateningly, but Binnie and Alf had already darted down the platform, jumped off the end, and disappeared. 'You tell them two to stop throwing rocks at the train, or I'll have 'em up on charges,' he shouted, his face red. 'Criminals! They'll end up in Wandsworth.'

Eileen was inclined to agree with him, but she couldn't let herself be sidetracked. 'Is it true the train didn't come at all yesterday?'

He nodded reluctantly. 'Trouble on the line, but they'll likely have fixed it by now.'

'But you don't know for certain?'

'No. You tell them two I'll set the constable on 'em if they come round here again.' He stomped back into the office.

Oh dear. They couldn't stay here all night, not knowing whether the train would come or not. Theodore's face was already pinched with cold, and with the blackout, station lights weren't allowed. If the train came after dark, it might not even see them waiting and wouldn't stop. She'd have to take him all the way back to the manor and try again tomorrow. But his ticket was for today, and she had no way to get in touch with his mother and tell her he wasn't coming. She peered anxiously down the track, looking for a glimpse of smoke above the bare trees.

'I'll wager the line was out 'cause there was a train wreck,' Binnie said, appearing from behind a pile of sleepers.

'*I'll* wager a Jerry plane flew over and dropped a bomb and the whole train blew up,' Alf said. They clambered up onto the platform. 'Boom! Arms and legs everywhere! And 'eads!'

'That's enough of that,' Eileen said. 'You two go back to school.'

'We can't,' Binnie protested. 'I told you, Alf's got a fever. His 'ead's—'

Eileen clapped her hand to Alf's perfectly cool forehead. 'He hasn't any fever. Now go.'

'We can't,' Alf said. 'School's let out.'

'Then go home.'

At the word, Theodore's face puckered up. 'Here, let's put your mittens on,' Eileen said hastily, kneeling in front of him. 'Did you ride on a train when you came to Backbury, Theodore?' she asked to distract him.

'*We* come on a bus,' Binnie said. 'Alf was sick all over the driver's shoes.'

'You get your 'ead cut off on a train if you stick it out the window,' Alf said.

'Come along, Theodore,' Eileen said. 'Let's go stand out by the edge where we can see the train coming.'

'A girl I know stood too close to the edge and fell onto the tracks,' Binnie said, 'and a train run right over her. Sliced her right in 'alf.'

'Alf, Binnie, I don't want to hear another word about trains,' Eileen said.

'Not even if it's comin'?' Binnie said and pointed down the tracks. The train was indeed bearing down on them, its massive engine wreathed in steam.

Thank goodness. 'Here's your train, Theodore,' Eileen said, kneeling to button his coat. She hung his gas-mask box around his neck. 'Your name and address and destination are on this paper.' She tucked it in his pocket. 'When you get to Euston, don't leave the platform. Your mother will come out to the train to fetch you.'

'What if she ain't there?' Binnie asked.

'What if she got killed on the way?' Alf said.

Binnie nodded. 'Right. What if a bomb blew 'er up?'

'Don't listen to them,' Eileen said, thinking, *Why can't it be the Hodbins I'm sending home?* 'They're teasing you, Theodore. There aren't any bombs in London.' *Yet.*

'Why'd they send us 'ere then?' Alf said, ''Cept to get us away from the bombs?' He stuck his face in Theodore's. 'If you go 'ome, a bomb'll prob'ly get *you.*'

'Or mustard gas,' Binnie said, clutching her throat and pretending to choke.

Theodore looked up at Eileen. 'I want to go home.'

'I don't blame you,' Eileen said. She picked up his suitcase and walked him over to the slowing train. It was full of soldiers. They peered around the blackout curtains in the compartments, waving and grinning, and jammed the platforms at both ends of the cars, some of them half hanging out over the steps. 'Come to see us off to the war, ducks?' one of them called to Eileen as the car slowed to a whooshing halt in front of her. 'Come to kiss us goodbye?'

Oh dear, I hope this isn't a troop train. 'Is this the passenger train to London?' she asked hopefully.

'It is,' the soldier said. 'Hop aboard, luv.' He leaned down, one hand extended, the other clutching the side railing.

'We'll take *good* care of you,' a beefy, red-faced soldier next to him said. 'Won't we, boys?' and there was an answering chorus of hoots and whistles.

'I'm not taking the train. This little boy is,' she said to the first soldier. 'I need to speak to the guard. Can you fetch him for me?'

'Through that mob?' he said, looking back into the car. 'Nothing could get through that.'

Oh dear. 'This little boy must get to London,' she said. 'Can you see that he arrives there safely? His mother will be at the station to meet him.'

He nodded. 'Are you certain you don't want to come as well, luv?'

'Here's his ticket,' she said, passing it up to him. 'His address is in his pocket. His name's Theodore Willett.' She handed the suitcase up. 'All right, Theodore, up you go. This nice soldier will take care of you.'

'No!' Theodore shouted, turning and launching himself into her arms. 'I don't *want* to go home.'

She staggered under his weight. 'Of course you do, Theodore. You mustn't listen to Alf and Binnie, they were only trying to frighten you. Here, I'll climb up the steps with you,' she said, trying to set him on the bottom rung, but he grabbed her around the neck.

'No! I'll *miss* you.'

'I'll miss you, too,' she said, trying to loosen his grip. 'But just think, your mummy will be there, and your own nice bed and toys. Remember how much you've been wanting to go home?'

'No.' He buried his head in her shoulder.

'Whyn't you just toss 'im onto the train?' Alf suggested helpfully.

'*No!*' Theodore sobbed.

'Alf,' Eileen said. 'How would *you* like to be tossed into the middle of a lot of people you didn't know to fend for yourself?'

'I'd like it fine. I'd make 'em buy me sweets.'

I'll wager you would, Eileen thought. *But Theodore's not as tough as you.* And, at any rate, she couldn't toss him. His hands were locked around her neck.

'*No!*' he shrieked, as she tried to pry his fingers loose. 'I want you to go with me!'

'I can't, Theodore. I haven't a ticket.' And the soldier who'd taken Theodore's suitcase had disappeared into the car to stow it, and there was no way to get it or the ticket back. 'Theodore, I'm afraid you must get on the train.'

'No!' he screamed, right in her ear, and tightened his grip around her neck, nearly strangling her.

'Theodore—'

'There, that's no way to carry on, Theodore,' a man's voice said, nearly in her ear, and Theodore was abruptly off her neck and in his arms. It was the vicar, Mr Goode. 'Of course you don't want to go, Theodore,' he said, 'but in a war we must all do things we don't want to do. You must be a brave soldier, and—'

'I'm *not* a soldier,' Theodore said, aiming a kick at the vicar's groin, which he deflected neatly by grabbing Theodore's foot.

'Yes, you are. When there's a war, everyone's a soldier.'

'You're not,' Theodore said rudely.

'Yes, I am. I'm a captain in the Home Guard.'

'Well, *she's* not,' Theodore said, pointing at Eileen.

'Of course she is. She's the major-general in charge of evacuees.' He saluted her smartly.

He'll never buy it, Eileen thought. *Nice try, Vicar*, but Theodore was asking, 'What sort of soldier am I?'

'A sergeant,' the vicar said. 'In charge of going on the train.' There was a *whoosh* of steam, and the train gave a lurch. 'Time to go, Sergeant,' he said, and handed him up into the arms of the red-faced soldier.

'I'm counting on you to see that he reaches his mother, soldier,' the vicar said to him.

'I will, Vicar,' the soldier promised.

'I'm a soldier, too,' Theodore informed the soldier. 'A sergeant, so you must salute me.'

'Is that so?' the soldier said, smiling.

The train began to move. 'Thank you,' Eileen called over the clank of the wheels. 'Goodbye, Theodore!' She waved to him, but he was talking animatedly to the soldier. She turned to the vicar. 'You're a miracle-worker. I could never have got him off by myself. Thank goodness you happened to be passing.'

'Actually, I was looking for the Hodbins. I don't suppose you've seen them?'

That explained why they'd vanished. 'What have they done now?'

'Put a snake in the schoolmistress's gas mask,' he said, walking out to the edge of the platform and looking over it. 'If you should happen to see them—'

'I'll see that they apologise.' She raised her voice in case they were under the platform. '*And* that they're punished.'

'Oh, I shouldn't be too hard on them,' he said. 'No doubt it's difficult for them, being shipped off to a strange place, so far from home. Still, I'd best go and find them before they burn down Backbury.' He took another searching look over the edge of the platform and left.

Eileen half expected Alf and Binnie to reappear as soon as he was out of sight, but they didn't. She hoped Theodore would be all right. What if his mother wasn't there to meet him, and the soldiers left him alone at the station? 'I should have gone with him,' she murmured.

'Then who'd take care of *us*?' Alf said, appearing out of no-where.

'The vicar says you put a snake in your schoolmistress's gas mask.'

'I never did.'

'I'll wager it crawled in there by itself,' Binnie said, popping up. 'P'raps it thought it smelled poison gas.'

'You ain't goin' to tell Mrs Bascombe, are you?' Alf asked. 'She'll send us to bed without our supper, and I ain't 'alf starved.'

'Yes, well, you should have thought of that,' Eileen said. 'Now, come along.'

They both stood stubbornly still. 'We 'eard you talkin' to them soldiers,' Alf said.

'Mrs Bascombe says nice girls don't talk to soldiers,' Binnie said. 'We won't tell if you don't tell 'er what we done.'

They've both long since grown up and been sent to prison, Eileen told herself. *Or the gallows.* She looked around, half hoping the vicar would reappear to rescue her, and then said, 'March. Now. It will be dark soon.'

'It's already dark,' Alf said.

It was. While she'd been wrestling Theodore onto the train and talking to the vicar, the last of the afternoon light had faded, and it was nearly an hour's walk to the manor, most of it through the woods. ''Ow'll we find our way 'ome in the dark?' Binnie asked. 'Ain't you got a pocket torch?'

'They ain't *allowed*, you noddlehead,' Alf said. 'The jerries'll see the light and drop a bomb on you. Boom!'

'I know where the vicar keeps 'is torch,' Binnie said.

'We are not adding burglary to your list of crimes,' Eileen said. 'We won't need a torch if we walk quickly.' She took hold of Alf's sleeve and Binnie's coat and propelled them past the vicarage and through the village.

'Mr Rudman says jerries 'ide in the woods at night,' Alf said. ''E says 'e found a parachute in 'is pasture. 'E says the jerries *murder* children.'

They'd reached the end of the village. The lane to the manor stretched ahead, already dark.

'Do they?' Binnie asked. 'Murder children?'

Yes, Eileen thought, thinking of the children in Warsaw, in Auschwitz. 'There aren't any Germans in the woods.'

'There is so,' Alf said. 'You can't see 'em 'cause they're 'idin', waitin' for the invasion. Mr Rudman says 'Itler's goin' to invade on Christmas Day.'

Binnie nodded. 'During the King's speech, when no one's expectin' it, 'cause they'll all be too busy laughin' at the King st-st-stammerin'.'

And before Eileen could reprove her for being disrespectful, Alf said, 'No, 'e ain't. 'E's goin' to invade tonight.' He pointed at the trees. 'The jerries'll jump outa the woods'—he lunged at Binnie—'and stab us with their bayonets!' He demonstrated, and Binnie began kicking him.

Four months, Eileen thought, separating them. *I only have to put up with them for four more months.* 'No one's going to invade,' she said firmly, 'tonight or any other night.'

''Ow do you know?' Alf demanded.

'You can't know something what ain't 'appened yet,' Binnie said.

'Why *ain't* 'e going to?' Alf persisted.

Because the British Army will get away from him at Dunkirk, Eileen thought, *and he'll lose the Battle of Britain and begin bombing London to bring the British to their knees. But it won't work. They'll stand up to him. It'll be their finest hour. And it will lose him the war.*

'Because I have faith in the future,' she said, and, getting a firmer grip on Alf and Binnie, set off with them into the darkness.

'The best laid plans ...'

ROBERT BURNS, 'TO A MOUSE'

BALLIOL COLLEGE, OXFORD — APRIL 2060

W hen Michael got back to his rooms from Wardrobe, Charles was there. 'What are you doing here, Davies?' he asked, stopping in the middle of what looked like a self-defence move, his left arm held stiffly in front of him and his right protecting his stomach. 'I thought you were leaving this afternoon.'

'No,' Michael said disgustedly. He draped his dress whites over a chair. 'My drop's been postponed till Friday, which they could have told me *before* I went and got my American accent, so I wouldn't have to run around Oxford sounding like a damned fool for four days.'

'You always sound like a damned fool, Michael,' Charles said, grinning. 'Or should I be calling you by your cover name so you can get used to it? What is it, by the way? Chuck? Bob?'

Michael handed him his dog tags. 'Lieutenant Mike Davis,' Charles read.

'Yeah, I'm keeping the names as close to my own as I can since the segments of this assignment are so short. What's your name for Singapore?'

'Oswald Beddington-Hythe.'

No wonder he's practising self-defence, Michael thought,

setting on the bed the shoes Wardrobe had issued him. 'When are you going, *Oswald*?'

'Monday. Why was your drop postponed?'

'I don't know. The lab's running behind.'

Charles nodded. 'Linna says they're simply swamped over there. Ten drops and retrievals a day. If you ask me, there are entirely too many historians going to the past. We'll be crashing into each other soon. I hope they postpone my drop. I've still got masses of things to learn. You wouldn't know anything about foxhunting, would you?'

'Foxhunting? I thought you were going to Singapore.'

'I am, but a good many of the British officers there were apparently County and spent all their time discussing their foxhunting exploits.' He picked up the dress whites Michael'd slung over the chair. 'This is a naval uniform. What was the US Navy doing at the Battle of the Bulge?'

'Not the Battle of the Bulge – Pearl Harbor,' Michael said. 'Then the second World Trade Center bombing, *then* the Battle of the Bulge.'

Charles looked confused. 'I thought you were going to the evacuation of Dunkirk.'

'I am. That's fourth on the list, after which I do Salisbury and El Alamein.'

'Tell me again why you're going all these extremely dangerous places, Davies.'

'Because that's where heroes are, and that's what I'm observing.'

'But aren't all of those events tens? And I thought Dunkirk was a divergence point. How can you—?'

'I'm not. I'm going to Dover. And only parts of Pearl Harbor are a ten – the *Arizona*, the *West Virginia*, *Wheeler Field*, and the *Oklahoma*. I'm going to be on the *New Orleans*.'

'But do you actually have to be *on* the boat with Lord Nelson or whoever it is? Couldn't you observe him from a safe distance?'

'No,' Michael said. 'One, the *New Orleans* is a ship, not a boat. Boats are what rescued the soldiers from Dunkirk. Two, observing from a safe distance is what historians were stuck doing *before* Ira Feldman invented time travel. Three, Lord Nelson was at Trafalgar, not Pearl Harbor, and four, I'm not studying the heroes who lead navies – and armies – and win wars. I'm studying ordinary people who you wouldn't expect to be heroic, but who, when there's a crisis, show extraordinary bravery and self-sacrifice. Like Jenna Geidel, who gave her life vaccinating people during the Pandemic. And the fishermen and retired boat owners and weekend sailors who rescued the British Army from Dunkirk. And Welles Crowther, the twenty-four-year-old equities trader who worked in the World Trade Center. When it was hit by terrorists, he could have got out, but instead he went back and saved ten people, and died. I'm going to observe six different sets of heroes in six different situations to try to determine what qualities they have in common.'

'Like an aptitude for being in the wrong place at the wrong time? Or owning a boat?'

'Circumstance is one factor,' Michael said, refusing to be baited. 'Also a sense of duty or responsibility, physical disregard for personal safety, adaptability—'

'Adaptability?'

'Yeah. One minute you're giving a Sunday morning sermon and the next you're helping pass five-inch shells up to the guns to shoot at Japanese Zeros.'

'Who did that?'

'The Reverend Howell Forgy. He was getting ready to do Sunday morning services on board the *New Orleans* when the Japanese attacked. They fired back, but the electricity to the ammunition hoists had been knocked out, and he's the one who organised the gun crews – in the dark – into a human chain to pass the shells up to the deck. And he's the one who, when one of the sailors said, "You didn't get to finish your sermon, Reverend. Why don't you finish it now?" answered, "Praise the Lord and pass the ammunition."'

'And you're certain being fired at by Japanese Zeros isn't a ten? I still can't see how you persuaded Dunworthy to approve a project like that.'

'You're going to Singapore.'

'Yes, but I'm coming back before the Japanese arrive. Oh, that reminds me, someone phoned for you earlier.'

'Who was it?'

'I don't know. Shakira took the message. She was here teaching me to foxtrot.'

'Foxtrot?' Michael said. 'I thought you had to learn about foxhunting.'

'I need to learn both. So I can go to the club dances. The British community in Singapore held weekly dances.' He put his arms in the self-defence positions he'd had them in when Michael came in and began stepping stiffly around the room, counting, 'Left and-two and-three-and-four and—'

'The British community in Singapore should have spent more time paying attention to what the Japanese were up to,' Michael said. 'Then they might not have been caught so completely flat-footed.'

'Like you Americans at Pearl Harbor, *Lieutenant Davis?*' Charles said, grinning.

'You said Shakira took the message. Did she write it down?'

'Yes. It's there by the phone.'

Michael picked up the slip of paper and tried to read it, but the only words he could make out were 'Michael' and, further down, 'to'. The rest of it was anybody's guess. There was something that might be 'dob' or 'late' or 'hots', and on the next line a '501' or 'scl'. 'I can't decipher this,' he said, handing it to Charles. 'Did she say anything about what it was about?'

'I wasn't here. I had to run to Wardrobe to be measured for my dinner jacket, and when I got back she told me there'd been a call for you and she'd written it down.'

'Where is she now? Did she go back to her rooms?'

'No, she went over to Props to see if they had a recording of

"Moonlight Serenade" for us to practise to.' He took the slip of paper from Michael. 'Here, let me try. Good Lord, she truly does have wretched handwriting. I think that's "sch".' He pointed at the 'sol'. 'And the next word might be "change". Schedule change?'

Schedule change. In which case the 'dob' might be 'lab'. 'They'd better not have postponed it again,' Michael said, calling the lab. 'Hi, Linna. Let me talk to Badri.'

'May I ask who this is?'

'It's Michael Davies,' he said impatiently.

'Oh, Michael, I'm dreadfully sorry. I didn't recognise you with that American accent. What is it you wanted?'

'Somebody called me earlier and left a message. Was it you?'

'No, but I only just came on duty. It may have been Badri. He's doing a retrieval. I can have him phone you as soon as he's finished.'

'Listen, can you check to see if the time of my drop's been changed? It was on the schedule for Friday morning at 8 a.m.'

'I'll check. Hang on a moment,' she said, and there was a brief silence. 'No, the time hasn't been changed. Michael Davies, Friday 8 a.m.'

'Good. Thanks, Linna.' He hung up, relieved. 'Whoever it was who called, it wasn't the lab.'

Charles was still poring over the message. 'Could it have been Dunworthy? I think this might be a D.'

The only reason Dunworthy would have called would have been to say he'd decided Pearl Harbor was too dangerous and he'd changed his mind about letting him go, in which case Michael didn't want to talk to him. 'That's not a D,' he said. 'It's a Q. Did Shakira say when she'd be back?'

Charles shook his head. 'I expected her by now.'

'And you say she's over at Props?'

'Or the Bodleian. She said she might try there or Research if the music archives didn't have it.'

Which meant she could be anywhere, and if he went looking

for her he was likely to miss her. He'd better stay here. He needed to check a few things anyway. He'd already done all the main research for Pearl Harbor – he knew the layout of the *New Orleans*'s decks, the names and ranks of the crew, and what Chaplain Forgy looked like. He'd memorised the rules of US Navy protocol, the location of every ship, and a detailed chronology of the events of December seventh. The only part he was worried about was getting onto the *New Orleans*. He was scheduled to go through to Waikiki at 10 p.m. on December sixth and take one of the liberty launches – which ran until midnight – out to the ship, but according to his research, Waikiki on a Saturday night had been full of drunk GIs and sailors spoiling for a fight, and an overeager shore patrol. He couldn't afford to be in the *New Orleans*'s brig when the Japanese attacked Sunday morning. Maybe he should see how far away from his drop the officers' club was and whether launches had run to and from it that night. They should have. There'd been a dance there. He could—

The phone rang. Michael leaped to answer it. 'Hullo, Charles,' Shakira said. 'Sorry I've been so long. I haven't been able to find any Glenn Miller. I've located a Benny Goodman—'

'This isn't Charles, it's Michael. Where are you?'

'You don't *sound* like Michael.'

'I just got an American L-and-A implant,' he said. 'Listen, when you were here, someone called for me—'

'I *wrote* it all down for you,' she said, sounding annoyed. 'The message should be there by the phone.'

'But what did they say?'

'I wrote it down,' she said, annoyed. 'The order of your drops has been changed. You're going to Dunkirk first. On Friday at 8 a.m.'

*'By your readiness to serve you have helped
the State in a work of great value.'*

QUEEN ELIZABETH, IN A TRIBUTE
TO THOSE WHO TOOK IN EVACUEES, 1940

WARWICKSHIRE – FEBRUARY 1940

It began to rain just as Eileen was about to hang out the laundry, and she had to string up the clothesline in the ballroom, amid the portraits of Lord Edward and Lady Caroline's ruffed and hoop-skirted ancestors, and hang the wet sheets in there, which would take twice as long. By the time she finished, the children would be home from school. She'd wanted to be gone before they arrived. Last time the Hodbins had followed her into the woods, and she'd had to postpone going to the drop for another week.

Again. The Monday before that she'd had to spend her half-day out fumigating the children's cots for bedbugs, and the Monday before that she'd had to take Alf and Binnie over to Mr Rudman's farm to apologise for setting his haystack ablaze. They'd claimed they'd been practising lighting signal fires in case of invasion. 'The vicar says unless everyone does their bit we can't win the war,' Binnie'd said.

I have an idea the vicar would make an exception in your case, Eileen had thought. But the Hodbins weren't the only thing preventing her from going. Ever since Christmas she'd spent what was supposed to have been her half-day out soliciting for the saving-stamps drive or working on some other project Lady Caroline had devised for 'assisting the war effort', which somehow never involved her doing anything, only her servants.

If I don't go through to Oxford soon, they'll think something's happened and send a retrieval team after me, Eileen thought. She needed to at least tell the lab why she hadn't checked in, and perhaps persuade them to open the drop more often than one day a week. 'Which means I need to finish hanging these wretched sheets before the Hodbins get home,' she said aloud to the portrait of an earlier Lady Caroline and her spaniels, and bent to take another sheet out of the basket.

The kitchen maid, Una, was standing in the door. 'Who was you talking to?' she asked, peering between the hanging lines.

'Myself,' Eileen said. 'It's the first sign of going mad.'

'Oh,' Una said. 'Mrs Bascombe wants you.'

What now? I'll never get away. She hastily hung up the last sheet and hurried down the back stairs to the kitchen.

Mrs Bascombe was cracking eggs into a bowl. 'Put on a fresh apron,' she said. 'Her ladyship wants you.'

'But today's my half-day out,' Eileen protested.

'Yes, well, you can leave after. Her ladyship's in the drawing room.'

In the upstairs drawing room? That meant someone had come to take their child home. They'd been steadily shedding evacuees since Christmas. If many more departed, she'd have no one left to observe. Which was another reason she needed to go to Oxford today, to see if she could persuade Mr Dunworthy into sending her somewhere else. Or cutting this assignment short and letting her go and do the assignment she truly wanted: VE-Day. Eileen hurriedly tied on a fresh apron and started out of the kitchen.

'Wait,' Mrs Bascombe said. 'Take her ladyship's nerve tablets with you. Dr Stuart brought them round.'

The tablets were aspirin, which Eileen doubted would do much for Lady Caroline's 'nerves', which in any case seemed to be mostly an excuse for insisting the evacuees be kept quiet. Eileen took the box from Mrs Bascombe and hurried to the drawing room, wondering whose parents were here. She hoped not the Magruders: Barbara, Peggy, and Ewan were the only three well-behaved children left. All the other children had been hopelessly corrupted by Alf and Binnie.

Perhaps it's their mother, she thought, brightening, but it wasn't, nor was it the Magruders. It was the vicar, and she would have been glad to see him except that he'd probably come because the Hodbins had committed some new crime.

'You asked for me, ma'am?' Eileen said.

'Yes, Ellen,' Lady Caroline said. 'Have you ever driven a motor car?'

Oh no, they stole the vicar's car and wrecked it, Eileen thought. 'Driven, ma'am?' she said cautiously.

'Yes. Mr Goode and I have been discussing Civil Defence preparations, particularly the need for ambulance drivers.'

The vicar nodded. 'In the event of a bombing incident or invasion—'

'—we will need trained drivers,' Lady Caroline finished. 'Do you know how to drive, Ellen?'

Except for chauffeurs, servants in 1940 hadn't had occasion to drive, so it hadn't been part of her prep. 'No, ma'am, I'm afraid I never learned.'

'Then you shall. I've offered Mr Goode the use of my Bentley to aid the war effort. Mr Goode, you may give Ellen her first lesson this afternoon.'

'This afternoon?' Eileen blurted out, unable to keep the dismay out of her voice, and then bit her lip. Nineteen-forties maids didn't talk back.

'Is that inconvenient for you?' the vicar asked her. 'I could just as easily begin the lessons tomorrow, Lady Caroline.'

'Absolutely not, Mr Goode. Backbury may come under attack at any time.' She turned to Eileen. 'When it comes to the war, we must all be prepared to make sacrifices. The vicar will give you your lesson as soon as we've finished here. And then you'll stay to tea, won't you, Vicar? Ellen, tell Mrs Bascombe that Mr Goode is staying to tea. And tell her she and Mr Samuels will have their lessons after tea. You may go.'

'Yes, ma'am.' Eileen curtseyed and ran back down to the kitchen. Now she really needed to go to the drop. It was one thing to not know how to drive, and another thing to be completely unfamiliar with 1940s motor cars. She needed to get some advance prep. She wondered if she should try to make it to the drop and back before the lesson. If she knew Lady Caroline, they'd be at least an hour. But if they weren't ... *Perhaps I can get Mrs Bascombe to have her lesson first*, she thought.

She found her putting cakes into the oven. 'The children just came in,' Mrs Bascombe said. 'I've sent them up to the nursery to take off their coats. What did her ladyship want?'

'The vicar's going to teach us all to drive. And Lady Caroline said to tell you he's staying to tea.'

'*Drive?*' Mrs Bascombe said.

'Yes. So that we can drive an ambulance in case of a bombing incident.'

'Or in case James is called up and she hasn't anyone to drive her to all her meetings.'

Eileen hadn't thought of that. She might very well be worried that her chauffeur would be called up. The butler and both footmen had been last month, and Samuels, the elderly gardener, was now manning the front door.

'Well, she's not getting me in any motor car,' Mrs Bascombe said, 'bombing incident or no bombing incident.'

Which meant Eileen couldn't exchange with her. It would have to be Samuels.

'When are we to find the time for these lessons? We've too much to do as it is. Where are you going?' Mrs Bascombe demanded.

'To see Mr Samuels. The vicar's to give me my first lesson

this afternoon, but as it's my half-day out, I thought perhaps I could exchange with him.'

'No, the Home Guard's meeting this afternoon.'

'But it's important,' Eileen said. 'Couldn't he miss—?'

Mrs Bascombe looked shrewdly at her. 'Why are you so eager to have your half-day out today? You're not meeting a soldier, are you? Binnie said she saw you flirting with a soldier at the railway station.'

Binnie, you little traitor. After I kept our bargain and didn't tell Mrs Bascombe about the snake. 'I wasn't flirting, I was giving the soldier instructions for delivering Theodore Willett to his mother.'

Mrs Bascombe looked unconvinced. 'Young girls can't be too careful, especially in times like these. Soldiers turning girls' heads, talking them into meeting them in the woods, promising to marry them—'

There was a loud thump overhead, followed by a shriek and a sound like a herd of rhinoceri. 'What are those wretched children doing now? You'd best go and see. It sounds like they're in the ballroom.'

They were. And the thumps had apparently been the sheet-filled clotheslines coming down. A huddle of children cowered in a corner, menaced by two sheet-draped ghosts with outspread arms. 'Alf, Binnie, take those off immediately,' Eileen said.

'They told us they was Nazis,' Jimmy said defensively, which didn't explain the sheets.

'They said Germans *kill* little children,' five-year-old Barbara said. 'They *chased* us.'

The damage seemed to be confined to the sheets, thank goodness, though the portrait of Lady Caroline's hoop-skirted ancestor was hanging crookedly. 'We told them we weren't allowed to play in here,' eight-year-old Peggy said virtuously, 'but they wouldn't listen.'

Alf and Binnie were still freeing themselves from the wet, clinging folds of sheet.

'Do the Germans?' Barbara asked, tugging on Eileen's skirt. 'Kill little children?'

'No.'

Alf's head emerged from the sheet. 'They do so. When they invade, they're going to kill Princess Elizabeth and Margaret Rose. They're going to cut their 'eads right off.'

'Are they?' Barbara asked fearfully.

'No,' Eileen said. 'Outside.'

'But it's rainin',' Alf said.

'You should have thought of that before. You can play in the stables.' She herded them all outside and went back up to the ballroom. She straightened the portrait of Lady Caroline's ancestor, rehung the lines, then began picking the sheets up off the floor. They'd all have to be washed again, and so would the dust sheets covering the furniture.

I wonder how badly it would affect history if I throttled the Hodbins, she thought. Theoretically, historians weren't able to do anything that would alter events. Slippage kept that from happening. But surely in this instance, it would make an exception. History would so clearly be a better place without them. She stooped to pick up another trampled sheet.

'Begging your pardon, miss,' Una said from the door, 'but her ladyship wants to see you in the drawing room.'

Eileen thrust the wet sheets into Una's arms and ran down to change into her pinafore again and then race back upstairs to the drawing room. Mr and Mrs Magruder were there. 'They've come for ... er ... their children,' said Lady Caroline, who obviously had no idea what the children's names were.

'For Barbara, Peggy, and Ewan, ma'am?' Eileen said.

'Yes.'

'We missed them so,' Mrs Magruder said to Eileen. 'Our house has been quiet as a tomb without them.' At the phrase 'quiet as a tomb', Lady Caroline looked pained. She must have heard the children.

'And now that Hitler's coming to his senses and realising

35

Europe won't stand for his nonsense,' Mr Magruder said, 'there's no reason not to have them with us. Not that we don't appreciate all you've done for them, your ladyship, taking them in and loving them like your own.'

'I was more than glad to do it,' Lady Caroline said. 'Ellen, go and pack Peggy's and ... the other children's things and bring them here to the drawing room.'

'Yes, ma'am,' Eileen said, curtseying, and walked quickly along the corridor to the ballroom. If she could find Una, she could have her get the Magruder children's things ready while she went to the drop. *Please let her still be in the ballroom.*

She was, still holding the damp wad of sheets. 'Una, pack the Magruders' things,' she said. 'I'm going out to fetch the children,' and fled, but when she ran outside, the vicar was standing there, next to Lady Caroline's Bentley.

'Vicar, I'm sorry, but I can't have my lesson now,' she said. 'The Magruders are here to fetch Peggy and Ewan and—'

'I know,' he said. 'I've already spoken to Mrs Bascombe and arranged for you to have your lesson tomorrow.'

I love you, she thought.

'Una will have hers today.'

Oh, you poor man, but at least she was free to go. 'Thank you, Vicar,' she said fervently, and walked quickly across the lawn in the misty drizzle towards the stables, then ducked behind the hothouse and ran out to the road and set off along it, hurrying so she wouldn't be overtaken by Una and the vicar in the Bentley.

Before she'd gone a quarter of a mile, it began to rain harder, but that was actually a good thing. Even the inquisitive Hodbins wouldn't try to track her down in this downpour. She turned off into the woods and hurried along the muddy path to the ash tree.

Please don't let me have just missed it opening, she thought. The drop only opened once an hour, and in another hour it would be dark. The drop was far enough into the woods that its shimmer couldn't be seen from the road, but with the blackout, any light was suspect, and the Home Guard, for lack of anything better to do, sometimes patrolled the woods, looking for German parachutists. If they or the Hodbins—

She caught a flicker of movement out of the corner of her eye. She turned quickly, straining to catch a glimpse of Alf's cap or Binnie's hair ribbon.

'What are you doing here?' a man's voice said from behind her, and she nearly jumped out of her skin. She whirled around. There was a faint shimmer next to the ash tree. Through it she could see the net, and Badri at the console. 'You're not supposed to go through till the tenth,' he was saying. 'Weren't you notified that your drop had been rescheduled?'

'That's why I'm here,' another man's voice said angrily as the shimmer grew brighter. 'I demand to know why it's been postponed. I—'

'This will have to wait,' Badri said. 'I'm in the middle of a retrieval—'

Eileen walked through the shimmer and into the lab.

*'At the time, we didn't know that it was a vital battle . . .
We didn't know we were quite so close to defeat, either.'*

SQUADRON LEADER JAMES H. 'GINGER' LACEY,
ON THE BATTLE OF BRITAIN

OXFORD – APRIL 2060

'They're sending you to Dunkirk?' Charles asked when Michael got off the phone. 'What happened to Pearl Harbor?'

'That's what I'd like to know,' Michael said. He stormed over to the lab to confront Badri.

Linna met him at the door. 'He's preparing to send someone through. Can I be of help?'

'Yes. You can tell me why the hell you changed the order of my drops! I can't go to the Dunkirk evacuation with an American accent. I'm supposed to be a reporter for the London *Daily Herald*. You've got to—'

'I think you'd better speak to Badri,' Linna said. 'If you'll wait here—' and walked quickly over to Badri. He was busily typing figures into the console, glancing up at the screens, typing again. A young man Michael didn't know stood behind him watching, obviously the historian who was going to be sent through. He was dressed in threadbare tweed flannels and wire-rimmed spectacles. *A 1930s Cambridge don*, Michael thought.

Linna leaned over Badri briefly and came back. 'He said it will

38

be at least another half-hour,' she reported. 'If you don't want to wait, he can ring you up at—'

'I'll wait.'

'Would you like to sit down?' she asked, and before he could say no, the telephone rang, and she went to answer it. 'No, sir, he's sending someone through right now,' he heard her say to the person on the other end. 'No, sir, not yet. He's going through to Oxford.'

Well, he'd been close. He wondered what he was researching in Oxford in the 1930s. The Inklings? The admission of women to the university?

'No, sir, it's just a recon and prep,' Linna said, into the phone. 'Phipps doesn't leave for his assignment till the end of next week.'

A recon and prep? Those were only used for especially complicated or dangerous assignments. He looked interestedly over at Phipps, who'd moved to the net. What could he be observing in 1930s Oxford that was that complicated? It couldn't be anything dangerous – he looked too pale and spindly.

'No, sir, he's only going to one temporal location,' Linna said into the phone. A pause while she consulted her console. 'No, sir. His only other assignment was to 1666.'

'Stand in the centre,' Badri said, and Phipps stepped under the draped folds and stood on the positioning marks, pushing his spectacles up on his nose.

'You want a list of all the historians currently on assignment and scheduled to go this week and next?' Linna asked the person on the telephone. 'Spatial locations or just temporal?' A pause. 'Historian, assignment, dates.' She scribbled it down, he hoped more legibly than Shakira had with the note she'd left him. 'Yes, sir, I'll get that for you straightaway. Do you wish to remain on the line?' she asked, and he must have said yes, because she laid the receiver down and scurried over to Badri, who was still getting Phipps into position, then over to an auxiliary terminal.

'All set?' Badri said to Phipps.

Phipps reached into his tweed jacket, checked something in the inside pocket, then nodded. 'You're not sending me through on a Saturday, are you?' he asked. 'If there's slippage, that will put me there on a Sunday, and—'

'No, a Wednesday,' Badri said. 'August seventh.'

'August seventh?' Phipps asked Badri.

'That's right,' Linna said, '1536,' and Michael looked over at her, confused, but she was back at the phone, reading off a printout. 'London, the trial of Anne Boleyn—'

'Yes, the seventh,' Badri said to Phipps. 'The drop will open every half-hour. Move a bit to the right.' He motioned with his hand. 'A bit more.' Phipps shambled obediently to the right. 'A bit to the left. Good. Now hold that.' He walked back over to the console and hit several keys, and the folds of the net began to lower around Phipps. 'I need you to note the amount of temporal slippage on the drop.'

'October tenth 1940,' Linna said into the phone, 'to December eighteenth—'

'Why?' Phipps asked. 'You're not expecting more slippage than usual on *this* drop, are you?'

'*Don't* move,' Badri said.

'There shouldn't be any slippage. I'm not going anywhere near—'

'Cairo, Egypt,' Linna said into the phone.

'Ready?' Badri asked Phipps.

Phipps said, 'No, I want to know—' and was gone in a shimmer of light.

Badri came over to Michael. 'I assume you received my message?'

'Yeah,' Michael said. 'What the hell's going on?'

'There's no need to swear,' Badri said mildly.

'That's what you think! You can't change my schedule at the last minute like this. I've already done the research for Pearl Harbor. I've already got my costume and papers and money and had an implant done so I sound like an American.'

40

'It can't be helped. Here's the new order of your drops.' Badri handed him a printout.

'Dunkirk evacuation,' he read out loud, 'Pearl Harbor, El Alamein, Battle of the Bulge, second World Trade Center attack, beginning of the Pandemic in Salisbury— You've changed all of them?' Michael shouted. 'You can't just move them around like this! They were in the order I gave you for a reason. Look,' he said, shoving the list under Badri's nose, 'Pearl Harbor and the World Trade Center and the Battle of the Bulge are all American. I scheduled them together so I could get one L-and-A implant. *Which I've already had*! How am I supposed to be a London *Daily Herald* war correspondent reporting on the evacuation from Dunkirk with this accent?'

'I apologise for that,' Badri said. 'We attempted to contact you before the implant. I'm afraid you'll have to have it reversed.'

'Reversed? And then what the hell do I do about Pearl Harbor? I'm supposed to be an American Navy lieutenant. You've got these alternating, for God's sake – British, American, British! This isn't an ordinary mission where I'm there for a year. I'm only going to be in each of these places a few days. I can't afford to spend it faking an accent and worrying about what to call things.'

'I understand,' Badri said placatingly, 'but—'

The door opened and a burly young man charged in. 'I want to speak to you,' he said to Badri and marched him over to the far corner of the lab. 'What the bloody hell do you think you're doing moving my drop up?' Michael heard him say, so apparently he wasn't the only one whose mission they'd been messing with.

He looked over at Linna. She was still on the phone. '—to February sixth, 1942,' she read from the printout.

'How the bloody hell do you expect me to be ready by Monday morning?' the burly guy shouted.

'Denys Atherton,' Linna droned on, 'March first, 1944—'

'I understand your vexation,' Badri said.

'My *vexation?*' the young man exploded.

Go ahead, Michael thought. *Hit him. Do it for both of us,* but he didn't. He stormed out, banging the door behind him so violently that Linna jumped. '—to June fifth, 1944,' she said into the phone.

Jesus, how many historians did they have going to World War II right now? Charles was right. They were going to start crashing into each other. He wondered if that was why they'd changed the order of his drops. But if that was the case, they'd have sent him to Salisbury or the World Trade Center.

Badri came back over to Michael. 'Can't you pose as an American reporter?'

'It isn't just the accent. It's the prep. I can't be ready in three days. I don't have any clothes or papers and I've only done the general research, not the—'

'We're aware you'll need time for additional prep,' Badri said placatingly, 'so we've moved the drop to Saturday—'

'You've given me one extra day? I'll need at least two weeks. And now I suppose you can't do that either.'

'No, no, of course we can reschedule,' Badri said, turning to the console, 'but you'll have to go with lab availability, and we're extremely heavily booked. Let me see,' he peered at the screen, 'the fourteenth might work ... no ... it will be at least three weeks. I think you'd do better to shorten the prep time with implants. The lab can arrange for you to—'

'I've already had my limit. You're only allowed three, and an L-and-A counts as two. And I had "Historical Events—1941", which will come in really handy at Dunkirk.'

'There's no need for sarcasm,' Badri said. 'The lab can arrange for a waiver so you can have an additional—'

'I don't want a waiver. I want you to change the order back the way it was.'

'I'm afraid that's impossible. And the next open date we have is May twenty-third, which will throw your other drops later.

There's a possibility we might be able to work you in sooner if there's a cancellation, but—'

The screen began blinking. 'Sorry. This will have to wait.'

'It can't. I—'

'Linna,' Badri said, ignoring him. 'Retrieval.'

The beeping became more insistent, and a faint shimmer appeared within the folds of the net. It brightened and spread, and Gerald Phipps was standing in the gauzy folds, pushing his spectacles up on his nose.

'I told you there wouldn't be any slippage,' he said.

'None at all?' Badri asked.

'Nearly. Twenty-two minutes. It only took me two hours to arrange everything. I posted the letters, made my trunk call, took the—'

'What about your return?' Badri asked. 'Did the drop open on time?'

'Not the first time, but there were boats on the river. They very likely kept it from opening.' He walked over to the console. 'When do I go through for my assignment?'

'Friday at half past ten,' Badri said, and he must not have changed his drop because Phipps nodded, said, 'I'll be here,' and started for the door.

'I'm still waiting for you to tell me why you can't change my drop back to Pearl Harbor,' Michael said before Badri could turn to the console.

'You must be sent in the authorised order—'

'I beg your pardon, Badri,' Linna interrupted. She was back on the phone. 'What was the slippage on Phipps's drop?'

'Twenty-two minutes,' Badri said.

'Twenty-two minutes,' she repeated into the phone.

'Okay, I'll make you a deal,' Michael said. 'I'll go to Dunkirk, and in exchange you send me to Pearl Harbor and the other sections I need the American accent for, and then to Salisbury and North Africa. Deal?'

43

Badri shook his head. 'I can only send historians in the authorised order.'

'Who did this authorising?'

'Badri,' Linna called, 'did Phipps's return drop open on schedule?'

'I'll be there in a moment, Linna,' Badri said, and the beeping started up again. 'I have another historian coming through, Mr Davies. Either you can go on Saturday, or I can postpone your drop to May twenty-third, which will move your Pearl Harbor drop to' – he turned to the console – 'the second of August, and your El Alamein drop to the twelfth of November.'

At which rate it would take him two years to finish his project. 'No,' he said. 'I'll be ready by Saturday.' *Somehow.*

He went straight to Props to tell them he needed a press card, a passport, and whatever other papers an American in England in 1940 needed, and that he had to have them by Thursday morning. When they told him that wasn't possible, he told them to take it up with Dunworthy and went over to Wardrobe, where he was told they couldn't measure him for a reporter's costume until he'd returned the dress whites, and went back to his rooms to begin the impossible task of memorising everything necessary for the assignment.

He didn't even know where to begin. He needed to find out who the civilian heroes of the evacuation had been, the names of their boats, when they'd arrived back in Dover, where the docks were and how to get access to them, where they'd gone after they got to Dover, where the train station was. And the hospital, in case the hero'd been injured. The list went on and on. And that was just so he could do his interviews. He also needed tons of background information on the evacuation and the war in general. And on local customs.

That was one good thing about having to be an American. It would give him an excuse for not knowing things. But he would still need to know what had happened during the months leading up to Dunkirk, especially since he was supposed to be a reporter.

First things first. He called up 'Heroes of Dunkirk' and got to work, hoping Charles and Shakira wouldn't suddenly arrive to practise the foxtrot.

They didn't, but Linna called. 'Don't tell me,' he said. 'You changed the order again.'

'No, you're still scheduled for the evacuation of Dunkirk, but we're having difficulty finding a drop site. Every one we've tried is indicating probable slippage of from five to twelve days, and Badri was wondering if—'

'No, I can't miss part of it, if that's what you're suggesting. The entire evacuation only lasted nine days. I *have* to be there by May twenty-sixth.'

'Yes, we know that. We were just wondering if you had any suggestions for a site. You know the events in Dover better than we do. Badri thought you might be able to suggest a location that might work.'

Nowhere near the docks obviously. And not the main part of town. It would be swarming with officers from the Admiralty and the Small Vessels Pool. 'Have you tried the beach?' he asked.

'Yes. No luck.'

'Try the beaches north and south of town,' he suggested, though he doubted that would work either with so many boats around. And England had been expecting to be invaded; the beaches were likely to be fortified. Or mined. 'Try something on the outskirts of Dover, and I'll hitch a ride in to the docks. There'll be plenty of cars headed that way.' And if it was a military vehicle, it might solve his problem of how to get onto the docks.

But Badri called back two hours later to say that none of those had worked. 'We need to go further afield. I need a list from you of nearby villages and other possible sites,' Badri said, which meant Mike had to spend the rest of the day in the Bodleian, poring over maps of 1940 England – looking for secluded spots within walking distance of Dover – instead of what he should be doing. At six he took the list to the lab, handed it to Badri (who was being shouted at by a guy in a doublet and tights whose schedule had been changed), and went back to the Bodleian to work on his heroes.

There were almost too many to choose from. In reality, every one of the solicitors and City bankers and other weekend sailors had been a hero to take their unarmed pleasure yachts and sailboats and skiffs into enemy fire, many of them making multiple trips.

But some had performed acts of extraordinary bravery – the badly injured petty officer who'd held off six Messerschmitts with a machine-gun while the troops boarded; the accountant who'd ferried load after load of soldiers out to the *Jutland* under heavy fire; George Crowther, who'd given up his chance at rescue to stay and help the ship's surgeon on the *Bideford*; the retired Charles Lightoller, who, not content with already having been a hero on the *Titanic*, had taken his weekend cruiser over and brought back one hundred and thirty soldiers.

But not all of them had come back to Dover. Some had gone to Ramsgate instead; some had come back on a different boat than the one they took over – Sub-Lieutenant Chodzko had gone over on the *Little Ann* and come home on the *Yorkshire Lass* – and one fishing boat captain had had three boats shot out from under him. And some hadn't come back at all. And for the ones who had returned to Dover, there were almost no details about which pier they'd docked at or when. Which meant he'd better have a bunch of backup heroes in case he couldn't find the ones he wanted to interview.

It took him all night. As soon as Wardrobe opened in the morning, he took his dress whites back and had them measure him for whatever the hell it was American World War II reporters wore, and then went back to Balliol to start in on the Dover research. Charles, attired in tennis whites, was just coming out the door. 'The lab phoned. You're to ring them back.'

'Did they say if they'd found a drop site?'

'No. I'm off to prep for Singapore. The colonials spent all their time playing tennis.' He waved his racket at Michael and left.

Michael called the lab.

'I can't find anything within a five-mile radius of Dover that will open before June sixth,' Badri said. 'I'm going to try London. You could take the train to Dover.'

And what if you can't find a drop site in London either? Mike wondered. That would mean the problem wasn't just finding a spot where nobody would see him come through – it was the evacuation itself. History was full of divergence points nobody could get anywhere near – from Archduke Ferdinand's assassination to the battle of Trafalgar. Events so critical and so volatile that the introduction of a single variable – such as a time traveller – could change the outcome. And alter the entire course of history.

He'd known Dunkirk was one of them; Oxford had been trying and failing to get to it for years. But he hadn't expected Dover to be one. If it was, there went one whole chunk of his assignment. On the other hand, it would mean he could go to Pearl Harbor, which he was actually ready for. And if Dover wasn't a divergence point, this delay gave him more time to prep. And more things he needed to learn. Such as which London station the trains to Dover left from and when. And he still had the overview of the evacuation to do. And the war. And everything else. In three days. On no sleep.

He wished he wasn't limited to a single implant. He could use half a dozen. He narrowed it down to the events of 1940, the events in Dunkirk and a list of the small craft that had participated, decided he'd pick when he got to Research, and went over there.

The tech shook her head. 'If you're going as a reporter, you'll need to know how to use a 1940s telephone. To file your stories,' she said. 'And a typewriter.'

Michael wasn't going to file any stories. All he was going to do was interview people, but if he did end up in a situation where he had to type something, that kind of ignorance could blow his cover, and there'd been Nazi spies in England in 1940. He didn't want to spend the evacuation in jail.

He went over to Props and borrowed a typewriter to see if he could fake it, but he couldn't even figure out how to get the paper in it. He went back to Research, talked the tech into putting an abridged version of typewriter skills and Dunkirk events in the same subliminal, had it, and dragged back to his rooms to get some sleep and then memorise everything else.

Charles was there, attired in a dinner jacket and practising putting on the carpet. 'Don't tell me,' Mike said. 'The colonials spent all their time playing golf.'

'Yes,' Charles said, lining up his putt. 'That is, when they weren't taking telephone messages for their roommates.'

'The lab called?'

'No, Props. They said to tell you they can't have your papers ready till next Tuesday.'

'Next Tuesday?' Mike bellowed. He called, told them in no uncertain terms that he had to have them by Friday at the latest, and slammed down the phone. It rang again immediately.

It was Linna. 'Good news,' she said. 'We've found you a drop site.'

Which meant Dover wasn't a divergence point after all. Thank God.

'Where is it?' he asked. 'In London?'

'No, it's just north of Dover, six miles from the docks. But there's a problem. Mr Dunworthy wanted to move one of the retrieval times up, so we gave them your Saturday slot.'

Great, Michael thought. *This'll give me a couple of extra days. I'll be able to memorise that list of small craft. And get some more sleep.* 'What day did you move it back to?'

'Not back,' she said, 'forward. You go through Thursday afternoon – tomorrow – at half past three.'

TO THE TRENCHES →

SIGN IN LONDON, 1940

OXFORD — APRIL 2060

'**I**n two days?' Eileen said, looking over Linna's shoulder at her console in the lab. She'd gone to see Mr Dunworthy as soon as she came through from Backbury and then come back to the lab to schedule her return. 'But I need to learn to drive. What about next week?'

Linna called up another schedule. 'No, I'm sorry, we haven't anything then either.'

'But I can't possibly learn to drive in two days. What about the week after next?'

Linna shook her head. 'That's even worse. We're totally swamped. Mr Dunworthy's ordered all these schedule changes—'

'Were they ones historians requested?' Eileen asked. Perhaps if she asked Mr Dunworthy—

'No,' Linna said, 'and they're all absolutely furious, which is something else the lab's had to deal with. I've done nothing but—' The telephone rang. 'Sorry.' She crossed the lab to answer the phone next to the console. 'Hullo? Yes, I know you were scheduled to go to the Reign of Terror first—'

The door of the lab opened and Gerald Phipps came in. *Oh no,* Eileen thought, *just what I need.* Gerald was the most tiresome person she knew. 'Where's Badri?' he demanded.

49

'He's not here,' Eileen said, 'and Linna's on the phone.'

'I suppose they've changed your date of departure as well,' he said, waving a printout at her. 'Is this for that silly VE Day assignment you're always on about?'

No, I'm not going to VE Day. Not unless I can persuade Mr Dunworthy to change his mind. Which seemed unlikely. When she went to see him, he'd refused not only to let her go, but to even listen to her worries about her evacuees all returning to London.

'No,' she said stiffly to Gerald. 'I'm observing World War II evacuees.'

He laughed. 'Are that and VE Day the most exciting assignments you could think of?' he asked, and for a moment she actually wished Alf and Binnie were there to set him on fire.

'The lab rescheduled your departure date?' she asked to change the subject.

'Yes,' he said, glancing impatiently over at Linna, who was still on the phone.

'No, I know you were supposed to do the storming of the Bastille first—' Linna said.

'But it can't be changed,' Gerald said. 'I've already been through and made all the arrangements. And got my costume from Wardrobe. If my arrival's changed from August, I'll need a whole new suit of clothes. I'm certain when I explain the circumstances, they'll change it back. This isn't an ordinary assignment where one can waltz in anytime. It was difficult enough getting it set up in the first place.' He launched into a long explanation of where he was going and the preparations he'd made.

Eileen only half listened. It was obvious he'd pounce on Linna the moment she got off the phone, and by the time he finished shouting at her and Eileen got to speak to her, Linna would be in no mood to move another departure date. And in the meantime, her two days were ticking away, and she hadn't even been to Oriel yet to sign up for lessons with Transport. 'I think I'd best come back later,' she interrupted Gerald to say, and started for the door.

'Oh, but I thought we could get together after this, and I could—'

Tell me more about your assignment? No, thank you. 'I'm afraid I can't. I'm going back almost immediately.'

'Oh, too bad. I say, will you still be there in August? I could take the train up to – where is it you are?'

'Warwickshire.'

'Up to Warwickshire some weekend to brighten your existence with tales of my derring-do.'

I can imagine. 'No, I'm afraid I come back at the beginning of May.' *Thank goodness.* She waved to Linna and walked quickly out of the lab before he could propose anything else. *First the Hodbins and now Gerald,* she thought, stopping outside the door to put on her coat and gloves.

But this wasn't February, it was April, and a lovely day. Linna'd said rain was forecast for late this afternoon, but for now it was warm. She took her coat off as she walked. That was the most difficult thing about time travel, remembering where and when one was. She'd forgotten she wasn't still a servant and called Linna 'ma'am' twice, and now she kept looking nervously behind her to make certain Alf and Binnie weren't following her. She reached the High, stepped into the street, and was nearly hit by a bicycle whizzing past.

You're in Oxford, she told herself, stepping hastily back up on the kerb, *not Backbury.* She crossed the street, looking both ways this time, and started along the sunlit High, suddenly jubilant. *You're in Oxford. There's no blackout, no rationing, no Lady Caroline, no Hodbins—*

'Merope!' someone shouted. She turned around. It was Polly Churchill. 'I've been calling to you all the way down the street,' Polly said breathlessly as she caught up to her. 'Didn't you hear me?'

'No ... I mean, yes ... I mean, I didn't realise you were calling me at first. I've been trying so hard to think of myself as Eileen O'Reilly these last months, I don't even recognise my own name anymore. I had to have an Irish name because of my posing as a maid—'

'And your red hair,' Polly said.

'Yes, and Eileen is all anyone's called me in months. I've practically forgotten my name is Merope, though I suppose that's better than forgetting one's cover name, which is what I kept doing the first week I was in Backbury, and on my very first assignment! How do you manage to remember your cover names?'

'I'm lucky. Unlike your Christian name, mine's been around for a good part of history, and I can always use it or one of its many nicknames. I can sometimes even use my last name. When I can't – Churchill's not really an option for World War II – I use Shakespeare.'

'Polly Shakespeare?'

'No,' Polly said, laughing, '*names* from Shakespeare. I had the plays implanted when I did that sixteenth-century assignment, and they're full of names. Especially the history plays, though for the Blitz it's going to be *Twelfth Night*. I'll be Polly Sebastian.'

'I thought you'd already gone to the Blitz.'

'No, not yet. The lab's had difficulty finding me a drop site that met all of Mr Dunworthy's requirements. He's such a fusspot. So since it's a multitime project, I did one of the other parts first. I only just got back yesterday.'

Eileen nodded. She remembered Polly having said something about observing the World War I Zeppelin attacks on London.

'I'm on my way to Balliol to report in to Mr Dunworthy,' Polly said. 'Is that where you're going?'

'No, I must go to Oriel.'

'Oh good, then we're going the same direction.' She took Eileen's arm. 'We can walk part of the way together and catch up on things. So you've been in Backbury observing evacuees—'

'Yes, and I have a question,' Eileen said earnestly. 'You've had loads of assignments. How do you keep from getting them all mixed together? It's not only the names. I'm already getting confused as to where I am and when.'

'You've got to forget you've ever been anywhere or anyone else and focus completely on the situation at hand. It's like acting. Or being a spy. You've got to shut out everything and *be* Eileen O'Reilly. Thinking about other assignments only ruins your concentration on the task at hand.'

'Even if you're doing a multitime assignment?'

'Especially if you're doing a multitime assignment. Focus entirely on the part or the assignment until it's over, and then shut *that* out and go on to the next. Why are you going to Oriel?'

'For driving lessons.'

'Driving lessons? You're not planning to *drive* to VE Day, are you? You'll never get through. The crowds—'

'This isn't for VE Day. If only it were. Mr Dunworthy refuses to send me.'

'But you—' Polly said and stopped, frowning.

'Had my heart set on going? That doesn't matter two pins to Mr Dunworthy. I met with him this morning, and he told me VE Day was already part of another assignment, and having two historians in the same temporal and spatial location was too dangerous, which is ridiculous. It isn't as if we'd run into each other – there were thousands of people in Trafalgar Square on VE Day. And even if we did, what does he think we'd do? Shout, "Oh, my, another time traveller!" or something? I don't suppose you know whose assignment he was talking about, Polly? I thought I might be able to persuade them to switch if they haven't already gone. Who else is doing World War II?'

'What?' Polly said blankly. She clearly hadn't heard a word Merope'd said.

'I said, who else has an assignment in World War II?'

'Oh,' Polly said. 'Rob Cotton, and I believe Michael Davies does.'

'Do you know what he's observing?'

'No, why?'

'I want to know who's going to VE Day.'

'Oh. I think he said something about Pearl Harbor.'

'When was Pearl Harbor?'

'The seventh of December, 1941. If it's not VE Day, where are you going that you need to learn how to drive?'

'Back to Warwickshire and the manor. I still have *months* to go on my assignment.'

'I wish I could have months. Mr Dunworthy's only allowing me to go to the Blitz for a few weeks. But I thought you were a maid. Servants didn't usually drive, did they?'

'No, Lady Caroline's insisting the staff learn so we can drive an ambulance if there's an incident.'

'But Backbury wasn't bombed, was it?'

'No, but Lady Caroline's determined to do her bit – or, rather, to make her staff do it for her. She's also made us learn to administer first aid and put out incendiaries. Next week she'll have us all learning to fire an anti-aircraft gun.'

'You sound better prepared for the Blitz than I am. I should have done my prep in Backbury.'

'No, you shouldn't have,' Eileen said. 'You'd have had to deal with the Horrible Hodbins.'

'What are Horrible Hodbins? Some sort of weaponry?'

'That's exactly what they are. A deadly secret weapon. They're the worst children in history.' She told Polly about the haystack fire and trying to put Theodore on the train and about Alf and Binnie's painting white stripes on Mr Rudman's Black Angus cows, '"So's 'e can see 'em in the blackout."'

'It's a pity they couldn't have been evacuated to Berlin instead of Backbury,' Eileen said. 'Two weeks of coping with Alf and Binnie, and Hitler would be *begging* to surrender.' They'd reached King Edward Street. 'I'd love to stay and chat, but I must get to Transport. You don't know when it closes, do you, Polly?'

'No. What automobile are you planning to learn on? A Daimler?'

'No, a Bentley. That's what Lady Caroline – or, rather, her chauffeur – drives. Why?'

'Nothing. I was going to warn you about the Daimler's gear-box, that's all – one has to yank the gear stick very hard to shift into reverse gear – but you're not going to be driving an actual ambulance, so it doesn't matter. Does Transport *have* a period Bentley?'

'I don't know, I haven't been there yet. I only came through this morning.'

'Do you have your driving authorisation form?'

'Driving authorisation?' Eileen said blankly.

'Yes. You must get it from Props before you go to Oriel.'

'You mean I've got to go all the way back to Queen's—?'

'No, I mean you've got to go to Balliol and get approval from Mr Dunworthy, and *then* you must go to Props.'

'But that will take all afternoon,' Eileen protested, 'and I only have two days. I'll never learn to drive in one day.'

'I don't understand. I thought the vicar was going to teach you to drive.'

'He is, but I've never even been in a 1940s automobile. I've got to learn how to open the door and switch on the ignition and—'

'Oh, I can easily teach you that in an hour or two. Come with me to Balliol. You can get your approval, and then I'll go with you and show you the ropes. And I'll speak to Mr Dunworthy about letting you do VE Day.'

'It won't do any good,' Eileen said glumly. 'I've already tried, and you know how he is when he's made his mind up—'

'True,' Polly said almost to herself. 'But he must change his mind sometimes if …'

'Polly!' They both turned and looked back. Seventeen-year-old sandy-haired Colin Templer came racing up to them with a sheaf of printouts. 'I've been looking for you everywhere, Polly,' he said breathlessly. 'Hullo, Merope.' He turned back to Polly. 'I finished the list of bombed Underground stations.'

'Colin's been helping me with my Blitz prep,' Polly explained to Eileen.

Colin nodded. 'Here.' He handed Polly several of the print-outs. 'This list is by station, but some of them were hit more than once.'

Polly looked through the pages. 'Waterloo …' she murmured, '… St Paul's … Marble Arch …'

Colin nodded again. 'It was hit on the seventeenth of September. There were over forty casualties.'

I hope they don't plan to stand here and go through the entire list, Eileen thought, looking at her watch. It was already half past three. Even if they could get in to see Mr Dunworthy immediately, they'd be at Balliol at least an hour, and if Transport closed at five—

'… Liverpool Street,' Polly said, '… Cannon Street … Blackfriars. Good Lord, this is every tube station in London!'

'No, only half,' Colin said, 'and most of them only had minor damage.' He handed her another set of pages. 'I also listed the dates so you'd know when not to be in them. I know Mr Dunworthy doesn't want you in the ones that were hit at all, but they're only dangerous for that day, and how are you going to get anywhere if you can't go to Victoria or Bank?'

'A man after my own heart,' Polly said and grinned at him. 'Don't tell Mr Dunworthy I said that.'

He looked horrified. 'You know I wouldn't, Polly.'

Hmm, Eileen thought.

'Is the list of air-raid and all-clear siren times here?' Polly asked, leafing through the pages. 'I haven't finished it yet,' he said, 'but here's the list of London landmarks that were damaged.' He handed her the rest of the pages. 'Did you know they bombed Madame Tussaud's Waxworks? And did you know it knocked the statue of Churchill over and took off Wellington's ear, but neither Hitler nor Mussolini got so much as a scratch? I call that unfair.'

'Yes, well, they got theirs later,' Polly said, looking through the pages. '*Thank* you, Colin. You've no idea how much help you've been.'

He reddened. 'I'll have the list of siren times to you in an hour or two. Where will you be?'

'Balliol.'

He dashed off.

'Thank you again, Colin! You're marvellous!' she called after him. 'Sorry,' she said to Eileen as they started walking again. 'He's been a wonderful assistant. All this would have taken me weeks.'

'Yes, well, it's amazing what a motivation love can be.'

'Love?' Polly shook her head. 'It's not me he's in love with, it's time travel. He's constantly after Mr Dunworthy to waive the age requirement and let him do an assignment now.'

'And what does Mr Dunworthy say?'

'You can imagine.'

'Being in love with time travel may explain why he's helping you with your prep,' Eileen said, 'but it doesn't explain why he blushes whenever you look at him. Or the way he says your name. Face it, Polly, he's head over heels.'

'But he's a child!'

'He's what? Seventeen? In 1940, seventeen-year-olds are lying about their age and joining up and getting killed by the Germans. And what does age have to do with anything? One of the evacuees at the manor when I first arrived wanted to marry me, and he was only three.'

'Oh dear, do you truly think—?' Polly looked back up the street. 'Perhaps I'd better not ask him to help me with any more research.'

'No, that would be cruel. He's trying to please and impress you. I think you should let him. You're only going to be here – how long?'

'Two weeks, if the lab can find me a drop site. I expected them to have found one by the time I got back, but they still haven't.'

'But they'll find you one eventually, and then you'll go to the Blitz – is this one real-time or flash-time?'

'Real-time.'

'And you'll be gone how long?'

'Six weeks.'

'Which is an eternity for a seventeen-year-old. By the time you come back, he'll have fallen in love with someone his own age and forgotten all about you.'

'I don't know, I was gone nearly that long last time ...' she said thoughtfully. 'And just because someone's young, it doesn't mean their attachment's not serious. On my last assignment—' She bit off whatever she had been going to say and said brightly, 'I think it's much more likely he's trying to impress me with his research skills so that I'll help him convince Mr Dunworthy to let him go to the Crusades.'

'The *Crusades*? That's even more dangerous than the Blitz, isn't it?'

'*Far* more dangerous, particularly when one knows where and when all the Blitz's bombs will be falling, which I will. And it's less dangerous than— Sorry, I've been doing all the talking. I want to hear about your assignment.'

'There's nothing much to tell. It's mostly washing up and dealing with children and irate farmers. I'd hoped I might meet the actor Michael Caine – he was evacuated when he was six – but I haven't, and— I just thought of something. You might meet Agatha Christie. She was in London during the Blitz.'

'Agatha Christie?'

'The twentieth-century mystery novelist. She wrote these marvellous books about murders involving spinsters and clergymen and retired colonels. I used them for my prep – they're full of details about servants and manor houses. And during the war she worked in a hospital, and you're going to be an ambulance driver. She—'

'I'm not going to be an ambulance driver. I'm going to be something far more dangerous – a shopgirl in an Oxford Street department store.'

'That's more dangerous than driving an ambulance?'

'Definitely. Oxford Street was bombed five times, and more than half its department stores were at least partly damaged.'

'You're not going to work in one of those, are you?'

'No, of course not. Mr Dunworthy won't even allow me to work in Peter Robinson, though it wasn't hit till the end of the Blitz. I can understand why he wouldn't let me ...'

Eileen nodded absently, listening to the bells of Christ Church tolling the hours. Four o'clock. They'd stood there talking to Colin longer than she'd thought. Perhaps instead of going with Polly, she should go to Oriel and find out when Transport closed.

'... John Lewis and Company ...' Polly was saying.

Or she could ask Polly to ask Mr Dunworthy to ring Props and approve the lessons over the phone for her.

'... Padgett's or Selfridge's ...'

I could go to Props, Eileen thought, pick up the authorisation form, *go to Oriel, and have Polly meet me there.*

'But I daren't dare push too hard,' Polly said, 'or he may cancel it altogether. He's thought this entire assignment was too dangerous from the beginning, and when he finds out—' She stopped, frowning again.

'Finds out what?' Eileen asked.

Polly paused. 'How many tube stations were hit,' she said finally, and Eileen had the feeling that hadn't been what she'd intended to say. 'I'm going to be spending my nights sleeping in the Underground stations.'

'The Underground stations?'

'Yes, there weren't enough shelters when the Blitz began, and the ones they had weren't particularly safe, so people began sleeping in the tube stations. I'm going to camp out there nights to observe the shelterers,' she said, and Eileen must have been looking as worried as she felt because Polly added, 'It's perfectly safe.'

'Provided you don't stay in one of the ones that were hit,' Eileen said dryly. They reached Balliol's gate. 'Polly, I'm not going to go in with you.' She told her her plan, then stepped up to the porter's lodge.

'Mr Purdy, do you know how late Transport stays open?'

'I've got their hours here somewhere,' the porter said, shuffling through papers. 'Six o'clock.'

Oh, good, there'd be time. 'Is Mr Dunworthy in his office?'

'I believe so,' Mr Purdy said. 'I only just came on duty, but Mr McCaffey said Mr Davies came through an hour ago looking for him, and he's still here, so I assume he found him.'

'Michael Davies?'

Mr Purdy nodded. 'Miss Churchill, you have a message from Colin Templer. He said to tell you he's looking for you and—'

'He found me,' Polly said, 'but thank you. Eileen, I'll tell Mr Dunworthy to ring you at Props—'

She shook her head. 'I'm coming with you.'

'But I thought you were going over to Props.'

'I am, but first I want to ask Michael if he's doing VE Day, and if he is, if he'll swap assignments with me. Or he may know who is.' She started across the quad with Polly in her wake.

Michael was sitting on the steps of Beard, tapping his foot. 'Are you waiting to see Mr Dunworthy, too?' Polly asked.

'Yes,' he said impatiently. 'I've *been* waiting for an hour and forty-five minutes. I can't believe this. First he louses up my assignment, and now—'

'What's your assignment?' Eileen asked.

'It *was* Pearl Harbor, which is why I sound like a damned American—'

'I thought you sounded odd,' Eileen said.

'Yes, well, I'll really sound odd in Dover. I'm doing the evacuation of Dunkirk. With less than three days' prep. That's why I'm here – to see if he'll move it back—'

'But—' Eileen said confused. 'They evacuated children from Dunkirk?'

'No. Soldiers. The entire British Expeditionary Force, as a matter of fact. Three hundred thousand men in nine days flat. Didn't you attend any of your first-year history lectures?'

'Yes,' she said defensively, 'but I didn't decide on World War II till last year.' She hesitated. 'The evacuation of Dunkirk *is* in World War II, isn't it?'

Michael laughed. 'Yes. May twenty-sixth to June fourth, 1940.'

'Oh, that's why I don't know about it—'

'But Dunkirk was one of the major turning points of the war,' Polly interrupted. 'Isn't it a divergence point?'

'Yes.'

'Then how can you—?'

'I'm not. I'm observing the organising of the rescue in Dover and then the boats as they come back with the soldiers.'

'You said you were supposed to go to Pearl Harbor,' Polly said sharply. 'Why did Mr Dunworthy cancel it?'

'He didn't,' Michael said. 'He just switched the order around. I'm doing several different events.'

'Is one of them VE Day?' Eileen asked.

'No. I'm observing heroes, so it's all crises – Pearl Harbor, the World Trade Center—'

'Are any of them near VE Day?' Eileen asked. 'In time, I mean?'

'No, the Battle of the Bulge is the closest. It was in December of 1944.'

'How long will you be there for that?' she asked.

'Two weeks.'

Then he wasn't the one doing VE Day. 'Do you know of any historians who are doing assignments in 1945?'

'Hmm, 1945 ...' he said, thinking. 'Somebody told me somebody was doing the V-1 and V-2 attacks, but I think those were in 1944—'

'Did Mr Dunworthy's secretary say how long it would be before you could get in to see him?' Polly interrupted. 'He needs to approve driving lessons for Merope – I mean, Eileen – and Props is only open till five.'

'No,' Michael said. 'All Mr Dunworthy's new secretary said was, was I willing to wait. I thought he meant a few minutes, not the whole damned afternoon, but it can't be too much longer, even if Dunworthy's reaming out a historian.'

'Why don't you go over to Oriel and reserve the Bentley, Merope – I mean, Eileen?' Polly said to her. 'We can tell Mr Dunworthy he needs to ring Props and authorise your lessons, and they can ring Transport. It will save time all around.'

'I will,' Eileen said. She turned to Michael. 'You don't know anyone else who's observing 1945?'

'No. Ted Fickley was supposed to be doing Patton's advance into Germany, but Dunworthy cancelled it.'

'Why?' Polly asked with that same alertness.

'I don't know,' Michael said. 'Ted said he couldn't get any reason out of the lab. All I know is Dunworthy's switched four drops and cancelled two others in the last two weeks.'

Eileen nodded. 'I was just over at the lab, and Linna said he'd made more than a dozen schedule changes. Gerald was there, and Mr Dunworthy had just postponed his drop.'

'Where was *he* going?' Polly asked her.

'I don't remember. It was something to do with World War II as well. Not VE Day, though.'

'Are *all* the drops he's changing World War II?' Polly asked Michael, sounding worried.

'No. Jamal Danvers was going to Troy. And my roommate, Charles, is scheduled to go to the lead-up to the invasion of Singapore, and Dunworthy hasn't changed his.'

'And he hasn't changed either of ours, Polly,' Eileen said. 'Polly's doing the London Blitz,' she explained to Michael. 'She's going to be a shopgirl in a big store in – where did you say?'

'Oxford Street,' Polly said.

'The *Blitz*?' Michael said, sounding impressed. 'Isn't *that* a divergence point?'

'Only certain parts of it,' Polly said.

'But it's definitely a ten. How did you talk Mr Dunworthy into it? I had a hell of a time talking him into letting me do Pearl Harbor, especially after what happened to Paul Kildow.'

'What happened to him?' Polly asked sharply.

'He got hit by shrapnel from a cannonball at Antietam,' Michael said. 'It was nothing, only a superficial wound, but you know how overprotective Dunworthy is. He refused to let him do any of the other battles in his assignment.'

'Perhaps that's why he's been cancelling drops,' Eileen said. 'Because he decided they were too dangerous. All the ones he's cancelled are battles and things, aren't they?'

'I need to go,' Polly said abruptly. 'I've only just remembered, I was supposed to have a fitting this afternoon. I must get to Wardrobe.'

'But I thought you were going to show me how to open the Bentley's doors and—'

'I'm sorry, I can't. Perhaps we can do it tomorrow.'

'But I thought you had to report in to Mr Dunworthy,' Eileen said. 'Do you want me to tell him—?'

'No. Don't. I'll come back after my fitting. I really must go. Michael, good luck at Dunkirk – I mean, Dover,' she said, and hurried off.

'What was that all about?' Michael asked, looking after her.

'I've no idea. She's seemed distracted all afternoon.'

'She is going to the Blitz.'

'I know, but she's done heaps of dangerous assignments. She's much more likely to be worried that Mr Dunworthy will cancel her drop. At least I needn't worry about him cancelling mine because it's too dangerous. Unless Alf and Binnie set fire to the manor or something.'

'Alf and Binnie?'

'Two of my evacuees. I'm observing the children who were evacuated from London.'

'Which was when?'

'September of 1939 to the end of the war. Didn't you attend any of your first-year history lectures?'

He laughed. 'I *meant*, when are you there?'

'Till May second, which is why I didn't know about Dunkirk.'

'If the evacuation lasted till the end of the war,' he said, 'maybe you can talk Dunworthy into letting you stay on to do VE Day. Or you could just not come back.'

She shook her head. 'The retrieval team would come after me. And even if I could elude them, staying would mean I'd have to put up with Alf and Binnie for another five—'

'Merope!' someone called.

Michael turned and looked across the quad. 'Someone's looking for you.'

It was Colin Templer. He loped up to them. 'Do you know where Polly is?'

'At Wardrobe,' Eileen said.

'I thought she said she was coming here.'

'She was. She did. She came to see Mr Dunworthy, but he's in with someone, and she couldn't wait.'

'What do you mean, he's in with someone? Mr Dunworthy's not here. He's in London. He won't be back till tonight.'

Eileen turned to Michael. 'But you said—'

'That damned secretary of his!' Michael exploded. 'He didn't say a word about Dunworthy's being gone. He just asked if I'd care to wait, and I assumed—'

'This is dreadful!' Eileen said. 'Now what am I going to do about my driving lessons?'

'*How* late tonight?' Michael asked Colin.

'I don't know,' Colin began, but Michael was already striding up the stairs and into Mr Dunworthy's office. 'You said Polly's over at Wardrobe?' Colin asked Eileen.

She nodded, and Colin took off at a run. Michael came back, shaking his head. 'He won't be back before midnight at the earliest. He went to see some temporal theorist named Ishiwaka. And here I wasted an entire afternoon – no offence,' he said. 'It's just that I didn't have enough time to get ready for this drop as it is, and now—'

'I know. I only have two days, and now I'll have to wait till tomorrow to get my driving lessons approved.'

'No, you won't,' he said, digging in his pockets. 'I got permission from him for lessons in piloting small craft when I thought I was going to Pearl Harbor. If he didn't fill it out ...' He pulled out a slip of paper and unfolded it. 'Good, he didn't. He just signed it. Here.'

'But won't you need it?'

'Not till I get back from Dover,' he said. 'I'll tell him I lost it and need another form.' He handed it to her.

'*Thank* you,' she said fervently. 'You've saved my life.' She looked at her watch. If she hurried, she could make it to Props and get the driving authorisation before they closed. 'I need to go.'

'So do I,' he said, walking her back to the gate. 'I need to go and memorise the map of Dover and the names of the ships that participated in the evacuation.'

They started out through the gate and nearly collided with Colin. 'I thought you were going to find Polly,' Eileen said.

'I was,' Colin said breathlessly. 'But when I got to Wardrobe, they asked me if I knew where you were, Mr Davies, and I said yes, and they said to come and tell you they need you to come and talk to them straightaway. They said they'd had to give your costume to Gerald Phipps and they need you to come in to try on a new one.'

OXFORD – APRIL 2060

B adri adjusted the folds of the net around Mike. 'I'm sending you through to 5 a.m. on May twenty-fourth,' he said.

Good, Mike thought. The evacuation wouldn't start till Sunday the twenty-sixth, and the civilian boats wouldn't start bringing soldiers back till the next day, so he'd have plenty of time to get to Dover and figure out how to get out to the docks.

'There may be slippage of an hour or two,' Badri said, 'depending on who's in the area and might see the shimmer.'

But when they sent him through a few minutes later, it was much darker than an hour or two before dawn should be – a total, blanketing darkness. He waited for his eyes to adjust, but there was no light to adjust to.

He couldn't see any stars *or* lights, though that could be due to the blackout. In May of 1940, no outdoor lights had been allowed, cars' lights had had to be masked, and windows had had to be covered with blackout curtains. The contemps had complained about how dangerous it had been to get around in the blackout, and now he could see – or, rather, not see – why. His first instinct was to put his hands out in front of him and feel his way forward, but this was the southeastern coast of England. He could be on the edge of a chalk cliff, and one step could send him plummeting to his death.

He stood still, listening. He could hear the faint sound of waves lapping the shore off to his right. From the twenty-third on, the fires of the burning town of Dunkirk had been visible from parts of the coast, but he couldn't see any red on the horizon. Or any horizon, for that matter. Which meant either this wasn't one of those parts or he'd come through earlier than the twenty-third, even though the whole point of picking this site was that it didn't have temporal slippage.

You can figure out the time later, he thought. *Right now you need to find out where you are.* The waves sounded level with him, not somewhere below. *Good.* He slid one foot slightly forward. Gravel. The shingle of a beach. Or a road down which someone would presently come driving with the shuttered headlights that only let the driver see a few feet ahead, in which case he needed to get off said road right away. But he couldn't hear any sound of an engine, and the road north of Dover wound along the tops of the cliffs, not down along the beaches.

He stooped and patted the gravel. It was damp. He swept his hand in a semicircle and could feel a patch of wet sand and what felt like a shell. Definitely a beach – though in 1940, an English beach was probably more dangerous than a road. It was likely to be mined or covered with barbed wire – or both – and in the dark he could easily trip and impale himself on a tank trap.

Props had sent a book of safety matches through with him. He debated lighting one to give him an idea of where he was. It should be all right. The beach had to be deserted. The drop couldn't have opened if there'd been anyone to see its shimmer. But that had been several minutes ago. A soldier might be patrolling or there might be a ship out there in the Channel. He couldn't see anything, but some vessels had run without lights to keep from being spotted by the Germans. And the shimmer would be visible for a long way over water. Even a match's tiny flame could be seen for miles. More than one World War II convoy had been sunk by submarines because a careless sailor had lit a cigarette.

So, no light. And unless he wanted to be blown up by a land mine, no wandering around in the dark. Which meant his only option was to stay put and hope dawn wasn't too far off. He lowered himself carefully down onto the sand and settled in to wait for dawn.

I could have been spending this time prepping in Oxford instead of sitting here in the dark, he thought. He could be memorising that list of naval ships that had participated in the evacuation he hadn't had time to, or finding out exactly where the returning troops had docked and how he was going to get access to the dock when the press wasn't allowed.

Damn Dunworthy and his schedule changes, he thought. The damp sand was soaking through his pants. He stood up, took his jacket off, folded it, sat down again, and resumed staring into the darkness. And shivering.

It was growing steadily chillier. *It's much too cold for May twenty-fourth,* he thought, and suddenly remembered every horror story he'd ever heard – the mediaeval historian they'd sent through to the wrong year who'd ended up smack in the middle of the Black Death; the one back in the early days of the net, when they'd still thought historians could affect events, who'd gone through to 1935 to shoot Hitler and found himself in East Berlin in 1970. And the historian who'd tried to go through to Waterloo – which was a divergence point just like Dunkirk – and ended up in America in the wilds of Sioux territory.

What if he wasn't in 1940 at all? Or what if, rather than being on an English beach, he was on one in the South Pacific, and the Japanese were about to invade? That would explain why he'd come through in the middle of the night – didn't the Japanese always sneak ashore before dawn?

Don't be ridiculous, he thought. *It's too cold to be the South Pacific.* So cold his legs were beginning to cramp. He rubbed them and then stretched them out. And jammed his foot against something hard. He jerked it back instantly. Had that been one of the metal struts of a tank trap? They sometimes had mines balanced on top, set to topple and explode at the slightest motion.

He scrambled to his knees and leaned forward, feeling cautiously along the sand to the base of whatever it was. *Rock*, he thought, relieved. Rock rising straight up out of the sand. The cliff? No, when he patted up its side, it was only slightly higher than his head and no more than four feet wide. It must be one of those freestanding rocks that occurred on beaches, the kind tourists climbed on. He manoeuvred around to sit with his back against it and straightened his legs again, cautiously this time.

It was a good thing, since he hit another rock. This one stood at an angle to the first one and was much wider and thicker. When he climbed up to feel how tall it was, the sound of the waves became suddenly louder, which explained why the drop site was here. The rocks could hide him – and the shimmer as the drop opened – from the beach.

But if they had, there wouldn't have been any slippage. The drop must be at least partly visible, either from the water or from the beach. Or somewhere above it. Civilian coastwatchers had been posted all along the eastern coast, and one of them might have their binoculars trained on the beach right now. Or would at 5 a.m., which was why he'd been sent through earlier.

Which means I'd better be careful when it begins to get light. If he didn't die of hypothermia first. Jesus, it was cold. He was going to have to put his jacket back on. He wished he had the one Wardrobe had given to Phipps. It was a lot warmer than this one. He stood up, legs protesting, put it on, and sat down again. *Come on*, he thought, *let's get this show on the road.*

Centuries crawled by. Mike took his jacket off and draped it over him blanket-style. He burrowed into the rock, trying to get warm, trying to stay awake. In spite of the cold, he could hardly keep his eyes open. *Isn't sleepiness the first sign of hypothermia?* he thought drowsily.

It's not hypothermia, it's time-lag. And the fact that you've been up all night and the night before that trying to get ready for this damned assignment. All so he could sit here in the dark and freeze to death. *I not only could have memorised the ships, I could have memorised the names of all the small craft, too, all seven hundred of them. And the names of all three hundred thousand soldiers they rescued.*

When the sky finally began to lighten several geologic ages later, he thought at first it was an illusion brought on by staring into the darkness too long. But that really was the outline of the rock opposite him he was seeing, tar-black against the velvet black of the sky, and when he stood up and peeked cautiously over the other rock towards the sound of the waves, the darkness was a shade greyer. Within minutes he could make out the line of white surf and behind him a looming cliff, ghostly pale in the darkness. A chalk cliff, which meant he was in the right place.

He wasn't between two rocks, though. It was a single rock, with a sand-filled hollow carved out of the middle by the tide, but he'd been right about its hiding him – and the shimmer – from the beach. He looked at the Bulova on his wrist. It said eleven-twenty. He'd set it for five just before he came through, which meant he'd been here more than six hours. No wonder he felt like he'd been on this beach for eons. He had.

And he couldn't see any particular reason why. He'd assumed someone had been in the vicinity at five, but there were no boats offshore or footprints on the beach. There weren't any beach fortifications either, no wooden stakes along the waterline to slow landing craft, no barbed wire.

Jesus, I hope the slippage didn't send me through in January. Or in 1938.

The only way to find out was to get off the beach. Which he needed to do anyway. If he was when and where he was supposed to be, the locals would think he was a German spy who'd just been put ashore by a U-boat and arrest him. Or shoot him. He needed to get out of here before full light. He put on his coat, brushed the sand off his trousers, peered over the rock in both directions, and then climbed out of the rock. He turned and looked up at the cliff. There was no one on top of it – at least the part he could see – and no way off the beach. And no way to tell which way Dover lay. He flipped a mental coin and set off towards the northern end, keeping close under the cliff so he couldn't be seen from above and looking for a path.

A few hundred yards from the rock he found one – a narrow zigzag cut into the chalk cliff. He sprinted up it, halting just short of the top to reconnoitre, but there was no one on its grassy top. He turned and looked out across the Channel, but even from up here he couldn't spot any ships. And no sign of smoke on the horizon.

And no farmhouses, no livestock, not even any fences, only the white gravel road he'd thought he might be on when he came through last night. *I'm in the middle of nowhere*, he thought.

But he couldn't be. The entire southeast coast of England had been dotted with fishing villages. *There's got to be one somewhere near here*, he thought, heading south to see what lay beyond the other headland. But if so, why hadn't he heard any church bells last night or this morning? *Let's just hope there is a village. And that it's within walking distance.*

It was. A huddle of stone buildings lay immediately beyond the headland, and beyond them a quay with a line of masted boats. There was a church, too. With a bell tower. The cliffs must have cut off the sound of the bells. He started down the road towards the village, keeping an eye out for a car he could hitch a ride in or, if he was lucky, the bus to Dover, but no vehicle of any kind came along the road the entire way.

It's too early to be up and around, he thought, and that went for the village, too. Its lone shop was closed, and so was the pub – the Crown and Anchor – and no one was on the street. He walked down to the quay, thinking the fishermen would likely be up, but there was no one there either. And though he walked out beyond the last house, there was no train station. And no bus stop. He walked back to the shop and peered in through the window, looking for either a bus schedule or something that would tell him which village this was. If he was really six miles north of Dover, it might be faster to walk it than wait for a bus. But the only sign he could see was a schedule for the Empress Cinema, which was showing *Follow the Fleet* from May fifteenth to the thirty-first. May was the right month, but *Follow the Fleet* had come out in 1937.

He went on to the Crown and Anchor and tried the door. It opened onto a dark hall. 'Hello? Are you open?' he called, and stepped inside.

At the end of the hallway was a stairway and a door leading into what must be the pub room. He could just make out settles and a bar in the near-darkness. An old-fashioned telephone, the kind with an earpiece on a cord, hung on the wall opposite the stairs, and next to it was a grandfather clock. Mike squinted at it. Five to eight. He hadn't come through at five, then. He set his Bulova, glad there was no one to see how clumsy he was at it, and then looked around for a bus schedule. On a small table next to the clock lay several letters. Mike bent over them, squinting to read the address of the top one. 'Saltram-on-Sea, Kent.'

That can't be right, he thought. Saltram-on-Sea was thirty miles south of Dover, not six miles north. The letter must be one that was being *mailed* to Saltram-on-Sea. But the tuppenny stamp in the corner had been cancelled, and the return address was Biggin Hill Airfield, which this obviously wasn't. He glanced cautiously up the narrow wooden stairs and then picked up the letters and shuffled through them. They were all to Saltram-on-Sea, and, clinching it, one of them was addressed to the Crown and Anchor.

Jesus, that meant there'd been locational slippage, and he'd have to take the bus, which meant he had to find out immediately when it went and where it stopped. 'Hello?' he called loudly up the stairs and into the pub room. 'Anyone here?'

No response, and no sound of any movement overhead. He

listened for another minute, then went into the semi-dark pub room to look for a bus schedule or the local newspaper. There wasn't one on the bar and the only thing on the wall behind the bar was another movie schedule, this one for *Lost Horizon*, which had come out in 1936 and was playing from June fifteenth through the thirtieth. *Christ, has there been temporal slippage, too?* he thought, going around behind the bar to see if there was a newspaper there. He had to find out the date.

There was a newspaper in the wastebasket, or a part of one. Half the sheet – the half with the name of the paper and the date, naturally – had been torn off, and the remaining half had been used to mop up something. He unwadded it carefully on the bar, trying not to tear the damp paper, but it was too dark in here to read the wet, grey pages.

He picked it up by the edges and carried it back out to the hall to read. 'Devastating Power of the German Blitzkrieg,' the headline said. Good. At least he wasn't in 1936. The main story's headline was missing, but there was a map of France with assorted arrows showing the German advance, which meant it wasn't the end of June either. By then, the fighting had been over for three weeks and Paris was already occupied.

'Germans Push Across Meuse.' They'd done that on May seventeenth. 'Emergency War Powers Act Passed.' That had happened on the twenty-second, and this had to be yesterday's newspaper, which would make this the twenty-third, which would mean the slippage had sent him through a day early, but that was great. It gave him an extra day to get to Dover, and he might need it. He read further down. 'National Service of Intercession to Be Held at Westminster Abbey.'

Oh no. That prayer service had been held on Sunday, May twenty-sixth, and if this was yesterday's paper, then it was Monday the twenty-seventh. 'Damn it,' he muttered. 'I've already missed the first day of the evacuation!'

'The pub doesn't open till noon,' a female voice said from above him.

73

He whirled, and his sudden jerk tore the wet newspaper in half. A pretty young woman with her hair in a pompadour and a very red mouth stood halfway down the stairs, looking curiously at the torn newsprint in his hands. And how the hell was he going to explain what he was doing with it? Or what he'd said about the evacuation. How much had she heard?

'Was it a room you were wanting?' she asked, coming down the rest of the stairs.

'No, I was just looking for the bus schedule,' he said. 'Can you tell me when the bus to Dover is due?'

'You're a *Yank*,' she said delightedly. 'Are you a flyer?' She looked past him out the door, as if expecting to see an aeroplane in the middle of the street. 'Did you have to bail out?'

'No,' he said. 'I'm a reporter.'

'A reporter?' she said, just as eagerly, and he realised she was much younger than he'd thought – seventeen or eighteen at the most. The pompadour and the lipstick had fooled him into thinking she was older.

'Yes, for the *Omaha Observer*,' he said. 'I'm a war correspondent. I need to get to Dover. Can you tell me what time the bus comes?' and when she hesitated, 'There is a bus to Dover from here, isn't there?'

'Yes, but I'm afraid you've only just missed it. It came yesterday, and it won't come again till Friday.'

'It only comes on Sundays and Fridays?'

'No. I told you, it came yesterday. On Tuesday.'

'An' if thou seest my boy, bid him make haste and meet me.'

WILLIAM SHAKESPEARE, *TWO GENTLEMEN OF VERONA*

OXFORD – APRIL 2060

Polly hurried out of Balliol's gate, up the Broad, and down Catte Street, hoping Mr Dunworthy hadn't glanced out of his windows and seen her standing in the quad talking to Michael and Merope. *I should have told them not to say anything about my being back*, she thought, but she'd have had to explain why, and she'd been afraid he might emerge from his office at any moment.

Thank goodness she hadn't gone blithely in and made her report. He already thought her project was too dangerous. He'd been protective of his historians since she was a first-year student, but he'd been absolutely hysterical about this project. He'd insisted on her drop site for the Blitz being within walking distance of Oxford Street, even though it would have been much easier to find a site in Wormwood Scrubs or on Hampstead Heath and take the tube in. It also had to be within a half-mile of both a tube station and whatever room she let. 'I want you to be able to reach your drop site quickly if you're injured,' he'd said.

'They *did* have hospitals in the 1940s, you know,' she'd said. 'And if I'm injured, how exactly will I walk half a mile?'

'Don't make jokes,' he'd snapped. 'It's possible to die on assignment, and the Blitz is an exceptionally dangerous place,' and launched into a twenty-minute lecture on the perils of blast from high-explosive bombs, shrapnel, and sparks from incendiaries. 'A woman in Canning Town got her foot entangled in the cord of a barrage balloon and was dragged into the Thames.'

'I am not going to be dragged into the Thames by a barrage balloon.'

'You could be struck by a bus which couldn't see you in the blackout, or murdered by a mugger.'

'I scarcely think—'

'Criminals thrived in the Blitz. The blackout provided them with cover of darkness, and the police were too busy digging bodies out of the rubble to investigate. The death of a victim found dead in an alley was simply put down to blast. I don't want to read your name in the death notices in *The Times*. A half-mile radius. That's final.'

And that hadn't been the only restriction. She was forbidden to rent a room in any house hit by a bomb before the end of the year, even though she'd only be there till the end of October, and the drop site had to be one that hadn't been hit at all, which eliminated three sites that would have worked nicely, but that had been destroyed in the last big raid of the Blitz in May 1941.

It was no wonder the lab still hadn't found a site. *I hope they locate one before Mr Dunworthy finds out I'm back*, she thought. *Or someone tells him.* She doubted if Mr Purdy would – he didn't even seem to realise she'd been gone – and hopefully Michael Davies would be too busy attempting to get his date changed and Merope'd be in too much of a hurry to get her driving permission for them to mention that they'd seen her.

She felt bad about ducking out on her promise to speak to Mr Dunworthy about Merope going to VE Day, but it couldn't be helped. And it wasn't as if time was an issue. Merope'd said she still had several months left to go on her evacuee assignment. *And I'll only be gone six weeks*, Polly thought. *I'll go and see him as soon as I'm safely back and persuade him to let her do it.*

If it was even necessary. He might already have changed his mind by then. In the meantime, Polly needed to keep out of Mr Dunworthy's way, hope the lab came up with a drop site soon, and be ready to go through the moment they did. To that end, she went to Props to get a wristwatch – this one radium-dialled, since the one she'd had last time hadn't been and had been nearly useless – a ration book and identity card made out in the name of Polly Sebastian, and letters of recommendation to use in applying for work as a shopgirl.

'What about a departure letter?' the tech asked her. 'Do you need anything special?'

'No, the same one I had last time will work – the Northumberland one. It needs to be addressed to Polly Sebastian and have an October 1940 postmark.'

The tech wrote that down and handed her thirty pounds.

'Oh, that's far too much,' she said. 'I'll have the wages I earn after the first week, and I don't expect my room and board to be more than ten and six a week. I'll only need ten pounds at the most.'

But the tech was shaking his head. 'It says here that you're to take twenty pounds for unforeseen emergencies.'

Authorised by Mr Dunworthy, no doubt, even though she had no business carrying that much money – it would have been a fortune to a 1940 shopgirl. But if she turned it down, the tech might report it to Mr Dunworthy. She signed for the money and the wristwatch, told the tech she'd pick up the papers in the morning, and went over to Magdalen to ask Lark Chiu if she could stay with her for a few nights, and when she said yes, sent her to Balliol to fetch her clothes and her research and sat down with the list of Underground shelters Colin had done for her.

Colin. She'd have to ask him not to say anything to Dunworthy. If he was still here. He'd probably gone back to school, which, in light of what Merope had said, might be just as well.

She memorised the Underground shelters and the dates and times they'd been hit and then started on Mr Dunworthy's list of forbidden addresses, which took her the rest of the night to commit to memory, even though it only included houses that had been hit in 1940, during the first half of the Blitz. Had every house in London been bombed by the time it was over?

The next morning she went over to Wardrobe to order her costume. 'I need a black skirt, white blouse, and a lightweight coat, preferably also black,' she told the tech, who promptly brought out a navy blue skirt.

'No, that won't work,' Polly said. 'I'm posing as a shop assistant, and department store employees in 1940 wore black skirts and white long-sleeved blouses.'

'I'm certain any dark skirt would do. This is a very dark navy. In most lights, one can't tell the difference.'

'No, it needs to be black. How long would it take to have a skirt like this made in black?'

'*Oh dear*, I've no idea. We're weeks behind. Mr Dunworthy suddenly made all sorts of changes in everyone's schedules, and we've had to reassign costumes and come up with new ones on no notice at all. When's your drop?'

'The day after tomorrow,' Polly lied.

'Oh dear. Let me see if I have anything else which might work.' She went into the dressing room and emerged after a bit with two skirts – one a 1960s mini and the other an i-com cargo kilt. 'These are the only blacks I could find.'

'*No*,' Polly said.

'The kilt's cellphone's only a replica. It's not dangerous.'

But the cellphone also hadn't been invented till the 1980s, and the cargo kilt itself hadn't been invented till 2014. She made the tech put in a rush order for a black skirt cut on the same pattern as the navy blue and then went over to the lab to tell them where she was staying and see if by some miracle they'd found a drop site.

The door of the lab was locked. To keep out historians irate at having had their drops cancelled? Polly knocked, and after a long minute a harassed-looking Linna let her in. 'I'm on the phone,' she said and hurried back to it. 'No, I know you were scheduled to do the Battle of the Somme first,' she said into it.

Polly went over to Badri at the console. 'Sorry to bother you. I was wondering if you'd found a drop site for me yet.'

'No,' he said, rubbing his forehead tiredly. 'The problem's the blackout.'

Polly nodded. The drop couldn't open if there was anyone nearby who might see it. Ordinarily the faint shimmer from an opening drop wasn't all that conspicuous, but in blacked-out London, even the light from a pocket torch or a gap in a house's curtains was instantly noticeable, and ARP wardens patrolled every neighbourhood, looking for the slightest infraction. 'What about Green Park or Kensington Gardens?'

'No good. They've both got anti-aircraft batteries, and the barrage balloons are headquartered in Regent's Park.'

There was an angry knock, and when Linna went to the door, a man in a fringed suede jacket and a cowboy hat stormed in, waving a printout. 'Who the bloody hell changed my schedule?' he shouted at Badri.

'I'll let you know as soon as I've found something,' Badri said to Polly, and this obviously wasn't the time to ask them to please hurry.

'I'll come back later,' she said.

'You can't cancel it!' the man in the cowboy hat shouted. 'I've been prepping to go to the Battle of Plum Creek for six months!'

Polly ducked past him and started for the door, waving at Linna, who was still on the phone. 'No, I realise you've already had your implants—' she was saying. Polly opened the door and went out.

And nearly fell over Colin, who was sitting on the pavement, his back to the lab's wall. 'Sorry,' he said and scrambled to his feet. 'Where have you been? I've been looking all over Oxford for you.'

'What are you doing out here?' Polly asked. 'Why didn't you come in?'

He looked sheepish. 'I can't. It's out of bounds. Mr Dunworthy's being completely unreasonable. I asked him to let me go on an assignment, and he phoned the lab and told them I wasn't to be allowed in.'

'Are you certain you didn't attempt to sneak into the net while someone else was going through?'

'No. All I did was say that on certain assignments someone my age could provide a different point of view from an older historian—'

'*What* assignment?' Polly asked. 'The Crusades?'

'Why does everyone keep bringing up the Crusades? That was something I wanted to do when I was a child, and I am *not*—'

'Mr Dunworthy's only trying to protect you. The Crusades are a dangerous place.'

'Oh, you're a fine one to talk about dangerous places,' he said. 'And Mr Dunworthy thinks every place is too dangerous, which is ridiculous. When he was young, *he* went to the Blitz. He went to all sorts of dangerous places, and back then they didn't even know where they were going. And the place I wanted to go wasn't remotely dangerous. It was the evacuation of the children from London. In World War II.'

Where she was going. Perhaps Merope was right.

'Speaking of dangerous,' he said, 'here are all the raids. I didn't know when you were coming back, so I did them from September seventh to December thirty-first. The list's awfully long, so I recorded it as well, in case you want to do an implant.' He handed her a memory tab.

'The times are when the bombing began, not when the air-raid alert sirens went. I'm still working on those, but I thought I'd better get the raid times to you in case you were going soon. And if you are, the raids generally began twenty minutes after the sirens sounded. Oh, and by the way, if you're on a bus, you may not be able to hear the sirens. The noise of the engine drowns them out.'

'Thank you, Colin,' Polly said, looking at the pages. 'You must have put in hours and hours of work on this.'

'I did,' he said proudly. 'It wasn't easy to find out what had been hit. The newspapers weren't allowed to publish the dates or addresses of specific buildings that were bombed—'

Polly nodded, still looking at the list. 'They couldn't print anything which might aid the enemy.'

'And a lot of the government's records were destroyed in the war and afterward, with the pinpoint and then the Pandemic. And there were lots of stray bombs. It's not like the V-1 and V-2 attacks, where they have the exact times and coordinates. I've listed the major targets and areas of concentration,' he said, showing her on the list, 'but there were lots of other things hit. The research said over a million buildings were destroyed, and this only lists a fraction of those. So just because the list says Bloomsbury, it doesn't mean you're safe wandering about some other part of London. Particularly the East End – Stepney and Whitechapel and places like that. They were the hardest hit. And the buildings on the list are only ones that were completely destroyed, not those that suffered partial damage or had their windows blown out. Hundreds of people were killed by flying glass or shrapnel from anti-aircraft shells. You need to keep as close to buildings as you can for protection if you're out during a raid. Shrapnel—'

'Can kill me. I know. You've been spending too much time with Mr Dunworthy. You're beginning to sound just like him.'

'I am not. It's just that I don't want anything to happen to you. And Mr Dunworthy's right about its being dangerous. Thirty thousand civilians were killed during the Blitz.'

'I *know*. I'll be careful, I promise.'

'And if you do get hit by shrapnel or something, don't worry. I promise I'll come and rescue you if you get in trouble.'

Oh dear, Merope *was* right. 'I promise I'll stay close to

buildings,' she said lightly. 'Speaking of Mr Dunworthy, you haven't told him I'm back, have you?'

'*No*. I haven't even told him *I'm* here. He thinks I'm at school.'

Good, then she needn't worry about him giving her away. 'Thank you for the list. It's enormously helpful.' She smiled at him, then remembered that wasn't a good idea under the circumstances. 'I'd best get on with my prep,' she said and started across the road.

'Wait,' he said, running to catch up with her. 'Is there any other research you need me to do? Besides the siren times, I mean? Do you need a list of the other shelters in case you can't get to an Underground station?' he asked eagerly. 'Or a list of the types of bombs?'

'No. You've spent too much time helping me already, Colin, and you've your own schoolwork to do—'

'We're out on holiday all this week,' he said, 'and I don't mind. Truly. It's good practice for when I'm a historian. I'll go and do them straightaway,' and he loped off down the street.

Polly went over to Research and had Colin's list of raids implanted so she wouldn't have to waste time memorising them, picked up her papers and letters from Props, and then went over to the Bodleian to study. She'd already memorised all this material once before, when she'd thought she was going to the Blitz first, but she'd forgotten most of it in the interim. She went over rationing, the blackout, the events a contemp in the autumn of 1940 would know about – the Battle of Britain, Operation Sea Lion, the Battle of the North Atlantic – and then committed the map of Oxford Street to memory. She debated doing the same with the Underground map, but those were posted in every tube station. Instead, she'd better memorise the numbers of the buses and—

'I've been looking all over for you,' Colin said, flopping down in a chair across the table from her. 'I forgot to ask you, where will you be living while you're there? There are thousands of shelters in London.'

'Somewhere in Marylebone, Kensington, or Notting Hill. It depends on where I can find a room to let.' She told him about Mr Dunworthy's walking-distance-from-Oxford-Street restriction.

'I'll begin with the shelters inside that radius, then,' he said, 'and if there's time, I'll map the rest of the West End. Oh, and when are you coming back? So I can mark the shelters you should stay out of.'

'October twenty-second,' she said.

'Six weeks,' he repeated thoughtfully. 'And then you're doing the Zeppelin attacks. How long will you be in 1915?'

'I don't know. It hasn't been scheduled yet. I can't afford to think about it just now. I've got to concentrate on making it through this one. Look, Colin, I've got a lot of studying to do. Were the dates all you needed?'

'Yes. No. I need to ask a favour of you.'

'Colin, I'd be glad to put in a good word for you with Mr Dunworthy, but I doubt very much if he'll listen. He's adamant about not letting anyone go to the past until they're twenty. And I know you've already been to the past and probably one of the most dangerous places you could ever go, but—'

'No, it's nothing like that.'

'It's not?'

'No. I want you to go real-time when you go to the Blitz, not flashtime.'

'I am,' she said, surprised. That certainly wasn't what she'd been expecting him to say. 'Mr Dunworthy insisted on a half hour on-and-off in case I'm injured, so it has to be real-time.'

'Oh good.'

What was he up to? 'Why do you want me to go real-time on this assignment?'

'Not on this assignment. On all your assignments.'

'All my—?'

'Yes. So I can catch up. In age. The thing is …' He paused and swallowed hard. 'The thing is, I think you're simply smashing—'

Oh dear. 'Colin, you're—' She stopped herself from saying 'a child' just in time. '—seventeen. I'm twenty-five—'

'I know, but it's not as though we were ordinary people. If we were, I agree, it would be rather off-putting—'

'And illegal.'

'And illegal,' he conceded, 'but we're not, we're historians. Or, at least you're a historian, and I will be, and we've got time travel, so I needn't always be younger than you. Or illegal.' He grinned. 'Listen, if I do four two-year assignments or six eighteen-month assignments, and I do them all flash-time, I can be twenty-five by the time you come back from the Blitz.'

'You can't—'

'I know, Mr Dunworthy's a problem, but I'll think of some way to convince him. And even if he prevents me from going to the past till I'm a third-year, I can still manage it so long as you don't do any more assignments flash-time.'

'Colin—'

'It's not like I'm asking you to wait years and years. Well, it would be years and years, but mine, not yours, and I don't mind. And it wouldn't have to be all that many years if you took me with you to the Blitz.'

'Absolutely not.'

'I don't mean to *do* the Blitz. If I get killed, I'll never catch up to you. I'd go north to where the evacuees went.'

'No,' Polly said. 'And I thought you wanted to catch up to me. If you go with me, our comparative ages will stay the same.'

'Not if I don't come back with you. I could stay till the end of the war – that would be five years – and then come back flash-time. That would make me twenty-two, and I'd only have two or three assignments to go. I could do those flash-time as well, so you wouldn't have to wait any time at all.'

She *must* put a stop to this. 'Colin, you need to find someone your own age.'

'Exactly. And you'll be my own age as soon as—'

'This is ridiculous. You'll change your mind a thousand times about what you want between now and when you're twenty-five. You changed your mind about wanting to go to the Crusades—'

'No, I didn't.'

'But you said—'

'I only tell people that so they won't try to talk me out of it. I fully intend to go there, *and* the World Trade Center. And I won't change my mind about this either. How old were you when you knew you wanted to be a historian?'

'Fourteen, but—'

'And you still want to be one, don't you?'

'Colin, that's different.'

'How? You knew what you wanted, and I know what I want. And I'm three years older than you were. I know you think this is some sort of childish calf love, that seventeen's too young to be in love with someone—'

No, she thought, *I know it's not,* and felt suddenly sorry for him.

Mistake. He clearly took her silence for encouragement. 'It's not as though I were asking for any sort of *commitment,*' he said. 'All I want is for you to give me a chance to catch up to you, and then, when we're both the same age – or, wait, do you like older men? I can shoot for any age you like. I mean, not seventy or something: I don't want to have to wait my entire life, but I'd be willing to do thirty, if you like older men—'

'Colin!' she said, laughing in spite of herself. 'I have no business letting you talk to me like this. You're seventeen—'

'No, listen, when I'm the right age, whatever it is, if you don't like me or you've fallen in love with someone else in the meantime – you haven't, have you? Fallen in love with someone?'

'Colin—'

'You *have*. I *knew* it. Who is it? That American chap?'

'What American chap?'

'Over at Balliol. The tall, good-looking one, Mike something.'

'Michael Davies,' she said. 'He's not an American. He had an American L-and-A implant. And he's just a friend.'

'Then which historian is it? Not Gerald Phipps, I hope. He's a complete stick—'

'I am not in love with Gerald Phipps, or any other historian.'

'Good, because we're absolutely *made* for each other. I mean, a contemp won't work, because either they've died before you were born, or they're *ancient*. And there's no point in falling in love with someone in this time because even if you start off at the same age, after a few flash-time assignments you'll be too old for *him*. And *they* can't come and rescue you if you get in trouble. So the only thing left's another historian, and as it happens, *I'm* going to be a historian.'

'Colin, you are seventeen—'

'But I won't be soon. You'll feel differently about this when I'm twenty-fi—'

'You are seventeen *now*, and I have work to do. This conversation is over. Now go away.'

'Not until you at least promise me you'll do your Zeppelin assignment real-time.'

'I'm not promising anything.'

'Well, then at least promise me you'll think about it. I plan to be devastatingly handsome and charming when I'm twenty-five.' He grinned his crooked grin at her. 'Or thirty. You can let me know which you'd prefer when I bring you the sirens list.' And he raced off, leaving Polly shaking her head and smiling.

She had a feeling he was right – with that reddish-blond hair and disarming grin, he was going to be fairly irresistible in a few years. And she wouldn't be surprised if ten minutes from now, he showed up with another question and more arguments as to why they were made for each other, so she took the maps back to Lark's rooms to memorise, stopping on the way to ask Wardrobe when her black skirt would be ready.

'Three weeks,' the tech said.

'*Three weeks?* I told you to put in a rush order.'

'That is a rush order.'

Which meant she'd better settle for the navy blue. She didn't want the lack of a skirt to keep her from going. *For want of a nail, the shoe was lost ...* she thought, quoting one of Mr Dunworthy's favourite adages.

She told the tech she'd decided the navy blue would work after all.

'Oh, excellent,' the tech said, relieved. 'Will you need shoes?'

'No, the ones I have will work, but I'll need a pair of stockings.'

The tech found her a pair, and Polly took the clothes over to Magdalen, memorised the map, and reread her notes on department stores. She was only halfway through them when the phone rang.

Colin, I do not have time for this, she thought. But it was Linna. 'We've found a site, believe it or not, but the problem is, I can't fit you in till a fortnight from now unless you can get here in the next half-hour. If you're not ready yet—'

'I'm ready. I'll be there,' Polly said and scrambled into her costume, nearly snagging her stockings in her haste. She grabbed her ration book, identity card, departure letter, and letters of recommendation, and crammed them into her shoulder bag. Oh, and her money. And Mr Dunworthy's twenty extra pounds. And her wristwatch.

And now all I need is to run into Mr Dunworthy, she thought, putting it on as she dashed out of Magdalen and hurried along the High, but her luck held, and she arrived at the lab with five minutes to spare. 'Thank goodness,' Linna said. 'I was wrong about that slot a fortnight from now. The next open time I have is the sixth of June.'

'D-Day,' Polly said.

'Yes, well, your D-Day's exactly five minutes from now,' Badri said, coming over. He positioned her in the net, taking measurements and then adjusting her shoulder bag so it was further inside the net. 'You're going through to 6 a.m. on the tenth of September.'

Good, Polly thought. *That will give me the entire day to find a flat and then go and apply for jobs.*

Badri adjusted the folds of the net. 'Ascertain your temporal-spatial location as soon as you go through, and note any slippage.' He went back to the console and began typing. 'And make certain you use more than one landmark to fix the location of your drop, not just a single street or building. Bombing can change the landscape, and it's notoriously difficult to judge distances and directions in a bombed-out area.'

'I know,' she said. 'Why do you want me to note the slippage? Are you anticipating more than usual?'

'No, the estimated slippage is one to two hours. Linna, ring up Mr Dunworthy. He wanted to be notified when we found a drop site.'

No, Polly thought, *not when I'm this close.*

'He's in London,' Linna called back. 'He went to see Dr Ishiwaka again. When I phoned his secretary with the slippage data, he said he won't be back till tonight.'

Thank goodness.

'All right, never mind,' Badri said. 'Polly, you're to report back to us as soon as you've located a place to live and been hired.' The draperies began to lower around her. 'And note exactly how much slippage you encounter when you go through. Ready?'

'Yes. No, wait. I forgot something. Colin was doing some research for me.'

'Is it something necessary for your assignment?' Badri asked. 'Do you need to postpone?'

'No.' She couldn't risk Mr Dunworthy cancelling her drop, and she had the times of the raids. Colin had said the sirens had generally gone twenty minutes before the raids began, and she could get the list from him when she came back through to tell them her address. 'I'm ready.'

The net immediately began to shimmer. 'Tell Colin—' she said, but it was too late. The net had already opened.

*Every owner of a motor vehicle should be ready, in
the event of invasion, to immobilise his car, bicycle,
or lorry the moment the order is given.*

BRITISH MINISTRY OF TRANSPORT POSTER, 1940

WARWICKSHIRE – SPRING 1940

The vicar came to give Eileen and the rest of the staff their first driving lessons the day after she returned from Oxford.

'Aren't you frightened?' Una asked Eileen.

'No,' she said, taking off her apron. 'I'm certain the vicar's an excellent teacher.' *And, thanks to my time in Oxford, I shall be an excellent pupil.*

In spite of her having had only two days and no help from Polly, she'd learned not only how to get into the Bentley, but how to start it and how to work the gear stick and the hand brake. Just before she'd come back, she'd driven it along the High, up Headington Hill, and safely back again. 'I rather think these lessons will be fun,' she told Una and went out to the car. But it wasn't the Bentley, it was the vicar's battered Austin.

'Her ladyship had a WVS meeting in Daventry,' the vicar explained.

And she didn't want her car damaged, Eileen thought.

'But driving one car is much like driving another,' the vicar said.

Not true. The clutch pedal on the Austin seemed to operate on an entirely different principle. It stalled no matter how slowly Eileen let it out – if she could even get it started in the first place. Either the engine refused to turn over, or she flooded it. When she finally did succeed in starting it and putting it in gear, it died before she'd gone ten yards. 'The old girl's rather temperamental, I'm afraid,' Mr Goode said, smiling at her. 'You're doing very well.'

'I thought clergymen weren't supposed to tell lies,' she said, and after three more tries she managed to nurse the Austin all the way to the end of the drive. But compared with Una, who couldn't even remember which foot to put on which pedal and burst into tears every time the vicar attempted to coach her, she was positively brilliant.

Samuels was even worse, convinced he could master 'that bloody car' by brute force and blasphemy, and Eileen was surprised the vicar didn't abandon the whole project, Lady Caroline or no Lady Caroline. But he kept grimly on, in spite of his students and the Hodbins, who'd decided it was the funniest thing they'd ever seen, and who raced home from school on lesson days to sit on the steps and heckle.

'What do they think they're doin'?' Alf would ask Binnie in a loud voice.

'Learnin' to drive, for when the jerries invade.'

Alf would watch the proceedings for a moment and then innocently ask, 'Whose side are they on?' and they would both collapse in merriment.

I must *get back to Oxford on my next half-day out and practise on an Austin*, Eileen thought, but she didn't make it. On Monday morning four new evacuees arrived, and she had no chance to get to the drop, and a week later evacuees they'd had before began to come back – Jill Potter and Ralph and Tony Gubbins – all of whom joined the Hodbins on the steps to watch the driving lessons and shout taunts.

'Get a 'orse!' Alf yelled during a particularly bad lesson of

Una's. 'You'd 'ave better luck teaching it to drive than this lot, Vicar!'

'I think the vicar should teach me to drive,' Binnie said. 'I'd be heaps better than Una.'

No doubt, Eileen thought, but a Hodbin version of Bonnie and Clyde, with Binnie driving the getaway car, was the last thing the vicar needed.

'If you truly want to help win the war, go and collect paper for the scrap drive or something,' she told the Hodbins, only to find out the next day they'd 'collected' Lady Caroline's appointment book, a first folio of Shakespeare, and all of Mrs Bascombe's recipes.

'They're impossible,' she told the vicar when he came for her next lesson.

'Our faith teaches us that no one is beyond the hope of re-demption,' he said in his best pulpit manner, 'although I must admit the Hodbins test the limits of that belief,' and proceeded to show her how to reverse the car. She felt guilty that he was spending so much time teaching her. He should be working with someone who'd be here when the war began in earnest, and she only had a few weeks left. She comforted herself with the knowledge that Backbury had had almost no need for ambu-lance drivers. It hadn't been bombed, and only one plane had crashed – in 1942, a German Messerschmitt west of the village. The pilot had died on impact and hadn't needed an ambulance. And at any rate, petrol rationing would soon prevent anyone from driving anything.

She doubted extra lessons would help Una or Samuels, and Mrs Bascombe was still staunchly refusing to be taught. 'I'm willing to do my bit to help win the war same as the next one,' she told the vicar when he tried to persuade her, 'but not in a motor car, and I don't care what her ladyship wants.'

'I don't mind motor cars,' Binnie said. 'You could give *me* lessons, Vicar.'

'What do you think?' he asked Eileen later. 'She *is* a quick study.'

Which was putting it mildly. 'I think she's dangerous enough on foot,' Eileen said, but after a week of her stealing signboards off front gates ('We *had* to,' she said when caught with Miss Fuller's Hyacinth Cottage sign, and showed Eileen a year-old Ministry of Defence directive ordering all signposts to be taken down), Eileen decided driving might be the lesser of two evils.

'But you're to do *exactly* as the vicar says,' she told Binnie sternly, 'and you're not to set foot in the Austin except during driving lessons.'

Binnie nodded. 'Can Alf 'ave lessons, too?'

'*No.* He's not allowed to be in the car with you at all. Is that clear?'

Binnie nodded, but when she and the vicar pulled up to the manor after her first tentative trip down the drive, Alf was leaning over the backseat. 'We found him at the end of the drive,' the vicar explained. 'He'd twisted his ankle.'

''E ain't able to walk at all,' Binnie said.

'A likely story,' Eileen said, opening the back door. 'You do not have a sprained ankle, Alf. Out. Now.'

Alf got out, wincing. '*Ow!* It 'urts!' Binnie helped him limp around to the servants' entrance, leaning heavily on her.

'They're quite good,' the vicar said, watching them. 'They should consider going on the stage.' He grinned at Eileen. 'Especially since the sprained ankle was a last-minute improvisation. We came round the curve rather suddenly and caught him preparing to spread tacks on the drive.'

'No doubt to puncture the Germans' tyres when they invade.'

'No doubt,' he said. He looked after Binnie, who was half-carrying Alf inside. 'But to prevent any further attempts on my tyres, I think it's best I keep him under my eye during future lessons. You needn't worry, I have no intention of letting him behind the wheel, and besides, he's not tall enough to reach the pedals.' He smiled. 'Binnie's actually quite good. I'm glad you suggested I give her lessons.'

Yes, well, we'll see, Vicar, Eileen thought, but even though Binnie drove much too fast – 'Ambulances *got* to go fast, to get to 'ospital before the people die,' she said – the lessons otherwise proceeded without a hitch, and Eileen was immensely grateful for at least some time when she needn't worry what the Hodbins were up to, because four new evacuees had arrived, one of whom was a bedwetter and all of whom had arrived in rags. Eileen spent every spare moment mending and sewing on buttons.

There weren't many spare moments, though. Lady Caroline had decided everyone should learn to use a stirrup pump, and announced that the vicar was going to give them lessons in how to disable a motor car by removing the distributor head and leads. In between, Eileen attempted to keep an eye on Alf and Binnie, who'd stopped heckling Una's driving lessons and moved on to more ambitious projects, such as digging up Lady Caroline's prize roses to plant a Victory garden, and Eileen began counting the days to her liberation.

When she had the time. Lady Caroline's son Alan arrived home on holiday from Cambridge with two friends, which meant even more laundry and beds to make up, and, as the war news grew worse, more and more evacuees arrived. By the end of March, there were so many the manor couldn't take them all. They had to be billeted in the surrounding villages, and in every cottage and farm in the area.

Eileen and the vicar used her driving lessons to pick up the draggled-looking children at the station. They were often sobbing and/or train-sick, and more than one vomited in the vicar's car as he and Eileen delivered them to their assigned billets – some of which were extremely primitive, with outhouses and stern foster parents who believed regular beatings were good for five-year-olds. If Eileen hadn't had her hands full with her own evacuees, she would have been more than able to view evacuees 'in a variety of situations'.

But there were up to twenty-five children, more than half of them their original evacuees who'd come back. By mid-April, all of them had returned except Theodore. *His mother probably couldn't get him onto the train*, Eileen thought, wearily making up more cots. *I can't believe I ever complained about not having enough evacuees.*

She was so busy she didn't even attempt to go to the drop, though she hadn't been through since February. Even if she'd had the time, it was nearly impossible to get away without being spotted by the Hodbins and followed, or lectured to by Mrs Bascombe on the dangers of meeting young men in the woods. And there was only a week of her assignment left.

Surely I can last a few more days, she thought, but when two more batches of evacuees arrived, all with head lice, she wasn't certain she'd make it. She spent the entire week washing their hair with paraffin.

It was after midnight on Sunday before she was able to lock herself in her room, rip open a section of her coat's hem, and take out the letter Props had sent with her, although it was probably just as well she hadn't been able to do it before. No hiding place was safe from the Hodbins.

The letter was addressed to her, and the return address was a nonexistent village in remote Northumberland. It and the postmark were smudged slightly to make them unreadable. She tore open the letter.

'Dear Eileen,' it read. 'Come home at once. Mother's very bad. I hope you are in time. Kathleen.'

It was to be found lying on her bed for Mrs Bascombe or Una to read after she'd gone. She debated hiding it under her mattress till tomorrow afternoon, then thought of the Hodbins and stuck it back inside the lining of her coat and basted the hem shut.

She got up at five on Monday and worked frantically all morning so everything would be in order before her half-day out began at one. She hoped they could find someone to replace her. She'd assumed Lady Caroline would simply hire another maid when she left, but yesterday Mrs Bascombe had said that Mrs Manning had been advertising for help for three weeks and hadn't had a single reply. 'It's the war. Girls who should be in service running off to join the Wrens or the ATS. Chasing after soldiers is all girls think of nowadays.'

Not all, Eileen thought, shrugging out of her uniform and into the blouse and skirt she'd arrived in. She retrieved the envelope from her coat lining, took the letter out, arranged them to look like she'd flung them down in haste, and pulled on her coat.

There was a knock on the door. 'Eileen?' Una said.

Oh, what now? Eileen opened the door a crack. 'What is it, Una?'

'Her ladyship wants to see you in the drawing room.'

Eileen couldn't tell Una she was just leaving, not when she'd supposedly packed and departed instantly after reading her sister's letter, too distraught to let anyone know. She'd have to go and see what Lady Caroline wanted. *It's probably another set of lousey bedwetters*, she thought, changing back into her uniform and hurrying along the corridor. *Or she's decided the staff should learn to operate an anti-aircraft gun.* Well, whatever it was, she wouldn't have to do it after today. She'd never have to stand there again with her hands folded and her eyes demurely down, taking orders and saying, 'You asked for me, ma'am?'

'You asked for me, ma'am?' she said.

'Yes,' Lady Caroline said grimly. 'Miss Fuller came to see me just now. While she was at the Women's Institute meeting yesterday, someone stole the hood ornament and the door handles off her Daimler.'

'Does she know who it was?' Eileen asked, even though she already knew the answer.

'Yes. She saw one of the culprits running away with them. It was Alf Hodbin. This sort of disgraceful behaviour cannot be allowed to continue. Heaven knows, I am eager to do my bit, as it were, but I cannot have criminals at the manor.'

'I'll see to it Alf returns them,' Eileen lied. 'Will that be all, ma'am?'

'No. The billeting officer, Mrs Chambers, is coming this afternoon. She's bringing three more children. Two of them were originally to be sent to Canada, but their parents decided the North Atlantic was too dangerous.'

It is, Eileen said silently, thinking of the *City of Benares*, which would be torpedoed and go down with more than a hundred evacuees aboard in September.

'Mrs Chambers assures me they're extremely well-behaved children,' Lady Caroline said.

Eileen doubted that, and even if they were, three days in the company of Alf and Binnie could turn an angel into a truanting, stone-throwing, distributor-stealing hooligan.

'You'll need to prepare cots for the children,' Lady Caroline said. 'I shan't be here this afternoon. Mrs Fitzhugh-Smythe and I have a Home Defence meeting in Nuneaton, so you will need to fill up the paperwork for Mrs Chambers when she arrives. She'll be here at three.'

And this is the last time you can make me do something on my half-day out, Eileen thought. 'Yes, ma'am. Will there be anything else?'

'Tell Mrs Chambers I'm sorry I wasn't able to be here,' she said, pulling on her gloves. 'Oh, and after you have the children settled, this cotton lint needs to be torn into strips and rolled for bandages. I promised they'd be done for my St John's Ambulance meeting tomorrow. And tell Samuels to have the car brought round.' She picked up her bag. 'You may go.'

That is just what I intend to do, Eileen thought, running down to tell Samuels and then pelting back up to her room. But before she could even get her uniform unbuttoned, Una appeared to tell her that Mrs Chambers was downstairs with three children.

'There must be some mistake,' Una said, nearly in tears. 'They can't be for here, can they?'

'Unfortunately, yes. Has her ladyship gone?'

Una nodded. 'What will we *do* with more children?' she wailed. 'We already have so many!'

And Una would never be able to manage the billeting forms. Eileen glanced at her watch. Half past two. The children wouldn't be home from school for another hour. *I'm already leaving her and Mrs Bascombe in the lurch,* Eileen thought. *At least I can get the new evacuees settled before I leave.*

'Go and make up three more cots in the nursery,' she said, 'and I'll go and speak with her. Where are they?'

'In the morning room. How will we manage thirty-two children with only the three of us?'

The two of you, Eileen corrected, hastening down to the morning room. Lady Caroline would simply have to exert herself and find a new maid. Or pitch in and do that bit for the war effort she was always talking about. She opened the door to the morning room. 'Mrs Chambers, her ladyship asked me to—'

Theodore Willett was standing there with his suitcase. 'I want to go home,' he said.

SALTRAM-ON-SEA – 29 MAY 1940

M ike stared at the girl. 'What did you say?' he asked. He had to have heard her wrong.

'I said, the bus came yesterday. It comes on Tuesdays and Fridays.'

Which meant today was Wednesday the twenty-ninth, and he'd already missed three days of the evacuation.

'It used to be every day,' she said, 'but since the war—'

'But Friday's the thirty-first,' Mike exploded. 'There has to be a bus before then.' The entire British Army would have been evacuated by then. He'd have missed the whole thing. 'What about Ramsgate? When's the next bus that goes there?'

'I'm afraid that's Friday, as well,' the girl said. 'It's the same bus, you see.' She'd retreated warily up a step, and he realised he'd been yelling.

'I'm sorry,' Mike said. 'It's just that I was supposed to be in Dover this afternoon to cover a story, and now I don't know how I'm going to get there. How far's the nearest train – I mean, railway – station?' If there was one in the next village, maybe he could walk to it.

'Eight miles,' Daphne said, 'but there haven't been any passenger trains from there since the start of the war.'

Of course there hadn't. 'What about a car? Is there one in the village I could rent – I mean, hire? Or someone I could pay to drive me into Dover? I could pay—' Oh Christ, what was the going rate for renting a car in 1940? '—three pounds.'

'Three pounds?' Her eyes widened. 'I always heard Yanks were rich.'

Which meant that was way too much. 'I'm not rich. It's just *really* important I get there today.'

'Oh. Mr Powney might be able to take you in his lorry,' she suggested, 'but I don't know if he's back yet.'

'Back?'

'He went to Hawkhurst yesterday to buy a bull,' she explained. 'He may have decided to stay over. He hates driving in the blackout. I'll ask Dad. Back in a moment.' She ran back up the stairs, glancing flirtatiously over her shoulder at him as she went. 'Dad?' he heard her say. 'Is Mr Powney back from Hawkhurst yet?'

'No. Who's that you're talking to, Daphne?'

'A Yank. He's a reporter.'

Mike couldn't hear the rest of the conversation. After a minute, Daphne ran back down the stairs. 'Dad says he's not back, but he should be sometime this morning.'

'And there's no one else here with a truck – I mean, a lorry? Or a motor car?'

'Dr Grainger has one, but he's not here either. He's visiting his sister in Norwich, and the vicar donated the tyres on his to the rubber drive. And what with the petrol rationing, I— Oh, here's Miss Fintworth,' she said as a thin, frowsy-haired woman came in. 'Our postmistress. Perhaps she'll know when Mr Powney's coming back.'

She didn't. 'Would you give this to him when he arrives?' she asked, handing Daphne a letter. Daphne stuck it with several others behind the bar, and Miss Fintworth went out, brushing past a toothless old man on his way in.

'Mr Tompkins will know,' Daphne said. 'Mr Tompkins,' she

called to him, 'do you know when Mr Powney's coming back?'

Mr Tompkins muttered something Mike couldn't make out at all, but Daphne apparently understood it. 'He says Mr Powney told him he planned to start back as soon as it was light. So he should be here by nine or half past.'

Nine-thirty, and then it would take them at least two hours to drive to Dover, which would put him there by noon. If Powney didn't have to put his new bull away first or milk the cows or feed the chickens or something.

'Here, I'll make you a nice cup of tea while you wait,' Daphne said, 'and you can tell me all about the States. You said you were from Omaha? That's in Ohio, isn't it?'

'Nebraska,' he said absently, trying to decide whether he should walk north of the village and try to hitch a ride or whether he was better off waiting here.

'That's in the Wild West, isn't it?' Daphne asked. 'Are there red Indians there?'

Red Indians? 'Not anymore,' he said. 'How many—?'

'Do you know any gangsters?'

She was clearly not a historian. 'Nope, sorry. How many vehicles go through here in a day, Daphne?'

'A day?'

'Never mind,' he said. 'I will have that cup of tea.'

'Oh good. You can tell me all about – where did you say you were from? Nebraska?'

Yes, but thanks to Dunworthy changing my schedule, I didn't have time to research it, so I don't know anything about it. It was obvious Daphne didn't either, but he'd still better avoid the subject. 'Why don't you tell me about the village instead?'

'I'm afraid there's nothing to tell. Scarcely anything happens in this part of the world.'

Less than fifty miles from here the British and French armies were being pushed into a desperate corner by the Germans, a makeshift armada was being organised to go and rescue them, and the outcome of the entire war depended on whether that rescue was successful or not, and she didn't know anything about it. He guessed he shouldn't be surprised. The news of it had been kept out of the papers till the evacuation was nearly over, and the only contemps who'd known about it were those who'd seen Dunkirk's smoke on the horizon or the trains full of wounded and exhausted soldiers arriving home.

And Saltram-on-Sea didn't have a train station. But it did have boats, and Mike was surprised the Small Vessels Pool hadn't been here. Its officers had driven up and down the Channel coast commandeering fishing boats and yachts and motor launches and their crews to go and pick up the stranded soldiers.

'I suppose you've been in lots of exciting places,' Daphne said, setting a cup of tea in front of him. 'And seen lots of the war. Is that why you need to get to Dover? Because of the war?'

'Yes. I'm writing a story for my paper on invasion preparations along the coast. How has Saltram-on-Sea prepared?'

'Prepared? I don't know ... we've the Home Guard ...'

'What do they do? Patrol the beaches at night?'

'No. Mostly they practise drilling.' She dropped her voice to a whisper. 'And sit in here bragging about what they did in the last war.'

So whatever had kept the drop from opening last night, it hadn't been the Home Guard. 'Do you have any coastwatchers?'

'Dr Grainger.'

Who was in Norwich, visiting his sister.

Mr Tompkins piped up from his table with a string of unintelligible syllables. 'What did he say?' Mike asked Daphne.

'He said our boys will never let Hitler get to France.'

Yes, well, right now Hitler was in France, had taken Boulogne and Calais, and was about to take Paris.

'Dad says our boys will chase Hitler back to Berlin with his tail between his legs,' Daphne said. 'He says we'll have the war won in two weeks.'

Doesn't anybody *ever see a disaster coming?* Mike wondered. This was just like Pearl Harbor. In spite of dozens of clues and warnings, the contemps had been caught completely off-guard. They hadn't seen the World Trade Center coming either, or Jerusalem, or the Pandemic. And at St Paul's, the day before a terrorist walked in with a pinpoint bomb under his arm and blew the cathedral and half of London to smithereens, the burning topic had been whether or not it was appropriate to sell *Light of the World* T-shirts in the gift shop.

At least the contemps here had the excuse that the news from France had been heavily censored. On the other hand, they'd been at war for over eight months, during which Hitler had sliced through half of Europe like a knife through butter. And Dunkirk was right across the Channel.

You'd think they'd have figured out *something* was up.

But apparently not. None of the farmers and fishermen who came in over the next hour discussed anything but the weather, and all Daphne was interested in talking about was American movie stars. 'I suppose you meet a lot of them, being a reporter. Have you ever met Clark Gable?'

'No.'

'Oh,' she said, sounding even more disappointed than when he'd told her there weren't any red Indians. 'He's my favourite film star,' and proceeded to tell him the entire plot of a movie she'd seen the week before, involving spies, amnesia, and an epic search for a lost love. 'He searched for her for years and years,' Daphne said. 'It was terribly romantic.'

And meanwhile, up in Dover, the Royal Navy's organising boats into convoys, and retired sailors and paddle-boat captains and fishermen are volunteering to man them, Mike thought, *and I'm missing it.* And it wasn't as if he could go back to Oxford and try again. Once a historian had been in a temporal location, he couldn't be in it again, and that wasn't just one of Dunworthy's overprotective precautions. It was a law of time travel, as a couple of early time travellers had found out the hard way. The night of the twenty-eighth and now the morning of the twenty-ninth were out of bounds to him forever.

Maybe I can do what's left of the evacuation and then go back and come through and do the first three days, he thought, but Dunworthy would never let him. If something went wrong and he was still here when his deadline on the twenty-eighth arrived, he'd be the one who was dead. And on a second try there might be even more slippage.

Nine o'clock, and then nine-thirty and ten, came and went with no sign of Mr Powney. *I can't afford to sit here all day*, Mike thought and told Daphne he was going to go and look around the village.

'Oh, but I'm certain Mr Powney will be along soon,' Daphne said. 'He must have got a late start.'

So did I, Mike thought. He told her he needed to interview some of the other locals on invasion preparations, made her promise to come find him if Powney arrived, and left the inn. Somebody *had* to have a vehicle in this place. It was 1940, for God's sake, not 1740. Somebody had to have a car. Or a boat, though he didn't like the idea of going out in the Channel, which was full of mines and U-boats. More than sixty of the seven hundred small craft that had participated in the evacuation had been sunk. He'd only go by boat as a last resort.

But even though he looked in every alley and back garden, he didn't see anything, not even a bicycle. And Dover was too far to make it on a bicycle. He walked down to the quay, where three fishermen, including toothless Mr Tompkins, were lounging and discussing – what else? – the weather.

'Looks bad,' one of them said without taking his pipe out of his mouth.

Mr Tompkins mumbled something unintelligible, and the other one, who smelled strongly of fish, nodded agreement.

'I need to get to Dover,' Mike said. 'Is there anyone here who'd be willing to take me there in his boat?'

'I doot yill fond onion heerbuts,' Mr Tompkins said.

Since he shook his head as he spoke, Mike interpreted that

as a no. 'What about one of you? I could pay ...' He hesitated. Three pounds was obviously too much. 'Ten shillings,' he said.

That was obviously too little. Tompkins and the fishy one immediately shook their heads. 'It's blowin' up a storm,' the pipe-smoker said.

The Channel had been 'as still as a millpond' the entire nine days of the evacuation, but Mike couldn't very well say that. 'I'll pay you a pound.'

'Nay, lad,' the fishy one said. 'Channel's too dangerous.'

Clearly none of these three would be volunteering to go to Dunkirk. He'd have to find somebody else. He started down the quay. 'Harold mot be able to run you up,' the pipe-smoker called after him.

'Harold?' Mike said, coming back.

'Aye, Commander Harold,' he said and the fishy one nodded.

A naval officer. Good. He'd know how to steer clear of U-boats and mines. 'Where can I find him?'

'Ye'll fand'm ont' *Lassie June*,' Mr Tompkins said. 'He's bin work nonner sin smale vises skill litter coom furnit buck.'

Mike turned to the pipe-smoker. 'Where can I find the – what did you say the name of his boat was?' but before he could answer, Mr Tompkins said, '*Tletty Gin*.' He pointed down the dock. 'She's doonthur at thind nix harbin ersees pride.'

Which meant God knew what, but there weren't that many boats lined up along the dock, and their names should be painted on their bows. He thanked the trio for their help, such as it was, and walked down the pier, looking at the tied-up boats: the *Marigold*, the *Princess Margaret*, the *Wren*. The names didn't sound very warlike, but then neither had the names of the yachts and barges and fishing smacks that were about to pull off the biggest military evacuation in history: the *Fair Breeze*, the *Kitty*, the *Sunbeam*, the *Smiling Through*.

But hopefully they'd been in better shape than this bunch. Most of them were ancient, none had been scraped or painted in recent memory, and one, the *Sea Sprite*, had its motor spread out in pieces on its deck. Obviously it wasn't going to Dunkirk, but some of the others would. Boats from every coastal village had been involved. He wished he'd had time to memorise the list of small craft that had been part of the evacuation so he'd know which, if any, of these had participated.

And which of them had made it back. The list had had asterisks next to the names of the ones that had been sunk. If he hadn't wasted a whole afternoon waiting to see Dunworthy, he'd know which was which.

He reached the end of the dock. No *Tletty Gin*. Or *Lassie June*. He started back along the row.

'Ahoy!' a voice called, and Mike looked up to see an elderly man in a yachting cap at the railing of a forty-foot launch. 'You there! Are you from the Small Vessels Pool?'

'No,' Mike said. 'I'm looking for a Commander Harold.'

The old man broke into a broad – and, thankfully, toothy – smile. 'I'm Commander Harold. You must be from the Admiralty. You've come about my commission. Thought I'd never hear from you. Come aboard.'

This was Commander Harold? He had to be seventy if he was a day, and no wonder he hadn't heard from the Admiralty about being commissioned. Mike peered at the bow, looking for the boat's name. There it was, so badly faded he could hardly make it out. The *Lady Jane*.

An unlucky name for a boat. Lady Jane Grey had only lasted as queen something like nine days before they'd chopped her head off, and the launch didn't look like it would last long either. It was covered with barnacles and hadn't been painted in years. 'Come aboard, lad,' the Commander was saying, 'and tell me about my commission—'

'I'm not from—'

'What are you standing there for? Come aboard.'

Mike did. Up close, the old man looked even older. His hair under the yachting cap was white and fine as thistledown, and his hand, snapping a salute, was gnarled with arthritis. 'I'm not from the Admiralty either,' Mike said hastily. 'I'm—'

'Suppose they've a new wartime department just for issuing commissions. In my day, His Majesty's Navy didn't have all these departments and regulations and forms to fill up. What would have happened to Lord Nelson at Trafalgar if he'd had to fill up all the forms they have nowadays?'

Nelson had been killed at Trafalgar, but it didn't seem wise to say that, even if Mike could have got a word in edgewise, which he couldn't.

'It's a wonder they ever manage to get their ships out of dry dock these days,' Commander Harold said, 'what with all the paperwork. Do you know how long it's taken for this commission to come through?' He didn't wait for an answer. 'Nine months. Put in for it the day after the war started, and it's taken you all this time. In my day, I'd already have been at sea. Well? What sort of ship have they given me? Battleship? Cruiser?'

'I'm not from the government at all. I'm a reporter.'

The Commander's face fell.

'For the *Omaha Observer*.'

'Omaha. That's in Kansas, isn't it?'

'Nebraska.'

'What are you doing in Saltram-on-Sea?'

'I'm writing a story on Britain's invasion preparations.'

'Preparations!' the Commander snorted. 'What preparations? Have you been out on the beach here, Kansas? It looks like a bloody holiday spot. No barricades, no tank traps, not even any barbed wire. And when I complained to the Admiralty, do you know what the young pup there said? "We're waiting for authorisation from headquarters." And do you know what I said? "If you wait much longer, you'll be asking Himmler!" Can you swim?'

'Swim?' Mike said, lost. 'Yes, I—'

'In my day, every man in His Majesty's Navy had to know how to swim, from the admiral on down. Now half of 'em've never even been to sea. They sit in London, typing up authorisations. Come here, Kansas, I want to show you something.'

'The reason I came was to ask you—' Mike began, but the Commander had already disappeared down a hatch. Mike hesitated. If Mr Powney showed up, Daphne wouldn't know where he'd gone. Mike didn't want to miss him. But he also needed to find out if the Commander would be willing to take him to Dover. If he would, it'd be the fastest way to get there, and it would solve the problem of how to get out onto the docks so he could interview the returning boats. And if they kept close to the shore, the Channel wouldn't be all that dangerous.

Mike looked over at the head of the quay. The three old men were still lounging there. They'd tell Daphne where he was. *If she can understand what they say*, he thought, and climbed down after the Commander.

It was dark inside the hatch. Momentarily blinded, Mike groped for the rungs as he climbed down the ladder and stepped off it.

Into a foot of water.

'What country, friends, is this?'

WILLIAM SHAKESPEARE, *TWELFTH NIGHT*

OXFORD – APRIL 2060

The shimmer was already so bright Polly couldn't see the lab or even the draperies, only the opening drop. She knew there wasn't enough time to tell Badri and Linna to give her apologies to Colin, but she made the attempt. 'Tell Colin what happened,' she shouted into the brightness, 'that there wasn't time to let him know. Tell him I'm sorry and that I said thank you for all his help, and I'll see him when I get back,' but it was too late. She was already through.

In a cellar. In the near-darkness, she could only just make out a brick wall and a black door from which the paint was peeling badly. There were brick walls on either side, too, and a low ceiling, and behind her, three steps leading up to the rest of the brick-paved cellar, which was filled with barrels and packing cases. Ordinarily a cellar would be a good place to come through, but this was the Blitz, when cellars had been used as shelters.

She stood still a moment, listening for the sound of voices – or snoring – in the part of the cellar she couldn't see, but she couldn't hear anything. She quietly tried the door. It was locked.

Wonderful. She'd come through in a locked cellar, and one that, as she peered more closely at it in the gloom, looked as though it had been locked a very long time. A spiderweb, with several dead leaves caught in it, was strung from the lower door hinge to the dirt floor, so unless there was a window she could climb out of, she'd have to wait here till the drop opened and make Badri find another site. And hope Mr Dunworthy didn't cancel her assignment in the meantime.

There'd better be a window, she thought, going up the steps. There was a scattering of dead leaves on them as well, and when she reached the top, she saw why. This wasn't a cellar. It was the narrow passageway between two buildings, and the locked door she'd tried was a recessed side door into a building. The ledge above the passage would at least partially keep the drop's shimmer from being seen from above, but what about the street at the end? If the shimmer could be seen from there, the drop would only be able to open when no one was about and would be effectively useless.

She squeezed down the passage past the stacked barrels to see, trying to protect her coat from being torn. And from getting filthy. The barrels' tops were thick with dust, and drifts of dry leaves crunched underfoot. *I hope I'm not in November instead of September*, she thought, wedging past the next-to-last barrel. *I'd better ascertain my temporal-spatial location. As soon as I've checked to see if the shimmer's visible from the street.*

But it wasn't a street. It was an alley, also paved in brick, and it was lined with the windowless backs of brick buildings – warehouses? Shops? She couldn't tell, but it didn't matter. What mattered was that even if the shimmer was visible from here, no one could see it from the buildings facing it, and at night the alley wouldn't have anyone in it.

She looked cautiously out into the alley. No one was in it. It was nearly as dark as the passage, too dark for 6 a.m. There must have been some slippage, or perhaps it was darker in the narrow alley than out on the street. She looked down the alley. The buildings at the alley's end were blurred.

Not slippage. Fog. Which meant it might be any time of day.

The coal-fire fogs of 1940s London could make midday as dark as night. But she was definitely in World War II because someone had drawn a Union Jack and scrawled, 'London kan take it!' in chalk on the brick wall next to the passage. And the chances were excellent that she'd come through exactly when she was supposed to have. There'd been a thick fog in the early morning hours of September tenth.

She walked to the near end of the alley, listened a few moments for approaching footsteps, and then looked cautiously out. There was no one in either direction as far as the fog let her see, and no vehicles on the wider road that she could dimly see off to her left, which meant the all-clear hadn't gone yet. Which meant there'd been scarcely any slippage at all.

But she still didn't know where she was. She needed to find out – and before the all-clear, if possible – but before she left the alley, she needed to make certain she could recognise it and the drop. She walked back down to the passage, committing the buildings to memory. The one nearest the street had large double doors, and the one next to it a ramshackle wooden staircase leading up two dangerous-looking flights to a door with the same black peeling paint as the door in the drop. Next to it was the passage, though if not for the chalked 'London kan take it' on the wall, she'd have missed it. The barrels hid not only the recess but the passage. An air-raid warden could look straight at it and not realise it was there.

If the wardens even checked the alley. It was as cobwebbed and leaf-strewn as the passage. Which was good.

She walked on down the alley, looking for other identifying features, but the buildings on both sides were of featureless brick except for the one second from the end, which was a black-and-white, half-timbered Tudor. Good: Tudor, 'London kan take it,' rickety staircase, brown double doors.

Which she wouldn't need, she realised as soon as she stepped out of the alley. A large poster was pasted on the wall next to the alley's entrance – a cartoon of Hitler, with his trademark moustache and hank of hair over one eye, peeking round the corner of a building above the words 'Be Vigilant. Report Anyone Behaving Suspiciously.'

It was good the all-clear hadn't gone. There'd be no one out on the streets to see her behaving suspiciously as she attempted to find out where she was. Which might be a problem. The contemps had taken down or painted over all of the street names at the beginning of the war to hinder the Germans in case of invasion. She'd have to hope she could find a landmark that would tell her where she was – a church spire or an Underground station or, if this was Kensington, the gates of Kensington Gardens. Not the railings – those had been taken down and donated to the scrap drive – but, depending on where she was, the Albert Memorial or the Peter Pan statue.

She needed to hurry. The fog was closing in, obscuring all but the nearest buildings, and shutting out what little light there was. *An authentic London pea-souper*, she thought, walking down to the wider road in the hopes of seeing a bit further. But the fog was even thicker here, and growing gloomier by the minute. She could scarcely see down to where the road curved off to the right. And she'd been wrong about the all-clear having gone, because two women emerged out of the fog like ghosts and crossed the road ahead of her, obviously on their way home from a shelter; one of them was carrying a pillow. They walked quickly down the road and were swallowed by the darkness.

Polly started down the road past the buildings that faced the alley where the drop was: a bakery, a knitting shop, and on the corner, a bay-windowed chemist's. They all looked shabby and in need of repair. She hoped that was due to war shortages and not because slippage had sent her through to the East End.

I need to make certain I'm not in Whitechapel or Stepney, she thought. That was where the raids on the tenth had been, and if there'd been locational slippage, and she was in the East End, she needed to go straight back to the alley and Oxford, Mr Dunworthy or no Mr Dunworthy.

She peered in the shops' windows, looking for a notice that would give her a clue to her location. There weren't any, but the presence of windows confirmed she was when she was supposed to be. None of them were broken, and only one shopkeeper had pasted crisscrossing strips of paper onto the glass to reinforce it. The Blitz couldn't have been going on more than a few days.

A ghostly black taxi went by, and a man in a Bowler hurried across the road ahead of her, walking even more rapidly than the women. *Late for work,* Polly thought, which meant it was even later than she'd thought. He had a newspaper under his arm. There must be an open newsagent's nearby. She could buy *The Times* and confirm this was the tenth, at the least. And ask the newsagent what road this was. She would need a newspaper, at any rate, to look for a flat.

But there was no newsagent she could see on this side of the road. She stepped to the edge of the pavement and peered into the gloom. If a bus came by, it would have a destination board, though the fog was making it so dark she wasn't certain she'd be able to read it. She might be able to hail it, though, and tell the conductor she'd got lost in the fog and ask where this was.

But no buses – or taxis, or motor cars – came by. She waited several minutes in the thickening darkness, listening for engine sounds, and then gave up and crossed the street. And wasn't even to the kerb before a bus roared by.

Idiot, she thought. If Mr Dunworthy had seen that, he'd have yanked her out of the Blitz so quickly it would have made her head spin. And in her attempt to leap out of its way, she'd missed seeing its destination board.

There was no newsagent's on this side of the road either – only a butcher shop and next to it a greengrocer's. T. Tubbins, Greengrocer, the lettering on the appropriately green awning read, and baskets full of cabbages stood on both sides of the door. It wasn't open yet, but on the right-hand window was an official notice of some sort.

Polly went closer to squint at it, hoping it was air-raid

instructions that would tell the address of the nearest shelter, or at the least have 'Borough of Marylebone' printed at the bottom, but it was merely a list of rationing rules.

Two shops further on was a tobacconist's, and it was not only open, but on the counter lay an array of newspapers. Behind it, a man with an appropriately tobacco-stained moustache said, 'May I help you, miss?'

'Yes,' she said, stepping into the doorway. 'I—' and an air-raid siren began to wind up into its distinctive wail. Polly turned and looked back out the door, bewildered.

'Earlier every night,' the man said bitterly.

'Earlier?' she repeated blankly.

He nodded. 'Last night it was half past seven. And now tonight the alert ...'

The alert. That was the up-and-down wail of the air-raid alert, not the all-clear. And at the realisation, everything she had seen clicked suddenly into place. It wasn't morning, it was evening, and the women she'd seen hadn't been coming home from a shelter, they'd been going to one.

'Better go along home,' the shopkeeper said, taking hold of the door.

'Oh, but,' she said, fumbling in her shoulder bag for her coin purse, 'I need a newspaper,' but he'd already shut the door.

'Wait!' she called through the glass. 'Where—?'

He shook his head, pulled the shade down, and locked the door. Another siren, nearer, started up. Colin had said she'd have twenty to thirty minutes before the raid began, but she could already hear the drone of planes in the distance. She needed to find a shelter. She had no business being out on the streets during a raid, especially if this was the East End. Or even if it wasn't. Colin was right – there'd been lots of stray bombs. And every one of these shops had plate-glass windows.

There's got to be a shelter somewhere near here, she thought. The women were going to it. She ran back up the road, looking for a notice or the red-barred symbol of an Underground station. But in the few moments she'd stood in the tobacconist's doorway, night and fog had descended like a blackout curtain. She couldn't see anything. And the planes were growing steadily nearer. They'd be overhead any moment.

Which meant this was the East End, and she needed to get back to the drop and out of here as soon as possible. But there was no way she could find her way back in this. She couldn't even see the pavement in front of her or tell if she was about to pitch off the kerb.

She took a cautious, exploring step forward, and crashed into someone. 'Oh, I'm terribly sorry,' she said. 'I didn't see you—' And she still couldn't. The person was only a solid mass of darkness against the more amorphous blackness of the road. She didn't even know it was a man till he spoke.

'Wot are you doing out in a raid, miss?' he growled. 'Why aren't you in a shelter?'

'I was looking for it,' she said, squinting at him, trying to make out his features. It was unsettling, conversing with someone she couldn't see. 'Which way is it?'

'Here,' he said, and apparently he could see her because he grabbed her by the arm and hustled her round the corner and down a side street.

And I hope this isn't one of the muggers Mr Dunworthy was talking about, she thought, clutching her shoulder bag as he dragged her down the narrow side street. Or was it an alley, which he was taking her into to rob her? *Or worse. If I get murdered my first night out, Mr Dunworthy will kill me.*

Her abductor hurried her through the dark for what seemed like miles and then stopped abruptly. 'Down there,' he ordered and gave her a push forward. As he did, there was a thud and an explosion, and the sky to the south lit momentarily, outlining the buildings around them in a garish yellow-white light and illuminating a flight of stone steps directly in front of her, leading down into darkness.

Was there a shelter at the bottom? Or waiting accomplices?

There was no shelter symbol on the wall next to the stairs.

There was a second explosion. She turned to face him, hoping it would illuminate the street behind him – and a path of escape. It did. It also illuminated the white letters on his tin hat.

An ARP warden. And seventy-five if he was a day.

'Down there,' he ordered her again, pointing down the now-invisible stairs. 'Quick.'

Polly obeyed, groping for the railing and feeling her way down the narrow, steep steps. There was another explosion, too close, but no corresponding light, and by the time she was halfway down she couldn't see anything. She glanced back up the steps, but it was just as dark up there. She couldn't even tell if the warden was still standing there to make certain she'd obeyed, or if he'd gone off to waylay someone else and drag him to a shelter.

If that was what was at the foot of these stairs. If there even was a foot – the steps seemed to go on and on. She worked her way down them, feeling for the edge of each one with her foot. After an eternity, she reached solid pavement and patted her way to a door. It was wooden, with an old-fashioned iron latch. She tried to open it, but it seemed to be locked. She knocked.

No response.

They didn't hear me, she thought and knocked again, harder.

Still no answer.

What if the warden got disoriented in the darkness and brought me to the wrong place? What if this is an alley, and this is a side door in a warehouse? she thought, remembering the cobwebbed black door in the drop. *What if there's no one on the other side?*

There was another explosion. *I can't stay here,* she thought, and began to grope her way back over to the stairs. A bomb hit nearly at the head of the stairs, and then two more, in rapid succession.

She turned back to the door. 'Let me in!' she called, pounding on the door with both fists, and then, when there was still no answer, taking off a shoe and pounding on the door with it, trying to make herself heard over the din of the raid.

The door opened. The sudden brightness from inside blinded her, and she put up her hand, still holding her shoe, to shield her eyes, and stood there squinting at the tableau inside. People sat against the walls on blankets and rugs, and a dog lay at the feet of one of the men. Three older women sat side by side on a high-backed bench, the middle one knitting – or rather, she had been knitting. Now she, like all the others, was staring at the door and at Polly. An aristocratic-looking elderly gentleman in the far corner had lowered the letter he was reading to look at her, and three fair-haired little girls had stopped in the middle of a game of *Snakes and Ladders* to stare at her.

There was no expression on any of their faces, no welcoming smiles – even from the man who'd let her in. No one moved or made a sound. They were frozen, as if they'd suddenly stopped in midsentence, and there was a feeling of fear, of danger in the room.

The thought flashed through her mind, *This isn't a shelter. The man who brought me here wasn't a real warden. He could have stolen that* ARP *helmet, and these people are only pretending to be shelterers.* But that was ridiculous. The man who'd let her in was obviously a clergyman. He was wearing a clerical collar and spectacles, and this wasn't Dickens's London. It was 1940.

It's me. There must be something wrong with the way I look, she thought, and realised she was still holding her shoe in her hand. She bent to slip it on, then looked back up at the assembly, and what she'd seen before must have been a trick of the light or her overactive imagination because now the scene looked perfectly normal. The white-haired woman smiled pleasantly at her and took up her knitting; the aristocratic gentleman folded his letter, returned it to its envelope, and put it in his inside coat pocket; the little girls returned to their game; and the dog lay down and put its head on its paws.

'Do come in,' the clergyman said, smiling.

'Shut the door,' a woman shouted, and someone else said, 'The blackout—'

'Oh,' Polly said, 'sorry,' and turned to shut the door.

'You'll get us all fined,' a stout man said grumpily.

Polly pushed the door shut, and the clergyman barred it, but apparently not fast enough.

'What are you trying to do?' a scrawny woman with a sour expression demanded. 'Show the jerries where we are?'

And so much for the fabled cheerful camaraderie of the Blitz, Polly thought. 'Sorry,' she said again, looking around the shelter for a place to sit. There was no furniture except for the bench. Everyone else sat on the stone floor or on blankets, and the only vacant spot was between the stout man who'd growled at her to shut the door and two young women in sequin-adorned dresses and bright red lipstick, who were busily gossiping.

'I beg your pardon, may I sit here?' she asked them.

The man looked annoyed, but grunted assent, and the young women nodded, scooted closer together, and went on chatting. ' … and then he asked me to meet him at Piccadilly Circus and go dancing with him!'

'Oh Lila, he didn't!' her friend said. 'You're not going to, are you?'

'No, of course not, Viv. He's far too old. He's thirty.'

Polly thought of Colin and suppressed a smile.

'I told him, you need to find someone your own age.'

'Oh Lila, you didn't,' Viv said.

'I did. I wouldn't have gone out with him at any rate. I only go out with men in uniform.'

Polly took off her coat, spread it out, sat down on it, and looked around at the room. It was obviously one of the shop or warehouse cellars pressed into service as a shelter when the Blitz began, though it didn't look as makeshift as she'd expected, considering the Blitz had begun only three days ago. Its contents, except for the high-backed bench, had been pushed to the far end, and the ceiling had been braced with heavy lengths of lumber. A stirrup pump, a bucket of water and an axe stood on one side of the door. On the other was a table holding a gas ring and a kettle, cups and saucers, and spoons.

The shelterers' arrangements didn't look makeshift either. The knitter had brought her yarn, a shawl and her reading glasses with her; the table was covered with an embroidered tea cloth; and the three little girls – whom Polly estimated as being three, four, and five – had not only their board game, but several dolls, a teddy bear and a large book of fairy-tales, which they were clamouring to have their mother read to them.

'Read us "Sleeping Beauty",' the eldest one said.

'No,' the littlest one piped up, 'the one with the clock.'

The clock? Polly wondered. *Which one is that?*

And apparently her sisters didn't know either. 'What's the clock story?' the eldest one asked.

'"Cinderella",' the littlest one said as if it were self-evident.

The middle girl took her thumb out of her mouth. 'That's the one with the shoe,' she said, and pointed at Polly.

And Polly supposed she had looked a bit like Cinderella, standing there in one shoe. And, just like Cinderella, she'd failed to ascertain her space-time location, with nearly as disastrous results. Except that no one had been dropping bombs on Cinderella.

And Badri had said there might be two hours of slippage, not twelve. The morning of the tenth must have been a divergence point for there to have been so much slippage. Or perhaps, in spite of its deserted appearance, someone had been in the alley or in a position where they could see the shimmer and kept it from opening. Whichever it was, she'd lost a full day of her already too short assignment.

She looked around at the others. The middle-aged woman sitting next to the knitter was the image of an early twentieth-century spinster, with her laced brown shoes and her greying hair pulled back into a bun and held in place with tortoiseshell combs. They could all have been taken from one of Merope's murder mysteries – the frail, white-haired old woman, the clergyman, the sour-faced, sharp-tongued woman, the gruff stout man who looked as if he might have been in the military. Colonel Mustard in the air-raid shelter with the service revolver. Perhaps that was why they'd struck her as sinister when she first saw them.

Or perhaps it was their calm self-possession. These were the fabled Londoners, of course, who'd faced the Blitz with legendary courage and humour, who hadn't even been fazed by the V-1 and V-2 attacks. But they'd had four and a half years of being accustomed to bombing before the rocket attacks. This was only the fourth night of the Blitz, and all the research she'd done had said they'd been terrified all that first week, especially till the anti-aircraft guns had started up on the eleventh, and that they'd only gradually learned to master their fear of the bombs.

But no one was saying, 'Where are *our* guns?' or 'Why aren't we hitting back?' and looking nervously up at the ceiling. They weren't paying any attention to the thud and *crump* of the bombs at all. It had apparently only taken the three previous nights for them to completely adapt to the raids. The white-haired woman glanced up, annoyed, at a particularly loud bang, then began counting stitches, and the clergyman returned to discussing next Sunday's service with a formidable-looking woman with iron-grey hair.

The scrawny, sour-faced woman was still scowling, but Polly had a feeling that was her permanent expression. The aristocratic gentleman was reading *The Times*, and the dog had gone to sleep. If not for the occasional muffled explosion overhead and Lila's talk of dating men in uniform, there'd have been nothing to indicate there was a war on.

And there was nothing to indicate where this was. Since there'd been temporal slippage and the net had sent her through twelve hours later than the target time, it was unlikely there'd been locational slippage as well. There was generally only one or the other. But the bombs were falling too near for this to be Kensington or Marylebone. Polly looked around at the shelter walls for the name or address of the shelter, but the only thing posted was a list of what to do in case of a poison gas attack.

She debated saying she'd got lost in the fog and asking where she was, but given the odd way they'd looked at her when she came in, she decided to listen to their conversations instead and hope they'd let fall some clue, though Lila's mention of meeting someone hadn't been any help. She could take the tube to Piccadilly Circus from anywhere, including the East End. And now she was explaining why she only dated soldiers – 'It's my way of doing my bit for the war effort' – and the women on the bench were discussing knitting patterns.

Polly focused on the clergyman, hoping he or the formidable-looking woman – whom he addressed as Mrs Wyvern – would mention the name of his church, but they were discussing flower arrangements. 'I thought lilies might be nice for the altar,' he said.

'No, the altar will be yellow chrysanthemums,' Mrs Wyvern said, and it was clear who was running things, 'and the side chapel bronze dahlias and—'

'Mice!' the littlest girl crowed.

'Yes,' her mother said. 'Cinderella's fairy godmother turned the mice into horses and the pumpkin into a beautiful carriage. "You may go to the ball, Cinderella," she said. "But you *must* be home by the stroke of midnight."'

'If that pill of a floorwalker hadn't made us stay after and do the display windows,' Viv grumbled, '*we'd* have been able to go to the ball.'

Floorwalker? Display windows? That meant Viv and Lila were shopgirls. But if that was the case Polly had been wrong about what shopgirls in 1940 wore and would have to go back through to Oxford and get a sequined dress before she went to apply for a position.

If she could find the drop again. She had no idea where it was from here.

'It wasn't only the floorwalker,' Lila said. 'It was your insisting we go home and change clothes first.'

'I wanted Donald to see my new dance frock,' Viv protested, and Polly breathed a sigh of relief. Those weren't their work clothes after all. But it was too bad Viv hadn't mentioned where they'd gone home to.

It's got to be Stepney or Whitechapel, Polly thought. The explosions were directly overhead. There was a *whoosh* and the muffled *crump* of an explosion very nearby, and then a horrid sound – a cross between a cannon going off in one's ear and a sledgehammer. 'What *is* that?' Polly said.

'Tavistock Square,' the stout man said calmly.

'No, it isn't,' the man with the dog corrected him. 'It's Regent's Park.'

'The anti-aircraft guns,' the clergyman explained, and the white-haired knitter nodded in confirmation.

The anti-aircraft guns? But they hadn't begun till the eleventh. And supposedly when they had, the contemps had been terrified by the unfamiliar noise and then relieved and overjoyed, shouting, 'Hurrah! That's givin' it to 'em!' and 'At least we're givin' a bit of our own back!' But these people hadn't noticed them any more than they noticed the bombs. The little girls were engrossed in 'Cinderella' and the dog hadn't even opened his eyes, so this couldn't be their first night. Which meant the guns had to have started on the eighth or the ninth.

Another gun started up with a deafening, bone-rattling *poom-poom-poom*. 'That's Tavistock Square,' the dog owner said, and, as another, even louder, joined in, 'And that's ours.'

The stout man nodded agreement. 'Kensington Gardens.'

Which meant she was in Kensington, thank goodness, or very near it. But it also meant that just because the raids had been mainly over Stepney and Whitechapel, it didn't mean Kensington hadn't been bombed as well. Colin had been right – there were *lots* of stray bombs. And lots of errors in people's memories, as witness the date the guns had begun. It had probably *seemed* like days before the guns had started up to the people in the shelters, even though it had only been a day or two after the Blitz began.

Which is why historians must do on-site research, Polly thought. There were simply too many errors in the historical record. Though she wouldn't tell Mr Dunworthy that when she checked in. Or that Kensington had been bombed on the tenth. Or how she'd been out on the streets in the middle of a raid. Actually, she'd better not tell him *anything,* except what her address was and where she was working.

She wished the newsagent hadn't shut his door before she had a chance to buy a newspaper so she could check the advertisements for available rooms tonight instead of wasting valuable time tomorrow. With all the restrictions Mr Dunworthy had put on where she could live, it could take her days to find a room, and she'd already lost one day.

She glanced over at the aristocratic gentleman, but he was still reading his *Times.* She looked around at the others, wondering if there was a newspaper in the stout man's coat pocket or tucked into the white-haired woman's knitting bag, but the only one she could see was the one the dog's owner had spread out to sit on, and he showed no sign of moving.

None of them did. They were clearly settling in for the night. The white-haired woman was putting away her knitting, the other women had covered themselves with their coats and leaned their heads back against the wall, and the mother had closed the fairy-tale book. 'And the prince found Cinderella and took her back to his castle—'

'And they lived happily ever after!' the littlest one burst out, unable to contain herself.

'Yes, they did. Now, time for bed,' she said, and the two older girls curled up on the floor beside their mother, but the littlest one stayed stubbornly upright.

'No! I want to hear another story. The one with the trail of bread crumbs,' which Polly assumed was 'Hansel and Gretel'.

'All right, but first you must lie down,' the mother said, and the little girl obediently put her head in her mother's lap. The stout man next to Polly folded his arms across his chest, closed his eyes, and immediately began to snore, and so did the man with the dog.

I'll have to wait till morning to look at the rooms to let, Polly thought, but a few minutes later the dog's owner stood up, bent and patted his dog, and walked over to the far end of the cellar, followed by his dog. He edged past the screen and bookcases and disappeared into the darkness.

He's going to the loo, Polly thought, got to her feet, and walked over to see if the spread-out newspaper was an old one or today's. If it was, when he came back, she'd ask him if she could look at the 'Rooms to Let' classifieds.

'You can't sit there,' the sour-faced woman who'd shouted at her when she came in called out. 'That space is saved.'

'I know,' Polly said. 'I only wanted to look at—'

'That newspaper belongs to Mr Simms.' She heaved herself up and started across the room as if to do battle.

'I'm sorry, I didn't realise—' Polly murmured and retreated to her own space, but the woman wasn't satisfied.

'Reverend Norris,' she said to the clergyman, 'that newspaper belongs to Mr Simms.'

'I'm certain the young lady didn't mean any harm, Mrs Rickett,' he said mildly.

She ignored him. 'Mr Simms,' she called to the dog's owner as he came back, 'someone tried to pinch your newspaper.' She pointed accusingly at Polly. 'She walked over, bold as brass, the minute you were gone.'

'I wasn't trying to steal it,' Polly protested. 'I only wanted to look at the rooms to let—'

'Rooms to let?' Mrs Rickett said sharply, obviously not believing her.

'Yes, I've only just arrived in London, and I need to find somewhere to stay,' Polly said, wondering if she should stand up again and go over to Mr Simms to apologise, but she feared that would only escalate the situation, so she stayed where she was. 'I do apologise, Mr Simms.'

'The newspaper's to mark my space,' he said.

'Yes, I know,' Polly said, though she hadn't known, and that was the problem. By walking over to his space she'd apparently broken some rule, and, from the looks everyone was giving her, a crucial one. Mrs Wyvern and the knitter were both glaring at her. Even the dog looked reproachful.

'Did she do something naughty, Mummy?' the littlest girl asked.

'Shh,' her mother whispered.

'I'm *dreadfully* sorry,' Polly said. 'I *promise* it won't happen again,' hoping an abject apology would put an end to it, but it didn't.

'Mr Simms has sat in that space every night,' the stout man said.

'Respecting another's shelter arrangements is vital,' Mrs Wyvern said to the clergyman. 'Don't you agree, Reverend?'

Help, Polly thought. *Colin, you said if I got in trouble, you'd come and rescue me. Well, now would be a good time.*

'If she wanted a newspaper,' Mrs Rickett said, 'she should have purchased one at a newsagent's—' and stopped, looking at the aristocratic gentleman. He'd stood up, holding his newspaper, which he'd folded in quarters, and was coming across the room.

He walked straight to Polly and held out his newspaper to her with grave courtesy. 'Would you care for my *Times*, dear child?' he asked her. He spoke quietly – but not so quietly that everyone in the room couldn't hear him, she noted – and his voice was as refined as his appearance.

'I—' Polly said.

'I'm quite finished with it.' He held it out.

125

'Thank you,' she said gratefully, and the incident was over. Mrs Rickett retreated sullenly to the bench, the white-haired woman took out her knitting again and began counting rows, the rector went back to his book, and Lila whispered, 'Don't pay Mrs Rickett any mind. She's an old cat,' and went back to talking about the dance she and Viv were missing.

The gentleman had managed to completely defuse the situation, though Polly wasn't certain how. She shot him a grateful look, but he'd retreated to his corner again and was reading a book. She looked down at the newspaper in her hand. He'd folded it open to the 'Rooms to Let' section for her. She started through the listings, looking for permissible addresses. Mayfair. No, too expensive. Stepney, no. Shoreditch, no. Croydon, no, definitely not.

Here was one. Kensington. Ashbury Lane, which might work. What was the address? *Please not six, nineteen, or twenty-one*, she said silently. Eleven. Excellent – an allowed address, within her budget, and near Oxford Street. Now if it was only near a tube stop. 'Convenient to Marble Arch,' the advertisement read. Which had taken a direct hit on September seventeenth.

She mentally crossed it off and continued down the list. Kensal Green. No, too far out. Whitechapel, no.

'The raid seems to be letting up,' Lila said.

The racket did seem to be diminishing. The explosions sounded further off, and one of the guns had stopped firing. 'Perhaps the all-clear will go early tonight, Viv,' Lila said, 'and we can still go to the dance,' but the moment she spoke, the barrage started up again.

'I *hate* Hitler,' Viv burst out. 'It's so *utterly* unfair, being trapped in this place on a Saturday night.'

Polly looked up sharply. *Saturday? It's Tuesday*. But even as she thought it, she was seeing the evidence that had been in front of her all along – the dance Lila and Viv had been planning to go to, the guns that hadn't started till Wednesday and that no one had remarked on, the braced ceiling, the *Snakes and*

Ladders game, the embroidered tea cloth – all signs they'd been coming here for more than three days. The clergyman and the woman's discussion of the order of service for Sunday.

For tomorrow.

She'd misread all the clues, just as she had on the street when she'd thought it was early morning. The guns hadn't started till the eleventh, after all, and of course the raids had sounded like they were overhead. Kensington had been bombed on Saturday. *But if it's Saturday,* she thought, *I've already missed four days.* And the crucial first few days of the Blitz when the contemps were adjusting to it. That's why they were all so calm, so settled in. They'd already adjusted.

And I missed it, she thought furiously. Badri said he expected two hours of slippage, not four and a half days. And it was actually even more than that. Tomorrow was Sunday. She wouldn't be able to look for work till Monday.

Which means I can't start work till Tuesday, by which time I'll have lost an entire week of observing shopgirls, and I only have six.

It can't be the fourteenth, she thought. She snatched up the newspaper and paged through it, looking for the front page. *I didn't have enough time to begin with.*

But it was. 'Saturday, September 14, 1940', the masthead read, and below it, appropriately enough, 'Late Edition'.

'For want of a nail, the shoe was lost. For want of a shoe,
the horse was lost. For want of a horse, the rider was lost.
For want of a rider, the kingdom was lost.'

PROVERB

SALTRAM-ON-SEA – 29 MAY 1940

It wasn't really a foot of water. it was only about four inches, but it covered the hold. Mike could see why the Commander had asked him if he could swim.

'Nothing to worry about,' the Commander said, seeing Mike's reaction. 'Just need to get the bilge pump started.' He splashed unconcernedly through the water and lifted a trapdoor. 'She's been sitting here all winter. An hour or two out in the Channel, and she'll be as good as new.'

An hour or two out in the Channel, and she'll be at the bottom of it, Mike thought. *And she won't need a U-boat to do it.* He looked around the hold. There was a tiny galley with a Primus stove against one wall and a scarred wooden table against the other. On it were a messy heap of papers, a half-empty bottle of Scotch, a flashlight, several large cork floats, and an opened can of either sardines or bait. Against the other wall were two lockers and a bunk with a tumble of grey blankets.

The Commander got down on his knees and reached down through the trap. The bilge pump coughed and then died.

There is no way I am going anywhere on this, Mike thought, *even to Dover. I'll just have to find another boat.* But the men on the dock hadn't exactly been full of suggestions. *Let's hope Powney's driving into town right now.*

Commander Harold did something else to the bilge pump, and this time it chugged for a full minute before dying. 'Needs a bit of oil is all,' he said. He splashed over to the galley, lit a fire under a coffeepot, and began rummaging through the pile of charts. 'The Navy's gone soft, that's what's wrong with it.' He unearthed an opened can of potatoes and then a doubtful-looking mug. 'You know what they feed 'em on board ship nowadays? Tea with milk and sugar! You wouldn't see Nelson drinking tea! Rum, that's what we drank, and hot coffee!' He poured a cup and handed it to Mike.

Mike took a cautious sip. It tasted like it looked.

'You should see what they sent – now, where did I put it?' the Commander said, attacking the mess on the table again. 'I know it's here somewhere – aha!' He fished a letter out of the heap and handed it to Mike with a triumphant flourish. 'The Small Vessels Pool sent that letter four weeks ago.'

The Small Vessels Pool. That was the 'Smale Vises School' Mr Tompkins had been mumbling about. And this was the letter they'd sent out at the beginning of May asking small craft owners if they'd be willing to volunteer their boats for service in case of invasion or other 'military emergency'.

'Sent one of their bloody forms along with it,' the Commander said. 'Six pages long! I wrote 'em back the very same day, volunteering the *Lady Jane* and me for service.'

I'll bet you didn't tell them about the broken bilge pump, Mike thought, *or the four inches of water in the hold.*

'And haven't heard a word since,' the Commander was saying. 'Four weeks! It took Hitler less than half that to take over Poland! If they're running the war in France the way they're running the Small Vessels Pool, they'll be surrendering to Hitler a fortnight from now!'

No, they wouldn't, thanks to a ragtag armada of motor

launches and fishing smacks and pleasure boats who'd arrived to rescue them in the nick of time. But the *Lady Jane* wouldn't be among them. It would never make it out of the harbour, let alone across the Channel and back. And there was no way he was going to let the Commander take him up to Dover in it. Which meant he'd better get back to the Crown and Anchor so he wouldn't miss Mr Powney. 'I've got to be going,' he said. 'Thanks for the coffee,' and tried to hand the mug back to the Commander.

'You can't go till you've seen the *Lady Jane*. This is her engine.' The Commander lifted another trapdoor to reveal an ancient-looking motor, black with grease. 'You won't find an engine like that nowadays.'

Mike could believe that.

'And you won't find a more seaworthy boat,' he said, splashing through the water to show Mike a locker containing grapples, a tangle of ropes, and a signal lantern. There was a bucket in the locker, too.

Good, Mike thought, because the water'd risen at least an inch since they'd been down here.

The Commander took him up on deck to show him the bridge. There was no sign of Daphne, and the three fishermen were still in the same place. The Commander showed him the bridge and the wheel and then dragged him to the rear of the boat to see the gunwales, the anchor, and the propellor, delivering lectures as he did on her seaworthiness and the modern Navy's shortcomings, then below again. 'I don't hold with all this modern navigation,' he said, pointing to a clock in the galley. 'In my day we used dead reckoning.'

The clock said five past six. How exactly was he going to navigate using dead reckoning with a stopped clock? Mike looked at his Bulova. It was nearly noon. Powney had to be back by now. Daphne was probably out looking for him. 'Thanks for the tour,' he said, 'but I've really got to be going.'

'*Going?* You can't go yet. You haven't finished your coffee. Or said why you were looking for me.'

Mike wasn't about to tell him he'd been looking for a boat to take him to Dover. 'That'll have to wait till later,' he said, wading towards the ladder. 'Right now I've got to …' He hesitated. He couldn't tell him about Mr Powney either. 'Get back to the Crown and Anchor—'

'The Crown and Anchor? If it's your dinner you're wanting, you can have it here. Sit down.' He forced Mike into a chair, handed him the mug of cold coffee, and rummaged through the heap on the table again. He came up with a pot, which he dumped the sardines into. 'In my day, every man in His Majesty's Navy knew how to cook and mend sail and scrub decks.' He dumped in the can of potatoes. 'Hand me that tin of bully beef.'

Mike handed it to him and he cut it open, dumped it in the pot in a solid block, stirred the mess with his knife, and set it on the Primus stove. 'Nowadays, all they know how to do is fill up forms and take tea breaks. Soft, that's what they are.' He rummaged again, came up with a tin plate and a crusted fork, and gave them to Mike. 'I'll wager Hitler's soldiers don't take tea breaks. Hand me your plate, Kansas.'

'No, I really can't stay. I've got to report in to my paper, and—'

'You can do that after dinner. Hand over your plate.'

'Grandfather!' a voice called, and a young boy poked his head down the ladder. 'Mummy says to come home to dinner.'

Rescued in the nick of time, Mike thought. 'I'll be going, then,' he said, standing up.

'You stay right there. Jonathan!' he shouted up at the boy. 'You go and tell your mother I'm having my dinner on board. Go on, then.'

The boy, who reminded Mike a little of Colin Templer, though he was even younger, stayed where he was. 'She said to tell you it's going to rain, and you'll catch your death.'

'You tell *her* I've been taking care of myself for eighty-two years and—'

'She said if you won't come, to put this on.' Jonathan came

down the ladder, handed the Commander a peacoat, and turned to Mike. 'Are you from the Small Vessels Pool?' he asked.

'No, I'm a reporter,' Mike said.

'A war correspondent,' the Commander said. 'Now, off with you. Tell your mother I'll be home when it suits me.'

'A war correspondent!' Jonathan stayed long enough to say. 'Have you seen lots of battles? I'm frightfully keen to get into the war. I'm going to enlist in the Navy as soon as I'm old enough.'

'If his mother'll let him,' the Commander said after he was gone.

'He's your grandson?'

'Great-grandson.' He tossed the peacoat on the bunk. 'He's a good lad, but his mother coddles him too much. Fourteen, and she won't even let him go out in the *Lady Jane* with me.'

I can't blame her, Mike thought.

'Won't let me teach him to swim either. He might drown, she says. And what the bloody hell does she think he'll do if he *doesn't* learn to swim? Here, give me your plate.'

'No, really, I have to go, too. I've got to write up my story.'

'In *my* day, reporters were on the front lines, reporting the real news. I'll wager that's where you'd like to be instead of in a backwater like this.'

I'd like to be in Dover, Mike thought.

'Not that anybody'd want to be in France now, with everything going to hell in a handbasket,' and was off again on a rant about the incompetence of the French, the Belgians, and General Gort. It was twelve-thirty before Mike was able to make his escape. Luckily, the Commander'd got so worked up over the softness of the BEF that he'd forgotten about Mike's having come to ask him something. And he'd forgotten about the stew.

But if I've missed Mr Powney ...

Mike sprinted back along the dock. The old men had disappeared. He hurried to the Crown and Anchor. Daphne was behind the bar, pouring ale from a pitcher for several customers. 'Mr Powney hasn't come back, has he?' Mike asked.

'No, I can't think what's keeping him.' She went over to the end of the bar, consulted with the ale drinkers, and came back. 'They say he might have gone straight home instead of stopping in.'

'Wouldn't he have had to come through the village?'

'No, his farm's south of here.'

'How far?' Mike asked, thinking, *Please let it be within walking distance.*

'Not far. Only three miles south by the coast road,' she said and drew a map for him. 'But it's much shorter if you cut across the fields, like this.'

That was probably true, but if Mr Powney hadn't gone home, Mike might miss him heading there and waste more time. And there was always the chance somebody else would come along – maybe the Army would show up to put in the beach defences – and he could hitch a ride with them.

So he kept to the road, but he didn't see a single vehicle the whole way to the turnoff to Mr Powney's.

There wasn't anybody at the farm either, though Mike tramped out to the barn and the outbuildings, looking for a farmhand he could ask who might know when Mr Powney was coming back, and he couldn't see anybody in the surrounding fields, except for a few cows.

Which means I'll have to take the same damned route back to make sure I don't miss him, Mike thought, looking longingly at the shortcut Daphne had mapped out for him. He hadn't prepped for an assignment with this much walking, and the farm had been much further from Saltram-on-Sea than Daphne'd said – the distance from the turnoff to the farm alone was a good mile – and he was tired and thirsty. And hungry.

He hadn't had anything to eat since he got here. *I should have had that kipper Daphne offered. Or some of the Commander's pilchard stew. Even it sounded almost good.*

I definitely should have had that cup of the Commander's

godawful coffee, he thought, yawning. *It would help keep me awake.*

The weather wasn't helping. In spite of everyone's prediction of storms, the afternoon was sunny and warm and filled with the sleep-inducing drone of bees. He trudged back along the farm track, fighting an overwhelming desire to lie down in the grass and take a nap. *When Mr Powney finally shows up, and I get in that truck, he thought, I intend to sleep all the way to Dover.*

But the road back was deserted all the way to Saltram-on-Sea, and there was no truck outside the Crown and Anchor, even though it was nearly three.

He must not be coming back today, Mike thought tiredly. He couldn't afford to wait for him any longer, with the evacuation racing irretrievably past. He had to get to Dover. *It'll have to be one of the boats*, he thought, heading out to the quay. Some of the fishing boats at least should be back by now, and surely he could talk one of them into running him up to Dover—

He stopped, staring. The quay was empty. Down at the end, the *Lady Jane* was still tied to the dock, but every other boat had vanished, including the *Sea Sprite*. Its engine had been lying in pieces on its deck. Where could it – where could they – all have disappeared to?

Dunkirk, he thought sickly. *The Small Vessels Pool was here while I was gone.* But it couldn't have been. The *Lady Jane* was still here. Commander Harold would have been the first to volunteer, and they couldn't possibly have got their boats ready so fast. There had to be some other explanation.

He sprinted down the quay to the *Lady Jane*. 'Commander Harold!' he called. 'Where's everyone gone?'

No answer. He ran aboard, called down the hatch, and when there was still no answer, climbed down the ladder to see if the Commander was down in the hold.

Maybe he missed it like I did, Mike thought, but the Commander wasn't asleep in his bunk. He must be at his grand-daughter's.

Mike ran over to the Crown and Anchor to ask Daphne where that was. The door to the inn was open, and next to it a bicycle was leaning against the wall. Mike went in—

—and nearly collided with the Commander, who was on the phone. 'Put me through to the officer in charge of the Small Vessels Pool! The one who was in Saltram-on-Sea this afternoon!' he was bellowing into it. 'Then put me through to the Admiralty! In London!' He spied Mike. 'Incompetents, the lot of them! And they're in charge of saying what's seaworthy and what's not!'

The Small Vessels Pool turned him down, Mike thought. *That's why he and the* Lady Jane *are still here.*

'Said they need our boats for a special mission,' the Commander bellowed. '*Special mission!* The French have botched it, and they need us to go and get our boys off before Hitler shows up. Say they need every boat they can get, and *then* tell me the *Lady Jane's* not seaworthy!'

Well, seaworthy or not, it was the only boat left in town. He was going to have to get the Commander to take him to Dover in it. 'Commander—' Mike began, but the old man went right on.

'Not *seaworthy*, and then they take the *Sea Sprite* and the *Emily B*! The *Emily B*!' he thundered. 'With a bad rudder and a captain who couldn't steer his way to the counter for a pint. And *then*, when I volunteered to pilot one of their convoys for 'em, told me I was too old! Too old? What do you mean, there's no one at the Admiralty?' he bellowed into the telephone. 'Don't they know there's a war on?'

'Commander—'

He waved Mike away. 'Well, then let me speak to the under-secretary! What *about*? About the war you're losing!' He slammed the earpiece into the cradle. 'Incompetent fool! I'll have to go the Admiralty myself!'

'Go?' Mike said, but the Commander had already stormed out the door past him.

'Commander, wait!' Mike called, starting after him. 'I need you to—'

'You're back,' Daphne said, blocking his way. 'Was Mr Powney at home?'

'No ... I need to—' he said, trying to get around her.

'You missed all the excitement,' Daphne said. 'An officer from the Small Vessels Pool was here—'

'I know – hang on, I've got to catch the Commander.' Mike pushed past her and outside, but the Commander, on the bicycle, was halfway down the street.

'Commander!' Mike shouted, cupping his hands around his mouth, and took off after him, but he was pedalling right past the quay. What the hell was he doing? *You can't ride that bicycle all the way to London.* It would take him a week, and besides, he was heading the wrong way. No wonder the Small Vessels Pool wouldn't let him lead a convoy. *And now what?* he thought, watching the Commander pedal out of sight, and then turning back towards the pub.

'Wasn't Mr Powney home?' Daphne asked, coming to meet him.

'No.'

'I can't imagine what's keeping him.' She linked her arm in his. 'You must be worn out, walking all that way.' She led him back into the inn. 'Come into the pub room, and I'll make you a nice cup of tea. The officer was a Navy lieutenant, and a very handsome one, though not nearly so handsome as you,' she said, glancing flirtatiously over her shoulder at Mike as she put the kettle on. 'He said, "I need every craft that can float to go to Dover straightaway."'

She prattled on about how the men had grabbed their gear, loaded their boats, reassembled the *Sea Sprite*'s engine, and set sail in less than two hours. *And I missed it,* Mike thought. *Like I missed the bus—*

Was that the sound of a car? Mike jumped up and ran for the door, Daphne right behind him, in time to see a battered roadster go roaring by with the Commander at the wheel, both hands clenching it and his eyes fixed firmly on the road, looking neither to right nor left. 'Wait!' Mike shouted and ran out into the street, waving both arms to signal him to stop, but he roared off, heading north, in a cloud of white dust, and out of sight.

Mike turned furiously to Daphne. 'You told me there was no one else in town with a car!'

'I forgot about the Commander's old roadster.'

Obviously.

'He hasn't driven it since the war started. Where do you suppose he's going?'

To London, Mike thought. *And then, when he can't find anyone at the Admiralty, to Dover. Where I have been trying to get since five this morning.*

'I *am* sorry,' Daphne said. 'He said he was going to put it up on blocks. But it's just as well. He's a dreadful driver. You're much better off going with Mr Powney. Are you very angry with me?' she said, pouting prettily.

'*Angry' isn't the word*, he thought. 'Is there anyone else here with a car you've forgotten about? Or a motorcycle. Anything. I have to get to Dover today.'

'No, no one else. But I'm certain Mr Powney will be home before tonight. The Home Guard meets on Wednesday nights, and he never misses.'

And he doesn't like to drive in the blackout, which means the soonest he'll be willing to take me is tomorrow morning, and it'll take all morning to get there. The evacuation would be half over.

He couldn't afford to waste any more time here. He'd already missed three days of the evacuation he could never get back. *I'm going to have to go back through to Oxford to make Badri find me a drop site closer to Dover.*

'Don't be angry,' Daphne was saying. 'I'll fry you a nice piece of cod for your tea, and Mr Powney will be here by the time you've eaten it.'

'No, I've got to go.' He stood up. 'I have to file my story with my paper in London.'

'But your tea's nearly ready. Surely you've time—'

Time's just what I don't have, he thought. 'No, I've got to get it in the afternoon edition,' he said and walked quickly out of the pub, out of the village, and up the hill, anxious to get to the drop before it got dark. The shimmer would be less visible in the daytime. Whichever boat had been offshore last night and prevented the drop from opening was halfway to Dover by now, but he wasn't taking any chances. And the earlier he left 1940, the earlier Badri could set the new drop for.

I won't care if it takes Badri a month to find me a new drop site, he thought, trudging up the hill. *It'll give me a chance to catch up on all the sleep I've lost.* Or get over his time-lag. Whichever it was, he could barely make it up the hill. Thank God he was nearly to the top. *I hope I don't fall asleep waiting for the drop to open and miss it—*

Half a dozen children stood on the edge of the cliff, right above the path down to the beach, talking excitedly and pointing out at the Channel. He looked where they were pointing. A smoky pall covered the horizon, and several black columns rose from it. The fires of Dunkirk.

Christ, what next? Maybe I can bribe them to go away, he thought, and started over to them, but they were already scrambling down the path. 'Wait!' Mike called, but it was no use. There were more children down on the beach, and several men. One of them had a pair of binoculars, and two of the kids were standing on Mike's rock for a better view.

They'd be there till sundown, and if the fires themselves were visible from here, half the night. And in the meantime, what the hell am I supposed to do? he thought. *Just stand here and watch my chance at observing the evacuation go up in smoke?* Boats full of rescued soldiers were already pulling into Dover.

He turned angrily and started back down to the village. There had to be some other way to get to Dover. The *Lady Jane* was still here. *Maybe Jonathan could pilot it. Or I could.* He could follow the coast. *And end up on the rocks. Or at the bottom of the Channel,* he thought, remembering the water in the hold, but he went out to the quay anyway. Jonathan might know somebody who had a motorbike. Or a horse.

But Jonathan wasn't on board. 'Ahoy! Jonathan!' Mike called down the hatch. 'Are you down there?'

No answer. Mike climbed down the ladder, stopping just above the water, which had got deeper since this morning. It was nearly up to the bottom rung. 'Jonathan?'

He wasn't there. *I'll have to go back to the Crown and Anchor and ask Daphne where he lives,* he thought wearily, looking over at the Commander's bunk. The grey wool blankets and filthy pillow looked incredibly inviting.

If I could just get an hour or two's sleep, he thought, suddenly overwhelmed with drowsiness, *I could think what to do, I could figure out something.* And by then Powney might be back. Or the Commander. He took off his shoes and socks, rolled up his trouser legs, waded over to the bunk, and climbed in.

Maybe I'd better start the bilge pump, he thought, but he was suddenly too tired to move. *This has to be time-lag. I've never felt this tired in my life.* He could hardly pull the wool blanket up over him. It smelled of tar and wet dog, and the tail of it was wet from where it had dragged in the water.

The Lady Jane *can't sink in an hour, can it?* he wondered, curling up on the bunk. The water sloshed as the boat rocked gently back and forth. *That's all I ask, an hour, and then, if the water level's still rising, I'll get up and start the pump.* And at some point he must have staggered over, still asleep, and done it because when he woke he could hear it chugging, and could no longer hear the water sloshing.

How long had he slept? He held his arm up to look at his watch, but it was too dark to read it. *Whatever time it is, I need to go see if Powney's back and then go find Jonathan,* he thought, and pushed the blanket off. He sat up and stepped down off the bunk.

Into over a foot of freezing water. The pump obviously wasn't working, even though it was wheezing away. Its chugging filled the hold, so loud it—

'Oh no!' Mike said and flung himself, splashing, across the hold and up the ladder. That wasn't the bilge pump. It was the engine. They were moving. He jerked the hatch open.

Onto more darkness. He blinked stupidly at it, waiting for his eyes to adjust, and at the rush of wind and salt spray against his face. 'Well, well, what have we here?' Commander Harold's voice said jovially. 'A stowaway?'

Mike could barely make him out in the darkness. He was at the wheel, in his peacoat and yachting cap. 'I had a feeling you'd try to get in on this,' he said.

'In on what?' Mike said, hauling himself up onto deck. He looked frantically back towards the stern, but he couldn't see anything, only darkness. 'Where are you going?'

'To bring our boys home.'

'What do you mean? To Dunkirk?' Mike shouted at him over the wind. 'I can't go to Dunkirk!'

'Then you'd better start swimming, Kansas, because we're already halfway across the Channel.'

'You may go to the ball, Cinderella,' her fairy godmother said,
'but you must take care to leave before the clock strikes twelve.'
'But what will I wear?' Cinderella asked. 'I cannot go in these rags.'

CINDERELLA

DULWICH, SURREY – 13 JUNE 1944

I t was late Tuesday afternoon by the time she reached Dulwich's First Aid Nursing Yeomanry post. No one answered her knock. *Of course not*, she thought, annoyed. *They're all out looking for V-1 fragments.* She'd planned to arrive on the morning of the eleventh so she'd have time to settle in, meet everyone, and watch them for two full days before the rockets began, but she hadn't counted on all the delays the invasion would cause. The D-Day landings in Normandy might have gone off with scarcely a hitch, but on this side of the Channel, chaos reigned. Every train and bus and road had either been crammed to capacity or restricted to invasion forces. It had taken her a day and a half to arrange transport to London with an American WAC delivering documents to Whitehall, and then at the last moment, the WAC had been ordered to Eisenhower's headquarters in Portsmouth instead, and when they got there, both car and driver had been commandeered by British Intelligence. She'd spent the next three days in the wilds of Hampshire, vainly attempting to get a seat on a train, and finally hitched a ride to Dulwich in a Jeep with some American GIs, but by then the first V-1s had already fallen, and she'd missed her chance to observe the post in 'normal' circumstances.

Though perhaps not. The government hadn't yet admitted that the explosions were the result of unmanned rockets, and wouldn't till three days from now. And none of the four V-1s that had hit last night had landed in Dulwich, so that if their post hadn't been one of those sent to the crash sites by the Ministry of Home Security to gather fragments so the government could determine exactly what sort of weapon they were dealing with, they still might not know. But they obviously had been sent out because there continued to be no answer to her knocking. The post was deserted.

It can't be, she thought. *This is an ambulance post. Someone has got to be manning the telephone.* She knocked again, more loudly. Still no answer.

She tried the door. It opened, and she went inside. 'Hullo? Anyone here?' she called, and when no one answered, went in search of the despatch room.

Halfway down the corridor she heard music – the Andrews Sisters singing 'Don't Sit Under the Apple Tree'. She followed the sound along the corridor to a half-open door. Inside, she could see a young girl in pigtails and trousers lying on a sofa reading a film magazine, one leg draped over the arm of the sofa. *A girl who obviously doesn't know about the V-1s yet*, she thought. *Good.* She pushed the door open. 'Hullo? I beg your pardon, I'm looking for the officer in charge.'

The girl shot to her feet, lunging for the phonograph and dropping the film magazine in a splaying of pages, then abandoned the effort and snapped to attention. Which meant she was older than she looked, even though she was standing there like a naughty child about to be sent to bed without supper. 'Lieutenant Fairchild, ma'am,' the girl said, saluting. 'Can I be of help, ma'am?'

'Lieutenant Kent reporting for duty.' She handed her her transfer papers. 'I've just been assigned to this post.'

'Assigned? The Major didn't say anything about ...' The girl frowned at the papers, and then grinned. 'Headquarters finally sent someone – I don't believe it! We'd given up all hope. Welcome to the post, Lieutenant – sorry, what did you say your name was?'

'Kent. Mary Kent.'

'Welcome, Lieutenant Kent,' Fairchild said, and extended her hand. 'I'm so sorry I didn't know who you were, but we've been short-handed for months, and the Major's been fighting to get HQ to send someone, but we'd given up hope of your ever arriving.'

So had I, Mary thought.

'I do wish you'd been here a month ago. We were absolutely swamped with officers who needed driving, what with the invasion and all. We weren't supposed to know what was going on – it was all terribly hush-hush – but it was obvious the balloon was about to go up. I got to drive General Patton,' she said proudly. 'But now they're all in France, and we haven't a thing to do. Not that we aren't glad to have you. And we shan't be idle long.'

No, Mary thought.

'The Major will see to that. There's no slacking off allowed at this post.' She glanced guiltily at the film magazine on the sofa. 'She insists we do our bit to win the war every moment of every day. And she'll have my head if she comes back and finds I haven't done my bit and shown you round the post. Hang on.' She laid the papers on the desk and went over to the door. 'Talbot!' she called down the corridor.

There was no answer. 'She must have changed her mind,' Fairchild said. 'And gone with the others to the applecart upset.'

What was an applecart upset? Some sort of ambulance call? She was obviously expected to know, but in all her researching of World War II slang she'd never heard the term.

'I should have thought they'd be back by now,' Fairchild said.

'Hang on.' She wedged the door open with her rolled-up magazine. 'So I'll be able to hear the telephone, though I doubt if it's needed. No one's rung up all day. This way, Kent.'

If no one had telephoned, then an applecart upset couldn't be a type of ambulance call. Could it be slang for an incident?

'This is our mess,' Fairchild said, opening a door, and she knew that term at least. 'And the kitchen's through there. And out here' – she propped open a side door and led her through – 'is our garage, though there's not much to see at the moment, I'm afraid. We've two ambulances, a Bentley and a Daimler. Have you ever driven a Daimler, Kent?' she asked, and when Mary nodded, 'What year was it?'

2060. 'I think it was a thirty-eight,' she said.

'I'm afraid that won't be much help, then. Our Daimler's positively *ancient*. I'm convinced Florence Nightingale drove it in the Crimean War. It's ghastly to start and worse to drive. And nearly impossible to turn in a tight space. The Major's put in for a new one, but no luck yet. This is the log,' she said, walking over to a clipboard hanging on the wall. She showed her the spaces for time, destination, and distance driven. 'And no detours for errand-running allowed. The Major's an absolute bear about wasting petrol. And about failing to sign the log before you take a vehicle out.'

'What if you're going to an incident?'

'An *incident*? Oh, you mean if a Spitfire crashes or something? Well, then of course one would go to it straightaway and fill out the log when one came back, but we get scarcely any of those. Most of our ambulance calls are for soldiers who've got in a fight or fallen down a flight of stairs when they were sloshed. The remainder of the time we drive officers. After you sign in, you take the keys to the despatch room,' she led her back inside to the room with the sofa and the phonograph, 'and hang them up here.' She showed her three hooks labelled 'Ronald Colman', 'Clark Gable' and 'Bela Lugosi'. 'We thought since the RAF crews name their aeroplanes, we'd name our ambulances.'

144

'I thought you said you had two ambulances.'

'We do. Ronald Colman is the Major's personal Bentley. She lets us use it when both ambulances are out or when we're to drive someone important.'

'Oh. I assume Bela Lugosi is the Daimler?'

'Yes, though the name doesn't begin to describe its evil nature. I wanted to name it Heinrich Himmler.' She led Mary down another corridor and opened the door on a long room with six neatly made cots. 'You'll bunk in here,' she said, walking over to the second cot to the right. 'This one's yours.' She patted it, then walked over to a wardrobe and opened its door. 'You can stow your things in here. You're allowed half, so don't let Sutcliffe-Hythe take more than her share. And don't pick up after her. She tends to strew her things about and expect other people to put them away. She only joined up four months ago, and before that, of course, she had servants to do for her.'

The casual way in which Fairchild said it confirmed what Mary'd already deduced – that in spite of the pigtails and film magazine, Fairchild was from an upper-class family, as was Sutcliffe-Hythe, and most of the young women in the First Aid Nursing Yeomanry. They'd qualified for the FANYs because, unlike lower-class girls, they knew how to drive. They also possessed the social skills to mingle with officers, which was why they'd ended up chauffeuring generals as well as driving ambulances.

'Let's see, what else do you need to know?' Fairchild said. 'Breakfast's at six, lights out at eleven. No borrowing someone else's towel or beau, and no discussing Italy. Grenville's fiancé's there, and she hasn't heard from him in three weeks. Oh, and don't mention anything to do with getting engaged to Maitland – you're not engaged, are you?'

'No,' she said, setting her duffel bag down on the bed.

'Good. Engaged girls are rather a sore point with Maitland just now. She's been trying to persuade the pilot she's seeing to propose, but so far she's not having any luck. I told her she

145

should take lessons from Talbot. She's been engaged four times since I've been here. Were you seeing anyone in – where were you stationed before this?'

'Oxford.'

'Oxford? Oh, then you must know—' She stopped and cocked her head alertly as a door slammed somewhere.

'Fairchild!' a voice called, and a vividly pretty brunette in a FANY uniform and cap burst in. 'You will not *believe* what I just heard.'

And so much for my observing pre-rocket behaviour, Mary thought.

'What are you doing here, Talbot?' Fairchild said. 'I thought you'd gone with Maitland and the others to the applecart upset.'

'No, but I should have done. I'm so sick of the Yellow Peril, I could scream.'

The Yellow Peril? What did Japan have to do with an ambulance post? *I should definitely have done more research on World War II slang.*

'I was at the motor pool,' Talbot said. 'The Major insisted I go and pick up Bela Lugosi,' and thank goodness Fairchild had explained about the ambulance names, or she'd be completely lost. Could the Yellow Peril be some sort of vehicle as well?

'I told the Major it wouldn't be ready,' Talbot went on, 'but she— Who's this?'

'Mary Kent,' Fairchild said. 'She's our new driver.'

'But you can't be!' Talbot cried, and Mary looked up sharply. 'Sorry. It's only that I had a wager with Camberley that even the Major couldn't get a new driver out of HQ. For a pair of stockings. Now what am I going to do? I lent my only good pair to Jitters, and she simply *shredded* them.'

'She means Lieutenant Parrish,' Fairchild explained. 'She's keen on jitterbugging.'

'I simply *must* have stockings. Philip's taking me to the Ritz on Saturday.'

No, he's not, Mary thought. *There'll be more than a hundred V-1s coming over on Saturday. You'll be transporting the wounded.*

'I don't suppose you've an extra pair you'd be willing to lend me, have you, Kent?' Talbot asked.

No, and even if I had, I wouldn't admit it. It would instantly expose her as the impostor she was. No woman in England had had presentable stockings by this point in the war. 'Sorry,' she said, pointing down at her much-mended cotton stockings. 'I'm sorry if I caused you to lose your wager.'

'Oh, well, it's my own fault for betting against the Major. I should know better. Have you met the Major yet, Kent?'

'No, she hasn't,' Fairchild said. 'The Major's in London. She was called to a meeting at HQ.'

'Well, when you do, you'll find she's extremely determined, particularly when it comes to obtaining equipment and supplies – and personnel – for our post.'

Fairchild nodded. 'She's convinced that the winning of the war rests entirely on our shoulders.'

'Though I'd scarcely call driving officers with roving hands vital to the war's outcome,' Talbot said. 'I hope you're skilled at fending off amorous advances, Kent.' She turned to Fairchild. 'When do you expect Maitland and the others back?'

'I rather expected they'd be back by now,' Fairchild said.

'Where was this applecart upset?'

'Bethnal Green.'

'Oh. I'm going to go bathe before they get back.' She took off her jacket and started for the door.

'Wait,' Fairchild said, 'you can't go yet. You still haven't told us what you heard.'

'Oh yes, I nearly forgot. I went to the motor pool, and they told me Bela would be ready tomorrow, which is what they *always* say.' She undid her skirt, stepped out of it, and began unbuttoning her blouse. 'And I said we *must* have it today, and that I'd be willing to wait.' She shrugged out of her blouse and stood there in her slip, her arms akimbo. 'But that was a mistake. All they wanted to do then was stand about and chat me up.'

I can imagine, Mary thought. Talbot was not only pretty, she had a stunning figure. It was easy to see why she'd been engaged four times. 'So I finally went across to the canteen to have a cup of tea, and Lyttelton was there waiting to drive a captain assigned to Coastal Defences back to Dover—'

She definitely knew about the V-1s. Coastal Defences had known that the Germans were planning to send over unmanned rockets for weeks. They'd been sworn to secrecy, but obviously the captain had told his driver, and she'd told Talbot.

'And you won't *believe* what she told me,' Talbot went on. 'She said that Captain Eden's *married*. To a WAAF.'

'Captain Eden who took you to Quaglino's last week?'

'And to the Savoy the week before that, and rang me up three days ago to ask me to a play.'

'The cad,' Fairchild said fervently.

'A complete bounder,' Talbot agreed. 'And it was a play I desperately wanted to see. On the other hand, he was a dreadful dancer, and this will give me a chance to go out with an American, who hopefully will be so smitten he'll present me with a pair of nylon stockings.' She slung a towel over her shoulder. 'Ta ta, I'm off to bathe,' she said and left.

'And I need to show you the rest of the post,' Fairchild said. 'You can unpack later. We haven't much time.'

And I haven't either, Mary thought, following her, because even though Talbot hadn't known about the V-1s, the returning girls definitely would. Fairchild had said they'd gone to Bethnal Green, and that was where the second V-1 had fallen, damaging a railway bridge. So she'd been right, they had been sent out to collect fragments. That meant an 'applecart upset' must be an incident. But why would Talbot have said she wished she'd gone with them?

'This is the common room,' Fairchild was saying, 'and that's the door to the cellar. Our air-raid shelter is down there.' She opened a door onto a steep descending staircase. 'Though we never use it. The siren's only sounded once in the past three months, and that was when some children broke into the Civil Defence post and cranked it up for a lark.'

There hadn't been any sirens last night? But that couldn't be right. The sirens had definitely sounded for all four V-1s. A ten-year-old planespotter had carefully written down the times of every alert and all-clear in his log. They must not have been able to hear them here in Dulwich.

'And now that our boys are in France, we shan't have to worry about any more air raids,' Fairchild said. 'The war can't last much longer—' She stopped, listening.

Mary heard the slam of a car door and then voices.

'The girls are back,' Fairchild said, hurrying into the corridor.

A trio of young women in FANY uniform were coming in from the garage, their arms full of clothing. 'I still say we should have got that ecru lace,' the first one, a chunky blonde, was saying to a tall redhead.

'It was too small,' the redhead said. 'Even Camberley couldn't get the zip up.'

'Grenville might have been able to let it out for her,' the blonde said.

'Were you successful, Reed?' Fairchild asked.

'Only partly,' the redhead said, coming into the despatch room and dumping the clothes she held onto the sofa. 'We were only able to snag one evening frock.'

'And Camberley was nearly killed getting that,' the blonde said. 'She had to fight two girls from Croydon's St John's Ambulance for it.'

'But I won,' the third one, a tiny, elfin-looking girl, said. She pulled a floor-length pink net frock out of the pile and held it up triumphantly. 'Champion of the St Ethelred Applecart Upset.'

Which solved one mystery. An applecart upset was slang for a clothing exchange. Exchanges had been common during the

149

war, a result of rationing and the shortage of fabric, which was all being used for uniforms and parachutes.

'It's a bit short,' the redhead Reed said, 'but there's a good deal of fullness in the skirt we can use to add a ruffle, and—' She stopped. 'Who's this?'

'Lieutenant Mary Kent,' Fairchild said. 'Kent, this is Captain Maitland,' she pointed at the chunky blonde and then at the redhead and the elfin one, 'Lieutenant Reed, and Lieutenant Camberley. Kent's our new driver. Headquarters sent her from Oxford.'

'You're joking!' Maitland said.

'I *told* you the Major'd pull it off,' Camberley said, 'even if it is a bit late. I'm afraid you've missed all the fun, Kent.'

'If you were stationed in Oxford,' Reed said, 'then you must know—'

'Never mind that,' Talbot said, coming in in a bathrobe with her hair wrapped in a towel. 'I want to see what you got. Pink? Oh no, I look dreadful in pink. It washes me out so. Still,' she said, snatching it up, 'it'll be better than the Yellow Peril for Saturday.'

'You're *not* wearing it on Saturday,' Camberley said. '*I* risked life and limb going up against those St John's girls, so *I* get to wear it first.'

'Evening frocks are in short supply,' Fairchild explained, 'so we all share. We've been making do with the Yellow Peril and the dress Sutcliffe-Hythe wore for her presentation at court. We dyed it lavender, but it came out rather streaky.'

'It can only be worn to very dark nightclubs,' Reed said.

'But I *must* wear the pink,' Talbot said. 'It's the Ritz. I've already worn the Yellow Peril there twice.'

'Who's taking you to the Ritz?' Reed demanded.

'I'm not certain yet. Possibly Captain Johnson.'

'Johnson?' Reed asked. 'Is he the handsome one with the dashing moustache?'

'*No*,' Talbot said, holding the pink frock up against her and looking at it in the mirror. 'He's the American one with access to the PX,' and Mary should have been delighted with the conversation. It was a perfect example of pre-rocket ambulance-post life. But why hadn't they heard about the V-1? Surely one of the Bethnal Green ambulance crew would have mentioned it.

Don't be silly, they weren't there, she told herself. They'd have been up since half past four, administering first aid and transporting victims – there'd been six casualties – to hospital. They wouldn't have then gone blithely off to a clothing exchange.

But even if they hadn't been there, surely someone would have mentioned hearing an explosion. Or the siren, if, as Fairchild said, they hadn't heard one for months. Unless, she thought, watching the FANYs pass around the pink frock and a pair of worn dancing slippers they'd obtained, they'd been so intent on finding clothes that they hadn't spoken to anyone else?

'Haviland was there, and you'll never guess what she told me,' Maitland said. 'Do you remember Captain Ward? We met him at that canteen dance – dark wavy hair? Well, Haviland said he's mad about me, but he's been afraid to ask me out.'

'I was able to find you a lipstick,' Reed was saying to Talbot. 'Crimson Caress.' She handed her a gold tube.

'Thank goodness,' Talbot said, taking off the cap and twisting it up to reveal a startling shade of dark red. 'Mine was down to nothing. Did you get the black gloves?'

'No, but Healey and Baker were there, and they said their post is putting on a ragbag in July and that they're certain they saw a pair in among the donations. They told me they'd save them for us.'

'What's the Bethnal Green post doing putting on a ragbag?' Fairchild asked.

'It's to raise funds for a new ambulance,' Maitland said.

'Oh no, don't let the Major find out, or she'll have us doing one,' Talbot moaned, but Mary scarcely heard her. Bethnal Green's FANYs *had* been there.

Could I have got the date the V-1 assault began wrong? she wondered, but the times and locations had been implanted straight from the historical records. But if the V-1 had hit the railway bridge, how could they have failed to mention it?

'Look,' Reed was saying, 'I got a pair of beach san—' She stopped, listening. 'I think I heard a motor,' she said, darted out of the room, and returned. 'The Major's back.'

It might as well have been an air-raid siren. Reed and Camberley scooped up the clothes and swept them out of the room. Fairchild lunged for the phonograph, unplugged it, slammed down the lid and thrust it into Maitland's hands. 'Take this back to the common room,' she ordered, and as Maitland left, wriggled into the jacket of her uniform. 'Kent, hand me the *Film News*. Quick,' she said, buttoning her jacket.

Mary dived to unwedge the rolled-up magazine propping open the door and hand it to Fairchild, who jammed it into a file cabinet drawer, then leaped back to the desk just in time to sit down and then stand up again as the Major entered.

From all the comments, Mary had been expecting a gorgon, but the Major was a small, slight woman with delicate features and only slightly greying hair.

When Mary saluted and said, 'Lieutenant Mary Kent, reporting for duty, ma'am,' she smiled kindly and said in a quiet voice, 'Welcome, Lieutenant.'

'I was just showing her round the post,' Fairchild said.

'That can wait. Assemble the girls in the common room. I have an announcement to make,' the Major said. Which meant the V-1s had hit on schedule after all, and the Bethnal Green FANYs, like the Coastal Defence officer, had been ordered not to say anything till an official announcement had been made. Which the Major was about to do.

And in the meantime she'd had the chance, in spite of having arrived late, to observe a cross-section of life at the post – a life which was about to change radically. It was already changing. The girls' solemn expressions as they gathered in the common room showed they knew something was up. Talbot had combed out her wet hair and got into uniform, and Fairchild had pinned her pigtails to the top of her head. They all stood at attention as the Major entered. 'We are now entering a new and critical phase of the war,' she said. 'I have just returned from a meeting at headquarters—'

Here it comes.

'—where our unit received a new assignment. As of tomorrow, we will be charged with transporting soldiers wounded in the Normandy invasion to Orpington Hospital for surgery.'

Coughs And Sneezes Spread Diseases

BRITISH MINISTRY OF HEALTH POSTER, 1940

WARWICKSHIRE – MAY 1940

It took Eileen nearly an hour to fill up the three evacuees' paperwork for Mrs Chambers, partly because Theodore announced he wanted to go home every thirty seconds. *So do I,* Eileen thought. *And if you hadn't arrived, I'd be back in Oxford now, persuading Mr Dunworthy to send me to* VE *Day.*

'I don't want to go home,' Edwina, the elder girl, said. She looked as though she'd fit right in with Binnie. 'I want to go in a boat like we was supposed to.'

'I want to go to the toilet,' Susan, the younger one, said. 'Now.'

Eileen took her upstairs, then came back down to sign several more forms. 'Do tell her ladyship thank you for all her hard work,' Mrs Chambers said, putting on her gloves. 'Her dedication to the war effort is truly inspiring.'

Eileen saw her out, then sent the children outside to play, took their luggage upstairs to the nursery, and ran up to her room for the third time. She changed out of her uniform, arranged the letter about her mother's illness and its envelope on the bed, and hurried downstairs. Ten past three. Good. The other children wouldn't be home from school till four, which meant she could take the road. She hurried around the corner of the house to the drive.

'Look out!' a man's voice called, and she looked up to see the Austin bearing down on her with the vicar in it and with – *oh no* – Una at the wheel. Eileen leaped aside.

'No, the brake, the brake!' the vicar shouted, 'That's the wrong—' and the Austin shot forward, straight at Eileen. Una flung her hands up, like someone drowning.

'Don't let go of the—' the vicar shouted, grabbing for the steering wheel. The Austin slewed wildly sideways, grazing the skirt of Eileen's coat, and screeched to a halt mere inches from the manor. He leaped out. 'Are you all right?' he said, racing over to Eileen. 'You're not hurt, are you?'

'No,' she said, thinking, *That would absolutely tear it, being killed on my last day here.*

'I'm having my driving lesson,' Una called unnecessarily from the car. 'Should I back up now?'

'No,' the vicar and Eileen both said.

'That will be all for today, Una,' the vicar told her.

'But, Vicar, it's only been a quarter of an hour, and her ladyship said—'

'I know, but I must give Miss O'Reilly her lesson now.'

'Oh, but I—' Eileen began and hesitated, attempting to think what to tell him. She couldn't tell him she'd just had word her mother was ill. He'd insist on driving her to the railway station. But she didn't have time for a driving lesson either.

'Please,' he whispered, 'don't make me get back in that car with her.'

Eileen nodded, suppressing a smile, and walked over to the Austin with him. Una reluctantly got out. 'But when will I have my lesson, Vicar?'

'On Friday next,' he said, getting in beside Eileen.

She started the car and started down the drive. 'You're braver than I am, Vicar. Nothing could induce me to get into a motor car with her again.'

'I plan to remove the distributor first,' he whispered back.

I'm going to miss you, she thought, and wished she could tell him goodbye instead of sneaking away, but she was going to have enough difficulty even doing that. She must think of some excuse to cut the lesson short. 'Vicar, I—'

'I know, you're much too busy to waste an hour on a lesson you don't need, and I've no intention of inflicting one on you. If you'll just drive till Una's safely in the house, and then keep out of her sight for the next hour—'

I can do better than that, Eileen thought, driving out through the manor gates and onto the narrow lane.

'There's a good spot to turn round just after the next curve,' he said.

She nodded and rounded the curve. Binnie and Alf were standing in the middle of the lane, making no effort to get out of the way. 'Look out!' the vicar cried, and Eileen jammed on the brakes and brought the car to a skidding stop. Alf continued to stand there, staring stupidly at the car.

Binnie came up to the passenger side. 'Hullo, Vicar.'

'Binnie, why aren't you in school?' Eileen demanded.

'We was sent 'ome. Alf took ill. Can we 'ave a ride, Vicar?'

'No,' Eileen said. 'You're to go straight back to school.'

Binnie ignored her. 'The schoolmistress said to take Alf 'ome, Vicar. 'Is 'ead's fearful hot, and 'e feels ever so bad.'

Eileen pushed the car door open, got out, and marched over to Alf. 'He's not ill, Vicar. This is one of their tricks. Alf, why did you steal Miss Fuller's hood ornament and door handles? And don't say you were disabling her car for the invasion.'

'We wasn't,' Binnie said. 'We was collectin' aluminium for the Spitfire Fund. To build a plane out of.'

'I want you to return them to Miss Fuller immediately.'

'But Alf's ill.'

'He's not ill.' Eileen clapped her hand to Alf's forehead. 'He's—' she began, and stopped. It was burning hot. She tilted his head up. His eyes were red and too bright, and his cheeks looked flushed under their layer of dirt. 'He does have a fever,' she told the vicar, feeling Alf's cheeks and hands.

'I told you 'e did,' Binnie said smugly.

Eileen ignored her. 'We must get him home, Vicar,' she said and bent over Alf. 'When did you begin to feel ill?'

'I dunno,' Alf said dully, and vomited all over her shoes.

''E was sick at school, too,' Binnie volunteered. 'Twice.'

The vicar instantly took charge. He handed Eileen his handkerchief, took off his coat, bundled Alf up in it, ordered Binnie to open the back door, and put him in the backseat, all in the time it took Eileen to wipe her shoes. 'Climb in the front seat, Binnie,' he said, 'so Eileen can sit with Alf.'

Binnie promptly got in the driver's seat. 'I can drive.'

'No, you can't,' the vicar said. 'Slide over.'

'But it's an emergency, ain't it? You said you was teachin' me to drive in emer—'

'Slide over,' Eileen said, 'now.' Binnie did. Eileen climbed in the back. Alf was huddled in the corner, his head in his hands. 'Does your head hurt?' she asked him.

'Yes,' he said and put his head in her lap. She could feel the heat through her coat.

'I'll wager it's typhoid fever,' Binnie said. 'I knew this boy what died of typhoid.'

'Alf hasn't got typhoid fever,' Eileen said.

'This boy who 'ad it ate a 'ard-boiled egg,' Binnie went on, undaunted, 'and 'is stomach blew up, just like that. You ain't s'posed to eat eggs if you've got typhoid fever.'

The vicar drove up to the manor and around to the kitchen door. He opened the door, took Alf from Eileen, and walked him into the kitchen, where Mrs Bascombe was kneading bread. 'If you're here to try to talk me into learning to drive, Vicar, you'd best save your breath. I've no intention of— Alf, what have you done now?'

'He's ill,' Eileen explained.

'We found him on the road,' the vicar said.

'He was sick all over Eileen's shoes,' Binnie put in.

'I think perhaps we'd better phone for the doctor.'

'Of course, Vicar,' Mrs Bascombe said. 'Una, take the vicar through to the library so he can use the telephone,' but as soon as they were gone, she turned on Alf. 'Doctor? What you need is a trip to the woodshed, Alf Hodbin. You've been at the jam cupboard again, haven't you? What else have you been stuffing yourself with? Cakes? Lamb pie?'

Oh, don't mention food, Eileen thought, looking worriedly at Alf's face. 'I don't think it's something he ate,' she said. 'He's feverish. I think he's ill.'

'P'rhaps 'e was poisoned,' Binnie said. 'By fifth columnists. The jerries—'

'What he needs is a dose of castor oil and a good shaking.' Mrs Bascombe grabbed his arm, and then stopped, frowning, and took a long hard look at him. 'Tell me where it hurts.' She pressed her hand against his forehead and then his cheeks. 'Are your eyes sore?'

Alf nodded. 'It's typhoid, ain't it?' Binnie asked.

Una came back in. 'Where's the vicar?' Mrs Bascombe demanded. 'Did he telephone for the doctor?'

Una nodded. 'He wasn't in. The vicar went to fetch him.'

Mrs Bascombe turned back to Alf. 'Does your head hurt?' He nodded. 'Has he had a runny nose?' she demanded of Eileen.

Alf always had a runny nose. Eileen tried to remember if he'd wiped it on his sleeve more than usual the past few days.

'It's been runnin' somethin' awful,' Binnie said, and Mrs Bascombe yanked up Alf's shirt and peered at his chest. It looked normal to Eileen, except for a long smear of dirt which he'd got God knew how. She'd given him a bath just last night.

'Is your throat sore?' Mrs Bascombe asked.

Alf nodded.

'Eileen, take Alf upstairs,' Mrs Bascombe ordered, 'and put him to bed. Make up a cot for him in the ballroom.'

'In the ballroom?' Eileen said doubtfully, remembering what had happened the last time the children had been in there.

'Yes. Binnie, come here and let me look at your chest. Do your eyes hurt?'

'Come along, Alf,' Eileen said and walked him up the stairs and into the nursery. 'Climb into your pyjamas. I'll be back straightaway,' she told him and ran back down to the kitchen. Mrs Bascombe was filling the kettle, and Binnie was looking interestedly at the pots and pans, no doubt waiting for a chance to steal them for the scrap drive. Eileen hurried over to Mrs Bascombe and whispered, 'Has Alf got something serious?'

Mrs Bascombe glanced over at Binnie, then set the kettle on the cooker, and struck a match. 'Make sure Alf's kept warm,' she said, lighting the burner. 'I'll bring you up a hot water bottle in a moment,' which meant she didn't want to say anything with Binnie there. Which meant it was serious, and obviously contagious. Not typhoid fever – that had been a waterborne disease – but there'd been all sorts of infectious diseases back before antivirals and some of them had been killers: typhus and influenza and scarlet fever.

He can't have scarlet fever, Eileen thought, running back upstairs. *I'm supposed to leave today.* She looked at the clock. It was four already, and who knew how long it would take the doctor to get here. If she didn't make it out to the drop before dark, she'd be trapped here an entire extra week. But if Alf was seriously ill—

Perhaps I can get him into bed, and then, as soon as Mrs Bascombe brings up the hot water bottle, run out to the drop and tell them I'm going to be late, she thought, going into the nursery. Alf was sitting listlessly on the edge of his cot, still in his clothes. Eileen took off her hat and coat and helped him into his pyjamas, looking anxiously at his chest as she buttoned the jacket. His chest was a bit pink, but she couldn't see a rash. 'Lie down while I make up a bed for you,' she told him and dragged one of the cots into the ballroom, made it up, then helped him across the corridor and onto the cot.

She heard a door slam below and voices. 'Go outside and play now,' Mrs Bascombe said.

The rest of the children must be home from school. 'I want to go and see Alf,' Eileen heard Binnie say.

'*I* want to go home,' Theodore Willett said.

'Outside,' Mrs Bascombe repeated.

'But it's raining,' Binnie protested. 'We'll catch our death.'

And whatever Alf had, it couldn't be that serious, because Mrs Bascombe said, 'No talking back. Outside, all of you.'

'I don't got to go outside, do I?' Alf asked worriedly.

'No,' Eileen said, covering him up. He looked very green. 'Are you feeling like you're going to be sick again?'

He shook his head weakly, but she fetched a basin, just in case. When she got back to the ballroom, Dr Stuart was there, and he was asking Alf the same questions Mrs Bascombe had. He looked at Alf's chest and then stuck a barbaric-looking glass thermometer in his mouth and took Alf's pulse, using two fingers and his watch. If this was something serious, Alf was in trouble. Nineteen-forties medicine was extremely primitive. Could a thermometer like that even detect a fever?

'He's been complaining of feeling cold,' Eileen said, 'and he's been sick twice.'

Dr Stuart nodded, waited an interminably long time, pulled out the thermometer, read it, and took a small pocket torch from his bag. 'Open wide,' he said to Alf and looked at the inside of his cheek with the light. 'Just as I thought. Measles.'

Not scarlet fever. *Thank goodness.* If he'd been really ill, Eileen wasn't sure she could have brought herself to leave. But measles was only a childhood disease of the time. 'Are you certain?' she asked. 'He hasn't any rash.'

'The measles won't appear for another day or so. Till then, he needs to be kept warm and the sickroom kept dark to protect his eyes. That's one advantage of the blackout. You needn't put up new curtains.' He put the torch back in his bag. 'His fever is likely to go up sharply until the measles come out.' He snapped his bag shut. 'I'll look in tonight. The most important thing is to keep him away from the other children. How many are here at the manor just now?'

'Thirty-five,' Eileen said.

He shook his head unhappily. 'Well, we'll hope most of them have already had measles. Alf, has your sister had them?' Alf shook his head weakly. The doctor turned back to Eileen. 'You've had them, I hope?'

'No,' she said, 'but I've been—' and remembered they hadn't had vaccines in 1940 except for smallpox. 'I mean, yes, I—' she stammered and stopped again. If she said she'd had them, he'd put her in charge of the sickroom and she'd never get away. The doctor was looking at her curiously. 'I haven't had measles,' she said firmly.

'Sit down,' he said, and opened his black bag. He took her temperature, looked at her throat, and examined the inside of her cheeks. 'No symptoms yet, but you've been in close contact. I'll tell Mrs Bascombe to send someone up to take over for you immediately. In the meantime, no more contact with the patient than absolutely necessary.'

She nodded, relieved. There was no reason now not to leave. Even if she stayed, she wouldn't be allowed near Alf or the other evacuees who caught the measles.

'I'll look in on him tonight,' Dr Stuart said and left.

'What'd 'e mean, 'ave someone take over?' Alf asked, sitting up on his cot. 'Ain't you goin' to take care of me?'

'I'm not allowed to,' Eileen said. 'I haven't had measles.' She started towards the door.

'You ain't leavin' *now*, are you?'

'No, I'm only going across to the nursery to fetch you another blanket. I'll be back straightaway.'

'You swear?'

'I swear. I won't leave till someone comes to relieve me.'

'Who?' he demanded.

'I don't know. Una or—'

'*Una?*' he said disbelievingly. 'Una'll let me die. *You're* the only one wot's nice to me'n Binnie,' and looked so woeful she almost felt sorry for him. Almost.

'Lie *down*,' she said, fetched him a blanket, and then went across to the nursery for her hat and coat and put them on the table just outside the ballroom door. One good thing about Alf's illness was that the resultant confusion in the manor should make it easier for her to slip away. When someone arrived to relieve her. Where was Una? Had the doctor forgotten to tell Mrs Bascombe to send her up? And what had happened to the hot water bottle Mrs Bascombe had said she'd bring him? Alf was shivering.

There was a knock on the door. *Finally*, Eileen thought and hurried to open it. 'I come to see 'ow Alf is,' Binnie said, peering into the ballroom.

'You're not allowed in here, Binnie. Your brother has the measles. You might catch them.'

'No, I won't,' Binnie said, attempting to sidle through the door. 'I've already 'ad 'em.'

'She's lyin',' Alf called from the cot.

'I am *not*. You was only a baby, Alf, that's why you don't remember. I was covered all over in spots.'

Well, that's a blessing, Eileen thought. All she needed was two ailing Hodbins. But she still didn't intend to let her in. 'Go and play.' She shut the door.

Binnie promptly knocked again. 'Alf don't like to be alone when 'e's ill,' she said when Eileen opened the door. ''E gets frightened.'

Alf has never been frightened of anything in his life. 'No one's allowed in.' Eileen shut the door again and locked it. 'Doctor's orders.'

Binnie knocked again. 'Go *away*,' Eileen said.

'Eileen?' Alf said.

'Binnie's *not* allowed in here.'

He shook his head. 'That ain't wot I—' he said and vomited again.

Eileen grabbed for the basin, but she shoved it under him a second too late. It went all over the sheets, the pillow, and his pyjamas as well. The knocking began again. 'Go *away*, Binnie!' she said, reaching for a towel.

'It's Una,' Una's voice said timidly.

Oh, for heaven's sake. 'Come in,' Eileen said.

'I can't. The door's locked.' Eileen handed Alf the towel and unlocked the door, and Una came in, looking frightened. 'Mrs Bascombe said I was to take over for you.'

Eileen was tempted to hand her the basin and walk out. 'Get Alf out of his pyjamas while I empty this,' she said. 'And don't let Binnie in.' She rinsed out the basin, got fresh sheets from the linen closet, and found a clean pair of pyjamas for Alf.

When she got back to the ballroom, Una was standing exactly where she'd left her. 'What's he got?' she asked nervously. 'Flu?'

'No,' Eileen said, standing Alf up and unbuttoning his pyjama top, taking it off him, and sponging his chest clean. 'Measles.' And, at the terrified look on Una's face, 'You have had the measles, haven't you?'

'Yes,' Una said. 'That is, I may have done. I'm not sure. But I've never *nursed* anyone with them.'

'The doctor will help you,' Eileen said, stripping the sheets off and remaking the cot. She helped Alf into bed and covered him up. 'Dr Stuart will be back later tonight. All you need to do is keep Alf warm.' She gathered up the soiled sheets and pyjamas. 'And keep the basin handy. And keep Binnie out.'

And she made her escape. But she still had the wad of soiled sheets, and she didn't dare take them down to the laundry, or Mrs Bascombe would hand her the hot water bottle or put her to work looking after the other children. She opened the door to the bathroom, dumped the sheets in the bathtub, and shut the door again, feeling guilty at leaving the mess, but it couldn't be helped. She *had* to get out of here.

She put on her coat and hat, listening for the children. Had they all come back inside, or only Binnie? And where *was* Binnie? Eileen couldn't afford to have her follow her. She heard a door slam below and Mrs Bascombe's voice saying, 'Go upstairs and get your things off, and then come straight back down for your tea. And you're not to go near the ballroom.'

'Why not?' she heard Binnie ask. 'I've *'ad* 'em.'

Good, they were all in the kitchen. For the moment. Eileen shot along the corridor and down the main staircase. If Lady Caroline was back or the doctor was still here, she'd simply pretend she had a question about Alf's care. But there was no one in the hall below. Good. In a quarter of an hour she'd be at the drop and on her way home. She ran down the stairs and across the large hall to the door and opened it.

Samuels was standing there, with a hammer in one hand and a sheaf of large yellow papers in the other. 'Oh,' Eileen gasped, 'has the doctor gone?' He nodded. 'Oh dear. Perhaps I can still catch him.' She started past him.

He stepped in front of her, blocking the way. 'You can't leave,' he said, looking pointedly at her hat and coat.

'I'm only going to fetch the doctor,' she said and attempted to sidle past.

'No, you're not.' He handed her one of the yellow sheets. 'By order of the Ministry of Health, County of Warwickshire,' it read at the top. 'No one's allowed in or out,' he said. He took the sheet back from her and nailed it up on the door. 'Except the doctor. This house and everyone in it's been quarantined.'

'Another part of the island.'

—WILLIAM SHAKESPEARE, *THE TEMPEST*

KENT – APRIL 1944

Cess opened the door of the office and leaned in. 'Worthing!' he called, and when he didn't answer, 'Ernest! Stop playing reporter and come with me. I need you on a job.'

Ernest kept typing. 'Can't,' he said through the pencil between his teeth. 'I've got five newspaper articles and ten pages of transmissions to write.'

'You can do them later,' Cess said. 'The tanks are here. We need to blow them up.'

Ernest removed the pencil from between his teeth and said, 'I thought the tanks were Gwendolyn's job.'

'He's in Hawkhurst. Dental appointment.'

'Which takes priority over tanks? I can see the history books now. "World War II was lost because of a toothache."'

'It's not a toothache, it's a cracked filling,' Cess said. 'And it'll do you good to get a bit of fresh air.' Cess yanked the sheet of paper out of the typewriter. 'You can write your fairy-tales later.'

'No, I can't,' Ernest said, making an unsuccessful grab for the paper. 'If I don't get these stories in by tomorrow morning, they won't be in Tuesday's edition, and Lady Bracknell will have my head.'

Cess held it out of reach. '"The Steeple Cross Women's Institute held a tea on Friday afternoon,"' he read aloud, '"to welcome the officers of the 21st Airborne to the village." Definitely more important than blowing up tanks, Worthing. Front-page stuff. This'll be in *The Times*, I presume?'

'No, the *Sudbury Weekly Shopper*,' Ernest said, making another grab for the sheet of paper, this time successful. 'And it's due at nine tomorrow morning along with four others, *which I haven't finished yet*. And, thanks to you, I already missed last week's deadline. Take Moncrieff with you.'

'He's down with a bad cold.'

'Which he no doubt caught while blowing up tanks in the pouring rain. Not exactly my idea of fun,' Ernest said, rolling a new sheet of paper into the typewriter, and began typing again.

'It's not raining,' Cess said. 'There's only a light fog, and it's supposed to clear by morning. Perfect flying weather. That's why we've got to blow them up tonight. It'll only take an hour or two. You'll be back in more than enough time to finish your articles and get them over to Sudbury.'

Ernest didn't believe that any more than he believed it wasn't raining. It had rained every day all spring. 'There must be someone else who can do it. What about Lady Bracknell? He'd be perfect for the job. He's full of hot air.'

'He's in London, meeting with the higher-ups, and everyone else is over at Camp Omaha. You're the only one who can do it. Come, Worthing, do you want to tell your children you sat at a typewriter all through the war or that you blew up tanks?'

'Cess, what makes you think we'll ever be allowed to tell anyone anything?'

'I suppose that's true. But surely by the time we have *grand*children, *some* of it will have been declassified. That is, if we win the war. Which we won't if you don't help. I can't manage both the tanks and the cutter on my own.'

'Oh, all right,' Ernest said, pulling the paper out of the

typewriter and putting it in a file folder on top of several others. 'Give me five minutes to lock up.'

'Lock *up*? Do you honestly think Goebbels is going to break in and steal your tea party story while we're gone?'

'I'm only following regulations,' Ernest said, swivelling his chair to face the metal filing cabinet. He opened the second drawer down, filed the folder, then fished a ring of keys out of his pocket and locked the cabinet. '"All written materials of Fortitude South and the Special Means unit shall be considered 'top top secret' and handled accordingly." And speaking of regulations, if I'm going to be in some bloody cow pasture all night, I need a decent pair of boots. "All officers are to be issued appropriate gear for missions."'

Cess handed him an umbrella. 'Here.'

'I thought you said fog, not rain.'

'Light fog. Clearing towards morning. And wear an Army uniform, in case someone shows up in the middle of the operation. You have two minutes. I want to be there before dark.' He went out.

Ernest waited, listening, till he heard the outside door slam, then swiftly unlocked the file drawer, pulled out the folder, removed several of the pages, replaced the file, and relocked the drawer. He slid the pages he'd removed into a manila envelope, sealed it, and stuck it under a stack of forms in the bottom drawer of the desk. Then he took a key from around his neck, locked the drawer, hung the key around his neck again under his shirt, picked up the umbrella, put on his uniform and his boots, and went outside.

Into an all-enveloping greyness. If this was what Cess considered a light fog, he shuddered to think what a heavy one was. He couldn't see the tanks or the lorry. He couldn't even see the gravel driveway at his feet.

But he could hear an engine. He felt his way towards it, his hands out in front of him till they connected with the side of the

Austin. 'What took you so long?' Cess asked, leaning out of the fog to open its door. 'Get in.'

Ernest climbed in. 'I thought you said the tanks were here.'

'They are,' Cess said, roaring off into blackness. 'We've got to go pick them up in Tenterden and then take them down to Icklesham.'

Tenterden was not 'here'. It was fifteen miles in the opposite direction from Icklesham and, in this fog, it would be well after dark before they even got there. *This'll take all night*, he thought. *I'll never make that deadline*. But halfway to Brede, the fog lifted, and when they reached Tenterden, everything was, amazingly, loaded and ready to go. Ernest, following Cess and the lorry in the Austin, began to feel some hope that it wouldn't take too long to get unloaded and set up, and they might actually be done blowing up the tanks by midnight. Whereupon the fog closed in again, causing Cess to miss the turn for Icklesham twice and for the lane once. It was nearly midnight before they located the right pasture.

Ernest parked the Austin among some bushes and got out to open the gate. He promptly stepped in mud up to his ankles and then, after he'd extricated himself, in a large cowpat. He squelched over to the lorry, looking around for cows, even though in this foggy darkness he wouldn't see one till he'd collided with it. 'I thought there weren't supposed to be any cows in this pasture,' he said to Cess.

'There were before, but the farmer moved them into the next one over,' Cess said, leaning out the window. 'That's why we picked this pasture. That, and the large copse of trees over there.' He pointed vaguely out into the murk. 'The tanks will be hidden out of sight under the trees.'

'I thought the whole idea was to let the Germans see them.'

'To let them see *some* of them,' Cess corrected. 'There are a dozen in this battalion.'

'We've got to blow up a *dozen* tanks?'

'No, only three. The Army didn't park them far enough

under the trees. Their rear ends can still be seen poking out from under the branches. I think it'll be easiest if I back across the field. Help me turn around.'

'Are you certain that's a good idea?' Ernest said. 'It's awfully muddy.'

'That'll make the tracks more visible. You needn't worry. This lorry's got good tyres. I won't get her stuck.'

He didn't. Ernest did, driving the lorry back to the gate after they'd unloaded the three tanks. It took them the next two hours to get out of the mudhole, in the process of which Ernest lost his footing and fell flat, and they made a hideous rutted mess out of the centre of the field.

'Göring's boys will never believe tank treads did that,' Ernest said, shining a shielded torch on the churned-up mud.

'You're right,' Cess said. 'We'll have to put a tank over it to hide it, and – I know! – we'll make it look as though it got stuck in the mud.'

'Tanks don't get stuck in the mud.'

'They would in this mud,' Cess said. 'We'll only blow up three quadrants and leave the other one flat, so it'll look like it's listing.'

'Do you honestly think they'll be able to see that from fifteen thousand feet?'

'No idea,' Cess said, 'but if we stand here arguing, we won't be done by morning, and the Germans will see what we're up to. Here, lend me a hand. We'll unload the tank and then drive the lorry back to the lane. That way we won't have to drag it.'

Ernest helped him unload the heavy rubber pallet. Cess connected the pump and began inflating the tank. 'Are you certain it's facing the right way?' Ernest asked. 'It should be facing the copse.'

'Oh, right,' Cess said, shielding his torch with his hand and shining the light on it. 'No, it's the wrong way round. Here, help me shift it.'

They pushed and shoved and dragged the heavy mass around

till it faced the other way. 'Now let's hope it isn't upside down,' Cess said. 'They should put a "this end up" on them, though I suppose that might make the Germans suspicious.' He began to pump. 'Oh, good, there's a tread.'

The front end of a tank began to emerge out of the flat folds of grey-green rubber, looking remarkably tanklike. Ernest watched for a moment, then fetched the phonograph, the small wooden table it sat on, and its speaker. He set them up, got the record from the lorry, placed it on the turntable, and lowered the needle. The sound of tanks rolling thunderously towards him filled the pasture, making it impossible to hear anything Cess said.

On the other hand, he thought as he wrestled the tank-tread cutter off the back of the lorry, he no longer had to switch on his torch. He could find his way simply by following the sound. Unless there were in fact cows in this pasture – which, judging by the number of fresh cowpats he was stepping in, there definitely could be.

Cess had told him on the way to Tenterden that the cutter was perfectly simple to operate. All one had to do was push it, like a lawn mower, but it was at least five times as heavy. It required bearing down with one's whole weight on the handle to make it go even a few inches, it refused to budge at all in grass taller than two inches, and it tended to veer off at an angle. Ernest had to go back to the lorry, fetch a rake, smooth over what he'd done, then redo it several times before he had a more-or-less straight tread mark from the gate to the mired tank.

Cess was still working on the right front quadrant. 'Sprang a leak,' he shouted over the rumble of tanks. 'Luckily, I brought my bicycle patch kit along. Don't come any nearer! That cutter's sharp.'

Ernest nodded, hoisted it over in front of where the tank's other tread would be, and started back towards the gate. 'How many of these do you want?' he shouted to Cess.

'At least a dozen pair,' Cess shouted, 'and some of them need to overlap. I think the fog's beginning to lift.'

The fog was not beginning to lift. When he switched on his torch so he could return the needle to the beginning of the record, the phonograph was shrouded in mist. And even if it should lift, they wouldn't be able to tell in this blackness. He looked at his watch. Two o'clock, and they still hadn't inflated a tank. They were going to be stuck here forever.

Cess finally completed the mired tank and slogged across the field to the copse to do the other two, Ernest following with the cutter, making tread tracks to indicate where the tanks had driven in under the trees.

Halfway there, the sound of tanks shut off. Damn, he'd forgotten to move the needle. He had to go all the way back across the pasture to start the record, and he'd no sooner reached the cutter again than the fog did indeed lift. 'I told you,' Cess said happily, and it immediately began to rain.

'The phonograph!' Cess cried, and Ernest had to rescue it and then the umbrella and prop it over the phonograph, tying it to the tank's rubber gun with rope.

The shower lasted till just before dawn, magnifying the mud and making the grass so slippery that Ernest fell down twice more – once racing to move the phonograph needle, which had stuck and was repeating the same three seconds of tank rumbling over and over, and the second time helping Cess repair yet another puncture. 'But think of the war story you'll have to tell your grandchildren!' Cess said as he wiped the mud off.

'I doubt whether I'll ever have grandchildren,' Ernest said, spitting out mud. 'I am beginning to doubt whether I'll even survive this night.'

'Nonsense, the sun'll be up any moment, and we're nearly done here.' Cess leaned down so he could see the tread marks, which Ernest had to admit looked very realistic. 'Make two more tracks, and I'll finish off this last tank. We'll be home in time for breakfast.'

And in time for me to finish the articles and run them over to Sudbury by nine, Ernest thought, aligning the tracker with the other tread marks and pushing down hard on it. Which would be good. He didn't like the idea of those other articles sitting there for another week, even in a locked drawer. Now that he could partially see where he was going and didn't need to stop and check his path with the torch every few feet, it should only take him twenty minutes to do the treads and load the lorry, and another three-quarters of an hour back home. They should be there by seven at the latest, which would give him more than enough time.

But he'd only gone a few yards before Cess loomed out of the fog and tapped him on the shoulder. 'The fog's beginning to lift,' he said. 'We'd best get out of here. I'll finish off the tanks and you start on stowing the equipment.'

Cess was right; the fog was beginning to thin. Ernest could make out the vague shapes of trees, ghostly in the grey dawn, and across the field a fence and three black-and-white cows placidly chewing grass – luckily, on the far side of it.

Ernest folded up the tarp, untied the umbrella, carried them and the pump to the lorry, and came back for the cutter. He picked it up, decided there was no way he could carry it all the way across the field, set it down, pulled the cord to start it, and pushed it back, making one last track from just in front of the tank's left tread to the edge of the field, and lugged it, limping, from there to the lorry. By the time he'd hoisted it up into the back, the fog was beginning to break up, tearing apart into long streamers which drifted like veils across the pasture, revealing the long line of tread marks leading to the copse and the rear end of one imperfectly hidden tank peeking out from the leaves, with the other behind it. Even though Ernest knew how it had been done, it looked real, and he wasn't fifteen thousand feet up. From that height, the deception would be perfect. Unless, of course, there was a phonograph standing in the middle of the pasture.

He started back for it, able to actually see where he was going for several yards at a time, but as he reached the tank, the fog closed in again, thicker than ever, cutting off everything – even the tank next to him. He shut the phonograph and fastened the clasps, then folded up the table. 'Cess!' he called in what he thought was his general direction. 'How are you coming along?' and the fog abruptly parted, like theatre curtains sweeping open, and he could see the copse of trees and the entire pasture.

And the bull. It stood halfway across the pasture, a huge shaggy brown creature with beady little eyes and enormous horns. It was looking at the tank.

'Hey! You there!' a voice called from the fence. 'What do you think you're doing in my pasture?' And Ernest turned instinctively to look at the farmer standing there.

So did the bull.

'Get those bloody tanks out of my pasture!' the farmer shouted, angrily jabbing the air with his finger.

The bull watched him, fascinated, for a moment, then swung his head back around. To look directly at Ernest.

LONDON – 15 SEPTEMBER 1940

The nice thing about time-lag was that one could sleep lying on a cold stone floor with bombs crashing and anti-aircraft guns roaring. Polly even slept through the all-clear. When she woke, only Lila and Viv were still there, folding up the blanket they'd sat on, and the sour-faced Mrs Rickett.

She's probably staying to make certain I don't take anything when I leave, Polly thought, picking up her satchel and the 'to let' listings, and wondering how early on a Sunday it was acceptable to show up to look at a room. She glanced at her watch. *Half past six.* Not as early as this. It was too bad she couldn't stay here and sleep. She still felt drugged, but Mrs Rickett, her thin arms folded grimly across her chest as she glared at Lila and Viv, was hardly likely to allow that.

They went out, giggling, and Mrs Rickett started over to Polly. *To hurry me along*, Polly thought, putting her coat on. 'I'll only be a moment—' she began.

'You said you were looking for a room?' Mrs Rickett said, pointing at the newspaper in Polly's hand.

'Yes.'

'I have one,' Mrs Rickett said. 'I run a boarding house. I intended to put it in the papers, but if you're interested it's at 14 Cardle Street. You can come along with me now and see it if you like. It's not far.'

And it was one of Mr Dunworthy's approved addresses. 'Yes,' Polly said, following her out the door and up the steps. 'Thank you.' She stopped and stared up at the building they'd come out of, its spire outlined against the dawn sky.

It's a church, she thought. That explained the clergyman's presence and the discussion about the altar flowers. The stairs they'd just come up were on the side of the church, and there was a notice board on the wall next to it. 'Church of St George, Kensington,' it read. 'The Rev. Floyd Norris, Rector.'

'My single rooms with board are ten and eight,' Mrs Rickett said, crossing the street. 'It's a nice, cosy room.' Which meant minuscule, and probably appalling.

But it's only six weeks. Or rather five, with the slippage, Polly thought. *And I'll scarcely ever be in it. I'll be at the store all day and in the tube shelters at night.* 'How far is the nearest tube station?' she asked.

'Notting Hill Gate,' Mrs Rickett said, pointing back the way they'd come. 'Three streets over.'

Perfect. Notting Hill Gate wasn't as deep as Holborn or Bank, but it had never been hit, and it was on the Central Line to Oxford Street. And it was less than a quarter of a mile from Cardle Street. Mr Dunworthy would be delirious. If the room was habitable.

It was, barely. It was on the third floor, and so 'cosy' the bed filled the room and Mrs Rickett had to squeeze past its foot to get to the wardrobe on the far side. The floor was liver-coloured linoleum, the wallpaper was darker still, and even when Mrs Rickett pulled the blackout curtains back from the single small window, there was scarcely any light. The 'facilities' were one flight up, the bathroom two, and hot water was extra.

But it met all of Mr Dunworthy's requirements, and she wouldn't have to spend valuable time looking for a room. She had a feeling Mrs Rickett would be a dreadful landlady, but having an address would make it easier for the department stores to contact her. 'Have you a telephone?' she asked.

'Downstairs in the vestibule, but it's for local calls only. Sixpence. If you need to make a trunk call, there's a phone box on Lampden Road. And no calls after 9 p.m.'

'I'll take it,' Polly said, opening her handbag.

Mrs Rickett held out her hand. 'That will be one pound five. Payable in advance.'

'But I thought you said it was ten and eight—'

'This room is a double.' *So much for the legendary wartime spirit of generosity*, Polly thought.

'You've no single rooms available?'

'No.'

And even if you did, you wouldn't tell me, but it was only for five weeks. She handed her the money.

Mrs Rickett pocketed it. 'No male visitors abovestairs. No smoking or drinking, and no cooking in your room. On weekdays and Saturdays, breakfast is at seven and supper at six. Sunday dinner's at one o'clock, and there's a cold collation for supper.' She held out her hand. 'I'll need your ration book.'

Polly handed it to her. 'When is breakfast?' she asked, hoping it was soon.

'Your board doesn't start till tomorrow,' Mrs Rickett said, and Polly had to resist the impulse to snatch the ration book back and tell her she'd look elsewhere. 'Here's your room key.' Mrs Rickett handed it to her. 'And your latch key.'

'Thank you,' Polly said, trying to inch to the door, but Mrs Rickett had a few more rules to deliver. 'No children and no pets. I require a fortnight's notice of departure. I hope you're not frightened of the bombs like my last boarder.'

'No,' Polly said. *Just so time-lagged I can hardly stand.*

'Your blackout curtains must be pulled by five o'clock, so if you won't be back from work by then, do them before you leave in the morning. You'll have to pay any fines for blackout infractions,' she said, and finally left.

Polly sank down on the bed. She needed to go and find the drop so she'd know where it was from here and from the church, then find the tube station and go to Oxford Street to see what time the stores opened tomorrow. But she was so tired. The time-lag was even worse than last time. Then, a good night's sleep had been all she needed to adjust. But even though she'd slept nearly eight hours last night in the shelter, she felt as exhausted as if she hadn't had any sleep at all.

And she wasn't likely to get much in the coming days. She couldn't count on being able to sleep through the bombing every night. The contemps had all complained about being sleep-deprived during the Blitz.

It would be smart to catch up on sleep while I can, she thought, though she actually had no choice. She was almost too drowsy to climb into bed. She kicked her shoes off, took off her jacket and skirt so they wouldn't get wrinkled, crawled into the creaking-springed bed, and fell instantly asleep.

She woke half an hour later and then lay there. And lay there. After what seemed like hours and was actually twenty minutes, she got up, cursing the unpredictable effects of time-lag, dressed, and went out. There was no one in the corridor and no sound from any of the rooms.

No one else seems to be having difficulty sleeping, she thought resentfully, but when she went downstairs she could hear voices from the direction of the dining room, and was suddenly starving.

Of course you're starving, she thought, letting herself out. *You haven't eaten in a hundred and twenty years.* There'd been a teashop on Lampden Road. Perhaps it was open. She walked back to St George's, counting streets and noting landmarks for future reference. And planning what she'd have to eat for breakfast. Bacon and eggs, she decided. It might be the last time she had the chance. Bacon was rationed, eggs were already in short supply, and she had a feeling Mrs Rickett's table would be spartan.

She reached the church. A woman carrying a prayer book was standing outside the front door. 'I beg your pardon,' Polly said, 'can you direct me to Lampden Road?'

'Lampden Road? You're on it.'

'Oh,' Polly said, 'thank you,' and walked rapidly up the road as if she knew where she was going. The woman was looking after her, her prayer book clutched to her bosom.

I hope she hasn't read one of those 'Report Anyone Behaving Suspiciously' posters, Polly thought.

The woman was right. This was definitely Lampden Road. Polly recognised its distinctive curve from the night before. The church must be nearer to the drop than she'd thought. She crossed a side street and saw the chemist's on the next corner, and, beyond it, the teashop, which unfortunately wasn't open. On up the street were the newsagent's and the greengrocer's she'd seen last night with the baskets of cabbages outside and 'T. Tubbins, Greengrocer' above the door.

Which meant the drop was only a few yards away in the next alley, even though she thought she'd come much further in the dark. The warden must have taken her some roundabout way. She turned towards the alley, wondering if she should go through right now and give the lab her address and report on the slippage. Badri had specifically asked her to note how much there was. She wondered if he'd been half-expecting something like this. Four and a half days' slippage had to be due to a divergence point, and the beginning of the Blitz had been rife with them. That was why she'd arranged to come through on the tenth rather than the seventh.

But if she reported in now, she'd need to go through again after she was hired at a department store, and she didn't want to give Mr Dunworthy additional opportunities to cancel her assignment.

I'll go tomorrow, after I've been hired, she thought, and checked the alley to make certain it was the right one. It was – she could see the barrels and the chalked Union Jack and 'London kan take it' on the wall – and then walked back to Lampden Road to look for an open restaurant.

There was nothing to the north but houses. She walked back down past St George's to the curve of the road, but there was nothing that way either except a shut-up confectioner's, a tailor's, and an ARP post with sandbags stacked on either side of the door.

I should have offered to pay extra to have my board begin today, she thought, and walked down to Notting Hill Gate Station, hoping the shelter canteens in the Underground stations had been set up by now and were open, but the only sign of food in the entire station was a currant bun being consumed by a small boy on the Central Line platform.

Surely there'll be a canteen open in Oxford Circus, she thought. *It's a much larger station,* but there wasn't, and Oxford Street was deserted. Polly walked down the long shopping street, looking at the shut shops and department stores: Peter Robinson, Townsend Brothers, massive Selfridge's. They looked like palaces rather than stores with their stately grey stone façades and pillars.

And indestructible. Except for the small printed cards in several stores' windows announcing 'safe and comfortable shelter accommodations', and the yellow-green gas-detecting paint patches on the red postboxes, there was no sign here that there was a war on. Bourne and Hollingsworth was advertising 'The Latest in Ladies' Hats for Autumn', and Mary Marsh 'Modish Dancing Frocks', and Cook's window was still calling itself 'The Place to Make Your Travel Arrangements'.

To where? Polly wondered. Obviously not Paris, which Hitler had just occupied, along with the rest of Europe. John Lewis and Company was having a sale on fur coats. *Not for long,* Polly thought, stopping in front of the huge square store, trying to memorise the building and the displays in its wide-fronted windows. By Wednesday morning, it would all be reduced to a charred ruin.

She walked past it towards Marble Arch, noting the stores' posted opening times and looking for 'Shop Assistant Wanted' cards in the windows, but the only one she saw was at Padgett's, which was on Mr Dunworthy's forbidden list even though it wouldn't be hit till October twenty-fifth, three days after the end of her mission.

She also looked for somewhere to eat, but every restaurant she saw had a Closed Sundays sign, and there was no one to ask. She finally spotted a teenaged boy and girl standing outside Parson's, but as she started over to them, Polly saw they were poring over a map, which meant they weren't from here either. 'We could go to the Tower of London,' the girl said, pointing at the map, 'and see the ravens.'

The boy, who didn't look any older than Colin, shook his head. 'They're using it for a prison, like in the old days, only now it's German spies, not royalty.'

'Will they cut their heads off?' the girl asked. 'Like they did Anne Boleyn?'

'No, now they hang them.'

'Oh,' she said, disappointed. 'I did so want to see them.'

The ravens or the cut-off heads? Polly wondered.

'They're good luck, you know,' the girl said. 'So long as there are ravens at the Tower, England can never fall.'

Which is why, when they're all killed by blast next month, the government will secretly dispose of the bodies and substitute new ones.

'It's so *unfair!*' the girl pouted. 'And on our honeymoon!'

Honeymoon? Polly was glad Colin wasn't here to hear that. It would give him ideas.

The boy pored over the map for several moments and then said, 'We could go to Westminster Abbey.'

They're here sightseeing, Polly thought, amazed. *In the middle of the Blitz.*

'Or we could go to Madame Tussaud's Waxworks,' the boy was saying, 'and see Anne Boleyn and Henry VIII's other wives.'

No, you can't. Madame Tussaud's was bombed on the eleventh, Polly thought, and then, *I should go sightseeing.* She couldn't look for a job till tomorrow, and she couldn't observe life in the shelters till tonight. And once she began working, she'd have almost no time to travel about London. This might be her only opportunity.

And there might be a restaurant open near Westminster Abbey or Buckingham Palace. *I can see where the bomb hit the north end of the palace and nearly killed the King and Queen,* she thought, walking back to the tube station. Or perhaps she should go and see something that wouldn't survive the Blitz, like the Guildhall or one of the Christopher Wren churches that would be destroyed on the twenty-ninth of December.

Or I could go and see St Paul's, she thought suddenly. Mr Dunworthy adored St Paul's. He was always talking about it, and perhaps if she told him she'd been to see it and all the things he'd raved about – Nelson's tomb and the Whispering Gallery and Holman Hunt's *The Light of the World* – and told him how beautiful she thought they were, she might be able to talk him into letting her stay an extra week. Or at least prevent him from cancelling her assignment.

No, wait, Mr Dunworthy had said an unexploded bomb had buried itself under St Paul's in September. But that had been early on the twelfth, which was this past Thursday, and he'd said it had taken them three days to dig it out, so it would have been removed on the fourteenth – yesterday. So the cathedral would be open again.

She started towards the Central Line and then changed her mind and took the Bakerloo to Piccadilly Circus instead. She could catch a bus from there and see some of London on the way. And there might be a restaurant in Piccadilly Circus.

There were more people in Piccadilly Circus than there had been on Oxford Street – soldiers, and elderly men hawking newspapers next to sandwich boards reading Latest War News – but there was nothing open here either. The statue of Eros in the centre of Piccadilly Circus had been boarded up. The Guinness clock and the giant signs advertising Bovril and Wrigley's Chewing Gum were still there, though not in their full electric glory. Their lightbulbs had been taken out when the blackout began.

Polly went a short way down Shaftesbury Avenue and then up the Haymarket, looking for an open café, then came back to Piccadilly Circus and found a bus to St Paul's. She climbed aboard and up the narrow spiral staircase to the upper deck so she could have a good view. She was the only one up there, and as soon as the bus started off, she could see why. It was freezing. She dug her gloves out of her pockets and pulled her coat closer about her, debating whether to go back down. But up ahead she could see Trafalgar Square, so she stayed where she was.

The broad plaza was nearly empty, and the fountains were shut off. Five years from now it would be crammed to bursting with cheering crowds celebrating the end of the war, but today even the pigeons had abandoned it. The base of Nelson's monument was swathed in a 'Buy National War Bonds' banner, and someone had stuck a Union Jack behind one of the bronze lions' ears. She looked at its paws, trying to see if they'd fallen victim to shrapnel, but that apparently hadn't happened yet. Then she craned her neck up to look at Nelson, high atop his pillar, his tricorn hat in his hand.

Hitler had planned to take the memorial – lions and all – to Berlin after the invasion and have it set up in front of the Reichstag. He'd also planned to have himself crowned Emperor of Europe in Westminster Abbey – he'd written it all down in his secret invasion plans – and then begin systematically eliminating everyone who got in his way, including all of the intelligentsia. And, of course, the Jews. Virginia Woolf had been on the 'elimination' list, and so had Laurence Olivier and C. P. Snow. And T. S. Eliot. And Hitler had come incredibly close to carrying his plans out.

The bus drove past the National Gallery and started down the broad Strand. There were many more signs of the war here – sandbags and shelter notices and a large water tank outside the Savoy Hotel for fighting fires. She didn't see any damage. *That will change tonight*, she thought. By this time tomorrow nearly every shop window they were passing would have been shattered, and there'd be an enormous crater in the spot the bus was driving over. It was a good thing she'd come today.

The bus turned onto Fleet Street. And ahead, for a brief moment, was St Paul's. Mr Dunworthy had spoken of its lead-coloured dome, standing high on Ludgate Hill above the city, but she could only catch intermittent glimpses of it between and above the newspaper offices lining Fleet Street. They'd all be hit several weeks from now, so badly that only one newspaper would manage to get out an edition the next morning. Polly smiled, thinking of its headline: 'Bomb Injured in Fall on Fleet Street'.

St Bride's was coming up. Polly leaned forward to see its wedding-cake steeple, with its decorated tiers and arched windows. On the twenty-ninth of December, those windows would be alight with fire. So would most of the buildings they were passing now. This entire part of London's old City had burnt that night in what history would call the Second Great Fire of London, including the Guildhall and eight Wren churches.

But not St Paul's, she thought, even though the reporters watching from here that night had thought it was doomed. The American reporter Edward R. Murrow had even begun his radio broadcast, 'Tonight, as I speak to you now, St Paul's Cathedral is burning to the ground.' But it hadn't. It had survived the Blitz, and the war.

But not the twenty-first century, Polly thought. Not the terrorist years. Nothing they were driving past had survived a terrorist with a martyr complex and a pinpoint bomb under his arm. She looked up at the dome again, which she could see looming ahead.

We're nearly there, she thought, but moments later the bus turned sharply to the right, away from it. She leaned over the side to look down at the street. It was blocked off with sawhorses and notices reading Prohibited Area.

There must be bomb damage ahead. The bus drove down two streets and turned east again, but that way was blocked, too, with a rope and a hand-lettered notice reading Danger, and when the bus stopped, a black-helmeted policeman came over to confer with the driver, after which he pulled the bus over to the kerb and passengers began to disembark. Was it a raid? She hadn't heard anything, but Colin had warned her that engine sounds sometimes drowned the sirens out, and everyone seemed to be getting off. Polly ran down the winding steps. 'Is it a raid?' she asked the driver.

He shook his head, and the policeman said, 'Unexploded bomb. This entire area's cordoned off. Where were you going, miss?'

'St Paul's.'

'You can't go there. That's where the UXB is. It fell in the road next to the clock tower and burrowed into the foundations. It's under the cathedral.'

No, it's not. It's already been removed, but she could scarcely tell them that.

'I'm afraid you'll have to go there another time, miss,' the policeman said, and the driver added, 'This bus can take you back to Piccadilly Circus, or you can take the tube from Blackfriars. It's just down there.' He pointed down the hill to where she could see an Underground station.

'Thank you. That's what I'll do,' Polly said and walked in the direction he'd pointed down to the first side street, then glanced back to see if they were watching. They weren't. She ducked down the side street and walked quickly to the next street and back up the hill, looking for a way through the barricade. She wasn't worried about being seen, except by the policemen. This area was all offices and warehouses. It would be deserted on a Sunday. That was how the fire on the twenty-ninth had got out of control. That had been a Sunday, too, and there'd been no one there to put out the incendiaries.

There was a policeman standing guard at the end of this street as well, so she cut over to the next one, which led into a maze of narrow lanes. It was easy to see why this had burned. The warehouses were mere feet apart. Flames could easily jump from building to building, from street to street. She couldn't see the cathedral's dome or west towers, but the lane she was on led uphill, and through the obscuring white paint on the kerb, she could make out 'Amen Corner'. She must be getting near it.

She was. Here was Paternoster Row. She started along it, keeping close to the buildings so she could duck into a doorway if necessary, and there was the front of St Paul's, with its wide steps and broad pillared porch.

But Mr Dunworthy had been wrong about how long it had taken to remove the UXB, because a lorry and two fire pumpers stood in the courtyard, and just past the end of the steps was a huge hole surrounded by heaps of yellow clay littered with shovels, winches, pick-axes, planks. Two men in clay-covered overalls were inching ropes down into the hole, two held fire hoses at the ready, and several more, some in clerical collars, watched in strained attention. The bomb was obviously still down there, and from the looks on the bomb squad's faces, liable to go off at any moment.

But it hadn't. They'd successfully got it out and taken it to Hackney Marshes to be detonated. Which meant it was perfectly safe to be here and go inside whether they had the bomb out or not. If she could only get past them without being seen.

She looked over at the cathedral doors at the top of the wide steps. They appeared too heavy to open quickly – and silently – even if they weren't locked.

A man's voice shouted, 'I can't— Where's that damned—?' and cut off abruptly, followed by a hollow, heart-stopping thud.

Oh God, they've dropped it, Polly thought, and then, *Mr Dunworthy was wrong about how long it took to get it out. What if he was wrong about the bomb going off as well?*

But if the bomb had gone off, the cathedral would have collapsed. There'd have been no valiant effort to save it on the night of December twenty-ninth, no morale-lifting photograph of it standing defiant above the flames and smoke, the symbol of England's determination and refusal to surrender. And the Blitz – and the war – would have gone very differently.

All those thoughts had gone through her head in the fraction of a second it had taken her to look over at the hole and realise the thud hadn't come from there. The men were still lowering the ropes inch by inch, still watching. She looked back at the porch. A man in a long black cassock and a tin helmet appeared from behind one of the pillars and hurried across the porch towards the hole, carrying a crowbar.

There's another door there, behind that pillar. Its opening was what I heard, she thought, and as soon as the clergyman reached the end of the porch and started down the side steps, she crept out of the doorway to look, keeping a sharp eye on the group of men. But no one looked up, not even when the clergyman handed the crowbar to one of the firemen.

Yes, there was the door, smaller than the central doors and obviously not locked, but there might still be someone inside, and if they caught her, what could she say, that she somehow hadn't noticed the barricades and the pumpers and the firemen? If she got arrested ... But she was so close. She started cautiously across the courtyard.

'Stop!' someone shouted, and Polly froze, but they weren't looking at her. They were staring intently down at the hole. The men had ceased to lower the ropes, and a fireman was down on one knee, his hands cupped around his mouth, shouting down into the hole. 'Try it to the left.'

It's stuck, Polly thought, and sprinted across the courtyard, up the broad steps and across the porch, and yanked on the door. It was so heavy she thought for a moment it was locked after all, but then it gave, and she was through it and easing the door silently shut behind her.

She was in a dark, narrow vestibule. She stood there for a moment, listening, but the only sound was the audible hush of a large building. She tiptoed out of the vestibule into the side aisle and looked out into the nave. A wooden admissions desk stood there, but no one was manning it, and there was no one in the north aisle.

Polly stepped out into the nave. And gasped.

Mr Dunworthy had said St Paul's was unique, and she'd seen vids and photographs, but they hadn't begun to convey how beautiful it was. Or how vast. She'd expected a narrow-aisled Gothic church, but this was wide and airy. The nave stretched away in a series of rounded arches supported by massive rectangular pillars, revealing vista after vista – dome, choir, chancel, altar – all of them lit with a rich, warm golden light that streamed from curved golden ceilings, from the golden-railed galleries, the gilt mosaics, the gold-tinged stone itself, turning the air itself golden.

'It's beautiful,' Polly murmured, and felt for the first time what its destruction really meant. *How* could *he?* she thought. *Even if he was a terrorist?* He'd walked into the cathedral one September morning in 2015 and killed half a million people. *And destroyed this.*

But it had only been there to destroy because the bomb underneath it at this very moment hadn't gone off, and because Hitler and his air force had failed to blow St Paul's up or burn it down.

Though they certainly tried, she thought, walking up the nave, her footsteps echoing in the vast open space. They'd dropped hundreds of incendiaries on its roofs, to say nothing of the V-1s and V-2s Hitler would send at it in 1944 and '45.

But St Paul's was ready for them. Tubs of water stood next to every pillar, and pick-axes and pails of sand were propped against the walls at intervals, next to coils of rope. On the night of the twenty-ninth, when dozens of incendiaries would fall on the roofs and the water mains would fail, they – and the volunteers wielding them – would be all that stood between the cathedral and destruction.

Polly heard a door shut somewhere far away and ducked into the south aisle behind one of the rectangular pillars, but no other sound followed, and after a cautious minute she emerged. If she wanted to see all the things Mr Dunworthy had spoken of, she'd best hurry. She might get tossed out at any moment.

She wasn't certain where the Whispering Gallery or Lord Nelson's tomb were. The tomb was presumably down in the Crypt, but she didn't know how to get to it. He'd said *The Light of the World* was the first thing he'd seen the first time he'd been in St Paul's, which meant it should be here in one of the side aisles. If it was still here. There were pale squares on the walls where paintings had obviously hung.

No, here it was, in a bay midway up the south aisle, looking just as Mr Dunworthy had described it. Christ, wearing a white robe and a crown of thorns, stood in the middle of a forest in a deep blue twilight, holding a lantern and waiting impatiently outside a wooden door, his hand raised to knock on it.

It's Mr Dunworthy, Polly thought, *wanting to know why I haven't checked in yet. No wonder he likes it so much.*

She wasn't particularly impressed. The painting was smaller than she'd expected and stiffly old-fashioned, and now that she looked at it again, Christ looked less impatient than unconvinced anyone was going to answer his knock. Which was probably the case, considering the door obviously hadn't been opened in years. Ivy had twined up over it, and weeds choked the threshold.

'I'd give it up if I were you,' Polly murmured.

'I beg your pardon, miss?' a voice said at her elbow, and she jumped a foot. It was an elderly man in a black suit with a waistcoat. 'I didn't mean to frighten you,' he said, 'but I saw you looking at the painting, and – I hadn't realised they'd opened the church again.'

She was tempted to say yes, that the bomb squad or the man in the cassock had given her permission to come in, but if he decided to check … 'Oh, was it closed before?' she said instead.

'Oh, my, yes. Since Thursday. We've had an unexploded bomb under the west end. They only just now got it out. It was a near thing there for a bit. The gas main caught fire and was burning straight for the bomb. If it had reached it, it would have blown up the lot of us, and St Paul's. I've never been happier in my life than to see that monstrous thing driven away. I'm surprised Dean Matthews decided to reopen the church, though. It was my understanding it was to have remained closed till they'd rechecked the gas main. Who—?'

'I'm so glad they did decide to open it, then,' Polly said hastily. 'A friend of mine told me I must see St Paul's when I came to London, particularly *The Light of the World*. It's beautiful.'

'It's only a copy, I'm afraid. The original was sent to Wales with the cathedral's other treasures, but we decided it simply wasn't St Paul's without it. It had hung here all through the last war, and we felt it was vital it be here through this one, particularly with the blackout and the lights gone out in Europe and Hitler spreading his nasty brand of darkness over the world. This reminds us that one light, at any rate, will never go out.'

He looked at it critically. 'I fear it's not a very good copy. It's smaller than the original, and the colours aren't as vivid. Still, it's better than nothing. See how the light seems to be fading, and how the artist has made Christ's face exhibit so many emotions at the same time: patience and sorrow and hope.'

And resignation, Polly thought. 'What is it a door to?' she asked. 'One can't tell from the painting.'

He beamed at her as if she were a bright pupil. 'Exactly. And you'll note the door has no latch. It can only be opened from the inside. Like the door of the heart. That's what is so wonderful

189

about the painting. One sees something different in it each time one looks at it. We like to call it our "sermon in a frame", although the frame's been taken to Wales as well. A lovely gilded wooden thing, with the Scripture which the painting depicts on it.'

'"Behold I stand at the door and knock,"' Polly quoted.

He nodded, beaming even more. '"If any man hear my voice and open the door I will come in to him." The artist's tomb is in the Crypt.'

With Lord Nelson's. 'I'd love to see it,' Polly said.

'I'm afraid the Crypt is closed to visitors, but I can show you round the rest of the church, if you've the time.'

And if Dean Matthews doesn't come in and announce the church is still closed and demand to know what I'm doing here, she thought. 'I'd love to see it, if it's no trouble, Mr—?'

'Humphreys. It would be no trouble at all. As verger, I often conduct tours.' He led her back down the aisle and over to the central doors where, presumably, he began those tours. 'This is the Great West Door. It's opened only on ceremonial occasions. On other days we use the smaller doors on either side,' he said, and she saw there was another door in the south aisle, the twin of the one she'd come through. 'The pilasters are of Portland stone,' he continued, patting one of the rectangular pillars. 'The floor where we are standing—'

Is where the Fire Watch stone will be, Polly thought, the memorial dedicated to the memory of St Paul's fire watch, the volunteers 'who by the grace of God saved this church'. And the only thing left after the pinpoint bomb.

'—is made of Carrara marble in a black-and-white checker-board pattern,' Mr Humphreys said. 'From here one can see the full length of the cathedral. It's built in the shape of the cross. To your right—' He walked over to the south aisle to a makeshift wooden partition just this side of the vestibule, 'is the Geometrical Staircase, designed by Christopher Wren. As you can see, it's currently boarded up, though a final decision on what to do hasn't been made.'

'What to do?'

'Yes, you see, the staircase offers the best access to the roofs on this end of the church, but at the same time it's extremely fragile. And irreplaceable. But if an incendiary were to fall on the library roof or the towers ... It's difficult to know what to do. Over here—' he walked up the south aisle to an iron grille, 'is the Chapel of the Order of St Michael and St George with its wooden prayer stalls. The banners which ordinarily hang above them have unfortunately been removed for safekeeping.'

The seventeenth-century cherubs had been, too, and the nave's chandeliers and most of the monuments in the south aisle. 'Some of them were too heavy to move, so we've put sandbags round them,' Mr Humphreys said, leading her past a stairway with a chain across it and a notice: To the Whispering Gallery. Closed to Visitors.

And so much for the Whispering Gallery, Polly thought as the verger led her into the wide central crossing beneath the dome, where there was another chained staircase.

'This is the transept,' he said. 'It forms the crosspiece of the cathedral.' He led her into it to show her the monument to Lord Nelson, or rather, the stack of sandbags hiding it, and several other piles of sandbags concealing statues of Captain Robert Scott, Admiral Howe, and the artist J. M. W. Turner. 'The south transept is chiefly interesting for the carved oak doorcase by Grinling Gibbons, which unfortunately—'

'Has been removed for safekeeping,' Polly murmured, following him from the transept into the choir and the apse, where he pointed out the organ (removed for safekeeping), the shrouded statue of John Donne (in a shroud of sandbags in the Crypt), the High Altar, and the stained-glass windows.

'We've been very lucky so far,' Mr Humphreys said, pointing up at them. 'They're too large to board up, but we haven't lost a single window.'

You will, Polly thought. By the end of the war they'd all have been smashed. The last one had been taken out by a V-2 that had crashed nearby.

Mr Humphreys led her back down the other side of the choir, pointing out the buckets of water and stirrup pumps lined against the wall. 'Our greatest worry is fire. The underlying structure's of wood, and if one of the roofs were to catch fire, the lead would run down into the cracks between the stones, and they'd burst as they did when the first St Paul's burned. It was utterly destroyed during the Great Fire of London, when this entire part of the city burned.'

And will again three months from now, Polly thought. She wondered if Mr Humphreys was part of the fire watch. He looked too old, but then again, the Blitz had been a war of old men and shopgirls and middle-aged women.

'But we shan't let that happen again,' he said, answering her question. 'We've formed a band of volunteers to keep watch for incendiaries on the roofs. I'm on duty tonight.'

'Then I shouldn't keep you,' Polly said. 'I should go.'

'No, no, not till I've shown you my favourite monument,' Mr Humphreys said, dragging her into the north transept. He made her look at the Corinthian columns and the oak doors of the north porch. 'And this is the monument to Captain Robert Faulknor,' he said, pointing proudly at another pile of sandbags. 'His ship was badly damaged. She'd lost most of her rigging and couldn't fire, and the *La Pique* was coming athwart her. Captain Faulknor courageously grabbed her bowsprit and lashed the two ships together and used the *La Pique*'s guns to fire on the other French ships. His brave action won the battle. Unfortunately he never knew what he'd accomplished. He was shot through the heart the moment after he'd bound the two together.' He shook his head sadly. 'A true hero.'

I'll need to tell Michael Davies about him, Polly thought, and wondered where he was now. He was to have left just after she did, which meant he was in Dover, observing the evacuation efforts. But here in this time, that had happened three months ago, and his next assignment, Pearl Harbor, which he'd leave for as soon as he returned from Dover, wouldn't happen here for more than a year.

'It's such a pity you can't see the monument,' Mr Humphreys said. 'Wait, I've just thought of something,' he said, and led her back down the nave. The cathedral had lost its golden glow and looked grey and chilly, and the side aisles were already in shadow. Polly stole a glance at her watch. It was after four. She hadn't realised how late it was.

Mr Humphreys was taking her to the admissions desk. It had a number of pamphlets on it, coloured prints of *The Light of the World* for sale for sixpence apiece, a box marked Donations to the Minesweepers Fund, and a wooden rack filled with picture postcards. 'I think we may have a photograph of Captain Faulknor's monument,' he said, searching through postcards of the Whispering Gallery, the organ, and a three-tiered Victorian monstrosity that had to be the Wellington Monument. 'Oh dear, we don't seem to have one of it. What a pity! You must come back and see it when the war's over.'

The side door clanged, and a sharp-faced young man came in, wearing a dark blue coverall and carrying a tin helmet and a gas mask. 'So they got the bomb out all right, did they, Mr Humphreys?' he asked the verger.

He nodded. 'You're a bit early, Langby. You don't come on duty till half past six.'

'I want to take a look at the chancel roof pump. It's been giving a bit of trouble. Have you the key to the vestry?'

'Yes,' Mr Humphreys said. 'I'll be there in a moment.'

'I'm keeping you from your duties,' Polly said. 'Thank you for showing me the cathedral.'

'Oh, but you mustn't go yet. There's one last thing you must see,' he said, leading her over to the south aisle.

No doubt another pile of sandbags, Polly thought, following him, but it wasn't. He'd led her back to *The Light of the World*, the painting now only dimly visible in the gloom.

Mr Humphreys said reverently, 'Do you see how, now that the light's fading, the lantern seems to glow?'

It did. A warm orange-gold light spread from it, lighting Christ's robe, the door, the weeds that had grown up around it.

'Do you know what Dean Matthews said when he saw that glow? He said, "He'd better not let the ARP warden catch him with that lantern."' Mr Humphreys chuckled. 'A fine sense of humour, the dean has. It's a great help in times like these.'

The door clanged open again and another member of the fire watch came in and walked swiftly up the nave. 'Humphreys!' Langby called from the transept.

'I'm afraid I must be going,' Mr Humphreys said. 'If you'd care to stay and look round a bit more ...'

'No, I should be getting home.'

He nodded. 'Best not to be out after dark if one can help it,' he said and hurried towards Langby.

He was right. It was a long way to Kensington, and she had to find somewhere open where she could get supper before she went back. There was no way she could make it through another night without having eaten. And the raids tonight began at 6:54. She needed to go.

But she stayed a few minutes longer, looking at the painting. Christ's face, in the dimming light, no longer looked bored, but afraid, and the woods surrounding him not only dark but threatening.

Best not to be out after dark if one can help it, Polly thought, and then, looking at the locked door, *I wonder if that's the door to an air-raid shelter.*

'Wouldn't it be lovely if it was true?'

LONDONER, 7 MAY 1945

LONDON – 7 MAY 1945

When the three girls turned onto the road that led to the Underground station, it was deserted.

'What if it was a false alarm and the war's not really over?' Paige asked.

'Don't be silly,' Reardon said. 'It was on the wireless.'

'Then where is everyone?'

'Inside,' Reardon said. 'Come along.' She started down the street.

'Do you think it could be another false alarm, Douglas?' Paige asked, turning to her.

'No,' she said.

'Do come on,' Reardon said, motioning them to hurry. 'We'll miss all the fun.'

But when they got inside the station, there was no one there either. 'They're down on the platform,' Reardon said, pushing through the wooden turnstile, and when there was no one on the platform either, 'They're all in London already, just like we'd be, if it weren't for Colonel Wainwright's gout. Why couldn't his big toe have waited till next week to get inflamed? Only just think,' Reardon smiled beatifically, 'we'll never have to put up with Colonel Wainwright again.'

'Unless the war's not actually over,' Paige said. 'Remember last week, when West Ham rang up and said General Dodd had told them it was all over? If this is another false alarm, we'll not only look like complete idiots, we'll be put on report. We should have rung up HQ in London and verified it.'

'Which would have made us even later,' Reardon said, 'and we've missed *hours* as it is.'

'But if it hasn't ended ...' Paige said doubtfully. 'Perhaps we should ring them up now, before we—'

'We'll miss the train and the end of the war,' Reardon said, looking down the track towards where the train was coming. 'It's eight o'clock. Don't you agree, Douglas?'

'Actually, it's twenty past eight,' Douglas said. *And every minute we stand here is one less minute I have to see the cele-brations*, she thought.

The train pulled in. Reardon said, 'Stop fretting and come along.'

Paige turned to Douglas. 'What do you think, Douglas?'

'It's not a false alarm,' she said. 'The Germans have surren-dered. The war's over. We've won.'

'Are you certain?'

More certain than you can possibly imagine, she thought. Here was something she'd never expected from her research, that it could be VE Day, and the contemps wouldn't know it. Or, rather, VE Day eve. VE Day, with its speeches by Churchill and the King and its Thanksgiving Services at St Paul's, had been – correction, wouldn't be till – tomorrow, but the celebrat-ing had begun today, and the party would go on all night.

'Douglas is certain,' Reardon was saying. '*I'm* certain. The war's over. Now get on the train.' Reardon grabbed Paige's arm and propelled her onto the car, and she got on with them.

The car was empty, too, but Paige didn't seem to notice. She was looking at the tube map on the wall of the car. 'Where should we go when we get there, do you think? Piccadilly Circus?'

'No, Hyde Park,' Reardon said. 'Or St Paul's.'

'Where do you think people will be, Douglas?' Paige asked.

All of the above, she thought, plus *Leicester Square and Parliament Square and Whitehall and every street in between*. 'Trafalgar Square is where one usually goes for that sort of thing,' she said, thinking of which place would have the easiest connection to her drop.

'What sort of thing?' Paige asked, and it was clear she thought nothing like this had ever happened before.

And she may be right, she thought. 'I meant it's where people have gathered in the past after military victories – the Battle of Trafalgar and the siege of Mafeking and all that.'

'This isn't only a military victory,' Reardon said. 'It's *our* victory as well.'

'If it's actually happened,' Paige said, peering out of the window as they pulled into the next stop, which was deserted as well. 'Oh dear, I'm afraid it is a false alarm, Douglas.'

'No, it's *not*,' she said firmly, though privately she was beginning to worry, too. Historical accounts had said the victory celebration had begun as soon as the news of the German surrender came over the wireless at three o'clock. Could they have got that wrong? Could everyone have doubted the news like Paige? There *had* been a number of false alarms, and everyone had been on tenterhooks for the last two weeks.

And it wouldn't be the first time the historical record had been wrong or incomplete. But VE Day was well documented. And the historical accounts said people should be pouring onto the train by now, waving Union Jacks and singing 'When the Lights Go on Again All Over the World'.

'If the war's over, then where is everyone?' asked Paige.

'At the next stop,' Reardon said imperturbably.

Reardon was right. When the doors opened, a veritable flood of people swept into their car. They were waving flags and rattling noisemakers, and two elderly gentlemen were singing 'God Save the King' at the top of their lungs.

'Now do you believe the war's over?' she and Reardon asked Paige, and she nodded excitedly.

More people pushed on. A little boy holding tightly to his mother's hand asked, 'Are we going to the shelter?'

'No,' his mother said, and then, as if she had just realised it, 'We're never going to the shelter again.'

People were still squeezing on. Many were in uniform, and some had red, white, and blue crêpe paper draped around their necks, including two middle-aged men in Home Guard uniforms, brandishing a copy of the *London Evening News* with the headline 'IT IS OVER' and two bottles of champagne.

The train guard squeezed and pushed his way through the crush to them. 'No alcoholic beverages allowed in the tube,' he said sternly.

'What do you mean, mate?' one of the men said. ''Aven't you heard? The war's over!'

''Ere!' the other one said, handing his bottle to the guard. 'Drink to the King's 'ealth! And the Queen's!' He snatched his friend's bottle and shoved it into the guard's other hand. He draped a chummy arm over the guard's shoulders. 'Why don't you come to the palace with us and toast 'em to their face?'

'*That's* where we should go,' Reardon said, 'to Buckingham Palace.'

'Oh yes,' Paige said excitedly. 'Do you think we might actually be able to see Their Majesties, Douglas?'

Not till tomorrow, she thought, *when the Royal Family will come out on the balcony no fewer than eight times and wave to the crowd.*

'Do you think the Princesses will be with them?' Paige asked.

Not only will they be with them, she thought, *but at one point they'll be out in the crowd, mingling incognito with people and shouting gaily, 'We want the King!'* but she couldn't say that. 'I should imagine,' she said, looking at the doors, where people were still squeezing on. If it took this long to load the train at every stop, it would take all night to get there.

I've already missed the beginning, she thought, *the RAF planes doing victory rolls over London and the lights being turned on.* And if there was going to be this much delay on the trains going back, she'd have to leave early to reach the drop on time, and she'd miss the end as well.

The train finally pulled out. Paige was still chattering on about the Princesses. 'I've always wanted to see them. Do you think they'll be wearing their uniforms?'

'It may not matter *what* they're wearing,' Reardon said as the train stopped again and more people squeezed on. 'We may be trapped in here forever. Which may not be all that bad. Douglas, look at that lieutenant who just got on! Isn't he handsome?'

'Where?' Paige said, standing on tiptoe to see.

'What do you think you're doing?' Reardon demanded. 'You've already bagged one. Don't be greedy.'

'I was only looking,' Paige said.

'You're not allowed to look. You're engaged,' Reardon said. 'Will he be here tonight?'

'No, he rang up night before last and said he wouldn't be back for a week at the least,' Paige said.

'But that was before,' Reardon said. 'Now that the war's over – Oh Lord, there are *more* people boarding! We'll pop!'

'We *must* try to get off at the next stop,' Paige said. 'I can't breathe.'

They nodded and when the train stopped again and a large man wearing a tin hat and an ARP armband began pushing towards the doors, they followed in his wake, squeezing between sailors and Wrens and navvies and teenaged girls.

'I can't see what station it is,' Reardon said as the train slowed.

'It doesn't matter,' Paige said. 'Only get off. I'm being squished. I feel like a pilchard in a tin.'

Reardon nodded and bent down to look out of the window.

'Oh good, we're at Charing Cross,' she said. 'It looks like we're going to Trafalgar Square after all, Douglas.'

The doors opened. 'Follow me, girls!' Reardon shouted gaily. 'Mind the gap!'

She scrambled off, and Paige did, too, calling, 'Coming, Douglas?'

'Yes,' she said, attempting to squeeze past the Home Guard, who for some reason had launched into 'It's a Long Way to Tipperary'.

'Sorry, this is my stop. I must get off here,' she said, but they didn't budge.

'Douglas! Hurry!' Reardon and Paige were shouting from the platform. 'The train's going to leave.'

'Please,' she shouted, trying to make herself heard over their singing. 'I must get through.' The door began to close.

'I am ashamed to say I told him it was the fault of the Germans.'

WINSTON CHURCHILL, ON HIS
GRANDSON'S GETTING THE MEASLES

BACKBURY, WARWICKSHIRE – MAY 1940

Binnie and the rest of the evacuees greeted the news that they were quarantined with an outburst of wild behaviour that made Eileen want to flee for the drop before the children's supper was half over.

'I was corn-teened for a month,' Alice announced. 'Rose n'me couldn't play outside or nothin'.'

'We ain't goin' to be quarantined for a month, are we, Eileen?' Binnie asked.

'No, of course not.' Measles only lasted a few days, didn't they? That's why they called them the three-day measles. Alice must be mistaken.

When Dr Stuart came back that night, Eileen asked him how long the quarantine was likely to last. 'It depends on how many of the children catch them,' he said. 'If Alf were to be the only case, which is unlikely, it will end a fortnight after his rash disappears, so three or four weeks.'

'Three or four *weeks*? But they only last three days.'

'You're thinking of German measles. These are red measles, which last a week or longer after the rash first appears.'

'And how long does it take for the rash to appear?'

'From three days to a week, and in some cases I've seen the rash last up to eight days.' And knowing Alf, he would be one of those cases. A week plus eight days plus a fortnight. They *would* be quarantined for a month. If no one else caught them. So she obviously couldn't wait until the quarantine was over. She had to go now. She wondered what the penalty for breaking quarantine was in 1940. During the Pandemic it would have got one shot, but surely that wouldn't be the situation with a childhood disease. Just in case, though, she waited till everyone was asleep and Samuels was snoring heavily in the porter's chair, which he'd dragged over in front of the front door, then tiptoed down the back stairs to the kitchen.

The door was locked. So were the French doors in the morning room, the windows in the library and dining room, and the side door leading off the billiards room.

'And the keys are here in my pocket,' Samuels said when she confronted him the next morning, 'and that's where they're going to stay. That Hodbin brat could get out of one of Houdini's traps, he could. I'm not letting him spread measles all over the neighbourhood. If it is measles. I say he's shamming so he can keep home from school.'

Eileen was inclined to agree with him. Alf not only drank all the broth she carried up for his breakfast, but asked for more, and when she came up for the tray, Una said he was bouncing on his cot and how did she get him to stop? And when the vicar came, he told her (shouting through the kitchen door since Samuels refused to let him in) that no one else who attended the village school in Backbury had come down with them.

When Eileen took up the lunch tray, she caught Alf leaning out of the ballroom door, flicking a wet facecloth at Jimmy and Reg. 'What are you doing out here?' she demanded.

'I'm washin' my face,' he said innocently.

'Get back in the nursery,' she ordered Reg and Jimmy. 'Alf, get back into bed.' She pushed him into the ballroom. 'Una, you can't allow Alf to – where's Una?'

'I dunno. Why ain't you takin' care of me?'

'Because you're contagious.' *And irritating beyond belief.* 'Climb into bed.'

'When can Binnie come see me?'

'She can't. Now lie down,' she said and went in search of Una. She wasn't in the bathroom or the nursery, where Binnie was leading the children in a noisy game of tag, and when Eileen glanced back in the ballroom, Alf was at the window, trying to open it, surrounded by the sheets he'd knotted together.

'Dr Stuart said I needed fresh air,' he said innocently.

Eileen confiscated the sheets, located Una in her bedroom changing out of her sopping wet dress – Alf had spilt the wash-basin on her – and sent her back downstairs to Alf.

'*Must* I?' Una begged her. 'Can't you nurse him? I'll give you my new film magazine.'

I know just how you feel, Eileen thought. 'I can't. I haven't had measles.'

'I wish I hadn't,' Una wailed.

Eileen took the sheets back down to the linen closet, briefly considering hanging them out of her bedroom window and escaping, but her room was four stories from the ground, and Dr Stuart would be here in another hour. After one look at Alf – and poor Una – he would almost certainly call off the quaran-tine, and she could walk out of the front door to the drop instead of risking life and limb.

But Dr Stuart telephoned to say he was delayed – one of the Pritchards' evacuees had fallen out of a tree and broken his leg – and by the time he arrived at three that afternoon, there was no longer any doubt of its being measles. Alf was covered from head to toe with unfakeable pink pinpoint dots, Tony and Rose were both complaining of sore throats, and before the doctor had even finished taking their temps, Jimmy had announced, 'I'm going to be sick,' and was. Eileen spent the rest of the afternoon setting up additional cots and cursing herself for not having climbed out of the window while she had the chance. Tony's brother Ralph and Rose's sister Alice fell ill during the night, and when Dr Stuart examined Edwina, she had white patches inside her mouth, even though she claimed she didn't feel ill. 'This would never have happened if we'd gone on the boat,' she said, annoyed.

Eileen wasn't listening. She was thinking about the drop. She couldn't go now, even if she could get past Samuels. She couldn't leave the children with only Una to care for them. Dr Stuart had promised to bring in a nurse, but the nurse wouldn't be available till the weekend, and by then the lab would have already sent a retrieval team to find out why she hadn't returned.

If they hadn't already. 'Is there a notice on the door saying we're quarantined?' she asked Samuels.

'Indeed there is, and one on the main gate.'

Which means when they do come through, they'll see what's happened, she thought, *and I needn't worry about getting word to them.* That was a blessing because she hadn't a moment to spare over the next few days, between carrying trays, washing sheets, and keeping the evacuees who hadn't yet caught the measles occupied.

Dr Stuart was determined to keep her out of the sickroom, even though Una was clearly overwhelmed, but when Reg and Letitia fell ill, he said, 'I'm afraid you're going to have to help out till the nurse arrives and the children break out. As soon as their rashes appear, they'll improve. Try to avoid close contact with them as much as you can.' And it was a good thing she wasn't really at risk because the children needed nonstop nursing. They all had fevers and nausea, and their eyes were red and sore. Eileen spent half her time wringing out cold compresses, changing sheets, and emptying basins, and the other half trying vainly to keep Alf in bed.

He hadn't felt ill since the first day, and he spent most of his time tormenting the other patients. The only thing that kept Eileen from killing him was the vicar's arrival. He called up to her that he'd brought extra linens and some jelly from Miss Fuller and chatted with her through the window for a bit.

'If it's any comfort, you're not the only ones quarantined. The Sperrys and Pritchards are as well. They've closed the school,' he told her. 'I'll leave the linens and jelly on the kitchen step. Oh, and I've brought the post.'

The post consisted of *The Times*, which reported that the Germans were driving into France and that Belgium might fall, a letter from Mrs Magruder saying yes, her children had had the measles, and a note from Lady Caroline. 'I am devastated at not being at home to assist you in this crisis,' she wrote.

'Ha!' Mrs Bascombe said. 'She's thanking her lucky stars she went to that meeting and was out of the house. Though if you ask me, it's a blessing she's not here. It's one less person to cook for and clean up after.'

She was right. They already had more than they could cope with. By the end of the week, eleven of the evacuees were down with the measles, the nurse Dr Stuart had promised still hadn't arrived, and when Polly asked him about it on his next visit, he shook his head grimly. 'She joined the Royal Nursing Corps last month, and all the other nurses in the area have already been engaged. There are a good many cases in the district.'

There are a good many cases here, Eileen thought, exasperated, and over the next few days the number grew even larger. Susan came down with measles and so did Georgie; they had to set up a second ward in the music room; and everyone – including Samuels, who saw his job as beginning and ending with keeping everyone from escaping the house – had to pitch in. Mrs Bascombe took over the housekeeping, the vicar brought medicine and calves' foot jelly, and Binnie carried trays and drove Eileen to distraction. 'Are they all going to die?' she asked her loudly, trying to peek into the ballroom.

'No, of course not. Children don't die of measles.'

'I know a girl what did. She 'ad a white coffin.'

After a day and a half of similar sentiments, Eileen reassigned

Binnie to kitchen duty. Mrs Bascombe tied one of her aprons on her and set her to work washing the dishes, hanging up the laundry in the now-deserted ballroom, and scrubbing the floor.

'It's not *fair*,' Binnie told Eileen indignantly. 'I wish *I* could have caught the measles.'

'Be careful what you wish for,' Mrs Bascombe, coming in from the larder, said. 'And be careful with those teacups. She's already broken four,' she told Eileen. 'And the Spode teapot. I don't know what Lady Caroline will say.'

Eileen wasn't particularly worried. Lady Caroline had only written once since that first time, to tell them that she'd be staying with friends till the quarantine was lifted and to send her 'my white georgette, my silver fox stole, and my blue bathing dress'.

The next few days were a blur – children in the vomiting stage, the spiking-fever stage, and the emerging-rash stage. Peggy and Reg got eye infections, and Jill developed a chesty cough that Dr Stuart warned Eileen to keep a sharp eye on. 'We don't want it to go into her chest,' he said, and added twice-a-day steam infusions under an improvised tent of blankets to Eileen's list of chores. Which was endless, in spite of everyone, including the little ones, helping out. Peggy and Barbara swept the nursery, Theodore made up his own cot, and Binnie toiled in the kitchen and endured Mrs Bascombe's lectures. Every time Eileen came down to the kitchen, Mrs Bascombe was shaking her finger at Binnie, saying, 'You call that peeling? You've taken off half the potato!' or 'Why haven't you finished putting away those dishes?' or the all-purpose 'Mark my words, you'll come to a bad end!' Eileen actually began to feel a bit sorry for her. On Thursday, when she went downstairs for mentholated spirits to put in Jill's steam kettle, Binnie was at the kitchen table with her head lying on her arms in an attitude of despair, a massive pile of to-be-cleaned vegetables next to her. 'Mrs Bascombe,' Eileen said, going out to the larder, 'you really mustn't be so hard on Binnie. She's doing her best.'

'So *hard*?' Mrs Bascombe said. 'Who's let her sit there at that table all morning while I did the washing up and the ironing because she complained of a headache? Who let her—?'

'Headache?' Eileen hurried back out to the kitchen and squatted next to Binnie's chair. 'Binnie?'

The girl raised her head, and there was no mistaking the too-bright eyes, the dark circles under them.

Eileen put her hand to Binnie's forehead. It was burning up. 'Do you feel like you're going to be ill?'

''Uh-unh. It's only my 'ead aches.'

Eileen led her upstairs to the ballroom. 'You'll feel better once you've had a lie-down,' she said, unbuttoning Binnie's dress.

'I've got the measles, ain't I?' she said plaintively.

'I'm afraid so,' Eileen said, lifting her singlet over her head. There was no sign of the rash yet. 'You'll feel better once they come out.'

But they didn't come out, and Binnie didn't manifest any of the other symptoms, except for the fever – which steadily climbed – and the persistent headache. She lay with her eyes squeezed shut and her fists jammed against her forehead as if to keep it from exploding. 'Are you certain it's the measles?' Eileen asked Dr Stuart, thinking of spinal meningitis.

'The rash takes longer in some children,' he reassured her. 'You'll see, Binnie will be all right by morning.'

But she wasn't, and her fever kept going up. When the doctor came in the afternoon, it was one hundred and two. 'Give her a teaspoon of this powder in a tumblerful of water every four hours,' the doctor said, handing Eileen a paper packet.

'For her fever?'

'No, it's to help bring the measles out. The fever will come down on its own once the rash appears.'

The powder was useless. It was three more days before Binnie broke out, and the measles gave her no relief. Her rash was bright red instead of pink, and covered every inch of her, even the palms of her hands. 'It *'urts*,' Binnie cried, moving her head restlessly on the pillow.

'She's got them hard,' the doctor said, which scarcely seemed a technical diagnosis. He took her temp, which was one hundred and three, and then listened to her chest. 'I'm afraid the measles have affected her lungs.'

'Her lungs?' Eileen said. 'You mean pneumonia?'

He nodded. 'Yes. I want you to make a poultice of molasses, dried mustard, and brown paper for her chest.'

'But shouldn't she be taken to hospital?'

'*Hospital?*'

Eileen bit her lip. Obviously people in this time didn't go into hospital for pneumonia, and why would they? There was nothing they could do for them there – no antivirals, no nanotherapies, not even any antibiotics except sulfa and penicillin. No, they didn't even have that. Penicillin hadn't come into common use till after the war.

'I shouldn't worry,' the doctor said, patting Eileen on the arm. 'Binnie's young and strong.'

'But isn't there something you can give her for her fever?'

'You might give her some licorice-root tea,' he said. 'And bathe her with alcohol three times a day.'

Teas, poultices, glass thermometers! It's a wonder anyone survived the twentieth century, Eileen thought disgustedly. She bathed Binnie's hot arms and legs after the doctor left, but neither that nor the tea had any effect on her, and as the evening wore on, she became more and more short of breath. She dozed fitfully, moaning and tossing from side to side. It was midnight before she finally fell asleep. Eileen tucked the covers around her and went to check on the other children. 'Don't leave me!' Binnie cried out.

'Shh,' Eileen said, hurrying back and sitting down beside her again. 'I'm here. Shh, I'm not leaving. I was only going to check on the other children.' She reached out her hand to feel Binnie's forehead.

Binnie twisted angrily away from her. 'No, you wasn't. You was goin' away. To London. I seen you.'

She must be reliving that day at the station with Theodore. 'I'm not going to London,' Eileen said soothingly. 'I'm staying right here with you.'

Binnie shook her head violently. 'I seen you. Mrs Bascombe says nice girls don't meet soldiers in the woods.'

She's delirious, Eileen thought. 'I'm going to fetch the thermometer, Binnie. I'll be back in just a moment.'

'I did so see her, Alf,' Binnie said.

Eileen got the thermometer, dipped it in alcohol, and came back. 'Put this under your tongue.'

'You can't leave,' Binnie said. She looked straight at Eileen. 'You're the only one wot's nice to us.'

'Binnie, dear, I need to take your temperature,' Eileen repeated, and this time Binnie seemed to hear her. She opened her mouth obediently, lay still for the endless minutes before Eileen could remove the thermometer, then turned over and closed her eyes.

Eileen couldn't read her temp in the near-darkness. She tiptoed over to the lamp on the table: one hundred and five. If her temperature stayed that high for long, it would kill her. Even though it was two in the morning, Eileen rang up Dr Stuart, but he wasn't there. His housekeeper told her he'd just left for Moodys' farm to deliver a baby, and, no, they weren't on the telephone. Which meant she was on her own – and there was absolutely nothing she could do. If her presence had affected events, the net would never have let her come through to Backbury.

But the alterations the net prevented were those which affected the course of history, not whether an evacuee lived through the measles. Binnie couldn't affect what happened at D-Day or who won the war. And even if she could, Eileen couldn't just stand here and let her die. She had to at least *try* to get her temperature down. But how? Rubbing her with alcohol had had no effect at all. Putting her in a tub of cold water? In her weakened state, the shock might kill her. She needed a medicine to bring down the fever, but they hadn't any drugs like that in 1940—

Yes, they do, she thought, *if Lady Caroline didn't take it with her.* She tiptoed out of the sickroom and ran along the corridor to Lady Caroline's rooms. *Please, please don't let her have taken her aspirin tablets with her.*

She hadn't. The box was on her dressing table, and it was nearly full. Eileen grabbed it up, put it in her pocket, and sped back to the sickroom. Her opening of the door wakened Binnie, and she sat up, flinging her hands out wildly. 'Eileen!' she sobbed.

'I'm here,' Eileen said, grabbing her hands. They were burning up. 'I'm here. I only went to fetch your medicine. Shh, it's all right. I'm here.' She took two of the tablets out of the box and reached for Binnie's water glass. 'I'm not going anywhere. Here, take this.' She supported Binnie's head while she took the tablet. 'That's a good girl. Now lie down.'

Binnie clutched at her. 'You can't go! Who'll take care of us if you leave?'

'I won't leave you,' Eileen said, covering Binnie's hot, dry hands with both of hers.

'Swear,' Binnie cried.

'I swear,' Eileen said.

LONDON – 17 SEPTEMBER 1940

B y Tuesday night, Polly still hadn't found a job. There weren't any openings 'at present', or, as the personnel manager at Waring and Gillow said, 'during this uncertainty'.

'Uncertainty' was putting it mildly. But then the contemps had been noted for understatement. Bombed buildings and people blown to bits were 'incidents'; impassable wreckage-strewn streets 'diversions'. The daytime air raids, which had interrupted her job search twice today, were christened 'Hitler's tea break'.

Only one person, a junior shop assistant at Harvey Nichols, was willing to say it baldly: 'They're not taking anyone new on because they can't see the point when the store mightn't be there in the morning. No one's hiring.'

She was right. Neither Debenham's nor Yardwick's would grant her an interview, Dickins and Jones wouldn't allow her to fill up an application form, and every other store was on Mr Dunworthy's forbidden list.

Which is ridiculous, Polly thought as her train reached Notting

Hill Gate. They'd all been hit at night, and only one – Padgett's – had had casualties, and it hadn't been hit till October twenty-fifth, three days after she was due to go back.

But Mr Dunworthy would already be furious that she hadn't checked in yet. She'd best not do anything to upset him further, which meant she needed to be hired at either Townsend Brothers or Peter Robinson. And hired soon. If she didn't check in tomorrow, Mr Dunworthy was likely to decide something had happened to her and send a retrieval team to pull her out. She bought the *Express* and the *Daily Herald* from the newspaper man at the top of the station stairs and hurried back to Mrs Rickett's, hoping tonight's supper would be better than last night's tinned beef hash, a watery mush of potatoes and cabbage with a few flecks of stringy red. It wasn't. Tonight the flecks were grey and rubbery – halibut, according to Mrs Rickett – and the potatoes and cabbage had been boiled to the point where they were indistinguishable. Luckily, the sirens went halfway through dinner, and Polly didn't have to finish it.

When she got to St George's, she immediately opened the *Herald* and looked through the 'To Let's for somewhere else to live, but all the rooms listed had addresses on the forbidden list. She turned the page to the 'Situations Vacant'. Companion wanted, upstairs maid, chauffeur. The *hired help have all gone off to war*, Polly thought, *or to work in munitions factories*. Nanny, maid of all work. Not a single ad for a shopgirl, and nothing in the *Express* either.

'Still no luck?' Lila asked. She was putting Viv's hair up on bobby pins.

'No, afraid not.'

'You'll get something,' she said, wrapping a lock of Viv's hair around her finger, and Viv added encouragingly, 'They'll begin hiring again when the bombing's stopped.'

I can't afford to wait that long, Polly thought, and wondered what they'd say if she told them 'the bombing' would go on for another eight months, and that even after the Blitz ended, there'd be intermittent raids for three more years and then V-1 and V-2 attacks to contend with. 'Have you tried John Lewis?' Lila asked, opening a bobby pin with her teeth. 'I overheard a girl on the way home saying they needed someone.'

'In *Better Dresses*,' Viv said. 'You'll have to be quick, though. You'll need to be there when it opens tomorrow.'

That'll be too late, Polly thought. Tonight was the night it had been hit.

She was spared from responding by the elderly gentleman, who came over to offer her his *Times* to her as he'd done every night thus far. She thanked him and opened it to 'Situations Vacant', but there was nothing in it either.

Lila had finished putting up Viv's hair, and they were looking at a film magazine and discussing the relative charms of Cary Grant and Laurence Olivier. Polly'd intended to observe shelterers in the tube stations, but St George's was even better. It had a diverse group of contemps – all ages, all classes – but it was small enough that she could observe everyone. And best of all, she could hear. When she'd come through Bank Station on Sunday on her way back from St Paul's, the din had been incredible, magnified by the curved ceilings and echoing tunnels.

Here, she could hear everything even above the *crump* of the bombs, from the mother reading fairy-tales to her three little girls – tonight it was 'Rapunzel' – to the rector and Mrs Wyvern discussing the church's Harvest Fête. And the same people came every night.

The mother was Mrs Brightford, and the little girls, in descending order, were Bess, Irene, and Trot. 'Her Christian name's Deborah, but we call her Trot because she's so quick,' Mrs Brightford had explained to Miss Hibbard, the white-haired woman with the knitting. The younger spinster was Miss Laburnum. She and Mrs Wyvern served on the Ladies' Guild of St George's, which explained all the discussions of altar flowers and fêtes. The ill-tempered stout man was Mr Dorming. Mr Simms's dog was named Nelson.

The only one whose name she hadn't found out was the elderly gentleman who gave her his *Times* each night. She'd pegged him as a retired clerk, but his manners and accent were upper-class. A member of the nobility? It was possible. The Blitz had broken down class barriers, and dukes and their servants had frequently ended up sitting side-by-side in the shelters. But an aristocrat would surely have somewhere more comfortable than this to go. He must have a particular reason for choosing this shelter – like Mr Simms, who came here because dogs weren't allowed in the tube. Or Miss Hibbard, who'd confided on their way over from the boarding house Sunday – she, Mr Dorming, and Miss Laburnum all boarded at Mrs Rickett's – that she came here for the company. 'So much more pleasant than sitting alone in one's room thinking what might happen,' she'd said. 'I'm ashamed to say I almost look forward to the raids.'

The elderly gentleman's reason obviously wasn't the company. Except to offer Polly his *Times*, he almost never interacted with the shelterers. He sat in his corner quietly observing the others as they chatted, or reading. Polly couldn't make out the title of his book – it looked scholarly. But appearances could be deceiving. The ecclesiastical-looking book the rector was reading had turned out to be Agatha Christie's *Murder at the Vicarage*.

Miss Laburnum was telling Mrs Rickett and Miss Hibbard about the bomb that had hit Buckingham Palace. 'It exploded in the Quadrangle just outside the King and Queen's sitting room,' she said. 'They might have been *killed*!'

'Oh my,' Miss Hibbard said, knitting. 'Were they hurt?'

'No, though they were badly shaken. Luckily, the Princesses were safely in the country.'

'Rapunzel was a princess,' Trot, on her mother's lap, looked up from the fairy-tale her mother was reading to say.

'No, she *wasn't*,' Irene said. 'Sleeping Beauty was a princess.'

'What about the Queen's dogs?' Mr Simms asked. 'Were they at the palace?'

'*The Times* didn't say,' Miss Laburnum said.

'Of course not. Nobody thinks of the dogs.'

'There was an advertisement in the *Daily Graphic* last week for a gas mask for dogs,' the rector said.

'I think Basil Rathbone's handsome, don't you?' Viv said.

Lila made a face. 'No, he's *much* too old. I think Leslie Howard's handsome.'

An anti-aircraft gun started up. 'There goes the Strand,' Mr Dorming said, and, as it was followed by the heavy *crump* of a bomb off to the east, and then another, 'The East End's getting it again.'

'Do you know what the Queen said after the palace was hit?' Miss Laburnum said. 'She said, "Now I can look the East End in the face."'

'She's an example to us all,' Mrs Wyvern said.

'They say she's wonderfully brave,' Miss Laburnum said, 'that she isn't afraid of the bombs at all.' Neither were they. Polly'd hoped to observe their adaptation to the Blitz as they progressed from fear to a determination not to give in to the nonchalant courage American correspondents arriving in mid-Blitz had been so impressed by. But they'd already passed those stages and reached the point where they ignored the raids completely. In eleven days flat.

They didn't even seem to hear the crashes and bangs above them, only occasionally glancing up when an explosion was particularly loud and then going back to whatever they'd been talking about. Which was often the war. Mr Simms reported the count of downed German and RAF aircraft every night; Miss Laburnum followed the royal family, recounting every visit 'our dear Queen' made to bombed-out neighbourhoods, hospitals, and ARP posts; and Miss Hibbard was knitting socks for 'our boys'. Even Lila and Viv, who spent most of their time discussing film stars and dances, talked about joining the Wrens. And Leslie Howard, who Lila thought was so handsome, was working with British Intelligence. He'd be killed in 1943, when the plane he was in was shot down.

Mrs Brightford's husband was in the Army, the rector had a son who'd been injured at Dunkirk and was in hospital in Orpington, and they all had relatives and acquaintances who'd been called up or bombed out – all of which they discussed in a cheerful, gossipy tone, oblivious to the raids, which came in waves, intensifying, subsiding, then intensifying again. Not even Mr Simms's terrier, Nelson, seemed particularly bothered by them, though dogs' ability to hear high-pitched noises was supposed to make it worse for them.

'Oh that's silly,' Lila was saying. 'Leslie Howard's *far* handsomer than Clark Gable.'

'"… and the witch said, 'You must give Rapunzel to me,'"'Mrs Brightford read. '"And she took the child from her parents …"'

Polly wondered if Mrs Brightford had refused to be separated from her little girls, or if they'd been evacuated and then come home again. Merope had said more than seventy-five per cent of them had been back in London when the Blitz began.

'Sounds like it's moving off to the north,' Mr Simms said.

It did seem to be moving off. The nearest of the anti-aircraft guns had stopped, and the roar of the planes had diminished to a low hum.

'"And the cruel witch locked Rapunzel in a high tower without any door,"' Mrs Brightford read to Trot, who was nearly asleep. '"And Rapunzel—"'

There was a sudden, sharp knock on the door. Trot sat up straight.

It's someone else caught out on the street by the warden, Polly thought, looking over at the door and then at the rector, expecting him to let them in.

He didn't move. No one moved. Or breathed. They all, even little Trot, stared at the door, their eyes wide in their white faces, their bodies braced as if for a blow.

That's how they looked when I was standing outside knocking that first night, Polly thought. *That's the expression they had on their faces in the moment before the door opened, and they saw it was me.*

She'd been wrong about their having adjusted to the raids. This terror had been there all along, just beneath the surface. She thought suddenly of the painting, *The Light of the World*, in St Paul's. *I wonder if that's why whoever's on the other side of the door isn't opening it. Because they're too frightened.*

More knocks, louder. Trot climbed straight up her mother's body and buried her face in her neck. Mrs Brightford pulled her other girls closer to her. Miss Laburnum pressed her hand against her bosom, the elderly gentleman reached for his umbrella, and he and Mr Dorming both stood up. 'Is it the Germans?' Bess asked in her piping voice.

'No, of course not,' Mrs Brightford said, but it was obvious that was what they were all thinking.

The rector took a deep breath and then crossed the room, unbolted the door, and opened it. Two young girls in ARP overalls and carrying tin helmets and gas masks tumbled through it. 'Shut the door!' Mrs Rickett said, and Mrs Wyvern echoed, 'Mind the blackout,' exactly as they had with Polly.

The girls shut the door, and Miss Laburnum smiled in welcome. Trot let go of her mother, Irene took her thumb out of her mouth to give the newcomers the once-over, and Viv scooted over closer to Lila to give them a place to sit. Mrs Rickett continued to glare suspiciously, but then she had done that to Polly, too.

The young women looked around the room at everyone. 'Oh dear, this isn't it either,' one said, disappointed.

'We were going to our post, and I'm afraid we've got lost in the blackout,' the other one said. 'Is there a telephone here we might use?'

'I'm afraid not,' the rector said apologetically.

'Then can you tell us how to get to Gloucester Terrace?'

'Gloucester Terrace?' Mr Dorming said. 'You are lost.'

They certainly were. Gloucester Terrace was all the way over in Marylebone.

'It's our first night on duty,' the first young woman explained, and the rector began to draw them a map.

'Are they Germans?' Trot whispered to her mother.

Mrs Brightford laughed. 'No, they're on our side.'

The rector gave them the map. 'Shouldn't you stay till this lets up?' the rector asked, but they shook their heads.

'The warden will have our heads for being late as it is,' the first one said, raising her voice to be heard above the din.

'But thanks awfully,' the other one shouted, and they opened the door and ducked out.

Michael Davies should have come here, not Dunkirk, if he wanted to observe heroes, Polly thought, looking after them. She'd just seen them in action. And it wasn't only the young women and their willingness to go out on the streets in the middle of a raid. How much courage had it taken for the rector to cross the basement and open that door, knowing it might be the Germans? Or for all of them to sit here night after night, waiting for imminent invasion or a direct hit, not knowing whether they'd live till the next all-clear? Not knowing. It was the one thing historians could never understand. They could observe the contemps, live with them, try to put themselves in their place, but they couldn't truly experience what they were experiencing. *Because I know what's going to happen. I know Hitler didn't invade England, that he didn't use poison gas or destroy St Paul's. Or London. Or the world. That he lost the war.*

But they didn't. They'd lived through the Blitz and D-Day and the V-1s and V-2s, with no guarantee of a happy ending.

'Then what happened to Rapunzel?' Trot asked as if nothing had happened.

'Tell us the rest of the story,' Bess and Irene chimed in and were both asleep before their mother had read a page, and Trot was struggling to keep her eyes open. They were too young to understand what was going on, of course, or what might happen. Polly was glad. And the others must feel the same protectiveness towards them that she did. Mrs Wyvern and Miss Laburnum dropped their voices to a whisper, and Mr Simms reached over to pull the blanket up over Bess's shoulders. Mrs Brightford smiled at him and went on reading. '"... and after many years of searching, the prince heard Rapunzel's voice ..."'

'Mummy,' Trot said, sitting up and tugging at her mother's sleeve. 'What if the Germans in vade?' she asked, pronouncing it as two words.

'They won't,' Mrs Brightford said. 'Mr Churchill won't let them.' She went on reading. '"And Rapunzel's tears, falling on the prince's eyes, restored his sight, and they lived happily ever after."'

'But what if they do? In vade?'

'They won't,' her mother said firmly. 'I'll always keep you safe. You know that, don't you, darling?'

Trot nodded. 'Unless you're killed.'

*'Meanwhile, it is important not to give the enemy any
information which would help him in directing his shooting
by telling him where his missiles have landed.'*

HERBERT MORRISON, HOME SECRETARY, 16 JUNE 1944

DULWICH, SURREY – 14 JUNE 1944

B y Wednesday morning, Mary was beginning to worry.
There'd still been no mention of Bethnal Green railroad
bridge or the other V-1s that had fallen the night of the twelfth.
If the first four V-1s had hit when her implant said they had,
they should have heard *something* by now.

But even though the last two FANYs – Parrish and Sutcliffe-
Hythe – had returned with a box of sticking plaster from Platt,
which was only four miles from where the first V-1 had fallen,
and Talbot had rung up Bethnal Green to ask them to save back
any dancing pumps that came in for her, there'd still been no
mention of explosions or of odd-looking planes with yellow
flames coming out of their tails.

There was nothing in the newspapers either, but Mary'd expected that. The government had kept the V-1s secret till after
the fifteenth, when more than a hundred rockets had come over
and made their existence impossible to keep quiet. But she'd
thought there might be something about a gas explosion, which
was the story they'd put out.

But there were no stories at all in the London papers, and the big news in the *South London Gazette* was the engagement of Miss Betty Buntin to Joseph Morelli, PFC, of Brooklyn, New York. And the FANYs' only topic of conversation was who got to wear the pink net frock first. If she'd been dropped into the post without any historical prep, she wouldn't even have been able to deduce there was a war on, let alone that they were under attack. And the next rockets wouldn't be launched till tomorrow night, so there was no way to introduce the subject.

She attempted it anyway. 'I was actually supposed to be here on Monday,' she said. 'Did I miss anything?'

'The invasion of Normandy,' Reed said, polishing her nails.

'And the applecart upset,' said Camberley, who was trying on the pink frock. 'We'd have got you that ecru lace if we'd known you were coming.' She turned to Grenville. 'I'll never be able to eat and breathe in this. It will have to be let out again.' She turned back to Mary. 'I say, Kent, you wouldn't happen to have any evening frocks, would you?'

'Don't tell them yes unless you're prepared to share them,' Fairchild said. 'But if you share yours with us, we'll share ours with you,' Camberley said. Parrish rolled her eyes. 'I'm certain she's simply panting for a chance to wear the Yellow Peril.'

'It might actually look nice on her, with her fair hair,' Camberley said.

'The Yellow Peril doesn't look nice on anyone,' Maitland said, but Camberley ignored her. '*Have* you a frock, Kent?'

'Yes,' Mary said, opening the duffel she still hadn't had a chance to unpack. 'Actually, I have two, and I'd be glad to share.' She lifted them out.

And knew instantly that she'd made a mistake. The FANYs were gaping at the frocks openmouthed. When she'd got them from Wardrobe, she'd purposely chosen ones that looked worn so she wouldn't stand out here, but next to the pink net, with its torn hem and obviously let-out seams, the light-green silk and the blue organdie looked brand-new.

'Where on earth did you get such heavenly things?' Fairchild asked, fingering the green silk.

'You're not having an affair with some rich American general, are you?' Reed said.

'No. My cousin gave them to me when she went out to Egypt. She's in the medical corps,' she said, hoping no one would say they knew a nurse in Egypt who constantly went to dances. 'I haven't had any occasion to wear them,' she added honestly.

'Obviously,' Parrish said, and Camberley looked as if she was going to cry.

'You're certain you're willing to share these with us?' she asked reverently. Which showed how much the war had changed these young women's lives. They came from wealthy families, they'd been debutantes, they'd been presented at court, and now they were overjoyed at the prospect of wearing out-of-fashion secondhand frocks. 'I haven't seen silk like this since before the war!' Sutcliffe-Hythe said, fingering the fabric. 'I do hope it doesn't end before I have a chance to wear this.'

It won't, Mary thought.

And much of the worst of it was still to come, but all the FANYs were convinced the war would be over by autumn. They'd even got up a betting pool on what day it would end.

'Oh, speaking of the war ending,' Fairchild said, 'you never did say what date you wanted for the pool, Kent.'

May eighth, 1945, she thought. But the calendar they were using only went through this October and most of the dates already taken were in late June and early July, even though the invasion had been less than two weeks ago.

'You can have the eighteenth,' Fairchild said, looking at the calendar.

The eighteenth was the day a V-1 had hit the Guards Chapel during a church service and killed 121 contemps. If that date and location weren't an error, too.

'Or August fifth.'

The day one had hit the Co-op Stores in Camberwell. But she

had to choose something. 'I'll take August the thirtieth,' Mary said, and as Fairchild wrote her name in the square, 'Yesterday, on my way here, I heard someone say something about hearing an explosion in—'

'Kent,' Parrish said, leaning in the door, 'the Major wants to see you in her office.'

'Don't say anything about the pool,' Fairchild warned her. 'Or about the war being nearly over. She's an absolute bear on the subject.' She thrust the calendar into a drawer.

Parrish walked her to the Major's office. 'The Major's convinced the war can still be lost, though it's difficult to imagine how. I mean, we've already taken the beaches and half the coast of France, and the Germans are on the run.'

But the Major was right. The Allied forces would shortly be bogged down in the hedgerows of France, and if they hadn't stopped the Germans at the Battle of the Bulge—

'You needn't look so nervy,' Parrish said, stopping outside the Major's door. 'The Major's actually not bad unless you're attempting to put one over on her.' She knocked on the door, opened it, and said, 'Lieutenant Kent is here, Major.'

'Send her in, Lieutenant,' the Major said. 'Have you found any blankets yet?'

'No, Major,' Parrish said. 'Neither Croydon nor New Cross has any they can spare. I have a call in to Streatham.'

'Good. Tell them it's an emergency. And send in Grenville.'

She does know about the V-1s, Mary thought. *That's why she's been so determined to stock up on supplies.*

Parrish left.

'What medical training have you had, Lieutenant?' the Major asked.

'I hold certificates in first aid and emergency nursing.'

'Excellent.' She picked up Mary's transfer papers. 'I see you were stationed in Oxford. With an ambulance unit?'

'Yes, Major.'

'Oh, then you will have met – what is it?' she asked as Parrish leaned in the door.

'Headquarters on the telephone, Major.'

The Major nodded and reached for the receiver. 'If you'll excuse me for a moment ...' she said, and into the telephone, 'Major Denewell here.' There was a pause. 'I am fully aware of that, but my unit needs those blankets. We begin transporting the wounded this afternoon.' She rang off and smiled at Mary. 'Now, where were we? Oh yes, your previous assignments,' she said, looking through her papers. 'And I see you drove an ambulance in London during the Blitz. Which part of London?'

'Southwark.'

'Oh, well, then you must know—'

There was a knock on the door. 'Yes, come in,' the Major said, and Grenville poked her head in.

'You wanted me, Major?'

'Yes, I want an inventory of all our medical supplies.'

Grenville nodded and left.

'Now, where were we?' the Major said, picking up the transfer papers again.

You *were about to ask me about someone I knew in London during the Blitz*, Mary thought, bracing herself, but the Major said, 'I see your transfer authorisation is dated June the seventh.'

'Yes, ma'am. I had difficulty obtaining transport. The invasion—'

The Major nodded. 'Yes, well, the important thing is that you're here now. We shall have our hands full over the next few days. Bethnal Green and Croydon will eventually also be transporting patients from hospital in Dover to Orpington, but for now we are the only unit assigned to transport duty. I'm sending you to Dover with Talbot and Fairchild this afternoon. They'll teach you the route. Has Fairchild shown you the schedule and the duty rosters?'

'Yes, Major.'

'Our job here is extremely important, Lieutenant. This war is not yet won. It can still be lost, unless every one of us does our part. I expect you to do yours.'

'Yes, ma'am, I will.'

'You're dismissed, Lieutenant.'

She saluted smartly, and started for the door, doing her best not to look like she was escaping. She put her hand on the door-knob. 'Just a moment, Lieutenant. You said you were stationed in Oxford—'

Mary held her breath. 'I don't suppose they have any blankets they can spare?'

'I'm afraid not. Our post was always short.'

'Oh well, ask in Dover if they have any. And tell Lieutenant Fairchild I know all about the pool and that I will not allow any premature declarations of victory at my post.'

'Yes, Major,' she said and went to find Fairchild, who wasn't at all alarmed that the Major knew.

'At least she didn't forbid us to have it,' she said, shrugging. 'Come along, we're leaving.'

They drove south through Croydon and then turned east, straight down the middle of what in two days would be Bomb Alley. *I should have had all the rocket times and locations implanted instead of just the ones in southeast London*, Mary thought, even though that wouldn't have been possible. There'd been far too many – nearly ten thousand V-1s and eleven hundred V-2s – so she'd focused on the ones which had hit the area around Dulwich, those that had hit London, and the area in between. *But not the area between Dulwich and Dover. Mr Dunworthy will have a fit when he finds out I've been in Bomb Alley*, she thought. But they would only be doing this till the V-1s began coming over. After that they'd have their hands full dealing with the incidents in their immediate area.

The route to Dover wove through a series of twisting lanes and tiny villages. She did her best to memorise it, but there were no signposts to go by, and on the return trip she had to devote all her attention to the patient they'd picked up. 'He's to have surgery on his leg,' the nurse said as he was loaded into the ambulance. She lowered her voice so he wouldn't hear. 'I'm afraid amputation may be necessary. Gangrene.' And when Mary climbed in the back with him, she could smell a sickening sweet smell.

'He's been sedated,' the nurse had told her, but before they were five miles out of Dover, he opened his eyes and asked, 'They're not going to cut it off, are they?' and what had nurses in 1944 said in answer to a question like that? What could anyone in any era say?

'You mustn't think about that now,' she said. 'You must rest.'

'It's all right. I already know they are. It's queer, isn't it? I made it through Dunkirk and El Alamein and the invasion without getting injured, and then a bloody lorry turned over on me.'

'You shouldn't talk. You'll tire yourself out.'

He nodded. 'Soldiers getting killed all round me on Sword Beach, and I didn't get so much as a scratch. Lucky all the way. Did I ever tell you about Dunkirk, Sister?' He must think she was his nurse in hospital at Dover.

'Try to sleep,' she murmured.

'I thought I wasn't going to make it off. I thought I was going to be left behind on the beach – the Germans were coming up fast – but my luck held. The chap who took me aboard had been pulled off Dunkirk two days before, and had come back to help get the rest of us off. He'd made three crossings already and the last one they'd nearly been torpedoed.'

He was still talking when they reached the War Emergency Hospital in Orpington. 'I nearly drowned, and he jumped in and saved me, hauled me aboard. If it hadn't been for him—'

Talbot opened the doors, and two attendants came out to unload the stretcher. Mary scrambled out, holding the plasma bottle aloft. An attendant took it from her. 'Good luck, soldier,' she said as they started into the hospital with him.

'Thank you,' he said. 'If it hadn't been for him, and for your listening to me—'

'Wait!' Fairchild said, leaping past Mary and inside. 'You can't take that blanket. It's ours.'

'Oh no,' Mary said to Talbot. 'I completely forgot to ask in Dover if they had any blankets.'

'I did. They didn't.'

Fairchild came back, triumphantly carrying the blanket. 'Did you ask if they had any extras to spare?' Talbot asked her.

'They don't. I nearly had to wrestle them to get this one back.'

'What about Bethnal Green?' Mary suggested. 'Could we go by the post there on the way home and check to see if they—?'

'No, we already asked them, the day of the applecart upset,' Talbot said.

Which meant she'd have to think of some other way to get to Bethnal Green to confirm the attack. Perhaps she could borrow a bicycle after she went off duty. But the Major sent her and Reed to Bromley after sticking plaster and rubbing alcohol, and early the next morning they set out for Dover again.

'And then you bear left at the bridge,' Fairchild said, teaching her the route. 'And then right just past those trees.' She pointed ahead to where two tanks sat in a pasture. 'That's odd. I thought all our tanks were in France.'

Mary wondered if they were real tanks. British Intelligence had used inflatable rubber tanks as part of their plan to deceive the Germans into thinking the invasion would be launched from southeast England. Perhaps they were left over from that.

A horrible thought struck her. British Intelligence had also attempted to fool the Germans as to where their V-1s had landed. They'd planted false stories and photos in the newspapers to make them alter their launch trajectories so the rockets would fall short of London. Which was why Dulwich and Croydon and Bomb Alley had been hit more than anywhere else.

What if Research had mistakenly put the falsified data into her implant instead of the actual times and locations? That would explain why no one had said anything about Bethnal Green – because the V-1 hadn't actually hit there. If that were the case, she was in trouble. Her safety depended on her knowing exactly where and when every V-1 and V-2 had landed.

As soon as we get back to the post, I've got to find out if that railway was damaged, she thought, but the moment they reached the post, the Major sent her and Fairchild off to Woolwich for the extra blankets she'd finally managed to procure, and it was dark before they got back. Which meant she'd have to wait and go to Bethnal Green tomorrow – unless the V-1s that hit tonight were on time. If they were, then the data in her implant was correct, and she could stop worrying. Unless of course one of them hit the post.

She fidgeted through the evening, waiting for 11:43, when the first one was supposed to have hit. The siren was supposed to have sounded at 11:31. She listened impatiently to the FANYs argue over who got to wear the green silk first, trying not to look at her watch every five minutes. She was immeasurably glad when eleven o'clock and lights-out came. She retired under the covers with a pocket torch to read her watch by and a magazine she'd borrowed from the common room. If anyone noticed the light, she'd say she was reading. She propped the magazine on top of the torch to shield the light and waited. Ten past eleven. Quarter past. The girls continued to argue in the dark. 'But Donald's never seen you in the Yellow Peril,' Sutcliffe-Hythe said, 'and Edwin's already seen me in it twice.'

'I know,' Maitland said, 'but I'm hoping Donald will propose.'

Twenty past. Twenty-five. Six more minutes, Mary thought, listening for the wail of the siren starting up, for the drone of the V-1. She wished she'd listened to a recording of one in the

Bodleian so she'd know exactly what they sounded like. Their distinctive rattle, which was supposed to sound like a backfiring motor car engine, had been loud enough that it had been possible to dive for the nearest gutter when one heard it and save oneself.

Twenty-nine. Half-past. 11:31. *My watch must be fast*, she thought, and held it up to her ear. *Oh, do come on. Sound the alert. I don't want to have to go back through to Oxford. What will I tell the Major? And Mr Dunworthy. If he finds out I've not only been driving Bomb Alley, but have a faulty implant, he'll never let me come back.*

11:32. 11:33 ...

'They'd make a beautiful target, wouldn't they?'

GENERAL SHORT, COMMENTING ON THE BATTLESHIPS
LINED UP AT PEARL HARBOR, 6 DECEMBER 1941

THE ENGLISH CHANNEL – 29 MAY 1940

Mike lurched to the rear of the boat. 'What do you mean, we're halfway across the Channel?' he shouted, peering out over the stern. There was no land in sight, nothing but water and darkness on all sides. He groped his way back to the helm and the Commander. 'You have to turn back!'

'You said you were a war correspondent, Kansas,' the Commander shouted back at him, his voice muffled by the wind. 'Well, here's your chance to cover the war instead of writing about beach fortifications. The whole bloody British Army's trapped at Dunkirk, and we're going to rescue them!'

But I can't go to Dunkirk, Mike thought. *It's impossible. Dunkirk's a divergence point.* Besides, this wasn't the way the evacuation had operated. The small craft hadn't set off on their own. That had been considered much too dangerous. They'd been organised into convoys led by naval destroyers.

'You've got to go back to Dover,' he shouted, trying to make himself heard against the sound of the chugging engine and the wet, salt-laden wind. 'The Navy—'

'The Navy?' the Commander snorted. 'I wouldn't trust those paper-pushers to lead me across a mud puddle. When we bring back a boatload of our boys, they'll see just how seaworthy the *Lady Jane* is!'

'But you don't have any charts, and the Channel's mined—'

'I've been piloting this Channel by dead reckoning since before those young pups from the Small Vessels Pool were born. We won't let a few mines stop us, will we, Jonathan?'

'Jonathan? You brought *Jonathan*? He's fourteen years old!'

Jonathan emerged out of the bow's darkness half dragging, half-carrying a huge coil of rope. 'Isn't this exciting?' he said. 'We're going to go and rescue the British Expeditionary Force from the Germans. We're going to be heroes!'

'But you don't have official clearance,' Mike said, desperately trying to think of some argument that would convince them to turn back. 'And you're not armed—'

'*Armed?*' the Commander bellowed, taking one hand off the wheel to reach inside his peacoat and pull out an ancient pistol. 'Of course we're armed. We've got everything we need.' He waved one hand towards the bow. 'Extra rope, extra petrol—'

Mike squinted through the darkness to where he was pointing. He could just make out rectangular metal cans lashed to the gunwales. Oh Christ. 'How much gas – petrol – do you have on board?'

'Twenty tins,' Jonathan said eagerly. 'We've more down in the hold.'

Which is enough to blow us sky-high if we're hit by a torpedo.

'Jonathan,' the Commander bellowed, 'stow that rope in the stern and go and check the bilge pump.'

'Aye, aye, Commander.' Jonathan started for the hatch.

Mike went after him. 'Jonathan, listen, you've got to convince your grandfather to turn back. What he's doing is—' he was going to say 'suicidal', but settled for, 'against Navy regulations. He'll lose his chance to be recommissioned—'

'Recommissioned?' Jonathan said blankly. 'What do you mean? Grandfather was never in the Navy.'

Oh Christ, he'd probably never been across the Channel either.

'Jonathan!' the Commander called. 'I told you to go and check the bilge pump. And, Kansas, go below and put your shoes on. And have a drink. You look like death.'

That's because we're going to die, Mike thought, trying to think of some way to get him to turn the boat around and head back to Saltram-on-Sea, but nothing short of knocking him out with the butt of that pistol and taking the wheel would work, and then what? He knew even less than the Commander did about piloting a boat, and there weren't any charts on board, even if he could decipher them, which he doubted.

'Get yourself some dinner,' the Commander ordered. 'We've a long night's work ahead of us.'

They had no idea what they were getting into. More than sixty of the small craft that had gone over to Dunkirk had been sunk and their crews injured or killed. Mike started down the ladder.

'There's some of that pilchard stew left,' the Commander called down after him.

I don't need to eat, Mike thought, descending into the hold, which now had a full foot of water in it. *I need to think.* How could they be going to Dunkirk? It was impossible. The laws of time travel didn't allow historians anywhere near divergence points.

Unless Dunkirk isn't a divergence point, he thought, wading over to the bunk to retrieve his shoes and socks.

They were in the furthest corner. Mike clambered up onto the bunk to get them and then sat there with a shoe in his hand, staring blindly at it, considering the possibility. Dunkirk had been a major turning point in the war. If the soldiers had been captured by the Germans, the invasion of England, and its surrender, would have been inevitable. But it wasn't a single discrete event, like Lincoln's assassination or the sinking of the *Titanic*, where a historian's making a grab for John Wilkes

232

Booth's pistol or shouting 'Iceberg ahead!' could alter the entire course of events. He couldn't keep the British Expeditionary Force from being rescued, no matter what he did. There were too many boats, too many people involved, spread over too great an area. Even if a historian wanted to alter the outcome of the evacuation, he couldn't.

But he could alter individual events. Dunkirk had been full of narrow escapes and near-misses. A five-minute delay in landing could put a boat underneath a bomb from a Stuka or turn a near-miss into a direct hit, and a five-degree change in steering could mean the difference between it being grounded or making it out of the harbour.

Anything I do could get the Lady Jane *sunk*, Mike thought, horrified. *Which means I don't dare do anything. I've got to stay down here till we're safely out of Dunkirk.* Maybe he could feign seasickness, or cowardice.

But even his mere presence here could alter events. At a divergence point, history balanced on a knife's edge, and his merely being on board could be enough to tilt the balance. Most of the small craft that had come back from Dunkirk had been packed to capacity. His presence might mean there wasn't room for a soldier who'd otherwise have been saved – a soldier who would have gone on to do something critical at Tobruk or Normandy or the Battle of the Bulge.

But if his presence at Dunkirk would have altered events and caused a paradox, then the net would never have let him through. It would have refused to open, the way it had in Dover and Ramsgate and all those other places Badri had tried. The fact that it had let him through at Saltram-on-Sea meant that he hadn't done anything at Dunkirk to alter events, or that whatever he'd done hadn't affected the course of history.

Or that he hadn't made it to Dunkirk. Which meant the *Lady Jane* had hit a mine or been sunk by a German U-boat – or the rising water in her hold – before she ever got there. She wouldn't be the only boat that had happened to.

I knew I should have memorised that asterisked list of small craft, he thought. *And I should have remembered that slippage isn't the only way the continuum has of keeping historians from altering the course of history.*

There was a sudden pounding of footsteps overhead and Jonathan poked his head down the hatch. 'Grandfather sent me to fetch you,' he said breathlessly.

'Get the bloody hell up here!' the Commander shouted over Jonathan's voice.

They've spotted the U-boat that's going to kill us, Mike thought, grabbing his shoes and wading over to the ladder. *That's why this is possible. Because the* Lady Jane *never made it to Dunkirk.* He clambered up it.

Jonathan was leaning over the hatch, looking excited. 'Grandfather needs you to navigate,' he said.

'I thought he didn't have any charts,' Mike said.

'He doesn't,' Jonathan said. 'He—'

'Now!' the Commander roared.

'We're here,' Jonathan said. 'He needs us to guide him through the harbour.'

'What do you mean, we're here?' Mike said, hauling himself up the ladder and out onto the deck. 'We can't be—'

But they were. The harbour lay in front of them, lit by a pinkish-orange glow that illuminated two destroyers and dozens of small boats. And behind it, on fire and half-obscured by towering plumes of black smoke, was Dunkirk.

Raid In Progress

NOTICE ONSTAGE IN LONDON THEATRE, 1940

LONDON – 17 SEPTEMBER 1940

B y midnight only Polly and the elderly aristocratic gentleman who always gave her his *Times* were awake. He had draped his coat over his shoulders and was reading. Everyone else had nodded off, though only Lila and Viv and Mrs Brightford's little girls had lain down, Bess and Trot with their heads in their mother's lap. The others sat drowsing on the bench or the floor, leaning back against the wall. Miss Hibbard had let go of her knitting, and her head had fallen forward onto her chest. The rector and Miss Laburnum were both snoring.

Polly was surprised. The historical accounts had said lack of sleep had been a major problem. But this group didn't seem bothered by the uncomfortable sleeping conditions or the noise, even though the raid was picking up in intensity again. The anti-aircraft gun in Kensington Gardens started up, and another wave of planes growled overhead.

She wondered if this was the wave of bombers that had hit John Lewis. No, they sounded nearer – Mayfair? It and Bloomsbury had both been hit tonight as well as central London, and after they'd finished with Oxford Street, they'd hit Regent Street and the BBC studios. She'd better try to sleep while she could. She would need to start off early tomorrow morning, though she wondered if the department stores would even be open.

London businesses had prided themselves on remaining open throughout the Blitz, and Padgett's and John Lewis had both managed to start up again in new locations after a few weeks. But what about the day after the bombing? Would the stores which hadn't been damaged be open, or would the whole street be out of bounds, like the area around St Paul's? And for how long? *If I haven't got a job by tomorrow night—*

Of course they'll be open, she thought. Think of all those window signs the Blitz was famous for: 'Hitler can smash our windows, but he can't match our prices', and 'It's bomb marché in Oxford Street this week'. And that photograph of a woman reaching through a broken display window to feel the fabric of a frock. It might even be a good day to apply for a position. It would show that the raids didn't frighten her, and if some of the shop-girls weren't able to make it into work because of bombed bus routes, the stores might hire her to fill in.

But she'd also have to compete with all those suddenly un-employed John Lewis shopgirls, and they'd be more likely to be taken on than she would, out of sympathy. *Perhaps I should tell them I worked there,* she thought.

She folded her coat into a pillow and lay down, but she couldn't sleep. The droning planes were too loud. They sounded like monstrous buzzing wasps, and they were growing louder – and nearer – by the moment. Polly sat up. The noise had wakened the rector, too. He'd sat up and was looking nervously at the ceiling. There was a *whoosh,* and then a huge explosion.

Mr Dorming jerked upright. 'What the bloody hell—?' he said, and then, 'Sorry, Reverend.'

'Quite understandable given the circumstances,' the rector said. 'They seem to have begun again.' Which was an under-statement even for a contemp. The gun in Battersea Park was going full-blast, and he had to shout to make himself heard. 'I do hope those girls are all right. The ones who were trying to find Gloucester Terrace.'

The gun in Kensington Gardens started in again, and Irene sat up, rubbing her eyes. 'Shh, go back to sleep,' Mrs Brightford murmured, looking over at Mr Dorming, who was staring at the ceiling. The raid seemed to be directly overhead, whumps and bangs and long, shuddering booms that woke up Nelson and Mr Simms and the rest of the women. Mrs Rickett appeared annoyed, but everyone else looked wary and then worried.

'Perhaps we shouldn't have let the girls go,' Miss Laburnum said.

Trot crawled into her mother's lap. 'Shh,' Mrs Brightford said, patting her. 'It's all right.'

No, it's not, Polly thought, watching their faces. They had the same look they'd had when the knocking began. If the raid didn't let up soon …

Every anti-aircraft gun in London was firing – a chorus of deafening *thump-thump-thumps*, punctuated by the thud and crash of bombs. The din grew louder and louder. Everyone's eyes strayed to the ceiling, as if expecting it to crash in at any moment. There was a screech, like tearing metal, and then an ear-splitting boom. Miss Hibbard jumped and dropped her knitting, and Bess began to cry.

'The bombardment does seem rather more severe this evening,' the rector said.

Rather more severe. It sounded as if the planes – and the antiaircraft guns – were fighting it out in the sanctuary upstairs. Kensington wasn't hit, she told herself.

'Perhaps we should sing,' the rector shouted over the cacophony.

'That's an excellent idea,' Mrs Wyvern said, and launched into 'God Save Our King'. Miss Laburnum and then Mr Simms gamely joined in, but they could scarcely be heard above the roar and screaming outside, and the rector made no attempt to go on to the second verse. One by one, everyone stopped singing and stared anxiously up at the ceiling.

A high-explosive bomb exploded so close that the beams of

237

the shelter shook, followed immediately by another HE, even closer, drowning out the sound of the guns, but not the planes droning endlessly, maddeningly overhead. 'Why isn't it letting up?' Viv asked, and Polly could hear the panic in her voice.

'I don't like it!' Trot wailed, clapping her small hands over her ears. 'It's loud!'

'Indeed,' the elderly gentleman said from his corner. '"The isle is full of noises",' and Polly looked over at him in surprise. His voice had changed completely from the quiet, well-bred voice of a gentleman to a deep, commanding tone that made even the little girls stop crying and stare at him.

He shut his book and laid it on the floor beside him. '"With strange and several noises",' he said, getting to his feet, '"of roaring ..." ' He shrugged his coat from his shoulders, as if throwing off a cloak to reveal himself as a magician. Or a king. '"With shrieking, howling, and more diversity of sounds, all horrible, we were awaked ..."'

He strode suddenly to the centre of the cellar. '"To the dread rattling thunder have I given fire",' he shouted, seeming to Polly to have grown to twice his size. '"The strong-bas'd promontory have I made shake!"' His resonant voice reached every corner of the cellar. '"Sometime I'd divide and burn in many places",' he said, pointing dramatically at the ceiling, the floor, the door in turn as he spoke, '"on the topmast, the yards, and bowsprit would I flame—"' He flung both arms out. '"Then meet and join."'

Above, a bomb crashed, close enough to rattle the tea urn and the teacups, but no one spared them a glance. They were all watching him, their fear gone, and even though the terrifying racket hadn't diminished, and his words, rather than attempting to distract them from the noise, were drawing attention to it, describing it, the din was no longer frightening. It had become mere stage effects, clashing cymbals and sheets of rattled tin, providing a dramatic background to his voice.

'"A plague upon this howling!"' he cried. '"They are

louder than the weather or our office",' and went straight into Prospero's epilogue and from there into Lear's mad scene, and finally *Henry V*, while his audience listened, entranced.

At some point the cacophony outside had diminished, fading till there was nothing but the muffled *poom-poom-poom* of an anti-aircraft gun off to the northeast, but no one in the room had noticed. Which was, of course, the point. Polly gazed at him in admiration.

'"This story shall the good man teach his son, from this day to the ending of the world",' he said, his voice ringing through the cellar, '"but we in it shall be remembered – we few, we happy few, we band of brothers."' His voice died away on the last words, like a bell echoing into silence.

'"The iron tongue of midnight hath told twelve",' he whispered. '"Sweet friends, to bed,"' and bowed his head, his hand on his heart.

There was a moment of entranced silence, followed by Miss Hibbard's 'Oh my!' and general applause. Trot clapped wildly, and even Mr Dorming joined in. The gentleman bowed deeply, retrieved his coat from the floor, and returned to his corner and his book. Mrs Brightford gathered her girls to her, and Nelson and Lila and Viv composed themselves to sleep, one after the other, like children after they'd been told a bedtime story.

Polly went over to sit next to Miss Laburnum and the rector. 'Who *is* he?' she whispered.

'You mean you don't *know*?' Miss Laburnum said.

Polly hoped he wasn't so famous that her failing to recognise him would be suspicious.

'He's Godfrey Kingsman,' the rector said, 'the Shakespearean actor.'

'England's greatest actor,' Miss Laburnum explained.

Mrs Rickett sniffed. 'If he's such a great actor, what's he doing sitting in this shelter? Why isn't he onstage?'

'You know perfectly well the theatres have closed because of

239

the raids,' Miss Laburnum said heatedly. 'Until the government reopens them—'

'All I know is, I don't let rooms to actors,' Mrs Rickett said. 'They can't be relied on to pay their rent.'

Miss Laburnum went very red. 'Sir *Godfrey*—'

'He's been knighted, then?' Polly asked hastily.

'By King Edward,' Miss Laburnum said. 'I can't imagine that you've never heard of him, Miss Sebastian. His Lear is *renowned*! I saw him in *Hamlet* when I was a girl, and he was simply marvellous!'

He's rather marvellous now, Polly thought.

'He's appeared before all the crowned heads of Europe,' Miss Laburnum said. 'And to think he honoured *us* with a performance tonight.'

Mrs Rickett sniffed again, and Miss Laburnum was only stopped from saying something regrettable by the all-clear. The sleepers sat up and yawned, and everyone began to gather their belongings. Sir Godfrey marked his place in his book, shut it, and stood up. Miss Laburnum and Miss Hibbard scurried over to him to tell him how wonderful he'd been. 'It was *so* inspiring,' Miss Laburnum said, 'especially the speech from *Hamlet* about the band of brothers.'

Polly suppressed a smile. Sir Godfrey thanked the two ladies solemnly, his voice quiet and refined again. Watching him putting on his coat and picking up his umbrella, it was hard to believe he'd just given that mesmerising performance.

Lila and Viv folded their blankets and gathered up their magazines, Mr Dorming picked up his Thermos, Mrs Brightford picked up Trot, and they all converged on the door. The rector pulled the bolt back and opened it, and as he did, Polly caught an echo of the tense, frightened look they'd had before Sir Godfrey intervened, this time for what they might find when they went through that door and up those steps: their houses gone, London in ruins. Or German tanks driving down Lampden Road.

The rector stepped back from the opened door to let them

through, but no one moved, not even Nelson, who'd been cooped up since before midnight.

'"Hie you, make haste!"' Sir Godfrey's clarion voice rang out. '"See this dispatch'd with all the haste thou canst,"' and Nelson shot through the door.

Everyone laughed.

'Nelson, come back!' Mr Simms shouted, and ran after him. He called down from the top of the steps, 'No damage that I can see,' and the rest of them trooped up the steps and looked around at the street, peaceful in the dim grey pre-dawn light. The buildings were all intact, though there was a smoky pall in the air, and a sharp smell of cordite and burning wood.

'Lambeth got it last night,' Mr Dorming said, pointing at plumes of black smoke off to the southeast.

'And Piccadilly Circus, looks like,' Mr Simms said, coming back with Nelson and pointing at what was actually Oxford Street and the smoke from John Lewis. Mr Dorming was wrong, too. Shoreditch and Whitechapel had taken the brunt of the first round of raids, not Lambeth, but from the look of the smoke, nowhere in the East End was safe.

'I don't understand,' Lila said, looking around at the tranquil scene. 'It sounded like it was bang on top of us.'

'What will it sound like if it is on top of us, I wonder?' Viv asked.

'I've heard one hears a very loud, very high-pitched scream,' Mr Simms began, but Mr Dorming was shaking his head.

'You won't hear it,' he said. 'You'll never know what hit you,' he added and stomped off.

'Cheerful,' Viv said, looking after him.

Lila was still looking towards the smoke of Oxford Street. 'I suppose the Underground won't be running,' she said glumly, 'and it'll take us ages to get to work.'

'And when we get there,' Viv said, 'the windows will have been blown out again. We'll have to spend all day sweeping up.'

'"What's this, varlets?"' Sir Godfrey roared. '"Do I hear talk of terror and defeat? Stiffen the sinews! Summon up the blood!"'

Lila and Viv giggled.

Sir Godfrey drew his umbrella like a sword. '"Once more into the breach, dear friends, once more!"' he shouted, raising it high. '"We fight for England!"'

'Oh, I do love *Richard the Third*!' Miss Laburnum said.

Sir Godfrey gripped the umbrella handle violently, and for a moment Polly thought he was going to run Miss Laburnum through, but instead he hooked it over his arm. '"And if we no more meet till we meet in heaven,"' he declaimed, '"then joyfully, my noble lords and my kind kinsmen, warriors all, adieu!"' and strode off, umbrella in hand, as if going into battle.

Which he is, Polly thought, watching him. *Which they all are.*

'How marvellous!' Miss Laburnum said. 'Do you think if we asked him, he'd do another play tomorrow? *The Tempest*, perhaps, or *Henry the Fifth*?'

LONDON – 18 SEPTEMBER 1940

It took Polly two hours to get to Oxford Street. Since Oxford Circus and Bond Street stations would both be closed from the attack on Oxford Street, she'd intended to take the tube to Piccadilly Circus, but the Circle Line trains weren't running at all, and when she attempted to take the District and then the Piccadilly, she couldn't get beyond Gloucester Road and had to leave the station and find a bus. But it only went as far as Bond Street, where a huge pile of rubble blocked the street. She had to walk the rest of the way, dodging barricades and a roped-off area with a notice saying Danger: Gas Leak.

Oxford Street was awash in water from the firemen's hoses and shattered glass. It took her another quarter of an hour to reach the gutted John Lewis, and when she did, it was much, much worse than she'd envisioned from the photos. The great brick arches gaped emptily onto a vast, blackened expanse of charred beams and girders, dripping with water. It looked less like a burned building than the wreck of some massive ocean liner. Here and there among the drowned wreckage were a half-burnt placard saying On Sale, a sodden glove, a charred clothes hanger.

At the rear of the store Polly could see a fireman playing a hose on the timbers, though the fire was long since out. Two other firemen wound a heavy hose onto a wooden reel, and a fourth walked towards the fire pumper still standing in the middle of the street. A middle-aged woman in trousers and a tin hat was stringing a rope around the area. There was broken glass everywhere, and brick dust, and when Polly looked up Oxford Street, it was shrouded in thick smoke.

She picked her way through the broken glass, stepping over hoses and between puddles. *This is pointless*, she thought. *There's no way any of the stores will be open, let alone hiring.* But two workmen were putting up a banner over Peter Robinson's main doors that read We're Open. Don't Mind Our Mess, as if they were under construction. And she could see a woman going into Townsend Brothers. Polly crunched through the glass behind her, stopping at the door to straighten her jacket and pick glass fragments out of the soles of her shoes before she went in.

She needn't have bothered. Two shopgirls were sweeping up more glass inside, and a third was showing lipsticks to the woman Polly had followed in. There was no one else on the floor, and no one in the lift except for the lift operator, who asked her, 'Didja see what Jerry did to John Lewis?' as she slid the gate across.

There was no one shopping on the fifth floor either. They obviously don't need any additional help, Polly thought, but the moment she walked into the personnel manager's office, he offered her the position of junior shop assistant in the lingerie department and escorted her personally down to the third floor to a pretty, brown-haired young woman. 'Where is Miss Snelgrove?' the manager asked her.

'She telephoned she'd be late, Mr Witherill,' she said, smiling at Polly. 'She said there was a UXB in the Edgware Road, and they'd cordoned the entire neighbourhood off, so she had to go through the park, and—'

'This is Miss Sebastian,' Mr Witherill cut in. 'She will be working the gloves and stockings counter.' And to Polly, 'Miss

Hayes will show you where things are and explain your duties. Tell Miss Snelgrove to report to me the moment she comes in.'

'Don't mind him,' Miss Hayes said after he'd left. 'He's a bit nervy. We've had three girls give notice this morning, and he's worried Miss Snelgrove might have legged it as well. She hasn't, more's the pity. She's our floor supervisor and *very* particular,' she confided, lowering her voice. 'I think *she's* the reason Betty quit, though she said it was because of what happened to John Lewis. Miss Snelgrove was always on at her about something. Have you worked in a department store before, Miss Sebastian?'

'Yes, Miss Hayes.'

'Oh good, then you'll have had some experience with stock and things,' she said, stepping behind the counter. 'And you needn't call me Miss Hayes when it's only us. Call me Marjorie. And you're …?'

'Polly.'

'Where did you work, Polly?'

'In Manchester, at Debenham's.' She'd picked Manchester because of its distance from London and because she knew there was a Debenham's there. She'd seen a photo of it gutted in a raid in December. But it would be just her luck to have Marjorie say, 'Really? *I'm* from Manchester.'

She didn't. She said, 'Do you know how to write up sales?'

Polly did. She also knew how to do sums, use carbon paper, work an adding machine, sharpen pencils, and every other possible task Research and Mr Dunworthy – who believed historians should be prepared for every *possible* contingency – thought a shopgirl might conceivably need to know.

The money had been the most difficult to learn. Really, their monetary system had been insane, and she'd expected that to give her the most trouble at work, but Marjorie told her all of Townsend Brothers' cash transactions were handled by the financial office upstairs. All Polly had to do was place the money and the bill in a brass tube, send it shooting along a system of pneumatic chutes, and it came back moments later with the correct change. *I needn't have learned all those guineas and half-crowns and farthings,* she thought.

Marjorie showed her how to bill a sale to a customer's account and write up a delivery order, which drawers the different sizes of gloves and silk and cotton lisle and woollen stockings were in, and how to line the hosiery boxes with a single sheet of tissue, lay the stockings in them, then wrap the box in brown paper, folding the ends under and tying them with string from a large bolt.

That was something neither Research nor Mr Dunworthy had thought of, but it didn't look too difficult. But when she made her first sale – Marjorie had been right, it had picked up; by eleven, there were half a dozen women shoppers, one of whom, an elderly lady, told Polly, 'When I saw what Hitler'd done to Oxford Street, I decided to buy a new pair of garters, just to show him!'– she made a complete botch of the wrapping. Her ends were uneven, her folds crooked, and when she tried to wrap the string around it, the wrapping came completely undone.

'I'm so sorry, madam. It's my first day,' she said, trying again, and this time she managed to hold the parcel together, but her knot was so loose the string slid off one end.

Marjorie came to her rescue, discarding the tangled string and starting with a new length, which she deftly tied around the parcel, and after the customer had departed, she said kindly, 'I'll take over the wrapping till you've got the hang of it.' But it was clearly something she should already know how to do, so in between customers Polly practised on an empty box, without much success.

At noon the 'very particular' Miss Snelgrove arrived. Polly hastily jammed the string she'd been practising with into her pocket and tucked in her blouse.

Marjorie hadn't been exaggerating about her. 'I expect the highest standards from those under me, a polite manner, and neatness of both work and appearance,' she told Polly, looking coldly at her navy blue skirt. 'Regulation wear for our shop assistants is a white blouse, a plain black skirt—'

I told Wardrobe that, Polly thought disgustedly.

'—and black, low-heeled shoes. Have you a black skirt, Miss Sebastian?'

'Yes, ma'am,' she said. *Or I will as soon as I check in with Mr Dunworthy tonight to tell him I have a position.*

'How long have you been in London?'

'I arrived last week.'

'You've experienced air raids then?'

'Yes, ma'am.'

'I cannot afford to have girls working under me who are nervy or easily frightened,' she said sternly. 'Townsend Brothers' employees must project an air of calm and courage at all times.'

Wanted: shop assistant, Polly thought. *Neat, polite, cool under fire.*

'Show me your sales book,' Miss Snelgrove commanded, and proceeded to show Polly everything Marjorie had already shown her, including how to wrap a parcel. She was even more expert at it than Marjorie, and more exacting. 'You must not waste string,' she said, tying the parcel tightly. 'Now you do it.'

Marjorie, over at the lingerie counter, looked at Polly in horror. *Wardrobe won't need to find me a black skirt*, Polly thought. *After I show her, I won't have a job*, and the air-raid siren went.

Polly had never been so glad to hear anything in her life, even though Townsend Brothers' shelter turned out to be an airless basement room with pipes running along the walls and nowhere to sit. 'Chairs and cots are reserved for customers,' Marjorie told her, and Miss Snelgrove said sternly, 'No leaning. Stand up straight.'

Polly hoped the raid would be a long one, but it was only half an hour before the all-clear went. By then, though, it was Polly's luncheon break, and then Miss Snelgrove's, and shortly after that Mr Witherill brought down 'Miss Doreen Timmons, who will take over Scarves and Handkerchiefs,' and Miss Snelgrove had to show her the procedures. And all of Polly's customers wanted their purchases delivered, so she was saved from any further wrapping. But obviously she couldn't count on new employees or air raids tomorrow. She'd have to perfect her wrapping skills in Oxford.

That's one advantage of time travel, she thought, starting home from work. *If it takes a week to master it, I can do it and still be on time to work tomorrow.*

She debated going straight to the drop, but she couldn't risk being seen going into the alley and followed. She'd have to wait till after the sirens had gone, the ARP wardens had made their rounds and the contemps were in their basements or the shelters. The raids tonight began at 8:45, which meant the sirens wouldn't sound till quarter past, and she couldn't go to the drop till after supper.

Which was a pity. The moment she opened the front door at Mrs Rickett's her nostrils were assailed by an unpleasant odour. 'It's kidney stew tonight,' Miss Laburnum said, and dropped her voice. 'I never thought I'd be eager to hear the sound of approaching bombers.' She leaned past Polly to look out of the door at the sky. 'Do you think there's a chance they'll be early tonight?'

Unfortunately, no, Polly thought, but as she started up the stairs to take off her coat and hat, the sirens went. 'Oh good,' Miss Laburnum said. 'Let me get my things and we'll walk over together. I'll tell you all about Sir Godfrey on the way.'

'No ... I ...' Polly stammered, bewildered that the sirens had gone so early. 'I ... There are some things I must do before I go. I need to wash out my stockings and—'

'Oh no, I won't hear of it,' Miss Laburnum said. 'It's far too dangerous. I read in the *Standard* about a woman who stayed behind to put out the cat and was killed.'

'But I'll only be a few minutes. I'll come as soon as—'

'Even a single minute can make all the difference, isn't that right?' Miss Laburnum said to Miss Hibbard as she hurried down the stairs, stuffing her knitting into her bag.

'Oh, my, yes.'

'But Mr Dorming isn't here,' Polly said. 'You two go on ahead, and I'll fetch him—'

'He's already gone,' Miss Hibbard said. 'He left the moment he heard what supper was. Come along,' and there was nothing for it but to go with them. She would have to wait till they reached St George's and then say she'd forgotten something and needed to go back. If the raids hadn't begun by then.

How could she have got the time wrong? she wondered, half listening to Miss Laburnum prattle on about how wonderful Sir Godfrey was, 'Though actually I prefer Barrie's plays to Shakespeare's, so much more refined.' The raids had begun at 8:45 on the eighteenth. But Hyde Park's siren was going, too, and as they crossed the street, Kensington Gardens' started up. Colin must have mixed the dates.

They were nearly to the church. 'Oh dear,' Polly said, 'I forgot my cardigan. I must go back.'

'I have a shawl you can borrow,' Miss Hibbard said, and before Polly could think of a response, Lila and Viv had come running up to tell her about John Lewis having been hit.

'Thank goodness I only found out about that job yesterday,' Lila said breathlessly. 'I'd never have forgiven myself if you'd got it and been working there when it was hit.'

'Oh, dear,' Miss Hibbard said, 'I believe I hear planes,' and hustled them all down the steps and into the shelter.

Polly debated making a break for it, but she would never succeed. Mrs Brightford, the little girls, Mr Simms, and his dog were all coming down the stairs, followed by the rector, who did a quick head count and bolted the door.

And now what was she supposed to do about a black skirt? And learning to wrap? She might be able to tell Miss Snelgrove she'd been caught by the sirens and hadn't been able to go home – *which is true*, she thought wryly – but what excuse could she give for producing such mangled packages? *I'll simply have to practise here*, she thought, checking her pocket to make certain she still had the length of string. She did. When Sir Godfrey offered her his *Times* (with no trace of the magnificence of the night before – he'd reverted completely to his role of elderly gentleman) she took it, and after everyone had gone to sleep – the bombing hadn't started till 8:47 after all, in spite of the sirens – she tiptoed over to the bookcase for a hymnal and attempted to wrap it in a sheet of the newspaper.

It was much easier to fold than the store's heavy brown paper, and she didn't have the pressure of a customer – or Miss Snelgrove – watching her, but she still made a botch of it. She tried again, holding the folded end against her middle to keep it from lapping open as she wrapped the string. That worked better, but the newsprint left a long black streak on her blouse.

'I expect neatness in your appearance,' Miss Snelgrove had said, which meant she'd have to wash out her blouse and iron it dry after the all-clear. The raids were supposed to be over by four, but as she'd learned tonight, that didn't mean the all-clear would sound then.

She took a new sheet of *The Times* and tried again. And again, cursing the uncooperative string and wondering why Townsend Brothers couldn't use cellophane tape instead. She knew it had been invented. She'd used it when—

A bomb exploded nearby with a sudden cellar-shaking crash, and Nelson leaped up, barking wildly. Polly jumped, and the newsprint tore across.

'What was that?' Miss Laburnum demanded sleepily.

'Stray five-hundred-pounder,' Mr Simms said, stroking his dog's head.

Mr Dorming listened and then nodded. 'They're on their way home,' he said and lay back down, but after a few minutes of silence, the raids abruptly started up again, the anti-aircraft guns beginning to pound, the planes roaring overhead.

Mr Dorming sat up again, and then the rector, and Lila, who

said disgustedly, 'Oh, not again!' The others, one by one, were waking up and staring nervously at the ceiling. Polly kept wrapping, determined to nail the skill down before morning. There was a clatter, like hail hitting the street above them.

'Incendiaries,' Mr Simms said.

A *crump*, and then a long, screaming *whoosh*, and a pair of explosions. It wasn't as deafening as it had been the night before, but the rector walked over to Sir Godfrey, who was reading a letter, and said quietly, 'The raids seem to be bad again tonight. Would you mind terribly, Sir Godfrey, gracing us with another performance?'

'I should be honoured,' Sir Godfrey said, folding up his letter, putting it in his coat pocket, and standing up. 'What will you have? *Much Ado*? Or one of the tragedies?'

'Sleeping Beauty,' Trot, on her mother's lap, said.

'Sleeping *Beauty*?' he roared. 'Out of the question. I am Sir Godfrey Kingsman. I do not do pantomime,' which should have reduced Trot to tears, but didn't.

'Do the one about the thunder again,' she said.

'*The Tempest*,' he said. 'A far better choice,' and Trot beamed.

He truly is wonderful, Polly thought, wishing she had time to watch him instead of having to practise wrapping.

'Oh no, do *Macbeth*, Sir Godfrey,' Miss Laburnum said. 'I've always longed to see you in—'

Sir Godfrey had drawn himself up to his full height. 'Do you not know calling the Scottish play by its name brings bad luck?' he boomed at her, then looked up at the ceiling and listened for a moment to the crashing and thud of bombs as if he expected one to come down on them in retribution. 'No, dear lady,' he said more calmly. 'We have had enough this fortnight of overreaching ambition and violence. There are fog and filthy air enough abroad tonight.'

He bowed sweepingly to Trot. '"The thunder one" it shall be, "full of sounds and sweet airs that give delight and hurt not." But if I am to be Prospero, I must have a Miranda.' He strode over to Polly and extended his hand to her. 'As forfeit for having mutilated my *Times*,' he said, looking down at the torn newspaper, 'Miss … ?'

'Sebastian,' she said, 'and I'm sorry I—'

'No matter,' he said absently. He was looking at her thoughtfully. 'Not Sebastian, but his twin Viola.'

'I thought you said her name was Miranda,' Trot said.

'It is,' he said, and under his breath, 'We shall do *Twelfth Night* another time.'

He pulled her to standing. '"Come, daughter, attend, and I shall relate how we came unto this island beset by strange winds."' He produced his book from his breast pocket and handed it to her. 'Page eight,' he whispered. 'Scene two. "If by your art, dearest father—"'

She knew the speech, but a shopgirl in 1940 wouldn't, so she took the book and pretended to read her line. '"If by your art, dearest father, you have put the wild waters in this roar,"' she read, '"allay them. The sky, it seems, would pour down stinking pitch—"'

'"Can'st thou remember a time before we came unto this cell?"' he asked.

'"'Tis far off,"' she said, thinking of Oxford, '"and rather like a dream than an assurance that my remembrance warrants—"'

'"What seest thou else,"' he said, looking into her eyes, '"in the dark backward and abysm of time?"'

Why, he knows I'm from the future, she thought, and then, *He's only speaking his lines, he can't possibly know,* and completely missed her cue. '"What foul play …"' he prompted.

She had no idea what part of the page they were on. '"What foul play had we that we came from thence?"' she said. '"Or blessed was't we did?"'

'"Both, both, my girl! By foul play, as thou sayst, were we heav'd thence, but blessedly holp hither,"' he said, taking hold of her hands, which still held the book, and launched into

Prospero's explanation of how they'd come to the island and then, without even a pause, into his charge to Ariel.

She forgot the book, forgot the role of 1940s shopgirl she was supposed to be playing, forgot the people watching them and the planes droning overhead – forgot everything except for his hands holding hers captive. And his voice. She stood there facing him enrapt—'spellstopp'd', as if he truly were a sorcerer – and wished he would go on forever.

When he came to '"I'll break my staff,"' he let go of her hands, raised his own above his head, and brought them down sharply, pantomiming the snapping of an imaginary staff, and the audience, who faced attack and annihilation nightly with equanimity, flinched at the action. The three little girls shrank against their mother, mouths open, eyes wide.

'"I'll drown my book,"' he said, his voice rich with power and love and regret, '"These our actors, as I foretold you, were all spirits and are melted into air, into thin air."'

Oh, don't, Polly thought, though what came next was Prospero's most beautiful speech. But it was about palaces and towers and 'the great globe itself' being destroyed, and he must have sensed her silent plea because he said instead, '"We, like this insubstantial pageant faded, leave not a rack behind,"' and Polly felt her eyes fill with tears.

'"You do look as if you were dismayed,"' Sir Godfrey said gently, taking her hands again. '"Be cheerful, child. Our revels now are ended,"' and the all-clear sounded.

Everyone immediately looked up at the ceiling, and Mrs Rickett stood up and began putting on her coat. 'The curtain has rung down,' Sir Godfrey muttered to Polly with a grimace and moved to release her hands.

She shook her head. '"It was the nightingale. It is not yet near day."'

He gave her a look of awe, and then smiled and shook his head. '"It was the lark,"' he said regretfully. '"Or worse, the chimes at midnight,"' and let go of her hands.

'Oh my, Sir Godfrey, you were so affecting,' Miss Laburnum said, crowding up to him with Miss Hibbard and Mrs Wyvern.

'We are but poor players,' he said, gesturing to include Polly, but they ignored her.

'You were *really* good, Sir Godfrey,' Lila said.

'Even better than Leslie Howard,' Viv put in.

'Simply mesmerising,' Mrs Wyvern said.

Mesmerising is right, Polly thought, putting on her coat and gathering up her bag and the newspaper-covered hymnal. *He made me forget all about practising my wrapping.* She glanced at her watch, hoping the all-clear had gone early, but it was half past six. *It is the lark,* she thought, feeling like Cinderella, *and I've got to go home and wash out my blouse.*

'I do hope you'll grace us with another performance tomorrow night, Sir Godfrey,' Miss Laburnum was saying.

'Miss Sebastian!' Sir Godfrey extricated himself from his admiring crowd and hurried over to her. 'I wished to thank you for knowing your lines – something my leading ladies scarcely ever do. Tell me, have you ever considered a career in the theatre?'

'Oh no, sir. I'm only a shopgirl.'

'Hardly,' he said. '"Thou art the goddess on whom these airs attend, a paragon, a wonder."'

'"No wonder, sir, but certainly a maid,"' she quoted, and he shook his head ruefully.

'A maid, indeed, and were I forty years younger, I would be your leading man,' he said, leaning towards her, 'and *you* would not be safe.'

I don't doubt that for a moment, she thought. He must have been truly dangerous when he was thirty, and thought suddenly of Colin, saying, 'I can shoot for any age you like. I mean, not seventy, but I'm willing to do thirty.'

'Oh, Sir Godfrey,' Miss Laburnum said, coming up. 'Next time could you do something from one of Sir James Barrie's plays?'

'Barrie?' he said in a tone of loathing. '*Peter Pan?*'

Polly suppressed a smile. She opened the door and started up the steps.

'Viola, wait!' Sir Godfrey called. He caught up to her halfway up the steps. She thought he was going to take her hands again, but he didn't. He simply looked at her for a long, breath-catching moment.

Thirty, nothing, she thought. *He's dangerous now.*

'Sir Godfrey!' Miss Laburnum called from inside the door.

He glanced behind him, and then back at Polly. '"We are too late met,"' he said. '"The time is out of joint,"' and went back down the stairs.

'Real planes, real bombs. This is no fucking drill.'

VOICE ON THE PA OF THE *OKLAHOMA*,
PEARL HARBOR, 7 DECEMBER 1941

DUNKIRK – 29 MAY 1940

Mike stared dazedly at the scene before him. The town of Dunkirk lay burning no more than a mile to the east of them, orange-red flames and clouds of acrid black smoke from the oil tanks billowing out over the docks. There were fires on the docks and on the beaches, and in the water. A cruiser lay off to the right, its stern angled out of the water. A tugboat stood alongside, taking soldiers off. South of it stood a destroyer and beyond it a Channel packet. It was on fire, too.

Flashes of light – from artillery guns? – played along the horizon, and the destroyers' guns answered with a deafening roar. There was an explosion on shore, and a billowing puff of flame – a gas tank exploding – and the far-off rattle of machine-gun fire.

'I can't believe it!' Jonathan shouted over the din, his voice bubbling over with excitement. 'We're actually here!'

Mike stared at the fire-lit harbour paralysed, afraid to let go of the railing, afraid to even move. Anything he did – or said – could have a catastrophic effect on events.

'This is great!' Jonathan said. 'Do you think we'll get to see any Germans?'

'I hope not,' Mike said, glancing up at the sky and then at the horizon, peering through the drifting smoke, trying to see if dawn was approaching. The harbour at Dunkirk had been an obstacle course of half-submerged wrecks, and they didn't have a hope of getting through it if they couldn't see. But they were more likely to be attacked by Stukas in daylight. And, Oh Christ, on the twenty-ninth the weather had cleared, and an offshore breeze had blown the smoke inland, away from the harbour, leaving the boats trying to load the soldiers sitting ducks. There was no breeze yet. But for how long?

'Kansas, don't just stand there!' the Commander shouted. 'You're supposed to be keeping the *Lady Jane* from ramming into something!'

Am I? Mike thought. *Or are you supposed to hit a trawler or a fishing smack and go down with all hands?* It was impossible to know what to do, or what not to do – like walking through a minefield blindfolded, knowing that every step could make the whole thing blow up in your face. Only this was worse, because so could standing still. Was shouting a warning what would alter the course of history, or keeping silent?

'Ship to starboard!' Jonathan shouted from the other side of the bow and the Commander turned the wheel, and they chugged past an oncoming minesweeper and into the harbour.

Mike saw he needn't have worried about their being able to see. The flames from the burning town lit the entire harbour. It was nearly as bright as day. Which was a good thing, because as they got closer in, there were more and more obstacles. A wooden crate floated by and, beyond it, straight ahead, lay a submerged sailboat, its mast sticking up out of the water.

'Go left!' Mike shouted, waving his arm wildly to the left.

'*Left?*' the Commander bellowed. 'You're on board ship, Kansas. It's port!'

'All right! Port! Now!'

The Commander turned the wheel just in time, missing the mast by inches, and Mike saw that by doing so, he'd set the

Lady Jane on a collision course with a half-submerged ferry. 'Right!' Mike shouted. 'I mean, starboard. Starboard!'

They didn't even have inches this time. They slid by with micrometers to spare. And were they supposed to have done that, or to have scraped a hole in the side? There was no possible way to tell, and no time to think about it. Ahead, under the water, was a huge paddle-wheel, and past it, on the left, a partly sunk rowboat, its prow pointed at the *Lady Jane* like a battering ram. 'Hard to starboard!' Jonathan shouted before Mike could, and they slid past.

There were more and more things in the scummy water: oars, oil drums, petrol cans. An Army jacket floated past and a piece of charred planking and a life-jacket. 'Are there any life-jackets – life-belts – on board?' he called to the Commander.

'Life-belts? I thought you said you could swim, Kansas.'

'I can,' he said angrily, 'but Jonathan can't, and if the *Lady Jane* hits something—'

'That's why I've got you navigating,' the Commander said. 'Now get to it. That's an order.'

Mike ignored him. He grabbed the boat hook to snag the life-jacket with and darted back to the railing, but they were already past it. He leaned over the side, hoping it wasn't the only one, but he couldn't see another. He saw a pair of trousers, its legs knotted to form a makeshift life-jacket, and a sock and a tangle of rope. And a body, its arms out at full-length like a crucifix. 'Look there!' Jonathan shouted from the other side of the bow. 'Is that a body?'

Mike was about to say 'yes' when he saw that what he'd thought was a corpse was only a military overcoat, the empty sleeves and tails of the belt drifting out at the sides. It had been abandoned by some officer as he swam out to one of the ships, along with the rest of his clothes probably, and his shoes, though those wouldn't float.

No, he was wrong. There was an Army boot, and a ladder and, amazingly, a rifle. They were nearly to the mouth of the harbour. The Commander manoeuvred past a drifting dinghy and a sail that had filled up with air, like a balloon, as the sailboat sank under it.

No, it wasn't a boat. It was the canvas cover of a truck that had been driven off the pier. Which meant they were getting into shallow water, where hopefully they could see the sunken wrecks before they ran into them.

'What do you think, Kansas?' the Commander said, surveying the harbour. 'What's our best bet?'

Turning around and heading home, Mike thought. The inner harbour had been an obstacle course of half-sunk boats and equipment the Army had pushed in the water to keep them from falling into enemy hands. Even if they got in, they'd never be able to get back out – the opening to it was so narrow a rowboat could block it. And if they tried the beaches, the *Lady Jane* was likely to be swamped by the thousands of soldiers who'd gathered there, waiting for rescue. Or to get stuck in the shallow water and have to sit there waiting for the next high tide.

'What did you say, Kansas?' the Commander asked, cupping his hand behind his ear. 'Which way do we head?'

There was a loud horn blast and a launch appeared out of the smoke, ploughing straight towards them. A young man in a naval uniform was standing in the bow. 'Ahoy!' he shouted, hands cupped around his mouth. 'Are you empty or loaded?'

'Empty!' Mike shouted back.

'Head that way!' he ordered, lowering one hand to point off to the east. 'They're loading troops off the mole.'

Oh Christ, the eastern mole. That was one of the harbour's most dangerous spots. It had been attacked repeatedly, and any number of ships had sunk trying to load troops off the narrow breakwater.

'What did he say?' the Commander called to Mike.

'He said go that way!' Jonathan cut in, pointing. The Commander nodded, snapped a salute, and headed the direction

Jonathan was pointing. The motorboat came around and roared past them, leading the way.

The breakwater stretched out beyond the inner harbour. *Well, at least we won't go aground,* Mike thought, but as they came closer, he saw that the mole had been bombed. Chunks of cement were missing from the breakwater, and doors and planking had been laid across the gaps. The naval officer pointed at the mole and, as soon as the Commander began to turn the *Lady Jane* towards it, waved and roared off.

The Commander began manoeuvring in towards the break-water, steering cautiously around a half-sunk tugboat and two jagged spars. The water was full of oil drums, oars, and still-burning planks. One had a name painted on it, *Rosabelle* – the name of a boat that had tried coming in here to take on soldiers, no doubt, and been blown to bits. 'Find a spot to tie her up,' the Commander ordered Mike, and he began looking for an open berth, but the whole length of the mole was blocked by dumped Army equipment and shattered boats. The rear end of a staff car driven off the side stuck up in the air.

Beyond it was a space of open water that looked like it might be wide enough for the *Lady Jane*. 'There!' Mike shouted, pointing, and the Commander nodded and steered towards it.

'Slow down,' Mike ordered, leaning halfway over the side, looking for underwater obstacles and expecting the Commander to tell him to use the nautical term, whatever the hell it was, but he was apparently as worried about tearing out the *Lady Jane*'s bottom as Mike. He cut the engine to a quarter of its speed and eased slowly into the dock.

'Look, there's another body!' Jonathan shouted, and this time it was a body, face-down, drifting lazily in the wash of the *Lady Jane*, and over by the mole was another one, this one floating upright, its head and shoulders out of the water and its helmet still on.

No, it wasn't a body – it was a soldier wading out to the boat, and behind him were two more, one holding his gun above his head. They obviously didn't intend to wait for the *Lady Jane* to dock and put out a gangway. There was a splash and then another one, and when Mike looked over at the mole, he saw another soldier had jumped off it, with a bedraggled dog. It paddled along beside him. Above them on the mole stood a dozen men, and further along the breakwater, a dozen more, running this way.

'Don't jump,' Jonathan shouted to them. 'We're coming in to get you,' and the Commander eased the *Lady Jane* up to the mole.

Jonathan tossed a line to the men. 'Tie her up!' the Commander called to them. 'Kansas, toss another line to those men in the water.'

Mike fastened a line to the gunwale, threw it down to them, and began hauling them up, hoping by doing so he wasn't rescuing someone who wasn't supposed to have been rescued. But he needn't have worried. Two of the men had climbed up over the side on their own while he was tying the rope, and the one he'd thrown the line to was busily tying it around the dog's middle to hoist him up. Saving a dog wasn't likely to alter events, and it couldn't get aboard by itself. Mike hauled it up and over the side, whereupon it shook itself all over him, everyone in range, and its owner, who'd just climbed on board.

He was apparently an officer because he promptly took over the rope. 'Kansas, help Jonathan get the gangway over to that dock,' the Commander ordered, and Mike complied, but the mole was too far above them, and, anyway, the soldiers had already taken matters in their own hands. They'd tied a ladder to the side and were climbing down it into the water and swimming over.

'Rig another line for them,' the Commander ordered Jonathan, and began untying petrol cans from the gunwales.

'Here, let me do that,' Mike said, carrying the heavy cans aft. Refilling the *Lady Jane*'s fuel tank was less likely to affect history than hauling up soldiers, some of whom wouldn't have made it without help.

'Give me your hand!' Jonathan shouted, leaning over the side. He came up with a soldier in full battle equipment, pack and helmet and all. 'I thought you were a goner!' Jonathan said, grabbing him by the straps on his pack and heaving him over the side.

'So did I!' the soldier said, dumping his pack on the deck and turning to help Jonathan heave the next soldier, and the next, on board. Mike emptied the petrol cans into the tank and then tossed them overboard. They bobbed away among the planks and clothing and bodies. He went back for two more, stepping around the soldiers who littered the deck.

They were continuing to clamber aboard. 'It's about time, guv'nor,' one of them said, flinging his leg over. 'Where the bloody hell have you been?' But most of them didn't say anything. They collapsed on the deck or sat down where they were, looking beaten and bewildered, their slack faces streaked with oil, their eyes bloodshot. None of them moved into the stern or onto the other side, and the deck began to tilt to port under their weight.

'Shift 'em to starboard,' the Commander shouted at Mike, 'or they'll have us over. How many more are there, Jonathan?'

'Only one,' Jonathan said, helping a soldier with a bandaged arm onto the deck. 'That's the lot.'

For the moment, Mike thought, looking up the mole. He could see soldiers converging on the land end of it from all directions. If they got here, they'd swamp the boat, but the Commander was already starting the engine. 'Cut the line,' he ordered Jonathan and pulled back on the throttle. The propellor began to turn and then stopped with a jerk.

'Propellor's fouled,' the Commander shouted. 'Probably a rope.'

'What do we need to do?' Jonathan asked.

'One of you'll have to go down and untangle it.'

And Jonathan can't swim, Mike thought. He looked desperately at the soldiers slumped on the deck, at the officer who'd taken over the task of hauling the soldiers up, hoping one of them would volunteer, but they weren't in any condition to do anything, let alone go back in the water.

Mike looked at Jonathan, who was bending over a soldier in a life-jacket, unfastening its ties. The soldier didn't resist, didn't even seem to know Jonathan was there. Jonathan, who was fourteen years old and who would die if the propellor wasn't unfouled, who would get his wish and be a hero in the war. *I got my wish too*, Mike thought. *I wanted to observe heroes, and here they are.*

Jonathan had succeeded in untying the life-jacket. 'I'll go, Grandfather,' he said, putting it on.

'No, I will,' Mike said, taking off his coat.

'Take your shoes off,' the Commander ordered. Mike obeyed. 'And watch for that flotsam in the water.'

Jonathan thrust the cork life-jacket into his hands, and Mike put it on and padded stocking-footed to the back of the boat. The Commander tied a line to the gunwale. 'Down you go, Kansas. We're counting on you.'

'You're sure the engine's off?' Mike said. 'I don't want the propellor to suddenly start up,' and went over the side.

The water hit him like an icy blow, and he gasped and swallowed water and then came up choking and clutching for the rope. 'Are you all right?' Jonathan called down.

'Yes,' he managed to say between coughs.

'Grandfather says he's stopped the engine.'

Mike nodded and worked his way around to the propellor shaft. He took a huge breath and ducked under. And immediately bobbed back up. 'What's wrong?' Jonathan called.

'It's the life-jacket,' Mike said, fumbling with the wet ties. 'It won't let me go under.' It seemed to take forever to get the ties unknotted and the jacket off. He let it float off, then thought, What if it gets tangled in the propellor? He went after it and tied it to the rope with numb fingers, then ducked under again.

It was totally dark under the water. He felt for the propellor, lost hold of the side, and then his sense of direction. He pushed up, and his head banged against something. *I'm under the boat*, he thought, panicking, and surfaced.

It wasn't the boat. It was merely a floating plank, and he was right where he'd gone under, next to the side. 'I can't see anything,' he shouted up to Jonathan. 'I've got to have a light.'

'I'll fetch a pocket torch,' Jonathan said and disappeared.

Mike paddled alongside, waiting. Jonathan reappeared, carrying a flashlight. He shone it out across the water.

'Shine it straight down on the propellor,' Mike ordered, pointing. Jonathan obeyed, and Mike took a breath and ducked under the water.

He still couldn't see anything. The flashlight lit a faint circle a few inches below the surface – no match for the oily water. He pushed back towards the surface. 'We need something brighter,' he shouted up to Jonathan, and it was suddenly light all around him.

He must have gone and got the signal lantern, Mike thought, and then, *Oh Christ, the Germans are dropping flares*. Which meant in five minutes they'd be dropping bombs. But in the meantime, he could see the propellor, and around it, a bulky wad of cloth. Another overcoat. One end of the belt trailed loosely through the water. Mike grabbed hold of the propellor blade and reached forward to disentangle the sleeve.

It fell away, and, Oh Christ, there was an arm in the sleeve, and what had fouled the propellor wasn't a coat. It was a body. It and the coat were tangled in the blades so that it looked like it was embracing the propellor. Mike tugged gingerly at the arm. The other end of the belt was wrapped around the blade and the body's hand. Mike unwound it, yanking on the end with the buckle to free it, and the soldier's head flopped forward, his mouth full of black water.

The greenish light was beginning to fade. Mike pulled the arm free of the blade, wondering how much longer he could hold his breath. He reached for the other arm. It wouldn't come. He yanked on it, his lungs bursting. He yanked again.

There was a flash and a shudder, and the body was flung violently against him, knocking the last of his air out of him. *Don't gasp*, Mike thought, struggling to close his mouth. *Don't breathe till you surface.* But he couldn't surface. The loose tails of the belt had wrapped around his wrist, entangling him as they had the propellor, dragging him under. He grabbed frantically at the belt to loosen it.

It unwound. He gave the body a violent push, and it fell away into the water, the belt trailing behind it like seaweed. Mike surfaced, choking. He couldn't see the *Lady Jane*. There was no sign of her, of anything except black water and burning wood and bobbing petrol cans. The sky lit up again, a nightmarish green, but he still couldn't see her. Just the looming black outline of the cruiser, and, beyond it, the destroyer.

I'm facing the wrong way, he thought, paddling in a circle to orient himself, and there was the *Lady Jane*, silhouetted against the burning town. Another flare fizzled down, illuminating Jonathan, still in the stern, waving the flashlight around erratically, searching for him.

'I'm here!' Mike called, and Jonathan swung the flashlight out onto the water behind him. 'Here!' Mike called again, and began to swim towards the boat. There was a *whoosh*, a blinding splash, and the water went up in a sheet of flame around him.

DULWICH – 15 JUNE 1944

At 11:35, four minutes after it was supposed to – though it seemed much longer to Mary – the alert finally sounded. 'What's happening?' Fairchild asked, sitting up in bed.

'Nothing,' Talbot said. 'Those horrid children have got at the siren again. Go back to sleep. It will stop in a bit.'

'Let's hope so,' Grenville said, burying her head in her pillow. 'And let's hope the Major realises what it is. I can't bear to spend the night in that wretched cellar,' but the siren continued its up-and-down whine.

'What if it's not a prank?' Maitland said, sitting up in bed and switching on her lamp. 'What if Hitler's surrendered and the war's over?'

'I do hope not,' Talbot murmured, her eyes shut. 'I need to win that pool.'

'It can't be surrender,' Fairchild said. 'They'd sound the all-clear if it was the end of the war.'

Shh, Mary thought, listening for the V-1. It was supposed to hit at 11:43 on Croxted Road, near the cricket grounds, which were directly west of here, so she should be able to hear it before it hit. The siren wound down. 'Finally,' Talbot said. 'If I get my

266

hands on those brats—' Maitland switched off her lamp and lay back down. Mary ducked back under the covers, switched on her torch, and looked at her watch.

11:41. Two more minutes. She listened intently for the engine's sound, but she couldn't hear anything. A minute. She should be able to hear the V-1 coming by now. Their stuttering jet engines made them audible for several minutes before they reached their targets, and it should pass directly over the post.

Thirty seconds, and still nothing. *Oh no, the V-1 isn't going to hit Croxted Road,* she thought. *Which means I have the falsified times and locations, and my assignment has just become a ten.*

There was a loud crash like thunder to the west, followed by a rumbling that shook the room. 'Good Lord, what was that?' Maitland said, fumbling for the lamp.

Thank goodness, Mary thought, looking at her watch. 11:43. She hastily switched off her torch and emerged from under the covers.

'Did you hear that?' Reed asked.

'I did,' Maitland said. 'It sounded like a plane. One of our boys must have crash-landed.'

'Alerts don't sound for downed planes,' Reed said. 'I'll wager it's a UXB.'

'It can't have been a UXB,' Talbot said disdainfully. 'How would they know in advance it was going to go off?'

'Well, whatever it was, it was in our sector,' Maitland said, and the phone in the despatch room rang.

A moment after, Camberley leaned her head in the door and said, 'Plane down in West Dulwich.'

'I told you it was a plane,' Maitland said, yanking on her boots. 'Civil Defence must have seen it was on fire and sounded the alert.'

'Where in West Dulwich?' Mary asked Camberley.

'Near the cricket grounds. Croxted Road. There are casualties.'

Thank God, Mary thought. Camberley disappeared. Maitland and Reed clapped their helmets on and hurried out. Camberley poked her head in again and said, 'The Major says everyone not on duty's to go down to the shelter.'

'How many planes does she expect will crash tonight?' Talbot grumbled.

A hundred and twenty, Mary thought, pulling on her robe. They trooped, grumbling, down to the cellar and then back up five minutes later when the all-clear went, shrugged out of their robes, and got into bed. Mary did, too, even though she knew the siren would go again in another – she glanced at her watch – six minutes.

It did. 'Oh, for goodness' sake,' Fairchild said, exasperated. 'What are they on about now?'

'It's a Nazi plot to deprive us of our sleep,' Sutcliffe-Hythe said, flinging back her bedclothes, and there was a *crump* to the southeast. *Croydon,* Mary thought happily, *and right on time.*

So was the next one, and the next, though none of them were close enough for her to be able to hear their engines. She wished again that she'd listened to a recording of one. She needed to be able to recognise the sound if she heard one coming when she was in Bomb Alley, but at least she knew what the explosions were. None of the other FANYs seemed to grasp the situation at all, even when Maitland and Reed returned from their incident with tales of flattened houses and widespread destruction. 'The pilot must have crashed with all his bombs still onboard,' Reed said, even though they'd heard four other explosions by then.

'Was it one of ours or theirs?' Sutcliffe-Hythe asked.

'There wasn't enough left of it to tell,' Maitland said, 'but it must have been a German plane. If it was one of our boys coming back, they'd have already dropped their load. The incident officer said he'd heard it come over, and it had sounded like it was having engine trouble.'

'Perhaps Hitler's running out of petrol and is putting kerosene in their fuel tanks,' Reed said. 'Coming back, we heard another one go over, stuttering and coughing.'

There was another rumbling boom to the east. 'At this rate, Hitler won't have an air force left by tomorrow,' Talbot said.

They're not planes, Mary said silently, *they're unmanned rockets*. And it was obvious she needn't have worried about arriving too late to observe their pre-V-1 behaviour – they were still exhibiting it.

They went back almost immediately to discussing the dance Talbot was going to the Saturday after next. 'I need someone to go with me,' she said. 'Will you, Reed? There'll be heaps of Americans there.'

'Then, no, absolutely not. I hate Yanks. They're all so conceited. And they step all over one's feet,' and launched into a story about a dreadful American captain she'd met at the 400 Club. Even Camberley's shouting down the cellar steps that there was another incident and Maitland and Reed's hurrying off to it didn't deter them. 'Why would you want to go to a dance with a lot of Yanks, Talbot?' Parrish asked.

'She wants one of them to fall madly in love with her and buy her a pair of nylons,' Fairchild said.

'I think that's disgraceful,' said Grenville, the one with the fiancé in Italy. 'What about love?'

'I'd *love* to have a new pair of stockings,' Talbot said.

'I'll go with you,' Parrish said, 'but only if you'll lend me your dotted swiss blouse to wear the next time I see Dickie.'

It had never occurred to Mary that the FANYs wouldn't tumble to what was going on once the rockets started – especially since, according to historical records, there'd been rumours since 1942 that Hitler was developing a secret weapon. Then again, historical records had said the siren had gone at 11:31.

And they would realise soon enough. By the end of the week there'd be 250 V-1s coming over a day and nearly eight hundred dead. Let them enjoy their talk of men and frocks while they could. It wouldn't last much longer. And it meant she was free to listen for the sirens and explosions and make certain they were on schedule.

They were, except for one that should have hit at 2:09 but didn't, and the last all-clear of the night, which went at 5:40 instead of 5:15.

'It hardly seems worthwhile to go to bed,' Fairchild said to Mary as they dragged back upstairs. 'We go on duty at six.'

But the sirens won't start up again till half-past nine, Mary thought, *and there won't be a V-1 in our sector till 11:39. I hope.*

She was worried about the one that hadn't hit at 2:09. It was supposed to have fallen in Waring Lane, which was even nearer than the cricket grounds. They should have been able to hear it.

Which meant it must have landed somewhere else. That fitted with British Intelligence's deception plan. On the other hand, the 2:09 was the only one that hadn't been at the right time and – as near as she could tell – in the right place, which meant it could also be only an error. Though a single error was all it would take to end her assignment abruptly. And permanently.

She was relieved when the 9:30 siren and the 11:39 V-1 were on schedule and even more when she saw the V-1 had hit the house it was supposed to – though when she saw the destruction, she felt guilty for having been so happy. Luckily, there were no casualties. 'We'd only just left the house, me and the wife and our three girls,' the house's owner told her, 'to go to my aunt's.'

'It's her birthday, you see,' his wife said. 'Wasn't that lucky?'

Their house had been blown so completely apart it was impossible to tell if it had been made of wood or of brick, but Mary agreed with them that it was incredibly lucky.

'If the bomber'd crashed five minutes earlier, we'd all have been killed,' the husband said. 'What was it? A Dornier?' Which meant they still thought all these explosions were caused by crashing planes.

But when they got back to the post, Reed greeted them with, 'The general I drove to Biggin Hill this morning says the Germans have a new weapon. It's a glider with bombs which go off automatically when it lands.'

'But a glider wouldn't make any noise,' Parrish, who was on despatch duty, said. 'And Croydon says they heard two come over this morning and they both had the same stuttering engines Maitland and Reed heard.'

'Well,' Talbot said, 'whatever they are, I hope Hitler hasn't got very many of them.'

Only fifty thousand, Mary thought.

'I drove a lieutenant commander last week,' Reed said, 'who said the Germans were working on—' She stopped as the siren sounded and they all trooped down to the cellar. '—on a new weapon. An invisible plane. He said they'd invented a special paint which can't be seen by our defences.'

'If our defences can't see them, then why do the sirens sound?' Grenville asked, and Fairchild said, 'If they can make them invisible, one would think they could make them silent as well, so we wouldn't hear them coming.'

They have, Mary thought. *It's called the V-2. They'll begin firing them in September, by which time surely it'll have dawned on you that these are rockets and not gliders or invisible planes.*

Or bombs shot from a giant catapult – a theory they discussed till the all-clear went half an hour later. 'Good,' Fairchild said, listening to its steady wail. 'Let's hope that's the last one for tonight.'

It won't be, Mary thought. *The alert will sound again in* – she glanced at her watch – *eleven minutes, if it was on schedule*, which she was beginning to be confident it would be. The explosions had been on time all day, and when she looked at the despatcher's log, there was a 2:20 a.m. ambulance call to Waring Lane. Which only left Bethnal Green. When the evening papers came out, she felt even more confident. Not only was the

Evening Standard's front page identical to the one she'd seen in the Bodleian, but the *Daily Express* said there'd been four V-1s on Tuesday night, though it didn't say where they'd landed.

The newspapers also settled the issue of what the V-1s weren't. *The Evening Standard*'s headline read, 'Pilotless Planes Now Raid Britain,' and they all described them in detail. The *Daily Mail* even had a diagram of the propulsion system, and the conversation in the shelter turned to the best way to avoid being hit by one.

'When the sound of the engine stops, take cover promptly, using the most solid protection available and keeping well away from glass doors and windows,' *The Times* advised, and the *Daily Express* was even more blunt: 'Lie face-down in the nearest gutter.'

'Keep watch on the flame in the tail,' the *Evening Standard* suggested. 'When it goes out, you will have approximately fifteen seconds in which to take cover,' which made the *Morning Herald*'s advice to go to the nearest shelter utterly impractical. But in general the press had it right. Though they couldn't agree on the sound the V-1s made and none of them mentioned a backfiring motor car. Descriptions varied from 'a washing machine' to 'the putt-putt of a motorbike' to 'the buzz of a bee'.

'A bee?' Parrish, who had heard one on an ambulance run, said. 'It's not like any bee I ever heard. A hornet perhaps. An extremely large, extremely angry hornet,' and Mary was forced to take her word for it. By the end of the first week of attacks, she still hadn't heard one nearby. That was the problem with being an ambulance driver. One went where the V-1 had already been, not where it was going.

But it wasn't their sound that mattered. It was the sudden silence, the abrupt cutting-off of the engine, and that would be easy to recognise. At any rate, she was bound to hear one soon. They were coming over now at the rate of ten an hour, and the FANYs were working double shifts, driving to incident after incident, administering first aid to the injured, loading them onto stretchers, transporting them to hospital, and – when they arrived at an incident ahead of Civil Defence, which often happened – digging victims, alive and dead, out of the rubble. And they were still ferrying patients from Dover to Orpington.

It was far more than they could handle, and the Major began lobbying HQ for more FANYs and an additional ambulance. 'Which she'll never get,' Talbot said.

That's true, Mary thought. Every available ambulance was being sent to France.

'Not necessarily,' Reed said. 'Remember, she got us Kent. And this is the Major,' and Camberley promptly started a betting pool on how long it would take her to obtain the ambulance.

The FANYs had shifted effortlessly from arguing over frocks to tying tourniquets and coping with grisly sights. 'Don't bother with anything smaller than a hand,' Fairchild told her, and as they waited with a stretcher while a rescue team dug a shaft down to a sobbing woman, Parrish said calmly, 'They'll never make it to her in time. Gas. Are you going to the dance with Talbot on Saturday?'

'I thought you were,' Mary managed to say, trying not to think about the gas. She could smell it growing stronger, and the woman's cries seemed to be getting correspondingly weaker.

'I was, but Dickie telephoned. He has a forty-eight-hour pass, and I was wondering if I might borrow your blue organdie, if you're not wearing it anywhere on – Oh look, they've got her out,' Parrish said and took off at a trot across the rubble with the medical kit, but it wasn't the woman, it was a dog, dead from the gas, and by the time they got the woman out, she'd died, too.

'I'll telephone for a mortuary van,' Parrish said. 'You didn't say whether you needed your organdie this weekend.'

'No, I don't,' Mary said, appalled at Parrish's callousness, and then remembered she was supposed to have driven an ambulance during the Blitz. 'Of course you can borrow it.'

Away from the incidents they never discussed what had happened there or their lives before the war. They were like

273

historians in that respect, focusing solely on their current assignment, their current identity. Mary had to piece together their backgrounds from clues they dropped in conversation and a copy of Debrett's she found in the common room.

Sutcliffe-Hythe's father was an earl, Maitland's mother was sixteenth in line to the throne, and Reed was Lady Diana Brenfell Reed. Camberley's first name was Cynthia and Talbot's Louise, though they never called each other by anything but their last names. Or nicknames. As well as 'Jitters' Parrish, there was a FANY at Croydon they referred to as 'Man-Mad', and they'd dubbed an officer several of them had gone out with 'NST', which Camberley explained meant 'Not Safe in Taxis'.

Maitland had a twin who was serving in the Air Transport Service, Parrish had an elder brother who'd been captured by the Japanese in Singapore and a younger one who'd been killed on HMS *Hood*, and Grenville's father had been killed at Tobruk. But to listen to their conversations, one would never have known that. They gossiped, complained about Bela Lugosi (which was refusing to start), about the dampness of the cellar, about the Major's habit of sending them after supplies when they were off-duty. 'She sent me to Croydon last night in the *blackout*, to fetch *three* bottles of iodine,' Grenville said indignantly.

'Next time, tell me and I'll go,' Sutcliffe-Hythe said from her cot. 'I'm not sleeping anyway with these wretched alerts going off every ten minutes.'

'Then you can go to the dance with me on Saturday,' Talbot said.

'I thought Parrish was going with you,' Reed said.

'She has a date.'

'I'd only yawn the whole evening,' Sutcliffe-Hythe said. She turned over and pulled the blanket over her head. 'Make Grenville go with you.'

'She won't,' Reed said. 'She's finally had a letter from Tom in Italy. She plans to spend tomorrow writing him.'

'Can't that wait till Sunday?' Talbot asked.

Reed gave her a withering look. 'You've obviously never been in love, Talbot. And she wants to make certain it reaches him before he's ordered somewhere else.'

'Well, then, it's up to you to go with me, Kent,' Talbot said, sitting down on the end of Mary's cot.

'I can't. I'm on duty Saturday,' she said, glad she had an excuse. If the dance was in Bomb Alley or one of the other areas that weren't in her implant—

'Fairchild will trade shifts with you,' Talbot said. 'Won't you, Fairchild?'

'Um-hmm,' Fairchild said without opening her eyes.

'But that's not fair to her,' Mary said. 'Perhaps she wants to go to the dance.'

'No, her heart belongs to the boy who used to pull her pigtails. Isn't that right, Fairchild?'

'Yes,' she said defensively.

'He's a pilot,' Parrish explained. 'He's stationed at Tangmere. He flies Spitfires.'

'He's her childhood sweetheart,' Reed put in, 'and she's made up her mind to marry him, so she isn't interested in other men.'

Fairchild sat up, looking indignant. 'I didn't say I was going to marry him. I said I was in love with him. I've loved him since I—'

'Since you were six and he was twelve,' Talbot said. 'We know. And when he sees you all grown up he's going to fall madly in love with you. But what if he doesn't?'

'And how do you know you'll still be in love with him when you see him again?' Reed said. 'You haven't seen him in nearly three years. It might have only been a schoolgirl crush.'

'It wasn't,' Fairchild said firmly.

Talbot looked sceptical. 'You can't know that for certain unless you go out with other men, which is why you need to go to the dance with me. I'm only thinking of your welfare—'

'No, you're not. Kent, I'd be delighted to switch shifts with you.' She punched her pillow into shape, lay down, and closed her eyes. 'Good night all.'

'Then it's settled. You're going with me, Kent.'

'Oh, but I—'

'It's your duty to go. After all, it's your fault I lost the pool and haven't any stockings.'

The siren went, making it impossible to talk. *Good*, Mary thought, *it will give me a chance to think of an excuse*, and when it wound down, she said, 'I haven't anything to wear. I lent both of my dancing frocks to Parrish and Maitland, and the Yellow Peril makes me look jaundiced.'

'The Yellow Peril makes everyone look jaundiced,' Talbot said. 'You won't need a dancing frock. This is a canteen dance. You can wear your uniform.'

'Where's it being held?' she asked, thinking, If *it's in Bomb Alley, I'll have to pretend I'm ill on Saturday.*

'The American USO in Bethnal Green.'

Bethnal Green. So she could finally go and look at the railway bridge and stop worrying over whether she could trust her implant. She should be able to sneak away from the dance easily – Talbot would be busy trying to wheedle nylons out of her Yanks – and it was perfect timing. The only V-1s that had fallen on Bethnal Green on Saturday were in the afternoon.

'Very well, I'll go,' she said, congratulating herself on her cleverness and wondering if she could persuade one of the soldiers at the dance to take her to Grove Road in his Jeep, but at two on Saturday afternoon Talbot said, 'Aren't you ready, Kent?'

'Ready? I thought the dance wasn't till tonight.'

'No. Didn't I tell you? It begins at four, and I want to be there before all the best Yanks are taken.'

'But—'

'No excuses. You promised. Now hurry, or we'll miss our bus,' and dragged her off to the bus stop.

Mary spent the ride to Bethnal Green listening anxiously for the sound of a washing machine or an angry hornet and looking for nonexistent street signs. One of the V-1s had fallen at 3:50 in Darnley Lane and the other at 5:28 in King Edward's Road. 'What street is the USO canteen in?' she asked Talbot.

'I can't remember,' Talbot said. 'But I know the way,' which was no help.

'This is our stop,' Talbot said. They descended on a street lined with shops.

Good, Mary thought. *This can't be Darnley Lane*. Darnley Lane was a residential street. She glanced at her watch. Five minutes to four. The 3:50 had already hit. She looked up and down the street. She couldn't see any sign of a railway bridge, so apparently this wasn't Grove Road either. She hoped it wasn't King Edward's Road. And that the Darnley Lane one had already hit. She didn't hear any ambulance bells, or an all-clear.

'It's a bit of a hike, I'm afraid,' Talbot said, setting off down the street.

Mary glanced up at the sky again, listening. She thought she could hear something to the southeast.

'What sort of men do you like?' Talbot asked.

'What?' The sound was a hum, rising to a steady wail. The all-clear. And seconds later, she heard a fire engine.

'I don't know why they even bother with an all-clear,' Talbot said exasperatedly. 'They'll only have to sound the alert again five minutes from now.'

No, not for an hour and a quarter, and by then they'd be at the dance, and she'd have been able to ask one of the USO people the canteen's address and make certain it wasn't on King Edward's Road. And she'd have been able to ask them how she could find Grove Road. 'Sorry, what were you saying before?'

'I was asking you what sort of men you like,' Talbot said. 'When we get there, I'll introduce you to some of the chaps I know. Do you like them tall? Short? Younger men? Older?'

Every man at this dance will be at least a hundred years too old for me, Mary thought. 'I'm not really interested in—'

'You're not in *love* with someone, are you?'

'No.'

'Good. I don't approve of people being in love during a war. How can anyone plan for the future when we don't know if we'll have one? When I was posted to Bournemouth, one of the girls got engaged to a naval officer who was on a destroyer guarding convoys. She worried herself sick about him, spent all her time devouring the newspapers and listening to the wireless. And then she was the one killed, driving an officer back to Duxton Airfield. And now with these flying bombs, any one of us might be killed at any minute.'

She turned down a narrow lane lined with shops with boarded-up windows. 'I tried to tell Fairchild that, the little goose. She's not really in love, you know. Where's my lipstick?' She fumbled in her bag for it as she walked. '*Where* is my compact? May I borrow yours?'

Mary obligingly dug in her bag. 'Never mind,' Talbot said, walking over to the one shop window which still had glass in it. She took the cap off her lipstick and twisted the base. 'It will never work. He's years older than she is.' She leaned forward to apply the lipstick in the window's reflection. 'You know the sort of thing, older boy worshipped by younger girl ...'

'Mmm,' Mary said, listening to the ragged *putt-putt* of an approaching motorcycle coming down the street they'd just left.

Talbot didn't seem to notice, even though she had to raise her voice over its noise. 'She has some fairy-tale notion that he'll see her in her uniform, all grown up, and realise he's always loved her, even though she still looks fifteen.' She was nearly shouting, the motorcycle was so loud. The sound echoed rattlingly off the shops in the narrow lane. 'She's determined to have her heart broken.' She pursed her lips as she applied the Crimson Caress. 'He's in the RAF, after all, not exactly the safest of jobs.'

The sound of the motorcycle grew deafeningly loud and then

shut off abruptly. *That's not a motorcycle. That's a V-1*, Mary thought.

And then, *It can't be, it's only quarter past four.*

And then, *What if my implant data's wrong after all?*

And then, *Oh God, I've only got fifteen seconds.*

'And what if he doesn't fall into Fairchild's arms as planned?' Talbot said, leaning towards the window to appraise the effect. 'Or his aeroplane crashes?'

Oh God, the glass! Mary thought. She'll be cut to ribbons. 'Talbot!' she shouted and made a running dive at her, tackling her, flinging her off the kerb. The lipstick flew out of her hand.

'Ow! Kent, what do you think you're—?' Talbot said.

'Stay down!' She pushed Talbot's head down into the gutter, flattened herself on top of her, and closed her eyes, waiting for the flash.

*'The girls won't leave without me, and I won't leave
without the King. And the King will never leave.'*

QUEEN MARY, ON BEING ASKED WHY SHE HADN'T
EVACUATED THE PRINCESSES TO CANADA

WARWICKSHIRE – MAY 1940

The aspirin tablets Eileen gave Binnie brought her fever
down partway and kept it down, but she was still gravely ill.
With each passing hour her breathing was more laboured, and
by morning she was calling wildly for Eileen, even though she
was there next to her. Eileen telephoned Dr Stuart.

'I think you'd best write to her mother and ask her to come,'
he said.

Oh no, Eileen thought.

She went to ask Alf their address. 'Is Binnie dyin', then?' he
asked.

'Of course not,' she said firmly. 'It's only that she'll get well
faster if your mother's here to care for her.'

Alf snorted. 'I'll wager she don't come.'

'Of course she will. She's your mother.'

But she didn't. She didn't even reply. 'Wicked,' Mrs Bascombe
said when she brought Binnie a cup of tea. 'No wonder they've
turned out the way they have. Is she breathing any easier?'

'No,' Polly said.

'This tea has hyssop in it,' Mrs Bascombe said. 'It will loosen her chest,' but Binnie was too weak to drink more than a few sips of the bitter-tasting tea and, worse, too weak to refuse to drink it.

That was the most frightening aspect of Binnie's illness. She didn't resist what Eileen did or even protest. All the fight had gone out of her, and she lay listlessly as Eileen bathed her, changed her nightgown, gave her the aspirin. 'Are you sure she ain't dyin'?' Alf asked her.

No, Eileen thought. *I'm not sure at all.* 'Yes, I'm certain,' she said. 'Your sister's going to be fine.'

'If she *did* die, what'd 'appen to 'er?'

'You'd better worry over what'll happen to you, young man,' Mrs Bascombe said, coming in from the pantry. 'If you want to get into heaven, you must change your ways.'

'I ain't talking about *that*,' Alf said and then hesitated, looking guilty. 'Would they bury 'er in the churchyard in Backbury?'

'What have you done to the churchyard?' Eileen demanded.

'Nuthin',' he said indignantly. 'I was talkin' about *Binnie*,' and stomped off, but the next day when the vicar brought the post, Alf called down to him, 'If Binnie dies, will she 'ave to 'ave a tombstone?'

'You mustn't worry, Alf,' the vicar said. 'Dr Stuart and Miss O'Reilly are taking very good care of Binnie.'

'I *know*. *Will* she?'

'What's all this about, Alf?' the vicar asked.

'*Nuthin'*,' Alf said and ran off again.

'Perhaps I'd best check the churchyard when I get home,' the vicar told Eileen. 'Alf may have decided tombstones would make excellent roadblocks when the Germans invade.'

'No, it's something else,' Eileen said. 'If it were anyone but Alf, I'd think he was worried about his sister being' – her voice caught – 'buried so far away from home.'

'There's no improvement?' he asked kindly.

'No.' And if there hadn't been two floors separating them, she'd have laid her head on his shoulder and sobbed.

He gave her a comforting smile and said, 'I know you're doing your best.'

But I'm afraid it's not good enough, she thought, and went to bathe Binnie's hot limbs and coax more aspirin into her, though she worried she might be making things worse, not better. But the next night when she didn't wake her to give the tablets to her – deciding it was better to let her sleep – her temp immediately shot up again. Eileen resumed giving it to her, wondering what she'd do when the tablets ran out.

I'll have to tell the vicar and hope he doesn't tell Dr Stuart, she thought. *Or tie my sheets together and go out of the window after some*, but it wasn't necessary. That afternoon Binnie's temp abruptly went down, leaving her bathed in sweat.

'Her fever's broken,' Dr Stuart said. 'Thank God. I feared the worst, but sometimes, with Providence's help, and good nursing' – he patted Eileen's hand – 'the patient pulls through.'

'So she will recover?' Eileen said, looking down at Binnie. She looked so thin and pale.

He nodded. 'She's through the worst of it now.'

And she seemed to be, though she didn't rally as quickly as the other children. It was three days before her breathing eased and a full week before she was able to sip a little broth on her own. And she was so ... docile. When Eileen read her fairy-stories, which Binnie usually despised, she listened quietly.

'I'm worried,' Eileen told the vicar. 'The doctor says she's better, but she just *lies* there.'

'Has Alf been in to see her?'

'*No*. He's liable to give her a relapse.'

'Or shake her out of her apathy,' he said.

'I think I'll wait till she's stronger,' Eileen said, but that afternoon, watching Binnie lying in her cot, gazing listlessly at the ceiling, Eileen sent Una to fetch Alf.

'You look 'xactly like a corpse,' he said.

Well, this was a good idea, Eileen thought, and was about

to escort him out when Binnie pushed herself up against the pillows.

'I do *not*,' she said.

'You do so. Everybody said you was goin' to die. You was out of your 'ead and everything.'

'I was not.'

Just like old times, Eileen thought and, for the first time since Binnie had fallen ill, felt a loosening of the tightness around her heart.

'She did almost die, didn't she, Eileen?' Alf said and turned back to Binnie. 'But you ain't goin' to now.'

Which seemed to reassure Binnie, but that night as Eileen put her into a fresh nightgown, she asked, 'Are you certain I ain't going to die?'

'Positive,' Eileen said, tucking her in. 'You're growing stronger every day.'

'What 'appens to people who die, when they 'aven't got no name?'

'You mean, when no one knows who they were?' Eileen asked, puzzled.

'*No.* When they ain't got a name to put on the tombstone. Do they still get to get buried in the churchyard?'

She's illegitimate, Eileen thought suddenly. Having an unmarried mother had been a true stigma for children in this era, with the child branded a bastard.

But the stigma hadn't extended as far as tombstones. 'Binnie, your name is your name, no matter whether your mother is married or not ...'

Binnie made a sound of complete disgust, and Eileen was certain that if she hadn't still been too weak to get out of bed, she'd have stomped from the room like her brother. As it was, she turned over onto her side and faced the wall.

Eileen wished the vicar was here. She racked her brain to recall any customs involving names and tombstones in 1940, but she couldn't think of anything. *Alf*, she thought. *He knows what this is all about,* and hastily gathered up the dirty linen. 'I'm taking these downstairs,' she told Binnie. 'I'll be back in a bit.'

No response. Eileen dumped the linens in the laundry and went to the ballroom, where Alf was wrapping Rose in bandages. 'I'm practisin' for the ambulance,' he said.

Alf, come with me,' Eileen said. 'Now,' and took him into the music room and shut the door. 'I want to know why Binnie's worried over her name being on a tombstone, and don't say you don't know.'

Something in her tone must have convinced him she meant business, because he muttered, 'She ain't got one.'

'A tombstone?'

'No, a *name,*' and at Eileen's bewildered look, 'Binnie ain't a real name. It's just short for 'Odbin.'

'Can you believe he told Binnie she didn't have a first name?' she told the vicar when he arrived the next day. 'And she apparently *believed* him.'

'Did you ask Binnie?' he said.

'What do you mean? You can't seriously think ... everyone has a first name. Just because they come from a poor—'

He was shaking his head. 'The Evacuation Committee's run into more than one slum child without a name, and the billeting officer's had to make one up on the spot. I'm not certain you realise how hard some of the children's lives were at home. Many of them had never slept in a bed before they came here—'

Or used a toilet, Eileen thought, remembering her prep. Some evacuees from the slums had urinated on the floors of their foster homes or squatted in a corner. And Mrs Bascombe had told her several of the evacuees at the manor had had to be taught to use a knife and fork when they'd first come. But a name! 'Alf has a name,' she argued, but the vicar wasn't convinced.

'Perhaps their father felt differently about a boy. Or perhaps it wasn't the same father. And you must admit, Mrs Hodbin – if she is a Mrs – hasn't shown much maternal instinct.'

'True. But still …' she said, and when she went in to talk to Binnie, tried to reassure her. 'I'm certain your name's not short for Hodbin,' Eileen told Binnie. 'That's only Alf teasing. I'm certain it's a nickname—'

'For *what*?' Binnie said belligerently.

'I don't know. Belinda? Barbara?'

'There ain't no "n" in Barbara.'

'Nicknames don't always have the same letters,' Eileen said. 'Look at Peggy. Her real name's Margaret. And there are all sorts of nicknames for Mary – Mamie and Molly and—'

'If Binnie's short for somethin', why ain't nobody ever said what?' she said, and was so sceptical Eileen wondered if their mother had made some comment that had put the idea in their heads. Whatever had, it was the last thing Binnie needed while she was recovering. After a fortnight her eyes had a shadowed look and she hadn't gained back any of the weight she'd lost.

Eileen said briskly, 'If you haven't got a name, then you must choose one.'

'*Choose* one?'

'Yes, like in "Rumpelstiltskin".'

'That wasn't choosin'. It was guessin'.'

Why did I think this would work? Eileen wondered, but after a minute, Binnie said, 'If I chose a name, you'd call me it?'

'Yes,' Eileen said, and was immediately sorry. Binnie spent the next few days trying on names like hats and asking Eileen what she thought of Gladys and Princess Elizabeth and Cinderella. But as maddening as the parade of names was, it did the trick. Binnie began to make rapid progress, growing rounder and more pink-cheeked by the day.

In the meantime, the Magruders proved conclusively they hadn't had the measles before, no matter what their mother had said, and Eddie and Patsy also broke out. By the evacuation of Dunkirk, Eileen had nineteen patients in varying degrees of spottiness and/or recovery.

Alf was thrilled about the ongoing rescue. 'The vicar says

they're going over in fishing boats and rowboats to get our soldiers,' he reported happily. 'I wish *I* could go.'

I wish I could, too, Eileen thought. *Michael Davies is in Dover reporting on the evacuation right now.*

'They're gettin' strafed and bombs dropped on 'em and everything,' Alf said, which at this point seemed infinitely preferable to caring for a score of feverish, fretful, moulting children. Once the rash went away, their skin developed brownish, peeling patches. 'Now you really look like a corpse,' Alf told Binnie. 'If you was at Dunkirk, they'd think you was dead and leave you behind on the beach, and the jerries'd *kill* you.'

'They would *not!*' Binnie shrieked.

'Out,' Eileen ordered.

'I can't go out,' Alf said reasonably. 'We're under quarantine.'

He was quite literally bouncing off the walls. Eileen found several portraits askew and Lady Caroline and her hunting dogs sprawled flat on the floor, and when she ordered them out of the ballroom, they retreated to Lady Caroline's bathroom, a fact Eileen didn't discover till water began dripping from the library ceiling.

'Alf and us were playing Evacuation from Dunkirk,' a sopping-wet Theodore explained.

The next time the vicar called up to the nursery window to ask if there was anything they needed, Eileen said yes rather desperately. 'Something to amuse the ones who aren't ill. Games or puzzles or something.'

'I'll see what the Women's Institute can come up with,' he said, and the next day delivered a basket full of donated books (*Little Lord Fauntleroy* and *The Child's Book of Martyrs*), jigsaw puzzles (St Paul's Cathedral and 'The Cotswolds in Spring'), and a Victorian board game called *Cowboys and Red Indians*, which inspired the Hodbins to lead the children on a whooping war-painted rampage through the corridors.

'And yesterday I caught Alf playing Burned at the Stake,' she called down to the vicar on his next visit, 'with Lady Caroline's Louis Quinze hat stand and a box of matches.'

He laughed up at her. 'I can see stronger measures are required.'

He was as good as his word. The next day the basket he brought contained ARP armbands, a logbook, a map and an official RAF chart showing the distinctive silhouettes of Heinkels, Hurricanes and Dornier 17s. Alf promptly became an ace aeroplane spotter, lecturing everyone on the difference between a Messerschmitt and a Spitfire – 'See, it's got eight machine guns on the wings' – and hanging out of the ballroom window and shouting, 'Enemy aircraft at three o'clock,' every time a plane appeared and diving to record the number, type and altitude in the logbook. The only plane most days was the one carrying the post to Birmingham, but that didn't discourage him, and comparative peace reigned for several days.

It was, of course, too good to last. Soon, Alf began flying bombing sorties through the kitchen. And the sickroom, and torturing Binnie. When she suggested Beauty for her name – 'You know, like in Sleeping Beauty' – Alf hooted, 'Beauty? Beast, more like! Or Baby, 'cause that's what you are, bawlin' when you was ill and beggin' Eileen not to leave. You made 'er swear and everythin'.'

'I never,' Binnie said indignantly. 'I don't even like her. She can go this minute for all I care.'

I would if I could, Eileen thought, but while she'd been intent on taking care of her evacuees, Samuels had boarded up all the doors except the one in the kitchen, moved his chair in front of that, and nailed shut the windows in every room but the ballroom, which was always full of children. And she only had ten more days. If no one else came down with the measles.

But if they did, surely Oxford would attempt to pull her out. She was surprised they hadn't already. Now that most of the children had recovered and Binnie was out of danger, Una and Mrs Bascombe could easily handle the situation, but there was no sign of the retrieval team and no message from them. 'No letters have come for me, have they?' she asked Samuels.

'No,' he said. Which must mean the quarantine was nearly over, and none of the other children were going to get the measles. Eileen began counting the days.

Two days before the quarantine was to be lifted, Lily Lovell came down with a roaring case, and ten days later Ruth Steinberg, and two weeks after that Theodore. 'At this rate, we'll still be quarantined at Michaelmas,' Samuels grumbled.

Eileen wasn't sure she could make it. Alf nearly fell out of the window trying to identify a plane, and Binnie began holding air-raid drills, standing at the top of the main stairway and giving her imitation of an air-raid siren. '*That* ain't the siren for air raids, you slowcoach,' Alf told her. 'You're doin' the all-clear. *This* is the air raid,' and let loose a bloodcurdling up-and-down yowl that Eileen thought would break Lady Caroline's crystal.

'They simply must go outside and run off some of their energy before they wreck the house,' she told Mrs Bascombe. 'It wouldn't be breaking quarantine if they stayed on the front lawn. If anyone came we could come inside straightaway.'

Mrs Bascombe shook her head. 'Dr Stuart will never allow it—'

There was an unearthly wail from the stairway. 'Air raid!' Theodore shrieked, giggling, and the children thundered through the kitchen towards the cellar steps, knocking a pan full of cakes off the table and onto the floor where Alf, wearing his ARP armband and a colander-helmet, stepped in the middle of it.

'Exactly how many more days is it till the end of quarantine?' Mrs Bascombe asked, helping Eileen pick up cakes.

'Four,' Eileen said grimly, reaching for one that had gone under the flour bin.

'All clear!' Binnie shouted from the cellar door, and the children roared back through the kitchen and up the stairs again, shrieking.

'No running!' Mrs Bascombe called futilely after them. 'Where's Una got to? Why isn't she watching them?'

'I'll go and find her,' Eileen said, dumping the last of the trampled cakes onto the baking pan and going upstairs. Knowing Alf and Binnie, she might be tied to a chair or locked in a closet.

She wasn't. She was lying on Peggy's cot in the ballroom. 'I think I've caught the measles,' she said. 'I feel so hot, and I have an awful headache.'

'You said you'd had them.'

'I know. I thought I had. I must have been wrong.'

'Perhaps it's only a cold,' Eileen said. 'Oh, Una, you can't have the measles!'

But she did. Dr Stuart confirmed it on his visit, and Una broke out the next day. Mrs Bascombe, determined not to let the quarantine be prolonged yet another month by Eileen's catching them, took over Una's nursing herself and forbade Eileen to go anywhere near her, which was just as well. She might have throttled her.

The children had to be kept quiet so as not to disturb Una – a nearly impossible task. Eileen tried telling fairy-stories to the children, but Alf and Binnie interrupted constantly and questioned every aspect of the story. ''Ow come they didn't just lock the door when the bad fairy tried to come to the christenin'?' they asked when she attempted to tell 'Sleeping Beauty', and ''Ow come the good fairy couldn't undo the whole spell 'stead of makin' 'er sleep a 'undred years?'

'Because she came too late,' Eileen said. 'The spell was already cast. She didn't have the power to undo it.'

'Or p'raps she weren't very good at spells,' Alf said.

'Then how come she's the *good* fairy?' Binnie demanded.

'Rapunzel' was even worse. Binnie wanted to know why Rapunzel hadn't cut off her hair herself and climbed down it, and Binnie promptly tried to demonstrate on Rose's braids.

Why did I wish she was her old self again? Eileen thought and announced they were going to do lessons instead.

'You can't!' Binnie protested. 'It's summer!'

'These are the lessons you missed when you were ill,' Eileen said. She made the vicar bring their schoolbooks, and he must have sensed she was near the breaking point, because he brought her a basket of strawberries and Agatha Christie's *The Murder of Roger Ackroyd*.

'I thought it might prevent *The Murder of Alf and Binnie Hodbin*,' he said. He also brought the post. And the war news. 'The RAF's holding its own, but the Luftwaffe has five times their number of planes, and now the Germans have begun attacking our airfields and aerodromes.'

She passed that on to Alf and got nearly an entire week of calm out of it. Then she caught him hanging out of the sitting-room window looking through Lady Caroline's opera glasses, which he promptly hid behind his back, dropping them in the process. 'I was only trying to see if it was a Stuka,' he said as she picked them up. There was an ominous tinkle of glass. 'It was your fault. If you hadn't scared me, I wouldn't have dropped them.'

Six more days, Eileen thought, hoping the manor wouldn't be reduced to a pile of rubble by then. But finally Dr Stuart proclaimed everyone clear, and had Samuels unboard the doors and take down the notices.

Five minutes later, Eileen was on her way to the drop. She didn't even set out the letter from her ailing mother in Northumbria. Mrs Bascombe would assume she simply hadn't been able to take any more, which was close to being true.

It was raining hard, but she didn't care. *I can dry off in Oxford*, she thought. *Somewhere where there are no children*. She walked swiftly to the road and cut into the woods. The trees were in full leaf and daisies and violets bloomed at their feet.

I hope I can find the drop, she thought, momentarily bewildered by the lush greenery, but there was the clearing and the ash tree. It was overgrown, and ivy and woodbine trailed everywhere. Eileen brushed the raindrops off the face of her watch, checked the time, and sat down to wait.

An hour went by and then another. By noon it was clear it wasn't going to open, but she sat there in the wet till nearly two, thinking, *Perhaps they didn't realise the quarantine was lifted this morning.*

At quarter past two the rain became a torrent, and she was forced to give up. She slogged back to the road and the manor. Binnie was standing in the kitchen door waiting for her. 'You're all wet,' she said helpfully.

'Really?' Eileen said. 'I hadn't noticed.'

'You look just like a drowned rat Alf caught once,' she said, and then accusingly, 'This ain't your 'alf-day out.'

My half-day out, Eileen thought. *That's why it didn't open. They're assuming I won't come through till Monday.*

But the drop didn't open on Monday either, even though Eileen had waited till the children were all inside having their tea so they couldn't follow her, and taken a roundabout route just to be certain.

The lab must not know the quarantine's over, Eileen thought, though the date it had ended would be in the Ministry of Health archives. But the lab might have sent through a retrieval team and they'd seen a notice that hadn't been taken down yet and concluded the manor was still under quarantine – though when she checked, all the notices had been removed.

And if the team had come to the manor, they'd have seen unmistakable signs that it had been lifted: children playing outside, cots being fumigated on the lawn, the grocer's boy going in and out of the kitchen. The retrieval team could easily have waylaid him on his way home and asked him about it.

And the evacuees' parents had all known the moment the quarantine had been lifted. Some of them had sent for their children the very next day, even though the Battle of Britain was in full cry, airfields and oil depots were being bombed, and the wireless was warning of invasion.

So were Alf and Binnie. ''Itler's sendin' over parachutists to get ready for it,' Alf eagerly told the vicar, who'd come to take

Eileen and Lily Lovell to the station. 'They're 'ere to cut tele-phone wires and blow up bridges and things. I wager they're 'idin' in the woods this very minute,' and even the vicar confided he feared the attack might come very soon.

But none of the invasion talk had any effect on the evacuees' parents. They were determined to have their children 'safely at home' – which presumably was a reference to their having sent them away only to have them catch the measles – and they couldn't be persuaded to leave them where they were. Eileen worried over what would happen to them in London.

When she wasn't worrying about where the retrieval team was. Since this was only her first assignment, she didn't know how long they waited before coming to get someone. Ten days? A fortnight? But this was time travel. Once they realised she was late, they'd have come through immediately.

There must be something wrong. It must be something else, a breakdown or something. *Alf and Binnie broke the drop*, she thought. Or they'd followed her and kept it from opening. She asked the vicar to resume Binnie's driving lessons so she could go to the drop without being observed. But it still didn't open.

Alf and Binnie aren't the only ones who could be watching, she thought. The Home Guard might be patrolling the woods for Alf's German parachutists, or the soldier Alf and Binnie'd seen talking to Una still might be hanging about.

In which case the lab would eventually realise that the drop wasn't going to open and send the retrieval team through somewhere else. Till then, she had more than enough to keep her occupied. Not only did she have the departing evacuees to deal with, but they had to clean and prepare the house for Lady Caroline, who'd written saying she was coming home.

And repair the damage the children had done. 'Oh, when she sees the library ceiling!' Una said.

And the Louis Quinze hat stand, and the opera glasses, Eileen thought, and prayed the retrieval team would arrive before Lady Caroline returned, but they didn't.

Lady Caroline had written that her son Alan would be accompanying her, but she arrived without him, and when Mrs Bascombe asked when he'd be coming, Lady Caroline told her he'd enlisted in the RAF and was training to be a pilot.

'He's doing his part to win this war,' she said proudly, 'and so must we,' and set the staff to learning the St John's Ambulance Emergency Medical Care manual from cover to cover. Which meant Eileen had to sandwich in the memorising of 'Shock: the shutting down by the body of peripheral systems in an attempt to survive', between attempting to keep the evacuees quiet, apologising to Mr Rudman, Miss Fuller and Mr Brown for Alf and Binnie's latest crimes, and taking children to the train.

Georgie Cox went home to Hampstead, in spite of the fact that a nearby aerodrome had been bombed, Edwina and Susan's grandfather came from Manchester to fetch them, and Jimmy's aunt in Bristol sent for him, which made Eileen hope that a relative – preferably one who didn't know them – would send for the Hodbins, but they didn't. *The Hodbins I shall have with me always*, she thought resignedly.

Sending the children off took nearly all of Eileen's time. She had to pack their things, walk them to the railway station, and wait on the platform with them, often for hours. 'It's all the troop trains,' Mr Tooley said, 'and now these air raids. The trains have to halt till they're over.'

The vicar kindly gave Eileen and the children lifts to the railway station when he could, but he was often busy attending the Invasion Preparedness meetings Lady Caroline had organised. Eileen didn't mind. Walking back gave her the opportunity to check the drop – when she could escape the Hodbins' watchful eyes, which wasn't often.

But today, seeing Patsy Foster off, Alf and Binnie had grown bored with waiting and left, and moments later the train had arrived, so Eileen was able to not only go to the clearing but spend the afternoon there on the off-chance the drop was only opening every hour and a half or two hours.

It wasn't, and there was still no sign that the retrieval team – or Una's soldier, or a German parachutist – had been here. What was keeping them? She thought suddenly of the train's being late and wondered if there was something going on in Oxford, the equivalent of troop trains or air raids, which was causing the delay.

If that was the case, then they might show up at the manor anytime, and she'd better be there. She hurried back through the woods. As she neared the lane, she caught a glimpse of someone standing on the other side of the lane. Eileen ducked behind a tree, and then peered cautiously out to see who it was.

It was Alf. *I knew it*, she thought. *He and Binnie have been spying on me. That's why it won't open*, but he wasn't looking into the woods. He was gazing up the lane in the direction of the manor as if waiting for someone. And when she stepped out onto the lane, he jumped a good foot. 'What are you doing here, Alf?' she demanded.

'Nuthin',' he said, putting his hands behind his back.

'Then what have you got in your hand?' Eileen said. 'You've been setting out tacks again, haven't you?'

'*No*,' he said, and oddly, it had the ring of truth. But this was Alf.

'Show me what you have there,' she said, holding out her hand.

Alf backed up against a bush, there was a suspicious thunk, and he held out both hands, empty. 'You've been throwing rocks at cars,' she said, but even as she said it, she was remembering that Alf had been gazing towards the manor, clearly waiting for a car to come from there, and it couldn't be Lady Caroline's Bentley. She was at a Red Cross meeting in Nuneaton, and the vicar had gone with her, so it couldn't be the Austin. 'Alf, who's at the manor?' she asked.

He frowned at her, trying to decide if this was a trick question. 'I dunno. Strangers.'

Finally, Eileen thought. 'Who did they come to see?'

'I dunno. I just seen 'em drive by.'

'In a car?'

He nodded. 'One like Lady Caroline's. But I wasn't goin' to throw rocks at it, I swear, only clods. I was practisin' for when the jerries invade. Me'n Binnie's goin' to throw rocks at their tanks.'

She wasn't listening. A car like Lady Caroline's. A Bentley. The retrieval team could have practised on one in Oxford, just as she'd done, and then come through, hired one, and driven it here to fetch her. She took off for the manor at a run.

The Bentley was drawn up to the front door. Eileen started up the steps, and then remembered she was still a servant, at least for a few more hours, and ran around to the servants' entrance, hoping Mrs Bascombe was in the kitchen. She was, with a bowl of batter in the crook of one arm, stirring it violently with a wooden spoon. 'Who's here?' Eileen asked, trying to keep the eagerness out of her voice. 'I saw a car out in front as I—'

'They're from the War Office.'

'But ...' *The War Office? Why would the retrieval team tell Lady Caroline that?*

'They're here to look over the house and grounds to see if they're suitable.'

'Clods don't hurt nothing,' Alf said at her elbow. 'It's only dirt.'

Eileen ignored him. 'Suitable for what?' she asked Mrs Bascombe.

'For the Army,' Mrs Bascombe said, stirring viciously. 'The government's taking over the manor for the duration. They're turning it into some kind of training school.'

The horns are to butt with and the mouth is to moo with.

LETTER FROM AN EVACUEE EXPLAINING
WHAT A COW IS, 1939

KENT – APRIL 1944

The bull stared at Ernest from across the pasture for a long, menacing moment. 'Worthing! Run! There's a bull!' Cess shouted from behind the lorry.

'Now look wotcha gone and done!' the farmer said. 'Y've upset me bloomin' bull. This is 'is pasture—'

'Yes, I can see that,' Ernest said without taking his eye off the bull.

The bull hadn't taken its little eyes off him either. Where the hell was the fog when you needed it?

The bull lowered its massive head. *Oh Christ, here he comes!* Ernest thought, pushing his back against the tank.

The bull began to paw the ground. Ernest shot a frantic look at the farmer, who was standing by the fence with his arms folded belligerently. 'Now y've torn it,' he said. 'He don't like what y've done to his bloomin' pasture, and nor do I. Look at this great mess of tracks. Y've chewed up the whole meadow with yer bloody tanks, and that's gorn 'n' made 'im mad.'

'I know,' Ernest said. 'What do you suggest I do now?'

'Run!' Cess shouted.

The bull swung its massive head around to see who'd said

296

that, and then turned back to Ernest. It snorted.

'Don't—' Ernest said, putting his hand out like a traffic policeman, but the bull was already barrelling across the grass straight at him.

'Run!' Cess bellowed, and Ernest took off for the end of the tank and around to the other side, as if crouching behind it was going to offer any protection.

The bull roared straight at the tank.

'Stop! Y'll do yourself a harm,' the farmer shouted, finally moving. 'Y're no match for a bloomin' tank. Stop!'

But the bull wasn't listening. It lowered its head and charged, its horns thrusting out like bayonets, and ploughed straight into the tank. Its horns went all the way in.

There was another endless moment, and then a high, thin wail, like an air-raid siren. 'Y've killed 'im,' the farmer shouted, pelting across the pasture, 'y'bloody bast—' And stopped, his mouth open.

The bull's mouth was open, too. It stood for a few more seconds, its horns impaled in the tank, then took a skittish step backward, freeing itself. The tank slowly shrivelled and shrank into a limp grey-green mass of rubber. The wail became a squeal and then faded away, and there was another long silence.

'Bloody hell,' the farmer said softly, and the bull looked like it wanted to say the same thing. It stared, stunned, at the collapsed tank.

'Bloody hell,' the farmer said again, as if to himself. 'No wonder the Panzers were able t'go straight through our boys in France.'

The bull raised its head and looked straight at Ernest, then gave a low bleat and turned and bolted for the safety of the fence. 'What in Gawd's name are you two playin' at?' the farmer demanded. 'Is this some sort o' bloody trick?'

'Yes,' Ernest said. 'We're—' and looked up at a faint droning sound.

'It's a plane!' Cess said unnecessarily and came galloping over to grab hold of the tank's deflated turret. 'Grab the rear end! Hurry!' They began dragging the tank over the wet grass to the trees.

'I don't know what the two o' you're up to—' the farmer began belligerently.

'Don't just stand there. Help us!' Ernest shouted over the drone, which was growing steadily louder. 'It's a German reconnaissance plane. We can't let them see this!'

The farmer glanced up at the clearing sky and then back at the tank and seemed, finally, to grasp the situation. He ran clumsily over and took hold of the tank's right tread and began helping them drag it over to the copse.

It was like trying to shift jelly. There was nothing solid to grab hold of, and it weighed a ton. The muddy, wet grass should have made the unwieldy mass easier to move, but the only thing it made slipperier was their footing, and when Ernest tried to yank the tank over a hillock, he slipped and fell flat in one of the tracks he'd just made. 'Hurry!' Cess shouted at him as he struggled to his feet. 'It's nearly overhead!'

It was, and all it would take was one photo of the deflated mass of rubber to blow Fortitude South wide open. Ernest planted his mud-caked boots, gave another mighty heave, and the three of them pushed, pulled, manhandled it in under the trees.

Cess looked up. 'It's one of ours,' he said. 'A Tempest.'

It was. Ernest could make out the distinct outline. 'This time,' he said. 'But next time it won't be.'

Cess nodded. 'We'd best get this on the lorry before another one shows up. Go and bring the lorry over here.'

'Not across this pasture,' the farmer said. 'Y've already torn it up bad enough already. To say nothin' of puttin' m'bull off his feed.' He gestured towards the bull, which was over by the fence, placidly chewing grass. 'And who knows what other damage y've done to 'im? I'm supposed to take 'im down to Sedlescombe next week to breed 'im, and now look at 'im.'

Since the bull had stopped chewing and was eyeing one of the cows beyond the fence, Ernest doubted that would be a problem, but the farmer was determined. 'I won't have 'im more upset than 'e already is,' the farmer said. 'You'll have to take that bloody tank back over to your lorry the same way you brought it over 'ere.'

'We can't,' Cess said. 'If a German reconnaissance plane sees us—'

'It won't see nothin',' the farmer said. 'Fog's comin' back in.'

It was, drifting thickly across the pasture to hide the grazing bull, the lorry, the tank tracks.

'And when you're done doin' that, you can take those bloody tanks with you, as well,' the farmer said, pointing to the ghostly outlines of the tanks sticking out from under the trees, and they spent the next quarter of an hour trying to explain the necessity of the tanks staying there till a German reconnaissance plane had photographed them.

'You'll be helping to defeat Hitler,' Cess told him.

'With a lot of bloody balloons?'

'Yes,' Ernest said firmly. And a bunch of wooden planes and old sewer pipes and fake wireless messages.

'His Majesty's Army will be glad to reimburse you for the damage to your field,' Cess said, and the farmer immediately perked up. 'And to your bull's psyche.'

Don't bring up the bull, Ernest thought, but the farmer smiled. 'I never seen nothin' like the look on 'is face when he gored that tank,' he said, shaking his head. He began to laugh, slapping his thigh. 'I can't wait to tell 'em down th' pub—'

'No!' they cried in unison.

'You can't tell *anyone*,' Ernest said.

'It's top secret,' Cess said.

'Top secret, is it?' the farmer said, looking even more pleased than he had at the prospect of being reimbursed. 'This to do with the invasion?'

'Yes,' Cess said, 'and it's terribly important, but we can't tell you anything more than that.'

'Y'don't 'ave to. I can puzzle it out on m'own. Invadin' at Normandy, are you, then? I thought so. Owen Batt said Calais, but I said no, that's what the Germans were expecting, and we're smarter than that. Wait till I—'

'You can't tell Owen Batt or anyone else,' Cess said.

'If you do, you could lose us the war,' Ernest said, and they spent another quarter of an hour standing there in the clammy fog getting the farmer to agree to keep the story to himself.

'I'll keep it dark,' he finally promised grudgingly, 'though it's a pity. The look on that bull's face—' He brightened. 'I can tell it after the invasion, can't I?'

'Yes,' Ernest said, 'but not till three weeks after.'

'Why not?'

'We can't tell you that either,' Cess said. 'It's top *top* secret.'

'And we can leave the tanks?' Ernest asked. 'We promise we'll come back for them as soon as they've been photographed.'

The farmer nodded. 'If it means doin' m' bit to win the war.'

'It does,' Cess said, and started for the lorry.

'Now, wait just a bloody minute. I said y' could leave the tanks, not drive all over me pasture. Y'll have to take that bust balloon back the way you brought it over 'ere.'

'But it'll take half an hour, and one of their planes might see us while we're doing it,' Cess argued. 'This fog might clear at any moment.'

'It won't,' the farmer said, and it didn't. It settled over the pasture and the woods like a heavy grey blanket that made it impossible to gauge direction, which resulted in their dragging, pushing and manhandling the deflated tank an extra hundred yards trying to find the lorry, during which effort Ernest fell down two more times.

'Well, at least it can't get any worse,' Cess said as they tried to shove the flopping mass up over the back of the lorry. At which point it began to rain again – a thin, bone-chilling rain that continued for the entire duration of their stowing the tank, loading the cutter and the pump and the phonograph and thanking the farmer, who, along with the bull, had watched the entire proceedings with interest. By the time they got back to Cardew Castle, they were drenched, frozen, and starving.

'Oh no, we missed breakfast,' Cess said, lifting the phonograph out. 'I'll never make it to luncheon. I could sleep for a week. What are you going to do, sleep or eat?'

'Neither,' Ernest said. 'I have to write up my news stories.'

'Can't that wait?'

'No, I've got to get them over to Croydon by four o'clock.'

'I thought you said they were due this morning.'

'They were, but as I missed the *Sudbury Weekly Shopper*'s deadline because I was nearly being killed by an angry bull, they'll now have to go in the *Croydon Clarion Call* instead.'

'Sorry.'

'It's all right. The ordeal wasn't entirely a loss. Our farmer friend back there gave me an idea for a letter to the editor.' He took the stack of phonograph records Cess handed him. '"Dear Sir, I woke Tuesday morning to find that a—" Whose tank brigade is supposed to be here now? American or British?'

'Canadian. The Canadian Fourth Infantry Brigade.'

'"To find that a squadron of Canadian tanks had destroyed my best pasture. They'd mashed the grass flat, frightened my prize bull—"'

'Not as much as it frightened you,' Cess said, handing him the bicycle pump.

'"—and left muddy tank tracks everywhere, all without so much as a by-your-leave."' He stuck the records under his arm and shifted the pump to his left hand so he could open the door. '"I realise we must all pull together to defeat the Germans, and that in wartime some sacrifice is necessary,"' He opened the door. '"But—"'

'Where have you two been?' Moncrieff demanded. 'We're late.'

'For what?' Ernest asked.

'Oh no,' Cess said. 'Don't tell me we've got to go and blow up more tanks. We've been up all night.'

'You can sleep in the car,' Moncrieff said, and Prism came in, dressed in tweeds and a tie.

'You can't go to the ball like that, Cinderella,' Prism said, taking the records and pump away from Ernest. 'Go on, get showered and dressed. You've got five minutes.'

'But I need to take my news stories over to—'

'You can do that later,' Prism said, dumping the records on the desk and propelling him towards the bathroom.

'But the *Sudbury Shopper*'s deadline—'

'This is more important. Go and wash that mud off and get dressed,' he said. 'And bring your pyjamas.'

'My pyjamas—?'

'Yes,' he said. 'We're going to see the Queen.'

*'I called to the other men that the sky was clearing, and then
a moment later I realised that what I had seen was not a rift
in the clouds, but the white crest of an enormous wave.'*

ERNEST SHACKLETON

LONDON – 19 SEPTEMBER 1940

Miss Laburnum raved about Sir Godfrey all the way back to
the boarding house in the chill dawn. 'How thrilling it must
have been for you, Miss Sebastian, performing with a great actor
like Sir Godfrey!' she gushed. '*A Midsummer Night's Dream* is
one of my favourite plays!'

Since they'd been doing *The Tempest*, Polly was glad Sir
Godfrey wasn't there to hear that.

'It's been such an exciting night,' Miss Laburnum said. 'I
won't be able to sleep!'

I will, Polly thought, but she didn't have time. She washed
out her *Times*-stained blouse, wishing she had a second one to
put on. She'd need to get one from Wardrobe when she went to
get her skirt.

She ironed her blouse more or less dry, ate a hasty breakfast
of badly scorched porridge, and set out for work, hoping the
Central Line had reopened – it had – and that Miss Snelgrove
would believe her story about being unable to go home because
of the raids, but when Polly arrived at Townsend Brothers, she
wasn't there. 'She's filling in up on fourth today,' Marjorie told

her. 'For Nan in Housewares. And she said for me to tell you that Townsend Brothers is moving up its closing time from six to half-past five because of the raids, starting tonight.'

Good, Polly thought. *That will give me more time to reach the drop.*

'Nan wasn't hurt in last night's raids, was she?' Doreen asked. 'They were bad in Whitechapel.'

'No, Miss Snelgrove would have said.'

'Perhaps Nan pulled a flit,' Doreen suggested.

'No, I don't think so. Miss Snelgrove didn't seem cross when she told me.' Marjorie grinned. 'I mean, more cross than usual.'

Doreen giggled. 'At least she's out of our hair.'

Yes, Polly thought, *but not for long*, and when Nan came back, Miss Snelgrove would expect Polly to have a black skirt and be able to wrap parcels, so in between customers, she totted up her sales so she could make a quick getaway at closing time. The raids didn't begin till 8:20, but obviously the sirens could go much earlier. *I'd best skip supper*, she thought, *and go straight to the drop from the tube station. I can't afford to be waylaid by Miss Laburnum tonight.* And when she got back to Oxford, she needed to get the list of siren times from Colin.

By four there was no one in the store. 'They don't want to be caught out when the sirens go,' Marjorie said, and Polly hoped that meant she could leave on time, but ten minutes before closing Miss Varley came in and wanted to see every single shade of stocking in stock, and, in spite of the earlier closing time, it was half past six before Polly had everything put away. She grabbed her coat and shot out of the store to the tube station, and then had to wait nearly twenty minutes for a train.

The sirens went while she was en route to Notting Hill Gate. She heard two women who got on at Lancaster Gate discussing them.

Good. She'd been afraid they might not go till later since the raids had mostly been over the East End. The ones over

Bloomsbury must be early in the evening. And if there weren't any delays, she'd have more than enough time to reach the drop before the raid started.

There weren't any, and when they pulled into Notting Hill Gate, it was only a quarter past seven. She hurried up the escalator and across to the exit. The grillework grates were pulled across it. 'No one's allowed to leave while a raid's in progress,' a tin-hatted guard told her.

'But I must go home,' Polly said, 'my family will be worried if I don't—'

'Sorry, miss,' he said and planted himself firmly in front of the gate. 'Those are the rules. No one's allowed out till after the all-clear. You go back down below where it's safe. The bombs'll be starting up any minute.'

No, they won't, she thought, but it was clear he wasn't going to relent, so she went back downstairs to look at the Underground map for other possible stations. Bayswater wasn't close enough for her to be able to walk to the drop before the first raid began, but High Street Kensington might work if it didn't have a gate. If there was only a guard, she might be able to sneak past him—

It had a gate, and a guard twice as determined not to let her go outside, and while she was arguing with him, the anti-aircraft guns started up. *I've got to face it*, she thought, *I'm stuck here for the night.*

No, she wasn't. She couldn't get to the drop, but she didn't have to spend the night here. She could take the tube to one of the deep stations and observe the shelterers. Balham would be the most interesting, but Mr Dunworthy would have a fit, even though it hadn't been hit till October fourteenth. And to go to Leicester Square, she'd have to change trains. She needed to be able to get back to Notting Hill Gate in the morning to tidy up before work. And, if the all-clear went early enough, go to the drop and through to Oxford to get her skirt before work. Which meant she needed a station on the Central Line. Holborn.

With its 150-foot-deep tunnels, Holborn had been one of the first tube stations the contemps had co-opted when the Blitz started. The government hadn't intended for them to be used as shelters. They'd been worried about sanitation and infectious disease. But their admonitions to 'Stay at Home – Build an Anderson Shelter' had gone largely unheeded, and there'd been no effective way to enforce the ban, not when there were stories of people being killed in Andersons and surface shelters. And not when all a person had to do was buy a ticket and ride to Holborn.

Which the entire city of London had apparently done tonight. Polly could scarcely get off the train, the platform was so jammed with people sitting on blankets. She picked her way carefully through them, trying not to step on anyone, and out to the tunnel. It was just as bad there, a solid mass of people, bedding and picnic baskets. One woman was boiling tea on a Primus stove and another was setting out plates and silverware on a tablecloth on the floor, which reminded Polly that she hadn't had supper. She asked the woman where the canteen was.

'Through there,' she said, pointing with a teaspoon, 'and down to the Piccadilly Line.'

'Thank you,' Polly said and made her way towards it through masses of people sitting against the tiled walls and standing in little knots, chatting.

The main hall was only slightly less mobbed. Polly rode down the long escalator to the canteen, which was much larger than Notting Hill Gate's and had china cups and saucers – 'Just bring them back when you're done, there's a dear,' the WVS volunteer behind the counter said – and Polly bought a ham sandwich and a cup of tea and walked about, looking at the contemps.

Historians had described the shelters as 'nightmarish' and 'like one of the lower circles of hell', but the shelterers seemed more like people on holiday than doomed souls, picnicking and gossiping and reading the papers. A foursome sat on camp stools playing bridge, a middle-aged woman was washing out stockings in a tin pot, and a wind-up portable gramophone was playing 'A Nightingale Sang in Berkeley Square'. Station guards were patrolling the platforms to keep order, but their only job seemed to be ordering people to put out their cigarettes and pick up their discarded wastepaper.

The government was right to have been concerned about sanitation. There was only one makeshift toilet on each level, with endless waiting queues. Polly saw several toddlers sitting on chamber pots and watched as a mother carried a pot over to the platform's edge and emptied it onto the tracks. Which no doubt accounted for the odour. Polly wondered what it would be like by the middle of winter.

There'd been some attempts to impose order – a lost-and-found, a first-aid post, and a lending library – but for the most part, chaos reigned. Children ran wild in the tunnels and played dolls and marbles and hopscotch in the middle of the tunnels and on the narrow strip of platform reserved for passengers getting on and off the trains. No one was making any effort to put them to bed, even though it was half past nine and a number of adults were unfolding blankets and plumping pillows, and one teenaged girl was putting cold cream on her face.

Which reminded Polly, she needed to find a place to sleep – or at the least, sit – which might be difficult. The few empty spaces along the walls were staked out with blankets for relatives and friends. The escalators would shut off when the trains stopped at half past ten. She might be able to snag one of their steps, though the wooden slats looked uncomfortable, but she had an hour to kill till then. She read the ARP and Victory Bonds posters pasted to the walls. One of them said Better Pot-Luck with Churchill Today than Humble Pie under Hitler Tomorrow.

Whoever composed that has obviously never eaten at Mrs Rickett's, she thought and went to look at the lending library. It consisted of a stack of newspapers, one of magazines, and a single row of worn paperbacks, most of which seemed to be murder mysteries.

'Book, dear?' the ginger-haired librarian asked her. 'This one's very good.' She handed Polly Agatha Christie's *Murder in Three Acts*. 'You'll never guess who did it. I never do with her novels. I always think I have the mystery solved, and then, too late, I realise I've been looking at it the wrong way round, and something else entirely is happening. Or perhaps you'd like a newspaper. I've got last evening's *Express*.' She pressed it into Polly's hands. 'Just bring it back when you're done with it so someone else can have a read.'

Polly thanked her and looked at her watch. She still had twenty minutes to fill. She got in the queue for the canteen again, keeping an eye on the escalators so she could dart to claim a step as soon as they stopped, and observing the contemps in the queue: a couple in evening dress, complete with fur cloak and top hat; an elderly woman in a bathrobe and carpet slippers; a bearded man reading a Yiddish newspaper.

A group of ragged, dirty urchins hovered nearby, playing tag and obviously hoping someone would offer to buy them a biscuit or an orange squash. The woman ahead of Polly carried a fretful toddler, and the one ahead of her had two pillows, a large black handbag, and a picnic basket. When she neared the front of the queue, she shifted the pillows to one arm, set the basket on the floor beside her and opened her handbag. 'I do so hate people who wait till they reach the counter to look for their money,' she said, digging in the bag. 'I *know* I had a sixpence in here somewhere.'

'*You're it!*' one of the urchins shouted, and a ten-year-old girl ran by, knocking against the handbag. Its contents, including the elusive sixpence, spilled out in all directions, and everyone except Polly stooped to gather up the lipstick, handkerchief, comb.

Polly was looking after the girl. *She knocked against her on purpose*, she thought and glanced back at the picnic basket. It was gone.

'Stop, thief!' the woman shouted, and the rest of the urchins scattered.

A station guard took off in hot pursuit, shouting, 'Come back here, you hooligans!'

He was back in moments, pulling a small boy along by the ear. 'Ow,' the boy protested. 'I didn't do nuthin'.'

'That's him,' the woman said, 'the one who stole my basket.'

'I dunno what you're talkin' about,' the boy said, outraged. 'I never—'

A workman came up, carrying the basket. He pointed at the boy. 'I saw him stowin' this behind a dustbin.'

'I put it there for safekeeping,' the boy said, 'till I could take it to the lost-and-found. I found it lyin' on the platform, without a soul round it.'

'What's your name?' the guard demanded.

'Bill.'

'Where's your mother?'

'At 'er work,' an older girl said, coming up, and Polly recognised her as the one who had knocked against the woman's handbag. She was wearing a dirty, too-short dress, and a filthy hair ribbon. 'Mum works in a munitions factory. Making *bombs*. It's dreadful dangerous work.'

'Is this your sister?' the guard asked the boy, and he nodded. 'What's your name?' he asked her.

'Vronica. Like the film star.' She clutched the guard's sleeve. 'Oh *please*, don't tell Mum about this, sir. She's enough worries already, what with our dad in the war.'

''E's in the RAF,' the boy put in. ''E flies a Spitfire.'

'Mum ain't 'eard from him in weeks,' the girl said tearfully. 'She's ever so worried.'

She's nearly as good as Sir Godfrey, Polly thought admiringly.

'Poor little tykes,' the woman murmured, and several of the people who'd gathered around glared at the guard. 'There's no harm done. After all, I've got my basket back.'

I think you'd better check the contents before you say that, Polly thought.

'Oh, *thank* you, missus,' the girl said, clutching the woman's arm. 'You're *ever* so kind.'

'I'll let you go this time,' the guard said sternly, 'but you must promise never to do it again.' He let go of the boy, and the two children instantly darted off through the crowd and down the escalator. Which had been switched off at some point during the altercation and was now crammed with people sitting and lying on the narrow steps.

Little wretches, Polly thought, *they cheated me out of my place,* and she made the rounds again, looking for an unoccupied space. There weren't any. Shelterers slept down on the rails after the trains stopped, but even though there were no historical accounts of anyone having been run over, it still struck her as a dangerous practice, to say nothing of all those emptied-out chamber pots.

She finally found an unoccupied space in one of the connecting tunnels between two already sleeping women. Polly took off her coat, spread it out and sat down. She set her shoulder bag next to her, then remembered the Artful Dodger and his sister and tucked it behind her back, leaned against it, and tried to go to sleep, which should have been easy. She hadn't slept at all last night and only a bit more than three hours the night before. But it was too bright and too noisy, and the wall was as hard as a rock.

She stood up, folded her coat into a pillow and lay down, but the floor was even harder, and when she closed her eyes, all she could think about was how upset Mr Dunworthy would be at her taking so long to check in and what Miss Snelgrove would say when she saw she still didn't have a black skirt. Which did no good. There wasn't anything she could do about either one at the moment.

She sat up and unfolded the *Express* the librarian had lent her. The ocean liner *City of Benares*, packed with evacuees, had been sunk by a German U-boat, the RAF had shot down eight German fighters, and Liverpool had been bombed. There was nothing about John Lewis – only a story headed 'Mass Bombing of City Continues' which said, 'Among the targets on Tuesday night were two hospitals and a shopping street' – but there was a John Lewis ad on page four.

Polly wondered if they'd forgotten to take it out of the paper, or if it was an attempt to deceive the Germans into believing it hadn't been hit. During the V-1 attacks, they'd planted false information in the papers about where the rockets had landed. She looked to see if there was an ad for Peter Robinson's, which had also been hit.

There wasn't. Selfridge's was having a sale on siren suits, a one-piece wool coverall, 'perfect for nights in the shelter – stylish and warm'. *That's what I need*, Polly thought. The cement floor was cold. She unfolded her coat, draped it over herself, put her head on her bag and tried again to sleep.

To no avail, even though at half past eleven the lights dimmed and conversation dropped to a murmur. She couldn't hear the bombs – the sound didn't penetrate this far underground. It was unnerving, not knowing what was going on up there. She lay there, listening to the shelterers snoring, and then sat up again and read the rest of the paper, including the 'Cooking in Wartime' column – it was clear Mrs Rickett got her recipes from it – the casualties list, and the personal ads.

They gave an intimate glimpse into what life was like for the contemps. Some were funny – *L. T., Apologise for behaviour at Officer's Club dance last Sat. Please say you'll give me another chance. Lt. S. W.* – and others heartbreaking – *Anyone having any information regarding Midshipman Paul Robbey, last seen aboard the* Grafton *at Dunkirk, please contact Mrs P. Robbey, 16 Cheyne Walk, Chelsea.* And there was no one who wasn't affected by the Blitz, as witness: *Lost, white cat, answers to Moppet, last seen during night raid 12 September. Frightened of loud noises. Reward.*

Poor thing, Polly thought, *trapped in a terrifying situation it couldn't understand.* She hoped it was all right. She read through the rest of the personals – *Homes wanted for evacuees* and *R. T., Meet me Nelson Monument noon Friday, H.* and *Ambulance drivers needed. Enlist in the* FANY *today* – and lay down again, determined to sleep.

She did, only to be wakened by a crying baby, a woman on her way to the loo, murmuring 'Sorry ... sorry ... sorry,' and then a guard saying sharply, 'Put that cigarette out. No smoking allowed in the shelter due to the fire danger.' The idea that the authorities were concerned about fire when half of London was on fire above them struck her as extremely funny, and she laughed to herself and fell asleep.

This time it was the guard shouting 'All clear!' that woke her. She put on her coat, yawning, and went down to the Central Line to catch the first westbound train, only to be met by a notice board: 'No train service between Queensway and Shepherd's Bush.' That included Notting Hill Gate, which ruled out any chance of getting to the drop before work. She would have to buy a skirt at Townsend Brothers before the store opened.

But the train took half an hour to arrive and then promptly stopped between stations. Twice. She scarcely had time to reach the store and wash her face and comb her hair in the employee loo before the opening bell. Her blouse was wrinkled and the back had a brown streak between the shoulder blades from where she'd sat against the wall. She brushed at it awkwardly, tucked the blouse in, and went out to the floor, praying Nan wasn't back.

She apparently was. Miss Snelgrove came over to Polly's counter immediately, her lips pursed in disapproval, and said, 'I believe I told you on being hired that Townsend Brothers' shopgirls wear black skirts and neat, clean white blouses.'

'Yes, ma'am, you did,' Polly said. 'I'm dreadfully sorry, but I've been unable to get home these past two nights because of the raids. I spent both nights in a shelter.'

'I will let it go today,' Miss Snelgrove said. 'I realise the current situation has created certain ... complications. However, it is our job to overcome them. Townsend Brothers cannot allow its standards to drop, no matter what the circumstances.'

Polly nodded. 'I'll have it by tomorrow, I promise.'

'See that you do.'

'Old bat,' Marjorie whispered to Polly as soon as she was gone. 'Have you got money enough for a skirt? If you haven't, I could loan you a bit.'

'Thanks, I can manage it,' Polly said.

'I'll cover your counter if you want to leave early so you can buy it before the shops close.'

'Would you?' Polly said gratefully. 'But won't we get in trouble?'

'I'll tell Miss Snelgrove Mrs Tidwell asked if we have the Dainty Debutante girdle in extra large. Looking for it will keep her in the workroom till well after closing.'

'But what if she finds it?'

'She won't. We only had one, and I've already sent it out to Mrs Tidwell.'

Marjorie was as good as her word, and Polly was able to leave half an hour early, which was wonderful since she'd decided the only way to ensure her making it to the drop was to walk. She couldn't risk being caught underground again, and a bus would have to pull over and stop if the sirens went. The raids weren't till nearly nine tonight, but after last night she wasn't taking any chances.

I hope it isn't raining, she thought.

It wasn't, but as she walked towards Marble Arch, fog began drifting in, and by the time she turned off Bayswater, it was even thicker than it had been the night she came through. She could only see a few houses' distance, and as she approached Lampden Road, ghostly outlines of its buildings. The fog made them look unfamiliar, at once far off and looming.

They were unfamiliar. She must have turned a street too soon, for these weren't the buildings that lined Lampden Road – the chemist's with its bow windows and the row of shops.

They were warehouses of some kind, windowless brick edifices with a single half-timbered house wedged in among them.

She walked towards them, looking for a familiar landmark, the curve of the road, or, if the fog was too thick for that, the spire of St George's. The fog had completely distorted distances. The warehouses still looked far away, even though she was nearly to the corner. And she should be able to see the spire from here. Could she have somehow got turned around? The street ahead couldn't be Lampden Road. It was much too broad—

She reached the corner and stopped, staring across the road. She had been right about the buildings being too far away. She was looking at the ones that faced the next street over. The entire row of buildings which should be in front of them was gone, collapsed into a tangled heap of roof slates and timbers and brick, exposing the backs of the buildings behind them.

It must have been an HE. And Badri had been right; it was easy to lose one's bearings after a bombing. She had no idea what part of the road this was. She looked down towards where St George's and the curve of the road should lie, but the fog was too thick – she couldn't see either one.

And nothing looked familiar. She looked across at the row of warehouses. They didn't seem damaged. And the second one from the corner had a wooden staircase angling down its back, and it hadn't fallen down, and if it was as ramshackle as the one in the alley next to the drop, one good hard push could have collapsed it, let alone the concussion from a bomb.

She turned to look at the buildings behind her on this side of the road. They hadn't been damaged either. Not even the windows of the butcher's shop had been broken. *Blast does do peculiar things*, she thought. The windows of the greengrocer's beyond the butcher's hadn't been broken either, and the baskets of cabbages sitting outside the door—

It can't be the same grocer's, she thought, running up the road towards it. But it was. The awning above the door said,

'T. Tubbins, Greengrocer.' *But if this is the same greengrocer's,
then—*

She stopped, staring not at the shop, but across the street at
the rubble and the row of warehouses behind it. At the narrow
passage between the second and third buildings from the end,
filled with barrels. And at the Union Jack chalked on the brick
wall and the words scrawled beneath it, clearly visible even
through the fog and the falling darkness: 'London kan take it.'

DUNKIRK, FRANCE – 29 MAY 1940

Mike must have been knocked unconscious by the bomb's concussion, because when he came to, the light from the flares had faded, and he was trussed up in a rope and being hauled up the side of the *Lady Jane*. 'Are you all right?' Jonathan asked anxiously.

'Yes,' he said, though he seemed to have trouble hanging on to the railing as Jonathan and one of the soldiers helped him over the side, their hands under his arms.

'Hypothermia,' Mike explained, and then remembered he was in 1940. 'It's the cold. Can I have a blanket?'

Jonathan ran off to get one while the soldier helped him over to a locker – he seemed to be having trouble walking, too – so he could sit down. 'Are you certain you're not hurt?' the soldier asked, peering at him in the darkness. 'That bomb looked like it fell bang on top of you.'

'I'm fine,' Mike said, sinking down onto the wooden locker. 'Go and tell the Commander I cleared the propellor. Tell him to start the engine.' Then he must have blacked out again for a few minutes because Jonathan already had the blanket around him and the engine had started up, though they weren't moving yet.

'We thought you were a goner,' Jonathan said. 'It took ages to find you. And when we did, you were floating face-down with your arms out, just like that body we saw. We thought—'

He looked up, and so did Mike. The sky overhead blossomed with flares, shedding greenish-white sparks as they fell.

'For what we are about to receive ...' one of the soldiers muttered.

'We've got to get out of here!' Mike said, getting up to go help the Commander guide the boat out of the harbour and then sitting shakily back down. 'Go and navigate! We've got to get out of here before they come back.'

'I think we're too late,' Jonathan said, and Mike looked frightenedly up at the sky, but Jonathan was pointing out across the water. 'They've seen us.'

'Who?' Mike staggered over to the railing and looked at the mole where soldiers were running towards them, wading, swimming out to the *Lady Jane* through the green-lit water. Hundreds of them, thousands of them. *Because I blacked out and they had to waste time rescuing me,* Mike thought. 'Go and tell your grandfather to cast off,' he shouted. 'Now!'

'And just *leave* them?' Jonathan asked, his eyes wide.

'Yes. We don't have any other choice. They'll swamp the boat. Go!' Mike shouted and gave him a push, then staggered back to the stern, hanging on to the rail for support, to pull up the rope they'd let down to him.

But it was too late. The soldiers were already climbing up it, hand over hand, grabbing for the sides, clambering over the rail. 'You'll swamp her!' Mike shouted, trying to untie the rope, but they weren't listening to him, they were swarming aboard like pirates, scrambling over each other, jumping down onto the deck.

'Move to the other side!' Mike shouted, clinging to the rail. He was still too wobbly to stand. 'You'll tip her over!' He shoved at them, trying to move them forward into the bow, but no one was listening.

The deck began to slant. 'Listen! Move—'

'Duck!' somebody yelled, and the men flattened themselves against the deck. The first bomb hit close enough to spray water all over them, and the second just as close on the other side. The hordes of soldiers still on the mole ran back along it, and the ones in the water began to swim back towards shore.

A few were still swimming out to them, still climbing aboard, but the bombs provided intervals, and the threat of strafing made it possible to convince some of the soldiers to go below. 'Space yourselves in the hold,' Mike told them, working his way along the rail. 'Not all on one side. And no moving around. Sit down and stay put.'

'Stop sending them forward!' Jonathan shouted back to him over the crowd. 'There's no room up here!'

'There's no room back here either!' Mike yelled. 'Tell the Commander to get out of here before we take on any more.' The launch was already riding perilously low in the water, and God knew how much water was in the hold by now. He could hear the bilge pump wheezing even over the sound of the engine. He should go below and make sure it didn't break down under the strain, but the soldiers were packed in too tightly to let him get through, or even away from the rail. Maybe that was why they weren't moving, because the Commander couldn't get to the wheel.

Someone grabbed at the neck of his shirt, yanking him back against the rail, and then clutched at his shoulder, using Mike to haul himself up over the side. It was a very young, very freckled soldier. 'Just made it,' he said. 'I was afraid you were going to leave without me. I say, it's a bit crowded, isn't it? We won't sink, will we?'

We will if we don't get out of here now, Mike thought, looking towards the bow. *Come on*, and the *Lady Jane* finally, finally began to move, backing out from the now-burning mole. There was a *whoosh* and a scream, and a bomb crashed down where they'd been moments before, spraying water over the bow.

'We made it,' the freckled soldier said jubilantly.

If we can make it out of the harbour, Mike thought, *and the Commander can find his way back to England. And the engine doesn't break down.* Or they didn't run into something.

He should be up in the bow, serving as lookout. 'Coming through,' he shouted, and tried to push his way forward, but he wasn't going anywhere – the soldiers were packed in too tightly – and as soon as he let go of the railing, the shakiness came back. *It's reaction,* he thought, grabbing for it again.

And relief. It was the force of the bomb that had knocked the body free, that had unfouled the propellor, not his attempts, and it was obvious the soldiers would have got on board with or without him. *So I don't have to worry about having affected the outcome of Dunkirk.*

'I didn't think anyone was going to come for us,' the freckled soldier said. 'Except the Germans. We could hear their artillery, there on the beach. They'll be here by morning.' He looked anxiously at Mike. 'Seasick, mate?'

Mike shook his head.

'I always get seasick,' the soldier said cheerfully. 'I hate boats. My name's Hardy. Private First Class, Royal Engineers. Bit crowded, isn't it?'

That was an understatement. They were crammed in as tightly as the pilchards in that can the Commander had made his stew with.

And I don't have to worry about having taken up anyone else's space on board, Mike thought. He wasn't taking up any space at all. They were so wedged in the other soldiers were holding him up. Which was a good thing. Without them and the rail, his legs would have buckled under him.

I should have eaten that stew when I had the chance, he thought. *And hung on to that blanket.* He'd lost it somewhere, trying to work his way forward, and his wet clothes were icy against his skin. He couldn't even feel his feet, they were so cold.

But the soldiers were even worse off. Many were shirtless and one was dressed only in boxer shorts and, of all things, a gas mask. He had a gash on the side of his head. Blood was dripping down his cheek and into his mouth, but he seemed oblivious. *He doesn't even know he's injured*, Mike thought.

'How far is it?' Private Hardy asked at his ear. 'Across the Channel?'

'Twenty miles,' Mike said.

'I was afraid I was going to have to swim for it.'

They were out of the harbour and into open sea. Mike could tell by how much colder the wind had got. He began to shiver. He tried to hug his chest, but his arms were wedged tightly to his sides. He wished fervently he still had that blanket and that Hardy would shut up. Unlike the other soldiers, his relief at being rescued had taken the form of talking compulsively. 'Our sergeant told us to head for the beaches,' he said, 'that there'd be ships to take us off, but when we got there, there wasn't a ship in sight. "We're for it now, Sergeant," I told him. "They've left us behind."'

The *Lady Jane* continued to plough through the darkness. *We've got to be at least halfway across*, Mike thought, *and it's got to be daylight soon*. He tried to free his arm to look at his Bulova and then remembered he'd left it up in the bow, along with his coat and shoes.

The sea grew rougher, and it began to rain. Mike hunched his shoulders against it, shivering. Hardy didn't even notice. 'You've no idea how it feels to sit and wait for days, not knowing if anyone's coming for you or if they'll be in time, not even knowing if anyone knows you're there.'

The night – and Hardy's voice – went on and on. The wind picked up, blowing the rain and the spray right into their faces, but Mike barely felt it. He was too exhausted to hold on to the railing, even held up as he was by the mass of soldiers.

'Our sergeant tried to send a Morse signal with his pocket torch, but Conyers said it was no use, that Hitler'd already invaded and there was no one to come. That was the worst, sitting there thinking England might not be there any longer. Oh, I say, look, it's getting light out.'

It was. The sky lightened to charcoal and then to grey. 'Now we'll be able to see where we are,' Hardy said.

So will the Germans, Mike thought, but there was no one else on the wide expanse of slate grey water. He scanned the waves, looking for a periscope, for the wake of a torpedo.

'It was odd,' Hardy droned on. 'I could bear the thought of being captured, or killed, so long as England was still there, but— I say, look!' He unwedged his hand to point at a smudge of lighter grey against the grey horizon. 'Aren't those the White Cliffs of Dover?'

They were. *I'll finally be where I've been trying to get for days*, Mike thought. *Talk about taking the long way around. But at least now I know where the small craft docked.* And he wouldn't have any trouble getting access to them. Or to the men coming back from Dunkirk. It had just never occurred to him he'd be one of them.

They were pulling into the harbour, manoeuvring their way through the maze of boats arriving, loading, setting out. 'Dear old England,' Hardy said. 'I never thought I'd see her again. And I wouldn't have if it weren't for you.'

'For me?' Mike said.

'And your boat. I'd completely given up hope when I saw your signal light.'

Mike jerked his head around sharply. 'Signal light?'

Hardy nodded. 'I saw it weaving about out there on the water, and I thought, that's a boat.'

The flashlight I made Jonathan shine on the propellor, Mike thought. *He saw the light from it when Jonathan was searching for me in the water.*

'If I hadn't seen it, I'd still be back on that beach with those Stukas. It saved my life.'

I saved his life, Mike thought sickly as the Commander guided the *Lady Jane* in towards the wharf. He wasn't supposed to have been rescued.

'We have injured aboard,' the Commander shouted to the sailor tying them up to the dock.

'Yes, sir,' the sailor said and took off down the wharf. Jonathan rigged a gangway. The soldiers began stumbling off the boat.

'Do you happen to know how one goes about finding one's unit?' Hardy asked. 'I wonder where I'll be sent next.'

North Africa, Mike thought, *but you aren't supposed to be there. You were supposed to have been killed on that beach. Or captured by the Germans.*

The sailor was back, leading orderlies with stretchers and an officer who knelt as soon as he was on deck and began bandaging a soldier's leg.

'Fetch us some petrol,' the Commander said to the sailor. 'We're heading back to Dunkirk as soon as we get this lot unloaded.'

'*No*,' Mike said, starting towards him. He swayed and nearly fell. Hardy grabbed him to steady him and helped him over to the locker to sit down. 'I'll fetch the captain,' he said, but the Commander was already heading towards him.

'I can't go back to Dunkirk,' Mike said to him. 'You've got to take me to Saltram-on-Sea.'

'You're not going anywhere, lad,' the Commander said. He turned and called, 'Lieutenant! Over here!'

'You don't understand,' Mike said. 'I've got to get back to Oxford and tell them what's happened. He wasn't supposed to make it back. He saw the light.'

'There, now, Kansas,' the Commander said, putting his hand around Mike's shoulder. 'Don't go upsetting yourself. *Lieutenant!*' he bellowed, and the officer who'd been tending the wounded stood up and started towards them.

'You don't *understand*,' Mike pleaded. 'I may have altered events. I've got to warn them. Dunkirk's a divergence point. I may have done something that'll make you lose the war,' but they weren't listening. They were all looking down at the deck, at the bloody mess that had been his right foot.

*'He hath fenced up my way that I cannot pass,
and He hath set darkness in my paths.'*

JOB 19:8

LONDON – 20 SEPTEMBER 1940

*I*t *can't have been hit,* Polly thought, looking stupidly across the expanse of rubble at the exposed drop. Mr Dunworthy would never have approved the drop if it had been. And Badri had said he'd insisted they find a site that had been untouched during the entire Blitz, not only during her six weeks.

But it wasn't hit, she realised. Only the buildings on the other side of the alley were, and they would have had Lampden Road addresses. Badri and his techs must only have checked the buildings on the passage's side of the alley, and it hadn't occurred to them that one side of an alley could be damaged and the other side untouched. They didn't know how erratic blast patterns could be. The passage – at least as far down it as she could see in the fog – looked undisturbed, and the rickety staircase on the back of the next building was still intact.

She needed to get a closer look. She walked across the road and up to the rubble, stepping carefully over a rope barrier with a small square sign suspended from it that read Danger – Keep Out.

Danger was right. On closer inspection the rubble was studded with jagged-ended timbers and broken roof slates, and was nearly head-high. Polly walked rapidly along the roped perimeter, looking for a way up onto the mound. But there wasn't any, though the rubble wasn't quite as deep on the north side, and a few feet in, there was a sort of path made of a door – which must have been flung on top of the mound by the force of the blast – and a torn piece of linoleum.

Polly took hold of a half-buried timber and climbed up onto the rubble. It was less solid than it looked. Her feet sank into the plaster and pulverised brick up to her ankles, and one of her stockings snagged on a large wooden splinter. She took another cautious step, and the whole mound seemed to shift.

She grabbed for a broken-off bedpost. Plaster and pebbles rattled down for several seconds, then stopped. She stepped forward cautiously, not letting go till she had to, and testing each hand and foot before she put her weight on the unsteady wreckage till she reached the piece of linoleum.

She'd been wrong. The linoleum hadn't been flung there by the bomb, and neither had the door. A rescue squad had laid them there, and they didn't lead to the drop. They led to a square-sided hole. Polly knew instantly what it was – a shaft dug to reach a victim, or a body, buried there. Which, presumably, they had got out.

She looked across at the passage. Glass was scattered in it, but no debris, and none of the barrels had been knocked over. They – and the drop's position in the recessed well – would both have helped protect the drop from blast.

If I can only get to it, she thought, testing the plaster-and-brick mass beyond the linoleum. It gave ominously under her foot. She needed something to walk on. Perhaps if she could shift the door in the direction of the drop …

But it was too heavy. So was the linoleum. She stood up and surveyed the mound, looking for a section of wall or a cupboard door she could use.

'You, there!' a man's voice shouted. 'What are you doing?' It was the ARP warden who'd dragged her to the shelter that first night. He was standing by the rope barrier, holding a pocket torch. 'This incident's out of bounds.'

Polly wondered fleetingly if she should make a run for it. He'd have a hard time catching her in this rubble, and it was nearly dark. Which meant she was liable to fall through and break a leg. 'Come down at once,' the warden said. He ducked under the rope, and started up onto the mound.

'I'm coming,' Polly said and started back towards the edge, picking her way carefully.

'What were you doing up there?' he demanded. 'Didn't you see the notice?'

'Yes,' Polly said, debating what to tell him. He didn't seem to have recognised her. 'I thought I heard a cat meowing.' She climbed down to where he was standing. 'I was—' Her foot slid, and the warden put out a hand to catch her. 'I was afraid it was trapped in the rubble.'

He looked worriedly past her. 'You're certain it was a cat and not someone calling for help?'

That was all she needed, for the warden to call a rescue crew and them to begin digging again. 'Yes, I'm certain,' she said hastily, 'and it wasn't trapped after all. Just as I got to where the sound was coming from, it ran away.'

'This incident's dangerous, miss. There's a good many holes and weak patches out there. If you was to fall through, nobody'd know you was out there. They wouldn't know to come looking for you. You could be out there for days, weeks even—'

'I know. I'm sorry. I didn't think.'

'You shouldn't be out this time of night,' he said. 'The sirens will be going any minute.'

She nodded. He held up the rope barrier for her, and she ducked under it.

'You need to get to shelter, miss.' That was the same thing he'd said to her last Saturday, and the same thought must have occurred to him because he frowned at her.

'Yes, straightaway,' she said, ducked quickly under the rope barrier, and started rapidly up the street.

'Wait!' he shouted, and came after her. 'Notting Hill Gate's this way,' he said, reaching for her arm.

She eluded his grasp. 'I live just up the street,' she said, pointing, hoping there hadn't been an incident up that way as well.

There was a drone of planes off to the east. The warden looked up. *Saved by the Luftwaffe,* Polly thought, and walked off quickly in the direction she'd pointed.

'See that you go straight there,' the warden called after her.

'I will, warden,' she said and kept going, resisting the impulse to look back to see if he was following her. She crossed the street and the next and then ducked into an alley. From this distance it would look to the warden as if she'd turned down a side street. If he was still watching.

He was.

Go and drag someone else off to St George's, she willed him, *or go and look for blackout infractions or something,* but he continued to stand there in the dusk. What if he stood there all night?

He'll have to leave when the raids begin and go and look for incendiaries, she thought, retreating into the alley. The raids weren't over Kensington tonight. They were over Bloomsbury and the East End. But as Colin had said, there were lots of stray bombs. She looked at her watch. Quarter to eight. Which meant she had over an hour to wait, and it was already frigid here in the alley.

If the warden would only leave, she could go to St George's and hide in the sanctuary till everyone was off the streets. It had to be warmer there than here. But the warden was still there, and it was already too dark down the alley to try to go that way. She'd crash into something and make the warden come running.

Leave, she willed the still-motionless figure. *Move.* And after a moment he did.

Oh no, he was coming this way. Polly backed further into the dark alley, looking for a doorway or a passage like the drop's to hide in. She could just make out a large metal dustbin in the darkness, and on the far side of it, a wooden crate. Polly sat down on the crate, tucking her feet back out of view, and waited, listening for footsteps.

After several minutes she heard some, but they were from the wrong direction and walking swiftly. Contemps going to a shelter. Another reason to stay here. She didn't want to run into Miss Laburnum again and be dragged off to St George's. She pulled her sleeve back and checked her watch again. Five past. She jammed her icy hands in her pockets and sat there, listening for planes.

It was an eternity before she heard them. A gun far to the east started up, and a brief interval later, she heard an HE hit, so distant it made only a faint *poomphing* sound. Polly stood up and felt her way along the side of the dustbin to the mouth of the alley to see if the warden was still there. She looked cautiously out.

Into blackness. It was as dark on the street as it had been in the alley. Darker. Between the fog and the blackout, there was no light at all. She'd never be able to find her way back to Lampden Road in this, let alone across that unstable, hazard-and shaft-strewn mound of rubble to the drop.

I'll have to go and fetch a pocket torch, she thought, but if she couldn't find her way back to the drop, she couldn't find her way to Mrs Rickett's.

But I can't afford to wait another night to go back to Oxford, she thought and flinched as there was another *whoosh* and *crump*, much nearer than the first, and then another. The gun in Tavistock Square started up, and a moment later a flare lit the street in a blue-white glow.

It flickered out, leaving behind a faint reddish glow and then fading, but almost immediately another one flashed to the west of it, arcing in a shower of shimmering white stars, and to the east, a reddish wavering glow lit the lower clouds. A fire, and now the searchlights were coming on, crisscrossing the sky, like giant pocket torches. Wonderful, there was more than enough light to get back to the drop by, and more than enough to see and avoid any rescue shafts.

And to see that the warden had gone. She ran quickly back to the drop, keeping a sharp eye out, but there was no one on the side streets or the part of Lampden Road she could see ahead. By the time she reached the incident, it was bright enough to be able to read the Danger – Keep Out notice. She took one last quick look round for the warden, then clambered up and over the rubble on all fours till she got behind the higher part of the mound and partially out of sight of the street, and then straightened up and moved more slowly.

The closer she got to the drop, the less stable the mound became. Whole sections went slithering down with every step. Polly backtracked a few yards to a tangle of broken-off joists and – holding on to them and then a large beam – worked her way to the wall, and then along it to the passage. When she jumped down into the mouth of the passage, she heaved a sigh of relief.

She'd been worried the blast had somehow penetrated to the drop, but the broken glass only extended a few feet in. There was a thin coat of plaster dust on the floor and the tops of the barrels, but nothing else.

Polly edged past the barrels and went down the steps into the narrow well. The stacked barrels and the ledge above blocked the light from the fires – but there was still more than enough light to see by. The passage and the barrels had protected the well completely. There wasn't even any dust on the steps, and the spiderweb on the hinge hadn't been disturbed. She tried the rusty doorknob in case the blast had jarred it loose, but it was still frozen, the door still locked.

The light show outside was growing more spectacular by the minute. The shimmer wouldn't be noticeable at all amongst the fires and glittering flares and crisscrossing searchlights. Which meant if the Luftwaffe would kindly keep this up for a few more minutes, she could go home to supper. And – finally – get her black skirt.

And a new pair of stockings. That last crawling scramble can't have done them any good. And I'll make Badri find me a new drop that isn't so uncomfortable to wait in, she thought, sitting down on the second-from-the-bottom step.

And a drop that wasn't so difficult to get to. This one might still be working, but it would be effectively nonfunctional most of the time, between sightseers gawking at the incident site and children scrambling over it searching for shrapnel, followed by construction workers and bulldozers swarming over the mound, clearing the site. And overly conscientious air-raid wardens checking for looters.

She hoped it wouldn't take Badri and his techs as long as last time to find another site. Having days – or, God forbid – weeks between encounters that to the contemps were only hours apart caused all sorts of problems. She was likely to forget the names of the people at St George's or Miss Snelgrove's instructions on filling up purchase-on-account slips.

But I'll have time to learn how to wrap parcels, she thought. *And to eat some decent meals.*

She wished the drop would open soon. The fires might be giving the sky a warm orangey glow, but the cement step she was sitting on was even colder than the alley had been.

I need to get a warmer coat as well, she thought, pulling on her gloves. She'd opted for a light one since she would only be here through part of October, but she hadn't thought about needing to sit in the drop, and the autumn of the Blitz had been one of the coldest and wettest on record.

It had to be getting near the half-hour mark – it felt as if she'd been sitting here for hours. *Which means it's probably been ten minutes,* she thought wryly, resisting the impulse to look at her watch. She knew all too well how slowly time moved when one was waiting for one's drop to open. That night in Hampstead Heath, it had seemed to take hours.

She waited what seemed like another quarter of an hour, pulled her sleeve back to look at her watch, and then stopped, frowning. She could scarcely see her sleeve or the door in front of her. Oh no. Was the raid letting up? If it was, the shimmer would be visible, and if anyone came out to check for incendiaries, the drop wouldn't be able to open. She went down the darkened passage to see.

The raid was still in full cry. The flares had stopped and the fire to the east had died down, which was why there was less light in the passage, but there were several fires to the north now, one close enough that she could see flames. There was a steady succession of shuddering explosions.

She looked at her watch, which here at the edge of the mound was light enough to read even without the radium dial. It read ten to ten, but she realised she had no idea what time she'd reached the drop. She'd left the alley a short time after 8:55, but it had taken her forever to get across the mound.

But she'd been able to see into the passage for at least part of that and hadn't seen any shimmer, and it had taken her several minutes to inspect the well for damage. And her foot had had time to fall asleep while she sat there on the steps. Even allowing for how slowly time went when one was waiting, half an hour had to have passed.

Polly scampered back to the well, afraid the drop would open before she got back, and in her haste scraped against one of the barrels, snagging her skirt.

I hope Mr Dunworthy's not in the lab when I arrive, she thought, hurrying down the three steps. *He'll think I'm an incident victim and cancel my assignment on the spot. Perhaps I should go to St George's and go through tomorrow after I've had a chance to tidy up.*

But she'd already waited too long to check in. And Miss Snelgrove would sack her if she showed up without a black skirt tomorrow. It had to be tonight. With luck, Mr Dunworthy would be off in London again, and she could persuade Badri and Linna not to tell him what had happened.

Why wasn't the drop opening? She pulled back her sleeve to look at her watch again and then ducked as a bomb screamed and then hit with a thunderous boom no more than a street away. And then another. And there was a crashing clatter as something hit the tangle of broken joists.

An incendiary, Polly thought, but there were no sparks, no blue-white flash of magnesium. It must have been a piece of shrapnel. *Mr Dunworthy will kill me if I get hit by shrapnel.*

The drone of the planes overhead became a roar, and there was another *whoosh*, and a *boom* that sounded as if it were directly across the street. 'The raids tonight are supposed to be in Bloomsbury,' Polly shouted up at the planes, 'not Kensington.' She thought of Colin, warning her about stray bombs, about the hundreds of minor incidents which hadn't made it into the historical record. 'You've got no business being out in a raid,' he'd told her.

You're right, she thought, crouching back into the corner of the steps. There was another *whoosh* and a window-rattling *boom* a few streets away, and then a long, rising scream that sent Polly ducking down, her hands over her ears. The sound crescendoed to eardrum-rupturing intensity, and there was an anticlimactic thud and then a terrific flash, and the whole building shook as if it would come apart.

Polly looked up at the brick walls on either side. *They're going to come crashing down*, she thought, *and no one will have any notion I'm in here. I've got to get out of here.*

'Open!' she shouted as if the techs in Oxford could hear her, and dived at the door. 'Open!' but another bomb was already falling, drowning out her voice.

The *whoosh* rose to a scream.

*'Since England, despite her hopeless military situation,
still shows no signs of willingness to come to terms,
I have decided to begin preparations for, and if
necessary to carry out, an invasion against her.'*

ADOLF HITLER, 16 JULY 1940

WAR EMERGENCY HOSPITAL – SUMMER 1940

When Mike came to, a nun in a white veil was standing over him. *Oh God*, he thought, *I'm in France. The Lady Jane left me behind on the beach at Dunkirk, and the Germans are coming.* But that couldn't be right. He remembered coming back across the Channel, remembered sitting there at the dock, looking down at his shredded—

'My foot,' he said, even though the nun wouldn't be able to understand English. He tried to raise his head to see it. 'It's bleeding.'

'There, there, you mustn't think about that now,' the nun said, and she had a British accent, so he must be in England.

But I didn't think the English had nuns. Hadn't Henry VIII burned down all the convents? He must not have, because the nun was bending over him, pulling the blanket up over his shoulders. 'You must rest,' she said. 'You've just come out of surgery—'

'Surgery?' he said in alarm. He tried to sit up, but the moment he raised his head off the pillow, a wave of dizzying nausea washed over him, and he fell back, swallowing hard.

333

'You're still feeling the effects of the ether,' she said, her hands firmly on his chest to keep him from attempting to sit up again. 'You must lie still.'

'No.' He shook his head, and that was a mistake, too. *I'm going to vomit all over her white habit*, he thought, and swallowed hard. 'You said they operated. Did they have to take off my foot?'

'Try to sleep,' she said, covering him up again.

'Did they?' he attempted to ask, but this time he did vomit, and while the nun was gone emptying the basin, he dozed off. And she was right, he must still be feeling the effects of the ether because he had strange drugged dreams – he was on the beach at Dunkirk with Private Hardy. 'I'd have been a goner without your light,' Hardy said. 'You saved my life,' but it wasn't true. The boats had all left, and the Germans were coming.

'It's all right,' Mike told him. 'We'll use my drop,' but it wouldn't open, and then he was in the water, trying to reach the *Lady Jane*, but she was already pulling away from the mole, she was already pulling out of the harbour, and when he tried to swim after her, the water was full of flames, it was so hot—

I must have a fever, he thought, waking briefly. *My foot must have got infected. Why aren't they giving me antibiotics?*

Because they hadn't been invented yet, and neither had antivirals or tissue regeneration. Had they even developed penicillin in 1940? *I have to get out of here. I have to get back to Oxford.* And he tried, but the nuns held him down and gave him an injection, and they must have had sedatives in 1940 because he ended up back in the flaming water. He couldn't see the *Lady Jane* anywhere, but there was a light, shining this way and that.

It's Jonathan's flashlight, he thought, and swam towards that, but he couldn't reach it. 'Wait!' he shouted, but the nun didn't hear him.

'No, no better, Doctor,' she said. 'I fear he's too ill to be moved,' but he must not have been, because when he woke up, after what seemed like days and days in his dream, he was in another bed, another, larger ward, with two long rows of white painted metal beds, and the nun was different, younger and with a white bibbed apron over her blue habit. But she said the same things: 'You must rest,' and 'His fever's up again,' and 'Go below and put your shoes on. We'll be in Dunkirk soon.'

'I can't go to Dunkirk!' he told her as she pulled the blanket up over him, but they were already there. He could see the docks and the flames from the town and the enveloping black smoke. 'You have to take me back!' he shouted. 'I'm not supposed to be here! It's a divergence point!'

'Shh, you're not going anywhere,' the nun said, and when he opened his eyes he was back in the bed, and she was standing next to it, holding his wrist, and the nausea and the splitting headache were gone.

'I think the effects of the ether have worn off,' he said.

'I should imagine so,' she said, and smiled. 'I'll fetch the doctor.'

'No, wait. How long—?' but she had already disappeared through the double doors at the end of the ward.

'Three weeks,' someone said, and Mike turned his head to look at the man in the bed next to him, or rather, boy – he couldn't be more than seventeen. His head was bandaged, and his left arm was in a cast held up at an angle by pulleys and wires.

'You mean three days?' Mike said.

The boy shook his head. 'It's been three weeks since they operated on you. That's why Sister Carmody smiled when you said you thought the effects of the ether had worn off.'

Three weeks? He'd been here three weeks? But that didn't make sense. Why hadn't the retrieval team come and got him?

'You've been rather out of it, I'm afraid,' the boy was saying. 'I'm Flying Officer Fordham, by the way. Sorry I can't shake your hand.' He raised his right arm, also in a cast, to show Mike, and let it fall back at his side.

'You said they operated on me? Did they amputate my foot?'

'I've no idea,' Fordham said. 'I'm not in a good position to see much except for the ceiling, which has a water stain in exactly the shape of a Messerschmitt, worse luck.'

Mike wasn't listening. He tried to raise his head up to see if his foot was still there, but the effort made him so dizzy he had to lie back and close his eyes to stop the spinning.

'Wretched angle to have an arm stuck at, isn't it?' Fordham was saying, gesturing at the arm in the pulleys with his right hand. 'I look as though I'm saluting *der Führer. Sieg heil!* Decidedly unpatriotic. It may keep the Nazis from shooting me when they invade, though. Till they find out who I am, at any rate.'

'What day is it?' Mike asked.

'No idea of that either, I'm afraid. It's easy to lose track in here, and unfortunately there's no stain in the shape of a calendar. The twenty-ninth, I think, or the thirtieth.'

The thirtieth? That would make it a full month. He must have heard him wrong. 'June *thirtieth?*'

'Oh, I say, you have been out a good while. It's July.'

'*July?*' *That's not possible*, he thought. Oxford would have sent a retrieval team as soon as he failed to return after the evacuation. 'Have I had any visitors?' he asked.

'Not that I know of, but I've been out of it a good deal as well.'

And the retrieval team wouldn't know where he was. They wouldn't know he'd gone to Dunkirk or that he was in a hospital, and it would never occur to them to look in a convent.

The nun was back with a doctor. He wore a white coat and had an antiquated stethoscope around his neck. 'Has he told you who he is yet?' he was asking the nun.

'No,' she said. 'I came as soon as I saw he was awake—'

'What day is it?' Mike demanded.

'Awake *and* talking,' the doctor said. 'How are you feeling?'

'What day is it?'

'August the tenth,' the nurse said.

'Good heavens, as late as that?' Fordham said.

'How are you feeling?' the doctor asked again, and the nurse cut in, 'What's your name?'

'There wasn't any identification on you when you were admitted,' the doctor explained.

So the retrieval team wouldn't have been able to find him even if it had occurred to them to look here.

'It's Mike,' he said. 'Mike Davis.'

The doctor wrote it on the chart. 'Do you remember what unit you were with?'

'Unit?' Mike said blankly.

'Or your commanding officer?'

They think I'm a soldier, Mike thought. *They think I was rescued from Dunkirk.* And why not? He'd been on a boat full of soldiers, and the fact that he hadn't been in uniform wouldn't mean anything. Half of the soldiers hadn't been either. He tried to remember what had happened to his papers. They'd been in his jacket, and he'd taken it off when he went in the water.

But why hadn't they realised he was an American? He remembered talking in his delirium. Maybe his L-and-A implant had stopped working. Implants sometimes went haywire when a historian got sick.

The doctor was waiting, his pen poised above the chart.

'I—' Mike began, and then hesitated. If his implant wasn't working, he shouldn't tell them he was an American. And if this was a military hospital, he shouldn't tell them he was a civilian. They'd throw him out. But military hospitals didn't have nuns.

'Never mind,' the doctor said before he could come up with a good answer. 'You've had a difficult time. Do you remember how you came to be wounded?'

'No,' Mike said. It must have happened when the explosion blew the dead soldier's body free of the propellor—

'He was hit by shrapnel,' the nun said helpfully, and to the doctor, 'He was in the water attempting to unfoul his ship's propellor when the ship came under attack, and he heroically dived in and freed it.'

The doctor said, 'Sister, may I speak to you for a moment?' He and the nun walked away, their heads together.

'—memory loss—' Mike heard him say, and 'extremely common in cases like this,' and '—concussion from the blast ... don't press him on it ... usually returns after a few days—'

Jesus, Mike thought, *they think I've got amnesia*. But maybe that was a good thing. It would give him a chance to figure out if his L-and-A had stopped working and whether this place only took military patients, and now that he'd told them his name, he might only need to stall for another day or two, and the team would come and get him out of here and safely back to Oxford. If it wasn't already too late, and they'd amputated his foot. If they hadn't, it could be repaired with nerve and muscle grafts and tissue regeneration, no matter how damaged it was, but if they'd already cut it off—

The nun and the doctor had finished conferring. 'Let's have a listen to your chest, shall we?' the doctor said, handing the chart to the nun; he stuck the ends of the stethoscope in his ears and pushed the blanket down and Mike's hospital gown up, baring his chest.

'Did you have to take my foot off?' Mike asked, careful to keep his accent neutral, neither English nor American-sounding.

'Take a deep breath,' the doctor said. He listened and then moved the stethoscope to a different spot. 'And another.' He looked up at the nun, nodding. 'A bit better. Not as much involvement in the left lung as there was.'

'Do I have pneumonia?' Mike blurted out, and his implant was obviously working now. His pronunciation of 'pneumonia' was unmistakably American.

The doctor didn't seem to notice. He was looking at the chart. 'Has his temperature come down at all?'

'It was one hundred and two this morning.'

338

'Good,' he said, handed the chart to the nun, and started to walk away.

'Do I have pneumonia?' Mike persisted. 'Did you amputate my foot?'

'You let us worry about the medical side of things,' the doctor said heartily. 'And you concentrate on—'

'Did you?'

'You shouldn't think about any of that now,' the nun said soothingly. 'Try to rest.'

'No,' Mike said, shaking his head. Mistake. The movement made him violently sick. 'I want to know the worst. It's important.'

The doctor exchanged glances with the nun and then seemed to come to a decision. 'Very well,' he said. 'When you were brought in, your foot was badly damaged, and you'd lost a good deal of blood. You were also suffering from exposure and shock, which meant we couldn't operate as soon as we would have liked, and by the time we did, there was a good deal of infection—'

Oh God, Mike thought, *they had to amputate the whole leg.*

'And after the first surgery you contracted pneumonia, so we had to wait longer than we wished to operate again. There was also considerable damage to the muscles and tendons—'

'I want to see it,' Mike said, and the nun glanced quickly at the doctor. 'Now.'

The doctor frowned and then said, 'Sister Carmody, if you'd help him to sit up,' and bent over to turn a crank at the foot of the bed.

The nun put her hand behind his back for support as the bed came up. His head swerved and spun. He swallowed hard, determined not to vomit. 'Are you feeling dizzy?' she asked.

Mike didn't trust himself to shake his head. 'No,' he said, watching as the doctor pulled back the blanket and sheet, revealing his pyjama-clad leg and his ankle and beyond it, a knobby lump of gauze in the general shape of a foot.

They didn't cut it off, Mike thought, weak with relief. He lay back limply against the nun's arm. *The foot bones are still there, and the rest can be repaired as soon as I get back to Oxford.*

'It will take some time to heal, but there's no reason you won't be able to walk again, though it will require additional surgeries. But just now you need to work on resting and regaining your strength. You're not to worry.'

Easy for you to say, he thought. *You're not a hundred and twenty years from home with an injured foot and primitive medical care and in an environment you haven't researched and that they will throw you out of as soon as they find out you're a civilian.*

And why didn't they know that? They knew about his unfouling the ship's propellor, which meant the Commander had brought him in. Then why hadn't he told them his name?

He might not have remembered it, Mike thought. He'd immediately christened him Kansas and called him that from then on, but that didn't explain why he hadn't told them he was a reporter.

Mike drifted off to sleep still trying to figure it out, and dreamed of the drop. It wouldn't open. 'It can't,' Private Hardy said. 'It doesn't exist.'

'Why not?' Mike said and saw it wasn't Hardy, it was the dead soldier who'd been tangled in the propellor. 'What's happened to the drop?'

'You weren't supposed to do it,' the dead soldier said, shaking his head sadly. 'You changed everything.'

Mike woke drenched in a clammy sweat. Oh God, what if his actions *had* altered events?

Saving a single soldier can't change the course of the war, he told himself. There were 350,000 soldiers on those beaches. But what if Hardy was supposed to have saved an officer's life there on the beach, an officer who'd be crucial to the success of D-Day? Or what if he was supposed to have been rescued by some other boat, or by one of the destroyers? What if he was the man who'd spotted the U-boat that would otherwise have torpedoed it, and without him it would be lost with all hands? And what if that destroyer had been one of the destroyers that had hunted down the *Bismarck*? What if they didn't sink it, and we ended up losing the war to the Germans?

That's why the retrieval team hasn't come, Mike thought, shivering uncontrollably. *Because—*

'Oh God,' he said to the dead soldier, 'who won the war?'

'No one as yet,' the nun on night duty said cheerfully, 'but I've no doubt we will in the end. Having a bad dream?' She took a thermometer out of her starched apron pocket, put it under his tongue, and laid her hand on his forehead. 'Your fever's back up.'

He felt a rush of relief. *It's the fever,* he thought. *You're not thinking clearly. You can't have altered events. The laws of time travel won't let you.* But they weren't supposed to have let him get anywhere near a divergence point either. And Hardy had said—

'Here, these will make you feel better,' the nun said, handing him two tablets and a glass of water. *Thank God,* he thought. At least they'd had aspirin. He swallowed them eagerly and lay back. 'Try to sleep,' she whispered and continued through the ward, her flashlight bobbing like Jonathan's had in the water, signalling Hardy.

Historians can't change history, Mike told himself, clenching his chattering teeth, waiting for the aspirin to take effect. *If my unfouling the propellor would have altered the course of the war, the net would have sent me through a month later. Or to Scotland. Or it wouldn't have let me through at all.*

And the reason the retrieval team's not here is because it never occurred to them to look in a convent.

But when Sister Carmody came to take his temperature in the morning, he asked her if he could see a newspaper so he could make sure the war was going the way it was supposed to. 'You must be feeling better,' she said, smiling her pretty smile. 'Do you think you could sit up and take some broth?' and when he nodded, hurried off, to return shortly with a bowl of broth.

'Did you bring the newspaper?' he asked.

'You mustn't worry yourself over the war,' she said brightly, helping him sit up and propping pillows behind his back. 'You must concentrate all your energy on getting well.'

'What energy?' he said. Sitting up in bed, even with her help, took a tremendous effort, and when Sister Carmody handed him the bowl, his hands shook.

'Let me help with that.' She took it from him. 'Has anything come back?' she asked, feeding him a spoonful of broth. 'Have you remembered what happened? Or the unit you were with?'

Maybe he should tell her he'd remembered so they'd transfer him to a civilian hospital where the retrieval team could find him. But what if they'd already checked the civilian hospitals and determined he wasn't there? And a different doctor might be determined to operate. 'No, not yet,' he said.

'You talked a good deal when you first came,' she said. 'You kept murmuring something about a "drop". We thought perhaps you might be a parachutist. Isn't that what they call it when they jump out of the plane, making a drop?'

'I don't know. Did I say anything else?'

'He said "Oxford",' Fordham said from the bed next to him.

'Oxford. Could that be where you're from?' the nun asked.

'I don't know,' Mike said and frowned as if trying to remember. 'It might be. I can't—'

'Well, you mustn't worry,' she said, and offered him another spoonful, but it was too much effort to even sip at it. He waved the spoon away and lay back against the pillows, exhausted, and he must have fallen asleep because when he opened his eyes, she was gone.

'Did you bring me a newspaper?' he asked when she came to take his temperature again.

'Your fever's back,' she said, writing it in the chart. 'I'll fetch you something for it.'

'Don't forget my newspaper,' he said, and when she returned

without it and with the blessed aspirin, he said slyly, 'I thought seeing a paper might help me to remember.'

'I'll see what I can do,' she said and left.

'Which is what she always says when I ask her out,' Fordham said. 'It means no.'

Asked her out? But he was a mere boy, and she was a nun—

'I don't blame her,' Fordham said. 'I couldn't exactly take her dancing, could I? And by the time I'm out of this bed, she'll already be engaged to one of the doctors,' but Mike had stopped listening.

She wasn't a nun, in spite of the wimple and veil, in spite of the title 'Sister'. She was a nurse. *Which I'd have known if I'd had time to research this era properly*. But if she wasn't a nun, then this wasn't a convent, and his theory of why the retrieval team hadn't found him didn't hold water. So where were they? They should have been here long before now.

Unless they didn't exist. Unless the net had malfunctioned and let him go through to somewhere he wasn't supposed to be and he had altered the course of events. Unfouling the propellor wasn't the only thing he'd done. He'd steered the Commander around that submerged sailboat, he'd helped sailors up over the side, he'd hoisted a dog on board. And in a chaotic system, any action, no matter how inconsequential, could affect—

'Sister Carmody!' he shouted, struggling to sit up. 'Sister Carmody!'

'What is it?' Fordham said, alarmed. 'What's wrong?'

'I've got to see a newspaper! Now!'

'I have yesterday's *Herald* here,' Fordham said. 'Will that do?'

'Yes.'

'The problem is how to get it to you. I can't reach far enough to get it over to you, I'm afraid. Can you get out of bed, do you think?'

I have to, Mike thought, but when he tried to sit up, hot and cold and nausea washed over him, and he had to lie back, swallowing hard.

'I could read it to you, if you like,' Fordham offered.

'*Thank* you.'

Fordham patted around on the bed for the newspaper and propped it up against his elevated arm. 'Let's see, a rector in Tunbridge Wells rang his church's bells in violation of the official edict that they're only to be rung to signal invasion—'

That's why I didn't hear the bells that night on the beach, Mike thought.

'—and was fined one pound ten,' Fordham said. 'There's been an overwhelming response to Lord Beaverbrook's Spitfire drive. They've collected five tons of aluminium saucepans alone. Sir Godfrey Kingsman is rehearsing a new production of *King Lear* at—'

'Isn't there anything about the war?'

'The war ... let's see ...' Fordham muttered. 'A barrage balloon broke loose from its moorings and drifted into the spire of St Albans Church and damaged some of the slates.'

'I meant, news about how the war's going.'

'Badly,' he said. 'As usual. The Italians hit one of our bases in Egypt—'

Egypt? Had Britain been in Egypt in August? He didn't know enough about the war in North Africa to know what was supposed to have been happening there then. 'What about the—?' He hesitated. Had they been calling it the Battle of Britain at this point? '—the air war?'

Fordham nodded. 'The Germans attacked one of our convoys yesterday, and the RAF shot down sixteen of their planes. We lost seven.' He turned the page, rattling the sheets. 'Good Lord, the Prime Minister —'

'What about the Prime Minister?' Mike said sharply. Oh God, what if something had happened to Churchill? England could never have won the war without him. If he'd been killed—

'He looks dreadful in this photograph. It's of him rejecting

Germany's latest peace proposal, but he looks like a suet pudding.'

Mike let out the breath he'd been holding. England was still refusing to surrender, the RAF was still holding off the Luftwaffe, and Churchill was all right.

Fordham had finished the news stories and was reading the personal ads: '*Anyone having information regarding the whereabouts of Pvt Derek Huntsford, last seen at Dunkirk, please contact Mr and Mrs J. Huntsford, Chifford, Devon.*' Fordham shook his head. 'He must not have made it back. He wasn't as lucky as you, poor chap.'

Lucky, Mike thought. *But at least he hadn't altered events. And the war was still on track.*

Fordham was reading another ad. '*To let, country home in Kent. Restful location …*'

Restful, Mike thought, and fell asleep.

He jerked awake to the up-and-down wail of sirens. And shouting. One of the patients, in pyjamas and bare feet, was waving a flashlight wildly around the dark ward. 'Wake up!' he shouted, shining the light full in Mike's face. 'They're here!'

'Who's here?' Mike said, trying to shield his eyes from the blinding light.

'The Germans, they've invaded. I only just heard it on the wireless. They're coming up the Thames.'

> *'I do not get panicky. I stay put. I say to myself: Our chaps*
> *will deal with them. I do not say: I must get out of here.'*

INVASION INSTRUCTIONS, 1940

WARWICKSHIRE – AUGUST 1940

The Army gave them till the fifteenth of September to vacate the manor, before which they had to cover all the furniture, crate Lady Caroline's ancestor and the other paintings, pack away the crystal and china, and keep Alf and Binnie from 'helping'. When Eileen went to take down the priceless mediaeval tapestry, she found them tossing it out of the window. 'We was tryin' to see if it was magic,' Binnie said. 'Like that flyin' carpet in the fairy-story you read us.'

They also had to make arrangements for the evacuees still at the manor. Mrs Chambers found new homes for the Potters, the Magruders, Ralph and Tony Gubbins and Georgie Cox. Mrs Chalmers came and took Alice and Rose, and Theodore's mother wrote to say that she would be up on Saturday. Eileen was relieved. She'd been afraid she'd have to send him kicking and screaming on the train again. 'I don't *want* to go home,' Theodore'd said when she told him his mother was coming. 'I want to stay here.'

'You can't stay 'ere, you noddlehead,' Alf said. 'Nobody's stayin' 'ere.'

'Where are *we* goin', Eileen?' Binnie asked.

'That hasn't been arranged yet.'

They'd written to Mrs Hodbin but hadn't had an answer, and no one in Warwickshire would take them. 'I've written to the Evacuation Committee,' the vicar said, 'but they're swamped with billeting requests just now. Everyone's afraid the Germans will begin bombing London soon.'

They will, Eileen thought, *and then there'd be no chance at all of placing Alf and Binnie.* More than a hundred thousand children had been evacuated from London after the Blitz began. They needed to find Alf and Binnie a home immediately.

Lady Caroline had sent Samuels ahead with her trunks to Chadwick House, where she was going to stay with the Duchess of Lynmere, which left Eileen, Una (who was useless) and Mrs Bascombe to finish preparations for the Army's arrival on their own. And no time for Eileen to check the drop or go to Backbury to ask if anyone had been inquiring after her. Or to look for another position.

If she could find one. A number of households were making 'wartime economies', which meant they were cutting back on the number of their servants, and there were no 'Housemaid Wanted's' in the *Backbury Bugler*. Una had announced she was joining the ATS, and Mrs Bascombe was going to Shropshire to help out a niece whose husband had joined up, so Eileen couldn't stay with either of them, and Backbury had no inn, even if she had enough money for one. And even if she did stay, there was no guarantee the drop would open or that a retrieval team would come. It had already been nearly four months.

You're going to have to find another way of getting home, she thought. She needed to go to London, find Polly, and use her drop. *If she's there.*

She wasn't coming till the Blitz. It would begin in September – Eileen didn't know the exact date. *I should have asked Polly*, she thought, but it had never occurred to her she'd still be here when Polly arrived. And the Army didn't take possession of the manor till the middle of September. The Blitz would surely have begun by then.

The idea of being in the midst of the bombing terrified her, but she couldn't think of anyone else she could go to. Michael Davies had been in Dover, but the evacuation of Dunkirk had been months ago. He'd have long since gone back by now. She thought Gerald Phipps was here – she remembered him saying something about August when she'd seen him in the lab – but she didn't know where. He'd told her, but she couldn't remember. It had begun with a D. Or a P.

She didn't know where Polly would be either. She'd said she was going to be working in a department store in Oxford Street and that Mr Dunworthy would only allow her to work in one that hadn't been bombed, and Eileen had a vague memory of her naming them. Which ones had she said? Eileen wished she'd paid more attention, but she'd been worrying about getting her driving authorisation. She remembered one had been a man's name.

She went down to the kitchen to ask Mrs Bascombe if she knew the names of any of Oxford Street's stores. 'You're not thinking of working in one of them places, are you?' Mrs Bascombe said.

'No, I've a cousin who does. I'm going to stay with her.'

'Two girls on their own in London? With all them soldiers about? You've no more business in the big city than Una has in the ATS. I'll tell you what I told her: You stay in service where you belong.'

She'd have to wait till she got to London to find out the name of the store. If she could get there. With the wages she had coming, she had enough for a second-class ticket, but she would need money to tide her over till she found Polly. Since it was the Blitz, she might be able to sleep in a shelter, but she would still need money for meals and bus fare.

But she would have to worry about that later. She had other, more pressing problems. Theodore's mother wrote to say that the aeroplane factory she worked in had gone to double shifts and she couldn't come for Theodore till the Saturday after next. They still hadn't heard from Alf and Binnie's mother, and when she went to the vicarage on the first of September to deliver a message from Lady Caroline, the vicar said, 'I can't find anyone to take them. Their reputation obviously precedes them. We may have to resort to the Overseas Programme. They can't have heard of them in the United States.'

'But wouldn't it be cruel to inflict the Hodbins on another country?'

'You're right. We can't afford to alienate our friends. We'll need all the help we can get before this war is over. You still haven't heard from their mother?'

'No.'

'I'm surprised. I thought she'd be the sort who'd want them back for their extra ration coupons. On the other hand, this is Alf and Binnie. Do let me know if you hear from her. In the meantime, I'll keep looking for someone to take them. You'll be here until the fifteenth, is that right?'

'Yes,' she said, and told him about going to London after that. 'My cousin works in a department store in Oxford Street.'

'Selfridge's?'

'No,' she said, though she seemed to remember Polly mentioning Selfridge's, too. 'It sounded like a man's name.'

'A man's name ...' he said thoughtfully. 'Peter Robinson?'

'No,' but as he said it, she thought, *One of the ones Polly mentioned began with a P.* Not Peter Robinson, but she'd know it if she heard it.

'A. R. Bromley?' the vicar said. 'No, that's in Knightsbridge. Let me see, what's in Oxford Street? Townsend Brothers ... Leighton's ... but I can't think of any ...' He brightened. 'Oh, I know. John Lewis?'

'Yes.' That was definitely it, and she was fairly certain Selfridge's was another. And when she got to Oxford Street she could find the one that began with a P. Polly was bound to be at one of the three, and she could ask her where her drop was, and go home.

If the retrieval team still hadn't shown up by then. It had occurred to her that they might be waiting to pull her out till the fifteenth, when her departure wouldn't be noticed in the bustle of the Army's arrival. But when she got back to the manor, the Army was already there. A staff car and a lorry were parked in the drive, and the next day soldiers began stringing barbed wire along the road and around the wood, making access to and from the drop impossible.

On the seventh, Lady Caroline sent for the vicar. Eileen showed him up to the dustcover-draped sitting room. 'Has Mrs Hodbin written yet, Ellen?' Lady Caroline asked Eileen.

'No, ma'am, but this came in the morning post.' Eileen handed her a letter from Theodore's mother.

'She says she can't come and fetch Theodore after all,' Lady Caroline said, reading it, 'and she wants us to send him home on Monday by train as we did last time.'

Oh no, Eileen thought.

Lady Caroline turned to the vicar. 'Have you found a new billet for the Hodbins, Mr Goode?'

'No, not yet. It may take several weeks to—'

'That's quite impossible,' Lady Caroline said. 'I've promised Captain Chase he can take possession on Monday morning.'

'*This* Monday?' he said, sounding as shocked as Eileen felt.

'Yes, and the Hodbins clearly can't stay here. There'll be no one here to care for them. They'll have to go home till you can find them a new billet. They can go to London with Theodore.'

Alf and Binnie loose on a train, Eileen thought. Visions of toppled luggage, rampaged dining cars and yanked communication cords danced before her eyes.

'No,' the vicar said, obviously imagining the same disasters. 'There'd be no one to meet them.'

'We can telephone Mrs Hodbin and tell her they're coming,' Lady Caroline said. 'Ellen, go and place a trunk call to—'

'They haven't a telephone,' Eileen said.

Lady Caroline looked annoyed.

'Couldn't you take them with you to Chadwick House, Lady Caroline?' the vicar ventured. 'Only until I find a place for them?'

'I couldn't possibly impose on my hosts like that. If you aren't willing to let them go alone, you must accompany them, Vicar.' She frowned. 'Oh dear, that won't work. Monday is the Home Defence meeting in Hereford, and it's essential that you attend. Someone else must accompany them instead, Mrs Chambers or—'

'I'll take them,' Eileen said. 'Begging your pardon, ma'am, but I'd planned to go to my cousin in London when I left here. I could escort the children.' *And with you paying my way, I'll be able to save my money to pay for lodging and food till I find Polly.*

'Excellent,' Lady Caroline said. 'It's the perfect solution, Vicar. Ellen can take them, and the only expense to the Evacuation Committee will be the Hodbins' fares. Theodore's mother has sent his ticket.'

The vicar must have seen the stricken look on Eileen's face, because he said, 'But if she's going as the children's escort, then—'

But Lady Caroline was already saying briskly, 'Go and tell the children to pack their things, Ellen. You can take the train on Monday.'

And you'd better hope the retrieval team doesn't show up before then, Lady Caroline, Eileen thought, going along to the nursery, *or I'll be out of here without so much as a backward glance, and you can take the Hodbins to London yourself.*

She packed the children's bags and her own the next day, said goodbye to Una and Mrs Bascombe, who were leaving on the bus, endured one last lecture on the dangers of talking to soldiers, fed the children their tea, put them to bed and then waited till they were asleep and the house was quiet to sneak out to the drop.

The moon was still up and she only had to use her torch once, to find a way through the barbed wire. The clearing looked enchanted, the ash tree's trunk silver in the moonlight. 'Open,' she murmured, 'please,' and thought she saw the beginnings of the shimmer, but it was only mist, and even though she waited two more hours, it didn't open.

It's just as well, she thought, picking her way back in the grey predawn light, *I couldn't really have abandoned poor Theodore to the Hodbins.*

She ran across the dew-wet lawn, let herself quietly into the kitchen, and started up the back stairs. Binnie was standing barefoot in her nightgown at the top of them. 'What are you doing up?' Eileen whispered.

'I seen you go out. I thought you was trying to sneak off on us.'

'I went out to see if any clothes had been left on the line,' Eileen lied. 'Go back to bed. We've a long train ride in the morning.'

'You *promised* you wouldn't leave us,' Binnie said. 'You *swore.*'

'I'm not leaving you. We're all going to London together. Now go back to bed.'

Binnie did, but when Eileen got up a few short hours later, she nearly fell over her, lying wrapped in a blanket in front of her door. 'Just in case you was lyin',' Binnie said.

Lady Caroline left at eight in the Rolls-Royce the Duchess had sent for her. *Without so much as offering us a lift*, Eileen thought furiously, and her anger helped her get the children dressed and assembled, and off to Backbury. The lane, which for the past week had been packed with military vehicles of all sorts, was utterly deserted. They didn't pass a single lorry on the hour-long, luggage-laden walk into town. Binnie whined that her suitcase was too heavy, Theodore demanded to be carried, and every time an aeroplane went over Alf insisted on stopping and marking it on his planespotter's map. 'I wish the vicar would come along and give us a ride,' Binnie said.

So do I, Eileen thought. 'He's not here,' she said. 'He's in Hereford.' But when they reached Backbury, Eileen took them past the vicarage on the off-chance that he hadn't left yet.

The Austin wasn't there. *I never got to say goodbye to him,* Eileen thought, bereft. Well, she supposed it served her right. After all, she'd been prepared to leave them all without a backward glance how many times? Including last night.

And you're only a servant, she told herself, hurrying the children through the village. It was nearly 11:41. She hustled them out to the station.

Mr Tooley came running out. *Oh dear, they hadn't missed it, had they?* 'I warned you ruffians not to come round here again—'

'They're with me, Mr Tooley,' Eileen said quickly. 'We're leaving for London on today's train.'

'Leaving? For good?'

She nodded.

'Them, too?'

'Yes. The train hasn't come yet, has it?'

Mr Tooley shook his head. 'I doubt it will today, what with the big bombing raids on London last night.'

Good, the Blitz had begun. Polly'd be there. 'What sort of bombers were they?' Alf asked eagerly. 'Heinkels? Junkers 88s?'

Mr Tooley glowered at him. 'You put any more logs across those tracks and I'll beat you to within an inch of your life,' he said, stormed back into the station, and slammed the door.

'Logs across the tracks?' Eileen said.

'It was a barricade,' Alf said. 'For when 'Itler invades. We was just practising.'

'We was goin' to move 'em afore the train came,' Binnie said.

One more day, Eileen thought. 'Sit down, all of you,' she said. She upended Alf and Binnie's suitcase and sat them down on it to wait for the train. *And please let it come soon.*

'I see it,' Alf said, pointing above the trees.

'I don't see nothin',' Binnie said, 'you're fibbing,' but when Eileen looked where he was pointing, she could see a faint blur of smoke above the trees. The train was definitely coming. It was a miracle.

'All right, gather up your things,' she said. 'Alf, fold up your map. Theodore, put your jacket on. Binnie—'

'Look!' Alf said excitedly, jumped off the platform, and ran towards the road with Binnie at his heels.

'Where are you—?' Eileen said, glancing anxiously up the tracks. 'Come back here! The train—'

It was approaching rapidly. She could see it emerging from the trees. 'Theodore, stay right here. *Don't* move,' she ordered him and took off for the platform steps. If those two made them miss the train …

'Alf, Binnie! Stop!' she shouted, but they weren't listening. They were running towards the Austin, which roared past them and skidded to a stop at the foot of the platform stairs.

The vicar leaped out and ran up the steps, carrying a basket. 'I'm so glad I caught you,' he said breathlessly. 'I was afraid you'd gone.'

'I thought you were in Hereford.'

'I was. I got stopped on the way home by a wretched troop convoy or I'd have been here earlier. I'm so sorry you had to walk all that way with the luggage.'

'It's all right,' she said, feeling suddenly that it was.

'I thought you said drivin' fast was only for emergencies,' Binnie said, bounding up onto the platform.

'You was going an 'undred miles an hour,' Alf said.

'Did you come to say goodbye to us?' Theodore asked.

'Yes,' he said to Eileen, 'and to bring you—' He stopped and glared at the train, which was nearly at the station. 'Don't tell me the train is actually on time. It hasn't been on time once since the war started, and now today of all days … At any rate, I brought you some sandwiches and biscuits.' He gave her the basket. 'And … Alf, Binnie, go and fetch the luggage,' and when they did, he said quietly, 'I rang the Children's Overseas Reception Board.' He handed her an envelope. 'I've arranged passage for Alf and Binnie on a ship to Canada.'

To Canada? That's where the *City of Benares* had been going when it was sunk by a U-boat. Most of the evacuees on board had drowned. 'Which ship?' Eileen asked.

'I don't know. Their mother's to take them to the Evacuation Committee's office – the address is in the letter – and they'll take them to Portsmouth.'

The *City of Benares* had sailed from Portsmouth.

'And this is for you as well.' He handed her an envelope with several ten-shilling notes inside. 'To cover your train fare and the children's expenses.'

'Oh, but I can't—'

'It's from the Evacuation Committee.'

You're lying, she thought. *It came out of your own pocket.*

'It isn't fair to ask you to pay your own way when you're doing the committee's job,' he said. He glanced over at Alf and Binnie. 'I'm certain you'll earn every penny.'

'The train's 'ere,' Alf said, and they both looked over at it.

It came to a whooshing stop.

'Thank you,' Eileen said, handing the envelope back to him, 'but I don't want you to have to—'

'Please,' he said earnestly. 'I know what a worrying time this has been for you, and I thought … I mean, the committee thought that at least you shouldn't have to worry about money. Please take it.'

She nodded, blinking back tears. 'Thank you. I mean, please convey my thanks to the committee. For everything.'

'I will.' He looked at her searchingly. 'Are you all right?'

No, she thought, *I'm a hundred and twenty years away from home, my drop's broken, and I have no idea what I'm going to do if I can't find Polly.*

'Whatever it is, you can tell me,' the vicar said. 'Perhaps I can help.'

I wish I could tell you, she thought.

'Come *along*,' Alf said, yanking on her sleeve. 'We gotta get on.'

She nodded. 'Children, gather up your things. Here, Binnie, take Theodore's duffel for him. Alf, take your—'

'I have them,' the vicar said, picking up the bags. With his help, she got them and Alf and Binnie up the steps onto the train. This one wasn't crammed with troops, thank goodness.

'Now you, Theodore,' she said.

Theodore balked. 'I don't want—'

Oh no, not again, Eileen thought, but the vicar was already saying, 'Theodore, will you show Eileen what to do? She's never been to London on the train before.'

'*I* have,' Theodore said.

'I know, so you must take good care of her.'

Theodore nodded. 'You go up the steps,' he instructed Eileen, demonstrating. 'Then you sit down—'

'You're a miracle worker,' Eileen said gratefully.

'Part of my job,' he said, smiling, and then soberly, 'London's extremely dangerous just now. Do take care.'

'I will. I'm sorry I won't be here to drive the ambulance after all your lessons.'

'It's all right. My housekeeper's agreed to fill in. Unfortunately, she shows the same aptitude as Una, but—'

'Come *along*,' Alf called from the top of the steps. 'You're makin' the train late!'

'I must go,' she said, starting up the steps.

'Wait,' he said, catching hold of her arm. 'You mustn't worry. It will all—'

'Come *on*!' Alf shouted, dragging her aboard. The huge wheels began to turn. 'I get to sit by the window—'

'Goodbye, Vicar!' Theodore shouted, waving.

'You do not get to,' Binnie said. 'Alf says 'e gets to sit by the window, but I want—'

'Shh,' Eileen said, leaning out. The train began to move. 'What?' she called back to the vicar.

'I *said*,' the vicar shouted, cupping his hands to his mouth, 'it will all come right in the end.' The train picked up speed, leaving him behind on the platform, still waving.

'And if we no more meet till we meet in heaven, then joyfully,
my noble lords and my kind kinsmen, warriors all, adieu! '

WILLIAM SHAKESPEARE, *HENRY V*

LONDON – 21 SEPTEMBER 1940

'Open the drop!' Polly cried, in her panic hammering on the peeling, nailed-shut door with both fists. 'Colin! Hurry!'

The scream of the bomb rose to a painful shriek. Polly clapped her hands over her ears. *Oh God, it's right on top of me*, she thought. *It's a direct hit*, and dropped to her knees, her head ducked against the eardrum-shattering sound, the expected blast.

But there wasn't any blast, only a deafening, bone-shaking *boom*, followed by the rattle of things falling and then fire-engine bells. They stopped nearly a quarter of a mile away.

Impossible, she thought, *that was on top of me*. So was the next one, and the next one, and even though she told herself, murmuring it like a prayer, that the drop hadn't been hit during the Blitz, it was impossible not to put her arms over her head when the bombs' descending screams began, and cower, terrified, against the foot of the door.

'Colin!' she sobbed. 'Hurry!'

After what seemed like an eternity but was only, according to the glowing dial of her watch, an hour and a half, the bombardment began to subside. Polly waited till the Kensington Gardens gun had stopped and then crept cautiously down the passage, almost afraid to look at what was left of it.

But the only sign of new damage was to the last two barrels at the alley end of the passage, which had toppled over. She pushed them out of the way and climbed a short way up onto the mound to look across the road. An incendiary had fallen in the middle of it and was sputtering and fizzing like an oversized child's sparkler, and in its light she could see the still-intact tobacconist's and could read 'T. Tubbins' above the door of the still-there greengrocer's. None of the shops was on fire. She couldn't even smell any smoke. The shops' unharmed roofs stood out sharply against the crimson sky, and she couldn't see any firespotters on top of them, and none on the warehouses on either side of the drop. But the drop still didn't open.

Perhaps the problem's the Luftwaffe, Polly thought, looking up at the narrow space between the buildings. *They can see the shimmer from up there and use it as a target.*

But the idea that bomber pilots could see a tiny light on the ground – a cigarette or a chink in the blackout curtains – had been proven to be a myth. Neither could be seen at all from ten thousand feet up. Which meant the shimmer wouldn't be visible either. And besides, the entire east and north of London were on fire, and the passage was nearly as bright as day. And half an hour later, when the planes were no longer overhead, the drop still showed no sign of opening.

An hour went by, then two. The raid intensified again and then let up, and the orange clouds faded to a sickly pink. The anti-aircraft guns stuttered to a stop. There was a long hush, broken only by the drone of a departing plane. It faded to a hum and then silence, and for several minutes Polly half expected to hear the all-clear. Then the whole thing started up again.

It stopped for good at three, exactly when Colin had said it would. But he, or the historical record, had got their location wrong. Those bombs had definitely fallen on Kensington, not

Marylebone. And not just in Kensington, but on Lampden Road.

Silence settled down over the site, but the drop still didn't open. By the time the all-clear went at half past five, Polly had had time to consider every possible and far-fetched reason for the drop's remaining shut, and discarded them all.

Except the obvious one. The drop had been damaged. In spite of the undisturbed barrels and the cobwebs, the blast that had flattened the row of buildings across the alley must have disrupted the drop's field somehow, destroyed the temporal connection. And there was no point continuing to sit here in the damp cold waiting for it to open. As soon as Badri – and Mr Dunworthy – realised what had happened, they'd set up a drop somewhere else and send a retrieval team for her.

If they can find me, she thought. *I should have checked in as soon as I found a room. Then they'd know where I live.*

But they had the list of approved streets and addresses, and this was time travel. They were no doubt already waiting for her at Mrs Rickett's.

I do hope she lets them in. She's so adamant about my not having male visitors. She hoped the team hadn't come through posing as soldiers, of whom Mrs Rickett had a very low opinion. Or as actors.

She stood up, stiff with cold and with sitting too long, and went down the passage. If she hurried, she might be able to reach the boarding house before Mrs Rickett got home from St George's and intercept the retrieval team. The fog, which had lifted during the raids, was closing in again, making it as dark as it had been that first evening when she came through, and shrouding the entrance and the rubble beyond. Polly worked her way as quickly as she could over the tangle of beams and bricks. She sank in almost to her knees once and had to grab for jutting timbers several times before she reached the edge.

She stepped down onto the pavement, and stopped to brush off her coat and see how bad her stockings were. Bad. She had wide ladders in both and a hole in the left one. Her knee was bleeding, and her skirt was a disaster. *My non-regulation navy blue skirt I promised Miss Snelgrove I wouldn't be wearing today*, she thought, and then remembered it didn't matter. She was going back to Oxford.

What time was it? She glanced at her wristwatch. The face was caked with pinkish dust. She wiped it clean with her finger. Ten past six. Oh dear, Mrs Rickett would be home from St George's by now and telling the retrieval team Polly wasn't there and that she had no idea where she was. If she hadn't simply slammed the door in their faces.

Polly ducked under the rope barrier and hurried down Lampden Road through the fog, hoping they were still at Mrs Rickett's, that she hadn't just missed them—

She halted, her mouth open, staring at the devastation before her. She'd been right: the raids hadn't been in Bloomsbury. They'd been here on Lampden Road. As far as she could see through the fog, everything had been flattened. She'd thought the shops in front of the drop had been destroyed, but it was nothing compared to this. Both sides of the road had been obliterated so completely she couldn't even guess what had originally stood here. Incident rope had been strung up across the debris-strewn road and along it as far as the fog let her see. It looked like a V-2 had hit it, but that wasn't poss—

'Dreadful, isn't it?' a voice behind her said. It was an elderly man in a wool cap, obviously on his way home from a shelter. He had a fringed pink silk cushion tucked under one arm and a large paper sack under the other. 'Parachute mine.'

A mine. That was why it had done so much damage. High-explosive bombs burrowed into the ground before going off, but mines exploded on the surface so that the full force of the blast hit the surrounding buildings.

'It must've been a thousand-pounder to take out all those shops,' the old man said, pointing back towards the rubble in front of the drop. 'And the church and—'

'The church?' She looked down the road, searching frantically for St George's spire. She couldn't see it. 'Which church? St George's?'

He nodded. 'Dreadful business,' he said, surveying the street. 'So many killed—'

Polly plunged past him. The incident rope caught at her legs and snapped, but she ran on, unheeding. The rope tangled in her legs and trailed out behind her as she raced down the debris-strewn road to the wreckage of the church.

No, not wreckage. There were no roof slates here, no rafters or pillars or pews to show it had ever been a church, only a flat expanse of pulverised bricks and glass. Except for the mangled metal railing of the steps which had led down to the basement shelter and which no one, no one could have got out of alive.

'So many killed,' the old man had said. Oh God, the rector and Miss Laburnum and Mrs Brightford. And her little girls.

This happened last night when I was in the drop, she thought. *I heard it hit.* They'd all have been there in the shelter. *And if I hadn't been in the drop, I'd have been there, too,* she thought sickly, and remembered her plan to hide in the sanctuary till everyone was off the streets. *I'd have been in that with them,* she thought, staring at the rubble. With Lila and Viv and Mr Simms. And Nelson.

And Sir Godfrey. They were all under there. 'We must get them out of there,' Polly said. She started towards the railing, thinking, *Why isn't the rescue squad here?* but even as she formed the thought, her mind was processing the fact that there wasn't any dust or smoke hovering above the wreckage, only the drifting fog, and that she'd looked for and hadn't seen the spire last night, was processing the already-strung rope and the depression in the centre of the mound that had to be a shaft dug by the rescue squad. And the old man, who knew the church had been hit, who knew the people in it had been killed.

He came trotting up, clutching his fringed cushion and his

paper sack. 'Hard to take in, isn't it, miss?' he said, coming over to stand beside her. 'Such a beautiful church—'

'When did this happen?' Polly demanded, but she already knew the answer. Not last night. Two nights ago. The rescue squad had already been here, had already dug out the bodies and taken them away in mortuary vans.

'Night before last,' the old man was saying, 'not more'n an hour after the sirens went.'

They were already dead when I was in the alley worrying about running into them on their way to the shelter, Polly thought bleakly. *And the whole time I was trapped in Holborn. St George's and the shops in front of the drop were hit the same night.* The back of her knees went suddenly weak, as if she had ventured too near the edge of a cliff.

'Least that's what the warden said yesterday morning,' the old man was saying. 'It didn't ... here, now, are you all right, miss?'

She stared blindly at him. The drop wasn't hit last night. It was the night before last. But it can't have been. If it was, then the—

Her knees buckled. The old man caught her, dropping his cushion and the paper sack onto the pavement as he did. 'Why don't you sit down here on the kerb for a moment,' he said, holding her up. 'Till you're feeling better, and then I'll take you home. Where is it you live, miss?'

He meant the boarding house. But Mrs Rickett and Miss Hibbard and Mr Dorming and Miss Laburnum were all dead. There was no one there to tell the retrieval team she lived there. And there'd been no one there yesterday, when—

'I must go to Townsend Brothers,' Polly said.

'That's not a good idea, miss,' the old man said. 'You've had a bad shock. The ARP post's just down the way. I'll be back in no time.'

In no time. *They're all dead,* she thought, *and they can't tell them where I am. They can't come and get me—*

'Oh dear,' the old man said, catching her and easing her down onto the edge of the kerb. 'Are you certain you aren't injured?' and when she didn't answer, 'You sit there, and I'll fetch the warden. He'll know what to do.' He tucked the fringed cushion against the small of her back, trotted off down the street, and disappeared into the fog.

Polly got to her feet and stumbled blindly off up the street. She had to get away before he came back with the warden. She had to get to Bayswater Road and find a taxi. And get to Townsend Brothers.

But no taxis were abroad, and no buses either. *Because of the fog,* she thought, but that wasn't the reason. There was a bus in the centre of the road half tipped into a large crater. It was empty. *I wonder what happened to the passengers,* Polly thought, but she knew. They were all dead. They'd been dead since yesterday, like Miss Laburnum and Trot and Sir Godfrey. Since yesterday.

Don't think about that, she told herself, willing her wobbly legs to walk past it, to walk up the foggy road. *Don't think about any of it. Find a taxi.*

She finally did, after what seemed like years of walking and wreckage and craters and fog. 'Townsend Brothers,' she told the cabbie as she opened the door. 'On Oxford Street.'

'Townsend Brothers?' he said, looking oddly at her.

She'd forgotten shopgirls didn't take taxis. But she had to. 'Yes,' she said. 'Take me there immediately.'

'But you're already there,' he said.

'Already—?' she said, looking bewilderedly where he was pointing, and there was Townsend Brothers. She looked at the boarded-up display windows, at the doors. And at the empty pavement in front of them.

The retrieval team wasn't there. She'd been so certain they would be, so certain that when they couldn't find out where she lived, they'd go to Oxford Street. *They've been delayed, that's all,* she told herself. *They couldn't find a taxi either. Or they thought there wasn't any point in coming till I arrived for work. They'll be here at nine.* She looked at her watch, but she couldn't make the hands mean anything. 'What time is it?' she asked the cabbie.

'Twenty past nine,' he said, pointing up the street at Selfridge's clock. 'You all right, miss?'

No. 'Yes,' she said, and realised she was still holding on to the open passenger door. She shut it and started towards the store.

They've already gone inside, she told herself, going in the staff entrance and up the stairs. *They're waiting for me in my department.* But they couldn't be. The store wasn't open yet, and when she reached third and opened the stairway door, there was no one over by her counter.

They're not here, she thought, and the sick dread she'd been trying to hold at bay since she saw the wrecked church, trying to keep from herself, washed over her in a drowning wave.

The drop had been damaged by the same parachute mine that destroyed St George's and killed— Oh God, Sir Godfrey and Trot and all the rest of them. They'd been killed and the shops flattened and the drop damaged all at the same time—the night before last, while she was in Holborn, standing in line at the canteen, talking to the librarian, sitting in the tunnel reading the newspaper. No, earlier than that. 'Not more'n an hour after the sirens went,' the old man had said. While she was trying to convince the guard to open the gate so she could go to the drop—

But it had already been out of commission. Already out of commission when she came to work yesterday morning. The retrieval team should have been here yesterday. They should have been waiting for her outside Townsend Brothers yesterday morning, not today. Yesterday.

'Polly!' she heard Marjorie say, but when she looked up, it was Miss Snelgrove, the floor supervisor, who was walking towards her. She looked appalled.

She's going to discharge me, Polly thought, *because I didn't get a black skirt.*

'Miss Sebastian,' Miss Snelgrove said. 'What—?'

'I couldn't get my skirt. I tried, but it wouldn't open—'

'You mustn't worry about that now,' Miss Snelgrove said, taking her arm as the old man had.

'And it's nearly half past nine.'

'You mustn't worry about that either. Miss Hayes,' Miss Snelgrove said to Marjorie, who'd come over. 'Go and tell Mr Witherill to telephone for a taxi,' but Marjorie didn't go.

'What happened, Polly?' she asked.

'They're not here,' Polly said. 'They're all dead.' She started blindly over to her counter.

Miss Snelgrove stopped her and steered her gently back towards the lifts. 'We'll find someone to fill in for you today,' she said, patting Polly kindly on the shoulder. 'You need to go home.'

Polly looked at her bleakly. 'You don't understand,' she said. 'I can't.'

It sounds perhaps callous – I don't know – but it
was enormously exciting and tremendous fun.

FLYING OFFICER BRIAN KINGCOME,
ON THE BATTLE OF BRITAIN, 1940

EN ROUTE TO LONDON – 9 SEPTEMBER 1940

The train wasn't quite as jammed as the one Eileen had sent Theodore home on in December, but every compartment was filled, and she had to wrestle the children and their luggage through three cars before they found space in a compartment with a portly businessman, two young women, and three soldiers. Eileen had to hold Theodore on her lap and sit across from Alf and Binnie. 'You two behave,' she told them.

'We will,' Alf promised and promptly began tugging on the sleeve of the stout man who had the window seat. 'I got to sit by the window so I can look for planes,' he said, but the man went on reading his newspaper, which read, 'German "Blitz" Tests London's Resolve.'

'I'm an official planespotter,' Alf said, and when the man still refused to move, Binnie bent towards Alf and whispered loudly, 'Don't talk to 'im. I'll wager 'e's a fifth columnist.'

The soldiers looked up.

'What's a fifth columnist?' Theodore asked.

'Here,' Eileen said, taking a packet from the basket the vicar had given them and handing it across to Alf and Binnie. 'Have a biscuit.'

'A fifth columnist's a traitor,' Binnie said, staring hard at the man.

He rattled his newspaper irritably.

'They look just like me 'n' you,' Alf said. 'They pretend to be readin' the papers, but they're really spyin' on people and then tellin' 'Itler.'

The two young women began whispering to each other. Eileen caught the word 'spy', and so, apparently, did the man, because he lowered his paper to glare at them and then at Alf, who was munching on a biscuit, and then retreat behind his newspaper again.

'You can tell fifth columnists by the way they hate children,' Binnie told Theodore. 'That's 'cause children are 'specially good at spottin' them.'

Alf nodded. ''E looks exactly like Göring, don't 'e?'

'This is intolerable!' the man exclaimed. He flung his newspaper down on the seat, stood up, yanked his valise down from the overhead rack, and stormed out. Binnie immediately moved into the now-vacant window seat, and Eileen expected an explosion from Alf, but he continued calmly munching his biscuit.

'You better not eat that,' Binnie said. 'You'll be sick.'

The soldier and the young women looked up alertly.

Alf dug another biscuit out of the packet and bit into it. 'I will not.'

'You will *so*. He's allus sick on trains,' she said to the soldiers. ''E threw up all over Eileen's shoes, didn't 'e, Eileen?'

'Binnie—' Eileen began, but Alf shouted over her, 'That was when I 'ad the measles. It don't count.'

'Measles?' one of the soldiers said nervously. 'They're not contagious, are they?'

'No,' Eileen said, 'and Alf isn't going to—'

'I don't feel well,' Alf said, clutching his middle. He made a gagging sound and bent over a cupped hand.

'I *told* you,' Binnie said triumphantly, and within moments the compartment had emptied and Alf had scooted over to the other window. 'Can I have a sandwich, Eileen?' he asked.

'I thought you got sick on trains,' Eileen said, moving Theodore off her lap and onto the seat beside her.

'I *do*, 'specially when I ain't 'ad nothin' to eat.'

'You just had two biscuits.'

'No, 'e ain't,' Binnie said. ''E 'ad six,' and the compartment door opened.

An elderly woman leaned in. 'Oh, good, there's room in here, Lydia,' she said, and she and two other elderly ladies came in. 'Little boy,' one of them said to Alf, 'you don't mind sitting next to your sister, do you? There's a good boy.'

'No, of course he doesn't mind,' Eileen said quickly. 'Alf, come sit here next to me.' She pulled Theodore onto her lap again.

'But what about my planespottin'?' Alf protested.

'You can look out of Binnie's window. And don't you dare pretend to be sick again,' she whispered. 'And *no* fifth columnists, or you shan't have any lunch.'

Alf looked as if he was going to object and then reached into his pocket and said to the ladies, 'Want to see my pet mouse?'

'Mouse?' one of them squeaked, and all three shrank back against the upholstered seat.

'Alf—' Eileen said warningly.

'I told 'im not to bring it,' Binnie said virtuously, and Alf took his fisted hand from his pocket. A long pink tail dangled from it. ''Is name's 'Arry,' he said, holding his fist out to the ladies.

Two of them shrieked, and all three scooped up their things and fled. 'Alf—' Eileen said.

'All you said was no being sick and no fifth columnists,' he said, sticking his fist back in his pocket. 'You never said nuthin' about mice.' He shut the compartment door, sat down by the window and pressed his nose to the glass. 'Look, there's a Wellington!'

'Alf, give me that mouse this instant.'

'But I gotta mark down where I seen the Wellington.' He pulled out the map the vicar'd given him and began to unfold it.

Eileen snatched the map away from him. 'Not till you give me that mouse.' She held out her hand.

'All right,' Alf said grudgingly, bringing it out of his pocket. 'It's only a bit of string.' He held a faded pink cord out in his open palm.

It looked oddly familiar.

'Where did you get this?'

'That carpet of Lady Caroline's,' Binnie said.

'It fell off,' Alf said.

Lady Caroline's priceless mediaeval tapestry. And when she finds out ...

But by then Eileen would be long gone, Lady Caroline would blame it on the Army, and Alf and Binnie would have been long since hanged for some other crime, so she settled for an admonition against frightening people and gave the three of them the sandwiches and bottles of lemonade in the basket, which they were happily drinking when a woman with iron-grey hair and a no-nonsense air opened the door.

'No,' Eileen said to Alf and Binnie.

The woman sat down across from Eileen, both hands on the handbag on her lap. 'You should not allow your children to have lemonade,' she said sternly. 'Or sweets of any kind.'

'Would you like to see my mouse?' Alf asked.

The woman turned a gimlet eye on him. 'Children should be seen and not heard.'

'It's to feed my snake with.' He showed her the dangling tapestry cord.

She looked coldly at it. 'I have been a headmistress for thirty years,' she said, taking hold of the cord and pulling it from his fist. 'Far too long to be fooled by schoolboy tricks regarding imaginary mice.' She handed the cord to Eileen. '*And* imaginary snakes. You need to be firmer with your children.'

'She isn't my mother,' Theodore piped up, and the head-mistress turned the gimlet eye on him. He shrank back against Eileen.

'They're evacuees,' Eileen said, putting her arm around him.

'All the more reason for you to use a strong hand with them.'

Alf put his hand on his stomach. 'I don't feel well, Eileen.'

'Alf allus gets sick on trains,' Binnie said.

'I shouldn't wonder,' the headmistress said to Eileen. 'This is what comes of giving them lemonade. A dose of castor oil will cure them.'

Alf promptly removed his hand from his stomach, and he and Binnie both scooted over to the corner.

'It's clear all three of your charges have been pampered and indulged far too much,' she said, glaring at Theodore.

Theodore. Who's had a luggage tag pinned to his coat and been handed over to strangers and shipped off to a strange place how many times?

'Coddling is not what children need,' the headmistress said. She turned to glower momentarily at Alf and Binnie, who were whispering in the corner. 'They need discipline and a firm hand, particularly during times like these.'

I'd have thought they needed more 'coddling' during a war, Eileen thought, *not less.*

'Being nice to children only makes them dependent and weak,' which weren't exactly the words Eileen would have used to describe Alf and Binnie. 'Spare the rod and spoil the child.'

'You mean *beating*?' Theodore asked tremulously, burrowing into Eileen's side.

'When necessary,' the headmistress said, looking over at Alf and Binnie with an expression that clearly indicated she thought it was necessary now.

Alf had stepped up on the seat to reach the luggage rack and Binnie was standing below to catch him. 'Alf, sit down,' Eileen said.

'I'm lookin' for my planespotter log,' he said, 'so I can write down the planes I seen.'

'Children should not be allowed to talk back to their elders,' the headmistress said. 'Or to clamber about like monkeys. You there,' she shouted to them, 'sit down at once,' and, amazingly, they both obeyed her. They sat down next to her, their hands folded on their laps.

'You see?' she said. 'Firmness is all that is required. These modern notions of allowing children to do whatever they – yowp!' She shot to her feet, flung her handbag at Eileen, and brushed madly at her lap as if it had caught fire.

'Alf, what did you do?' Eileen said, but he and Binnie were already on their knees scrabbling to retrieve something off the floor. Alf jammed it in his pocket.

'Nuthin',' he said, standing up and holding out his empty hands.

'We was just sittin' there,' Binnie said innocently.

'Horrid children,' the headmistress said furiously and wheeled on Eileen. 'You are obviously unfit to have children in your care.' She snatched her handbag out of Eileen's hands. 'I intend to report you to the Evacuation Committee. *And* the conductor.' She snatched up her suitcase and her parcels and turned on Alf and Binnie. 'I predict you two will come to a bad end.' She swept out of the compartment.

'I only wanted to show her it wasn't 'maginary,' Alf said, pulling a green garden snake out of his pocket.

'And it served 'er right,' Binnie added darkly.

Yes, it did, Eileen thought, but she said, 'You had no business bringing a snake on the train.'

'I couldn't leave 'im all alone at the manor,' Alf said. ''E might've got shot. 'Is name's Bill,' he added fondly.

'Will we be thrown off the train?' Theodore asked fearfully, and as if in answer, the train began to slow. Alf and Binnie dived for the window.

'It's awright,' Binnie said, 'we're comin' into a station.' But at the end of ten minutes, the train hadn't started up again, and when Eileen went out in the corridor (after warning the children not to *move* while she was gone) she saw the headmistress out on the platform shaking her finger at the stationmaster, who was looking anxiously at his pocket watch.

Eileen retreated hastily back inside the compartment. 'Alf, you must get rid of that snake this minute.'

'Get rid of Bill?' Alf said, appalled.

'Yes.'

''Ow?'

'I don't care,' she began to say, then had a horrible image of it slithering down the corridor. 'Put it out of the window.'

'Out the *window*? 'E'll be run over!' and Theodore began to cry.

One more day, Eileen thought, *and I will never have to see these children again.*

The train was beginning to move. The stationmaster must have persuaded the headmistress to allow them to stay on board. Or perhaps she'd stormed off to take a later train. 'You can't throw Bill out now we're movin',' Binnie said. 'It'd kill 'im for sure.'

'It ain't Bill's fault 'e's 'ere,' Alf argued. 'You wouldn't like it if you was somewhere you wasn't s'posed to be and somebody tried to kill you.'

Which is exactly the situation I'll be in when I reach London, Eileen thought. 'Very well,' she said, 'but you must put him out the next time we stop. And till then, he stays in your haversack. If you take him out, it's out of the window.'

Alf nodded, climbed on the seat, stowed the snake away, and jumped down. 'Can I 'ave some chocolate?'

'No,' Eileen said, looking anxiously at the door, but when the guard appeared, it was only to punch their tickets, and there were no other intrusions, not even when the train stopped at Reading and passengers swarmed aboard.

Word must have spread, she thought, wondering how long

it would take the Hodbins to become notorious throughout London. A week.

But in the meantime, Theodore could sit beside her instead of on her lap, and she didn't have to listen to the headmistress's lectures, so when the train butcher came through, she relented and bought them apples.

She should have known better. They immediately demanded sandwiches, followed by boiled sweets and sausage rolls. *I'll be bankrupt before we reach London*, she thought, *and let's hope Alf doesn't really get sick on trains*, but he was busy marking Xes on his map and pointing out nonexistent planes to Theodore.

'Look, there's a Messerschmitt! ME's have got five-hundred-pound bombs on 'em. They can blow up a whole train. If they dropped one on you, they wouldn't be able to find your body or nuthin'. *Ka-bloom!* You'd disappear, just like that.'

The two of them pressed their noses to the window to search for more planes. Binnie was engrossed in a film magazine one of the young women must have left behind. Eileen picked up the stout man's newspaper to see if there was an ad for John Lewis or Selfridge's which would give their addresses.

Both stores were open till six. Good. With luck, she'd be able to deliver the children and make it to both before they closed. But what if Polly didn't work at either department store? Eileen scanned the ads, looking for the other name Polly'd mentioned. Dickins and Jones? No. Parker and Co.? No, but she was more convinced than ever the name had begun with a P. Was it P. D. White's?

No, here it was. Padgett's. *I knew I'd remember it when I saw it.* Padgett's was open till six, too, and from the addresses, it looked as if they were only a few streets apart. With luck, she could check all three before closing. She hoped there wasn't a raid tonight. Or if there was, that it wasn't over Oxford Street. The idea of being in an air raid was terrifying. *I should have researched the Blitz so I'd know where and when they were*, she thought. But it had never occurred to her that she would need to know those things.

Polly had said the Underground stations had been used as shelters. She could go there if there was a raid. But not all of them were safe – she remembered Colin giving Polly a list of the ones which had been hit, but she couldn't remember which ones he'd said.

Once I find Polly, I'll be all right, Eileen thought. *She knows everything about the Blitz.* Thank goodness she knew what name Polly was using and could ask for Miss Sebastian instead of—

'Polly,' Binnie said.

'What?' Eileen asked sharply, thinking for an awful moment that she'd spoken her thoughts aloud.

'What about *Polly*? For my *name*. Polly 'Odbin. Or Molly. Or Vronica.' She shoved the magazine at Eileen and pointed at a photo of Veronica Lake. 'Do I look like a Vronica?'

'You look like a toad,' Alf said.

'I do not,' Binnie said and whacked him with the magazine. 'Take it back.'

'I won't!' Alf shouted, shielding his head with his arms. 'Toad 'Odbin! Toad 'Odbin!'

One more day, Eileen thought, separating them. *I'll never make it.* 'Alf, do your planespotting,' she ordered. 'Binnie, read your magazine. Theodore, come here and I'll tell you a story. Once upon a time there was a princess. A wicked witch locked her in a tiny room with two evil monsters—'

'Look,' Alf said, 'a barrage balloon!'

'Where?' Theodore asked.

'There.' Alf pointed out the window. 'That big silver thing. They use 'em to keep the jerries from dive-bombing.'

That meant they must be nearing London, but when Eileen looked out of the window, they were still in the country, and she couldn't see anything that remotely resembled a barrage balloon.

'You seen a cloud,' Binnie said, but the only clouds were faint, feathery lines crisscrossing the expanse of vivid blue. Looking out at the sky and the passing fields and trees and quaint villages, with their stone churches and thatched cottages, it was difficult to imagine they were in the middle of a war.

Or that they would ever get to London. The afternoon wore on. Alf marked nonexistent Stukas and Bristol Blenheims on his map, Binnie murmured, 'Claudette ... Olivia ... Katharine 'Epburn 'Odbin,' and Theodore fell asleep. Eileen went back to reading the paper. On page four, there was an ad encouraging parents to enroll their children in the Overseas Programme. 'Have the comfort of knowing they're safe,' it read.

Unless they're on the *City of Benares*, she thought, looking worriedly at Alf and Binnie. Today was the ninth. If Mrs Hodbin took them to the office tomorrow and they left for Portsmouth on Wednesday, they might very well end up on the *City of Benares*. It had sailed on the thirteenth and been sunk four days later.

'I'm hot,' Binnie said, fanning herself with her magazine. It was hot. The afternoon sun was streaming in, but pulling down the shade wasn't an option. It had been designed for the blackout and shut out all light. And it would deprive Alf of his planespotting, and he'd think up some other mischief.

'I'll open the window,' Alf said and jumped up on the plush seat. There was a sudden jerk, a whoosh of releasing steam, and the train began to slow sharply.

'What did you do?' Eileen said.

'Nuthin'.'

'I'll wager he pulled the communication cord,' Binnie said.

'I never,' Alf said hotly.

'Then why's the train stoppin'?' she asked.

'Did you let Bill out?' Eileen demanded.

'No.' He rummaged in his haversack and held up the wriggling snake. 'See?' He shoved it back in and jumped down. 'I'll wager we're comin' to a station.'

He darted for the door. 'I'll go and see.'

'No, you will not,' Eileen said, grabbing him. 'You three stay here. Binnie, watch Theodore. I'll go and see.' But no station was visible in either direction from the corridor, only a meadow with a stream meandering through it. Several people had come out into the corridor, including the headmistress. Oh dear, she was still on the train.

'Do you know what's happening?' one of the passengers asked.

The headmistress turned and glared directly at Eileen. 'I suspect someone pulled the communication cord.'

Oh God, Eileen thought, ducking back into the compartment. *They'll put us off the train in the middle of nowhere.* She shut the door and stood there with her back to it.

'Well?' Binnie demanded. 'Are we at a station?'

'No.'

'Why'd we stop, then?'

'I'll wager it's an air raid,' Alf said, 'and the jerries are goin' to start droppin' bombs on us any minute.'

'We've probably stopped to let a troop train pass,' Eileen said, 'and we'll start again in just a bit.' But they didn't.

The minutes wore on, the compartment grew hotter, and the number of passengers milling about in the corridor increased. Eileen tried to distract the children with a game of I Spy.

'I'll wager there's a spy on the train and that's why we've stopped,' Alf said. 'I *knew* that man who wouldn't let me sit by the window was a fifth columnist. 'E's goin' to blow up the train.'

'I don't *want*—' Theodore began.

'There is *not* a bomb on the train,' Eileen said, and the guard came in, looking grim.

'Sorry to inconvenience you, madam,' he said, 'but I'm afraid we must evacuate the train. You need to collect your things and leave the train.'

'Evacuate?'

'I *told* you,' Alf said. 'There's a bomb, ain't there?'

The guard ignored him. 'What was your destination, madam?'

'London,' Eileen said. 'But—?'

'You'll be taken by bus the rest of the way,' he said and left before they could ask any more questions.

'Gather up your things,' Eileen said. 'Alf, fold up your map. Binnie, hand me my book. Theodore, put on your coat.'

'I don't *want* to blow up,' Theodore said. 'I want to go home.'

'You won't blow up, dunderhead,' Binnie said, standing on the seat to take down their luggage. 'If it was a bomb, they wouldn't let you take anything with you,' which made sense.

And it's a good thing there isn't one, Eileen thought, wrestling the three of them and the luggage out into the corridor and down to the end of the car, *or we'd never make it out in time*.

The other passengers were already off the train and standing on the gravel next to the tracks. The headmistress was shouting at the guard. 'Are you telling me we're expected to walk all the way to the nearest village?'

It was obvious that that was exactly what was expected. Several passengers had already set off across the meadow carrying their bags. 'I'm afraid so, madam,' the guard said. 'It's not far. You can see the steeple of the church just beyond those trees. A bus should arrive within the hour.'

'I still don't understand why you can't take us on to the next station. Or back to—'

'I'm afraid we can't do that. There's another train behind us.' He leaned towards her, lowering his voice. 'There's been an incident on the line ahead.'

'I *told* you there was a bomb,' Alf said. He shoved his way past the headmistress. 'What'd 'e blow up?'

The guard glared at him. 'A railway bridge.' He turned back to the headmistress. 'We greatly regret the inconvenience, madam. Perhaps this boy could help you carry your bags.'

'No, thank you, I will manage on my own.' She turned to Eileen. 'I warn you that I have no intention of sharing a bus with a snake,' she said and set off grimly across the meadow after the others.

'Was it a Dornier what dropped the bomb?' Alf, undaunted, asked the guard. 'Or a Heinkel III?'

'Come *along*, Alf,' Eileen said and dragged him away.

'If the train'd been a few minutes earlier,' he mused, 'we'd've been on that bridge when they dropped the bomb.'

And you and your snake were the ones who made the train late, Eileen thought, remembering the headmistress shaking her finger and the stationmaster looking anxiously at his watch. Which she supposed meant she should be grateful, but somehow she couldn't manage it. The grass in the meadow was knee-high and impossible to walk through while carrying luggage. Theodore made it a quarter of the way and then demanded to be carried. Alf refused to carry Theodore's duffel, and Binnie dawdled behind.

'Stop picking flowers and come along,' Eileen said.

'I'm pickin' a name,' Binnie said. 'Daisy. Daisy 'Odbin.'

'Or Skunk Cabbage 'Odbin,' Alf said.

Binnie ignored him. 'Or Violet. Or Mata.'

'What sort of flower's that?'

'It ain't a flower, slowcoach. It's a *spy*. Mata 'Ari. Mata 'Ari 'Odbin.'

'I'm hot,' Alf said. 'Can't we stop and rest?'

'Yes,' Eileen said, even though the rest of the passengers were far ahead. Or perhaps that was just as well, considering. She set Theodore down. 'Alf, they won't let you take your snake on the bus. You need to let it go.'

''Ere?' Alf said. 'There ain't nothin' for Bill to eat 'ere.' He pulled the writhing snake not out of his haversack, but out of his pocket. ''E'll starve.'

'Nonsense,' she said. 'This is a perfect place for him. Grass, flowers, insects.'

It *was* a perfect place. If she hadn't been trekking three children and all this luggage across it, she would have loved standing here knee-deep in the fragrant grass, the breeze ruffling her hair, listening to the faint hum of bees. The meadow was golden in the afternoon light and full of buttercups and Queen Anne's lace. A copper dragonfly hovered above a spray of white stitchwort, and a bird flashed past, dark blue against the bright blue sky.

'But if I leave Bill 'ere, 'e might get bombed,' Alf said, dangling the snake in front of Binnie, who was unimpressed. 'The Dornier might come back and—'

'Let him go,' Eileen said firmly.

'But 'e'll be lonely,' Alf said. 'You wouldn't much like bein' left all alone in a strange place.'

You're right, I don't. 'Let him go,' she said. 'Now.'

Alf reluctantly squatted and opened his hand. The snake slithered enthusiastically off into the grass and out of sight. Eileen picked up Theodore's duffel and her own suitcase, and they set off again. The other passengers had disappeared. She hoped they'd tell the bus to wait for them, though that was probably a fond hope, considering the headmistress's attitude.

'Look!' Alf shouted, stopping so short Eileen nearly ran into him. He pointed up at the sky. 'It's a plane!'

'Where?' Binnie said. 'I don't see nuthin'.' For a second Eileen couldn't either, then saw a tiny black dot. 'Wait, now I see it!' Binnie cried. 'Is it comin' back to bomb us?'

Eileen had a sudden image of a vid in one of her history lectures, of refugees scattering wildly as a plane dived towards them, strafing them. 'Is it a dive-bomber?' she asked Alf, dropping her suitcase and clutching Theodore's hand, ready to reach for Binnie and Alf with the other and run.

'You mean a Stuka? I can't tell,' Alf said, squinting at the plane. 'No, it's one of ours. It's a 'Urricane.'

But they were still out in the middle of a meadow, with a stopped train – a perfect bombing target – only a few hundred yards off. 'We need to catch up to the others,' she said. 'Come along. Hurry.'

No one moved. 'There's another one!' Alf said deliriously. 'It's a Messerschmitt. See the iron crosses on its wings? They're goin' to fight!'

Eileen craned her neck to look up at the tiny planes. She could see them both clearly now, the sharp-nosed Hurricane and the snub-nosed Messerschmitt, though they looked like toy planes. They circled each other, swooping and turning silently as if they were dancing instead of fighting. Theodore let go of her hand and went over to stand by Alf, looking up at the graceful duet, his mouth open, transfixed. And rightly so. They were beautiful. 'Get 'im!' Alf shouted. 'Shoot 'im down!'

'Shoot 'im down!' Theodore echoed.

The toy planes banked and dipped and soared silently, trailing narrow veils of white behind them. *Those weren't clouds I saw from the train.* They were vapour trails from dogfights just like these. I'm watching the Battle of Britain, she thought wonderingly.

The Messerschmitt climbed and then dived straight at the other plane. 'Look out!' Binnie shouted.

There was still no sound, no roar as the plane dived, no machine-gun rattle. 'Missed!' Alf shouted, and Eileen saw a minuscule spurt of orange halfway along the Hurricane's wing.

''E's hit!' Binnie shouted.

White smoke began to stream from the wing. The Hurricane's nose dipped. 'Pull up!' Alf shouted, and the tiny plane seemed to straighten out.

That means the pilot's still alive, Eileen thought.

'Get out of there!' Binnie yelled, and it seemed to obey that, too, fleeing north, white smoke trailing from its wing. But not fast enough. The Messerschmitt banked sharply and came around again.

'Behind you!' Alf and then Theodore shouted. 'Watch out!'

'Look!' Binnie's arm shot up. 'There's another one!'

'Where?' Alf demanded, 'I don't see it,' and Eileen suddenly did. It was above the other two planes and coming in fast.

Oh God, don't let it be German, Eileen thought.

'It's a Spitfire!' Alf yelled, and the Messerschmitt cockpit exploded into flame and black smoke. ''E got 'im!' he said deliriously. The Messerschmitt keeled over and went into a spiralling dive, smoke billowing from it, still graceful, still noiseless in its deadly descent.

It won't even make a sound when it hits, Eileen thought, but it did – a quiet, sickening thud. The children cheered. 'I knew the Spitfire'd save 'im!' Alf exulted, looking back up at the two planes.

The Spitfire was circling above the Hurricane, which still streamed white smoke. As they watched, the Hurricane went into a long, shallow dive across the endless expanse of blue sky, and vanished beyond the trees. Eileen closed her eyes and waited for the impact. It came, faint as a footstep.

I want to go home, she thought.

''E bailed out,' Alf said. 'There's 'is parachute.' He pointed confidently at the empty blue and white sky.

'Where?' Theodore asked.

'I don't see no parachute,' Binnie said.

'We must go,' Eileen said, picking up her suitcase and taking Theodore's hand.

'But what if 'e crash-landed and needs first aid?' Alf asked. 'Or a ambulance? The RAF are wizard pilots. They can land anywhere.'

'Even with their wing on fire?' Binnie said. 'I'll wager 'e's dead.'

Theodore clutched Eileen's hand and looked imploringly up at Eileen. 'You don't know that, Binnie,' Eileen said.

'My name ain't Binnie.'

Eileen ignored that. 'I'm certain the pilot's fine, Theodore,' she said. 'Now come along. We'll miss the bus. Alf, Binnie—'

'I told you, I ain't Binnie no more,' Binnie said. 'I decided on my new name.'

'What is it?' Alf asked disdainfully. 'Dandelion?'

'No. Spitfire.'

'Spitfire?' Alf hooted. ''Urricane, more like. 'Urricane 'Odbin.'

'*No*,' Binnie said. 'Spitfire, 'cause they're what's goin' to beat old 'Itler. Spitfire 'Odbin,' she said, trying it out. 'Ain't that a good name for me, Eileen?'

'All lost!'

WILLIAM SHAKESPEARE, *THE TEMPEST*

LONDON – 21 SEPTEMBER 1940

M iss Snelgrove told Polly she was in no condition to work and insisted on her lying down. 'Miss Hayes can take charge of your counter,' she said.

'Shouldn't she go home?' Doreen asked, coming over.

'She can't,' Marjorie said, and whispered something to her. *How does she know about the drop being damaged?* Polly wondered.

'Come along,' Miss Snelgrove said and took her down in the lift to Townsend Brothers' basement shelter. 'You need to rest,' she said, pointing to one of the cots normally reserved for customers, and when Polly still stood there, 'Here, take off your coat.' Miss Snelgrove unbuttoned it for her and laid it over a chair.

'I'm sorry I couldn't get a black skirt,' Polly said. She hadn't projected an air of calm and courage either. All employees were supposed to be cool under fire. 'And I'm sorry I—'

'You mustn't worry about that now,' Miss Snelgrove said. 'You mustn't worry about anything except having a good sleep. You've had a bad shock.'

A bad shock, Polly thought, sitting down obediently on the cot. Sir Godfrey and Miss Laburnum and all the others dead and the drop not working. And the retrieval team not here. They were supposed to be here yesterday. Yesterday.

'Take off your shoes, there's a good girl. Now, lie down.' She patted the cot's pillow.

I shouldn't have left the old man's fringed pink pillow there on the pavement, Polly thought. *It'll be stolen. I should have put it inside the incident perimeter.*

'Lie down, that's a good girl,' Miss Snelgrove said. She covered Polly with a blanket and switched off the lights. 'Try to rest.'

Polly nodded, her eyes filling with tears at Miss Snelgrove's surprising kindness. She closed her eyes, but the moment she did, she saw the wrecked church, and it seemed to her that she was not looking at the church but at the people in it, mangled and smashed and splintered – the rector and Mrs Wyvern and the little girls. Bess Brightford, aged six, died suddenly, from enemy action. Irene Brightford, aged five. Trot—

'You won't hear it,' Mr Dorming had said. 'You'll never know what hit you.' Was that true? She hoped fervently that it was, that they hadn't had time to realise they were trapped, to feel the church crashing down, to know what was going to happen to them.

Like I do, Polly thought sickly. She pushed the panic forcibly back down. *You're not trapped. Just because the drop is damaged doesn't mean they can't pull you out. There's plenty of time.*

But that was just it. Oxford didn't need any time. They had all the time in the world. Even if they had to repair the drop, and it took weeks – or months – they could still have been here as soon as it happened. *So where are they?*

Perhaps they couldn't find me, she thought, the panic pushing up into her throat again. She hadn't checked in, hadn't told them her address. *And there was no one at Mrs Rickett's to tell them she lived there.*

But Mr Dunworthy would have made the retrieval team check every room and flat listed under 'To Let' in the newspapers. And they knew she was working on Oxford Street. Mr Dunworthy would have made them check every department of every store.

But I'm not in my department, she thought, and flung the blanket off. She sat up and reached for her shoes, but before she could put them on, Marjorie came in carrying a cup of tea and a parcel. 'Did you manage to sleep for a bit?' she asked.

'Yes,' Polly lied. 'I feel a good deal better. I'm ready to come back up to the floor now.'

Marjorie looked at her measuringly. 'I don't think that's a good idea. You're still looking very peaky.' She handed Polly the tea. 'You need to rest, and besides, there's no need to. We're not at all busy.'

'Has anyone been in asking for me?' Polly interrupted.

'You mean from the ARP or Civil Defence? No, no one's been here. Did they have to dig you out?' Marjorie asked curiously, and Polly realised they thought her boarding house had been bombed.

'No, it wasn't where I lived,' Polly tried to explain. 'It was the shelter. At St George's. They had a shelter in the basement where I spent the raids. I wasn't there—'

But if she hadn't tried to go to the drop, if she hadn't been caught in the tube station – or if she'd gone through to Oxford earlier in the week to check in – she would have been there with them when the parachute mine exploded, when the church came crashing down, crushing—

'How lucky you weren't there,' Marjorie was saying.

Lucky, Polly thought. 'You don't understand, they—' she said, and had a sudden stabbing image of them sitting there in the cellar in the moment before they died: Miss Hibbard knitting, Mr Simms petting Nelson, Lila and Viv gossiping, Bess and Irene – with her thumb in her mouth – and Trot huddled against their mother, listening to a fairy-tale. 'They ... there were three little girls ...'

'How dreadful,' Marjorie said, setting the parcel down on the floor and sitting on the cot next to Polly. 'No wonder you ...

you really shouldn't be here. Where do you live? I'll ring up your landlady and tell her to come and take you home.'

Home. 'You can't,' Polly said.

'But I thought you said—'

'She's dead. Mrs Rickett was at St George's. And all her boarders – Miss Hibbard and Mr Dorming and Miss Laburnum …' Her voice faltered. ' … there's no one there to tell—'

'And that's why you said you can't go home. I suppose you can't. I don't know what happens to the roomers when a boarding house's owner is killed,' Marjorie said, as if to herself. 'I suppose someone else takes over … do you know if Mrs Rickett had any family?'

'No.'

'But if they would decide to sell … And, at any rate, you can't stay there all alone, after— Is there anyone you can go and stay with? Have you any family or friends here in London?'

No, Polly thought, feeling the panic rise again. *I'm all alone here, in the middle of a war, and if the retrieval team doesn't come for me—*

Marjorie was looking at her with concern. 'No,' Polly said. 'No one.'

'Where are your family? Do they live near London?'

'No. In Northumberland.'

'Oh. Well, we'll think of something. In the meantime, here, drink your tea. It will make you feel better.'

Nothing will make me feel better, Polly thought, but she needed to persuade Marjorie that she was recovered enough to come back up to the floor, so she drank it down. It was weak and barely lukewarm. 'You're right, that helped,' she said, handing the cup to Marjorie, and attempted to stand up, but Marjorie stopped her.

'Miss Snelgrove said you were to rest,' she said firmly.

'But I'm feeling *much* better,' Polly protested.

Marjorie shook her head. 'Shock takes people in odd ways. Mrs Armentrude – she's my landlady – her niece was on a bus that got hit, and Mrs Armentrude said she seemed perfectly fine, and then an hour later went all white and shaky. She had to be taken to hospital.'

'I'm not in shock. I'm only a bit banged up, and I want—'

'Miss Snelgrove said you were to rest,' Marjorie repeated, 'and that I was to give you this.' She handed Polly the parcel. It had perfectly even ends, and the string around it was taut and tied in a precise bow.

'Is this to practise wrapping on?' Polly asked.

'No, of course not,' Marjorie said, looking at her oddly. 'You *are* shocky, no matter what you say. Here.' She took the package back from Polly. 'Let me open it for you.'

It was a black skirt. 'Miss Snelgrove said it cost seven and six, but that you're not to worry about paying her the money and the ration points till you're on your feet again.'

'Seven and six?' Polly said. That was nothing at all. A pair of stockings cost three times that. 'It can't have—'

'She said she bought it at Bourne and Hollingsworth's bomb sale. Water damage.' She handed it to Polly.

It was clearly not from a bomb damage sale. It was brand-new and spotless and, Polly guessed, had come straight from Townsend Brothers' Better Ladies Wear department and cost five pounds at the least. Polly held the skirt in both hands, too overcome to speak. 'Tell her it was very kind of her,' she said finally.

Marjorie nodded. 'She can be almost human on occasion. But she'll have my head if I stay down here any longer.' She took the skirt gently from Polly and draped it over a chair back. 'Is there anything else I can do for you?'

'Yes. Tell her I'm ready to come back to my counter.'

'I most certainly will not. You're not thinking clearly and you're still white as a sheet. And there's no need for heroics. This is Townsend Brothers, not Dunkirk. Now, lie down.'

Polly did, and Marjorie tucked a blanket around her. 'Now stay there.'

Polly nodded, and Marjorie stood up to leave. 'Wait,' Polly said, grabbing her wrist, 'if anyone asks for me, if they ask if I work here, you'll tell them where I am?'

'Of course,' Marjorie said, giving her that odd look again.

'And you'll ask Miss Snelgrove if I can come back to the floor this afternoon?'

'Not unless you promise to try to sleep,' Marjorie said and left. She was back in a few minutes with a sandwich and a glass of milk. 'Miss Snelgrove says you're to rest till three,' she said, 'and then she'll see. And you're to eat something.'

'I will,' Polly lied. The thought of food made her ill. She lay back down and tried to sleep as ordered, but it was no use. What if the retrieval team didn't ask Marjorie if she was there? What if they walked through the department, pretending to be browsing, and when they didn't see her, concluded she didn't work there and left? She flung off the blanket, got up, grabbed the skirt, and went into the ladies' to tidy up.

And was horrified by the sight of herself in the mirror. No wonder Miss Snelgrove had given her a skirt. Hers was not only dirty and brick dust-covered, but one entire side was torn. She must have caught it on a jagged timber. And no wonder they were all being so nice to her – she looked ghastly. Her hair and face were white with plaster dust, and her cheeks streaked with tears. Blood from her knee had trickled all down her leg and clotted her torn stockings.

They both had wide ladders in them, and several holes. She washed the blood off, but they still looked dreadful, so she stripped them off and stuck them in her handbag. It would be all right – young women had gone bare-legged because of the shortage of stockings.

But that was later on in the war, not in 1940. Marjorie was right, she wasn't thinking clearly. She'd have to keep behind her counter and hope the customers didn't notice. Her blouse wasn't too bad. Her coat had partially protected it. She sponged the smears off as best she could, put on the new skirt, washed her face, and combed her hair. She needed to put on lipstick – she looked so white – but when she did, it simply made her look paler. She wiped most of it off and went back up to her counter.

'What are you doing here?' Marjorie said when she saw her. 'It's only two o'clock. You were to rest till three. Miss Snelgrove!' she called before Polly could stop her, and Miss Snelgrove hurried over, looking concerned.

'Miss Sebastian, you should be resting,' she said reprovingly.

'No, please, let me stay.'

'I don't know,' she said doubtfully.

'I feel much better now. Truly,' Polly said, trying to think what would persuade her. 'And Mr Churchill says we must soldier on, that we can't give in to the enemy.'

'Very well. But if you feel at all ill or faint—'

'Thank you,' Polly said fervently, and as soon as Miss Snelgrove had ordered Marjorie to keep an eye on her and had gone over to the lift to greet Miss Toomley, looked around the floor, searching for anyone who might be the retrieval team.

Marjorie had been telling the truth. They had scarcely any customers at all, and the ones who came in as the afternoon wore on, she recognised as regular shoppers: Miss Varley and Mrs Minnian and Miss Culpepper. Miss Culpepper wanted to try on pigskin gloves, then decided on woollen ones instead. 'The newspapers say it may be an exceptionally bad winter,' she said.

You're right, it may be, Polly thought, tying up the gloves for her and watching the lifts, willing the arrows above their doors to stop on third, willing the doors to open and the retrieval team to step out.

But no one came, and by five the floor was deserted except for Miss Culpepper, who had decided to buy a flannel nightgown as well and was over at Marjorie's counter. All the other girls were putting boxes away or leaning on their counters, watching the clock above the lifts.

That's why the retrieval team hasn't come up, Polly thought. Because everyone was watching. Everyone would see them come out, would see her run towards them, would see the look of relief on her face. *They're waiting downstairs till the store closes so they can speak to me alone.*

As soon as the closing bell rang, Polly hurried into her coat and hat, down the stairs and out of the staff entrance, but there was no one waiting there. *They're around front*, she thought, walking rapidly out to the street and over to the main doors, but the only person there was the doorman, helping an elderly woman into a taxi.

He closed the door and spoke to the driver. It pulled away, and the doorman turned to Polly. 'Can I assist you, miss?'

No, she thought. *No one can help me.* Where *were* they?

'No, thank you,' she said. 'I'm waiting for someone.'

He nodded, tipped his visored cap at her, and went back inside.

The retrieval team doesn't know that Townsend Brothers moved up their closing time, Polly thought, watching the shoppers walking quickly along the street and hailing taxis, the shopgirls and lift boys streaming from the staff entrance and hurrying towards the bus stop and the steps down to Oxford Circus. That's why they're late. They'll be here at six. But as the minutes went by, the dread she'd been trying to hold off all day began to creep in like the fog that first night when she came through.

Where are they? she asked herself, shivering from the cold and her bare legs. She went out to the edge of the pavement and leaned out, trying to see up the street. *What's happened to them? What if they don't come at all?*

A hand closed on her arm. '*There* you are!' Marjorie said breathlessly. 'I've been looking everywhere for you. Why did you run out like that? Come along. You're to come home with me tonight. Miss Snelgrove's orders.'

'Oh, but I can't,' Polly said. If the retrieval team came—

'You can't go back to your boarding house when there's no one there. Miss Snelgrove and I agree you shouldn't be alone.'

'But I need—'

'We can go and fetch your things tomorrow. I'll lend you a nightgown tonight, and tomorrow we'll go over together and see about finding you a place to live.'

'But—'

'There's nothing that can be done tonight. And tomorrow you'll feel stronger and be better able to face things. Tomorrow's Sunday. We'll have all day to—'

Sunday, Polly thought, remembering the rector and Mrs Wyvern planning the flowers for the altar. The altar that had crashed, along with the rest of the church, onto Sir Godfrey and Miss Laburnum and Trot—

'You see?' Marjorie said, taking her arm. 'You're not fit to be alone. You're shaking like a leaf. And I promised Miss Snelgrove I'd take care of you. You don't want me to get sacked, do you?' She smiled encouragingly. 'Come along. It's past six. My bus will be here—'

Past six, and the retrieval team still wasn't here. *Because they aren't coming*, Polly thought, staring numbly at Marjorie. *And I'm trapped here.*

'I know. It's dreadful, what's happened,' Marjorie said sympathetically.

No, you don't know, Polly thought, but she let Marjorie lead her back along the street to the bus stop.

'Miss Snelgrove said I was to cook you a good hot meal,' Marjorie said as they joined the queue, 'and see that you got a good night's sleep. She would have taken you home with her, only her sister and her family were bombed out, and they're staying with her. And I have lots of room. The girl I used to share with moved to Bath. Oh good, here's the bus.' She pushed Polly onto the crowded bus and down into an empty seat.

Polly leaned over the woman in the seat next to her to look out of the window at Townsend Brothers, but the front of the store was deserted, and when the bus passed Selfridge's, the clock read quarter past six.

'We'll be home in no time,' Marjorie said, standing over her. 'It's only three stops.' But immediately after the bus had passed Oxford Circus, it pulled over to the side and stopped, and the driver got off.

'Diversion,' he said when he got back on. 'UXB,' and turned down a side street and then another and another.

'Oh dear, we should have taken the Underground,' Marjorie fretted, looking worriedly at Polly. 'I'm sorry, Polly.'

'It's not your fault.'

The bus stopped again. The driver conferred with an ARP warden and then set out again.

'Where *are* we going?' Marjorie said, leaning past Polly to peer out of the window. 'This is ridiculous. We're nearly at the Strand. We'll never get home at this rate.' She pulled the bell for the driver to stop. 'Come along. We're taking the Underground.'

They descended into a nearly dark street. Polly could see a church spire off to the left above the buildings. 'Do you know where we are?' she asked.

'Yes. Charing Cross is that way.'

'Charing Cross?' Polly said, and felt her legs begin to buckle again. She grabbed for the lamppost they were passing.

'Yes. The tube station's not far,' Marjorie said, still walking. 'That's the spire of St Martin-in-the-Fields, and beyond it is Trafalgar Square. I hope the Piccadilly Line's running. It's been hit twice this week. Yesterday there was a bomb on the tracks between— Polly, are you all right?' She hurried back to her. 'I'm so sorry. I didn't think. I shouldn't have mentioned a bomb—' She looked wildly around the deserted street for assistance. 'Here, come and sit down over here.'

She led Polly over to a shop and sat her down on the steps leading up to the door. A door. *How appropriate,* Polly thought. *But it's no use. It won't open. My drop's broken.*

'Is there anything I can do?' Marjorie said anxiously. 'Should I go and fetch a doctor?'

Polly shook her head.

'You mustn't despair,' Marjorie said, sitting down next to her and putting her arm around her. 'We'll get through this.'

Polly shook her head.

'I know, it seems like this horrid war will last forever, but it won't. We'll beat old Hitler and win this war.'

You're right, you will, Polly thought. She raised her head and looked off towards the spire of St Martin-in-the-Fields. *I know. I was in Trafalgar Square the day the war ended. But you're wrong about my getting through this, unless my retrieval team pulls me out before my deadline. A historian can't be in the same temporal location twice. And they should have been here yesterday. Yesterday. This is time travel.*

'You'll see,' Marjorie said, tightening her hold, 'things will work out all right in the end,' and east of them a siren began to wail.

WAR EMERGENCY HOSPITAL – SUMMER 1940

The patient shook the rails at the foot of Mike's bed. 'Hurry!' he shouted. 'The Germans are coming! It's the invasion! We must get out of here!'

Oh God, Mike thought, *we lost the war. I did affect events.*

'What is it? What's happening?' Fordham said sleepily from the next bed.

'The invasion's begun!' the patient said, and the doors to the ward burst open, but it was only the night nurse. She ran over to Mike's bed and put her hand on the patient's arm.

'You shouldn't be out of bed, Corporal Bevins,' she said calmly. 'You need your rest. Come, let's go back to bed.'

'We can't,' Bevins said, shining his flashlight full in her face. 'They're marching into London. We must warn the King.'

'Yes, yes, someone will warn His Majesty.' She gently took the flashlight away from him. 'Let's go back to bed now.'

'What's happening?' the patient next to Fordham asked.

'The Germans are invading,' Fordham said. 'Again.'

'Oh, that's all we bloody need,' the patient said and stuck his pillow over his head.

'I must get back to my unit!' Bevins cried, his voice rising. 'They'll need every man!'

'Shell shock,' Fordham said to Mike. 'It's the sirens that set him off. This is the third time this fortnight.' He closed his eyes. 'He'll be all right as soon as the all-clear goes.'

But I won't, Mike thought, lying there, trying to slow his pounding heart. *What if they do invade? Or you read in to-morrow's newspaper that Churchill was killed in a raid on an airfield?*

The all-clear went, its steady, sweet note as reassuring as Sister Gabriel's voice murmuring, 'You mustn't worry about that now,' as she led Bevins back to bed. 'You must try to sleep,' she said, tucking him in. 'Everything's all right.'

Is it? Mike thought, and in the morning made Fordham read him the rest of his *Herald.* The RAF had shot down sixteen planes, and the Germans had only downed eight, but that didn't prove anything. The RAF had had far fewer than the Luftwaffe to lose, and he knew from his first-year lectures that they'd come within a hair's-breadth of losing the Battle of Britain. And the war.

In the afternoon, a middle-aged woman in a green WVS uniform came into the ward, pushing a cart full of books and magazines, and Mike waylaid her and asked if she had any newspapers. 'Oh yes,' the volunteer, whose name tag read 'Mrs Ives', chirped. 'What would you like? *The Evening Standard? The Times?* The *Daily Herald?* It has a lovely crossword.'

'All of them,' he said, and the next several days scanned them for the number of planes downed, which were posted like baseball scores – Luftwaffe 19, RAF 6; Luftwaffe 12, RAF 9; Luftwaffe 11, RAF 8.

The hell with the names of the small craft, he thought. *I should've memorised the daily stats for the Battle of Britain.* Without them, the numbers meant nothing, though they were worryingly large, and he read the other news feverishly, look-ing for something, anything, that would prove events were still on course. But he only knew the events up to Dunkirk. Had the Germans blown up a passenger train? Had they shelled Dover? Had Hitler announced he intended to have completed the conquest of England by the end of summer?

He didn't know. All he knew was that the news over the next week was uniformly bad: 'Convoy Sunk', 'British Troops Withdraw from Shanghai', 'Airfields Sustain Major Damage'. Had things really gone that badly or was this a sign that the war had gone off-track, that he'd altered the course of—

'You mustn't fret about the war,' Sister Carmody said severely, taking the *Express* he was reading away from him. 'It's not good for you. Your fever's back up. You must concentrate all your energy on getting well.'

'I am,' he protested, but she must have instructed Mrs Ives not to let him have any more newspapers because when he asked her for the *Herald* the next day, Mrs Ives chirped, 'How about a nice book instead? I'm certain you'll find this interesting,' and handed him a massive biography of Ernest Shackleton.

He read it, figuring if he did, Mrs Ives might relent and let him have a newspaper, and that even a boring biography had to be better than lying there worrying, but it wasn't. Shackleton and his crew had got stranded in the middle of the Antarctic with no way to let a rescue team know where they were and the polar winter closing in fast. And one of Shackleton's crew had frozen his foot and had to have part of it cut off.

And even after Mike had finished it and lied to Mrs Ives about how much he'd liked it and how much better he was feeling, she still wouldn't let him have a newspaper. And he had to get his hands on one soon because today was the twenty-fourth, and the twenty-fourth had been one of the war's major divergence points.

It was one he'd learned about when he was studying time travel theory. Two Luftwaffe pilots had got lost in the fog and been unable to find their target, so they'd jettisoned their bombs over what they thought was the English Channel and was actually Cripplegate in London. They'd hit a church and a historic statue of John Milton and killed three civilians and injured twenty-seven others, and as a result, Churchill had ordered the bombing of Berlin, and an enraged Hitler had called a halt to the battle with the RAF and begun bombing London.

In the nick of time. The RAF had had fewer than forty planes left, and if the pilots hadn't got lost, the Luftwaffe could have wiped out the remaining air forces in two weeks flat – some historians said within twenty-four hours – and marched unopposed into London. And with Britain out of the way, Hitler would have been able to concentrate all his military might on Russia, and the Russians would never have been able to hold Stalingrad. 'For want of a nail ...'

If Cripplegate was bombed, it might not prove conclusively that he hadn't altered events, but it would prove he hadn't knocked the war off course, that history was still on track. The story wouldn't be in the papers till tomorrow, or possibly today's late editions, but the weather forecast would be. He could at least see if fog was predicted. It was clear right now.

But it'll come in in the late afternoon, he thought, waiting anxiously for Mrs Ives's arrival.

But she didn't come, Fordham didn't have the *Herald,* and the sky was still clear when Sister Gabriel pulled the blackout curtains shut.

Even if saving Hardy did alter events, it can't have affected the weather, he told himself. But in chaos systems everything affected everything else in complicated and unpredictable ways. If a butterfly flapping its wings in Montana could cause a monsoon in China, then saving a soldier at Dunkirk could affect the weather in southeast England.

There were no sirens during the night, and the next morning the sky was still clear.

The fog could have been limited to London, he told himself.

When Sister Gabriel brought his breakfast, he asked her, 'What happened last night? I thought I heard bombs.'

It was impossible to hear a bomb in Cripplegate from Dover, of course, but he hoped she'd say, 'No, but London got it last night,' and then elaborate.

She didn't. She gave him the same look she always gave Bevins and took his temperature. She looked at the thermometer, frowning. 'Try to rest,' she said and left him to wait anxiously for Mrs Ives. What if Mrs Ives didn't come again today? What if she never came back, like Mr Powney?

She did, but not till late afternoon. 'I've been down on first since yesterday morning,' she said, 'assisting with the new patients. Nearly a dozen pilots. One of them crash-landed, and he—' she caught herself. 'Oh, but you don't want to hear about that. How about a nice book?'

'No, reading books makes my head ache. Can't I have a newspaper? Please.'

'Oh dear, I really shouldn't. The nurses said you weren't to read anything troubling ...'

Troubling. 'I don't want to read the war news,' he lied. 'I just want to work the crossword puzzle.'

'Oh,' she said, relieved, 'well, in that case ...' and handed him the *Herald* and a yellow lead pencil, and then stood there while he opened it to the puzzle. He'd have to at least pretend to work it. He started reading the clues. Six across: 'The man between two hills is a sadist.'

What? Fifteen across: 'This sign of the Zodiac has no connection with the fishes.' What kind of clues were these? He'd worked crosswords when he'd studied the history of games, but they'd had straightforward clues like 'Spanish coin' and 'marsh bird', not, 'The well brought-up help these over stiles.'

'Do you need any help?' Mrs Ives asked kindly.

'No,' he said and quickly filled in the first set of spaces with random letters. Mrs Ives moved on down the ward with her cart. As soon as she left, Mike quickly flipped to the front page. 'London Church Bombed', the headline read. '3 Killed, 27 Injured', and there was a photo of the half-destroyed Church of St Giles, Cripplegate, complete with the toppled statue of Milton.

Thank God, he thought, though he couldn't be certain till he'd seen what the response to the bombing was, which meant convincing Mrs Ives to keep on giving him the paper.

But when he asked the next day, she said, 'Oh, the crossword's done you good. Your colour's much improved,' and handed over the *Express* without any argument.

On the twenty-seventh the headline read, 'RAF Bombs Berlin!' and the next day, 'Hitler Vows Revenge for Berlin Bombing'. He breathed a massive sigh of relief. But if he hadn't altered events, then what had happened to the retrieval team?

They don't know where I am, he thought. It was the only explanation. But why not? Even if they hadn't been able to find out anything in Saltram-on-Sea, they'd known he'd intended to go to Dover. They'd have scoured the town, checked the police station and the morgue and all the hospitals. How many were there? He hadn't had time to research that because of wasting that afternoon waiting for Dunworthy. 'How many hospitals are there here?' he asked Sister Gabriel when she brought his medicine.

'Here?' she said blankly. 'In England?'

'No, here in Dover.'

'I say, you have been out of it,' Fordham said from his bed. 'You're not in Dover.'

'Not in—? Where am I? What hospital is this?'

'The War Emergency Hospital,' Sister Gabriel said. 'In Orpington.'

LONDON – 10 SEPTEMBER 1940

It took Eileen until two the next day – shuffled from bus to train to bus again – to get the children to London, by which time she'd spent more than half of the money the vicar had given her on sandwiches and orange squash and reached the end of her patience with Alf and Binnie.

I am delivering them to their mother, and then I never want to see them again, she thought when they finally arrived at Euston Station. 'Which bus do we take to get to Whitechapel?' she asked the station guard.

'Stepney's closer than Whitechapel,' Binnie said. 'You should take Theodore home first and then us.'

'I'm taking you to your house first, Binnie,' Eileen said.

'*Not* Binnie. I *told* you, my name's Spitfire. Any rate, our mum won't be there.'

'And if you take Theodore first,' Alf said, 'we could help you find his street. You'll likely get lost on your own.'

'I don't want to go—' Theodore began.

'Not one word,' Eileen said. 'Out of any of you. We're going to Whitechapel. Which bus do we take for Whitechapel?' she asked the guard.

'I don't know as you can get there at all, miss,' he said. 'It was hit hard again last night.'

'I told you we should go to Stepney,' Binnie said.

'What sort of bombers were they?' Alf inquired.

'Shh,' Eileen said and asked the guard for the bus number.

He told her. 'Though I doubt they're running. And even if they are, the streets'll be blocked off.'

He was right. They had to take three different buses and then get out and walk, and by the time they reached Whitechapel, it was half past four. Whitechapel's slums looked like something out of Dickens – narrow, dark lanes and soot-blackened, ramshackle terrace houses. A pall of smoke hung over the area, and off in the distance Eileen could see flames. She felt guilty at the idea of abandoning Alf and Binnie to this, and even guiltier when she saw a terrace that had been bombed. One wall still stood, curtains at its blown-out windows, but the rest of it was a mound of timbers and plaster. Part of an upended kitchen chair stuck out of the mound, and she could see pieces of broken crockery and a shoe. Alf whistled. 'Will ya look at that!' he said and would have climbed onto it – in spite of the rope barrier – if Eileen hadn't caught hold of his shirt collar.

There was another mound of rubble on the corner and, at the end of the next street they crossed, the blackened skeletons of an entire row of houses.

What if when we get there, Alf and Binnie's home has been hit? Eileen thought worriedly, but when they turned in to Gargery Lane, all the houses were intact, though they looked as if a good hard push could topple them, let alone a bomb. 'We can find our way from 'ere,' Alf said. 'You needn't go with us.'

She was sorely tempted, but she'd promised the vicar she'd hand them over to their mother personally. 'Which one is yours?' Eileen asked him, and Alf pointed cheerfully at the flimsiest-looking block of all.

And it must be theirs because when she knocked on the front

door, the woman who answered growled, 'I thought we'd got rid of the two of you. You stay away from my Lily.'

When Eileen asked if Mrs Hodbin was home, she snorted. '*Mrs* Hodbin? That's rich, that is. She's no more a missus than I'm the Queen.'

'Have you any idea when she might be home?'

She shook her head. 'She never come home last night.'

Oh no, what if she'd been killed in the bombing? But neither the woman nor Alf and Binnie seemed worried. 'I told you you should take Theodore home first,' Binnie said.

'I've brought Alf and Binnie home—' Eileen began.

'Spitfire,' Binnie corrected.

'—Alf and his sister home from Warwickshire for the Evacuation Committee,' Eileen said to the woman. 'Can I leave them with you till their mother returns?'

'Oh no, you're not going to land me with them two. For all I know, she's gone off with some soldier again, and then where would I be?'

In exactly the same position I am, Eileen thought. 'Well, is there someone who could watch—?'

'We ain't babies,' Alf protested.

'We can stay by ourselves till Mum comes back,' Binnie said. 'If this old cow'll give us our key—'

'A good beating, that's what I'll give you,' the woman said, 'both you and that brother of yours. And if you was mine, I'd give you a lot worse.' She shook her fist at Eileen. 'And don't you try goin' off and leavin' 'em, or I'll call a policeman,' she said, and slammed the door in their faces.

'I ain't afraid of no police,' Alf said staunchly.

'And we don't need no key,' Binnie said. 'We got lots of ways of getting' in 'thout that old cow knowin'.'

I can imagine, Eileen thought. 'No, I promised the vicar I'd deliver you to your mother. Come along. We're going to Stepney.' *And please let Theodore's mother be home.*

She wasn't. When they reached Stepney, after an even longer

and more roundabout trek, her neighbour, Mrs Owens, said, 'She's left for the night shift. You've only just missed her.'

Oh no. 'When do you expect her home?'

'Not till the morning. They're working double shifts at the factory.'

Worse and worse.

'But Theodore's welcome to stay the night with me,' Mrs Owens said. 'Have you had your tea?'

'*No*,' Binnie said vehemently.

'We're not 'alf starved,' Alf said.

'Oh, you poor lambs,' she said, and insisted on making them cheese on toast and pouring Eileen a cup of tea. 'Theodore's mother will be *so* glad to see him. She's been that worried, what with all the bombings. She's been expecting him since yesterday afternoon,' and listened, clucking sympathetically, as Eileen told her what had happened.

It was wonderful, sitting there in the warm, tidy kitchen, but it was growing late. 'We must be going,' she said when Mrs Owens urged a second cup of tea on her. 'I must get Alf and Binnie home to Whitechapel.'

'Tonight? Oh, but you can't. The sirens'll go any minute. You'll have to leave that till the morning.'

'But—' Eileen said, her heart quailing at the thought of setting out with Alf and Binnie to find a hotel, if Stepney even had such a thing. And the cost!

'You must all stay here,' Mrs Owens said.

Eileen gave a sigh of relief.

'Theodore's mother gave me her key,' Mrs Owens went on. 'I'd have you here, but there's no Anderson, only that cupboard.' She pointed at a narrow door under the stairs.

What is she talking about? Eileen wondered, following her next door with the children in tow. *And who's Anderson?*

'The children can sleep in here,' Mrs Owens said, showing them into the sitting room. 'That way you won't have to get them down the stairs.' She opened a linen closet and brought out blankets. 'It's a bit dampish for my old bones, that's why I didn't have one put in. Still, going out to the back garden's better than going all the way to Bethnal Green in the blackout. Mrs Skagdale, two doors down, she fell off the kerb and broke her ankle night before last when the sirens went.'

The air raids, Eileen thought. *She's talking about the air raids*. And an Anderson was some sort of shelter. She hadn't researched shelters. The whole point of sending the children to Backbury had been to get them away from the need for shelters. Mrs Owens had said it was in the back garden. While Mrs Owens took the children upstairs to fetch pillows, Eileen ran outside to look at it.

At first she couldn't find it, and then she realised the large grassy mound by the back fence was it. It was a corrugated iron hut which had been sunk into the ground, with dirt piled around it on three sides and on top of its curved roof. Grass was growing on top.

Like a grave, Eileen thought. The end that hadn't been banked with dirt had a metal door. She opened it, and Mrs Owens was right: it did smell damp. She peered in, but it was too dark to see anything.

I need to ask if Mrs Willett has a torch, she thought, and went back inside, where she found Alf and Binnie whaling away at each other with the pillows. 'Stop that immediately and put on your nightclothes,' she said, apologised to Mrs Owens, and asked her about the torch. Mrs Owens found it and a box of matches for her. 'For the hurricane,' she said cryptically and made Eileen promise to come and ask if she needed anything else.

'Should I take the children out to the Anderson now?' Eileen asked her anxiously at the door.

'Oh no, there'll be plenty of time once the sirens go. A quarter of an hour at least.' She looked up at the darkening sky. 'If they go. I've a premonition Hitler's told them to stay home tonight.'

Good, Eileen thought, and went back inside to separate Alf and Binnie, who were battling over the right to sleep on the sofa. She pulled the blackout curtains together and helped Theodore into his pyjamas, then trooped them all upstairs to the loo and back down to the sitting room, put Theodore on the sofa – 'Because it's his house, Alf' – made up beds for Alf and Binnie on the floor, set the torch by the back door, switched off the lamp, and sat down in the overstuffed chair, listening for the sirens and hoping she'd recognise them when she heard them. She hadn't researched sirens either. Or bombs.

She'd only just decided it was safe to take her shoes off when she heard the sirens, and then, before she could get her shoes back on, the ominous buzz of approaching planes. And immediately after, the distant *crump* of a bomb. 'Binnie! Alf! Wake up! We've got to go to the Anderson.'

'Is it a raid?' Alf said, instantly alert. He leaped up and then stood there looking up at the ceiling, listening. 'That's a Heinkel III.'

'You can do that in the Anderson. Hurry. Take your blanket with you. Theodore, wake up.'

Theodore rubbed his eyes sleepily. 'I don't want to go to the Anderson.'

Of course. She wrapped the blanket around him and picked him up in her arms. There was a *boom*, and then another, much louder. 'They're comin' nearer,' Alf said happily.

'Let's go. Hurry,' Eileen said, trying to keep the panic out of her voice. 'Binnie, fetch the torch—'

'My name's *Spitfire*.'

'*Fetch* the torch. Alf, open the door – no, switch off the lamp first.' She got the torch and matches from Binnie, and they ran out of the back door and across the grass, the torch's beam lighting a wobbly path in front of them.

'The ARP warden'll get you for showin' a light,' Alf said. 'You could go to prison.'

Binnie reached the Anderson first. She opened the low door, stepped in, and backed out again. 'It's wet!'

'In,' Eileen said, 'now,' and pushed her through the door. She grabbed Alf, who was standing on the grass staring up at the dark sky, shoved him through the door and stepped through after him. And into four inches of icy water.

It's flooded, she thought, grabbing the torch and shining it down on the water and then along the walls to see if water was coming in somewhere. So this was what the neighbour meant by dampish.

'My shoes and socks are soaking,' Binnie said.

'I want to go back *inside,*' Theodore said.

'We can't, not till the raid's over.' She had to shout over the noise of the bombs and the Heinkel IIIs or whatever they were, their sound a heavy growl. Perhaps shutting the door would shut some of the racket out. She handed Binnie the torch and pulled the door shut and fastened it.

It didn't help. The curved tin roof seemed to magnify and reverberate the sound, like shouting into a megaphone. How had people slept in these? She took the torch back from Binnie and shone it around the shelter. There were two very narrow bunks on each side, with shelves at the end by the door. On one sat an oil lamp with a glass chimney.

The hurricane, Eileen thought, lifting Theodore onto a top bunk, then waded over to light the lamp. It cast a dim, shadowy light.

'Look,' Binnie said, pointing. 'There are spiders.'

'*Where?*' Theodore cried.

'In the water.'

Eileen replaced the glass chimney over the flame and switched off the torch. 'It's all right. They've all drowned.'

'*Drowned?*' Theodore wailed.

'I think the water's gettin' deeper,' Binnie said.

'No, it isn't,' Eileen said firmly. 'Get in your bunks. Binnie, you take that one.' She pointed to a lower bunk. 'Alf, you climb up on top.'

'I want to go back inside,' Theodore said. 'I'm cold.'

'Here's your blanket,' Eileen said, picking it up. It was sopping wet. The tail must have dragged in the water. She took off her coat and tucked it around him.

'There's no room in 'ere,' Binnie said from her bunk. 'I can't even sit up.'

'Then lie down and go to sleep,' Eileen said.

'With all *that* goin' on?' Alf asked.

He had a point. The noise of engines and explosions was growing louder. There was a *whoosh* and then an explosion that shook the Anderson. The hurricane lamp rattled.

'Are we going to *drown?*' Theodore asked.

No, we're going to be blown to bits, Eileen thought. And Binnie was right, there was no room in these bunks. She curled up on the lower one, shivering, her feet in their wet stockings tucked under her.

I should have knocked on Mrs Owens' door and run and left them standing there, she thought, her teeth chattering. *I could have been home by now.*

'I gotta go to the loo again,' Alf said.

WAR EMERGENCY HOSPITAL – AUGUST 1940

Mike stared at Sister Gabriel. 'I'm in Orpington?' he repeated stupidly. Orpington was just south of London. It was *miles* from Dover.

'Yes, you were brought here from Dover for surgery,' Sister Gabriel explained.

'When?'

'I'm not certain.' She picked up his chart to look.

'I am,' Fordham said. 'It was the sixth of June.'

D-Day, Mike thought. *Oh God, it's 1944. I've been here four years.*

'I remember because it was only two days after I was admitted,' Fordham went on, 'and the orderlies kept banging against my traction wires as they got you into bed.'

'Yes, the sixth,' Sister Gabriel said, looking at his chart, and it was obvious the date meant nothing to them. It wasn't 1944, it was still 1940. Thank God. June the sixth. That meant he'd been brought here a week after Dunkirk, so that by the time the retrieval team had talked to the Commander and then come to Dover looking for him, he'd have been long gone, and with no name to trace him by.

That's why the retrieval team's not here, he thought

409

jubilantly, and then, *I've got to let them know where I am.* He grabbed the blankets to fling them off and get out of bed.

'I say, what do you think you're doing?' Fordham said, startled, and Sister Gabriel rushed over to stop him.

'Oh, you mustn't try to get out of bed,' she said, putting her hand on his chest. 'You're still far too weak.' She pulled the covers back up.

'What is it? Have you remembered something about your coming here?'

'No, I ... I didn't realise I wasn't in Dover.'

'It must be difficult, not being able to remember,' Sister Gabriel said sympathetically. 'Could you have been in the RAF?'

Oh no, had his L-and-A implant stopped working again?

'There are lots of American flyers in the RAF,' she went on. 'You could have been shot down, and that's why you were in the water.'

He shook his head, frowning. 'It's all so foggy.'

'Never mind. You're in very good hands here.' She handed him his crossword puzzle and pencil. 'And you're much safer here than in Dover.'

No, I'm not, he thought. *And I have to get word to them.* But how? He couldn't send a telegram to 2060. The only way to get a message to Oxford was via the drop, and if he could get there to send it, he wouldn't need to send a message. He could go through himself.

He tried to think what the retrieval team would have done when they couldn't find him in Dover. They'd have gone back to Saltram-on-Sea. It, and the Commander, would be their only lead. *I have to get word of where I am to him so he can tell them.* But how? The Commander obviously didn't have a phone or he wouldn't have had to use the one at the inn to call the Admiralty.

Maybe I could call the inn, he thought, and *leave a message with the barmaid* – what was her name? Dolores? Deirdre? He couldn't just call and ask for the brunette with the trick of glancing flirtatiously over her shoulder, not with her father there. And besides, he didn't trust her to remember to deliver the message. She hadn't been able to remember that the Commander had a car, even when he'd been in desperate need of one.

Maybe he could send the Commander a telegram. But he had no idea how to go about it. And no money. And if he asked Fordham or one of the nurses if they could send one for him, they'd conclude he'd regained his memory and ask all kinds of inconvenient questions.

Maybe I can ask Mrs Ives, he thought. *She doesn't know I'm supposed to have amnesia. Fordham goes down for X-rays this afternoon. I'll ask her then.*

But when she arrived, Fordham was still there. 'Anything else you need?' Mrs Ives asked cheerily after she'd given Mike his newspaper.

Yes, Mike thought, *I need an attendant to come and take Fordham*. 'Can you help me with this crossword clue?' he asked, picking one at random. '"Mount where the PM goes on Sunday mornings." Nine letters. I can't figure it out.'

'Oh, that's Churchill,' she said.

'*Churchill?*'

'Yes, our new prime minister.'

And here, finally, was the attendant with the gurney. He and the nurse began unhooking Fordham from his pulleys. 'But how is Churchill the name of a mount?' Mike asked, to stall.

'A mount is a hill ...'

'Careful,' Fordham said as they put him on the gurney. 'Don't— Christ!— Sorry, Mrs Ives.'

'I quite understand,' she said and returned to the puzzle. 'And the place one goes on Sunday mornings is "church", and together they spell out Church-hill. Churchill.'

'So the clues are riddles?' Mike said.

Mrs Ives nodded.

Fordham yelped in pain. 'Sorry, just a momentary twinge.

Go ahead, driver. To the photographer's studio!' and was finally wheeled off towards the ward's double doors.

'I need to get word to someone,' Mike said as soon as the gurney was out of earshot, 'and I was wondering if you—'

'Could write a letter for you?' Mrs Ives said. 'I'd be delighted.' She began gathering stationery from her cart.

'No, I wanted to send a telegram—'

'Oh dear, no, telegrams are such horrid things, always bringing bad news, especially now with the war. You don't want to frighten the poor person you're sending it to. A letter's much better.' She picked up a fountain pen. 'I'll be glad to post it for you.'

'But I need to get word to this person right away—'

'A letter will be nearly as quick as a telegram,' she said, sitting down beside the bed. 'Now, to whom is it to be sent?'

'I can write it myself. I just need—'

'Oh, I don't mind. It's my way of doing my bit for the war effort. And you mustn't tire yourself out. You must conserve your strength towards getting *well*.'

There wasn't time to argue with her. Fordham might be back any minute. 'It's to Commander Harold,' he said.

She wrote, 'Dear Commander Harold,' in a neat, spidery hand.

'I am in the War Emergency Hospital in Orpington,' Mike dictated. 'I was brought here from Dover for surgery on my foot.' And now what? He needed to phrase it so it didn't give away the fact that he'd been feigning his amnesia, or that he was a civilian. If they found that out and moved him to another hospital, it would defeat the whole point of writing.

Mrs Ives was looking up at him expectantly.

'I'm too tired to write any more right now,' he said, rubbing his hand across his forehead. 'Just leave it, and I'll finish it later.'

'I'll be glad to come back,' she said, folding the letter and sticking it in her pocket.

No, Fordham would be there then, listening. 'Just put, "Please write,"' Mike told her. The important thing was to tell the Commander where he was, and hopefully he'd write back and tell him if anyone had been there, looking for him. 'And sign it "Mike Davis".'

She wrote that, folded the letter in thirds, put it in an envelope, licked the flap, tore a stamp off a sheet, licked that, and pressed it onto a corner of the envelope. And it was just as well she'd written the letter for him – he'd have had no idea how to get the envelope shut or the stamp on. She wrote Mike's name and the hospital's address in the left-hand corner and 'Commander Harold' in the centre. 'What's the Commander's address?' she asked.

'I need you to find that out for me. He lives in a village called Saltram-on-Sea. It's in Kent. Or possibly in Sussex.'

'The postmaster will know,' she said. 'Saltram-on-Sea will get it to him.' She wrote 'Saltram-on-Sea' and, under it, 'England', and stuck it in her uniform pocket. 'I'll post it when I leave tonight.'

I hope she knows what she's doing, Mike thought. 'How long do you think it will take to get there?'

'Oh, it should arrive with tomorrow's morning post, though with the war, one never knows. It might not arrive till the afternoon post, but it will definitely be there by tomorrow,' she said, which meant it would get there Wednesday or, since it didn't have the Commander's address, possibly Thursday. That meant the retrieval team could be here by Friday. Which meant he'd better work on getting better, and fast, so that when they showed up, they'd be able to get him out of here without having to resort to stealing a stretcher and an ambulance. To that end, he forced himself to eat everything on his tray, and practise sitting up in bed for longer than five minutes at a stretch.

It was harder than he expected. He was still incredibly weak, and even trying to sit on the side of the bed left him drenched in sweat. 'There's still some lung involvement,' the doctor said,

listening to his chest. 'How's the memory? Anything returning?'

'Bits and pieces,' Mike said cautiously. Had Mrs Ives told him
about the letter?

Apparently not, because the doctor said, 'Don't try to force it.
Take it slowly. And that goes for you trying to get up. I don't
want you having a relapse.'

And when Sister Carmody came to take his temperature, she
told him the doctor had scolded her for allowing him to sit up.
'He says you're not to get up till next week.'

By which time I'll be back in Oxford, he thought, but by
Friday, there was still no sign of them, and no letter. 'It must
have been delayed,' Mrs Ives said. 'The war, you know. I'm certain it will come tomorrow,' but it wasn't in the post Saturday
morning, either. Obviously Mrs Ives had been wrong, and
'Saltram-on-Sea, England' hadn't been enough of an address.
He was going to have to send a second letter and make Mrs Ives
find out the county this time, but the first thing she said was,
'Perhaps instead of writing back to you, he's planning to come
and see you on the weekend.'

That possibility hadn't even occurred to Mike. Oh God, the
thought of the Commander roaring in and announcing to the
nurses that he was an American reporter. *I have to tell them my
memory's come back*, Mike thought.

'When are weekend visiting hours, Mrs Ives?' he asked her.

'From two o'clock to four, both today and tomorrow.'

That meant he wouldn't have time to have his memory come
back in pieces. It would have to be all at once. *I'll have to say it
was triggered by something*, he thought, and, as soon as Mrs Ives
left, started through the *Herald*, looking for a story he could say
had sparked the memory: 'Airfield Bombed', 'Londoners Hold
Gas Attack Drills', 'Invasion May Be Imminent'. But nothing at
all about Dunkirk or Americans. He turned to the inside pages.
An ad for John Lewis, funeral notices, wedding announcements:

Lord James and Lady Emma Siston-Hughes announce the engagement of their daughter Jane—

Jane. Perfect. He pretended to read for a few minutes, then rang the bell excitedly. 'What is it?' Fordham asked. 'What's wrong?'

'I've remembered who I am!' Mike rang the bell again.

Sister Carmody came bustling up. 'I know who I am,' Mike said, handing her the paper and pointing to the announcement. 'I saw the name Jane and it suddenly all came back – how I got to Dunkirk, what I was doing there, how I got injured. I was on the *Lady Jane*. And I'm not a soldier.'

'Not a soldier?'

'No, I'm a war correspondent. I was in Dun—'

'But if you're not a soldier, you're not supposed to— I'll fetch the doctor.' She hurried off, clutching the *Herald*.

She returned almost immediately with the doctor in tow. 'I understand your memory is beginning to return,' he said.

'*Has* returned – just like that.' Mike snapped his fingers, hoping to God memories actually did come back that way. 'I was reading the *Herald*,' he said, taking the paper from Sister Carmody and showing them the announcement, 'and as soon as I saw the name Jane I remembered everything. I work for an American paper, the *Omaha Observer*. I'm their London correspondent. I went over to Dunkirk with Commander Harold on his boat, the *Lady Jane*, to report on the evacuation.' He glanced ruefully at his foot. 'I got more of a story than I bargained for.'

The doctor listened to Mike's account – bringing the soldiers aboard, the propellor, the Stuka – calmly and impassively. 'I told you not to worry,' he said at the end of it. 'That your memory would come back.' He turned to Sister Carmody. 'Would you tell Matron I need to speak with her, please?'

She shot Mike a stricken look. 'Doctor, could I have a moment?' she asked, and they retreated to the centre of the ward for another of those whispered conferences. '... it isn't his fault,' he heard Sister Carmody say, and, '... couldn't it wait till his foot? ... pneumonia ...'

The doctor sounded just as unhappy: '... nothing I can do ... regulations ...'

He must have told her again to go get Matron because she crossed her arms belligerently across her chest and shook her veiled head. '... won't have any part in it ... miracle he survived being moved the first time ...' and the doctor took off for the double doors with her in pursuit.

And now, Commander, Mike thought, *you'd better show up today.*

He didn't. A steady stream of visitors – girlfriends, mothers, men in uniform – came that day and the next to sit beside patients' beds, but no Commander.

I shouldn't have jumped the gun, Mike thought, watching Sister Carmody as she shooed visitors out. 'Are they going to transfer me to another hospital?' he asked her.

'You mustn't worry,' she said. 'Try to rest.'

Which means yes, he thought, and spent the night trying to think of ways to keep that from happening. And imagining all the things that could have happened to his letter. The postmistress had given it to the barmaid to give to the Commander, and she'd stuck it behind the bar and forgotten it. The Commander'd dropped it in the water in the hold. Or lost it among the charts and pilchards on that mess of a table.

'*Still* no letter?' Mrs Ives *tsk-tsked* when she brought him his *Herald* on Monday morning. 'I do hope nothing's happened,' which set off a whole new fit of worrying. The train carrying the letter had been bombed. Saltram-on-Sea had been bombed. The retrieval team had been bombed—

This wasn't doing any good. Mike picked up the *Herald* and opened it to the crossword. Even trying to figure out ridiculous riddles was better than squirrel-caging.

One across was 'sent to a place where no message can get out'. Ten down was 'the calamity one feared has arrived'. Mike flipped back to the front page. 'Invasion Thought Imminent', the headline read. 'German buildup along the English Channel indicates—'

Sister Carmody plucked it out of his hands. 'You've a visitor,' she said. 'A young lady.'

It's the retrieval team, he thought, relief washing over him so violently he could hardly hold the comb and mirror the nurse handed him 'to tidy up for her' with. He'd been expecting a male historian, but a female made more sense. Nobody would think to question a young woman coming to see a patient. *Maybe it's Merope*, he thought hopefully. *Thank God Fordham's down for X-rays again. We won't have to talk in code.*

The nurse took the mirror and comb from him, helped him into a maroon bathrobe, smoothed his blanket, and went to get his visitor. The doors swung open and a young woman in a green dress and jauntily angled hat came into the ward.

It wasn't Merope. It was a brunette with swept-up hair, rouged cheeks and very red lipstick. With her open-toed shoes and short-skirted dress she looked just like the other wives and girlfriends who'd visited, but she was definitely one of the retrieval team. She was carrying a cardboard box with a string handle that had to be a gas mask, and, in spite of all the historical accounts describing the contemps carrying them, he hadn't seen a single one since he got here.

I hope it doesn't attract attention, he thought, but the only kind of attention she was getting was whistles as she proceeded through the ward. 'Oh, please say it's me you've come to visit!' the soldier three beds up from Mike called to her as she walked past his bed, and she paused, looking back over her shoulder to smile flirtatiously at him.

It's the barmaid, Mike thought. He hadn't recognised her with her hair up and all that makeup. *It's Doris or Deirdre or whatever the hell her name is. Not the retrieval team.* And she must have seen the disappointment in his face, because her own face fell.

417

'Dad said I shouldn't come, that I should write you a letter, but I thought …' Her voice faltered.

'No, no,' Mike said, trying to look pleased to see her. And to remember her name. *Deborah? No, it had an "e" at the end.* 'I'm glad you came, Deirdre.'

She looked even more disappointed. 'Daphne.'

'Daphne. Sorry, I've been kind of fuzzy since the—'

She looked immediately sympathetic. 'Oh, of course. The nurse told me about the shock making you lose your memory and how you've only just got it back, and how badly injured you were, your foot … how is …?' she stammered, glancing at the outline of his foot under the covers and then away. 'You said in your letter you'd had surgery on it. Were they able to—?' she began, and then stopped, biting her lip.

'My foot's healing well. The bandages are supposed to come off next week.'

'Oh good.' She thrust the cardboard box at him. 'I brought you some hothouse grapes. I wanted to bake you a cake, but it's so difficult to get sugar and butter, what with the rationing—'

'Grapes are just what the doctor ordered. Thanks. And thank you for coming such a long way to see me,' he said, trying to figure out a way to bring the conversation around to asking her if anyone had come into the pub inquiring about him. 'Did you come by bus?'

'No, Mr Powney took me to Dover, and I took the train from there,' she said, taking off her gloves and laying them across her lap.

Mr Powney. So he'd finally shown up.

'I couldn't come before because of the pub being busy on the weekend. Dad wanted me to write, but I didn't like to, you being injured and all.' She picked up her gloves again and twisted them. 'I thought it would be better to tell you in person.'

The retrieval team had been there. What story had they told her? That they were looking for him because he was AWOL?

Was that why the Commander hadn't told them where he was? 'Tell me what?' he asked.

'About the Commander and his grandson Jonathan,' she said, twisting the gloves in her hands.

'What about them? Daphne?'

She looked down at the tortured gloves. 'They were killed, you see. At Dunkirk.'

*'We cannot tell when they will try and come. We
cannot be sure that in fact they will try at all.'*

WINSTON CHURCHILL, 1940

LONDON – 21 SEPTEMBER 1940

Polly looked past Marjorie at the spire of St Martin-in-the-Fields. Beyond it lay Charing Cross. And Trafalgar Square. *You're wrong*, she thought, *it won't come out right in the end. Not for me.* Another siren, to the south, began to wail, and then another, their sound filling the dark street where they sat on the steps.

'There's the siren,' Marjorie said unnecessarily. 'We shouldn't stay here.'

I can't do anything else, Polly thought. *My drop's broken, and the retrieval team didn't come.*

'The bombers will be here any minute. Can you walk, do you think, Polly?' Marjorie asked, and when she didn't answer, 'Shall I try to find someone to help?'

And expose them to the dangers of the raid that would begin in a few minutes? Polly was already endangering Marjorie, who was selflessly trying to help her. And the bomb that had destroyed St George's wasn't the last one that would be dropped. There would be more parachute mines and HEs and deadly shrapnel tonight. And the next night. And the next.

And Marjorie and Miss Snelgrove and the old man who sat

me down on the kerb at St George's are in as much trouble as I am. The only difference is that they don't know the date of their deaths. The least she could do was not get them killed for trying to help. 'No,' she said, forcing her voice to sound steady, 'I'm all right.' She got up from the steps. 'I can make it to the tube station. Which way is it?'

But when Marjorie pointed down the darkened street and said, 'That way. We can cut through Trafalgar Square,' she had to clench her fists and hold them tightly at her sides to keep from grabbing Marjorie's arm for support.

You can do this, she told herself, willing her legs to support her. You *saw it before, on the way to St Paul's.* But she hadn't known then that she was trapped here.

You have to do it.

It won't look anything like it did that night.

She needn't have worried, it was too dark to see anything. The lions, the fountains, the Nelson Monument were only outlines in the blackness. But Polly kept her eyes carefully fixed ahead, concentrating on reaching the station, finding a token in her handbag, getting on the descending escalator.

The station didn't look as it had that night either, filled with celebrating people. It looked like every other tube station Polly'd been in since she got here, jammed with passengers and shelterers and running children.

And it was safe. It had been hit on September tenth, but wouldn't be hit again till the twenty-ninth of December. And on the noisy, crowded platform, conversation would be impossible. She wouldn't have to answer Marjorie's questions, to keep up the pretence that she was all right.

But Marjorie didn't look for an unoccupied space where they could sit. She didn't even spare a glance for the shelterers. She went straight down to the Northern Line and towards the northbound tunnel. 'Where are you going?' Polly asked.

'Bloomsbury,' Marjorie said, pushing her way through the tunnel. 'That's where I live.'

'Bloomsbury?' There were raids over Bloomsbury tonight. But the sirens had already gone. The guard wouldn't let them out of the station when they got there. 'Which is your station?' Polly asked, praying it wasn't one of the ones that had been hit.

'Russell Square.'

The streets bordering Russell Square had been pummelled with bombs in September, and the square had been hit by a V-1 in 1944, but the station itself wouldn't be hit till the terrorist attacks of 2005. They'd be safe there.

But when they reached it, the gates hadn't been pulled across. 'Oh good, Russell Square's siren hasn't gone yet. They don't close the gates till then,' Marjorie said, and started outside. 'I'm glad. I promised Miss Snelgrove I'd give you supper, and one can't get so much as a cup of tea here.'

'Oh, but I don't want to—'

'I *told* you, you're not imposing. In fact, you may well have saved me.'

'Saved you? How?'

'I'll tell you all about it when we reach my boarding house. Come along. I'm starving.' She took Polly's arm and struck off down the darkened street.

As they walked, Polly tried to remember what parts of Bloomsbury had been hit on the twenty-first. Bedford Place had been almost completely destroyed in September and October, and so had Guildford Street and Woburn Place. The British Museum had been hit three times in September, but except for the first time, on the seventeenth, the specific dates hadn't been on Colin's list. And a Luftwaffe dive-bomber had crashed in Gordon Square, but she didn't know the date of that either.

Marjorie led Polly down a series of winding streets, stopped in front of a door, knocked, and then used her latchkey. 'Hullo?' she called, opening the door. 'Mrs Armentrude?' She listened a moment. 'Oh good, they've all gone to St Pancras. She leaves early to get a good space. We'll have the house to ourselves.'

'Don't you go to St Pancras?'

'No,' she said, leading the way up a flight of carpeted stairs. 'There's a gun in Tavistock Square that goes all night long so it's impossible to get any sleep.'

Which meant this wasn't near Tavistock Square.

'So which shelter do you go to?'

'I don't.' They went up another carpeted flight and then an uncarpeted one and down a dark corridor. 'I stay here.'

'There's a shelter here, then?' Polly asked hopefully.

'The cellar,' Marjorie said, opening the door onto a room exactly like Polly's except for an enamel stand with a gas ring, a worn chintz-covered chair with a pair of stockings draped over the back, and a shelf with several tins and boxes and a loaf of bread on it. Apparently Mrs Armentrude wasn't as strict as Mrs Rickett. *Oh God, Mrs Rickett was dead. And so was Miss Laburnum. And—*

'Though I don't know but what our cellar's more dangerous than the bombs.' Marjorie pulled the blackout curtain across the single window and then switched on the lamp by the bed. 'I nearly broke my neck two nights ago running down the stairs when the sirens went.' She picked up the kettle. 'Now sit down. I'll be back in a trice.'

She disappeared down the corridor. Polly went over to the window and peeked out between the blackout curtains, hoping the light from the searchlights would let her see if they were near the British Museum or the Royal Academy of Dramatic Arts, which had also been hit in the autumn, but the searchlights hadn't switched on yet.

She could hear Marjorie returning. She let the curtain fall and stepped hastily away from the window. When Marjorie came in with the kettle, she asked, 'Is this Bedford Place?'

'No,' Marjorie said, setting the kettle on the gas ring.

It could still be Guildford Street or Woburn Place, though, but at the moment Polly couldn't think of any reason she could give for pressing Marjorie further.

'Sit down,' Marjorie said, striking a match and lighting the gas under the kettle and getting a teapot and a tin of tea down from the shelf. 'The tea will be ready in no time,' she said, as casually as if they weren't in the middle of Bloomsbury, in a house that might very well be bombed tonight.

And she had to survive not only tonight, but tomorrow night and all the other nights of the Blitz – the twenty-ninth of December and the eleventh of January and the tenth of May. She felt the panic welling up. 'Marjorie,' she said to stop it from washing over her, 'at the station you said my coming here had saved you. From what?'

'From doing something I knew I shouldn't,' Marjorie said, smiling wryly. 'This RAF pilot I know – hang on.' She switched off the light, opened the curtains, retrieved a bottle of milk and a small piece of cheese from the windowsill, pulled the curtains across, and switched the lamp back on again. 'He's been after me to go out dancing with him, and I'd told him I'd meet him tonight—'

And if she'd met him, I wouldn't be here and in danger of being bombed. 'You can still go,' Polly said. *And I can go back to Russell Square—*

'No, I'm glad you kept me from going. I should never have said yes in the first place. I mean, he's a pilot. They're all terribly fast. Brenda, that's the girl I used to share with, says they're only after one thing, and she's right. Lucille in Kitchenwares went out with a rear-gunner, and he was all over her.' Marjorie reached up on the shelf for two teacups. 'He refused to take no for an answer, and Lucille had to—'

There was a high-pitched whistle, and Polly looked over at the kettle, thinking it had come to a boil, but it was a siren. 'That tears it,' Marjorie said disgustedly. 'The Germans don't even let us have our tea.' She switched off the gas ring and the lamp. 'They're coming sooner every night, have you noticed? Only think what it will be like by Christmas. Last year was bad enough, and we only had the blackout to deal with – dark by half past three in the afternoon.'

And I'll still be here, Polly thought. *And when New Year's comes, I won't even know when and where the raids are.*

'Come along,' Marjorie was saying. 'I'll show you our "safe and comfortable shelter accommodations".' She led the way back downstairs, across the kitchen, and down to the cellar.

She hadn't been exaggerating about its dangerousness. The steps were perilously steep and one was broken, and the beams in the low-ceilinged cellar looked as if they might give way at the mere sound of a bomb, let alone a direct hit. It should be on Mr Dunworthy's forbidden list.

St George's hadn't been on his list. Why not?

Because you were supposed to be staying in a tube shelter, she told herself. But St George's hadn't been on Colin's list either.

An anti-aircraft gun began pounding away at the droning planes, both of them as loud and as close as they'd sounded when she sat in the drop, waiting for it to open and unaware that the retrieval team should already have been there, that Miss Laburnum and the little girls were already dead.

And Sir Godfrey, who'd saved her life that first night when she'd gone over to look at Mr Simms's newspaper, who'd said, '"If we no more meet until we meet in heaven—"'

'Do the guns frighten you?' Marjorie asked. 'They used to drive my flatmate Brenda completely mad. That's why she left London. She's always after me to leave as well. She wrote last week and said if I'd come to Bath, she was certain she could get me on at the shop where she works. And when something like this happens – I mean, the church and all those people – it makes me think perhaps I should take her up on it. Do you ever think about chucking in the whole thing and getting out?'

Yes.

'At least it would be better than sitting here, waiting to be killed. Oh, I am sorry,' Marjorie said, 'but, I mean, things like that do make one think. Tom – that's the pilot I told you about – says in a war you can't afford to wait to live, you've got to take what happiness you can find because you don't know how much time you've got.'

How much time you've got.

'Brenda says that's only a line of chat, that the men use it on all the girls, but sometimes they mean it. The Navy lieutenant Joanna – she used to work in China and Glassware – went out with, he said the same thing to her, and *he* meant it. They eloped, just like that, without a word to anyone. And even if Tom is only feeding me a line, it is true. Any one of us could be killed tonight, or next week, and if that's the case, then why not go out dancing and all the rest of it? Have a bit of fun? It would be better than never having lived at all. Sorry,' she said, 'I'm talking rot. It's sitting in this wretched cellar. It makes me nervy. Perhaps I *should* go to Bath, only everyone at work would think I was a coward.' She looked up suddenly at the ceiling. 'Oh good, the all-clear's gone.'

'I didn't hear it,' Polly said. She could still hear explosions and guns. 'I don't think it went.'

But Marjorie had stood and was starting up the stairs. 'That's what we call it when the gun in Cartwright Gardens stops. It means the planes have left off this part of Bloomsbury. We can finally have our tea.' She led the way back up to her room, relit the gas ring, and set the kettle on it.

'Now take off your things,' she said. She opened the closet and took a chenille robe off a hook. 'And get into this, and I'll wash out your blouse and sponge your coat off.' She thrust the robe at her. 'Give me your stockings, and I'll rinse them out, too.'

'I must mend them first,' Polly said, pulling them from her handbag. Marjorie took them gingerly from her and looked them over. 'I'm afraid these are beyond mending. Never mind. I'll lend you a pair of mine.'

'Oh no, I can't let you do that.' Marjorie would need to hold on to every stocking she had. On the first of December the government would stop their manufacture, and by the end of the war they'd be more priceless than gold. 'What if I were to ladder one of them?'

'Don't be silly,' Marjorie said, 'you can't go without stockings. Here, give me your blouse.'

Polly handed it to her, took off her skirt, and wrapped the robe – which felt wonderfully cosy – around her.

The kettle boiled. Marjorie ordered Polly to sit down in the chair. She made the tea and brought Polly a cup, then took down a tin of soup from the shelf and got an opener, a spoon and a bowl out of the top bureau drawer, keeping up a steady stream of chatter about Tom, who had also told her that he might be posted to Africa any day, and that when two people loved each other, it couldn't be wrong, could it? 'Drink your tea,' Marjorie ordered.

Polly did. It was hot and strong.

'Here,' Marjorie said, handing her a bowl of soup. 'I've only got one bowl and one spoon, so we'll have to eat in shifts.'

Polly obligingly took a swallow, trying to recall when she'd eaten last. Or slept. *The night before last in Holborn with my head lying on my handbag*, she thought. No, that didn't count. She'd only dozed, wakened every few minutes by the lights and voices and the worry that that band of urchins would come back and try to rob her. She hadn't really slept since Wednesday night, in St George's.

In St George's, with Mr Dorming, his hands on his stomach, snoring, and Lila and Viv wrapped in their coats, their hair in bobby pins, and the rector, asleep against the wall, his book fallen from his hand. *Murder at the Vicarage*—

'You haven't finished any soup at all,' Marjorie said reprovingly. 'Do take a few more bites. It will make you feel better.'

'No, you take your turn.'

Marjorie took the bowl and spoon from her. 'I'll go and wash these up. I'll be back straightaway,' and Polly must have fallen asleep because Marjorie was back in the room covering her with a blanket, and the anti-aircraft gun had started up again.

'Shouldn't we go down to the cellar?' Polly asked drowsily.

'No, I'll wake you if it comes near us. Go back to sleep.'

Polly obeyed, and when she woke, it was five and the all-clear was going, and the answer was clear, too. The reason the retrieval team hadn't been there was because they were looking for her in the tube stations. There were far fewer stations on Mr Dunworthy's approved list than there were Oxford Street shops, and if they had described her to the guard at Notting Hill Gate, he would have remembered her.

They'd gone to Notting Hill Gate that morning, but she'd been in Holborn, and that afternoon she'd left work early and walked home so she wouldn't be caught in the station by the sirens, and they'd have had no way of knowing she would go to the drop. And tonight she'd been in Charing Cross and Russell Square.

They'd been waiting in Notting Hill Gate this entire time. They were waiting there now. *I must go and find them*, she thought, and had started out of the chair before she remembered that Marjorie had washed her blouse, and that the trains wouldn't begin running till half past six.

I'll rest here till then, she thought, *and then I'll go and find them*, but she must have dozed off again because when she woke, it was daylight and Marjorie was dressed and standing at an ironing board, pressing a blouse. Polly's own blouse, neatly washed and pressed, lay on the made-up bed. 'Good morning, Sleeping Beauty,' Marjorie said, smiling at her over the iron.

Polly looked at her watch, but it had stopped. 'What time is it?'

'Half past four.'

'Half past *four*?' Polly pushed the blanket aside and stood up.

'Perhaps I shouldn't have let you sleep so long, but you looked all-in … What are you doing?' she asked as Polly reached for her blouse.

'I must go,' Polly said, pulling it on and buttoning it with fumbling fingers.

'Where?' Marjorie said.

Home, she thought. 'To the boarding house,' she said, pulling on her skirt. 'I must find out if I still have a room there.' She tucked in her blouse and sat down to put on her shoes. 'And if I haven't, I must find another.'

'But it's Sunday,' Marjorie said. 'Why don't you stay here tonight and come to work with me tomorrow, and we could go over together after work?'

'No, you've already done too much for me, letting me stay and pressing my blouse for me. I can't impose any further.' She pulled on her coat.

'But … can't you wait? I'll go with you. You shouldn't go there alone.'

'I'll be all right.' Polly grabbed up her hat and bag. 'Thank you – for everything.' She hugged Marjorie briefly and hurried out of the room and down the stairs.

Halfway down, Marjorie called after her, 'Wait, you forgot the stockings,' and ran down the stairs with them fluttering in her hand.

To avoid a time-consuming argument, Polly took them and jammed them into her coat pocket. 'Which way is Russell Square Station?'

'Turn left at the next crossing, and then left again,' Marjorie said. 'If you'll only wait a moment, I'll fetch my coat and—'

'It's not necessary. Really,' Polly said and was finally able to get away. She ran all the way to Russell Square, but when she reached it, there was an endless queue of shelterers laden with camp cots and dinner baskets and bedrolls. 'Is there a separate queue for passengers?' she asked a woman wheeling a pram full of dishes and cutlery.

'Just go to the head of the line and tell 'em you're meetin''

429

someone,' the woman said, 'and that if you're late, you'll miss 'im.'

I will, Polly thought, thanking the woman and going over to the guard. He nodded and let her through, and she hurried to the lift and down to the southbound platform. A chalkboard stood in the doorway. 'Southbound service temporarily suspended,' it read.

There must have been damage on the line, she thought, consulting the Underground map. She'd need to take a northbound train to King's Cross and catch the Metropolitan Line and then the District Line. She prayed it hadn't been knocked out, too.

It had, but only between Holland Park and Shepherd's Bush. She took the train to Notting Hill Gate and hurried towards the escalators. 'Oh my God, look!' a young woman's voice squealed from the far side of the hall as she crossed it, 'It's Polly!' and a second voice echoed, 'Polly!'

Oh, thank God, she thought, relief washing over her. *They're here. Finally.*

'Polly Sebastian! Over here!' they called from the direction of the escalators.

It can't be the retrieval team, Polly thought as she turned. *They'd never call attention to me or to themselves like that.*

It wasn't. It was Lila and Viv.

'Never give up. No one knows what's going to happen next.'

L. FRANK BAUM

LONDON – 22 SEPTEMBER 1940

'**P**olly! over here!' Lila called again from across the tube station, and Viv echoed, 'Here.'

It couldn't be them – no one could have survived in that flattened tangle of rubble – but there they were, elbowing their way towards her carrying mugs of tea and sandwiches. 'Where – how—?' Polly stammered. 'I thought you were dead.'

'You thought *we* were dead?' Lila said. 'We thought *you* were dead! Viv, go and tell them we've found her,' she ordered, and Viv handed Polly the sandwich and tea she was holding and took off back through the crowd.

'You said "they". Does that mean—?'

But Lila wasn't listening. 'What *happened* to you?' she demanded. 'We were convinced you'd gone to St George's. Where have you *been* all this time? It's been three days!'

Polly heard Viv say, 'We came up to the canteen to buy a sandwich, and there she was,' and looked over at the escalator. Viv was leaning over it, chattering to someone coming up. 'We couldn't believe our eyes!' and it was the rector she was talking to.

Polly started through the crowd towards them, but the little girls – Bess and Irene and, oh, thank *goodness*, Trot – were already pelting towards her. Irene ran full tilt into her, and Trot hugged her legs. 'You aren't killed!' she said happily.

'I *knew* she wasn't,' Bess said.

The rector came up. 'Praise God you're safe.'

Irene was tugging on her arm. 'Come along,' she said. 'We must show you to Mother.'

'Trot, let go,' Bess said, taking hold of her other arm. 'You'll bowl her over.' And the three of them dragged her down the escalator, Trot clinging to her skirt, and out to the northbound District Line platform, shouting, 'Mother, look what we've found!'

And there at the end of the platform were Mrs Brightford and Miss Laburnum and Mr Dorming – all of them rising from where they'd been sitting to gather around her, exclaiming and smiling and talking at once in a happy jumble: 'Where have you *been*? ... gave us such a fright ... so worried ... Sir Godfrey refused to leave ... and when you didn't come back to Mrs Rickett's ...'

Trot was tugging on her mother's skirt. 'She isn't killed, Mummy.'

'No, she isn't,' Mrs Brightford said, beaming. 'And we're very, very glad.'

'I told you you were all worried for nothing,' Mrs Rickett said to the rector. 'Didn't I say she'd turn up?'

'But you ... I don't understand ... the man at the church—' Polly stammered. 'I saw the wreckage—' And yet here came Miss Hibbard, carrying her knitting, tears streaming down her face, and trotting towards Polly on a leash was Nelson. 'But pets aren't allowed in public shelters,' Polly said, thinking, *This must be a dream.*

'The London Underground Authority's given him a special dispensation,' Mr Simms said, and she couldn't be dreaming. She could never have imagined something like that.

'Oh, I'm so glad to see you! We feared you'd been killed,' Mrs Wyvern said, stepping forward to embrace her, and she couldn't have imagined that either.

They were really here and not buried in the rubble of the church. 'You're not dead. You're all here,' Polly said, looking around happily at Mrs Rickett and the rector and Nelson and—

Where was Sir Godfrey? She looked wildly around at the people on the platform. 'Sir Godfrey refused to leave,' they'd said, and the old man at St George's had shaken his head and murmured, 'Such a pity. So many killed.'

'Where's Sir Godfrey?' Polly demanded. She darted back along the platform, pushing her way past passengers, looking for him, stepping over shelterers, thinking, *Oh God, that rescue shaft was for him*—

And saw him coming through the archway from the tunnel, his *Times* tucked under his arm.

Thank God, he's all right, Polly thought, but he wasn't. He looked beaten, battered – as if St George's *had* crashed down on him – and years older than that night they'd done *The Tempest*. His face was lined and ashen.

Trot shot past her through the milling passengers, shouting, 'Sir Godfrey! Sir Godfrey!' He looked down at Trot and then up. And saw Polly. 'She's not dead!' Trot said happily.

'No,' he said, his voice cracking, and took a step towards Polly.

'Sir Godfrey,' she tried to say, but nothing came out.

'"I saw her as I thought dead,"' he murmured, '"and have in vain said many a prayer upon her grave."' He reached forward to take her hands and then stopped and looked questioningly at her. '"What rich gift is this?"'

'What?' Polly said blankly and looked down at her hands. She was still holding Viv's sandwich and tea mug. 'I've no idea ... I must have ...' she stammered, and held them helplessly out to him.

He shook his head. '"I am too far already in your gifts—"'

'Oh good, you've found him, Miss Sebastian,' the rector said, coming up with Miss Laburnum and the others. They crowded around them. Nelson pushed forward, tail wagging.

'Sir Godfrey, isn't it wonderful?' Miss Hibbard said. 'Finding Miss Sebastian safe and well?'

'Indeed,' he said, looking at her solemnly. '"It is a most high miracle. Though the seas threaten, they are merciful. I have cursed them without cause." Welcome, thrice drowned Viola.'

'You should have seen Sir Godfrey!' Lila said. 'He was simply *beside* himself.'

'They had dogs and everything,' Viv said.

'What I want to know is where you've been all this time,' Mrs Rickett demanded sourly.

'Yes, do make her tell us where she's been, Sir Godfrey,' Miss Laburnum urged.

'But shouldn't we go back to our own corner first?' Mr Simms suggested. 'Someone's liable to take our space.'

'We are rather in the way here,' the rector said, and led the way back along the crowded platform through the jostling passengers, Bess and Trot holding Polly by the hand.

'It's not so cosy here as the shelter in St George's, I'm afraid,' Miss Laburnum said.

'And it's rather noisy,' Mrs Brightford added, 'though when the trains stop, it's a bit better.'

'*I* like it,' Lila whispered to Polly as they followed the rector. 'There's a canteen and—'

'And lots of nice-looking men,' Viv finished.

They reached the end of the platform. 'Now, sit down,' Miss Laburnum said, gesturing to Lila and Viv to make room for Polly, 'and tell us all about your adventures.'

Sir Godfrey gently took the mug and sandwich – which she was still unaccountably holding – from her and handed them to Viv. Polly sat down. So did everyone else, moving their camp stools and blankets to form a circle around her. 'What happened to you?' Lila asked. 'Why didn't you come back to Mrs Rickett's?'

'Tell us *everything*,' Trot said.

'Aye, Miranda,' Sir Godfrey said. '"Where hast thou been preserved? Where lived? How found thy father's court?"'

'She didn't,' Trot said. 'We found *her*!'

'Hush, darling,' her mother said. 'Let her speak.'

'"Aye, speak, maid,"' Sir Godfrey ordered. '"Give us particulars of thy preservation, how thou hast met us here who three days since were wrecked upon this shore."'

She couldn't tell them she'd spent a night in the drop. Instead, she said the sirens had gone when she was still at work, and she'd had to spend the night in Townsend Brothers' basement shelter. 'And the next morning there wasn't time to go home before work, and that night it happened again. And when I came home on Saturday morning, I saw the church, and they said people had been killed. I thought you were all dead. Who *was* killed?'

'Three firemen and an ARP warden,' the rector said. 'And the entire bomb disposal squad.'

Miss Hibbard shook her head sadly. 'Poor brave men.'

'The mine's parachute had caught on a cornice of the building next to the vicarage,' Mr Dorming explained. 'They were trying to cut it down when it went off.'

'But I still don't see how you—'

'We'd all been evacuated,' Mr Simms explained.

'We'd no more than arrived at St George's when the ARP warden knocked on the door,' Miss Laburnum said, 'and told us we had to leave immediately.'

'Sir Godfrey refused to go without you,' Lila said. 'He said you wouldn't know about the bomb and we must wait till you arrived, but the warden said they'd cordoned off the area.'

'They took us to a makeshift shelter in Argyll Road,' Miss Laburnum said, 'and we were no sooner there than it went off. If we'd waited even a few minutes longer—' She shook her head.

'As soon as the raid let up, they sent us here,' Lila said, 'and the tube authorities wouldn't let Nelson in—'

'And Mr Simms said he couldn't just leave him outside in the middle of a raid,' Viv put in eagerly.

'Sir Godfrey told the guard he was an official member of our

435

acting troupe,' Mr Simms said, 'so then they *had* to let him in.' He patted Nelson's head affectionately.

'We were certain you'd be here,' Mrs Brightford said.

And she had been, but then she'd gone to Holborn to observe the shelterers.

'Sir Godfrey went to Bayswater and Queensway stations to see if you might have been sent there,' Miss Hibbard said, 'but you hadn't.'

'And then,' Miss Laburnum said, 'when you didn't come back to the boarding house the next morning ...'

The boarding house. She'd told herself the retrieval team hadn't been able to find her because they'd been killed, that there'd been no one at Mrs Rickett's to tell them she lived there. But they weren't dead. They *would* have been there to tell the retrieval team. So where *were* they?

'We feared the worst,' Miss Laburnum said.

So do I, Polly thought, and felt the panic begin to stir again.

'We were afraid there were areas which hadn't been cordoned off and you hadn't seen the *Danger – Keep Out* notices in the dark,' the rector said, 'and had come along to the church.'

'And been *killed*,' Trot said.

'Sir Godfrey insisted the rescue squad search through the wreckage of the entire church,' Lila said.

That rescue shaft I saw wasn't for them, Polly thought. *It wasn't for Sir Godfrey. They were looking for me.*

'They told him it was no use,' Viv said, 'that the entire weight of the sanctuary and the roof had collapsed directly onto the shelter, and no one could have survived under there, but Sir Godfrey refused to give up. He was determined to find you, no matter how long it took.'

Like Colin, Polly thought. The problem wasn't only that the retrieval team hadn't come, it was that Mr Dunworthy and Colin hadn't. They'd have moved heaven and earth to find her. 'Mrs Rickett, did anyone come to the boarding house looking for me?' she asked.

'*Everyone* was looking for you,' Mrs Rickett said reprovingly. 'Sir Godfrey spent all day yesterday *and* today searching the hospitals for you. You could at least have attempted to notify us that you were unharmed.'

'How could she have notified us?' Lila said. 'She thought we were *dead*.'

Mrs Rickett glared at her.

'What matters is that you're alive and safe and we're all here together,' the rector said in his peacemaking voice. 'All's well that ends well, isn't that right, Sir Godfrey?'

'Indeed. "And if it end so meet, the bitter past, more welcome is the sweet." Or to quote our fair Trot, "And they all lived happily ever after."'

'Except for the fact that Hitler was still trying to kill them,' Mr Dorming said dourly.

And except for the fact that the retrieval team hasn't been to the boarding house. Where are they? What if something terrible's happened? But she had thought something terrible had happened to the group, and here they all were, safe and sound.

You were foolish to panic, she told herself. *There could be lots of reasons why the retrieval team hasn't found you yet.* Perhaps they'd gone to the boarding house before Mrs Rickett and the others had got back home. Or perhaps the streets around it had been cordoned off, and only residents had been allowed through. Or Badri had had difficulty finding a drop site for the team. It had taken him six weeks to find her one.

But she kept coming back to the fact that this was time travel. No matter how long it took Oxford to locate another drop or check every department store and Underground station, they could still have returned to Oxford, sent a second team through and had them waiting for her outside Townsend Brothers that first morning.

Unless they couldn't get there, she thought, remembering how much difficulty she'd had getting to St Paul's that Sunday and to Oxford Street the day after John Lewis, and how the indomitable Miss Snelgrove hadn't made it into work that same day. If Badri *had* had difficulty locating a new drop site and, as a result, the retrieval team had had to come through in the East End or Hampstead Heath, or somewhere outside London altogether, they might still be there, unable to get into the city because the trains and buses weren't running. Or they might have made the mistake of entering a roped-off area or trying to cross a mound of rubble and had been arrested for looting.

Or, more likely, it had taken them two full days of dealing with daytime raids and diversions and damage on the Underground lines to reach Oxford Street, by which time she'd have gone home with Marjorie. And rather than face the trek back, they'd decided to simply wait till Monday. In which case they'd be at Townsend Brothers tomorrow morning.

But they weren't, even though Polly stayed at her counter through her lunch and tea breaks to make certain she didn't miss them.

Marjorie was overjoyed that Sir Godfrey and the others hadn't been killed. 'I *told* you things would work out all right in the end,' she said.

Not quite, Polly thought, hoping the retrieval team would be at the boarding house when she got home, but they weren't there either. 'Did anyone come and ask for me today?' she asked Mrs Rickett.

'If they had, I would obviously have told you,' she said, offended. 'Who were you expecting? I hope I needn't remind you of the rules against having gentlemen in your room.'

The team wasn't at Notting Hill Gate either, though Polly searched every tunnel and platform.

'Mrs Wyvern and the rector and I have had the most ingenious idea,' Miss Laburnum said when Polly came back from searching. 'We *shall* have our own theatrical troupe!'

'Here in the shelter,' Mrs Wyvern said. 'We'll do public dramatic readings. It will be excellent for civilian morale—'

'And not only dramatic readings,' Miss Laburnum interrupted.

'We shall put on a play! Sir Godfrey will star, and we shall all be in it.'

'I did amateur theatrics when I was up at Oxford,' the rector said. 'I played the Reverend Chasuble in *The Importance of Being Earnest*.'

'What a coincidence!' Mrs Wyvern said. 'I played Cecily in that play at school,' something Polly found impossible to picture.

'We can do Barrie's *The Little Minister*,' Miss Laburnum enthused.

Sir Godfrey will love that, Polly thought. And even if they didn't drive him away by doing Barrie, the theatres would reopen in another fortnight, and he'd be returning to the West End.

'Isn't putting on a play a wonderful idea?' Miss Laburnum asked her.

'I ... are you certain Sir Godfrey will be willing?'

'Of course,' Mrs Wyvern said. 'It's his chance to aid the war effort.'

'*The Little Minister*'s such a lovely play,' Miss Laburnum said. 'Or we could do *Mary Rose*. Do you know the play, Miss Sebastian? It's about a young woman who vanishes and then reappears years later, not a day older, and then vanishes again.'

She must have been a historian, Polly thought.

But Mary Rose's retrieval team had obviously come and fetched her. *Unlike mine. Where* are *they?*

They weren't waiting for her outside the station the next morning. Or at Mrs Rickett's. Or outside Townsend Brothers. Which meant the problem had to be something besides diversions and transportation delays.

Slippage, she thought. There had been four and a half days' slippage on her drop, which she'd assumed had been because of a divergence point. Could there have been another divergence point the day the drop had been damaged – or on subsequent days – which would have kept their drop from opening? The Battle of Britain was over and the attack on Coventry wasn't till mid-November. The Luftwaffe had begun dropping the nasty bundles of HEs and incendiaries called Göring breadbaskets around then, but the retrieval team's presence couldn't have affected that. Had Churchill or General Montgomery had a near-deadly encounter? Or the King?

Miss Laburnum and Miss Hibbard followed the Queen's activities faithfully. When Polly got to Notting Hill Gate that night, she asked them if the Royal Family had been in the news lately.

'Oh my, yes,' Miss Laburnum said, and told her Princess Elizabeth had been on the wireless with an encouraging message for the evacuated children, which wasn't exactly what Polly was looking for.

'The Queen visited the East End yesterday,' Miss Hibbard said. 'The bombed-out families, you know. There was a woman there who was trying to get her little dog out of the rubble. Poor thing, it was too frightened to come out. And do you know what the Queen did? She said, "I've always been rather good with dogs," and she got down on her hands and knees and coaxed it out. Wasn't that lovely of her?'

Mrs Wyvern said doubtfully, 'It doesn't seem quite dignified for a queen to—'

'Nonsense, she did just what a queen should have done,' Mr Simms said. 'Isn't that right, Nelson?' He scratched the dog's ears. 'She was doing her bit for the war effort.'

But the rescue of a dog wasn't likely to affect the war's outcome one way or the other. And Buckingham Palace wouldn't be bombed again till March.

Polly borrowed Sir Godfrey's *Times* and read the headlines and then went to Holborn and looked through the library's supply of the previous week's *Heralds* and *Evening Standards*, looking for other events it might have been necessary to keep historians away from.

The National Gallery had been hit, but a historian couldn't affect where bombs fell. An incendiary bomb had started a small fire in the House of Lords that a few minutes' delay could have turned into a major blaze. A historian could have affected that, but the retrieval team would have had no reason to be there or at St Thomas's Hospital, which was hit the same night. A land mine had landed on Hungerford Bridge. If it had gone off, it would have killed everyone in the War Office, including Churchill. That was a possibility, though that divergence point would only have lasted for the time it took to remove the bomb. Polly couldn't find anything which might have kept the net from opening for the five days since her drop had been damaged.

Though the event wouldn't have to be the sort of thing that made the papers. In London now, a few minutes' delay in getting to a shelter or in boarding a train could make a life-or-death difference. And it could be the sort of action that set a domino-like chain of events in motion that would take several days or weeks to play out. And in the meantime, there was nothing she could do but wait.

Or find some other historian who was here – and not in the Blitz – and use his drop. Who might be here now? Merope had said Gerald Phipps was doing something in World War II, but she hadn't said what or when. Michael Davies was doing Dunkirk. He might be here. But Dunkirk had been over for nearly four months. He was probably in Pearl Harbor by now, or at the Battle of the Bulge, neither of which did her any good. He'd mentioned his roommate, but he'd been doing Singapore, also of no help. Polly frowned, trying to remember if he and Merope had mentioned anyone else who—

Merope. Might she still be in Backbury? When Polly'd seen her in Oxford, she'd said she still had months left on her assignment, but that might mean anything. She tried to remember if Merope had said anything else about how long her assignment was. Most of the children had been evacuated in September and October 1939. If Merope had been on a yearlong assignment, there was a chance she might still be there.

I need to write to her immediately, Polly thought. But what was her name? Eileen Something. An Irish name. O'Reilly or O'Malley. Or Rafferty. She couldn't remember. She couldn't remember the name of the manor either. Had Merope even mentioned it?

There would scarcely be more than one manor near Backbury. But what if there were? And even if there was only one, she couldn't send a letter addressed only to 'Eileen the Irish Maid at the Manor near Backbury'.

I'll have to go up to Backbury and find her, she thought. She'd need to go up there to use her drop at any rate, and going would be quicker than writing and then waiting for a letter back.

But what if she's not there? Polly thought. *I'll have given up my job – and the best chance the retrieval team has of locating me – for naught. And what if it is a divergence point that's standing in their way, and they come the moment I'm gone?* She'd better stay here.

But every day that went by increased the chance of Merope's going back to Oxford and Polly's missing her. And she needn't quit her job to go and find her – she could show Miss Snelgrove Props's letter saying that her mother was gravely ill and that she needed to come at once. Miss Snelgrove could scarcely refuse to let her go in that sort of situation, and she'd been extremely understanding the day the shelter had been destroyed. And as far as the retrieval team went, Polly could tell Marjorie to tell anyone who came in asking for her that she worked there and when she'd be back.

And making the journey to Backbury would be better than sitting here fretting over what would happen if the retrieval team didn't come by her deadline. But, given her recent run of luck, they'd arrive as soon as she left. Especially if the divergence point they were being kept from interfering with was the big attack on Fleet Street, which would happen on Wednesday night.

I'll give it till Thursday, she thought. *Surely they'll be here by then.* But they weren't.

WAR EMERGENCY HOSPITAL – SEPTEMBER 1940

'Commander Harold and Jonathan were killed at Dunkirk?'
Mike said to Daphne. 'No, they weren't. They made it
safely back to Dover. I was with them. The Commander helped
put me on the stretcher—'

'That's when you were hurt?' Daphne asked. 'On that first
journey?'

'Yes – first journey?'

She nodded. 'When the *Lady Jane* turned up missing, the
Commander's granddaughter – Jonathan's mother – was afraid
they'd gone to Dunkirk. She asked Dad to go down to Dover to
find out what he could, and the Admiralty told him they'd gone
to Dunkirk on their own and brought troops back and then set
off again immediately, but that they didn't make it back that
time. They didn't know what had happened to them, but we
do know they made it over to Dunkirk that second time. Mr
Powney saw them.'

'Mr Powney? The farmer who'd gone to buy the bull?'

'Yes. That's why he didn't come back that day. He never
made it to Hawkhurst. On his way there he found out about the

rescue effort and went to Ramsgate to volunteer. They put him on a coastguard cutter, and he made three journeys and rescued ever so many soldiers.'

'And he saw the Commander and Jonathan?'

'Yes, in Dunkirk. On the thirtieth. They were loading troops onto the *Lady Jane* under heavy fire. He hailed them, but they were too far away to hear him. And the *Daffodil* saw them leaving the east mole, but they weren't seen after that. The officer who talked to Dad said it was likely a torpedo got them on the way back. Or a mine.'

Or a Stuka, Mike thought, remembering the shriek of the diving plane. *Or another corpse in the propellor.*

'When your letter for him came, Miss Fintworth – she's our postmistress – didn't know what to do. She couldn't give it to Jonathan's mother – she'd gone to her people in Yorkshire after she got the bad news – and she didn't like to send it back since it was plain you didn't know what had happened, so she brought it to Dad to ask him what to do. I hope you don't think we did wrong by opening it, but Dad said it might be urgent, being from a hospital and all, and when we read it and found out you'd been injured at Dunkirk, we thought you must have been with them. We knew you didn't know' – she gave the gloves another twist – 'how things had ended, or you wouldn't have written to the Commander, but we thought perhaps you were there when the *Lady Jane* was hit and then got separated from them somehow and were rescued, and that you knew what had happened.'

No, but I know why they died, he thought. Because he'd untangled their propellor. He'd made it possible for them to go back again.

Daphne was looking questioningly at him.

'No, I was injured on that first run,' he managed to say. 'I didn't know they'd gone over there again. I'm so sorry.'

'It's not your fault,' she said, looking down at her gloves. 'Dad says it was the Commander's foolhardiness got them killed. The

444

Small Vessels Pool had turned the *Lady Jane* down, you see. Dad says he should have listened to them.'

'He wanted to help,' Mike said. 'A lot of boats went over on their own, and it was a good thing. The Army was in a pretty bad spot.'

'And you went along to help them. I think it was marvellous of you to do that, being a Yank and everything. It was very brave. The officer told Dad that the Commander and Jonathan brought home nearly a hundred of our boys. He said they were true heroes.'

They were, he thought. *You wanted to observe heroism, and you got your wish.* 'Absolutely. They showed a lot of courage.'

Daphne nodded solemnly. 'You were a hero as well. The nurse told me about your untangling the propellor and all that. She said you should have a medal.'

A medal, he thought bitterly, for being where he wasn't supposed to be, for murderously altering events. *If I hadn't unfouled that propellor, that bomb would have hit the* Lady Jane *and damaged her rudder. They wouldn't have been able to make that second trip—*

Daphne was looking worriedly at him. 'I've tired you out,' she said, standing up and beginning to pull on her gloves. 'I should go.'

'No, you can't.' He hadn't been able to ask her about the retrieval team yet. 'Can't you stay a little longer?'

She hesitated, looking uncertainly in the direction of the doors. 'The nurse said I was only to stay a quarter of—'

'Please.' He reached for her hand. 'It's so nice having a visitor. Tell me what's been happening in Saltram-on-Sea.'

'Oh, all right then,' she said, looking pleased. 'We did have a bit of excitement last week. The Germans dropped a bomb in Mr Damon's field. We thought it was the invasion starting. Mr Tompkins was all for ringing the church bells, but the vicar wouldn't let him till we knew for certain. Mr Tompkins said it would be too late by then – that they'd already have sent in

445

saboteurs and spies, and they'd be landing soon – and they had a grand row, standing in front of the church.'

Spies. That gave him the opening he needed. 'I suppose you're all on the lookout for strangers, then?' he asked.

'Oh yes. The Home Guard patrols the fields and the beach every night, and the mayor sent round a notice telling us to report any strangers in town to him immediately.'

'And have you had any? Strangers?'

'No – there were a good many reporters in town just after Dunkirk to speak to Mr Powney and the others—'

'Did any of them come in the pub and talk to you?'

'You sound as though you're jealous,' she said, cocking her head flirtatiously at him.

'No, I ...' he stammered, caught off-guard, '... I thought someone might have come looking for me from my newspaper. I told my editor I was going to Saltram-on-Sea and that I'd send him a story about the invasion preparations, and I thought when he didn't hear from me, he might—'

'What does he look like, your editor?'

'Brown hair, medium height,' he improvised, 'but he may have sent someone, another reporter or— Has anyone asked about me?'

'No. They might have spoken to Dad, I suppose. If they did, he very likely told them you'd gone back to London. That's what we thought you'd done.'

Which might mean the team was looking for him in London. 'Daphne, if my editor or anyone else does come, will you tell them where I am and what's happened? And ask your father if anyone inquired about me. If they did, write and tell me.'

'Oh, I will. I'll write to you even if no one comes. And I'll come and visit you again if Dad can spare me.' Again that flirtatious glance at him. 'Next time I'll manage a cake, I promise.'

The matron came in and announced that visiting hours were over. Daphne stood up. 'Thank you for coming,' Mike said, 'and for the grapes. And for telling me about the Commander and Jonathan. I'm so sorry.'

She nodded, her made-up face suddenly sad. 'Miss Fintworth says not to give up hope, that they may still be alive, but if they are, why haven't they come home or written to us or anything?'

'Time,' Matron said sternly.

'Goodbye. I'll come again soon, and you needn't worry, I won't go out with anyone but you,' Daphne said, planted a lipsticky kiss on his cheek, and hurried out to more whistles.

'You lucky devil,' one of the patients called out.

Lucky. I killed an old man and a fourteen-year-old boy. Here he'd been worried about saving Private Hardy's life, and instead— *I should have refused to go in the water. I should have told the Commander I'd lied before, that I couldn't swim.* Instead, he'd unfouled the propellor, and it had affected events, all right. It had got the Commander and Jonathan killed. And what else had it affected? What other damage had he done?

He lay awake well into the night, going over and over it, like an animal pacing its cage, and when he closed his eyes, trying to shut it out, he saw Jonathan and the Commander, heard the Stuka diving and the water splashing up where they'd been only moments before. If he hadn't unfouled the propellor, the bomb would have hit the bow. They'd have begun taking on water, and one of the other boats would have come over to take everyone off and transfer them to—

But there hadn't been any boats anywhere nearby, and there'd been dozens of Stukas. And with a damaged bow, they'd have been a sitting duck. On its next pass, the Stuka would have hit them amidships and killed everybody on board. Was that what was supposed to have happened? What *would* have happened if he hadn't been there?

He sat up in bed, considering the implications of that possibility. If they were supposed to have been killed, if the *Lady Jane* had had an asterisk next to it on that list he hadn't memorised,

447

then he'd altered events not by getting them killed, but by saving them.

And a chaotic system had built-in mechanisms for countering alterations. It had negative loops that could tamp down effects or cancel them out altogether. History was full of examples. Assassins missed, guns misfired, bombs failed to go off. Hitler had survived an attempt on his life because the bomb had been put on the wrong side of a table leg. A telegram warning of the Pearl Harbor attack had been sent in time to have the ships take defensive measures, but it had got put in the wrong decoding pile and hadn't arrived till after the attack.

And if the Commander and Jonathan weren't supposed to have been rescued, that would have been easy to correct. Had their deaths on that second trip been part of a negative loop, of a cancellation? If it was, then he might not have done any damage after all. And that was why he'd been allowed to go to Dunkirk, because his actions hadn't had a lasting effect on the outcome. But it still left Jonathan and the Commander dead. And what about Private Hardy?

Unless his saving of him had been cancelled out, too. Hardy'd been drenched when he climbed aboard. He might have got pneumonia and—

He was the one who told the nurses I unfouled the propellor, Mike thought suddenly. He'd assumed it had been the Commander, but Daphne'd said they'd set out again immediately, and that would explain why the hospital hadn't known his name. But why would Hardy have gone with him to the hospital?

Because he was being admitted, too. Hardy hadn't said anything about being injured, but he might not have realised he was.

Just like me, Mike thought, and when Sister Carmody came in to open the blackout curtains in the morning, he said, 'Can you find out something for me? I need to know if a patient was admitted to the hospital in Dover the same day I was. His name was Hardy.'

She looked at him doubtfully. 'You're certain this is something you've remembered and not something you read about?'

'*Read* about?'

'Yes. Amnesia patients' memories are often confused. And, you know, "Kiss me, Hardy" and all that.'

'What?' he said, completely lost.

'Oh, I forgot, you're an American. When Lord Nelson was fatally injured at the Battle of Trafalgar, his last words were "Kiss me, Hardy,"' she explained. 'Hardy was captain of the *Victory*. He was with Lord Nelson when he died. But if you didn't know that, then it can't have been something you read, can it?'

'No. Can you find out? Please. It's important,' and his urgency must have communicated itself to her because when she brought his breakfast, she told him she'd rung up Dover, but that no one named Hardy had been admitted when he was.

Which didn't prove anything. He could have got sick later. *Or been injured on his way back to his unit*, he thought, remembering the bombed train he'd read about. Or in Dover. The docks had been shelled. Hardy could have helped put Mike in the ambulance, told the driver about the fouled propellor, and been killed five minutes later. This was a war. There were hundreds of ways to cancel things out. But if Mike's altering of events had been cancelled out and he hadn't lost the war, then why wasn't the retrieval team here? He wished he'd reminded Daphne to ask her father as she left. He was afraid she'd forget.

But she didn't. A letter arrived by the Tuesday afternoon post. 'I asked Dad,' she wrote on scented paper, 'but he said no one's been in the pub asking about you.'

But that didn't mean they hadn't been there. She'd said there'd been lots of reporters in the town after Dunkirk, and 'We all thought you'd gone back to London.' The team could have asked Mr Tompkins or one of the fishermen and then have gone to London to look for him, with no idea they should be checking military hospitals. But, even in 1940, London had been a huge place. How would they have gone about trying to find him?

Polly Churchill will be there as soon as the Blitz starts next week, he thought. They'd try to contact her to see if he'd been in touch with her. Which meant *he* needed to get in touch with her. But how? She'd said she was going to work in an Oxford Street department store, but he didn't know which one, or even what name she'd be here under. He'd have to go to London and find her.

But if he was able to get to London, then he was able to get to his drop. And the last thing he wanted to do was find himself in the middle of the Blitz. He needed a way to contact the retrieval team now, from here, before he was thrown out. When he'd asked Sister Carmody about his status, she'd said, 'Matron spoke to the Admiralty, and they said, since the crews on all the small craft had to sign on for a month's service in the Navy before they left for Dunkirk, you have a perfect right to be here.'

But that had been the small craft formed into convoys at Dover. He hadn't signed on for anything, and it was only a matter of time before they found that out – another reason he needed to contact the retrieval team now.

Just like they'd be trying to do if they thought he was in London. They'd be trying to communicate with him. They'd send a message telling him where they were and asking him to get in touch with them. Like those personal ads he'd read: *If anyone has information regarding the whereabouts of time traveller Mike Davis, last seen at Saltram-on-Sea, please contact the retrieval team,* and a phone number to call.

Only the message would be in code, like, *Mike, all is forgiven. Please come home,* or something. He picked up the *Herald* and began reading through the personal column: *Wanted, country home willing to take Pekingese dog for duration of bombings. L. Smith, 26 Brown Street, Mayfair.* No. *Lost in Holborn Underground Station. Brown leather handbag. Reward.* No. *For sale, garden sets. Iris, lilies, poinsettias.*

Poinsettias. Right before Pearl Harbor, the US Navy'd intercepted a phone call from a Tokyo newspaper to a Japanese dentist in Honolulu: 'Presently the flowers in bloom are fewest out of the whole year. However, the hibiscus and the poinsettias are in bloom.' It had been a coded message telling Japan that the battleships and destroyers were all in port, but not the aircraft carriers. And the retrieval team would know he was scheduled to go to Pearl Harbor next.

But the address in the ad was in Shropshire, and there was no phone number. And five ads below it was a nearly identical one for 'dahlias and gladiolas'. All the other ads were standard *Found* and *For Sale* ones. No *Wishes to Contact* or *Anyone having information regarding the whereabouts of* messages. But this was only the *Herald*. They might have put a message in *The Times* or the *Evening Standard*. Tomorrow he'd have to talk Mrs Ives into getting him the other papers. And find out how to go about putting a personal ad of his own in: *Dunworthy, contact Mike, War Emergency Hospital, Orpington. Time is of the essence*, or maybe *just R. T., contact M. D.*

He scanned the *Herald* to see how much an ad cost, and then remembered his money was in his jacket. The jacket he'd left on the deck of the *Lady Jane*. And if he asked Mrs Ives to help him, she'd ask all kinds of questions. He'd better wait till he was out of the hospital.

But he couldn't *get* out till he could walk. Which meant his first priority was to get back on his feet. He wangled a postcard from Mrs Ives – it took him fifteen minutes to talk her out of writing it for him – and wrote to the poinsettias address, requesting more information and giving the hospital's address, just in case it was a message, and then tried to talk his nurses into letting him up.

They refused to consider it, even with crutches. 'You're still mending,' they said and handed him *The Times*. He combed it for messages, but the only *Please Contact* was *Will the young lady in the red polka-dotted frock at the dance at Tangmere*

Airfield last Saturday please contact Flt. Lt. Les Grubman.

There were several more *garden sets* ads, and on Friday a letter arrived from the poinsettias address, with an attached price list and seed catalogue.

Mike decided to take matters into his own hands and get up on his own, but Sister Carmody caught him before he was even out of bed. 'You know you mustn't put any weight on that foot till it's completely healed,' she told him.

'I can't stand to stay in this bed another minute,' he said. 'I'm going crazy.'

'I know just what you need—'

'A nice crossword puzzle?' he asked sarcastically.

'Yes,' she said, handing him the *Herald* and a pencil. 'And some fresh air and sunlight.' She went out and returned in a few minutes with a cane-backed wheelchair and took him and his *Herald* up to the sun-room, though it wasn't very sunny. It had tall windows, but there were black Xes of tape on the panes, sandbags were piled against them, and the green net curtains gave an underwater look to the room. The high-backed chairs were wicker, but they'd been painted dark brown and had darker green velvet cushions. In one of them sat a red-faced man with a neck brace, reading the *Daily Telegraph*.

As well as the chairs there were massive oak tables and bookcases and curio cabinets and equally massive and dark potted plants. There was barely room for Mike's wheelchair as Sister Carmody pushed him over to the sandbagged windows. She parked him next to a massive table and opened the window. 'There, some nice fresh air for you,' she said.

The red-faced man cleared his throat irritably and rattled his newspaper.

'Is there anything else I can do for you?' she whispered.

'No,' Mike said, looking speculatively at the heavy furniture. If he were alone in here, he might be able to lean on it and—

'Would you like me to stay and read to you?' Sister Carmody asked.

'No, I want to work on my crossword.'

She nodded and took a bell from her pocket and set it on the table with only a slight ringing, but the newspaper rattled irritably again.

'Matron's just outside the door,' she whispered. 'Ring if you need anything. If your pencil falls to the floor, you're not to try to pick it up. You're to ring for Matron. You're not to get out of that chair. I'll be back for you in time for lunch,' she said and tiptoed out.

It would take Red Face at least till lunch to read his *Telegraph*. Mike would have to hurry him along. He opened the *Herald*, folded it noisily in half and then in quarters so the crossword was on top. 'One across,' he said loudly. '"Likely to make waves."' He tapped his pencil on the table. 'Make waves ... betides? ... no, it's eight letters. Hurricane?'

Throat clearing and ominous rattlings.

'Sorry,' Mike called to him. 'You wouldn't know what "likely to make waves" is, would you? Or "serving task with no end in sight"? Seven letters?'

Red Face snapped his newspaper shut, stood up, and stalked out. Mike bent intently over the crossword again for a few minutes, in case Matron came in, then rolled his wheelchair over closer to a huge potted palm and grabbed the trunk with one hand, testing to see if it was as sturdy as it looked.

It was. When he put his other hand around the trunk and raised himself slowly to standing, the fronds didn't even move. He cautiously transferred some of his weight to his bad foot. So far, so good. The pain wasn't nearly as bad as he'd thought it might be. He reached for the nearest bookcase, still holding on to the palm tree, and took a careful step towards it.

Oh Christ. His nails dug into the wood of the bookcase. He balanced there, breathing out in hisses through his clenched teeth, trying to get the courage to take another step, praying Matron didn't choose this moment to come in.

All right, next step. It'll never get any better if you don't do this, he told himself. He repositioned his hand on the bookcase, unclenched his teeth, and took another step. *Jesus.*

It took him half an hour to get two chairs', another bookcase's, and a curio cabinet's length from his wheelchair, by which time he was drenched in sweat.

I shouldn't have come this far, he thought. If he heard Matron coming, there'd be no way he could make it back to his wheelchair in time.

He began working his way back, incredibly grateful for the Victorians' penchant for teeter-proof furniture. *Bookcase, potted palm, wheelchair.* He sank gratefully into it and sat there, panting for several minutes, then tackled the crossword, looking for something, anything, he could fill in quickly. 'Island creature Peter Pan author shot'? What the hell could that be? 'Doctor's warning Hitler would ignore'?

He gave up and scrawled in some words. Just in time. Sister Carmody came in smiling. 'Did you make progress?' she asked.

'Yes.' He tried to fold the puzzle to the inside before she could look at it, but she'd already snatched it from him. 'Actually, no. I fell asleep. The fresh air made me drowsy.'

'And it's given you a good colour,' she said, pleased. 'If it's fine tomorrow, I'll bring you up here again.' She handed him back the newspaper. 'You've got eighteen down wrong, by the way. It's not "deception".'

That's what you think, he said silently, but if he was going to pull this off, he couldn't afford to have her get suspicious, so he spent the rest of the day figuring out crossword clues for the next time she took him up.

On Saturday the Blitz began with the bombing of the docks and the East End, and for the next two days everyone was too busy with incoming casualties to take him to the sun-room. But on Tuesday, Sister Carmody wheeled him up again, and he immediately filled in the answers he'd prepared in advance and then got out of his chair. This time he made it further, though he still couldn't walk more than a few steps without the furniture's support, and every step hurt like hell.

On Wednesday a foursome was playing bridge, and on Thursday he was taken down for X-rays, but on Friday the sun-room was deserted. It had turned cold and threatened rain. 'Are you positive you'll be warm enough in here?' Sister Carmody asked, draping a wool blanket around his shoulders and another one over his knees. 'It's dreadfully cold.'

'I'll be fine,' he insisted, but she still hesitated.

'I don't know. If you were to catch cold—'

'I won't. I'll be fine.' *Go.*

She went, after extracting a promise that he would 'ring for Matron' if he felt the slightest chill, and he scrawled in the crossword answers he'd worked out the night before – 4 across: divebomber, 28 down: cathedral, 31 across: escape – pushed the blankets aside, listened a moment to make sure she wasn't coming back, and started his circuit.

Bookcase, window – his foot had stiffened up over the last three days. He had to force himself to put his weight on it. Clock, potted palm, high-backed chair.

'Tsk, tsk, tsk,' a voice said from the depths of the chair. 'I thought you were supposed to keep your weight off that foot, Davis.'

LONDON – SEPTEMBER 1940

Eileen refused to take Alf back into the house to use the loo. 'They're dropping bombs out there,' she said. 'You'll simply have to wait till it's over.' And when he predictably declared he couldn't, she felt about in the water under the bunks to see if the Anderson shelter was provided with a chamber pot.

It was, but Alf refused to use it. 'In *front* of you 'n' Binnie?' he said, at which point Binnie said she had to go, too, and Theodore said, his teeth chattering, that he was cold. Eileen was shivering, too, and her wet feet felt like ice.

I was wrong, she thought. *We won't be blown to bits, we'll freeze to death*, and as soon as there was a lull in the bombing, darted back into the house with the children. She took the torch, but they didn't need it. The garden was bright from the fires around them. Even inside the house there was more than enough light to find their way.

How could Polly have wanted to observe this? Eileen wondered, rummaging for blankets and attempting to hurry the children along. 'The bombers will be back soon,' she said, hustling them down the stairs, but the planes were already here. A bomb whistled down, shaking the house, as they hurried through the kitchen to the back door.

'I'm scared,' Theodore said.

So am I, Eileen thought, handing the blankets to Binnie and scooping Theodore up and running with him to the Anderson and into the shock of the icy water. 'Binnie, hold the blankets up so they don't get wet – where's Alf?'

'Outside.'

Eileen dumped Theodore on the upper bunk and ran back outside. Alf was standing in the middle of the grass, gazing up at the red sky. 'What are you *doing*?' she shouted over the drone of the bombers.

'Tryin' to see what sort of planes they are,' he said, and there was a shuddering boom up the street and a flickering red glow. 'A fire!' he shouted, and started to run towards it.

Eileen grabbed him by the shirttail, shoved him through the door, and yanked it shut as another thunderous boom shook the shelter. 'That's it,' she said. 'Now go to sleep,' and amazingly, they did.

But not before Binnie complained about her blanket being scratchy and Alf argued, 'It's a spotter's job to find out whether they're Dorniers or Stukas.' But once they were wrapped in the dry blankets, they – and Eileen – slept till another siren went.

This one had an even, high-pitched tone which she was afraid signalled a poison gas attack. She shook Binnie awake to ask her. 'That's the all-clear,' Binnie said. 'Don't you know nuthin'?' and there was a loud, reverberating knock on the door.

'I'll wager it's the warden, come to arrest you now the raid's over,' Alf said, emerging from his blanket. 'I told you you ain't s'posed to shine a torch in the blackout.'

But it wasn't a warden. It was Theodore's mother, overjoyed to see Theodore and oblivious to the water, though when they'd all trooped back inside, she insisted Eileen take off her wet stockings and put on a pair of her own slippers. 'I can't tell you how grateful I am to you for bringing my dear boy all this way to me,' she said, making Horlicks for all of them. 'Do you live in London, then?'

Eileen told her her cousin had just come to London to work in an Oxford Street department store. 'But she didn't say which one. I wrote to ask her, but her answer hadn't arrived when we left, so I don't know where she lives or works.'

The neighbour, Mrs Owens, came in then and said the Browns had been bombed out. 'Was anyone hurt?' Mrs Willett asked.

'Only Mrs Brown's littlest, Emily. She was a bit cut up, but the house is a complete ruin,' she said, and Eileen shivered, remembering that irresponsible trip back to the house.

'You've caught a chill,' Mrs Willett said to her. 'You must lie down. What a time of it you've had, your first night in London. You must stay and make up the sleep you lost.'

'I can't. I must take Alf and Binnie to their mother and then go and find my cousin,' Eileen said. *So I won't have to spend another night in that Anderson. Or this century.*

'Of course,' Mrs Willett said, 'but you must at least stay to breakfast, and if you don't find your cousin immediately, you must come back and stay with us. And if there's anything either of us can do to help—'

'If I could give this as an address where I can be reached, in case I need to leave my cousin a message—?'

'Of course. And I'm certain Mrs Owens would let you give her telephone as a number where you can be reached.'

Eileen thanked her, though she hoped she wouldn't need either, or the offer to 'stay as long as you like', which she extended again as Eileen left. 'I want to go with Eileen,' Theodore said.

'Come along, Alf, Binnie,' Eileen said, anxious to be gone before Theodore asked her if she was coming back. 'Let's go and find your mother.'

'She won't be there,' Alf predicted.

She wasn't, and the person who answered Eileen's knock this time – a worn-out-looking woman with a squalling infant in her arms and two toddlers hanging on her skirts – wouldn't even open the door all the way. When Eileen asked if Alf and Binnie could stay with her, she shook her head. 'Not after what they done to my Mickey.'

'Well, do you know when—?' Eileen began, but the woman had already shut the door and locked it. *I am never going to get rid of these children. They're going to be attached to me for ever.*

'What now?' Alf asked.

I have no idea, she thought, standing irresolutely on the pavement. She needed to find Polly. But even if she found her, she couldn't go through the drop till she'd disposed of Alf and Binnie.

But she could at least locate Polly and find out where the drop was and then, when Mrs Hodbin finally made it home, she could go straight to it. 'Come along,' she said. 'We're going shopping.'

'With all this lot?' Binnie asked, holding up their bags.

She was right. They could scarcely walk into a department store like this. 'We'll ask her if you can at least leave your things here,' she said, starting up to the door.

'No! They'll pinch our stuff,' Binnie said.

'I know a place,' Alf said. He grabbed the bags, tore off up the street with them to the bombed house, clambered up onto the rubble, and behind a still-standing wall. He reappeared immediately, without their luggage, and jumped down off the rubble to the pavement. 'Where are we goin' shoppin'?' he asked.

'Oxford Street,' she said. 'Do you know how to get there?'

They did, and she was almost glad they were along to navigate the tube station and find the right platform and get off at the right stop. They weren't in the least intimidated by the size of Oxford Circus station or its network of tunnels and two-storey-long escalators, or by the masses of people. Had people actually slept here during the raids? How did they manage to keep from being trampled?

The pavement outside was just as crowded as the tube station had been, with motor cars and taxis and enormous double-decker buses roaring past. *I'm glad I only had to drive on country lanes,* Eileen thought, standing on the corner, looking in vain for the stores Polly'd named. There were scores of shops and department stores in this bit alone, and the line of them stretched as far as she could see in both directions. Thank goodness she knew which three Polly might be working in. If she could find them. She scanned the names above the doors – Goldsmiths, Frith and Co., Leighton's—

'What're you lookin' for?' Alf asked.

'John Lewis,' she said, and then, so they wouldn't think that was a person, 'It's a department store.'

'We *know*,' Binnie said. 'It's this way,' and dragged Eileen down the street.

They passed department store after department store – Bourne and Hollingsworth, Townsend Brothers, Mary Marsh – and all of them were enormous buildings with at least four floors. Selfridge's, on the other side of the street, covered an entire block. *Let's hope Polly's not working there,* Eileen thought. It would take a fortnight to find her.

But Padgett's was nearly as large, with even more grandiose Greek columns along its front. John Lewis, two streets down, had columns as well, plus unboarded-up display windows. Eileen corralled Alf and Binnie – who'd gone next door to Lyons Corner House to look at the pastries in the window – and tried to clean them up a bit. She tied Binnie's sash and straightened her collar. 'Pull up your socks,' she told them, rummaging in her handbag for a comb.

'I'm 'ungry,' Binnie said. 'Can we go in here?'

'No,' Eileen said, yanking the comb through her tangles. 'Tuck in your shirt, Alf.'

'We ain't 'ad nothin' to eat in *hours*,' Alf complained. 'Can't we—?'

'No,' she said, trying to hold him still so she could give him a quick spit bath with her handkerchief. 'Come along.'

She took their hands and led them over to the entrance. And stopped, stymied. There was no door, only a sort of glass-and-wood cage, divided into vertical sections. 'Ain't you never seen a revolving door?' Alf said, and darted into one of the sections, pushing on it to make it turn, followed by Binnie, giving a running commentary on how to do it. Eileen trusted neither it *nor* the Hodbins, but in spite of a momentary feeling of being trapped, she made it through and inside the store.

And what a store! Hanging brass-and-glass lamps and carved wooden pillars and polished floors. The counters were of oak, and behind them rows of brass-handled drawers went all the way to the high ceilings. On each counter stood an elegant lamp and behind each one an equally elegant young woman.

Oh dear, Eileen thought. John Lewis was clearly too good for a housemaid and two slum children – and the problem wasn't just that they stood out in their shabby clothes. Eileen had intended to pretend to look at merchandise till she'd located someone she could ask, but that wasn't going to be possible. Except for several hats on a brass hat stand, and some folded scarves on one of the counters, no merchandise was on display. She was obviously supposed to ask to see things, and the salespeople just as obviously wouldn't believe she could afford anything in the store.

Her assessment was rapidly borne out by a middle-aged man in a frocked coat and striped pants bearing down on the three of them with an appalled expression. 'May I assist you, madam?' he asked, sounding as appalled as he looked.

'Yes,' she said. 'I'm looking for someone who works here. Polly Sebastian?'

'Works *here*? As part of the cleaning staff?'

'No, as a shopgirl.'

'I think you must have the wrong store, madam,' he said, his tone of voice clearly saying, 'We would never hire anyone who knew the likes of you.'

He won't even check to see if she works here, Eileen thought, *and he won't let me look for myself either.* In another minute he'd be escorting them to the revolving door, and there'd be no way he'd let them back in. *I should never have brought Alf and Binnie with me,* she thought, and had a sudden inspiration. 'These children are evacuees,' she said. 'They're staying with Lady Caroline at Denewell Manor. I'm her maid. She sent me to London to have them outfitted with new clothes. I was told to ask for Miss Sebastian.'

'Oh, of course,' he said, all smiles now. 'You'll want our children's department. That's on the third floor. This way, if you please,' he said, leading the way, and for a moment she was afraid he intended to go with them, but he stopped outside a lift. A boy not much older than Binnie leaned out and asked, 'Which floor, miss?'

'Third,' Eileen said and stepped in with the children. The boy reached forward to shut the wooden door, pull the brass gate across, and push down on the lever. The lift started up.

'Second floor, men's wear and shoes,' the boy recited mechanically. 'Third floor, children's wear, books, toys.' He pulled the gate open, opened the door, and held it for them while they exited.

Eileen had worried they'd immediately be confronted by another striped-pants person, but the one on this floor was assisting a woman and her daughter.

Good, Eileen thought, taking Alf and Binnie by the hand and starting across the floor in the opposite direction, but Alf and Binnie dug in their heels and refused to move. 'We're 'ungry,' Binnie said.

'I told you—'

'So 'ungry we might say something we ain't s'posed to,' Alf said.

'Like Lady Caroline didn't really send you.'

Why, you wretched little blackmailers. But she didn't have time to argue with them. Striped Pants was coming this way.

'Very well, I'll take you to Lyons for lunch,' she whispered. '*After* I finish here.'

'Lunch *and* a sweet,' Binnie said.

'Lunch and a sweet. *If* you help me find my cousin.'

'We will,' Alf said, and they were as good as their word. When Striped Pants asked Eileen if he could assist her, Alf said promptly, 'We're Lady Caroline's evacuees,' and looked appropriately pathetic.

'You'll want our children's department then,' Striped Pants said. 'This way.'

And what do I do when I get there? Eileen wondered, half sorry she'd invented the evacuee story. Now she couldn't ask the shopgirls if Polly worked here, and what excuse could she give for not buying anything when they reached Children's Wear?

But Alf came through for her. 'Eileen, I feel like I'm goin' to be sick,' he said, clutching his stomach, and Striped Pants led them hastily to the ladies' lounge instead.

Once inside, Alf said, 'I know a better way to go up and down without no floorwalker seein' us.'

A floorwalker, that was what Striped Pants was.

'Come on,' Alf said, and led her – with Binnie acting as lookout – over to a door marked *Stairs* and through it into a stairwell. Eileen followed them, trying not to think about why he and Binnie were both so familiar with department stores and revolving doors and lifts. Blackmail *and* shoplifting.

But she had to admit using the stairs was a stroke of genius. It was possible to stand inside their windowed doors and survey the entire floor before emerging. If Polly had been there, Eileen would have seen her.

But she wasn't. Eileen searched all six floors, including the basement, part of which had been fitted up as a shelter, but there was no sign of her. 'Can we have our lunch now?' Binnie begged.

'*And* a sweet,' Alf added.

'Yes,' Eileen said, steering them out of the store and next door to Lyons. 'You've earned it,' though when she saw the prices she regretted agreeing to the sweet. 'No, you may not have the four-course meal,' she told Alf, who had found the most expensive thing on the menu. 'I said lunch.'

'But it's already past three,' Binnie said. 'We should get lunch *and* tea.'

'Past three?' Eileen said, looking over at the clock, but Binnie was right. It had taken the better part of the afternoon to search John Lewis. She'd planned on doing Padgett's after the children ate, but it was even larger than John Lewis, and she had to deliver Alf and Binnie or be stuck with them for another night. And by the time she got them to Whitechapel and came back, the raids would be starting.

She hurried them through their lunch and pudding, out of Lyons and back up the street towards Oxford Circus. 'Marble Arch is nearer,' Binnie said, pointing in the other direction.

She was right. Marble Arch was only a short distance from Lyons and an even shorter one from Padgett's. Eileen made a mental note to use Marble Arch when she came back.

If she had time to come back. *What if their mother's still not there and I have to take them back to Theodore's with me?* she thought, waiting on the platform for their train. But when they reached Gargery Lane, she was – a blowsy woman in a frayed silk kimono who'd clearly been awakened by Eileen's knocking. Her blonde pompadour was mussed and her makeup smeared.

'What're you two doing here?' she demanded when she saw Alf and Binnie carrying the luggage Alf had just retrieved from the bombed house. 'Threw you out, did they?'

Eileen explained about the manor being taken over, but Mrs Hodbin wasn't interested. 'Have you got their ration books?'

'Yes,' Eileen said, handing them over. 'They both had the measles this summer, and Binnie was very ill.'

But Mrs Hodbin wasn't interested in that either. She snatched the ration books, ordered Alf and Binnie inside and banged the door shut.

Eileen stood there a moment, feeling oddly ... what? Cheated, because Mrs Hodbin hadn't let her say goodbye to them? That was ridiculous. She'd been trying for the last three days to rid herself of them. *And now you're free to go and find Polly and her drop and go home,* she told herself, hurrying down the stairs and up the street, past the bombed-out houses. *I hope they'll be all right.*

She stopped short, remembering the vicar's letter. Oh no, she'd forgotten to give it to Mrs Hodbin. She rummaged through her handbag, found it, and started back towards the Hodbins', and then stopped again, trying to decide what to do. It was dangerous here in Whitechapel, but far more dangerous on board the *City of Benares*, and Mrs Hodbin had looked as if she'd be glad to be rid of Alf and Binnie. If she took them to the Overseas Programme office today or tomorrow, they'd almost certainly end up on the *City of Benares*.

You don't know that, she told herself. *You don't even know that she'd want them to go. She grabbed for those ration books awfully quickly.* And Alf and Binnie could just as easily be killed here. But here they'd have a chance. In the dark waters of the Atlantic ... Besides, if she did go back, Mrs Hodbin might not even open the door. And she didn't have time. She had to get to Oxford Street before Padgett's closed.

Eileen put the envelope in her handbag, caught the tube to Marble Arch, walked to Padgett's and began searching it. Without Alf and Binnie to deal with, she should be able to check the floors and ask her questions much more quickly.

But by the time the closing bell rang, she'd only completed the main floor, the mezzanine and the first floor. For a terrified moment she thought that the closing bell was a siren, and her first panicked instinct was to hurry back to Stepney and the Anderson, but she'd so hoped to be safely back in Oxford by tonight. She forced herself to go to the staff entrance at the side of the store and stand there watching the shopgirls coming out, chattering. But Polly didn't appear, and no one she asked knew her.

The sirens went while Eileen was on her way to Marble Arch. There were people camping out in the tunnels and on the platform and she was tempted to join them. That way she might be able to catch Polly on her way to work, but she was already too mussed and her clothes too wrinkled for the posh stores. She decided to go back to Stepney, where she could tidy up and set out again early in the morning.

But the raids had damaged two of the main streets in Stepney, so she had to walk nearly two miles to catch the bus in the morning, and just as she reached Oxford Circus, the sirens went, and she had to spend a cramped three-quarters of an hour in the basement shelter of Peter Robinson's.

She didn't reach Padgett's till nearly noon. She walked purposefully in past the doorman, took the lift to the third floor and then the stairs to the fifth and began working her way down, checking each department before she asked for Polly, in case she'd remembered her name wrong.

By half-past twelve, she'd worked her way down to the ground floor and still hadn't found her. *If Polly's not on this floor, I'll have to try Selfridge's*, she thought, walking towards the stationery department. But as she was asking the shopgirl if Polly Sebastian worked there, two saleswomen emerged chattering from the stairwell, obviously just back from lunch, and the one behind the stationery counter began putting on her hat.

It's lunchtime, Eileen thought. She hadn't seen everyone after all. She'd have to search the store again after they were all back from lunch. And she might have missed Polly at John Lewis as well. She'd have to search it again, too.

But there was no sign of her at either store, and no one who knew her. That left Selfridge's, which stretched for miles, with all sorts of pillars and alcoves and recesses that made it impossible to see more than one department at a time. By closing time she'd only finished searching two of its six floors and wasn't convinced she'd seen every part of those two. She went out to find Selfridge's staff entrance, but by the time she did, employees were already streaming out and obviously had been for some time.

A siren began its up-and-down whine nearby. *I want to go home*, Eileen thought, then smiled ruefully, thinking, *You sound just like Theodore.* At least she wouldn't have to put up with this for weeks on end, as he would. *You've only got to stand it one more night.*

But she wasn't certain she could. The raids were so heavy Mrs Owens abandoned her cupboard and came out to join Theodore and Eileen in the Anderson despite the dampness, and it was only the older woman's presence and Theodore's trembling little body pressed against her that kept Eileen from cowering in the corner and screaming. The bombs sounded as if they were right in the garden, though when Mrs Willett arrived home from the factory, she said Stepney had been largely spared, that most of the bombing had been over Westminster and Whitechapel.

I hope Alf and Binnie are all right, and that I did the right thing in not giving that letter to Mrs Hodbin. Today was the thirteenth. If she sent the letter now, it probably wouldn't arrive till after the *City of Benares* had sailed, and no other evacuee ship had sunk after that. And they'd be far safer in Canada than in London. Eileen borrowed a stamp from Theodore's mother, wrote Mrs Hodbin's address on the envelope, intending to post the letter on the way to the tube station, and then changed her mind at the last moment. If the *City of Benares* hadn't sailed ...

She'd hoped to get to Selfridge's before it opened so she could watch the employees arriving, but her train was delayed twice because of damage on the line. When she finally reached Selfridge's, she devised a new strategy: She took the lift up to the personnel office to ask if Polly was employed there. 'Sorry,' the secretary said as she walked in. 'We've already filled the opening for a waitress in our Palm Court Restaurant.'

'Oh, but I'm not—' Eileen began.

'I'm afraid we have no openings for sales assistants either.' She turned back to her typewriter.

'I'm not looking to be hired,' Eileen said. 'I'm trying to locate someone who works here. Polly Sebastian.'

The secretary didn't even stop typing. 'Selfridge's does not give out information regarding its employees.'

'But I must find her. You see, my brother Michael's in hospital, and he's asking for her. He's an RAF pilot. His Spitfire was shot down,' she added, and the secretary not only looked up Polly's name in the employee files for her, but, when she couldn't find it there, checked the list of recent hires.

She also asked a number of difficult-to-answer questions about which airfield Michael was stationed at, so when Eileen went to John Lewis, she said he'd been injured at Dunkirk.

The secretary there couldn't find Polly's name in the files either, and at Padgett's the secretary said, 'I'm only temporary. I usually work in the perfume department, but Miss Gregory's secretary was killed, and I was called in to substitute, so I don't know about the personnel files, and Miss Gregory's not here just now. If you'd care to leave your name, I can have her ring you when she returns.'

Eileen gave her her name and Mrs Owens' telephone number and went back to Selfridge's to ask the shopgirls in each department if they knew anyone named Polly Sebastian who worked on their floor, but none of them recognised the name. 'She'd only just have started,' she told one in the millinery department. 'She has fair hair and grey eyes,' but the young woman was shaking her head.

'They haven't hired anyone new since July,' she said, 'even though several girls have left, and now I doubt they will, what with the raids causing business to fall off.'

Which presented a whole new problem – what if Polly had been unable to get hired by any of the stores she'd mentioned? Presumably she'd have got a job at some other store. But which one? There were dozens of department stores and shops on Oxford Street. It would take weeks to search them all. Polly had said Mr Dunworthy had insisted she work in one that hadn't been bombed, but except for the three she'd heard Polly mention, she had no way of knowing which ones those were. 'Are you certain it was Padgett's and not Parson's?' the shopgirl was asking.

'Yes,' Eileen said, 'her letter said she was coming to London to take a job at Padgett's.'

'Did she say when? Perhaps she hasn't started yet.'

She hadn't thought of that either. Polly might not even be here yet. Eileen didn't know how long the Blitz had lasted, but she thought it was several months, and Polly'd said her assignment was only for a few weeks. She might not be coming till next week. Or next month.

'Are you all right, ma'am?' the shopgirl was asking.

No, Eileen thought. 'Yes,' she said, thanked her for her help, and started towards the lifts.

'I hope you find her,' the shopgirl called after her.

I hope I find her soon, Eileen thought. She had only money enough for two or three more days' tube fares and meals, even if Theodore's mother let her stay on. 'Stay as long as you like,' she'd said, but she'd meant 'till you find your cousin in a day or two', not weeks.

But if Polly wasn't here in 1940 yet or was working in one of the dozens of smaller shops, it might take much longer to find her. Eileen would have to find work. But doing what? Her only experience was as a servant, but going into service was the worst thing she could do. She'd have a half-day out at most and no freedom to come and go.

Perhaps I can get hired at Lyons Corner House, she thought, but when she inquired there, the personnel office told her they were only hiring for the evening shift, which meant she'd have to work during the raids, and she didn't know whether Lyons had been hit or not.

She spent the rest of the day searching Parson's, just in case that was the name Polly'd said, made a list of every shop and department store on Oxford Street so she could tick them off as she searched them, and then bought a newspaper and, on the train home to Stepney, circled all the *Situations Vacant* ads with Oxford Street addresses.

There were only four, and none were for Selfridge's, Padgett's or John Lewis. The best was *Waitress wanted. Wisteria Tea Shoppe. 532 Oxford Street. 1 to 5 p.m. shift.* It was several streets away from the department stores, but only a few doors down from Marble Arch tube station, so if the raids began before her shift ended, she could take shelter there. And the hours were perfect. She could spend all morning looking for Polly, work her shift, and then go and watch the staff entrances as the shopgirls left.

I'll take the earliest bus so I can be first in line, she thought as she walked to Theodore's house, but he met her at the door with, 'A lady telephoned for you.'

It's Polly, she thought. *She went to Padgett's to apply, and Miss Gregory told her I'd been there and gave her my number.* 'What was the name of the lady who rang up?' she asked.

'I don't know,' Theodore said. 'A lady.'

'Did she leave her address, or a telephone number?'

Theodore didn't know that either. She took him next door to ask Mrs Owens, thinking, *Please don't have let Theodore have been the one who spoke to her*, but Mrs Owens had taken the call. 'What a pity. You only just missed her.'

'What did she say?' Eileen asked eagerly.

'Only that she wished to speak with you, and that you were to ring her at this number.' She gave it to Eileen.

'May I use your phone to ring her? I'm afraid if I go down to the phone box, Padgett's will have closed.'

'Of course.' Mrs Owens showed her to the phone. 'Theodore, come with me into the kitchen and have your tea.'

Good, Eileen thought, giving the operator the number. *With them not here in the room, I'll be able to ask Polly where her drop is.* 'Hullo, this is Eileen O'Reilly,' she said.

'Yes, this is Miss Gregory from Padgett's Department Store. You left your name and number with us.'

'That's right.' *Polly must be there in the office with her.*

'I phoned to tell you that we have an opening in our sales staff.'

'An opening?' Eileen said blankly.

'Yes, to start immediately. As a junior assistant in our notions department.'

They were offering her a job. Miss Gregory must have found the information she'd left and thought it was an application. But she'd so hoped it was Polly, that she was on her way home. 'Are you available, Miss O'Reilly?' Miss Gregory was asking.

Yes, she thought bitterly. But she couldn't afford to pass up this job. It was in one of the stores where Polly might already be working, and near the others, and even if Polly didn't work there, Eileen would be in the heart of Oxford Street and – on her lunch break – able to systematically go up one side of Oxford Street and down the other, searching every department store. 'Yes,' Eileen said, 'I'd very much like the job.'

'Excellent. Can you begin tomorrow morning?' Miss Gregory asked, and when Eileen said yes, told her when and where to report and what to wear.

'Are you *going*?' Theodore asked, his voice rising threateningly when she rang off.

Not yet, Eileen thought. 'No,' she said, and smiled at him. 'I'm going to stay here and work at Padgett's.'

LONDON – 26 SEPTEMBER 1940

Polly's retrieval team still hadn't come by Thursday night. *I can't stand this waiting. I'll give it till Saturday, and then I'm going up to Backbury*, she thought, listening to Miss Laburnum and the others argue over which play to do.

Surprisingly, Sir Godfrey had agreed to the idea of a full-scale theatrical production. 'I'd be delighted to assist in such a worthy cause,' he'd said. 'We must do *Twelfth Night*. With Miss Sebastian as Viola.'

'Oh, I had my heart set on one of Barrie's plays,' Miss Laburnum said.

'Perhaps *Peter Pan*,' Mrs Brightford suggested. 'The children could be in it.'

'Nelson could play Nana,' Mr Simms said.

Sir Godfrey looked aghast. '*Peter Pan?*'

'We can't,' Polly said quickly. 'We've no way to manage the flying.'

Sir Godfrey shot a grateful glance at her. 'An excellent point. On the other hand, *Twelfth Ni*—'

'It must be a patriotic play,' Mrs Wyvern said decisively.

'*Henry V,*' Sir Godfrey said.

'No, not enough women. We must do a play with women in it so everyone in our little troupe can participate.'

'And with a dog,' Mr Simms said.

'*Twelfth Night* has lots of women,' Polly said. 'Viola, the Lady Olivia, Maria—'

'I think we should do the clock one,' Trot said.

'What a good idea!' Miss Laburnum exclaimed. 'We can do Barrie's *A Kiss for Cinderella*!'

'Is there a part for a dog in it?' Mr Simms asked.

'What about a murder mystery?' the rector said.

'*The Mousetrap*,' Sir Godfrey said dryly.

When I get to Backbury, I must tell Merope that Sir Godfrey likes Agatha Christie, Polly thought, and then realised he was referring to *Hamlet*. And probably plotting the murder of Miss Laburnum.

She half listened to them propose possible plays, trying to decide when to go. If she waited till after work on Saturday, she wouldn't need to ask Miss Snelgrove for time off or run the risk of missing the retrieval team while she was gone. But she seemed to remember Merope saying her half-day off was Monday and that that was when she went through to Oxford to check in. If it took Polly longer than planned to get to Backbury, she ran the risk of Merope's not being there when she arrived.

Or not being there at all. Merope's assignment had to be nearly over. What if she was going back for good on Monday? I'd better not wait till Saturday night, Polly thought.

'I saw three copies of *Mary Rose* in a secondhand bookshop last week,' Miss Laburnum said. 'Such an affecting play ... That poor boy, searching for his lost love those years ...' She put her hand to her bosom. 'I shall make an expedition to Charing Cross Road on Saturday.'

And I shall make one to Backbury, Polly thought. *I'll go on Saturday and come back on Sunday.* She needed to find out about trains. It was too late to go to Euston to look at the schedule. The Underground trains had already stopped for the night. She would have to do it in the morning.

But when the trains began running again at half past six the next morning, there was a notice board saying the Central Line was out of service due to 'damage on the line', so instead she had to ask Marjorie to watch her counter while she ran up to the book department and consulted an ABC railway guide.

The earliest train on a Saturday was at 10:02, with connections at Reading and Leamington. It didn't get in to Backbury till ... Oh no, after ten o'clock at night. That meant she wouldn't be able to go to the manor till Sunday morning. And depending on how far from Backbury it was, it might take her the better part of the day to walk there and back.

And if Merope had already gone back, she couldn't afford to miss the return train. And, according to the ABC, the only one from Backbury on Sunday went at 11:19 a.m.

I shall to have to go tonight, she thought. *If there's a train.*

There were three, the first one at 6:48. *If I go straight to Euston from work, I should be able to make the 6:48*, she thought, starting down to her counter to relieve Marjorie.

Marjorie. If Merope was in Backbury, Polly wouldn't be coming back, which meant that before she left she needed to buy Marjorie stockings to replace the ones she'd borrowed. But she hadn't enough money with her for them and her train fare. She'd have to go back to Mrs Rickett's for Mr Dunworthy's emergency money, and take the 7:55 instead, but that had a benefit. She'd be able to tell Mrs Rickett where she was going. And if she was delayed for some reason, she could take the 9:03.

She hurried back to her counter. Marjorie was busy with a customer. Polly brought Doreen over to write up the purchase and, when Marjorie finished waiting on her customer, took the stockings over to her. 'They're lovely,' Marjorie said, 'but it wasn't necessary for you to do that.'

Yes, it is, Polly thought. *You've no idea how scarce stockings are about to become. You may well have to make these last for the remainder of the war.*

'Thank you,' Marjorie said. She leaned over the counter towards Polly. 'You'll never guess who was here while you were gone,' she whispered, and before Polly's heart could turn over, 'The airman I told you about who's always after me to go out with him. Tom. He wanted me to go out dancing.'

'And are you going?' Polly asked.

'No, I told you, he's terribly fast.' She frowned. 'Though perhaps I should have. As he said, in times like these people need to seize happiness while they can.'

Which was also a very old line. 'I need to ask you something,' Polly said. 'Is it Miss Snelgrove I need to speak to about getting tomorrow off, or Mr Witherill?'

'A day off?' Marjorie echoed. She sounded horrified.

'Yes. I've had a letter from my sister, you see. My mother's ill, and I must go home.'

'But you can't go tomorrow. Saturday's Townsend Brothers' busiest day of the week. They'll never allow it.'

It had never occurred to Polly that she might not be able to get the day off, especially with an excuse like an ailing mother. She could just leave, of course, but if Merope wasn't in Backbury, working here was her best chance of being found by the retrieval team.

'Miss Snelgrove's already had her quota of human kindness for the week,' Marjorie was saying. 'And Mr Witherill will be convinced you're doing a flit.' She looked at Polly sharply. 'You're not, are you? Not that I'd blame you. Sitting in that horrid cellar last night, listening to the bombs, I thought, "When the all-clear goes, I'm going to go straight to Waterloo Station, take the train to Bath, and move in with Brenda."'

'I'm not running away.' Polly pulled out the letter from Props and handed it over, making certain Marjorie saw the Northumbria postmark on the envelope. 'It's her heart. Surely if I tell Miss Snelgrove—'

But Marjorie was shaking her head. 'Don't say anything to her *or* Mr Witherill,' she ordered, handing the letter back. 'Tomorrow morning, I'll say you rang me up and said you weren't feeling well. Will you be back by Monday?'

'Yes, unless ...' Polly said hesitantly. She hated to get Marjorie into trouble if she didn't return.

'I'll cover for you Monday as well. If you need to stay on longer, you can always write from home and tell them.'

'But what about tomorrow? You'll be left short-handed.'

'I'll manage. No one's buying girdles just now. They take too long to put on when there's a raid. Do you leave tonight?'

Polly nodded. 'Thank you so much for covering for me. If anyone should come in asking for me, tell them I'll be back on Monday, or Tuesday at the latest.'

Marjorie leaned confidingly on the counter. 'Who *is* this mysterious person you're always hoping will come in and ask for you? A man?'

I don't know, Polly thought. It was likely the retrieval team would be female, but not certain.

'Is he a pilot?'

'No. A cousin of mine is coming to London and might look me up,' she said and walked quickly back to her own counter before Marjorie could ask any more questions.

At quarter past five, she began tidying up, hoping she might be able to leave early, but just before the closing bell Miss Snelgrove demanded to see her sales book.

Marjorie came over, already in her hat and coat. 'I'm leaving now, Miss Snelgrove,' she said, and turned to Polly. 'Are you feeling all right? You look rather pale.'

'I'm fine,' Polly said, then realised Marjorie was attempting to help her set up her alibi for tomorrow. 'It's only a headache, and my throat's been a bit sore this afternoon.' She put her hand to her throat, but Miss Snelgrove didn't look impressed. Marjorie was right; she'd used up her quota of kindness for the week.

'Where is your sales receipt for Mrs Scott?' Miss Snelgrove demanded.

Polly had wanted to say goodbye to Marjorie – it was, after all, the last time she might ever see her – but by the time Miss Snelgrove finished reprimanding Polly for smudging her carbons, she'd already gone, and it was probably for the best. Polly couldn't afford to have her ask what her cousin's name – or gender – was. And at any rate, there was no time for goodbyes. It was already quarter to six.

She had to leave. And to make the 6:48, she'd have to take a taxi to Mrs Rickett's. If she could find one. There weren't any parked in front of Townsend Brothers or on the street. She finally ran to Padgett's and had its doorman hail her one, but it took several minutes, and by the time they reached Mrs Rickett's, it was twenty past. Polly told the cabbie to wait, and raced inside, hoping Miss Hibbard would be in the parlour so she wouldn't have to deal with either Mrs Rickett or the talkative Miss Laburnum, but there was no one there, or in the dining room, though the supper dishes still lay on the table. The sirens must have gone early again – the raids tonight didn't start till nine.

She pelted up the stairs to her room to get her money, ran back downstairs, leaped in the taxi, and said, 'Euston Station. And hurry. I've a train to catch.'

'I'll get you there,' he said and roared down Cardle Street to Notting Hill Gate and past the Underground station.

Oh no, Polly thought, *I didn't tell them I'm leaving.* When she'd realised the siren had sounded, she'd forgotten all about it. *I should have left a note.*

It was too late now. It was already twenty to. She'd be lucky to catch her train as it was. But she was seeing the tears streaming down Miss Hibbard's face and the look on Sir Godfrey's ashen face before he saw her. She was remembering her own knees giving way when she saw the wrecked church.

I can't do that to them again, she thought, *not when they'll have to face so many real deaths in the four and a half years ahead.* She leaned forward and tapped the cabbie on the shoulder. 'I've changed my mind,' she said. 'Take me to Notting Hill Gate Underground Station.'

'But what about your train, miss?'

'I'll take the next one,' she said.

He made a U-turn and headed back. 'Do you want me to wait again?' he asked, pulling up in front of the station.

With the sirens already having gone, the guard wouldn't let her out of the station. 'No, I'll take the tube from here,' she said, handed him the fare, and ran inside and down to the platform.

'Oh good, the warden told you,' Miss Laburnum said the moment she saw her.

'Told me what?'

'About the gas leak.'

'A delayed-action bomb went off two streets over and ruptured a gas main,' Miss Hibbard said, coming over with her knitting. 'During supper.'

A gas leak! A spark from the taxi's ignition could have blown us both skyhigh.

The rector and Mrs Rickett were there, and Mrs Brightford and her girls, all spreading out their blankets. 'I'm glad you're here,' Miss Laburnum said. 'We've been discussing the play.'

'I can't stay,' Polly said. 'I only came to tell you I won't be here tonight.'

'Oh, but you must,' Miss Laburnum said.

'We've decided the only fair thing to do is put it to a vote,' Mrs Wyvern said.

Oh dear, that meant Barrie. Poor Sir Godfrey.

'But Sir Godfrey wants us to wait till Sunday. First he wants us to see a scene from *Twelfth Night*. The one where Viola longs to tell him of her love, but she can't because she can't reveal her true identity – and he wants you to play Viola.'

He was obviously counting on her to help him talk them out

of Barrie. But she *had* to catch the 7:55. 'I'm afraid someone else will have to play Viola. I—'

'Oh, but Sir Godfrey *insists* you do it. He says you're perfect for the part.'

'I can't. I've had a letter from my sister. My mother's ill, and I must go home. I only came to tell you so you wouldn't think—'

'You were killed,' Trot said promptly, and Polly was very glad she'd come, even though it meant she'd missed the 6:48.

'Yes,' she said, 'and to tell you I won't be back till Sunday night at the earliest. It all depends on how my mother is. Tell Sir Godfrey I'm sorry I couldn't stay, but my train—'

'Of course, you must go. We quite understand,' the rector said, and the others, excepting Mrs Rickett, nodded sympathetically.

'Thank you. For everything. Goodbye,' she said and hurried off down the platform and along the tunnel, sorry she hadn't been able to tell Sir Godfrey goodbye, though that was probably for the best. Lying to Miss Laburnum and the rector was one thing, but Sir Godfrey wasn't fooled nearly so easily. And she wasn't certain she could have turned him down if he'd asked her to stay and play the part of Viola to his Orsino.

And I must make the 7:55, she thought, hurrying across to the escalator, glancing at her watch as she pushed through the crowd. Quarter past. If there wasn't too long a wait between trains, she should be able to—

'Miss Sebastian, wait,' Sir Godfrey called. He caught up to her. 'I've just been told that you are leaving us.'

'Yes. I've had a letter saying my mother's ill.'

'And so you must away to Northumbria?'

'Yes.'

'Forever?'

I should have pretended I didn't hear him calling me, she thought. And it didn't matter what she told him, he could see right through her. 'I don't know.'

A look like pain crossed his face, and he said quietly, abandoning his theatrical language, 'Are you in some sort of trouble, Viola?'

Yes, she thought. *And you were right. Viola's the perfect role for me. I am in disguise. I can't tell you the truth.*

'No,' she said, hoping she really was the actress he'd said she was. 'It's only that I'm so worried over my mother. My sister says she's not in any danger, but I'm afraid—'

'That she's not telling you the truth?'

'Yes,' she said, meeting his gaze steadily. 'She knows how difficult it is for me to take time off from my job. That's why I must go, to see if she's all right. If it isn't anything serious, I'll return on Sunday, but if she's really ill, I may have to stay for several weeks, or months.'

And you don't believe a word I'm saying, she thought.

But all he said was, 'I wish her a speedy recovery and you a speedy return. If you are not here for the vote Sunday night, I fear I shall be doomed to performing *Peter Pan*, a fate which surely you would not wish on me.'

Polly laughed. 'No. Goodbye, Sir Godfrey.'

'Goodbye, fair Viola. What a pity I never got to act *Twelfth Night* with you, though perhaps it's just as well. I should have hated to find myself playing Malvolio, smiling and cross-gartered. And sadly mistaken in thinking the lady cared for him.'

'Never,' Polly said. 'You could never play any part but Duke Orsino.'

He clutched his chest dramatically. 'Oh, to be twenty-five again!' He pushed her onto the escalator. 'Now, begone. Swiftly, that we may meet again. Sunday night at Notting's Gate when the Luftwaffe roars. Fail me not, fair maid! My life and your good name upon it!' he said and disappeared into the crowd before she could reply.

She hurried towards the Central Line platform. It was already twenty to. *I'll never make it to Euston in time*, she thought. *Unless by some miracle it's late.*

480

It was, and it was a good thing – the sirens started up as the 7:55 was pulling out of the station. But even though they'd escaped that, they still spent most of the night stopped due to raids, and most of Saturday forced onto sidings by troop trains, which meant she missed the train from Leamington. The next one wasn't till morning. 'There's *nothing* tonight?'

The ticket agent shook his head. 'The war, you know.'

And if the morning train was delayed like the one she'd just been on, she wouldn't make it to Backbury till Monday afternoon, by which time Merope would have left for Oxford to check in. Or would have gone back altogether. 'Is there a bus to Backbury?'

The agent consulted a different schedule. 'There's a bus to Hillford, and another that leaves for Backbury from there tomorrow morning at seven.'

It would mean spending the night in the station in Hillford, but at least she would be in Backbury by Sunday, not Monday, and, unlike a train, a bus couldn't be shunted onto a siding for hours while a succession of troop trains passed.

It could, however, be stopped at railway crossings while those same troop trains crawled by. And at roadblocks, where overzealous Home Guard officers insisted on checking everyone's papers. She needn't have worried about spending the night in the station. It was nearly seven in the morning before they reached Hillford.

The bus for Backbury was stopped by a troop train only once and for only half an hour. When the driver called out 'Backbury,' it was just a bit after eight. 'What time's the next bus from here back to Hillford?' Polly asked as she got off.

'Twenty past five.'

'In the *afternoon*?'

'Only two buses a day on Sunday. The war, you know.'

Yes, I do know. But at least there was a train from Backbury. She was glad she'd checked the ABC and found out when it went. Taking the 11:19 would get her back to London far faster than the bus. If she could get to the manor and back in three hours.

And if she could find it. The driver had stopped among a small huddle of shops and cottages. She couldn't see a manor house. Or a railway station. She turned back to ask the bus driver, 'Can you direct me to the manor?' but he'd already shut the door and was pulling away.

I'll have to ask one of the villagers, she thought, but there was no one in sight. They might be in church. It was Sunday, and even if Backbury didn't have an early mass, the local equivalent of Mrs Wyvern might be there arranging the altar flowers. But when she pushed open the door and looked in the sanctuary, she couldn't see anyone. 'Hullo?' she called. 'Anyone there?'

The only response was a distant whistle. *So I know which direction the railway station is,* she thought, going back outside and following the sound and the plume of smoke. She arrived at the station platform in time to see a troop train race by at top speed.

Why couldn't they have moved that quickly last night? she thought, walking over to the station, though it could hardly be called that. It was no larger than a potting shed. There was probably no point in knocking, but when she did, there was the sound of a cough and then a shuffle and an unshaven and obviously hungover – or drunken – man opened the door.

'I beg your pardon, sir,' Polly said, taking a step back so he didn't fall on her. 'Can you direct me to the manor?'

'*Manor?*' he said, weaving and squinting blearily at her. Definitely drunk.

'Yes. Can you tell me how to get there?'

He waved vaguely. 'Road just beyond the church.'

'Which way?'

'Only goes one way,' he said and would have shut the door if she hadn't grabbed it and held it open.

'I'm looking for someone who works at the manor. One of

the maids. Her name's Eileen. She cared for the evacuees at the manor. She has red hair and—'

'Evacuees?' he said, his eyes narrowing. 'You ain't here about those bloody Hodbin brats, are you?'

Hodbin? That was the name of the evacuees who'd given Merope so much trouble.

'You'd better not be bringin' 'em back.'

'I'm not. Does Eileen still work at the manor?' she asked, but he'd already slammed the door, and it would have been on her hand if she hadn't snatched it away at the last second. 'Can you tell me how far it is?' she called through the door, but got no answer.

It can't be that far. Merope walked it, Polly thought, going back to the church and then along the road beyond it. It was more a lane than a road – and the sort of lane that looked as if it would peter out in the middle of a field – but there was nothing else resembling either a road or a lane, and it led only south. It was also rutted with tyre tracks, and Merope had been going to take driving lessons.

But it sounded from what the stationmaster had said that the Hodbins were no longer here, and if the evacuees had gone home, Eileen would have, too. From what Eileen had said, though, the Hodbins might have been sent home in disgrace. Or shipped off to a reform school.

The lane led past a hayfield and then into woods. There was a scent of rain in the air. *Rain*, Polly thought, *that's all I need. Merope had better be here, after all this.*

Where was the manor? Polly'd already come at least a mile, and there was still no gateway, or, in spite of all the tyre tracks, a vehicle in which she could catch a ride. There were only woods. And more woods.

Merope – correction, Eileen; she had to remember to call her Eileen – had said her drop site was in the woods, near the manor house. If she wasn't there, perhaps Polly could still find it, though if she'd gone back it would no longer be working.

The lane curved to the left. *It can't be much further,* Polly thought, trudging along the ruts, but there was still no sign of a manor house through the woods, or any other house, for that matter, and the lane seemed to be narrowing. And ahead, the woods had been fenced off with barbed wire.

It is going to peter out in a field, she thought. *I must have come the wrong way.*

No, wait, there was the manor's gateway ahead, with its stone pillars and wrought-iron gate. And a sentry box, complete with a bar to keep vehicles out. And a uniformed sentry.

'State your name and business,' he said.

'I'm Miss Sebastian. I was looking for someone, but I must have come the wrong way. I was trying to find the manor.'

'This is it.'

And it had obviously been taken over by the Army. It was a good thing she hadn't tried to find the drop on her own. She might have been shot. 'How long has the Army been here?' she asked.

'I'm afraid you'll have to ask Lieutenant Heffernan that. I've only been here two weeks.'

'You don't know if any of the staff stayed on after the manor was taken over, do you?'

'You'll have to ask Lieutenant Heffernan.' He stepped back into the sentry box and picked up the telephone. 'A Miss Sebastian to see Lieutenant Heffernan. Yes, sir,' he said. He hung up and came back out. 'You're to go up.' He raised the bar so she could pass through. 'Follow the drive up to the house and ask for Operations.' He handed her a pasteboard visitor's pass. 'It's just through there,' he said, pointing between a pair of new-looking barracks.

'Thank you,' Polly said and started up the gravel drive, even though there was no point. Merope's assignment had obviously ended with the takeover of the manor. Unless the remaining evacuees had been transferred to another village and she'd gone with them. But Lieutenant Heffernan couldn't tell her anything about the evacuees.

'I didn't arrive till after the school was in operation,' he said.

'When did the Army take over the manor?'

'August, I believe.'

August. 'Did any of the staff stay on here?'

'No. Some of them may have gone with the lady of the manor. I believe she went to stay with friends.'

In which case she'd only have taken her personal maid and chauffeur.

'I can give you her ladyship's address,' he said, looking through a stack of papers. 'It's here somewhere ...'

'No, that's all right. Do you know if the evacuees who were here returned home or were billeted somewhere else?'

'I'm afraid I don't. I believe Sergeant Tilson was here then. He might be able to help.'

But Sergeant Tilson hadn't been there either. 'I didn't come till September the fifteenth, and the evacuees had already gone back to their parents by then.'

'To their parents? In London?'

He nodded.

Then Merope definitely hadn't gone with them. 'What about the staff?'

'From what Captain Chase said, they went home to their families as well.'

'Captain Chase?'

'Yes. He was in charge of setting up the training school. He'd be able to tell you – he was here when they all left – but I'm afraid you just missed him. He left for London early this morning and won't be back till Tuesday.' He frowned. 'The vicar in the village might be able to tell you where they went.'

If I can find him, Polly thought. But if she could make it back to Backbury before eleven, he'd be at the church, preparing for the service. She quickly took her leave of the sergeant – and the sentry, who solemnly raised the bar again to let her out – and hurried back along the road.

It was already past ten. *I'll never make it walking,* she thought, and it was too far to run. And just outside the gate, it began to rain in earnest, turning the lane into a muddy mire. She had to stop twice to scrape the caked mud off her shoes with a stick.

They'll already be in church, she thought when she finally splashed into the village. She spotted the vicar, half running, half walking along the side of the church towards the vestry door, clutching a sheaf of paper, his robe flying out behind him.

'Vicar!' she called, running after him. 'Vicar!' Or was he the vicar? Now that she grew closer, he looked awfully young. Perhaps he was the choirmaster, and those papers were the morning's anthems. 'Sir! Wait!'

She caught up to him just as he was going in. 'What is it, miss?' he said, his hand on the half-open vestry door. His eyes swept over her damp hair, her muddy shoes. 'What's happened? Has there been an accident?'

'No,' she said, out of breath from running. 'I've just been out to the manor. I came in on the bus this morning—'

'Vicar!' A small boy poked his head out of the half-opened door. 'Miss Fuller said to tell you they've finished the prelude.' He tugged at the vicar's sleeve.

'Coming, Peter,' he said, and to Polly, 'Has something happened at the training school?'

'No. I only wanted to ask you a question. I—'

'It's time for the invocation,' Peter hissed.

'I must go,' the vicar said regretfully, 'but I'll be glad to speak with you as soon as the service is over. Would you care to join us?'

'*Vicar, it's time!*' Peter said, and dragged him into the church.

And that's that, Polly thought and walked out to the station to wait for the train. *Unless the stationmaster knows where the evacuees have gone.*

But he'd apparently spent the last three hours drinking. 'Whaddya want?' he demanded, and it was obvious he didn't recognise her from this morning.

'I'm waiting for the 11:19 to London.'

'Won't be here f'r 'ours,' he said, slurring his words. 'Bloody troop trains. Always late.'

Good. She could go back to the church, wait for the end of the service, and ask the vicar after all. And if the 11:19 was as late as every other train she'd been on, she could also ask everyone else in the village. She hurried back to the church through the rain and slipped into the back of the sanctuary.

Only the first few rows of pews had people in them – several white-haired ladies in black hats, a handful of balding men, and young mothers with children. They were just finishing singing 'O God, Our Help in Ages Past'. Polly tiptoed in and sat down in the last pew.

The vicar looked up from his hymnal and smiled welcomingly at her, and one of the white-haired ladies, who looked like a cross between Miss Hibbard and Mrs Wyvern, turned around and glared. Miss Fuller, no doubt.

She's the person I should speak with, Polly thought. The captain had suggested the vicar, but she doubted if he was on intimate terms with the hired help at the manor. But this was a tiny village. Miss Fuller and the other elderly women would know all the comings and goings of everyone. If Polly could get past that disapproving glare.

But even if she couldn't, the boy Peter was likely to know about the evacuees, or could at least point out the schoolmistress to her. She'd be certain to know. And in the meantime, if it wasn't exactly warm in the sanctuary, it was at least dry, and hopefully the vicar's sermon wouldn't be too long, though she doubted it from the thickness of his sheaf of papers, which he was now arranging on the top of the pulpit.

He finished arranging them and gazed out over the congregation. 'The Scriptures say that our true home is not in this world, but the next, and that we are only passing through …'

Truer words, Polly thought.

'Thus it is with this war,' he said. 'We find ourselves stranded in an alien land of bombs and battles and blackouts, of Anderson shelters and gas masks and rationing. And that other world we once knew – of peace and lights and church bells chiming out over the land, of loved ones reunited and no tears, no partings – seems not only impossibly distant, but unreal, and we cannot quite imagine ourselves ever getting back there. We mark time here, waiting …'

For church to be over, for the train to arrive, for the retrieval team to come, Polly thought. The vicar's sermon was cutting a little too close to the bone. Why couldn't he have preached on begats or something?

'… hoping that this ordeal will pass, but secretly fearing that we shall never see that land of milk and honey – and sugar and butter and bacon – again. That we will be trapped in this dreadful place forever—'

A whistle cut sharply across his words. Peter got onto his knees to look out of the window, and Miss Fuller glared at him. Polly looked down at her watch: 11:19. The train. But the stationmaster had said it was always late.

It's another troop train, she thought, but she could already hear it slowing.

'Just as we have faith that one day the war will be over,' the vicar said, 'we have faith that one day we shall attain heaven. But just as we cannot hope to win this war unless we "do our bit" – rolling bandages, planting Victory gardens, serving in the Home Guard – so we cannot hope to attain heaven unless we also do our bit—'

Polly hesitated, caught in an agony of indecision. This was today's only train, and the bus wouldn't come till after five. If it was on time.

But someone here might know where Merope went. *You know where she went*, Polly thought, *and you know what they'll tell you: that all the evacuees went back to London and she left as soon as they were gone. She's been back in Oxford for weeks. Which means her drop isn't working anymore, and even if it was, you don't know where it is and can't get to it without being shot at, so there's no point in staying here.*

And if you miss that train, there'll be no way you'll make it back to London before Tuesday – or Wednesday – and Marjorie can't cover for you for ever. You'll lose your job, and when the retrieval team comes, they won't be able to find you.

'We must act—' the vicar said. The whistle, much closer, blew again.

Polly stood up, shot the vicar an apologetic glance, opened the church door, and ran for the train.

Those in the convent are desperate.

CODED MESSAGE TO THE FRENCH RESISTANCE, 5 JUNE 1944

WAR EMERGENCY HOSPITAL – SEPTEMBER 1940

Mike had had no idea anyone was sitting there in the high-backed wicker chair. When the voice said, 'I thought you were supposed to keep your weight off that foot, Davis,' it startled him so much he let go of the chair back, came down full on his bad foot, nearly fell, and had to clutch wildly at the potted palm to stay upright.

At the same time, a wild hope surged through him. *It's the retrieval team*, he thought. *Finally.*

The man was wearing hospital-issue pyjamas and maroon bathrobe, but he could have got those from Wardrobe. 'Patient' would be a perfect disguise for getting into the hospital, and he was the right age for a historian. And he'd waited till they were alone in the sun-room to speak.

'Sorry, old man, I didn't mean to give you a fright,' he said, leaning over the arm of the chair to smile at Mike.

'You know my name,' Mike said.

'Oh, right, we haven't been properly introduced, have we?' He extended his hand. 'Hugh Tensing. I'm on the third floor.'

And you're not the retrieval team, Mike thought. Now that he looked closer, he saw Tensing was much too thin, and he had the drawn, strained look of an invalid.

'You're Mike Davis, the American war correspondent,' Tensing was saying. 'You repaired a broken propellor with your bare hands and singlehandedly rescued the entire BEF, according to Nurse Baker. She can't stop talking about you.'

'She's wrong,' Mike said. 'The propellor wasn't broken. It was just fouled, and all I did was pull—'

'Spoken like a true hero,' Tensing said. 'Modest, humble even though you were injured in the line of duty—'

'I wasn't—'

'I see, it's all a fabrication. You weren't actually in Dunkirk at all,' Tensing said, smiling. 'You were in your newspaper office in London when a typewriter fell on your foot. Sorry, it won't wash. I know you're a hero. I've seen you take dangerous risks.'

'Dangerous—?'

'Just now. Openly defying your nurse's orders. And Matron's wrath. You're *far* braver than I am.'

'Yes, well, I'm not brave enough to risk being caught,' Mike said, 'and they may be here any minute, so I'd better make my way back to where I'm supposed to be.' He let go of the palm tree and stretched out his hand to grab the windowsill.

'No, wait, don't go,' Tensing said. 'I wasn't hiding from you just now. I was hiding from *my* nurse, hoping she'd think someone had taken me back to the ward so I could do the same thing you were doing. As a matter of fact, I was treading exactly the same circuit when your nurse wheeled you in and nearly caught me red-handed. Or is it red-footed?'

Mike glanced down at Tensing's feet, but there was no cast.

'Back injury,' Tensing said. 'For which they have prescribed—'

'Bed rest,' Mike guessed.

'Exactly. "You must be patient. Your recovery will take time", which utterly fails to comprehend that the one thing I don't have—'

'—is time.'

'Exactly. A man after my own heart.' He grinned. 'And because you are, I've a proposition for you. I can see you want the same thing I do – to get back in the war.'

You're wrong, Mike thought, *I want to get out of it. Before I do any more damage.*

'The last time I was caught trying to hasten my recovery,' Tensing went on, 'I was denied sun-room privileges for three weeks, all because I lacked an adequate warning system. I therefore propose a partnership.'

A partnership, Mike thought grimly. *I shouldn't even be talking to you, let alone helping you 'hasten your recovery'. What if you get back in the war a month earlier than you would have, thanks to me, and kill somebody you're not supposed to and change the outcome of the war?*

'I propose,' Tensing was saying, 'that one of us guard the door while the other walks, and give a warning if someone comes in. It won't require any effort. They'll glance in the door and see you reading or— What were you doing just now?'

'Working a crossword puzzle.'

'They'll see you solving a crossword and assume all's quiet on the western front and go away again.'

'And if they don't?'

'Then you'll call out a warning and I'll sink into the nearest chair and give an excellent imitation of a patient napping. And then as soon as they're gone, we'll switch places, and I'll stand guard while you walk, and we'll both be recovered and out of here in no time. What do you say?'

No, Mike thought, *I can't risk it.*

On the other hand, the sooner he got out of this hospital and this century, the better, for him and the century. 'All right,' he said, 'but how do we arrange to both be here at the same time?'

'Leave that to me. I think half past ten's best. Earlier than that and Colonel Walton's likely to be in here reading the *Daily Telegraph*. Shall I make the rounds first, or would you rather?'

'No, you go. I can only manage a few minutes at a time,' Mike said and began hobbling back to his wheelchair. 'What should our code be? "The dog barks at midnight"? Isn't that what spies always use?'

Tensing didn't answer.

Mike looked back, wondering if he'd already walked off to the other side of the room and couldn't hear him, but he was still sitting in the wicker chair, frowning. 'Tensing? I said—'

'Yes. Sorry. I was trying to think of an appropriate code. Just call out one of your crossword clues. Tell me when you reach your chair.'

'I'm there,' Mike said, lowering himself into it. He picked up his crossword, rolled himself over by the door, and then looked over at Tensing beginning his circuit. Tensing didn't have to hold on to the furniture, but twice he had to stop, his hands tightening into white-knuckled fists.

What if he has internal injuries, Mike worried, *and has no business doing this? What if my helping him walk makes his injury worse?*

Tensing made two halting trips around the edges of the room and then said, 'Your turn,' and took his place at the door while Mike worked his way over to the windows and back.

'How did you come to take up crosswords?' he asked as Mike grabbed for a bookcase. 'I thought Americans preferred base-ball.'

'They wouldn't let me have the newspaper otherwise, and I wanted to read the war news,' Mike said, reaching for a chair back. 'I'm not really very good at your crosswords.'

'Most Americans can't solve them at all.' There was a silence and then he said, 'Six across: barrage.'

'What?' Mike said, stopping.

'Nightly gunfire full of anger.'

'Is that the code? Do you hear someone coming?'

'No, it's the answer to six across.'

'Oh,' Mike said, limping over to the potted palm.

'"Rage" is a synonym for "anger'.'

'Is *that* the code?'

'No, sorry. Perhaps we'd better go with "the dog barks at midnight" after all. I was explaining the clue. "Rage" is a synonym for "anger", and "full of" means one word inside another. "Going the wrong way" means it's an anagram, and so does "muddled".' His voice changed. 'Thirty-eight down: caught in the act.'

That *had* to be the code. Mike pushed off violently from the bookcase to the potted palm, clamping his jaw against the pain, and flung himself into his wheelchair. '*Go*,' he said, propelling his chair rapidly to the door, and Tensing rolled his into the wilderness of wicker – handing off Mike's crossword as he went by – and disappeared behind a curio cabinet.

Mike barely had time to reach for his pencil before a nurse appeared.

She scanned the room suspiciously. 'Have you seen Lieutenant Tensing?' she asked Mike.

'He's over there,' Mike whispered, nodding towards the far end. 'Why don't you come back later? I think he's asleep.'

'Good,' she said. 'He needs rest. You haven't seen him trying to get out of his chair, have you?'

'No,' Mike said and would have asked her about his injury, but Sister Gabriel came to take him back before he could.

He spent all afternoon worrying about it. What if there was a bullet lodged in Tensing's spine, or a piece of shrapnel, and walking would dislodge it? Or what if Tensing was shell-shocked, like Bevins, and likely to hurl himself off a cliff as soon as he was walking well enough to get to one?

'I met a patient named Tensing today in the sun-room,' he said to Sister Carmody when she came with his tea. 'What's he in for?'

'You make us sound like a prison,' she scolded. 'We're not allowed to discuss patients' injuries.'

'Was he a pilot?'

'No, he's something to do with the War Office,' she said, wringing out the sponge in the basin.

'The War Office?' Mike said. 'How'd he get injured working a desk job?'

'I don't know. Perhaps he was in a motor car accident or something. He's got five cracked ribs and a sprained back,' she said and then looked appalled. '*Please* don't tell Matron I told you that. I could get in trouble.'

So could I, he thought. But if Tensing worked in the War Office, at least Mike wouldn't be helping him go back into battle. And walking wouldn't hurt a sprained back and cracked ribs.

Tensing was good as his word about getting him to the sun-room. An orderly appeared every day at ten-thirty to take Mike up. He'd worried about his nurses getting suspicious, but they were swamped with new patients, most of them RAF pilots. And with Tensing standing guard, he was able to get in nearly an hour of exercise every day. By the middle of the next week he was walking – all right, limping – unassisted half the length of the room. And, with Tensing's helpful hints, filling in the *Daily Herald* puzzle in forty minutes flat.

Tensing was doing even better. He was walking not only in the sun-room, but the length of the wards and then up and down stairs with his doctors' approval. 'At this rate, you'll be out of here in a week or two,' Mike told him when Tensing came down Wednesday in robe and slippers to see him in the ward.

'No,' he said, pulling over a chair, 'I'm being discharged to-morrow morning. I got word this afternoon.' He sat down and leaned forward, lowering his voice. 'Sorry to break up our partnership, old man, but duty calls, and you're doing splendidly. You'll be out of here in no time.'

'You're going back to your old job?' Mike said, thinking, *What if the War Office gets bombed? Right now London's as dangerous as the front.*

'My old job?' Tensing said, looking disconcerted.

'Yes, in the War Office.'

'Oh. Yes. It's not a glamorous job, I know, filling up forms, but it must be done. And London's rather exciting these days, with the raids and all.'

'Is that how you got injured before? In a raid?'

'Nothing so dramatic, I'm afraid. A typewriter fell on me.' He shook Mike's hand. 'I hope we meet again.'

We won't, Mike thought, but he nodded. 'Good luck.'

Tensing shook his head. 'Wrong response. The correct answer is "nineteen across: clumsy curtain wish",' and went out.

It took Mike ten minutes to figure out that the answer was 'Break a leg'. He wrote it on a slip of paper and handed it to Sister Carmody when she came over to his bed, but before he could ask her to take it to Tensing, she asked, 'Are you feeling well enough for a visitor?'

'A visitor?' It couldn't be Daphne. In her last letter she'd written that there'd been an influx of soldiers to the coast, 'with the invasion coming', and as a result, the pub was so busy she was unable to get away, which he'd decoded as meaning she'd found someone new to flirt with. *Thank God.*

'Yes, it's a new patient,' Sister Carmody said. 'As soon as he was admitted, he asked if you were here.'

So he'd been right about the retrieval team coming disguised as patients. 'Where is he?' He started to swing his feet over the side of the bed, and then remembered he was supposed to still be bedridden.

'I'll send him in,' Sister Carmody said, and almost immediately the ward doors swung open and a man with a freckled face, a bandaged shoulder and a cast on his arm came striding jauntily into the ward. It was Hardy.

'Do you remember me?' he said. 'Private David Hardy? From Dunkirk?'

'Yes,' Mike said, looking at his cast. *I'd hoped you'd died, that you hadn't had the chance to do any damage.*

'I wouldn't have been surprised if you didn't remember,'

496

Hardy was saying. 'You were pretty badly off. How's your foot? Did they have to cut it off?'

'No.'

'They didn't? I thought it'd definitely have to come off,' he said cheerfully. 'It looked like bloody hell.'

'How'd you get that?' Mike asked, pointing at Hardy's cast.

'Dunkirk,' Hardy said. 'Messerschmitt. It was coming straight at us, and I dived for the deck and came up hard against the side. Smashed my shoulder blade to bits. That's why I'm here, to have surgery on it because it's not healing properly, and the moment I arrived I asked, "Is there a patient here who mangled his foot unfouling a propellor at Dunkirk?" and they said yes. I can't tell you how glad I was. The hospital in Dover hadn't any record of your ever having been admitted, even though I'd seen you into the ambulance myself, so I thought you must have died on the way to hospital. And then when they said they were sending me to Orpington, I thought perhaps that was what had happened to you, and here you are. I'm awfully glad I found you. I wanted to thank you for saving my life. If it hadn't been for you, I'd be in a German prison camp. Or worse.'

He beamed at Mike. 'And I wanted you to know what a good day's work you did when you rescued me. As soon as I'd had a hot meal and a sleep, I went back over on the *Mary Rose*, and then, when she was sunk, the *Bonnie Lass*. I made four trips altogether and personally got five hundred and nineteen men safely on board and back to Dover.' He grinned happily at Mike. 'And all because I saw that light of yours.'

'No ships in sight. Something must have gone wrong.'

CAPTAIN JOHN DODD, ROYAL ARTILLERY, AT DUNKIRK MAY 1940

EN ROUTE TO LONDON – 29 SEPTEMBER 1940

Polly's journey back to London was even worse than the one to Backbury had been. The train had no empty seats, and she had to stand squashed in the corridor – the only advantage of which was that she couldn't fall down when the train swayed or stopped so the inevitable troop trains could pass.

When she changed trains at Coventry, she managed to snag a seat, but at the next stop scores of soldiers poured onto the train, all with enormous kitbags which they crammed onto the overhead racks and then, when those were filled, set on the already crowded seats, squashing Polly into a smaller and smaller space.

Colin warned me about the dangers of blast and shrapnel, but not about the possibility of being smothered. Or stabbed to death, she thought, attempting to shift the kitbag on her right, which appeared to have a bayonet in it from the way it was poking her in the side.

And why had the train had to arrive in Backbury on time, today of all days? No other train had been on time during the entire war. If it had been put onto a siding by even a single troop train, she'd have had time to speak to the vicar and find out for certain if Merope had gone back to Oxford.

Of course she's gone back, she argued. *She left when the Army took over the manor.* Her assignment had obviously been designed to end then. With everyone leaving, her disappearance wouldn't even have been noticed. They'd have assumed she'd taken another job or gone home to her family, like the sergeant said. But what if she hadn't left for Oxford? What if the evacuees had been sent to another village, and Merope'd gone with them?

No, the sergeant had said the children had gone back to London, and even if they'd been sent to another manor, it would have had its own staff to care for them. And the last thing Merope would have wanted to do was to go with the Hodbin children. And to leave her drop. If she'd been told to accompany them, she'd have made some excuse and gone to the drop and through to Oxford as soon as possible.

Either way, she was gone, which meant Polly was stuck here till someone came to fetch her. But it also meant she could stop imagining that the net was broken, or worse, and that they wouldn't be able to come and get her before her deadline. Merope's drop was obviously working or she couldn't have gone back.

Which meant the problem had to be a divergence point – or a series of them – and the team would be here as soon as they were over. Or they might already be over, and the team was waiting for her at Townsend Brothers, though it was highly unlikely they'd have come on the one day she'd been gone.

If it was only one day. At this rate it would take her a week to get back to London. The change from Coventry had been so late and there'd been so many delays that by six o'clock they still hadn't reached Oxford, which meant she might as well have stayed till the service was over, talked to everyone in Backbury, and taken the bus back. But after Reading they made better time, and by ten one of the soldiers reported, 'We're coming into Ealing. We should be in London soon.'

The train pulled out of the station and then stopped. And sat. 'Is it another troop train?' Polly asked.

'No. Air raid.'

Polly thought of the vicar's sermon. 'We fear we will be trapped in this dreadful place forever,' he'd said. *Truer words*, she thought, leaning her head against the kitbag and trying to catch a bit of sleep.

It was a good thing Marjorie had said she'd cover for her if she wasn't there at the opening bell. They didn't make it to Euston Station till half past eight the next morning, after which she still had to run the obstacle course of London-After-a-Big-Raid. Neither the Piccadilly nor the Northern Line was running; the bus she needed to take was lying on its side in the middle of the road; and there were notices saying Danger UXB barring access to every other street.

It was half past eleven before she reached Townsend Brothers. Marjorie would almost certainly have told Miss Snelgrove about Polly's ailing mother by now. She'd have to ask Marjorie exactly what she had told her, so they could coordinate their stories.

But Marjorie wasn't there. When Polly got to the floor, Doreen hurried over to her and demanded, 'Where *have* you been? We thought you'd gone off with Marjorie.'

'Gone off?' Polly said, glancing over at Marjorie's counter, but a plump brunette she didn't recognise was standing behind it. 'Where?'

'No one knows. Marjorie didn't say a word to anyone. She simply didn't come in this morning. Miss Snelgrove was *livid*, what with not knowing whether you'd be in and us so busy. Customers have been coming in in *droves*.' She pointed at the brunette. 'They had to send Sarah Steinberg down from Housewares to fill in till they can hire someone.'

'Hire someone? But just because Marjorie didn't come in doesn't mean she's given her notice. She might have had difficulty getting here. I had a dreadful time coming from the station. Or something might have happened to her.'

'That was the first thing we thought of, what with the raids last night,' Doreen said. 'And when Miss Snelgrove rang her landlady, she said Marjorie hadn't come in last night, and she'd rung the hospitals. But she rang back a bit ago and said she'd checked Marjorie's room, and all her things were gone. Marjorie was always on about going to Bath to live with her flatmate, but I never thought she'd actually do it, did you?'

'No,' Polly said. Marjorie hadn't said a word about leaving. She'd promised to cover for her and to tell the retrieval team where she was. What if they'd been here this morning?

'Did anyone come in—?' she began, but Doreen cut her off.

'Quick, Miss Snelgrove's coming,' she whispered. She scuttled off to her own counter, and Polly started towards hers, but too late. Miss Snelgrove was already bearing down on her.

'*Well?*' she demanded. 'I trust you have a good reason for being two and a half hours late?'

That all depends on what Marjorie told you on Saturday, Polly thought. Had she said she was ill or visiting her mother?

'*Well?*' Miss Snelgrove repeated, folding her arms belligerently across her chest. 'I trust you're feeling better.'

She'd told her she was ill, then. *I hope.* 'No, actually, I'm still a bit gippy. I rang up to say I wouldn't be in today, but they said you were dreadfully short-handed, so I thought I'd best try to come in.'

Miss Snelgrove was not impressed. 'To whom did you speak?' she demanded. 'Was it Marjorie?'

'No, I don't know who it was. I didn't know about Marjorie till I got here. I was so surprised—'

'Yes, well, go and tell Miss Steinberg she can go back to her department. And I believe you have a customer.'

'Oh yes, sorry,' Polly said and went over to her counter, but Miss Snelgrove continued to watch her like a hawk, so she didn't have a chance to ask Sarah if anyone had come in asking about her this morning, and no chance to talk to Doreen either till Miss Snelgrove went on her lunch break.

As soon as she was out of sight, Polly darted over to Doreen's counter and asked her, 'Marjorie didn't say whether anyone had come in asking for me before she left, did she?'

'No, I didn't even have a chance to talk to her,' Doreen said. 'We were swamped, what with you being out ill and all, and then, just before closing, Miss Snelgrove said I'd made a mistake in my sales receipts, and I had to tot them all up again and by the time I'd finished, Marjorie'd gone.' She looked speculatively at Polly. 'Who were you expecting? Did you meet someone?'

'No,' Polly said. She repeated the story she'd told Marjorie about her cousin coming to London. 'And you didn't see her talking to anyone?'

'No, I told you, we were frightfully busy. There was a story in the Saturday morning papers about the government rationing silk because the RAF needed it for parachutes, and everyone in London came in to buy up nightgowns and knickers. She could at least have said goodbye,' Doreen said indignantly. 'Or left a note or something.'

A note. Polly went back to her counter and searched its drawers and her sales book and then, pretending to rearrange the merchandise, the drawers of stockings and gloves, but all she found was a scrap of brown wrapping that read cryptically '6 bone, 1 smoke' – presumably a reminder of stocking colours to be ordered. Or the description of a bomb site. But no note.

Even though it was unlikely Sarah would have seen the note and pocketed it, Polly ran upstairs to Housewares on her tea break to ask her. She hadn't, and no, no one had come in asking for Polly this morning before she got there. Sarah hadn't talked to Marjorie on Saturday either. Neither had any of the other girls except Nan, and Marjorie hadn't mentioned anyone inquiring after her.

'Face it, luv, he's not coming,' Doreen said as they covered their counters.

'What?' Polly said, startled. 'Who?'

'This boyfriend you've asked everyone in the entire store about. What's his name?'

'I haven't got a boyfriend. I told you, my cousin—'

Doreen didn't look convinced. 'This chap didn't ... you're not in trouble, are you?'

Yes, Polly thought, *but not the sort you mean*. 'No,' she said, 'I told you, I haven't got a boyfriend.'

'Well, you haven't one now, that's certain. He's left you in the lurch.'

No, they haven't, Polly thought, but there was no one standing outside the staff entrance, and no one in front of Townsend Brothers. Polly waited as long as she could, hoping the team didn't know about the earlier closing hour, but darkness – and, consequently, the raids – were coming earlier now that it was nearly October. In another week, the raids would begin before people left work.

Sir Godfrey was waiting for her at Notting Hill Gate when she stepped off the train. He took her arm. 'Viola! I have tragic news. You weren't here to vote with me last night, and so we are condemned to do that sentimental ass Barrie.'

'Oh dear. Not *Peter Pan*?'

'No, thank God,' he said, escorting her to the escalator and down, 'though it was a near thing. Mr Simms not only voted for it but demanded Nelson be allowed to vote as he would be playing Nana. And after I intervened to get the wretched dog allowed down here in the first place! Foul traitor!'

He smiled at her and then frowned. 'Don't look so heartbroken, child. All is not lost. If we must do Barrie, *The Admirable Crichton*'s at least amusing. And the heroine shows great courage in adversity.'

'Oh good, you're back,' Miss Laburnum said, coming down the escalator. 'Has Sir Godfrey told you we're doing *The Admirable Crichton*?' and before Polly could answer, 'How is your dear mother?'

Mother? Polly thought blankly and then remembered that was where she was supposed to have gone. 'Much better, thank you. It was only a virus.'

'Virus?' Miss Laburnum said, bewildered.

Oh God, hadn't viruses been discovered in 1940? 'I ...'

'Virus is a variety of influenza,' Sir Godfrey said. 'Isn't that right, Viola?'

'Yes,' she said gratefully.

'Oh dear,' Miss Laburnum said. 'Influenza can be dreadfully serious.'

'So it can,' Sir Godfrey said, 'but not with the proper medicine. Have you given Miss Sebastian her script?'

Miss Laburnum fluttered off through the crowd to fetch it. 'If she asks you what sort of medicine,' Sir Godfrey whispered to Polly, 'tell her gin.'

'Gin?'

'Yes. A most efficacious remedy. Tell her your mother came to so fast she bit the bowl off the spoon.'

Which was from Shaw's *Pygmalion* and meant that he knew perfectly well that she'd lied about going to see her mother. She braced herself for his asking where she *had* been, but Miss Laburnum was back with a stack of small blue clothbound books.

She handed one to Polly. 'Alas, I was unable to locate sufficient copies of *Mary Rose* to enable us to perform it,' she said, leading them out to the platform, 'though I'm certain I saw several in the bookshops only last week.'

They reached the group. 'Miss Sebastian's mother is much improved,' she announced, and went over to give the rector his copy.

'I hope you appreciate the sacrifice I've made for you,' Sir Godfrey whispered to Polly. 'I spent three pounds ten buying up every copy of *Mary Rose* on Charing Cross Road to save you from sentimental claptrap like "Goodbye, little island that likes too much to be visited."'

Polly laughed.

'Attention, everyone,' Mrs Wyvern said, clapping her hands. 'Does everyone have a script? Good. Sir Godfrey is to play the title role, Miss Sebastian is to be Mary—'

'Mary?' Polly said.

'Yes, the female lead. Is there a problem?'

'No, it's only ... I didn't think we were doing *Mary Rose*.'

'We're not. We're doing The Admirable Crichton. You are playing Lady Mary.'

Sir Godfrey said, 'Barrie was inordinately fond of the name Mary.'

'Oh,' Polly said. 'I'm not certain I should be given such a large part, with my mother and everything. If I were to have to leave suddenly ...'

'Miss Laburnum can act as your understudy,' Sir Godfrey said. 'Go on, Mrs Wyvern.'

Mrs Wyvern read the rest of the cast list. 'Sir Godfrey has also kindly agreed to direct. The play is about Lord Loam, his three daughters, and their fiancés. They and their servants are shipwrecked—'

Shipwrecked, Polly thought. *How appropriate.*

'—on a desert island. And the only person among them with any survival skills at *all* is their butler, Crichton, so he becomes their leader. And *then*, when they've resigned themselves to remaining on the island forever, they're rescued—'

Resigning myself's not an option, Polly thought. *I can't afford to sit here and wait for rescue. If I'm not off the island when my deadline arrives ...*

But there was nothing to do but sit and wait for the retrieval team to come. Or for her drop to open. If the problem was a divergence point, then the drop might not have been damaged, and its failure to open was only temporary. If so, the retrieval team might not have come because it wasn't necessary. She could go home on her own.

So when the all-clear went the next morning, Polly stayed behind, saying she wanted to learn her lines. She gave them half an hour to get home and then went to the drop.

Workmen had begun clearing the site, so the passage was even more visible from Lampden Road, but there was no one about.

The passage and the well looked just as they had the night she'd waited there except for a heavy coat of plaster dust, no doubt churned up by the work going on outside. There weren't any footprints in the dust, so none of the men clearing the site had discovered the passage, which was lucky, but there weren't any footprints on the steps leading down to the drop either, or any other sign that the team had come through the drop.

Polly sat down on the steps to wait, staring at the peeling black door and thinking about *The Light of the World*. And about Marjorie. It seemed so unlike her to have left when she'd promised to cover for Polly. And without telling anyone. But perhaps she'd been afraid if she told people, they'd attempt to talk her out of it – or say she'd lost her nerve and was running away – so she'd waited till Polly was gone and the store was especially busy to slip away.

If Merope had been in Backbury, you'd have disappeared just as precipitously, Polly told herself. *As you will now if your drop opens.*

But it didn't. It didn't open the next morning either, or that night. Which meant either the divergence point was still occurring, or her drop *had* been damaged after all. But even if it had and the retrieval team had to come through somewhere else, they might still come here looking for clues to her whereabouts.

She scribbled her name and 'Townsend Brothers' on a scrap of paper, folded it, and wedged it half under the peeling black door and, after work the next day, ran up to Alterations and stole a piece of French chalk.

It rained that night, preventing her from going back to the drop, so she went to Holborn and, on the pretext of borrowing an Agatha Christie mystery from the lending library, told the frizzy-haired librarian all about the acting troupe and *The Admirable Crichton*, mentioning her own name twice and Notting Hill Gate three times. 'I work at Townsend Brothers in the stockings department during the day,' she said, 'so acting makes a nice change. You must come see our play. We're on the northbound District Line platform.'

She did the same thing at work the next day during her lunch and tea breaks. After work she wrote her address and Mrs Rickett's phone number on the back of her sales receipt book and, although it was still misting slightly, went to the drop.

She'd forgotten about the men clearing the site. She had to crouch in the same alley in which she'd hidden from the warden till the last workman left before scrambling over what remained of the mound of rubble to the passage.

The only footprints were the ones she'd made last time, and her note was still there. Polly retrieved it and took out the piece of chalk she'd stolen, then stood there a moment, looking at the door, deciding what message to leave. She couldn't write what she wanted – 'Help! I'm stranded in 1940. Come get me.' Just because the workmen hadn't found the passage yet didn't mean they wouldn't.

Instead, she chalked, 'For a good time, ring Polly', and Mrs Rickett's telephone number on the door, and down in the corner – where it would only be noticed by someone expressly looking for it – the barred-circle symbol of the Underground and 'Notting Hill Gate'. She went out into the passage, drew an arrow on the barrel nearest the steps, then squatted down and wrote on the side facing the wall, 'Polly Sebastian, Townsend Brothers', and the address of the boarding house, and then sat down on the steps and waited a full hour, just in case the drop was operational now.

It apparently wasn't. She gave it ten more minutes and then went out to the alley, rubbed out her footprints, sprinkled plaster dust over the floor, and scrawled 'Sebastian Was Here' on the warehouse wall above 'London kan take it', and went to Notting Hill Gate.

Miss Laburnum met her at the top of the escalator. 'Did the young woman find you?' she asked.

Polly's heart began to thud. 'What young woman?'

'She didn't tell me her name. She said she'd come from Townsend Brothers. What do you think, white lace for Lady Mary in act one, and then blue for the shipwrecked scenes? I always think blue shows up nicely onstage—'

'Where did she go?' Polly said, looking around at the crowd. 'The young woman?'

'Oh dear, I don't know. She ... oh, there she is.'

It was Doreen. She was red-faced and out of breath. 'Oh, Polly,' she gasped, 'I've been looking for you everywhere. It's Marjorie. Her landlady telephoned Miss Snelgrove just after you left – Marjorie wasn't in Bath after all.'

'What do you mean?' Polly demanded. 'Where was she?'

'In Jermyn Street,' Doreen said, and burst into tears. 'When it was bombed.'

Danger: Land Mines

NOTICE ON ENGLISH BEACH, 1940

WAR EMERGENCY HOSPITAL — SEPTEMBER 1940

H ardy stood there by Mike's bed, beaming at him. 'You've got five hundred and nineteen lives saved to your credit,' he said, a grin on his freckled face. 'That's a war record to be proud of.'

If I didn't lose the war, Mike thought sickly. *If one of those men it's my fault were saved didn't alter some critical event at El Alamein or D-Day or the Battle of the Bulge and change the course of the war.* And it was ridiculous to think they hadn't. The continuum might be able to cancel out one or two changes, but there was no way it could make up for 519 soldiers – no, 520, counting Hardy – being rescued who weren't supposed to have been.

'I didn't mean to tire you out,' Hardy said uncertainly. 'I only thought you might want cheering up. Can I do anything for you—?'

You've already done more than enough, Mike wanted to snap at him, but it wasn't Hardy's fault. He'd been trying to do the right thing when he went back to Dunkirk. He'd had no way of knowing what the consequences would be.

'I should let you get some rest,' Hardy said, but that was impossible. Mike had to get out of here. He had to get back to the drop and warn Oxford about what he'd done. If it wasn't already too late, and that was why the retrieval team wasn't here – because he'd lost the war and they didn't exist.

But Hardy had said he'd thought he was dead. Maybe when the retrieval team couldn't find any trace of him, they'd concluded that, too. Or maybe they were still looking for him in London.

And even if it was too late, he had to try. Which meant getting out of this damned hospital. But how? He couldn't just sneak out. For one thing, he hadn't mastered getting down stairs yet, and even if he could, he wouldn't get a hundred yards in a bathrobe and slippers. Besides, he didn't have any papers. Or money. At the very least, he had to have train fare to Dover and bus fare from there to Saltram-on-Sea. And shoes.

And he had to convince the doctors to let him out of here, which meant he had to be walking better than he was now. Mike waited till after Hardy'd gone and the night nurse had made her rounds, then got up and practised hobbling the length of the ward for the rest of the night, and then showed the doctor his progress.

'Astonishing,' his doctor said, impressed. 'You've made a much faster recovery than I thought possible. We should be able to operate immediately.'

'Operate?'

'Yes. To repair the tendon damage. We couldn't till your original wound had healed.'

'No,' Mike said. 'No operation. I want to be discharged.'

'I can understand your wanting to get back in the war,' the doctor said, 'but you need to understand that without further operations, there's very little chance you'll regain the full use of your foot. You're risking the possibility of being crippled for life.'

And I'm risking a hell of a lot more than that if I stay here, Mike thought, and spent the next several days trying to convince the doctor to discharge him and practically going crazy with waiting. It didn't help that there were sirens and the ever closer sound of bombs every night, and that Bevins kept sobbing, 'It's the invasion. You must get out immediately.'

I'm trying, Mike thought, stuffing his pillow over his head.

'Hitler's coming!' Bevins shrieked. 'He'll be here any moment!' and it was hard to see how he wouldn't. According to the papers, the Luftwaffe was hammering London every night. The Tower of London, Trafalgar Square, Marble Arch Underground station and Buckingham Palace had all been hit, and thousands of people had already been killed.

'It's dreadful,' Mrs Ives said when she brought him the *Herald*, whose headline read, 'Nightly Raids Show No Signs of Letting Up – Londoners' Resolve Unwavering'. 'My neighbour was bombed out last night and—'

'How do I go about getting new identity papers?' Mike interrupted. 'Mine were destroyed at Dunkirk, and I don't know what happened to my clothes.'

'The Assistance Board is in charge of those things, I believe,' she said, and the next morning a young woman showed up at his bedside with a notebook and dozens of questions he didn't know the answer to, from his passport number to his shoe size.

'It's changed recently,' he said. 'Especially the right foot.'

She ignored that. 'When was your passport issued?'

'All my papers were arranged for by my editor at my newspaper,' he said, hoping she'd assume things were done differently in the States.

'What is your editor's name?'

'James Dunworthy. But he's not there anymore. He's on assignment in Egypt.'

'And the name of your paper?'

'The *Omaha Observer*,' he said, thinking, *They'll check and find there's no such newspaper, no such passport, and I'll find myself in the Tower of London with all the other enemy agents.* But when she came back that afternoon, she had an emergency identity card, ration book, and a press pass.

'You need to fill up this form and send it and a photograph to the US Embassy in London to get a new passport,' she said. 'I'm afraid it may take several months. The war, you know.'

Bless the war, he thought.

'Until then, here is your temporary passport and visa.' She handed them to him. 'I've left clothing for you with Matron.'

And bless you.

'Have you given any thought to where you'll be going after you're discharged?' she asked.

He hadn't thought of anything else. He needed to get back to Saltram-on-Sea and the drop, but he had to get there without any of the locals spotting him, especially Daphne. He couldn't risk her getting more attached to him. She might turn down a date with the man she was supposed to marry, or feel jilted when he left and swear off reporters. Or Americans. Hundreds of English women had married American soldiers. Daphne might well have been one of them. And he'd already done enough damage as it was. He needed to get out of here without doing any more.

He'd have to go to Dover and then take the bus down to Saltram-on-Sea and hope that the driver would be willing to let him out above the beach. And that he could manage the path down to the drop.

'I thought I'd go to Dover,' he told the Assistance Board woman. 'I have a reporter friend there I can stay with,' and the next morning she brought him a train ticket to Dover, a chit for lodging, and a five-pound note 'to assist you till you get settled'. 'Is there anything else you need?'

'My hospital discharge papers,' he said, and she truly *was* a miracle worker – the doctor signed them that afternoon. Mike promptly rang for Sister Gabriel and asked for his clothes.

'Not till Matron countersigns your papers,' she said.

'When will that be?' he asked. Today was Wednesday and, as he knew from bitter experience, the bus to Saltram-on-Sea only ran on Tuesdays and Fridays – so he had to get there by Friday.

'I'm not certain. Tomorrow, perhaps. You needn't act so glad to leave us.'

Sister Carmody was more sympathetic. 'I know what it's like to want to get back into the war and be forced to wait. I put in for duty in a field hospital *months* ago,' she said, and promised to talk to Matron.

She was as good as her word. She was back in less than an hour with the package of clothes the Assistance Board had left. 'You're being discharged today,' she said. The package contained a brown tweed suit, white shirt, tie, cufflinks, socks, underwear, wool overcoat, fedora, and shoes that were unbelievably painful to get onto his bad foot, let alone walk in.

They'll never let me out of here when they see me trying to hobble in these, Mike thought, and if the hospital hadn't had a policy of taking departing patients downstairs in a wheel-chair and putting them into a taxi, they wouldn't have. As it was, Sister Carmody handed him a pair of crutches at the last moment. 'Doctor's orders,' she said. 'He wants you to keep the weight off your foot as much as possible. And here's something for the train,' she added, giving him a brown paper parcel. 'From all of us. Do write and let us know how you're doing.'

'I will,' he lied, and told the taxi driver to take him to Victoria Station. On the way there, he opened the package. It was a book of crossword puzzles.

He took the first train to Dover he could get and, as soon as he arrived, found a pawnbroker and hocked the cufflinks and overcoat for four pounds. He would have sold the crutches, too, but they had come in handy, getting him a seat in the packed-solid train. Hopefully, they'd also persuade the bus driver to let him out at the beach.

If he could find out where to catch the bus from. Nobody seemed to know, not even the stationmaster. Or the pawnbroker. He tried to think who would. The hotels should. He knew where they were, thanks to that map of Dover he'd memorised all those months ago in Oxford, but they were all too far from the pawnbroker's to walk to with his bad foot. He hailed a taxi, wrestled his crutches into it, and got into the backseat. 'Where to, mate?' the cabbie asked.

'The Imperial Hotel,' Mike said. 'No, wait.' The cabbie would know where the bus went from. 'I need to catch the bus to Saltram-on-Sea.'

'There's no bus that goes there. Hasn't been since June. The beach is closed.'

'Closed?'

'Because of the invasion. It's a restricted area. No civilians allowed, unless you live there or you have a pass.'

Oh Christ. 'I'm a war correspondent,' he said, pulling out his press pass. 'How much would *you* charge to take me to Saltram-on-Sea?'

'Can't, mate. I haven't got the petrol coupons to go all that way, and even if I did, that coast road's full of rocks. I've got to make these tyres last the war.'

'Then where can I hire a car?'

The cabbie thought a moment and then said, 'I know a garage that might have one,' and drove him there.

The garage didn't have any cars. They suggested 'Noonan's, just up the street'. It was considerably further than that. By the time Mike reached it, he was really glad he hadn't sold his crutches.

The garage owner wasn't there. 'You'll find 'im at the pub,' a grease-covered boy of ten told him, but that was easier said than done. The pub was as crammed as the boat coming back from Dunkirk. There was no way to get through the crush on his crutches. Mike left them at the door and hobbled into the mass of workmen, soldiers, and fishermen. They were all arguing about the invasion. 'It'll 'appen this week,' a stout man with a red nose said.

'No, not till they've softened up London a bit more,' his friend said. 'It won't be for at least another fortnight.'

The man next to him nodded. 'They'll send in spies first to get the lay of the land.'

Which one of these was the garage owner? 'Excuse me,' Mike said. 'I'm looking for the man who owns the garage next door. I need to hire a car.'

'A *car*?' the stout man said. ''Aven't you 'eard there's a war on?'

'What do you want to hire a car for?' his friend asked.

'I need to drive down to Saltram-on-Sea.'

'To do what?' he said suspiciously, and his friend asked, narrowing his eyes, 'Where are you from?'

Oh Christ, they thought he was a spy. 'The States,' he said.

'A Yank?' the man snorted. 'When are you lot going to get in the war?'

And a tiny, timid-looking man in a bowler hat said belligerently, 'What the bloody hell are you waiting for?'

'If you could just point out the garage owner—'

''E's over there, at the bar,' the stout man said, pointing. ''Arry! This Yank wants to talk to you about hirin' a car.'

'Tell him to try Noonan's!' he shouted back.

'I already did,' Mike called, but the garage owner had already turned back to the bar.

This was hopeless. He'd have to see if he could find a farmer he could get a lift with. *Maybe Mr Powney's in town buying another bull,* he thought, and started for the door and his crutches.

'Hold on there,' the stout man said, and pointed at Mike's foot. 'How'd you get that?'

'Stuka,' Mike said. 'At Dunkirk,' and felt the unfriendliness go out of the room.

'Which ship?' the little man in the bowler asked, no longer belligerent, and the garage owner left the bar and was coming over.

'The *Lady Jane*,' Mike said. 'It wasn't a ship. It was a motor launch.'

'Did she make it back?'

'The trip I was on, yes, but not the next one,' he tried to say, but before he could get it out, they were bombarding him with questions:

'Torpedo sink her?'

'How many men were you able to take off?'

'When were you there?'

'Did you see the *Lily Belle*?'

'Give him a chance,' the garage owner shouted. 'And a pint. And let him sit down, will you? Nice lot you are, makin' a hero of Dunkirk stand and not even offering him a drink.'

Someone produced a bench for him to sit on and someone else a glass of ale. 'Going 'ome, are you?' the stout man asked.

'Yes,' Mike said. 'I just got out of the hospital.'

'I wish I could help,' the garage owner said, 'but all I've got are a Morris without a carburettor and a Daimler without a magneto, and no way to get either one.'

'He can borrow my car,' the tiny man who'd been so belligerent volunteered. 'Wait here,' he said, and was back in a few minutes with an Austin.

'Here's the ignition key. There's an extra tin of petrol in the boot if you run out.' He looked doubtfully at Mike's foot. 'Are you certain you can work the pedals?'

'Yes,' Mike said quickly, afraid the little man would offer to drive him down. 'I can pay you for the gas. And the hire of the car.'

'Oh no, I wouldn't think of it,' he said. 'The registration papers are in the glove box, in case you need to show them at a checkpoint. You can leave the car here at the pub when you come back.'

I'm not coming back, Mike thought guiltily. 'I don't know what I'd have done without you,' he said. 'You've saved my life.'

'Don't give it another thought,' the man said, patted the hood of the car, and started back into the pub. 'I was there, too. At Dunkirk. On the *Marigold*.' He went inside.

Mike put his crutches in the backseat, got in, and drove off, incredibly grateful the little man hadn't stayed to watch him try to start the car or struggle with the gear lever.

He never would have lent it to me if he'd seen this, he thought, lurching onto the coast road. *I should have taken driving lessons like Merope.*

He drove south, looking out at the beaches he passed. If he had been a spy, he'd have had a discouraging report to make to Hitler. The beaches bristled with concertina wire and sharpened stakes and rows of concrete pylons and large signs reading, This Area Mined: Enter at Your Own Risk. He hoped they hadn't mined the beach at Saltram-on-Sea or put in obstacles like the ones he saw as he neared Folkestone.

There was a checkpoint at Folkestone, and another at Hythe, both manned by armed guards who questioned him and examined his papers before letting him through. 'Have you seen any suspicious strangers on the road?' they asked him at the second checkpoint, and when he told them no, said, 'If you see any unauthorised persons on a beach or behaving suspiciously, asking questions or taking photographs, contact the authorities.'

That's why the retrieval team hasn't come, Mike thought as he drove, *because Badri hasn't been able to find a drop site.* The whole coast had been crawling with soldiers, coast watchers and aircraft spotters ever since Dunkirk. Not only that, but every single farmer and driver and pub-frequenter was watching for paratroopers and spies. There was no way the retrieval team could have come through anywhere inside the restricted area without being noticed, and if they'd come through outside it, they'd have run into the same problems getting to Saltram-on-Sea he was having. No wonder they hadn't found him yet.

I didn't alter the future, he thought jubilantly. *I didn't lose the war. And if I can just get to the drop without changing anything else, I'll be home free.*

If I can get down to the beach, he amended, looking at the chalk cliffs, which were getting steeper with every mile. On the plus side, the military was apparently counting on those cliffs being enough to stop the tanks. The only defences on the beaches below were two lines of stakes and some barbed wire.

It had begun to rain just outside Hythe. Mike peered through the windshield at the white road and occasional glimpses of grey ocean beyond the cliffs, looking for landmarks he recognised. The road moved away from the Channel again and then back, climbing. He had to be getting close—

There it was. The road went up a small hill, and at the top he could see all the way to Saltram-on-Sea and past it. He pulled the car off onto the grass and got out, scowling for the benefit of anybody who might be watching, and slammed the door angrily. He yanked up the hood and bent over it. He wished he knew how to make steam billow up, so it would look like the car had overheated, but he had no idea how a gasoline engine worked, and he didn't dare risk its really conking out.

He pretended to adjust a few things and then smacked the fender hard with his hand as if fed up and limped over to the edge of the cliff and looked disgustedly out at the grey Channel and the grey sky, and then down at the beach. A sharp jut in the cliffs blocked his view of the drop, but he could see most of the rest of the beach. There were the same stakes and barbed wire here, but no machine-gun nests, no guard posts. Good.

Unless the beach was mined. But the drop was only a little way from the cliff's edge, and mines were much more likely to be near the water's edge, or in between the tank traps. They were expecting an invasion from the beach, not from the land.

It was windy here on top of the hill, and freezing standing in the misty rain. He pulled the collar of his jacket up around his neck, wishing he hadn't sold his overcoat. Especially if it took a while for the drop to open. But it shouldn't. The good thing about all this barbed wire and the wretched weather was that he wouldn't have to worry about anyone being out in it, including coast watchers. And if there were any boats out in that choppy water, which he doubted, their crews' eyes would be trained on the Channel, not on the beach. So he should have a clear shot.

If he could get to the drop. He walked a little further, trying to see around the jutting cliff, but it was still in the way. He went back to the car, got in, pretended to try the ignition, then got out again and limped north along the road as if looking for a house where he could ask for help.

When he judged he was past the jutting cliff, he hobbled out to the edge again.

The drop was clearly visible from here. He could see the rock's two sides sticking jaggedly up out of the sand. And between them in the middle, right on top of the drop site, a six-inch artillery gun.

*'And there sprang up all around the park briars and brambles,
twined one within the other, so that no one could pass through.'*

SLEEPING BEAUTY

LONDON – OCTOBER 1940

Polly stared sickly at Doreen, standing there sobbing in the middle of the bustling tube station, oblivious to the people pushing past them. 'Hit?' she repeated, thinking, *Marjorie's dead. That's why she didn't tell anyone she was leaving.*

'And the worst part ...' Doreen said, trying to talk through her tears, 'oh, Polly, she was in the rubble for three days before they found her!'

Marjorie's poor mangled body had lain there for three days. Because no one knew she was there. Because no one even knew she was missing. 'But her landlady said she'd left,' Polly said, 'that she'd taken her things. Why—?'

'I don't know,' Doreen said. 'I asked her, but she said they won't let her in to see Marjorie—'

'Let her – she's alive?' Polly said, grabbing both of Doreen's arms. 'Where is she?'

'In hospital. Mrs Armentrude – that's her landlady – said she's very badly hurt ... her insides ...'

Oh God, Polly thought, *she has internal injuries.*

'Mrs Armentrude said she had a ruptured spleen ...'

A ruptured spleen, Polly thought. Oh, that wasn't nearly so bad. It was still dangerous, but they'd known how to deal with a ruptured spleen, even in 1940. 'Did she say anything about infection?'

Doreen shook her head. 'She said some of her ribs were broken and ... and ... her arm!' And broke down completely.

People didn't die from broken arms in any century, and if peritonitis hadn't set in, Marjorie might be all right. 'Here, my dear,' Miss Laburnum was saying, offering Doreen a lace-edged handkerchief. 'Miss Sebastian, would you like me to fetch your friend a cup of tea from the canteen?'

'No, I'm all right,' Doreen said, wiping at her cheeks. 'I'm sorry. It's only that I feel so dreadful that I was angry at her for going off and leaving us shorthanded, when all the time ...' She began to cry again.

'You didn't know,' Polly said, thinking, *We should have. I should have known she wouldn't have gone off to Bath without telling me, that she wouldn't have let me down when she'd said she'd cover for me—*

'That's what Miss Snelgrove said,' Doreen sniffled, 'that it was no one's fault. That even if we'd known Marjorie was still in London, we wouldn't have known where she was. I don't know what she was doing in Jermyn Street. She must have been on her way to the railway station when the raid began.'

But Jermyn Street's nowhere near Waterloo Station, Polly thought. *It's in the opposite direction.*

'Imagine, thinking you'll be safely out of London soon, and then ...' Doreen began to cry again. 'I only wish there were something we could do, but Mrs Armentrude said she's not allowed any visitors.'

'Perhaps you could send her flowers,' Miss Laburnum suggested, 'or some nice magazines.'

'Oh, that's a good idea,' Doreen said, cheering up. 'Oh, Polly, Marjorie will be all right, won't she?'

'Yes, of course she will,' Miss Laburnum said, and Polly looked gratefully at her. 'She's in good hands now, and you mustn't worry. Doctors can do marvellous things. Why don't you stay here in the shelter with us tonight?'

'I can't, thank you,' Doreen said to Miss Laburnum and turned to Polly. 'Miss Snelgrove asked me to tell everyone, and Nan still doesn't know. I must find her and tell her.'

'But you can't,' Polly said. 'The sirens will be going any minute now, and you've no business being out in a raid.'

'It's all right. Nan's usually at Piccadilly,' Doreen said, and looked vaguely around at the notices painted on the wall. 'Does the Piccadilly Line run from here?'

'You take the District to Earl's Court and change from there,' Polly said. 'I'll go with you. Miss Laburnum, tell Sir Godfrey I've gone to help a friend locate someone.'

'Oh, but we were to rehearse the shipwreck scene tonight,' Miss Laburnum said. 'Sir Godfrey will be so cross.'

She was right. He'd thrown himself into the role not only of butler, but of director, and bellowed at everyone, including Nelson. And if she missed a rehearsal—

'No, no, you needn't go with me,' Doreen was saying. 'I'm much better now. Thank you both.' She handed Miss Laburnum back her handkerchief and hurried off.

'How dreadful!' Miss Laburnum said, looking after her. 'To be trapped like that without anyone knowing where you are. You mustn't feel badly, Miss Sebastian. It wasn't your fault.'

Yes, it was. I should have known something was wrong, but I was too busy worrying about whether she'd spoken to the retrieval team. I am so sorry, Marjorie.

She went to the hospital the next morning, but all they would tell her was that 'the patient is stable', and that she wouldn't be able to have visitors 'for some time'.

'Perhaps Miss Snelgrove will be able to find out more from the doctors,' Doreen said, passing round a card for everyone to sign with cheerful comments like 'Hitler o, Marjorie 1.'

Polly was doubtful, given Miss Snelgrove's less than charming manner, but she returned full of information. They had operated successfully to remove Marjorie's spleen; there appeared to be no other damage except for the arm and four broken ribs, and she was expected to make a full recovery, though it would be at least a fortnight before she was able to return to work. She'd lost a good deal of blood.

'She was under several feet of rubble,' Miss Snelgrove said. 'It took the rescue squad nearly a day to dig her out after they found her. She was lucky to have been found at all. The house was listed as empty in the ARP warden records. The elderly woman who owned it had shut it up and gone to the country when the bombings began.'

And what was Marjorie doing in an abandoned house? Polly wondered.

'—so the rescuers hadn't even looked for anyone. If an air-raid warden making his rounds hadn't heard her calling from under a section of collapsed wall—' Miss Snelgrove shook her head. 'She was very lucky. She was apparently in a sort of recessed doorway.'

Like the drop, Polly thought, remembering that night with the bombs falling all around. If the wall had collapsed on the passage, no one would have known she was there either.

'Did they let you in to see her?' Sarah Steinberg, who'd been sent down to fill in for Marjorie, asked.

'No, she's still much too ill to have visitors,' Miss Snelgrove said. 'I gave Matron your magazines and your card, and she promised to deliver them to her.'

'And you're certain she's going to be all right?' Doreen asked.

'Quite sure,' Miss Snelgrove said briskly. 'She's in excellent hands, and nothing can be gained by worrying. We must concentrate on the task at hand.'

For the next week, Polly tried to do just that – concentrating on selling stockings, wrapping parcels, learning her lines and her blocking – but she kept seeing Marjorie buried in the rubble: frightened, bleeding, waiting for someone, anyone, to come and dig her out. And if she'd been unconscious or unable to call for help, she'd still be there, and no one would ever have known what happened to her.

'Lady Mary!' Sir Godfrey roared at her. 'That's your cue!'

'Sorry.' She said her line.

'No, no, no!' Sir Godfrey bellowed. 'You are not on a picnic. You have been shipwrecked. Your vessel has been blown off-course, and no one has any idea where you are. Now, try it again.'

She did, but her mind was on what Sir Godfrey'd said: 'No one has any idea where you are.'

They'd thought Marjorie'd gone to Bath when she was actually buried under a wall in Jermyn Street. Could the same thing have happened with Polly's retrieval team? Could they have seen or heard something that made them reach an erroneous conclusion about where she was? Could they be off looking for her on Regent Street or in Knightsbridge? Or another city?

But she hadn't gone off without telling anyone where she was going, like Marjorie, and she hadn't been blown off-course. She was exactly where she'd told the lab – and Colin – she'd be: working in a department store on Oxford Street and sleeping in a tube station that had never been hit. And Doreen's having come to Notting Hill Gate to tell her about Marjorie proved that Townsend Brothers knew how to find her if the retrieval team asked for her. And this was time travel—

'Wrong, wrong, wrong!' Sir Godfrey bellowed. Polly scrambled to find her place, but this time he was yelling at the rest of the cast. 'Your chances of rescue are nearly nonexistent. You're far from the shipping lanes, and when word of the loss of your ship reaches England, you will almost certainly be given up for dead.'

Given up for dead. What if, rather than thinking she was somewhere else, the retrieval team thought she was dead? When Doreen had first told her about Marjorie, she'd thought she was dead, and when she'd seen the wreckage of St George's, she'd thought Sir Godfrey and the others were. And they'd thought she was dead, too. Sir Godfrey had insisted that the rescue squad dig for her. What if, during that time the retrieval team had come, and the rector had told them she was dead? Or what if he'd—?

'Miss Laburnum,' she whispered, 'after St George's was destroyed, did you—?'

'Lady Mary, did you have some comment on this scene?' Sir Godfrey asked, his voice dripping with sarcasm.

'No. I'm sorry, Sir Godfrey.'

'As. I. Was. Saying,' Sir Godfrey said, emphasising each word, 'only the butler, Crichton, and *Lady Mary*' – he glowered at her – 'have realised the gravity of their plight at this point, and it is that which provides the humour, such as it is, in this scene. Lady Agatha, you stand here,' he said, taking Lila by the arm and moving her to the end of the platform, 'and Lord Brocklehurst, you're seated here in front of her on the sand.'

Polly took advantage of his repositioning the cast to ask Miss Laburnum, 'When I was missing, did the rector send my name to the newspaper for the casualties list?'

Miss Laburnum shook her head. 'Mrs Wyvern thought it was our duty to send in a death notice,' she whispered, 'but Sir Godfrey wouldn't hear of it. He—'

'*Mary!*' Sir Godfrey thundered. 'If you don't mind, I'd like to rehearse this scene *before* the end of the war.'

'Sorry.'

They started through the scene. Polly forced herself to concentrate on saying her lines and getting through her blocking without incurring Sir Godfrey's wrath again, but as soon as rehearsal was over, she took the tube to Holborn's lending library to look at its old newspapers. Mrs Wyvern might not have notified officials of her death, but that didn't mean the incident officer – or one of the ARP wardens – hadn't. Or she might have been mentioned in the account of the church's destruction. And if the retrieval team had seen 'Polly Sebastian, died suddenly of enemy attack' in *The Times*—

But the oldest paper the library had was three days old. 'You haven't any from further back?' she asked the librarian.

'No,' she said apologetically. 'Some children came round several days ago collecting for the scrap paper drive.'

She'd have to go to *The Times* office herself. But when? The newspaper morgue wasn't open Sundays, her only day off, and her lunch break wasn't long enough for her to go all the way to Fleet Street and back. And Polly didn't dare phone in again and say she was ill. Miss Snelgrove was convinced anyone who asked for time off was decamping like Marjorie.

But she had to see those casualty lists, so after rehearsal the next night she borrowed Sir Godfrey's *Times* to find a death notice she could use, borrowed a handkerchief from Miss Laburnum, and waited for Friday night when the raids over Clerkenwell would hopefully prevent Miss Snelgrove from getting to work on time the next morning.

They did. Polly grabbed the handkerchief and ran upstairs to Personnel to ask Mr Witherill if she could be gone for the morning. 'To attend my aunt's funeral.'

'You must obtain permission from your floor supervisor.'

'Miss Snelgrove's not here.'

He glanced over at his secretary, who nodded confirmation. 'She telephoned to say the trains weren't running, and she was going to attempt to take a bus.'

'Oh. Your aunt, you say?'

'Yes, sir. My Aunt Louise. She was killed in a raid.' She dabbed at her eyes with the handkerchief.

'My condolences. When is the funeral?'

'Eleven o'clock at St Pancras Church,' Polly said, and if Mr Witherill (or, more likely, Miss Snelgrove) checked the funeral notices, they would find 'Mrs James (Louise) Barnes, aged 53, St Pancras Church. 11 a.m. No flowers'. 'Very well,' he said, 'but I expect you to return immediately after the funeral.'

'Yes, sir, I will,' Polly said and ran down to tell Doreen where she was going and to tell anyone who inquired after her that she'd be back by one, took the tube to Fleet Street, and walked quickly to *The Times* office, hoping ordinary people were allowed access to the morgue.

They were. She asked for the morning and evening editions from September twentieth through the twenty-second and was shocked to be handed the actual newspapers – though this was of course before digital copying, or even microfilm. She paged through the large sheets, looking for the death notices and reading down through them – 'Joseph Seabrook, 72, died suddenly of enemy action. Helen Sexton, 43, died suddenly. Phyllis Sexton, 11, died suddenly. Rita Sexton, 5, died suddenly'.

Polly's name wasn't on any of the lists, and the news article was only a brief paragraph headed 'Beloved Eighteenth-Century Church Blitzed'. There were no details, no photo, not even the name of the church.

Good, she thought. She returned the papers to the desk and went on to the *Daily Herald*, checking the news story about St George's – 'Fourth Historic Church Destroyed by Luftwaffe in Failed Campaign to Demoralise Brits' – and the death notices. Her name wasn't there either, or in the *Standard*, which was all she had time to check. She would have to check the others later.

She raced back to Townsend Brothers, stopping at Padgett's to rub a bit of rouge around her eyes in the ladies' lounge and splash water on her eyelashes, cheeks and handkerchief. And a good thing she had. Miss Snelgrove had arrived and clearly did not believe she'd been to a funeral.

And Colin wouldn't believe I was dead either, she thought, *even if he did see my death notice.* Colin would refuse to give up. He'd insist they continue looking for her just as Sir Godfrey had.

Then where are they? she thought, writing up purchases and waiting for Miss Snelgrove to leave so she could ask Doreen whether anyone had asked for her while she was gone. *Why aren't they here?* It had been nearly four weeks since the drop was damaged and five since she should have checked in.

She had to wait till after the closing bell to speak to Doreen. Doreen told her no one had come in, and then asked her about Marjorie. 'Miss Snelgrove said she won't be well enough to have visitors for at least a fortnight,' she said. 'You don't think it means she's getting worse, do you?'

'No, of course not,' Polly lied.

'I keep thinking about her lying in that rubble and us not knowing what had happened,' Doreen said, 'thinking she was safely in Bath when all the time ... I feel so guilty not sensing she was in trouble.'

'You had no way of knowing,' Polly said, which seemed to reassure her. She went off to cover her counter, but Polly stood there, lost in thought.

No way of knowing. What if the reason the retrieval team hadn't come wasn't divergent points, or their thinking she was dead, or any of the other things she'd imagined? What if it was simply because the lab didn't know they needed to send a team? That they didn't know anything was wrong? *Like I didn't know Marjorie was lying in the rubble.*

The lab had been swamped with retrievals and drops and schedule changes, and Mr Dunworthy had been busy as well, meeting with people and going off to London. Could they all have been so busy and distracted they'd forgotten she was supposed to check in? Or could something have happened to Michael Davies at Dover or Pearl Harbor, and everyone's attention was on pulling him out, and they'd put every other retrieval on hold?

If that was the case, they wouldn't find out her drop wasn't working till the day she was supposed to be back. Which meant they'd be here on the twenty-second, and all she needed to do was last a few more days. No, she was forgetting Colin. No matter what was distracting other people, he wouldn't have forgotten

528

about her. He'd have been at the lab every day, demanding to know whether she'd checked in. And when she didn't, he'd have gone straight to Mr Dunworthy.

No, wait, he couldn't. He wasn't allowed in the lab.

That wouldn't stop him, Polly thought. Unless Colin himself was the distraction. He'd been determined to go on assignment so he could 'catch up' to her. What if he'd gone through the net without permission to the Crusades or something, and they'd had to send a retrieval team to fetch him, or Mr Dunworthy had gone after him? And in all the resultant chaos they'd completely forgotten about her? It was all too likely a scenario, and she spent the time till the twenty-second worrying about Colin. And Marjorie.

October twenty-second came and went without the retrieval team appearing. *It will take them time to find me*, she told herself, ignoring the laws of time travel and the trail of bread crumbs she'd so carefully laid. *They'll be here tomorrow.*

But they weren't, nor on the twenty-fourth. Or outside Notting Hill Gate the next morning. *And it's a good thing I didn't apply for that position at Padgett's*, Polly thought, walking past the store on her way to Townsend Brothers. Tonight was the night it had been bombed. A direct hit by a thousand-pound HE had demolished the building, and because it had been hit just after closing and there were still people in the building, there'd been three deaths.

Polly stopped to take a last look at the store's grandiose columns, at its glass display windows and the mannequins dressed in wool coats and small-brimmed felt hats. 'End-of-Summer Sale', a banner read. 'Last chance to buy at these prices'.

Or to do anything else, Polly thought, wondering who the three fatalities had been. Late shoppers? Or junior sales assistants who'd had to stay behind to add up their sales receipt books or wrap parcels?

I'd best put my hat and coat behind the counter tonight and take the tube instead of the bus. Unless the retrieval team's waiting for me when I get to work, she thought, walking the last three streets to Townsend Brothers.

But they weren't there. *Where are they?* Polly thought sickly, going up to third. *Where are they?*

There was four and a half days' slippage when I came through, she told herself, uncovering her counter. If they'd tried to come through on the twenty-second and had encountered the same amount of slippage, they wouldn't be here till tomorrow night.

And what will you tell yourself the day after tomorrow when they still haven't come? And the next day? And the day before your deadline? She looked anxiously over at Doreen and Sarah, who were discussing where they were going after work tonight. *I wish I knew*, Polly thought.

But they didn't know either. They were making plans to go see a film in Leicester Square, but if Padgett's had been hit just after closing, then the sirens would go just as they were leaving. They might have to spend the night in Oxford Circus Station.

Or be blown to bits on their way there, or on the way home. They had no more idea what would happen or whether they'd make it through alive than she did, and they had the threat of invasion and losing the war to worry about as well. And if they were Jewish, like Sarah ...

And they have no retrieval team or Mr Dunworthy – or Colin – to rescue them, Polly thought, ashamed. Yet they managed somehow to not give way to anxiety or despair, to wait cheerfully on Miss Eliot, who was berating Sarah for Townsend Brothers' being out of woollen vests, and on Mrs Stedman, who'd brought her unevacuated toddlers with her today.

If they could put on a brave face, surely she could, too. She was, after all, an actress. Starring opposite a knighted actor in a play by J. M. Barrie.

'Courage, Lady Mary,' she murmured and went to rescue Doreen from the toddlers. She showed them how the pneumatic tubes worked and then walked them – holding tightly on to their small hands – over to Miss Snelgrove to ask if she'd heard anything about Marjorie's having visitors.

'I telephoned this morning,' Miss Snelgrove said, 'but Matron said she was still too ill to see anyone,' which sounded ominous, and apparently Miss Snelgrove thought so, too, because she added, 'You must try not to worry.'

Polly nodded, took the toddlers back to their mother and a grateful Doreen, and went to wait on Mrs Milliken and a succession of ill-tempered customers. Difficult Mrs Jones-White came in, followed by Mrs Aberfoyle and her nippy little Pekingese, and elderly Miss Pink, who was notorious for asking to examine every single piece of merchandise in every single drawer and then not buying anything.

'Every unpleasant person in London has decided to shop at Townsend Brothers today,' Doreen whispered on her way to the workroom.

'I know,' Polly said, wrapping Miss Gill's purchases. She'd told Polly she wanted them sent and then changed her mind and decided to take them with her. It took Polly till closing to wrap them all, by which time Miss Gill had changed her mind again.

'Thank heavens,' Doreen said when the closing bell rang, and began covering her counter.

Polly put on her coat and was reaching for her hat when Miss Snelgrove came over. 'You waited on Mrs Jones-White earlier?'

'Yes, she purchased two pairs of stockings. She wanted them sent,' Polly said, thinking, *Please don't say she's changed her mind and wants her purchases wrapped, too.*

'Mrs Jones-White has decided she wishes—'

'Oh!' Doreen gave a strangled cry and rushed past Polly's counter towards the lifts.

'Where are you going, Miss Timmons?' Miss Snelgrove said, annoyed, and then, in an entirely different tone of voice, 'Oh my!' and started after her towards the lift.

A young woman was stepping off it. She moved stiffly, as if she hurt, and her arm was in a sling. It was Marjorie.

531

Here Comes the Navy – with the Army!

HEADLINE OF STORY ABOUT THE
EVACUATION OF DUNKIRK, JUNE 1940

LONDON – 25 OCTOBER 1940

Marjorie stepped off the lift and started across the floor towards Polly, who was still putting on her coat. 'Marjorie!' Polly breathed and ran over to her.

Doreen got there first. 'When did you get out of hospital?' she was asking. 'Why didn't you tell us?'

Marjorie ignored Doreen. 'Oh, Polly!' she said. 'I'm so glad to see you!' She looked dreadful, thin and with dark shadows under her eyes, and when Polly embraced her, she flinched. 'Sorry,' she said. 'I'm afraid I've got four broken ribs.'

'And no business being here,' Polly said. 'You don't look as though you should even be out of hospital.'

'I'm not,' Marjorie said and laughed shakily.

Miss Snelgrove came over. 'What are you doing here, Marjorie? Your doctor should never have allowed—'

'He didn't,' Marjorie said. 'I … It was my idea to come.' She put her hand to her forehead, swaying slightly.

'Miss Sebastian, fetch her a chair,' Miss Snelgrove ordered, and Polly started towards her counter, but Marjorie clutched her sleeve.

'No, please, Polly,' she pleaded. 'Stay with me.'

'I'll fetch it,' Doreen volunteered.

'Thank you,' Marjorie said, still holding on to Polly. Doreen left, and Marjorie turned to Miss Snelgrove. 'Could you possibly go and tell Mr Witherill I'm here? I'd intended to go up to Personnel to speak to him about coming back, but I'm afraid I'm not feeling—'

'You mustn't worry over that,' Miss Snelgrove said kindly. 'I can assure you your place will be here whenever you're ready to return.' Doreen brought the chair, and Marjorie sank into it. 'And you're to take as much time as you need.'

'Thank you, but if I could just speak to Mr Witherill—'

'Certainly, my dear.' Miss Snelgrove patted her hand and started towards the lifts.

'What did you do to her?' Doreen said, looking wonderingly after her. 'She's been an absolute *bear* these last few weeks.' She turned to Marjorie. 'You still haven't told us what you were doing in Jermyn Street.'

'Doreen, could I possibly have a glass of water?' Marjorie said faintly. 'I'm sorry to be such a bother ... '

'I'll bring it straightaway,' Doreen said and scurried off.

'Oh, you shouldn't have come,' Polly said, concerned.

'I had to.' She clutched Polly's arm. 'I sent her for the water so I could speak to you alone. I've been so worried. Did you get into trouble?'

'Trouble?'

'Because I wasn't here to tell Miss Snelgrove you weren't coming in,' she said, near tears. 'I'm so sorry. I only remembered this morning. I heard two of the nurses talking, and one of them said she needed to leave early and asked the other to cover for her, and I thought, Oh no, I was supposed to cover for Polly if she wasn't back on time Monday. I came as soon as I could. I had to sneak out of hospital—'

'It's all right,' Polly said. 'You mustn't upset yourself. Everything's fine.'

'Oh, then you *did* make it back in time for work on Monday.'

Colour flooded back into her cheeks, and she looked so relieved Polly didn't have the heart to tell her she hadn't. 'I was so afraid Miss Snelgrove would sack you.'

She'd have liked to, Polly thought. 'No, I wasn't sacked.'

'And your mother was all right?'

Polly nodded.

'Oh good,' Marjorie said. 'I was so worried that you'd had to stay and I'd let you down.'

'You let *me* down?' Polly said. 'I let *you* down. I thought you'd gone to Bath. I should have known you wouldn't leave London without telling me. I should have told the authorities you were missing. I should have made them look—'

Marjorie was shaking her head. 'They couldn't have found me. I didn't tell anyone where I was going.'

'Where *were* you going?' Polly asked, and then regretted it because Marjorie looked stricken. 'It's all right,' she said hastily. 'You needn't talk about it if you don't want to.' She looked over at the lifts. 'I can't imagine what's taking Doreen so long with the water. I'll go and see what's keeping her.'

'Thank you. Did your friend find you?'

Polly froze. 'My friend?'

'Yes. She came the day you were gone. Eileen O'Reilly—'

Merope. They'd sent Merope. Of course. She not only knew Polly, she knew the historical period. But how ironic. While Merope'd been here looking for her, she'd been up in Backbury looking for *her*. 'She said you were at school together,' Marjorie said.

At school. 'We were,' Polly said. 'She came in the Saturday I was gone?' That had been nearly four weeks ago.

'Yes. I told her you'd be back on Monday,' Marjorie said. 'Didn't she come in?'

'No. What else did she say?'

'She asked if you worked here, and I said yes, and she asked where she could find you.'

'What did you tell her?'

'She was so anxious to contact you, I told her you'd gone to Northumbria to visit your mother.'

And Merope, hearing the explanation the lab had them use to cover their disappearance at the end of an assignment, must have concluded she'd already gone back through to Oxford, and that was the reason Merope hadn't come back on Monday.

'She gave me her address,' Marjorie said, 'but I'm afraid I haven't got it. I'd put it in my pocket, and when they rescued me, they had to cut my clothes off because of all the blood … The nurse said they had to be discarded.'

'And you don't remember the address?'

'No,' she said, looking stricken again. 'It was in Stepney. Or Shoreditch. Somewhere in the East End. I only glanced at it, you see. I intended to give it to you on Monday morning. I remember where she said she works, though.'

'Works?' Polly said bewilderedly.

'Yes, because it's here on Oxford Street, too. Padgett's.'

'Here,' Doreen said, hurrying up with a glass of water. 'Sorry, I had to go up to the lunchroom for it, and when I told them it was for you they wanted to know how you were doing.' She handed it to Marjorie. 'You've got to tell us what happened. We all thought you'd done a flit, didn't we, Polly? Why did you go without—?'

'Marjorie,' Polly cut in, 'are you certain she said Padgett's?'

'Yes, she said she worked on—' She glanced over at the lifts. Miss Snelgrove and Mr Witherill were emerging from the centre one. They'd be here in another moment.

'She worked on—' Polly prompted.

'On the third floor. In Notions. I remember, because it was the same as our floor, and when I first came to Townsend Brothers, that's the department I—'

'Miss Hayes,' Mr Witherill said, coming over to Marjorie, 'on behalf of Townsend Brothers, allow me to welcome you back.'

'I assured her her position would be here whenever she's ready to return,' Miss Snelgrove said.

Polly edged away from them, trying to make sense of what Marjorie had just told her. It had to have been a cover story. Mr Dunworthy would never have allowed Merope to work in a department store on the forbidden list even for the few days it took to locate Polly. She'd only said it to establish a bond with Marjorie, and the East End address was where she and the new drop site really were.

But that made no sense. The East End was just as dangerous as Padgett's. And when Merope'd found out she hadn't gone back through to Oxford, why hadn't she come back to Townsend Brothers?

Unless she wasn't part of a retrieval team at all. Unless her drop hadn't opened either, and she'd come to London to find Polly, just as Polly had gone to Backbury to find her. And when she said she was living in Shoreditch and working at Padgett's, she was telling the truth.

At Padgett's, which had been hit – oh God, tonight. And there'd been casualties.

I've got to find her and get her out of there, Polly thought, starting blindly for the lift. But it was up on sixth. She looked back over at Miss Snelgrove. At any moment she and Mr Witherill might look up and see her leaving. Polly walked swiftly over to the door to the stairs, pushed through it and ran down the three flights of stairs and outside.

It was raining hard, but she didn't have time to button her coat or even pull up her collar. She ran bareheaded towards Padgett's, fighting her way through people coming out of the shops, pushing past umbrellas and people hurrying head-down against the rain and not looking where they were going. If only she'd researched exactly what time Padgett's had been hit …

But I didn't think I'd be here then, she thought, sidestepping a pram and trying to remember what she'd read about Padgett's. There'd been three casualties, and the reason for that was that it had been hit early, during the first raid. And the raids tonight had begun at 6:22. Which meant the sirens might go any moment.

Two more streets, she thought, splashing across a street, and the sirens went. People began heading for shelter. Polly zigzagged through them and arrived at Padgett's entrance. A doorman stood under the pillared porch, arguing with a woman and a small boy.

'Hail me a taxi at once,' the woman was ordering the doorman.

'The sirens have gone, madam,' he said. 'You and your son need to take shelter. Ow!' he yelped as the boy kicked him in the shins.

Polly darted past them to the revolving door and pushed on it, but it wouldn't budge. 'Sorry, miss,' the doorman said, turning from the woman. 'Padgett's is closed.'

'But I'm supposed to meet a friend here,' Polly said, trying to peer through the door into the store. 'She—'

'She'll have gone,' he said. 'And, as I was telling this lady, you need to take shelter—'

'I know, but I'm not looking for a customer. My friend's employed here. On third. She—'

'I *must* get to Harrods before it closes,' the woman cut in, and the little boy pulled his foot back for another kick.

The doorman sidestepped quickly and said to Polly, 'You want the staff entrance.'

'Where's that?'

'I insist you obtain a taxi for me immediately,' the woman said. 'My son is leaving for Scotland on Thursday, and it's essential he be properly outfitted—'

Polly couldn't wait to find out where the staff entrance was. She ran down to the side of the building and around to the rear, looking for it. Shopgirls were coming out, hesitating in the doorway to see how hard it was raining and to open their umbrellas, looking anxiously up at the sky at the planes, which sounded as if they were coming closer.

'How tiresome!' one of them said as Polly darted past her. 'I wanted to buy a chop for my tea on the way home. Now it will have to be shelter sandwiches. Again. Doesn't Jerry ever take a night off?'

Townsend Brothers' staff entrance was guarded, but Padgett's didn't seem to be, thank heavens. Polly pushed past the shop-girls and their umbrellas to the entrance and slipped through the door.

And collided with a guard standing just inside. 'Where are you going?' he demanded.

She'd have to pretend she worked here. 'I forgot my hat,' she said, hurrying past him as if she knew where she was going. She couldn't see any stairway, only a long corridor lined with doors. Which one led to the stairs?

'Here, wait!' the guard said behind her, and the last door on the left opened, revealing a stairway and, at its foot, two young women, pulling on their gloves. Polly ducked past them through the door and ran up the stairs. As the door swung shut, she heard the guard shout, 'Here! Where do you think you're going?' and then the sound of footsteps running awkwardly after her. She raced up the stairs past the door marked Mezzanine, and up to first. He'd be coming any second. She opened the door to first and ran out onto the floor, hoping there was no one still here.

There wasn't. The lights had been switched off and the display cases covered for the night. Polly dived behind the nearest counter and crouched there, watching the door to the stairs. After a moment, it opened and she could hear footsteps. She pressed closer behind the counter, holding her breath, and the footsteps retreated and the door closed.

She waited another long minute, listening. She couldn't hear anything but the hum of the planes, still distant but moving steadily closer. She looked over at the lift. She could operate it – she'd watched the lift boys at Townsend Brothers do it – but the dial above its door said it was on Ground. It couldn't come up to First without an operator. And if she went back to the stairs, and the guard had gone on up the stairwell, she'd run straight into him.

She ran across the floor, hoping there were stairs on the far side, and there was. She darted up them, counting floors. *One and a half. Two. No, mezzanine. Mezzanine and a half. Two.* Why couldn't Merope have worked on the ground floor?

The drone of the planes was substantially louder. She hoped the sound was being somehow magnified by the narrow stairwell. If it wasn't ... *Two and two-thirds ... three.* She opened the door silently and peered out onto the floor. She couldn't see any sign of the guard. Or of Merope anywhere on the darkened floor. The sound of the planes was less loud here than in the stairwell, but only marginally, and far off to the east Polly could hear the faint *crump* of a bomb.

She slipped through the door and started across the floor, looking for the notions department. 'Merope!' she called. 'Where are you?'

No answer. Polly remembered her saying she hadn't recognised Polly calling her name that day in Oxford, and if anyone else was here, they'd know her by the name Eileen, too. 'Eileen!'

Still no answer. *She's not here*, Polly thought, running through the linen department. *Or the planes are drowning out my voice.* 'Eileen!' she shouted more loudly. 'Eileen O'Reilly!'

A hand clamped on her arm. Polly whirled, trying to think what excuse to give the guard. 'I know you said the store was closed, but—' She stopped, her mouth open in astonishment.

It wasn't the guard. It was Michael Davies.

*'In view of the present situation, all parents whose children
are still in London are urged to evacuate them without delay.'*

GOVERNMENT NOTICE, SEPTEMBER 1940

LONDON – 25 OCTOBER 1940

'I do believe that every single unpleasant person in London
has decided to shop in Padgett's today,' Miss Peterson whispered to Eileen in the stockroom, and Eileen had to agree. She'd
spent all afternoon waiting on Mrs Sadler and her wretched
son Roland, who was being belatedly evacuated to Scotland on
Thursday.

And it's too bad it's not Australia, Eileen thought, bringing
out yet another blazer for Roland to try on. He refused to extend
his arm so she could get it into the sleeve and, when his mother
turned away to look at the waistcoats, he kicked Eileen hard in
the shins. 'Ow!'

'Oh, did I knock into you?' Roland said sweetly. 'I beg your
pardon.'

And I thought Alf and Binnie were bad, Eileen thought. They
were angels compared to Roland. 'How is this, madam?' she
asked Mrs Sadler after she'd finally managed to force the jacket
onto him.

'Oh yes, the fit's much better,' Mrs Sadler said, 'but I'm not
certain of the colour. Do you have it in blue?'

'I'll see, madam.' Eileen limped into the curtained storeroom, her ankle throbbing, to fetch the blazer in blue and then brown, and wrestle them onto the resisting Roland.

Why am I always stuck dealing with horrible children? she thought. *I should never have let them transfer me up here from Notions, shorthanded or not.* And now it was perfectly obvious why they'd been shorthanded in Children's Wear. *When I get back to Oxford, I am never doing another assignment involving children. Even if it means giving up* VE *Day.*

'This blue is much nicer,' Mrs Sadler said, fingering the lapels, 'but I'm afraid it won't be warm enough. Scotland's winters are very cold. Have you something in wool?'

The first four blazers he tried on, Eileen thought. 'I'll see, ma'am,' she said and made another trip to the storeroom, thinking, *Why couldn't I have searched the stores on the other side of Oxford Street first?* If she had, she wouldn't have missed Polly. She'd still have been at Townsend Brothers when she went there, and they could have gone through to Oxford together. Instead, Polly was gone, and she was stuck here at Padgett's waiting on six-year-old psychopaths till either someone came for her or she saved enough money to return to Backbury.

She'd written to the vicar on the pretext of telling him she'd safely delivered the children, so he knew where she was staying and could tell the retrieval team, but if she were in Backbury, they wouldn't have to come to London looking for her.

And it was far safer there. Stepney was bombed constantly, and Oxford Street had already been hit twice. The first time John Lewis had been gutted, which meant it hadn't been the store Polly had mentioned. She must have got it muddled with the similar-sounding Leighton's, and Townsend Brothers was where she'd got the idea it was a man's name.

Thank goodness she hadn't been hired at John Lewis. But nowhere on Oxford Street was truly safe. If she'd been on her way to the tube station when John Lewis's windows blew out ...

But at this point she hadn't managed to save enough money to go to Backbury. She needed not only train fare, but enough to pay her expenses once she got there. Mrs Willett wasn't charging her to stay since she watched Theodore at night and since they'd spent every night thus far in the Anderson. But she was charging Eileen board, and there were also her lunches and tube fare. She would have to work another full fortnight before she could afford to go.

And it looked as though it might take Mrs Sadler that long to decide on a blazer. 'No, I'm afraid that isn't warm enough either,' she was saying. 'Haven't you anything heavier? A tweed, perhaps?'

Eileen went on yet another search, wishing Mrs Sadler would make up her mind so she could get her purchases written up before Padgett's closed. The air raids had been starting earlier and earlier this past week, and it was a long way to Stepney. And if she was forced to spend the night in town, Theodore would have to stay next door with Mrs Willett's neighbour, and Eileen didn't trust her to take him out to the Anderson.

She'd had to stay in Padgett's shelter the night before last, and when she reached home, Theodore'd told her they'd spent the night at Mrs Owens' kitchen table playing cards. 'She's teaching me to play gin rummy,' he reported proudly. 'And when the bombs get very bad, we hide in the cupboard under the stairs,' and when Eileen had confronted her, Mrs Owens had said, 'That cupboard's safer than a bit of tin, I don't care what the government says.'

Eileen hoped Alf and Binnie's mother didn't have the same cavalier attitude towards shelters. Whitechapel was bombed nearly every night. She hoped she'd done the right thing in not giving Mrs Hodbin the vicar's letter. It was too late to give it to her now. After the *City of Benares*'s sinking, they'd suspended overseas evacuations, and she'd heard on the wireless this week there was a severe shortage of places for evacuees.

'No, this tweed's much too rough,' Mrs Sadler said. 'Roland is extremely sensitive.'

Sensitive, my foot, Eileen thought.

'Haven't you anything in camel's hair?'

The closing bell rang while Eileen was searching for it. *Thank goodness*, she thought, but Mrs Sadler remained oblivious, even though all around them customers were departing and shop assistants were covering their counters and putting on their coats and hats.

'I'm afraid Padgett's is closing, ma'am,' Eileen said. 'Would you like me to send the things you've purchased thus far and decide on a blazer tomorrow?'

'No, that won't do at all,' Mrs Sadler said. 'Roland leaves next Thursday, and if it should need to be altered …'

Eileen's supervisor, Miss Haskins, hurried up. 'Is there a problem, Mrs Sadler?'

Thank goodness, Eileen thought. *Tell her the store is closing*, but Mrs Sadler had already launched into the tale of her decision to evacuate Roland to Scotland. 'Everyone said I should send him to the country, but what's to keep the Germans from bombing Warwickshire as well as London? I want to know that he's truly safe. In my opinion, the Queen's simply being foolhardy not to send the Princesses to Scotland. After all, one must put the safety of one's children first, no matter how painful the separation may be.'

'Painful' is the word, Eileen thought. Roland had taken the opportunity of his mother's not watching him to pinch Eileen hard on the arm.

'… so you can see how important it is I complete Roland's shopping today,' Mrs Sadler was saying.

'Yes, of course. Miss O'Reilly, you don't mind staying, do you?' Miss Haskins didn't wait for an answer. 'Miss O'Reilly will be happy to assist you,' she said, and to Eileen, 'Remember to switch off the lights in your department when you leave.'

'Yes, ma'am,' Eileen said. Miss Haskins left, and a moment later, the lights on the rest of the floor went off, leaving Children's Wear a small island of light.

Eileen managed to fight Roland into the camel's hair blazer

without suffering further injury. 'It's an excellent fit,' she said, neatly dodging Roland's aimed foot. 'And very warm—' She stopped and listened as a siren sounded.

'It *is* a good fit ...' Mrs Sadler said consideringly.

Eileen was constantly amazed at the coolness of Londoners during raids. They didn't seem at all bothered by the sirens or the sound of the anti-aircraft guns, and when they went to the shelters, they strolled along as though they were window-shopping. Her first few days in London, Eileen had thought it was because they'd had more experience with them than she had. 'You'll get used to them soon,' Theodore's mother had said when she flinched at the *crump* of the bombs, but she still panicked every time she heard the sirens, even when she knew she wasn't in any danger, like here in Padgett's.

'Madam, the sirens have gone,' she said, looking up at the ceiling. She thought she could hear the faint buzz of planes.

Roland apparently heard them, too. 'Mummy, listen,' he said, tugging at Mrs Sadler's arm. 'Bombers.'

'Yes, dear. And I *do* like it, but I don't know ...'

It was obvious why it had taken Mrs Sadler over a year to evacuate her son. She'd obviously dawdled over that decision the way she was dawdling now over this blazer. *You accused the Queen of being foolhardy*, Eileen thought. *What would you call this? For all you know, Padgett's could be bombed at any moment.*

'Madam, we can't stay here,' she said. 'It's not safe.'

'The question is, will it be warm enough?'

For goodness' sake, he's not going to Antarctica.

'But it is the best we've seen ... Very well, I'll take it.'

Thank goodness. 'Excellent, madam. I'll have it and your other purchases sent round first thing tomorrow morning.'

'Perhaps it would be best if I took them with me.'

No, no, no. If you take them, they'll need to be wrapped, and those are definitely planes.

'You're certain they'll be delivered by tomorrow morning?'
Mrs Sadler was saying. 'Roland—'

Is leaving for Scotland on Thursday. I know. 'Absolutely certain, madam. I'll see to it personally.' She walked them over to
the lifts, where the lift operator was waiting impatiently, then
dashed back to her counter, wrote up the sales slip, pinned it to
the stack of clothes, and started into the storeroom with them.

Oh no, here they came again. 'Did you forget something,
Mrs Sadler?' Eileen asked.

'No, I decided I want to see Roland in the blazer and the woollen waistcoat. It will be very cold in Scotland. Roland, unbutton
your coat.'

'I won't,' Roland said.

'I know you're tired, darling,' Mrs Sadler said, 'but we're
nearly finished.'

Truer words, Eileen said silently, glancing nervously up at
the ceiling. The planes sounded very close, and it was a long
way from here to the tube station.

Where is the retrieval team? she thought for the thousandth
time since she'd arrived in London. *If they don't get here soon,
there'll be nothing left for them to retrieve.*

'Won't you please put the blazer on for Mother?' Mrs Sadler
said. 'There's a good boy.'

He was anything but. He twisted his head violently as Eileen
attempted to put the waistcoat on him and, when she held out
the blazer, folded his arms belligerently across his chest. 'I don't
like her,' he said. 'She twisted my arm before.'

You little liar, Eileen thought, wishing Alf and Binnie were
here. 'I'll be very careful,' she said, and, under her breath, 'Hold
your arm out before I break it.'

He promptly extended it and she got the blazer on him.

'There. It's a perfect fit.'

'You're quite right. It is.' Mrs Sadler stood back, looking
doubtfully at him. 'But now that I see them together, I don't
know ...'

'I could hold them for you,' Eileen said before she could ask to see anything else.

'Oh, I don't know,' she said doubtfully. 'I had hoped to finish his shopping today ... but if you haven't any brown ... yes, I think having you hold them will be best.'

Thank God, Eileen thought, even though it meant she'd have all this to do again tomorrow. She unblazered and unwaistcoated Roland, forgetting in her eagerness to have them gone to watch out for him. He stomped down hard on her instep, and when she yelped, said innocently, 'Oh, did I tread on your foot? I am sorry.'

'Come, Roland,' Mrs Sadler said. 'We must hurry.'

She's finally noticed we're in the middle of an air raid, Eileen thought, *and about time*. The searchlights had gone on, and the anti-aircraft guns were starting up.

'Do hurry, darling. We must go to Harrods and see what they have.'

Harrods is closed, Eileen thought, but she wasn't about to say that, or anything else that might delay them. She saw them to the lift again, and then hobbled over to switch off the department's lights, wondering if Roland had broken her foot.

And just when I need to make a run for the tube shelter, she thought, limping back to her department. Another gun, nearer than the last, began firing, and she heard an explosion.

If I don't leave soon, I'll have to spend the night here again. And perhaps that would be best. The planes sounded as if they were headed straight for Oxford Street, and at least she was safe here in Padgett's. She scooped up the blazer and waistcoat, dumped them in the storeroom, and covered her counter.

And heard voices from over by the lifts. *Oh no*, Eileen thought, *they're back again.* She quickly switched off the lamp on her counter and ducked into the storeroom. She wouldn't put it past Mrs Sadler to send Roland in here to look for her. She limped to the back and hid behind the last row of shelves, straining to hear above the increasing drone of the planes.

The voices were coming closer. *I am not going out there, no matter what,* she thought. She pressed herself into the corner and prepared to wait them out.

'I am coming home if I can.'

POSTSCRIPT ON A POSTCARD WRITTEN BY AN EVACUEE

LONDON – 25 OCTOBER 1940

For an endless minute standing there in Padgett's, Polly couldn't absorb what Michael Davies was saying or even the fact that he was there, she'd been so focused on finding Merope. She simply stood there gaping at him while he shook her arm and shouted that they had to get out of there.

'What are you doing here?' she managed finally. 'Why aren't you at Pearl Harbor?'

'It's a long story. I'll tell you later. The question is, what are you doing here? Didn't you hear the sirens? Come on!'

You're the retrieval team, she thought, dazed. *You're finally here.* She felt suddenly light and buoyant, as if an enormous weight she hadn't known she was carrying had been lifted. 'Oh my God, Michael, I ...' she stammered, 'I am so glad to see you!'

'*You're* glad?' An anti-aircraft gun started up. 'Listen, we can't stay here. We've got to get to shelter. Does this store have one?'

'Yes, but we can't use it. It was demolished.'

'Demolished? What do you—?'

'Padgett's is going to be bombed tonight.'

'*Tonight?* What time?'

'I don't know. At some point during one of the first raids.'

'Then let's get out of here,' he said and began pulling her back towards the stairwell.

'No! We've got to find Merope first.'

'*Merope?* What's she doing here? She was supposed to have gone back ages ago.'

'I don't know, but she works here on this floor. In Notions.' She wrenched free of him and ran across the darkened floor, calling, 'Eileen!'

There she was, standing next to a counter. 'Merope!' Polly cried, but it wasn't her – it was a mannequin, draped in lengths of fabric, her hands modishly posed. Polly raced past her, past bolts of fabric and rows of sewing machines, looking for Notions.

And this was obviously it – here was the buttons cabinet and the threads case – but the counter was shrouded, like all the others, in green baise, and its counter lamp was switched off. 'Merope? Eileen? Are you here?' she called, but there was no answer, no movement. 'She's not here,' she reported to Michael as he came up.

He was limping. 'What happened?' she asked. 'Did you hurt your foot?'

'Yes, but not recently. I'll tell you later. Right now we need to get out of here.'

'Not without Merope.'

'Who told you she worked here?'

'A girl I work with. Why?'

'Because I've been here the whole afternoon, looking for you, and I didn't see her.'

'But – you looked on this floor? Here in the notions department?'

'Yes. She wasn't here.'

'She might have been on her tea break or—'

'No, I was here over an hour. And then I stationed myself where I could watch the staff entrance when the store closed. That was what I was doing when I spotted you. She didn't come out the staff entrance.'

'Then she must still be here. She must work in some other part of the store,' Polly said, even though Marjorie'd said she was certain about her working in Notions. On third. 'Or she may have been sent to another floor to fill in.'

'Even if she was, she'd have left by now.' He looked up at the ceiling. 'We've got to get out of here. Listen to those planes. They'll be here any minute—'

'Not till we've searched the other floors.'

'We don't have time—'

'We will if we split up. You go back down to first and work your way up, and I'll—'

'Absolutely not. It took me almost a month to find you. We're not getting separated again. Come on.' He grabbed her arm and hurried her across the floor. 'We'll take the elevator.'

'You mean the lift?' Polly said. 'But—'

'Don't worry, I know how to run it. That's how I got up here.' He pushed her into the open lift.

'But they aren't supposed to be used during raids.'

'The raid hasn't started yet.' He pulled the metal grille across and reached for the lever. 'Which floor?'

She looked up at the numbers above the door. 'The top one. Seven. We'll work our way down.'

'Along with the bombs,' he said, yanking the lever across. The car began to ascend. 'Seven's nothing but offices. We'll start with six.'

She nodded, watching the arrow creep past four to five and then six. 'Do you remember what was on six?'

'Sixth floor. China, kitchenwares, home furnishings,' he chanted in a lift boy's singsong. 'Here we are, madam.' The lift jolted to a stop. 'Sorry.' He slid the gate back and reached to open the door.

'Careful,' Polly whispered. 'If the guard's out there—'

'He's not. He's down on the ground floor looking for me.' He opened the door onto a roar of planes. 'Or if he has any survival instincts, he's in a shelter. It doesn't look like she's—'

'You take that side and I'll take the other,' Polly said and ran through the darkened departments, past the place settings and sofas, shouting Merope's name over the rumble of the planes, but she wasn't there.

Or on fifth. 'She's not here,' Mike said, hobbling over to her, 'and we've got to go. The planes—'

'Fourth,' Polly said grimly.

They got back in the lift. 'If there's no one here either,' he said, opening the door, 'we're going to have to—'

'She's here,' Polly said. 'Look. The lights are still on.' But the light was coming from the searchlights and an orange glow from a fire somewhere. Between them, they lit the entire floor and it was obviously deserted.

'She's not here either,' Michael said.

'We still must check,' she said stubbornly and started out of the lift.

He grabbed her arm. 'There's no time. You've got to face it, she's not here. Even if she does work here, we must have missed her somehow. Maybe she took one of the other elevators down while we were coming up. There's nobody here. The store's completely empty.'

'No, it's not. There were casualties. Three people were killed—'

'Yes, and two of them will be us if we don't get out of here *right now.*'

He was right. The planes were nearly overhead. And Merope obviously wasn't here. Marjorie must have got the name of the store muddled—

Marjorie, who nobody had known was on Jermyn Street. What if Merope had stayed late to tidy her shelves? Or had come back for something she'd forgotten? There'd been three casualties—

Polly wrenched violently free of Michael and ran out across the floor. 'Merope!' she shouted above the drone of the planes.

There was a loud *crump*, and the tall windows lit up. She flinched. 'Eileen!'

'Polly!' Mike shouted, hobbling after her. 'Get away from the windows!'

She ignored him, running on towards what had to be the children's wear department. There was a tiny mannequin in a frilly dress. 'Eileen!' she called, running past it towards a row of infants' cots.

'We've got to go!' Mike shouted. 'She's not here—' There was another explosion, closer, and Mike's voice cut off.

Polly wheeled, but he wasn't hurt: He was standing there, staring back towards Children's Wear as if he'd heard something. 'What is it?' Polly asked.

And Merope was running towards them from the door of a storeroom, her face radiant with smiles. She threw herself into Polly's arms. 'Polly, oh, my goodness, I've never been so happy to see anyone in my life!' She ran over to hug Michael. 'And you're here, too! This is wonderful! I'd nearly given up hope. Where have you *been*?'

The *poom-poom-poom* of an anti-aircraft gun started up, so close it rattled the windows, and Michael said, 'We can discuss that later. Right now we've got to get out of here.'

'There's a shelter here,' Merope said. 'In the basement—'

'No, we must get out of the store,' Polly said.

'Oh. Then I'll get my coat and—'

'There isn't time. Come on!' Michael shouted over the deafening sound of the planes. 'Where's the closest way down?'

'There's a stairway over there,' Merope said, pointing.

'The elevator will be quicker,' Mike said and started back across the floor.

Polly opened her mouth to say, 'But the raid's begun. Wouldn't the stairs be safer?' but it was four flights, and with that limp he clearly couldn't move that fast. She followed him, dragging Merope along with her. 'Hurry.'

Merope was limping, too. 'Is your foot injured?' Polly shouted as they ran.

'No. A perfectly horrid child trod on my instep.'

'The ones you were telling me about in Oxford?'

'Alf and Binnie? No, they're amateurs compared to this little wretch. I hope one of these bombs falls on him,' she said, glancing anxiously up at the ceiling. The planes were very near. Another anti-aircraft gun roared into action, and the windows lit up with a garish green. A flare. 'I don't think there's time to go to a shelter. We'll have to use Padgett's. It's all right. It's been reinforced.'

Polly shook her head. 'Padgett's is going to be bombed.'

'It is?' Merope turned frightened eyes to her. 'But you said … *When?*'

'I don't know,' Polly said. 'Any minute.'

'But you said Padgett's hadn't been bombed.'

'I did not. Hurry! We can talk about this later.'

But Merope continued to chatter as Polly dragged her, hobbling, to the lift. 'That's why I took the job here, because you said it was safe. You said you were going to work in a department store, Selfridge's or Padgett's or—'

Oh God. I said those were the ones Mr Dunworthy forbade me to work in, Polly thought, but this was no time to go into it. Or into why Merope hadn't come back to Townsend Brothers that Monday. Or what she was still doing here. 'We'll sort it all out later,' she said.

Merope nodded. 'After we're back in Oxford. When I found out you'd already gone, I was afraid I'd never see Oxford again. I didn't know what to do—'

Michael was already inside the lift. 'Come on!' he yelled.

There was a loud *crump*, half a mile away, and a bright flash. Polly pushed Merope into the lift ahead of her, and pulled the brass gate across for Michael. 'Go,' she said.

He yanked the lever all the way back, and the lift began to descend. 'I still can't believe you're here,' Merope chattered to Michael. 'I heard voices, but I thought Mrs Sadler and her horrid son Roland had come back, so I hid in the storeroom, and then I heard someone calling Polly's name. When I think I nearly didn't come out—'

There was a loud *boom*, and then a leaden *thunk*, and the lift jerked to a stop. They weren't at a floor. Beyond the metal gate there was only blank wall.

We're trapped, Polly thought, and then, *There were three casualties. We rescued Merope only to trap her here.*

'What happened?' Merope asked, but Michael didn't answer. He pushed hard on the lever, then pulled it back. The lift began to ascend. Michael let it go up for a moment and then reversed the lever. The lift started down.

Polly held her breath. *Second floor*, that's it, she thought, willing it to descend, *and now first—*

The lift jerked to a stop again, and this time it sounded final. Michael yanked with both hands, but the lever wouldn't budge. He pulled the gate open and looked up. The floor was three feet above them. 'Polly, I need you to climb up and open the door,' he said, bracing his body against the side wall. He laced his fingers together. 'Climb onto my hands,' he ordered.

Polly nodded and stepped up, reaching for the edge of the floor above. He hoisted her up, Merope giving support, and she got one knee onto it.

'Now stretch your hand over to the door handles,' Michael ordered. 'That's it. Now slide them apart,' which was easier said than done. She had almost no leverage. She managed to pull the doors a few inches apart, but her knee slipped, and she nearly fell.

'No problem,' Michael said. He lowered her back down. 'That was a good first try. If only we had a stick or something to push it open with,' he said, looking around, but Padgett's lifts didn't have so much as a stool for the lift operator. 'Okay, let's try it again.'

'Let me try this time,' Merope said, kicking off her shoes. She stepped lightly onto his hands, squeezed herself into the narrow opening, her legs dangling as she heaved herself through it and up onto the floor, and stood up. She slid the doors all the way open from the outside to the instant accompaniment of guns and bombs. Merope looked nervously over her shoulder and then knelt down, her hand extended. 'Now you, Polly. Boost her up, Michael.'

He did, and Merope grasped Polly's free hand and pulled her up over the edge. A bomb exploded somewhere nearby, and Merope flinched and said frightenedly, 'How near do you think—?'

'Near. Help me pull Michael out,' Polly said. *If we can*, she thought. *I should have boosted him up.* 'Take hold of my ankles,' she ordered Merope, lying down flat on the floor and extending her arms down to Michael.

'That won't work,' Michael shouted up. 'I'm too heavy. Listen, you two go on.'

Merope leaped to her feet and ran stocking-footed into the darkness. Polly stared after her, furious. She was obviously frightened, but they couldn't abandon Michael. 'Merope—!'

'You, too,' Michael shouted up to her. 'I'll fix it and meet you downstairs.'

'I'm not going without you.'

'There's no time to argue,' he said. 'You need—' but Merope was back, dragging a chair.

'Sorry,' she said breathlessly. 'I had to go all the way to the ladies' lounge for it. Help me with it.' Together, they lowered the chair down to him, and he stepped awkwardly up onto the seat.

'Wait,' Merope shouted. 'My shoes!'

'There isn't time to—' Polly began, but he'd already stepped off the chair, jammed them in his pockets, and climbed back up.

Merope knelt next to Polly, and they heaved him up and out. 'Where's the nearest stairway?' he asked Merope.

'There,' she said, and they fled across the firelit floor, Michael hobbling behind them.

'I can't wait to get out of this horrid place and back to Oxford,' Merope said as they ran. 'Do you know what the first thing I'm going to do when we get there is?'

If we get there, Polly thought, hurrying them along. The planes were directly above them now. Bombs whistled all around them, and the floor lit up with bright, deafening flashes. They dived into the stairwell and racketed down the stairs.

'I'm going to tell Mr Dunworthy I am never doing another assignment involving children,' Merope said.

Polly glanced back at Michael. He was keeping up, though he was leaning heavily on the stair railing.

'I thought you'd never find me, Polly,' Merope said. 'When I found out you'd gone back, I—'

They reached the ground floor. Polly opened the door, and they plunged along the side of the store through a barrage of flashes and explosions, their hands up to shield their heads, and across the street.

When they came up onto the pavement on the far side, Merope and Michael stopped, panting. 'No, we're still too close,' Polly said, grabbing Merope's arm and pulling her along the street with Michael limping after, trying to keep away from the windows of the shops and at the same time in the protection of the buildings. They should have stayed on the same side of the street as Padgett's. The blast would spread out in an arc, and here there were no walls between them and the force of the concussion. And she had no idea how far the blast from the explosion would reach.

'I'm sorry,' Merope gasped after a hundred yards, 'I've *got* to stop a moment.'

Polly nodded and pulled them around the next corner into the shadow of a building to catch their breath. 'Thank you,' Merope panted, leaning against the wall.

Michael was bending down, his hands on his knees, breathing

hard. 'I wish I could … say it was … letting up,' he said, looking up at the sky, 'but I think it's … getting worse.'

'But if we go to a shelter,' Merope objected, 'we'll be trapped there all night. Shouldn't we go straight to the drop?'

The drop. She'd been so fixed on getting Merope out of Padgett's, on getting them to safety, she'd forgotten about Michael being the retrieval team. He was here to take her – to take them – back to Oxford, to safety. *Home.*

'Yes, of course. You're right,' she said. She turned to Michael. 'Let's go to the drop.'

'Great,' he said. 'Where is it?'

'What?'

'Your drop. Where is it? Is it far from here?'

They were both looking at her expectantly. 'You're not the retrieval team, Michael?' Polly said.

'The retrieval team? No.'

I should have known, Polly thought dully. All the clues were there: his injured foot, his not knowing Merope was here, his remark that he'd been searching for her for almost a month.

'Wait, I don't understand,' Merope said, looking bewilderedly from one to the other. 'Neither of you is the retrieval team? But then what are you doing here, Michael?'

'I can't get to my drop,' he said. 'I came to London to find Polly so I could use hers—'

'So did I,' Merope said, 'but when I went to Townsend Brothers, they told me you'd gone back, Polly, so I—'

'Look, we can discuss all this in Oxford,' Michael said impatiently. 'Right now we need to get to your drop, Polly. How far—?'

'It's in Kensington,' Polly said, 'but we can't use it either. *Why* can't you get to your drop?'

An HE crashed down up the street, spewing glass everywhere. The three of them instinctively put their hands up to shield their faces. 'We've got to get to a shelter,' Michael said. 'Which one's nearest?'

'Oxford Circus,' Polly said and led them at a trot along the street to the entrance and down the steps. The iron grille had already been pulled across. The guard had to open it for them. 'You lot are cutting it close,' he said as they ran in. 'You'd best get below straightaway.'

They didn't need any encouraging. They ran for the turnstiles. 'I haven't any money,' Merope said. 'My handbag—'

Polly fumbled in her bag for extra tokens. Another HE thudded nearby, shaking the station.

'Are you certain it's safe in here?' Merope said, looking nervously up at the ceiling.

'Yes,' Polly said, handing her and Michael tokens. 'Oxford Circus wasn't hit till the end of the Blitz.' She pushed through the turnstile and ran over to the escalators.

'Oh, that's right,' Merope said, behind her. 'I forgot. You know where all the bombs fell.'

Till the first of January, Polly thought, stepping onto the long escalator. *Which means we'd better have got to Michael's drop by then.*

What did he mean, he couldn't get to it? She turned to ask him, but he was several steps above them, limping down to where they were, leaning heavily on the moving rubber rail. 'Are you all right?' Merope asked. 'You didn't sprain your ankle chasing me in Padgett's, did you?'

'No,' Michael said, coming down onto the step with Merope, 'I— It was hit by shrapnel. At Dunkirk.'

Dunkirk? Polly felt a twinge of panic. Was that why he couldn't get to his drop, because it was in Dunkirk? If it was, they wouldn't be able to reach it till the end of the war, and that was too late. But his drop couldn't be in Dunkirk. And he couldn't have been there either.

'What were you doing in Dunkirk?' Merope was asking.

'Shh,' Michael said, pointing below them. They were to the foot of the escalator, which was so jammed with people they had difficulty getting off, and once they did, even more difficulty getting through the crowd. The entire hall was packed solid with people. Everyone on Oxford Street – and Regent Street and New Bond Street – had fled down here when the bombing began, and they all had parcels and shopping bags and wet umbrellas to add to the crush.

The tunnels were just as bad, and Polly knew from experience that the platforms would be even worse. 'This is impossible,' Michael said. 'We've got to find a place where we can talk. What about another tube station? The trains are still running, aren't they?'

She nodded and led them through the crowd, saying over and over, 'Sorry, we're trying to get to our train, sorry …'

'No use going out to the platform, dearie,' a woman in the archway to the Central Line platform said. 'The Central Line trains aren't running.'

'What about the Bakerloo Line?' Polly asked.

The woman shrugged. 'No idea, dearie.'

'We'll have to go back upstairs,' Polly told Michael and Merope. If they could get there, if they could even get out of this entryway and into the tunnel—

'*There's* a space!' Merope cried and, before Polly could stop her, ran out onto the platform. When Polly and Michael caught up to her, she was standing happily on a blue blanket held down at each corner by a shoe.

'We can't sit here,' Polly said, remembering that first night at St George's when she'd got in trouble with everyone for—

The troupe. She'd completely forgotten about them. When she didn't come, they'd think something had happened to her, and Sir Godfrey would—

'*Why* can't we sit here?' Merope said. 'Whoever was sitting on it before has gone off to the canteen or the loo or something, and it'll take them hours to get back in this crowd.'

'And this is as good a place to talk as we're going to get,' Michael said.

He was right. The people on both sides were deep in

conversation and didn't even notice when Merope sat down on the blanket and curled her legs up under her. Mike eased himself down, putting his hand on her shoulder for support, and wincing as he crossed his legs. 'Now,' he said, leaning forward and lowering his voice, 'I want to hear about your drop, Polly. Why isn't it—?'

Merope cut in, 'No, first you must tell us what happened to your foot. What were you doing at Dunkirk? I thought you were going to Dover.'

'I was,' he said, 'but I came through on a beach thirty miles south of it—'

Oh thank God. His drop *wasn't* in Dunkirk. It was on this side of the Atlantic.

'—and before I could get to Dover I was shanghaied—'

'*Shanghaied?*'

'It's a long story. Anyway, I ended up taking part in the evacuation from Dunkirk, where I got this.' He pointed at his foot. 'They did surgery and managed to save it, but the tendons are damaged, which is why I've got the limp.'

'But why didn't you go back to Oxford to have it repaired?' Merope asked.

'I told you, I can't get to my drop.'

'Why not?' Polly asked. 'Is the beach patrolled?' If that was the only problem, the three of them should be able to come up with some way to distract the guard.

'No, it doesn't have to be. There's an artillery gun emplacement right on top of the drop site.'

Which will be there till the end of the war, Polly thought.

'But then why didn't they send a retrieval team for you?' Merope whispered.

'They may have, and couldn't find me. I was unconscious when I was brought in and didn't have any papers on me, so the hospital didn't know who I was, and before I could tell them I was moved to Orpington.'

Polly looked up at him. 'Orpington?'

'Yeah, it's in southeast London. They'd never have thought to look for me there. Listen, we can discuss what happened to me later.' He lowered his voice. 'Right now we need to figure out what to do about a drop. Polly, are you sure yours isn't working?'

'Yes.' She told them about the incident.

'Blast can do odd things,' Michael agreed. 'I know that from my prep. It can kill people without leaving a mark on them. Which leaves yours, Merope,' he said, turning to her. 'What did you mean when you said you can't get to your drop either? And please don't say there's an artillery gun on it.'

'No, but the Army's taken over the manor for training.'

'Was the drop on the manor grounds?'

'No, in the woods, but the Army's conducting shooting practice in them.'

'And they've strung barbed wire all round it,' Polly said.

Merope looked at her, surprised. 'How do you know that?'

'I went to Backbury to look for you. That's where I was the day you came to Townsend Brothers. We just missed each other.'

'But why did they say you'd gone to Northumbria? I thought—'

'Later,' Michael said impatiently. 'Is the fence guarded? Do you think we'd be able to cut through it? Or crawl under?'

'Possibly,' Merope said. 'But that's not the only problem. I think my drop must have been somehow damaged, too. It wouldn't open, even before the Army came. After the quarantine, I tried to go through over a dozen times, but—'

'After the *quarantine*?' Michael said.

'Yes, my assignment was supposed to be over the second of May, but Alf got the measles, and the manor was quarantined for nearly three months—'

Her assignment had ended the second of May? Polly'd assumed it had ended when the Army took over the manor. 'When did you leave the manor?' she asked.

'The ninth of September.'

May second to September ninth. That was four months. She'd been at the manor for *four months* after her assignment had ended. 'And no retrieval team came for you?' Michael asked.

'No, unless they came while we were quarantined and Samuels wouldn't let them in.'

But even if they'd been unable to get to her during the quarantine – and surely they could have managed that – they'd had more than a month after that to pull her out, and there wasn't the excuse of their not knowing where Merope was, as there was with her and Michael. Oxford had known exactly where to find her.

But it wasn't just that. Mr Dunworthy would never have left Merope to cope with an epidemic, and he definitely wouldn't have left Michael here with an injured foot.

And this was time travel. Even if it had taken them months to locate Michael in hospital, Oxford could have sent a second team to be there when he landed in Dover and take him to the new drop site and back to Oxford.

'But my drop can't have been damaged by blast,' Merope said. 'The manor wasn't bombed. So what can have happened?'

'I don't know,' Michael said.

I do, Polly thought sickly. She'd known it from that morning at St George's when she'd realised the retrieval team should have been outside Townsend Brothers the day before. That was why her knees had buckled – because she knew what their not being there meant. But she'd kept inventing excuses to keep from facing the truth. Which was that something terrible had happened in Oxford, and the retrieval team wasn't coming.

Nobody's coming, she thought.

'But if we can't use any of our drops,' Merope was saying, 'what do we do now?'

LONDON – 25 OCTOBER 1940

'How will we get home if both Polly's and my drops are broken?' Merope asked, trying to shout over the noise on the platform and at the same time keep the shelterers on the adjacent blankets from hearing.

'We don't know for sure that they are broken,' Mike said. 'You said there were soldiers at the manor. They might have been close enough to your drop to prevent it from opening.'

Merope shook her head. 'They didn't come till a month after the quarantine ended.'

'How far into the woods was your drop?' Michael asked. 'Could it be seen from the road? Or could one of your evacuees have followed you? What about yours, Polly? Are you sure yours was damaged, or could an air-raid warden have been somewhere where he could see the shimmer? Or a firespotter?'

'It doesn't *matter*,' Polly wanted to scream at him. 'Don't you understand what's happened?'

I've got to get out of here, she thought, and stood up. 'I have to go.'

'Go?' Michael and Merope said blankly.

'Yes. I'd promised I'd meet some of the contemps. I must go and tell them I can't come.'

'We'll come with you,' Michael said.

'*No*. It'll be faster if I go alone,' she said and fled into the crowd.

'Polly, wait!' she heard him call, and then say, 'No, you stay here, Merope. I'll go get her,' but she didn't look back. She ploughed through the crowd, around outstretched feet, over blankets and hampers, through the archway and down the tunnel, desperate to get away, to find somewhere where she could be alone, where she could absorb what Michael and Merope had just told her. But there was nowhere here that wasn't jammed with people. The central hall was even worse than the tunnel had been.

'Polly, wait!' Michael called. She glanced back as she ran. He was gaining on her in spite of his limp, and the hall was packed so tightly she couldn't push through. Where—?

'You there, stop!' someone shouted, and two children shot past her, darting between people with a station guard in hot pursuit. The crowd parted in their wake, and Polly took advantage of the momentary opening to run after them as they raced towards the escalators. The crowd closed in behind her.

The urchins, who looked suspiciously like the boy and girl who'd stolen that picnic basket in Holborn, racketed down the escalator to the next level and into the southbound tunnel with the guard and Polly a few steps behind.

They rounded a corner. 'Stop, you two!' the guard shouted, and two men who'd been standing among a group against the wall joined the chase. Polly stepped quickly into the space the men had left, flattening herself against the wall, breathing hard.

She leaned out past the remaining men to look back the way she'd come, but Michael didn't appear in the stairway. *I've lost him*, she thought. She was safe for the moment.

Safe, she thought dully. *We're in the Blitz, and we can't get out. And nobody's coming to get us.* She put her hand to her stomach as if to hold the sickening knowledge in, but it was already spilling out, engulfing her.

Something terrible – no, *worse* than terrible – something *unthinkable* had happened in Oxford. It was the only possible explanation for her drop and Merope's drop both failing to open, for their retrieval teams not being here, for Mr Dunworthy not being here. He would never have left Michael lying wounded in hospital, never have left Merope stranded in the middle of an epidemic, never have left her here knowing she had a deadline. He'd have yanked her out the moment, the instant, he realised Merope's drop wasn't working, and he wouldn't have sent a retrieval team to Mrs Rickett's or Townsend Brothers or Notting Hill Gate. They'd have been waiting for her in the passage when she came through that first night. And the fact that they hadn't been could mean only one thing.

Mr Dunworthy must be dead, she thought. She wondered numbly what had happened. Something no one had seen coming, like Pearl Harbor? Or something even worse – a terrorist with a pinpoint bomb, or a second Pandemic? Or the end of the world? It had to have been something truly catastrophic, because even if the lab and the net had been destroyed, they could have built a new one, and this was *time travel*. Even if it had taken them five years, or fifty, to construct a new net, to recalculate their coordinates, they could still have pulled her out that first day, could have pulled Michael and Merope out before the quarantine started, before Michael injured his foot. Unless there was no one left alive who knew they were here.

Which meant everyone was dead, Badri and Linna and Mr Dunworthy. And, *oh God*, Colin.

'Are you all right, dearie?' a round, rosy-cheeked woman across the tunnel from her said. She was looking at Polly's hand, still pressed against her stomach. 'You mustn't be frightened. It always sounds like that.' She gestured up at the ceiling, from which the sound of bombs was very faintly audible. 'The first night I was down here, I thought we were for it.'

We are, Polly thought bleakly. *We're stranded in the middle of the Blitz, and no one's coming to get us. We'll still be here when my deadline arrives.*

'You're quite safe,' the woman was saying. 'The bombs can't get us down here – did you find them?' she broke off to ask the guard, who was coming back along the tunnel, looking disgruntled.

'No. Vanished into thin air, they did. They didn't come back this way, did they?'

'No,' the woman said, and to Polly, 'These children, left to run wild …' She clucked her tongue. 'I do hope we see an end to this war soon.'

You might, Polly thought. *I can't. I've already seen it.* And had a sudden vision of the cheering crowds in Charing Cross, of—

That was how you knew, she thought suddenly, *before Eileen even told you her drop wasn't working, how you knew that morning at St George's before you even went to Townsend Brothers, before you knew the retrieval team hadn't come.*

Till this moment she'd never made the connection, not even that night Marjorie took her home with her and they'd ended up at Trafalgar Square. She'd kept the knowledge carefully from herself, afraid to touch it, to even look at it, as if it were a UXB which might go off. Which it was. It was the final proof that in fact the terrible something had happened, that no one had come in time. Unless … Oh God, she hadn't even thought of that possibility. She'd assumed … but that was even worse …

'Are you feeling ill, dearie?' the woman was asking. 'Come, sit down.' She patted her blanket. 'There's room.'

'No, I must go,' Polly said in a strangled voice and darted back down the tunnel and across to the escalators. She had to get back to the platform and ask Merope—

'Polly!' a woman's voice called from behind her. It was Miss Laburnum, struggling towards her through the milling mob with two carrier bags. She looked flushed and harried, her hair straggling out of its bun.

566

I'll pretend I didn't see her, Polly thought, but the crowd had closed in, cutting off escape.

'I'm so glad to see you're late for rehearsal as well,' Miss Laburnum said. 'I was afraid I was the only one. I went out to Croxley to borrow a butler's livery from my aunt for our play. I got a lovely costume for when you're shipwrecked. Here, hold this.' She handed Polly one of the bags and began digging through the other. 'It's in here somewhere.'

'Miss Laburnum—'

'I know, we're already horribly late. The train back was delayed – bomb on the line,' she said, giving up her rummaging. 'Never mind, I'll show it to you at rehearsal.'

'I can't go with you,' Polly said, and tried to hand her back the bag.

'But why not? What about rehearsal?'

'I—' What excuse could she give? My fellow time travellers are here? Hardly. Some school friends? No, Merope had already told Marjorie Polly was her cousin.

Marjorie. 'My friend who was in hospital – do you remember?' she said. 'You were with me the night I found out she'd been injured?'

'Yes,' Miss Laburnum said and seemed to look at her strained face for the first time. 'Oh my *dear*, your friend hasn't—?'

'No, she's much better, so much that she can have visitors now, and I promised I'd—'

'Oh, but you can't go to see her in the midst of a raid.'

In her worry over everything else, Polly'd forgotten all about the bombs falling above them right now. 'No, no, I'm not going to visit her. I promised her I'd go to St Pancras to tell her landlady the good news, and take her a list of things Marjorie wants her to bring to her in hospital.'

'Oh, of course. I quite understand.' She took the bag from Polly. 'But you'll be there tomorrow?'

Yes. Tomorrow and tomorrow and tomorrow. 'Tell Sir

Godfrey I'll be at rehearsal,' Polly said and hurried away. She had to get to Merope and ask her—

A hand clamped onto her shoulder. 'I've been looking for you everywhere,' Michael said angrily. 'Why did you run off like that?'

'I told you, I needed to tell the contemps I promised to meet that I couldn't come,' Polly said, but he wasn't listening.

'Don't pull a stunt like that again! I just spent the last three and a half weeks looking all over London for you. I can't afford to lose you again.'

'I'm sorry.' *And sorry you found me before I was able to find out—*

'Michael,' she said, 'when did you leave for your Dover assignment?'

'Right after I saw you in Oxford.'

Thank goodness, she thought. But this was time travel. He could have gone to Pearl Harbor flash-time. 'You weren't able to persuade Mr Dunworthy to change your schedule back?' she asked to be certain.

'No, I never even got in to see him.' He looked curiously at her. 'Why?'

'I wondered, that's all. We'd best go find Merope. She'll be worried.' She started off through the crowd, hoping she might be able to lose him again.

'No, wait,' Michael said, clamping a hand on her arm. 'I need to know—'

'Polly!' Merope shouted. They both turned to look. She was coming down the escalator, elbowing past people to reach the bottom, to get to them.

'Michael! Oh, thank goodness! I've been looking for you everywhere. The man whose blanket it was came back and made me leave. He said it was his spot and that his wife had been queuing since noon to save it, and there was nowhere else to sit so I came looking for you, but I couldn't find either of you *anywhere*, and I was afraid I'd never see you again!' she said, and burst into tears.

'Don't cry,' Michael said, putting his arm around her. 'It's all right. You did find us.'

'I know,' she said, pulling away from him and wiping at her cheeks. 'I'm sorry. I haven't cried the entire time I've been here, not even when I found out you'd gone back to Oxford, Polly. I mean, I know you didn't, but I thought you had, and that I was all alone here ...' She began to cry again.

'You're not alone now,' Michael said, handing her a handkerchief.

'Thank you,' she said. 'I know. It's ridiculous to cry now. It must be reaction. I'm sorry I lost our place to sit—'

'It's all right, we'll find another one,' Michael said. 'What about the next level up, Polly?'

'We can try it,' Polly said and started towards the escalator.

'Wait!' Merope said, clutching Polly's hand. 'What if we get separated?'

'She's right,' Michael said. 'We need to decide on a meeting place. What about at the foot of the escalators?'

'Can it be the furthest level down?' Merope asked nervously, glancing up to where the muffled *crump* of bombs could be heard.

'Fine,' he said. 'If we get separated again or anything happens, we go straight to the foot of the escalators on the lowest level and wait there for the others. Right?'

Merope and Polly nodded, and they got on the escalator. But the level above was just as crowded. 'After the trains stop, we might be able to sneak up to the surface,' Polly said. 'There shouldn't be anyone in the station but the guard.'

'But what about the raids?' Merope asked fearfully.

'Oxford Circus wasn't hit—'

'You said Padgett's wasn't hit either,' Merope said accusingly, and Mike shook his head in warning at Polly and said, 'I don't think upstairs is a good idea. Isn't there anywhere down here?'

'No,' Polly said, looking around at the entrances to the tunnels, trying to think which platform might—

She frowned. There, emerging from the southbound tunnel, were the two urchins the guard had been chasing. How had they got up here? The guard had said they'd vanished into thin air. 'Hang on, I have an idea. Stay there,' she said and, before the other two could object, darted into the tunnel.

Halfway along it was a grey metal door marked Emergency Exit and under it, No Unauthorised Admittance. A couple was sitting in front of it on a plaid rug, righting several overturned dishes and mopping up spilled tea.

Polly ran back out to Michael and Merope. 'I think I've found something,' she said. She handed Merope her handbag.

'Why are you giving this to me?' Merope asked.

'You'll see. Come along.' She led them into the tunnel and stopped a few yards short of the door. 'Tell the couple you're an Underground official,' she whispered to Michael, 'and that you need to go inside, and then follow my lead.'

He did. 'Official business.'

'We're looking for two children,' Polly said. 'They stole my bag.'

'I told you, didn't I, Virgil?' the woman said. 'They're thieves, I said.'

'They're not in there,' Virgil said. 'They come barrelling out, knocking our things all about, a bit ago.'

'Broke my plate with the pansies, they did.'

'They went that way,' Virgil said and pointed. 'But you'll never catch 'em, not those two.'

'We plan to set a trap for them,' Mike said, 'if you'll just let us through,' and the couple immediately began packing up the hamper and moving it and themselves away from the door.

'I hope when you do catch them, you lock them up,' the woman said as they opened the door and went through. 'Young hooligans!'

'Why is it everywhere I go there are horrible children?'

Merope said as soon as they were inside. She stopped and looked at their dimly lit surroundings. They were on a landing, and above and below it an iron staircase spiralled out of sight.

Polly crossed the landing to look up and then down the steps, but apparently no one besides the children had discovered the stairwell yet, and hopefully Virgil and his wife would keep anyone else out, at least on this level. There were obviously doors on other levels or the children couldn't have used it as a shortcut. And if it was an emergency staircase, that meant it went all the way to the surface, hundreds of feet up.

'This is perfect,' Merope said, going up several steps and sitting down. 'Now we can *talk* and not worry about people hearing us. I have so much to *tell* you—'

'Shh,' Michael said, looking up the staircase. 'We need to see if anyone else is in here first. I have a feeling sound carries a long way. Polly, you check up above, and you check below,' he said to Merope, who obligingly scrambled to her feet and ran down the steps. At least no one would be able to sneak up on them. Merope's footsteps clattered loudly down the iron treads.

Polly started up, but before she'd climbed three steps, Michael's hand clamped round her wrist. 'Shh,' he mouthed silently. 'Stay here. I've got to talk to you.' He waited, listening, as the clank of Merope's footsteps faded away below them.

Oh no, he's realised why I asked him when he left for Dover, Polly thought. *He's going to ask me if I have a deadline, and if I tell him, he'll begin asking questions—*

'Was John Lewis supposed to be bombed?' Michael said. The question was so utterly different from what she'd expected that she could only gape stupidly at him. 'Was it?'

'Yes—'

'What about Buckingham Palace? Were the King and Queen supposed to have almost been killed like that?'

'Yes. Why are you—?'

'What about the other raids? Have they been where they were supposed to be?'

'Yes.' *It's a good thing we're not having this conversation out in the station or we'd be arrested for being German spies,* she thought. 'Why are you asking me all this?'

'Because Dunkirk's a divergence point.'

'But—'

'Shh.' He put his finger to his lips. Polly listened. There was a faint clanking from below them.

'She's coming back,' Michael said. He released her wrist and motioned for her to go up the stairs, and she ran up them on tiptoe, trying not to make any noise. And to make sense of what he'd said. Had he seen something which didn't match what he'd read about the Blitz? Or the evacuation of Dunkirk?

Could he think that his having been at Dunkirk had altered history, and that was why their drops wouldn't open? But it was impossible, and if he weren't so unnerved over all the bad news he'd had tonight, he'd realise how ridiculous a theory like that was.

And what about you? she thought. *Is that why you're imagining the worst, too? Because, as Miss Snelgrove would say, you've had a bad shock? Perhaps the situation's not as bad as you think.*

Or perhaps it was worse. She had to talk to Merope. Alone. But how? Send Michael on some errand? He'd already scolded her for going off without them.

She went up as far as the next landing with a door and opened it a tiny crack to peer out. A row of toddlers lay wrapped like cocoons in blankets in front of the door. Good, no one could get in that way.

She ran up two more flights, peered up into the long darkness above, then ran back down to where Merope and Michael were sitting. 'All clear,' she said, sitting down on the step beside them. 'Was there anyone down below, Merope?'

'No. Now, Michael, I want to hear—'

'Not Michael. And not Merope. You're Eileen O'Reilly and

I'm Mike Davis, and you're Polly – what last name are you using?'

'Sebastian.'

'Sebastian,' he repeated. 'I wish I'd known that. I'd have been able to find you a lot sooner. You're Polly Sebastian, and those are our names for as long as we're here. Even when we're alone. Understood? We can't afford to have somebody overhear us calling each other by some other name.'

Merope nodded. 'Yes, Michael – I mean, Mike.'

'Good,' he said. 'Now, the first thing we have to do—'

'—is get something to eat,' Polly said. 'I haven't had any supper. Have either of you?'

'I haven't eaten since breakfast,' Merope – correction, Eileen – said. 'I spent my entire lunch break waiting on Mrs Sadler and that wretched son of hers. I'm starving!'

'Can't this wait, Polly?' Michael – Mike – said.

'No, I don't know how long the canteen stays open.'

'Okay, but we shouldn't all go. One of us needs to stay here. Polly, you hold down the fort, and Eileen and I'll go,' and before she could think of a reason she needed to be the one to accompany Eileen, they'd started down the stairs.

'Oh, I just thought of something,' she heard Eileen say below. 'I haven't any money.'

And now you haven't got a job either, Polly thought. She wondered if Mike had one. Probably not – he'd just got out of hospital. *How are we going to live?* she wondered.

Below her she heard the door shut and, after a moment, the clank of feet on the stairs. Was it the children who'd used this stairway before? *Or a guard?* she thought, remembering the No Admittance notice.

It was Mike. 'I told Eileen I wasn't sure I had enough money. I gave her two shillings and told her to go get in line, and I'd be there in a minute.'

'Oh.' Polly reached for her bag.

He stopped her. 'It was just an excuse so we could finish our

573

conversation. You didn't answer my question before. Has any-thing been hit that wasn't supposed to be?'

'No. Mike—'

'What about something that was supposed to be hit that wasn't?' he persisted. 'Or some night when there were supposed to be raids and there weren't?'

'There were raids every night till November,' Polly said, 'and they've all been on schedule. Is this because you were at Dunkirk?'

'I wasn't just there. I did something that may have altered events.'

'But you know as well as I do that we can't do that. The time travel laws won't let us.'

'The time travel laws don't let historians anywhere near a divergence point either, but I was right there in the middle of one.'

'And you think that's why our drops won't open? But that's impossible. If your being there would have changed things, the net would have kept you from getting there.'

'That's just it. It sent me through thirty miles from where I was supposed to be and five days late, so I missed the bus and couldn't get to Dover.' He told her the story of how he'd ended up in Dunkirk. 'The slippage was trying to stop me. If I hadn't got on the *Lady Jane*—'

'But if your being at Dunkirk was going to alter events, it *would* have stopped you. It would have sent you through after the evacuation. Or to Wales or somewhere. Historians can't change the course of history. You know that.'

'Then why did you look so horrified when I told you I'd been to Dunkirk?'

Careful, Polly thought. 'Because you'd just told me none of our drops were working. And that your retrieval team hadn't come to pull you out when you were injured. Even if it took them a long time to find you in hospital—'

'No, you don't understand. They'd never even *think* to look in

574

hospitals. Nobody knew I'd gone to Dunkirk except the captain of the boat and his grandson, and they were both killed.'

Killed? Polly thought, but he was already hurrying on. 'I'd told the people in the village that I was going back to London to file my story, and nobody in the hospital knew who I was. Anyway, the point is, there was no way for the retrieval team to find me.'

'Mike, it's *time* travel. No matter how long it took for them to find you, they could still have been there.'

'Not if they're still looking for me. I've spent the last three and a half weeks looking for you in stores on Oxford Street and couldn't find you. Which store *do* you work in?'

'Townsend Brothers.'

'I was on every floor of Townsend Brothers *twice* and never found you, and neither did Merope – I mean, Eileen – and she works four streets away. And you couldn't find Eileen even though you went to Backbury.'

'But this is—'

'I know, time travel. And part of time travel is slippage.'

'*Five months'* worth?'

'No, just enough for our retrieval teams to lose the trail. If they came through after I was moved from the hospital in Dover or Eileen left for London—'

He was right. They'd have no way of knowing Eileen was working at Padgett's, and if the hospital hadn't known who Mike was, they could easily have lost the trail. 'But what about all those weeks when Eileen was quarantined?' she asked. 'They knew exactly where she was then.'

'I don't know. Maybe the quarantine was some kind of divergence point. Measles can kill people, right? Maybe the retrieval team wasn't allowed to come through because they'd have caught the measles and infected some general who played a critical role at D-Day.'

It sounded just like the arguments she'd used these last few weeks as she'd tried to convince herself they'd be here any day.

She wondered if that was what Mike was doing, trying to convince himself. And it still didn't explain the drops.

'I never said mine wasn't working,' Mike said. 'I just said I couldn't get to it. And the same goes for Eileen's. If there were evacuees in the woods, they could have kept it from opening, or someone from the village could have—'

There was a pounding on the door below them. 'Stay here,' Mike said and ran down to see who was knocking.

It was Eileen. 'I only had enough money for sandwiches and two teas,' Polly heard her say. 'But I thought we could share.' She heard them start up the stairs. 'The queue was endless.'

Polly waited where she was, thinking over what Mike had said. If there'd been two or three days' slippage on her team's drop, they'd have come through before she found a job, and when they went to Townsend Brothers, they'd have been told she didn't work there. And they wouldn't have been able to find her at night because she was at St George's rather than a tube shelter. Mike was right. They might still be looking for her.

Eileen came up the stairs, carrying waxed-paper-wrapped sandwiches, followed by Mike with cartons of tea. 'Cheese sandwiches were the cheapest thing they had,' she said, passing them out. 'What happened to you, Mike? Why didn't you come?'

'Polly and I were discussing what we're going to do.'

'Which is what?' Eileen said, unwrapping her sandwich and taking a huge bite out of it.

'Well, first we're going to eat our supper.' He took the lid off the carton of tea.

'And you're going to tell me how you got shanghaied,' Eileen said, 'and Polly, you're going to tell me why you told me Padgett's was safe.'

She did, and then they recounted their adventures. Polly was horrified to find out that Mike had been living in Fleet Street and that Eileen had been living in Stepney. '*Stepney?*' she said. 'It had one of the highest casualty rates of all of London. No wonder you're frightened of the bombs.'

'We have to get you out of there immediately,' Mike said.

'She can move in with me,' Polly said. 'My room's a double.'

'Good. And ask your landlady if she has any vacant rooms. It'll make it a lot easier for us to be found if we're all at the same address.'

And safer, Polly thought. She didn't say that. Eileen was looking better now that she'd had something to eat, but as she told them about her attempts to find Polly, it was clear she'd had a bad time these last few weeks, and when Mike said she needed to go fetch her things first thing in the morning, she looked absolutely stricken. '*Alone?*' she said. 'But what if we get separated again?'

'We won't,' Polly reassured her and wrote out Mrs Rickett's address for her and Mike. 'I work on the third floor of Townsend Brothers. And if I'm not there—'

'I know,' Eileen said. 'I'm to go to the foot of the escalator on the lowest level of Oxford Circus.'

Mike laid out what they were to do. Polly was to make a list for him and Eileen of when and where the raids were for the next week, and Eileen was to write to the manor and everyone she'd known there and give them Mrs Rickett's address. 'So if your retrieval team comes, they'll know where you are,' Mike said. 'And write to the postmistress in Backbury. And the stationmaster.'

'I've met the stationmaster,' Polly said. 'I don't think there's anything to be gained by writing to him.'

'Well, the local clergyman then.'

'I wrote to the vicar as soon as I arrived in London to tell him I'd delivered the children to their parents,' Eileen said.

The vicar knew Eileen was in London, Polly thought. And if that wretched train had been late like the stationmaster said it always was and she'd been able to stay till after the service, she'd have found Eileen a month ago, and Eileen would never have been in danger of being killed at Padgett's.

'Write to him again,' Mike was saying. 'And contact the parents of the other evacuees you delivered.'

'Alf and Binnie?' Eileen said, sounding horrified.

'Yes, and whoever was in charge of the evacuation. We need every contact we can think of. And we need to find a drop—'

He stopped, listening. A door opened somewhere above them and then slammed, and someone rattled down the steps. Whoever it was must be running. The footsteps clanked down towards them at an enormous rate, and they could hear giggling.

Those children who were running from the guard, Polly thought. 'I do hope the raids won't last very long tonight,' she said loudly.

The footsteps halted abruptly and then clanked back up the steps. The door opened and slammed again. 'They're gone,' Mike said. 'Now where were we?'

'You said we need to find a drop,' Eileen said.

'Right, preferably one that isn't under the gun, so to speak,' he said cheerfully.

He was sounding and looking much better, too. She must have convinced him that he hadn't altered events. *I wish he'd managed to convince me that nothing's happened to Oxford,* she thought.

'We need to find one of the other historians who's here besides us,' Mike went on.

'There was someone who was going to the Battle of the Bulge,' Eileen said.

'That was me,' Mike said. 'And I'm glad this didn't happen while I was there. The Ardennes in winter would have been a nasty place to be stuck.'

'Whereas this ...' Polly said, spreading her hands to indicate the dim stairwell.

'At least no one's shooting prisoners here,' he said, 'and it's not snowing.'

'It might as well be,' Eileen said, hugging her arms to herself. 'I wish I had my coat. It's simply *freezing* in here.'

Mike took off his suit jacket and draped it around her shoulders.

'*Thank* you,' Eileen said. 'But won't you be cold—? Oh, I just thought of something,' she said, sounding dismayed. 'How am I going to buy another coat? And pay Theodore's mother the room and board I owe her? All the money I had was in my handbag. I was supposed to collect my pay packet tomorrow, but if Padgett's—'

'Was the store totally destroyed?' Mike asked. 'Maybe—'

Polly shook her head. 'Direct hit. A thousand-pound HE.'

'Has it already been hit?' Eileen asked, glancing up at the stairs spiralling above them.

'Yes, I don't know exactly when. I wasn't supposed to still be here when it hit, so I don't know the details. Only that it was early this evening and that there were three fatalities.'

'But if it *had* already been hit, wouldn't we have heard it?' Eileen asked. 'Or the fire bells or something?'

'Not in here,' Polly said. 'Don't worry about the coat. Mrs Wyvern – she's one of the people I sit with in the shelter – helps distribute clothing to people who've been bombed out. I'll see if I can arrange a coat for you from her.'

'Do you think you could talk her out of one for me, too?' Mike asked. 'I hocked mine.'

Polly nodded. 'You'll both need one – 1940 was one of the coldest and rainiest winters on record.'

'Then let's try not to spend more time in it than we have to,' Mike said. 'There's at least one historian here now. Both times I was in the lab, Linna was on the phone giving someone a list of historians currently on assignment. I only heard snatches, but one of them was October 1940.'

'Are you certain it wasn't me?' Polly asked. 'I was supposed to go back on October twenty-second.'

He shook his head. 'October was the arrival date. The departure date was December eighteenth.'

'Which means whoever it is is here right now,' Eileen said. 'You didn't hear the name?'

'No, but I also met a guy in the lab. He was there doing a recon and prep drop. I don't know the date of his assignment, but the recon and prep was to Oxford on July second, 1940. His name was Phillips or Phipps—'

'Gerald Phipps?' Eileen said.

'I didn't hear his first name. Do you know him?'

'Yes,' Eileen said, making a face. 'He's insufferable. When I first told him about my assignment, he said, "A maid? Is that the most exciting assignment you could find? You won't get to see the war at all".'

'Which tells us *he* would,' Polly said.

'And that his assignment *was* exciting,' Mike added. 'Did he tell you where he was going?'

'Yes. It began with a D, I think. Or a P. Or possibly a T. I wasn't really listening.'

'And he didn't tell you what he'd be observing?' Mike asked, and when Eileen shook her head, 'Polly, what was happening in July?'

'In England? The Battle of Britain.'

'No, I don't think that's it. He was wearing tweeds, not an RAF uniform.'

'But you said it was a set-up,' Polly argued. 'Perhaps he had to arrange for a transfer to an airfield.'

'He *did* say he'd posted some letters and made a trunk-call,' Mike said. 'What airfields begin with a D?'

'Detling?' Polly suggested. 'Duxford?'

'No,' Eileen said, frowning. 'It might have been a T.'

'T?' Mike said. 'You said a D or a P.'

'I know.' She bit her lip thoughtfully. 'But I think it may have been a T.'

'Tangmere?' Polly said.

'No ... I'm sorry. I'd know it if I heard it.'

'We need a list of English airfields,' Mike said.

'But I can't imagine Gerald as a pilot,' Eileen said.

'Yeah, I know,' Mike said. 'He's scrawny, and when I saw him, he was wearing spectacles.'

'And he's a dreadful grind,' Eileen said. 'Maths and—'

'He might be posing as a course plotter or a radio operator,' Polly suggested. 'That's much more likely than his being a pilot. The life expectancy for pilots during the Battle of Britain was three weeks. Mr Dunworthy would never have allowed it. And if he was a course plotter or a dispatcher he could observe the Battle of Britain without being in as much danger, though the airfields and sector stations were bombed as well. But if he *was* here to observe the Battle of Britain, then he may already have gone back.' She turned to Eileen. 'He didn't say how long he was staying?'

'No. At least I don't think so,' she said, frowning in concentration. 'I was late for my driving lesson, and, as I said, he's insufferable. All I was thinking about was getting away from him. If I'd known this was going to happen, I'd have listened more carefully.'

'Yes, well, if we'd known we were going to be stuck here, we'd all have behaved differently,' Mike said grimly. 'Never mind, we can easily find out the airfields. Do either of you know who this other person who's here from October to December could be? Or do you know of anyone else who might be here?'

'Robert Glabers said he was doing World War II,' Polly said.

'He is,' Mike said. 'The testing of the atomic bomb in New Mexico in 1945, which doesn't help us.'

Yes it does, Polly thought. *It gives me the chance to ask Eileen the question I need to.* 'Nineteen forty-five,' she said thoughtfully. 'Nineteen forty-five. What about the person who did VE Day whom you were going to switch with, Eileen? Did you persuade Mr Dunworthy to let you go?'

'We need someone right now,' Mike said impatiently. 'Why are you two talking about 1945?'

'Did you?' Polly persisted.

'No, I couldn't ever get in to see him. And now, with all this, he probably won't even consider letting me go.'

Thank God, Polly thought, *she didn't go to VE Day. She doesn't have a deadline, thank God. And neither does Mike. But then—*

'Do you think this October person could be here in London?' Mike asked.

'No, if Badri'd had to find two drops in London, I'm certain he'd have mentioned it; he had so much difficulty finding mine. But I can't think of anything else besides the Blitz a historian would be doing in October, at least in England.'

'Then it sounds like Gerald's a better bet,' Mike said. 'If we can just figure out which airfield he's at. Tomorrow we'll get a map—'

He stopped again at muffled sounds from below.

The children again, Polly thought, but there were no clanking footsteps or giggling. 'False alarm,' Mike said.

'Wait.' Polly clattered down the steps and opened the door. The couple that'd been in front of it had gone, and across the tunnel people were folding blankets and putting dishes and empty bottles into baskets. Polly opened the door a bit wider and called to a young girl sitting on the floor putting on her shoes, 'Has the all-clear gone?'

The girl nodded, and Polly ducked back inside the stairwell and ran up to tell Mike and Eileen.

'Jesus,' Mike said, looking at his watch, 'it's nearly six. We've stayed up all night talking.'

'And I've got to be at work in three hours.' Polly stretched and brushed off her skirt.

Eileen took Mike's coat from around her shoulders and gave it back to him. 'Okay,' Mike said, 'Eileen, you're going to go get your belongings and try to remember which airfield Gerald told you.' He gave her money for her tube fare. 'Polly, you make that list of raids for us, and I want you to show me where the drop is before you go to work.'

They left the stairwell. Everyone in the tunnel had packed up and gone except for two very dirty urchins picking over the left-behind food scraps, and they fled the moment Polly opened the door.

The main hall was nearly deserted as well. 'What train do you take to Stepney, Eileen?' Polly asked.

'Bakerloo to District and Circle.'

'We take the Central Line,' Polly said, and at Eileen's worried expression, 'We'll walk you to your platform.'

That was easier said than done. The people on the Bakerloo platform were still in the process of packing up. One group had gathered around an ARP warden who'd obviously just come in from outside. He was covered in soot, and his coverall was torn. 'How bad is it?' a woman asked him as they started past. 'Did Marylebone get it again?'

He nodded. 'And Wigmore Street.' He took off his tin hat to wipe his face with a sooty handkerchief. 'Three incidents. One of the firemen said it was pretty bad out Whitechapel way, too.'

'What about Oxford Street?' Mike asked.

'No, it was lucky this time. Not a scratch on her.'

The colour drained from Mike's face.

'Are you certain—?' Eileen began, but Mike was already limping down the tunnel. He was nearly to the escalators before Polly caught up with him.

'That warden wouldn't necessarily have seen Padgett's,' she said. 'You heard him, he was on Wigmore Street all night. That's north of here, and it's still dark. And when there's an incident, there's all this smoke and dust. One can't see anything.'

'Or there isn't anything to see,' he said, starting up the escalator.

'I don't understand,' Eileen said, catching up to them as they reached the top. 'Wasn't Padgett's hit?'

Mike didn't answer her. He limped across the station to the exit and up to the street.

It was still dark out, but not dark enough that Polly couldn't

583

see the black roofs of Oxford Street's stores against the inky sky. There was no sign of destruction, and no broken glass in the dark street. 'It's freezing out here,' Eileen said, shivering in her thin blouse as they stood looking down the street. 'If it was hit, wouldn't it be burning?'

Yes, Polly thought, but there was no sign of flames, no reddened sky, not even any smoke. The air was damp and clean.

'Are you certain you got the name of the store right?' Eileen asked, her teeth chattering. 'It wasn't Parmenter's that was hit? Or Peter Robinson?'

'I'm certain,' Polly said.

'Perhaps you got the date wrong,' Eileen suggested, 'and it won't be hit till tomorrow night. Which means I can fetch my coat. And my handbag.' She set off down the dark street.

'Did you?' Mike asked. 'Get the date wrong?'

'No. All the Oxford Street raids were implanted. We just can't see it from here.' Which was true, but they'd be able to see the fire engines and hear the ambulance bells. And see the blue light of the incident officer. 'When we get a bit further down, we'll see it,' she said firmly and set off after Eileen.

'Or I changed the course of events somehow so it didn't get hit,' Mike said, limping alongside her. 'I didn't tell you what I did at Dunkirk—'

'It doesn't matter *what* you did; historians can't alter events. Padgett's was hit by an HE, not an incendiary. They don't necessarily cause fires, and if it happened early last night, the fire could have been out for hours—'

Ahead of them, Eileen called, 'Padgett's is still there. I can see it,' and Mike took off towards her at an awkward, hobbling run.

It can't be, Polly thought, racing after and then past him, but it was. Before she'd run halfway she could make out Lyons Corner House in the darkness, still intact, and beyond it the first of Padgett's pillars.

Eileen was nearly there. Polly ran after her, straining to see through the darkness. There were the rest of Padgett's pillars, and the building beyond it. *No,* she thought. *It can't still be there.*

It wasn't. Before she was even to Lyons Corner House, she could see the side wall of the building beyond Padgett's, half destroyed, and the empty space between it and Lyons.

Eileen had reached the front of the store. 'Oh no,' Polly heard her gasp.

She turned to call back to Mike, 'It's all right. It was hit,' and ran on to the store. Or the space where it had been. The pillars – and beyond them a deep pit – were all that was left. The HE had totally vaporised the department store, which meant it had been a thousand-pounder. *And when we read the newspapers tomorrow, it will say that, and that there were three fatalities.*

They had strung up rope at the edge of the pavement, blocking off the incident, and Eileen stood motionless just outside it, staring. In relief or shock? Polly couldn't tell – it was too dark to see the expression on her face.

Polly reached her side. 'Look,' Eileen said, pointing, and Polly saw she wasn't staring at what was left of Padgett's. She was staring at the glass-strewn pavement between the pillars. And at what Polly hadn't seen before because it was too dark.

The pavement was strewn with bodies, and there were at least a dozen of them.

> *'Be careful. Should you omit or add one single word,*
> *you may destroy the world.'*

THE TALMUD

OXFORD STREET – 26 OCTOBER 1940

Polly squinted at the bodies sprawled across the pavement. Even though she could only just make them out in the darkness, she could see that their arms and legs had been flung into tortured angles.

Mike limped up. 'Oh Christ,' he breathed. 'How many are there?'

'I don't know,' Eileen said. 'Are they dead?'

They had to be. It wasn't light enough to see their faces – or the blood – but it was impossible for necks to turn that far. They had to be dead. *But they can't be*, Polly thought. *There were only three fatalities.* Which meant some of them had to be alive, in spite of the angles of the necks, the severed arm. 'Mike, go fetch help!' she said.

He didn't seem to hear her. He stood there frozen, staring past Polly at the bodies. 'I knew it,' he said dully. 'This is my fault.'

'Eileen!' Polly said. *'Eileen!'*

She finally turned, a look of disbelief on her face. 'Go back to the station and fetch help,' Polly ordered. 'Tell them we need an ambulance.'

Eileen nodded dumbly and stumbled off.

'Mike, I need a torch,' Polly said, and ducked under the rope. She crunched across the broken glass to the bodies, but as she ran she was already processing the scene.

It was all wrong. The bodies should be under the rubble, not flung free of it. They must have been standing at the windows looking out when the bomb hit, but no Londoner in his right mind would do that. And where was the rescue squad? They'd clearly been here. They'd put up rope around the incident. And gone off again?

They wouldn't just leave them lying there, she thought, kneeling beside a woman. Not even if they were all dead, which they clearly were. The woman's arm, still in its coat sleeve, had been blown off. It lay, bent stiffly at the elbow—

Polly sat back on her heels. 'Eileen! Come back!' she called. 'Mike! It's all right. They're mannequins. They must have been blown out of the display windows.'

'You, there!' a deep voice called from beyond the rope. 'What are you doing?'

Good Lord, it's that same ARP *warden who caught me going to my drop,* Polly thought a little wildly, but it wasn't. It wasn't even a man. It was a woman wearing ARP overalls.

'Come out of there at once!' she said. 'Looting's a punishable offence.'

'We weren't looting,' Polly said, putting the arm down and standing up. 'We thought the mannequins were bodies. We were trying to help.' She pointed at Eileen, who'd come running back. 'She works here. She was afraid it might be someone she knew.'

The warden turned to Eileen. 'You work at Padgett's?'

'Yes, I'm Eileen O'Reilly. I work on the fifth floor. In Children's Wear.'

'Have you reported in?'

Eileen looked at the gaping hole where Padgett's had been. 'Reported in?'

'Round there,' the warden said, leading them on to the corner and pointing down the side street, where Polly could see a blue incident light and people moving about. 'Mr Fetters,' the warden called.

'Wait,' Mike said, 'were there any casualties?'

'We don't know yet. Come along, Miss O'Reilly,' she said and led Eileen over to Mr Fetters, who'd apparently come here straight from bed. He was wearing pyjamas under his coat, and his grey hair was uncombed, but he sounded brisk and efficient. 'I need to know your name, floor and department,' he said.

Eileen told him. 'I was transferred up from Notions last week,' she said.

Which explained why she hadn't been on third.

'Oh, excellent,' Mr Fetters said. 'You were one of the ones we were worried about. Someone said they thought you might still have been in the building.' He checked off her name, and then turned expectantly to Polly. 'And you are—?'

'I'm— We're friends of Miss O'Reilly's. Neither of us works at Padgett's.'

'Oh, I beg your pardon,' he said with dignity in spite of the pyjamas, and turned back to Eileen. 'Who was still on your floor when you left?'

'No one. I was the last one out.'

Literally, Polly thought.

'Miss Haskins and Miss Peterson both left before I did. Miss Haskins had asked me to switch off the lights.'

'Did you see anyone on your way out? Do you know if Miss Miles or Miss Rainsford had gone?'

And there are two of the three casualties, Polly thought.

'Are they unaccounted for?' Eileen asked.

'We haven't been able to locate them as yet. I'm certain they're in a shelter and perfectly all right.' He smiled reassuringly. 'You need to go see Miss Varden,' he pointed at her, 'and give her your address and telephone number so we can contact you when we're ready to reopen.'

Eileen nodded.

'Wait,' Mike said to her, 'what floors did Miss Miles and Miss Rainsford work on?'

'They were both on fifth,' Eileen said. 'I do hope they're all right,' and went off with Mr Fetters.

The moment she was gone, Mike said accusingly, 'You said there were supposed to be three fatalities.'

'There will be,' Polly said. 'They've only been searching a few hours. They'll find—'

'Find *who*?' he said. 'You heard Eileen. Those two women worked on fifth. We were *on* fifth. There was no one there.'

'I know,' Polly whispered, drawing him back around the corner, out of sight and earshot of the others, 'but that doesn't mean they weren't in the store. They might have gone down to the basement to the shelter—'

He wasn't listening. 'There are only two,' he said in that driven voice. 'There were supposed to be three.'

'There may have been someone in the offices. Or it may have been a charwoman. Or the guard who chased us. Just because they haven't found all the casualties yet doesn't mean there weren't any. It was sometimes weeks before all the bodies at an incident were found, and you saw that pit. This doesn't prove your being at Dunkirk affected—'

'You don't understand, I saved a soldier's life. Private David Hardy. He saw my light—'

'But one soldier—'

'It *wasn't* one soldier. After I saved him, he went back to Dunkirk and brought back four boatloads full of soldiers. Five hundred and nineteen of them. And don't tell me changing what happened to that many soldiers didn't alter history. It's a chaotic system. A goddamn *butterfly* can cause a monsoon on the other side of the world. Changing what happened to five hundred and twenty soldiers is sure as hell going to change something! I just hope to God what I changed wasn't who won the war.'

'It wasn't.'

'How the hell do you know?'

Because I was there the day we won it, she thought. But telling him that meant telling him she had a deadline, and he was still reeling from finding out about the drops and the retrieval teams. 'Because the laws of time travel say it's not possible,' she said. 'And historians have been travelling to the past for nearly forty years. If we were altering events, we'd have seen the effects long before now.' She put her hand on his arm. 'And the men you saved were British soldiers, not German pilots. They couldn't have affected Padgett's bombing.'

'You don't know that,' he said angrily. 'It's a chaotic system. Every action's connected to every other action.'

'But they don't always have an effect,' she said, thinking of her last assignment. 'Sometimes you do things that you think will alter the course of events, but in the end they don't. And you said yourself there should be discrepancies, and there haven't been.'

'You're certain? There hasn't been any event that was supposed to have happened that didn't? Or that happened earlier or later than it was supposed to?'

'No,' she said, and thought suddenly of the UXB at St Paul's. Mr Dunworthy had said it had taken the bomb squad three days to remove it, which would have been on Saturday, not Sunday. But Mr Dunworthy could have made a mistake about the date, or there could have been an error in the historical records he'd read.

'No, none at all,' she said. 'And even in a chaotic system there must be connections. The butterfly flapping its wings can only cause a monsoon because both involve air movement. The lines of connection between your soldiers and the number of casualties in Padgett's simply aren't there. And besides, five hundred and twenty British soldiers not dead and not in prisoner-of-war camps would help the war effort, not hurt it.'

'Not necessarily. In chaotic systems, positive actions can cause bad results as well as good, and you know as well as I do that the war had divergence points where any action, good or bad, would have changed the entire picture.'

I'm going to have to tell him about VE *Day, even if it does mean his finding out about my deadline,* she thought. *It's the only way to convince him.* But once he found out she had a deadline, he'd—

'Polly! Mike!' Eileen's voice called, sounding frantic, and they hurried back around the corner. 'I came to tell you—'

'What is it?' Mike said. 'Have they found bodies?'

'No, and everyone except Miss Miles and Miss Rainsford has been accounted for.'

'What about the guard at the staff entrance?' he asked.

'He's here. He was the one who told them he thought I was in the building. He thought you might have been, too, Polly, but I told him that as soon as you got to fourth you realised I'd gone and left. The bomb apparently hit just after we got out.'

And if we hadn't been able to get the lift door open, Polly thought, *or if we'd run into the guard on the way down—* She looked anxiously at Eileen, wondering if she was thinking the same thing.

Eileen was shivering, though that could be due to her thin blouse and the damp, chill air. *We should have done that looting we were accused of and stolen that coat off the mannequin.*

'You're sure *everybody's* been accounted for? Even the charwomen?' Mike demanded, his voice rising the way Eileen's had in the tube station. *He's just as near the edge as she is,* Polly thought. *He's in no shape to hear more bad news.* 'Yes, everyone,' Eileen said, 'but that isn't what I came to tell you. It was two words.'

'*What* was?' Mike asked impatiently.

'The name of the place Gerald was going. It was two words. I was speaking to Miss Varden about Miss Miles, and she said she lived in Tegley Place, and when she said it, I thought, *The airfield Gerald told me he was going to was a two-word name.*'

'Middle Wallop?' Polly said.

Eileen shook her head.

'West Malling?'

'No. I'm positive one of the words began with a T. Or a P—' She stopped, looking past Polly. 'Oh, thank goodness, it's Miss Miles!' She ran to meet the young woman coming across the street.

'What happened?' Miss Miles said, staring at the scattered mannequins.

'Padgett's was bombed last night—' Eileen began, but Mike cut in, 'Was Miss Rainsford still in the building when you left last night?'

'No,' Miss Miles said, still staring blindly at the sprawled bodies.

'No, you don't know? Or no, she wasn't in the building?' Mike shouted, and Eileen turned to look at him incredulously, but his anger had roused Miss Miles from her trance.

She turned from staring at the mannequins and said, 'She wasn't here yesterday. Her brother was killed the night before last.'

'You'd best tell Mr Fetters that,' Eileen said, and to Mike and Polly, 'I'll be back straightaway,' and led Miss Miles off towards the others.

'Well?' Mike said before the two girls were even out of earshot. 'You heard her. Everybody's been accounted for. Which means there weren't any fatalities.'

'It doesn't mean that at all,' Polly said. 'They could have been passers-by. On my way to Padgett's I saw a woman and her little boy insisting the doorman get them a taxi. They might still have been waiting for it when the bomb hit,' she said, though if that were the case, their bodies would have been blown out onto the pavement like the mannequins. 'No one knew *we* were in Padgett's. There might have been other people who—'

'Or the continuum might have been altered,' Mike said, looking like he was going to be sick, 'and we're going to lose the war. And don't tell me it's impossible.'

It is impossible, she thought, but she said, 'If England lost the war, then Ira Feldman's parents would have died in Auschwitz or Buchenwald, and he'd never have invented time travel, and Oxford would never have built the net, and we couldn't have come through.'

'You're forgetting something,' he said bitterly.

'What?'

'We came through the net before I saved Hardy.'

And I was at VE *Day before he saved Hardy*, she thought, but—

'Why else would there be a discrepancy?' he said.

'You don't know that it's a discrepancy. You don't know you saved Hardy, either.'

'What do you mean? I told you—'

'Perhaps it wasn't your light he saw. Perhaps it was a light from some other boat, or a reflection off the water. Or a flare.'

'A flare,' he said, and some of the colour came back into his face. 'I hadn't thought of that. There *were* flares.'

'In any case, we can't know anything for sure till we've found Gerald and seen whether his drop is working.'

'Or yours is,' he said.

Now was no time to tell him of her multiple trips to the drop. 'I'll take you there tonight after work,' she said. 'I think right now you should go with Eileen to Stepney. She's had too many shocks to deal with to go by herself,' and before he could object, called 'Eileen!' and walked briskly over to where she stood talking to Miss Miles. Eileen's teeth were chattering, and she was hugging her arms tightly to herself. 'Here, take my coat,' Polly said, unbuttoning it.

'But—'

'I won't need it. I'm going to Mrs Rickett's to see about your moving in with me, so I can get my suit jacket.' She put the coat on Eileen. 'I'll see you when you return from Stepney. Come to Townsend Brothers, and we'll plan our next move.'

Now she was the one shivering in the chill predawn air.

'I'd best go if I'm to get to Mrs Rickett's and back in time for work. I'll see you in a bit. I'm on third,' she reminded her. 'The stockings counter. Take care,' and hurried off towards the tube station.

The train to Notting Hill Gate was empty, and she was grateful. She needed time to think what to do. If she told Mike why she was positive they'd won the war, it would stop him worrying about having altered events.

But she'd have to tell him all of it. Saying she'd been at VE Day wouldn't convince him. He'd just say the continuum hadn't changed till later, after he'd rescued Hardy. She'd have to tell him why that wasn't true. And both of them had had as many shocks as they could take for one night.

Eileen had already broken down once, and when the knowledge of how narrowly she'd escaped death in Padgett's sank in, she might give way altogether.

And Mike, for all his Admirable Crichton-like taking charge, was in worse shape than Eileen. He'd obviously been brooding for weeks over the possibility of having lost the war. Telling him about VE Day might send him right over the edge.

But so could thinking he'd caused the nightmare the world would have become if Hitler and his monstrous Third Reich had won – concentration camps and gas chambers and ovens and who knew what other horrors. Hitler had planned to set up a gallows outside the Houses of Parliament and execute Churchill and the King and Queen. And Princesses Elizabeth and Margaret Rose, aged fourteen and ten.

I'm going to have to tell him, she thought. *I'll do it as soon as he and Eileen get back from Stepney*, and the train immediately jerked and slowed.

Are we coming into the station? she wondered, peering forward out of the window, but she couldn't see anything. The train ground to a halt and sat there. And sat there.

What was causing the delay? A bomb on the line like the one on Miss Laburnum's train from Croxley, or a tunnel collapse?

Or a simple mechanical problem? There was no way to tell, any more than the three of them could tell if their drops' failure was due to a catastrophe in Oxford or Mike's having rescued a soldier at Dunkirk. Or only something minor, like slippage or their retrieval teams having difficulty finding them.

The train started up, gathered speed, racketed along for perhaps a minute, and halted again. *I'll never get out of here,* she thought and smiled bitterly. Mike had already convinced himself that he was responsible for all this. What if she told him and he still didn't believe her? What if it only made matters worse? And what if he told Eileen? Surely there was some other way to convince him he couldn't have altered events besides telling him about VE Day.

But by the time the train reached Notting Hill Gate three quarters of an hour later, she hadn't thought of one. She walked quickly along the tunnel and onto the escalator, glancing at her watch. Half past eight. She scarcely had time to get to Mrs Rickett's and back, let alone go see Mrs Wyvern about coats. She hurried over to the turnstile.

'Finally bringing the curtain down, are they?' the guard asked as she started through.

'What? Is the troupe still down there rehearsing?'

He nodded.

'*Thank* you,' she said fervently and ran back down to the District Line. With luck, Mrs Rickett *and* Mrs Wyvern would both be there, but when she reached the platform, she couldn't see either of them. The rest of the troupe was still doing a scene. 'No, no, *no*,' Sir Godfrey was saying to Lila, 'not like that. You need to sound more cheerful.'

'*Cheerful?*' Lila said. 'I thought you said we were supposed to play this scene like we didn't know what was going to happen to us.'

'I did,' Sir Godfrey said, 'but that is no reason to convince the audience you will all be dead by the final curtain. This is a comedy, not a tragedy.'

That remains to be seen, Polly thought.

'Miss Laburnum,' Sir Godfrey said. 'Kindly give Lady Agatha her cue.'

'"Here comes Ernest,"' Miss Laburnum read from the script and caught sight of Polly. 'Miss *Sebastian*,' she said, hurrying over. 'Did you find her?'

For a moment Polly had no idea what she was talking about – so much had happened since she'd seen Miss Laburnum at Oxford Circus – and then remembered she'd told her she had to deliver a message to Marjorie's landlady. 'Yes, I mean ... no,' she stammered. It obviously couldn't have taken her all night to deliver a message. 'Something happened. Has Mrs Rickett gone home?'

'Yes, she went ahead to cook breakfast.'

'Breakfast,' Mr Dorming snorted. 'Is that what you call it?'

'Miss Laburnum, do you know if she has any rooms to let?' Polly asked.

'Lady Mary, here at last!' Sir Godfrey said, his voice rich with sarcasm. 'May I remind you that this is *The Admirable Crichton*, not *Mary Rose*, and that, consequently, vanishing for long periods of time and then reappearing is not—' His face changed. 'Something's happened. What is it, Viola?'

She couldn't say 'Nothing.' He wouldn't believe her. And she'd have to tell the troupe something to account for Eileen's moving in with her.

'She was delivering a message for a friend in hospital,' Miss Laburnum was whispering to Sir Godfrey. 'I'm afraid something may have happened to her friend.'

'No,' Polly said, 'it isn't Marjorie. It's Padgett's. It was bombed last night.'

'Padgett's?' Miss Laburnum said. 'The department store?' And the others instantly gathered round, asking questions: 'When?' 'How badly?' 'You weren't injured, were you?'

'But I thought you worked at Townsend Brothers,' Lila said.

'I do, but my cousin works – worked at Padgett's, and she and I were to meet there after work—'

'Oh my *dear*,' Miss Laburnum said, 'I do hope she wasn't—'

'No, she's all right, but the store was bombed just after closing, and we'd only just left—' Which hopefully accounted for the fear Sir Godfrey had seen in her face. 'It was completely destroyed.'

More questions. Was it incendiaries or an HE? How big an HE? Were there any casualties?

Polly answered them the best she could, keenly aware of how much time this was taking and of Sir Godfrey's searching look. She spent a full quarter of an hour assuring them she was all right before they began to gather up their things.

Polly looked at her watch, trying to decide if she had enough time to get to Mrs Rickett's and back.

'I don't understand,' Miss Laburnum said. 'Why did you ask about a room if it was your cousin's place of employment which was bombed?'

'I was meeting her so we could look for a room for her. The boarding house where she lived was bombed out, and now Padgett's has been as well,' which was a totally implausible story. It was a good thing Sir Godfrey had gone over to pick up his coat and his *Times*. 'I was hoping Mrs Rickett might have a room to let.'

'But couldn't she stay with you? Your room was meant to be a double, wasn't it?'

'Yes, but a friend of ours, Mr Davis, was bombed out, too.'

Miss Laburnum's eyebrows went up. 'A friend?'

Oh no. She'd immediately assume some sort of hanky-panky. 'Yes,' she said, and then shamelessly, 'He was injured at Dunkirk.'

'Oh, poor boy,' Miss Laburnum said, instantly sympathetic. 'There's no vacancy at Mrs Rickett's at present, but I believe Miss Harding has one. She's in Box Lane.'

Which wasn't on Mr Dunworthy's forbidden list. Perfect. Now if she could just get over to Box Lane and put a deposit on the room.

'And you'd best look for a room for your cousin,' Mr Dorming growled on his way out. 'She's already been bombed out. You don't want to put her through Mrs Rickett's cooking as well, do you?'

He went out. Polly thanked Miss Laburnum and started after him, but Sir Godfrey stopped her. 'Viola, what is it? What's really happened?'

'I told you,' she said, not meeting his eyes. 'My cousin—'

'Viola could not speak either, to tell Orsino of her sorrow or the brother she had lost,' he said. 'But silence has its dangers as well. Whatever is troubling you, you can tell—'

'Sir Godfrey, I'm so sorry to interrupt,' Miss Laburnum said, 'but I *must* speak to you. It's about shoes.'

'*Shoes?*'

'Yes, in the third act, on the island after the shipwreck, everyone's supposed to go unshod, but the station floor's so unsanitary, so I was thinking perhaps beach sandals—'

'My dear Miss Laburnum,' Sir Godfrey said, 'at this point we will not ever *reach* the third act. Lord Loam is incapable of remembering his lines. Lady Catherine and Tweeny are incapable of remembering their blocking. Lady *Mary*,' he said, looking at Polly, 'persists in nearly getting herself blown up, and the Germans may invade at any moment. We have far more pressing problems at hand than footwear.'

You're right, we do, Polly thought. *Not knowing what airfield Gerald is at, and not having coats or jobs or roofs over our heads. And trying to keep from being arrested as German spies. Or killed by shrapnel or stray parachute mines.*

'Oh, but Sir Godfrey,' Miss Laburnum protested, 'if we don't do it now—'

'If and when we reach a point where it becomes necessary to decide whether going unshod is a threat to our health, we will discuss it. Until then, I'd suggest you concentrate on persuading Lady Catherine not to *titter* each time she says a line. There is no point in fretting over things which may never come to pass. "Sufficient unto the day is the evil thereof," my dear Miss Laburnum.'

And there's my answer, Polly thought gratefully. *Mike and Eileen have more than enough to deal with without my adding to it. We need to concentrate on getting Eileen out of Stepney and Mike out of Fleet Street and both of them into warm coats. And on finding Gerald Phipps. If we do, and his drop is working, I won't have to tell them at all.*

'"Sufficient unto the day",' Miss Laburnum was saying. 'Is that from *Hamlet*?'

'It is from the *Bible*!' Sir Godfrey roared.

'Oh, of course. And it's excellent advice, but with winter nearly here and so many shortages, beach sandals may prove difficult to find, and if we don't purchase them now—'

'I don't mean to interrupt, Sir Godfrey,' Polly said, taking pity on him, 'but I must ask Miss Laburnum something.'

'Pray do, Viola,' he said with a grateful look at her. '"Mark what I spake to thee",' and fled.

'Do you have the address of Mrs Wyvern's assistance centre?' Polly asked. 'I must speak with her about getting coats for my cousin and Mr Davis.'

'Coats?'

'Yes, they lost theirs in the bombing.' She hoped Miss Laburnum wouldn't ask her which one. 'I thought Mrs Wyvern might be able to help.'

'Oh, I'm certain she will. What sizes?'

'My cousin's my size, though a bit shorter. When I gave her my coat, it was too long. I'm not certain about Mr Davis—'

'Gave her *your* coat? But what are *you* doing for one?'

'I'll be all right. Townsend Brothers is only a short way from Oxford Circus—'

'Oh, but it's dreadfully cold out. You'll catch your death. You must take mine.' She began unbuttoning it. 'I have an old brown tweed at home I can wear.'

'But what about you? It's a long walk to Mrs Rickett's. I hate to take—'

'Nonsense,' she said briskly. 'It's our duty to help each other, especially in time of war. As Shakespeare says, "No man is an island".'

And thank goodness Sir Godfrey wasn't here to hear that.

'"Each is a piece of the whole, a part of the main,"' Miss Laburnum said, handing Polly the coat. 'Now is there anything else you need?'

The name of the airfield Gerald's at, Polly thought, and looked around for Lila and Viv, but they'd left.

She glanced at her watch. She couldn't afford to go after them. It was nearly nine, and she couldn't risk losing her job by being late. Room and board and train fares to airfields would all take money. But asking Mrs Rickett about Eileen's sharing her room couldn't wait till after work. 'There is something you could do for me, if you would,' Polly said. 'If you could tell Mrs Rickett what happened and—'

'Ask her if your cousin can stay with you? Of course. You go on to work, my dear. I'll take care of everything.'

'*Thank* you,' Polly said gratefully, and raced off, arriving at Townsend Brothers with seconds to spare. 'Where did you go off to last night?' Doreen asked as she uncovered her counter. 'Marjorie wanted to speak to you.'

'I had an appointment,' she said, and, to avoid questions – *Which is all I seem to do*, she thought – she asked, 'Did Marjorie tell you what she was doing on Jermyn Street the night she was injured?'

'No, Miss Snelgrove wouldn't let us ask her anything. She said she was too ill to have us yammering at her. She insisted on escorting her back to the hospital herself. What sort of appointment? With a man? Who is he?'

Luckily, Sarah arrived just then, full of the news of Padgett's, and Polly didn't have to answer her. On the other hand, she couldn't bring the conversation round to airfields either. She had to wait till the opening bell had rung and Doreen came past with a stack of lingerie boxes on her way to the workroom. When she did, Polly said, 'I met an airman in the shelter night before last, and we rather hit it off.'

'I *knew* it. Appointment, my eye.' Doreen set the boxes down and leaned her elbows on the counter. 'I want to hear all about him. Is he good-looking?'

'Yes, but there's not much to tell. His leave was up, and he was on his way back to his airfield. We were only able to talk for a few moments, but he asked me to write to him, only I can't remember which airfield he was stationed at. It began with a D, I think, or a T.'

'Tempsford?' Doreen said. 'Debden?'

'I'm not certain,' Polly said. 'The name might have had two words.'

'Two words?' Doreen said thoughtfully. 'High Wycombe? No, that doesn't begin with a T or a D. Oh, look out, here comes Miss Snelgrove.' She scooped up her boxes and scurried into the stockroom.

Polly tore off a scrap of brown wrapping paper, jotted the names down so she wouldn't forget them and stuck the list in her pocket. With any luck, she'd be able to get others from the shopgirls at lunch, and one of them would ring a bell with Eileen. She and Mike should be here soon. Stepney was less than three-quarters of an hour away, and she doubted if Eileen had much to pack.

But they still weren't there by eleven, and Polly realised belatedly that she didn't know Mike's address, or the name of the people Eileen was staying with. And Padgett's employee records had just been blown to bits. *Where are they?* she thought. *It shouldn't take four hours to go to Stepney and back.*

She watched the clock and the stairways and the lifts, trying not to worry, trying to believe they would walk in any moment, safe and sound, that they were going to find Gerald Phipps and his drop was going to open and they would go back to Oxford where Mr Dunworthy would let Eileen go to VE Day. To believe their retrieval teams were going to walk in any moment and say, 'Where have you *been*? We've been looking *everywhere* for you!'

But as the minutes crept by and Mike and Eileen still didn't come, doubts began to drift back in like the fog that first night she'd come through. Even if the measles epidemic had been a divergence point and kept the retrieval team from coming for Eileen till after she'd left for London, Lieutenant Heffernan would have said they'd been there. And if the measles *had* been a divergence point, why had Eileen been allowed to come through in the first place?

And this was *time travel*. Polly might have failed to find out where Eileen was from the vicar because she had a train to catch, but the retrieval team wouldn't have. They had literally all the time in the world.

And if Oxford hadn't been destroyed, if Colin wasn't dead, where *was* he? He had promised to come and rescue her if she got in trouble.

'If you can,' Polly murmured. 'If you're not killed.'

The arrow above the lift door stopped at three and she looked over at the lift, half expecting to see Colin standing there. But it wasn't him. Or Mike and Eileen. It was Marjorie. 'Oh, Polly!' she cried. 'Thank goodness! I heard Padgett's was hit, and I was so afraid ... is your cousin all right?'

'Yes,' Polly said, grabbing her arm quickly to support her. She looked even whiter and more ill than yesterday.

'Oh, thank heavens,' Marjorie breathed. 'No, I'm all right. It was just that I was afraid ... I mean, I sent you there, and if something had happened to you ...'

'It didn't,' Polly assured her. 'I'm quite all right, and so is she. You're the one we're concerned about,' she said reprovingly. 'You can't keep escaping from hospital and dashing over here. You're an invalid, remember.'

'I know. I'm sorry,' Marjorie said. 'It was only ... when I heard people had been killed—'

'Killed?' Polly said, thinking, *Thank goodness. I can tell Mike that, and he'll stop worrying.*

'Yes,' Marjorie said, 'one of them died on the way to hospital. That's how I found out about it. I heard the nurses talking. The other four were dead when they found them.'

LONDON – 17 SEPTEMBER 1940

The shimmer blinded him for a moment, and he took a stumbling step forward. And nearly killed himself. He was on a narrow spiral staircase, and only a last-moment grab for the iron railing kept him from pitching down it. He cracked his knee hard, barked both shins, and made a clanging, echoing racket in the process.

A brilliant beginning, he thought, nursing his bruised knee and looking at his surroundings. The staircase was in a narrow windowless shaft that extended up – and down – for further than he could see, and he was apparently the only person in it, or at any rate no one had come to investigate the noise he'd made. And now that its echoes had stopped, he couldn't hear anything.

Nothing could get through those walls, he thought, looking at the dimly lit stone. If the railing hadn't been of iron, he'd have thought he was in the tower of a castle. Or the dungeon. In which case he should climb up to get out. But hopefully going in either direction would bring him to some clue as to where – and when – this was, and down was easier than up, especially since his knee hurt.

He started down the stairs. Three turns down brought him

to a bare lightbulb set in a wall socket, which meant he was in the correct century, but there was nothing to indicate what the staircase was part of, or where it led. If anywhere. He'd already come down a hundred steps, and there was still no end in sight.

I should have gone up, he thought, making another turn in the spiral, and there below him was a door. 'Let's hope it's not locked,' he said, his voice echoing in the narrow space, and opened the door.

Onto a mob scene. Scores of people scurrying past in both directions, women in knee-length frocks, men in trench coats, uniformed soldiers, sailors, WAAFs, Wrens, all of them walking quickly, purposefully, down a brightly lit, low-ceilinged tunnel. There was an arrow painted on the wall and the words 'To the trains' and below it, with an arrow pointing in the opposite direction, 'Way Out'.

This is an Underground station, he thought, and started down the tunnel towards a poster on the wall. 'Do your bit for the war effort', it read. 'Buy Victory Bonds. Defeat Hitler'.

I made it. I'm actually here in London in World War II, he thought, grinning from ear to ear – an expression which was completely inappropriate for an air raid (and a war), but he couldn't help himself. And at any rate no one was paying any attention to him. They pushed past him, totally intent on getting wherever it was they were going – workmen in overalls, businessmen with toothbrush moustaches and furled umbrellas, mothers with children in tow. And every one of them was wearing a hat. The men all had bowlers, fedoras, woollen caps.

He should have worn a hat. The rest of his clothes seemed all right, but he hadn't realised how universal hats had been in this era. Even the little boys were wearing cloth caps. *I'll stand out like the impostor I am*, he thought, searching the crowd for anyone with a bare head.

There was one – a blonde in a WVS uniform – and walking just behind her was a grey-haired man. He began to relax a bit. The man was carrying a pillow under his arm.

He must be one of the shelterers, he thought, though no one was sitting down or lying along the tunnel. *Perhaps they only sleep out on the platforms, or this isn't one of the stations they used for a shelter. Or they haven't started using the stations yet.*

Whenever this was. He'd set the net so he'd come through at 7 p.m. on September 16, 1940. *I need to make certain I did*, he thought, hurrying down the tunnel, and then remembered he'd need to be able to find his way back to the drop and went back to take a hard look at the door he'd come through. It was black-painted metal, stencilled in white: Stairs to Surface. To Be Used in Case of Emergency Only, which explained the seemingly endless number of steps. And the reason it had been empty.

Near the foot of the door someone had scratched 'E.H.+ M.T.' He made a mental note of the initials, of a peeling corner on the Victory Bonds poster, and of a second poster reading 'Don't Leave It to Others: Enrol Today'. And a notice at the end of the tunnel that said 'Central Line'.

But no mention of what station it was. He needed to find that out, and the date and time of day, before he did anything else. The time should be easy. Nearly everyone was wearing a watch, and he could ask about the station at the same time, but just as he was about to tap a man with an ARP armband on the shoulder, he saw a notice: 'Be alert for spies. Report all suspicious behaviour'.

Did asking what station one was in count as suspicious behaviour? He didn't see why it would be – he could claim he'd got off at the wrong stop or something – but he'd already made an error about the hat. What if there was something else suspicious about his clothes? He'd better not do anything to attract attention to himself.

And it was more important to find out the date and the station. The name would be posted out on the platform. He started in the direction of the To the Trains arrow, and then stopped and elbowed his way back to a bench, where an elderly man sat snoring, the newspaper he'd been reading open on his chest. 'London Damaged by Bombs', the headline read. He leaned closer to see the date. September seventeenth. Not the sixteenth. He must have made an error in the settings.

And the seventeenth was the day Marble Arch had been hit. He needed to find out what station this was immediately. He hurried on towards the platform.

Halfway down the tunnel was an Underground map. Perhaps it had a *You Are Here* arrow marked on its crisscrossing multi-coloured lines.

It didn't. He was going to have to go on out to the platform. Two children had come up next to him to look at the map – a small boy with a dirty face and an older girl with a half-untied sash and hair ribbon. Children usually took questions, no matter how odd, in stride. He said to the boy, 'Can you tell me—?'

'I didn't do nuthin',' the boy said defensively and backed away. 'I was only standin' 'ere, lookin' at the map.'

'We was seein' which train to take,' the girl said.

So much for not attracting attention. 'I only wanted to know what station this is.'

'Coo, 'e don't know where 'e is,' the girl crowed, and the boy regarded him through narrowed eyes.

''Ow much'll you pay us if we tell you?'

'Pay?' How much did one pay an urchin in 1940 for information? Tuppence? No, that was Dickens. Sixpence?

'We'll tell you for a shilling,' the girl said.

'All right,' he said and fumbled in his pocket for coins, hoping he could recognise a shilling, but he didn't need to, the boy instantly plucked it out of the coins in his open hand.

'This 'ere's St Paul's,' he said.

Good. This wasn't Marble Arch. But if it was St Paul's Station, that meant he was just along the street from the cathedral itself. From St Paul's! *I must go and see it*, he thought. *Just for a moment.*

If he could. During raids, they'd shut the gates to keep people from going outside. 'Do you know what time it is?' he asked.

''Ow much'll you pay if—?' the boy began to say, but the girl poked him on the arm, pointing up the tunnel, and both of them took off at a dead run.

He turned to see what had spooked them and saw a uniformed guard coming. 'Was them two giving you trouble, lad?'

'No,' he said, 'I was only asking them for directions.'

The guard nodded grimly. 'I'd check my money if I was you, lad. And your ration book.'

The last thing he needed was an official scrutinising his papers, but the guard was standing there waiting. He pulled out his ration book, rifled quickly through the pages, and stuck it back into his pocket before the guard could get a good look. 'All there ...' he said, and Oh blast, how did one address a station guard? Sir? Officer? He decided he'd better not risk either. 'No harm done,' he said, and walked quickly away as if he knew where he was going.

It turned out to be the right direction. He rode up the long, wooden-slatted escalator to the station entrance. Good, the gates were open. But as he started through the turnstile, a siren began winding into an up-and-down wail. It was a horrible sound. No wonder they call it the devil's tritone, he thought. But at least now he knew what time it was. On September seventeenth, the sirens had gone at 7:28 p.m. He'd spent several minutes in the staircase and the station, and and at least ten dealing with the children and the guard. That meant he'd come through at exactly the right time, so he had definitely made an error on the date.

Another guard was pulling the accordion-like metal gate across the exit. *Blast. If those children hadn't demanded payment, he thought. Now I've missed—*

But there was still a narrow open space. He darted through it, through the throng of people hurrying into the station, up the steps, and outside onto a twilit narrow street with tall brick buildings on either side.

But no St Paul's. He turned to look behind him, but he still couldn't see it. He craned his neck, trying to catch a glimpse of the dome above the buildings.

'You'd best get under cover, lad,' a workman paused to say before hurrying past him into the station. 'Jerry'll be here any minute,' and the man was right. He had no business being out in the middle of an air raid, but the chance to actually *see* St Paul's was too good to pass up, and there'd been a twenty-minute gap between the sirens and the actual raids.

And all he wanted was a look. He loped to the opposite end of the station and looked down a side street. Not there, and how difficult was it to find an enormous cathedral with a towering dome? Had those urchins lied to him? He sprinted up to the next corner.

And there she was, at the end of the street, looking just as she did in photographs – the dome, the towers, the broad pillared porch – but far more beautiful. He wondered if he had time to go inside, just for a moment.

The siren was winding down. He thought he heard the faint hum of a plane and looked up at the darkening sky. Another siren started up and then another, further off, each slightly out of sync with the others and drowning out any other sound with their discordant whine. He couldn't see any planes and he still had at least a quarter of an hour, but the people on the street were hurrying now, their heads ducked as if they expected a blow any second. He'd better get back to the Underground station. He couldn't afford to get killed. He had to do what he'd come to do. He took one long, last look at St Paul's and turned to run back.

And collided full-force with a young woman in a Wren's uniform. The bundles she'd been carrying flew in all directions.

'I'm so sorry, I didn't see you,' he said, stooping to pick up a brown-paper-and-string-wrapped parcel.

'It's all right,' she said, reaching for the messenger bag that had fallen from her shoulder when they collided. As she picked it up, it opened, spilling its entire contents – compact, handkerchief, ration book, coins, lipstick. The lipstick rolled across the pavement and into the gutter and he leaped after it, retrieved it and handed it to her, apologising again.

She jammed the lipstick into her purse, looking anxiously up at the sky. He could definitely hear planes now, a heavy hum, and a distant *whump!* that had to be a bomb. The Wren began gathering up her things more hurriedly. He scrambled to pick up another parcel and her handkerchief. An elderly man in a black suit stopped to help, and so did a naval officer, both of them stooping to pick up the scattered coins.

There was a deafening *boom!*, much louder than the *whump!* After several seconds there was another and then another, in a steady rhythm. *The anti-aircraft guns*, he thought, hoping he was out of range of the shrapnel from their shells, and then handed the Wren her comb and her ration book. The black-suited man handed her several coppers and hurried off up the street.

'Will you be all right then?' the naval officer asked her, handing her the last of her coins, and she nodded.

'I'm just down there,' she said, pointing vaguely off to her left, and the naval officer tipped his hat and walked away up the street towards St Paul's.

There was another *whump!*, much nearer, and the sky lit briefly. He handed her the last of her parcels, and she hurried off. 'I am sorry,' he called after her.

'No harm done,' she called back.

He turned and began to lope back to the station. There was another *whump!*, and then a loud thud and a huge crash, and the entire sky lit up. He broke into a run.

For the riveting conclusion to

BLACKOUT

be sure not to miss

Connie Willis'

ALL CLEAR

coming from Gollancz

in 2011

ACKNOWLEDGMENTS

I want to say thank you to all the people who helped me and stood by me with *Blackout* as it morphed from one book into two and I went slowly mad under the strain: my incredibly patient editor, Anne Groell, and my long-suffering agent, Ralph Vicinanza; my even longer-suffering secretary, Laura Lewis; my daughter and chief confidante Cordelia; my family and friends; every librarian within a hundred-mile radius; and the baristas at Margie's, Starbucks, and the UNC student union who gave me tea – well, chai – and sympathy on a daily basis. Thank you all for putting up with me, standing by me, and not giving up on me or the book.

But most especially, I want to thank the marvellous group of ladies at the Imperial War Museum the day I was there doing research – women who, it turned out, had all been rescue workers and ambulance drivers and air-raid wardens during the Blitz, and who told me story after story that proved invaluable to the book and to my understanding of the bravery, determination, and humour of the British people as they faced down Hitler. And I want to thank my wonderful husband, who found them, sat them down, bought them tea and cakes, and then came to find me so I could interview them. Best husband ever!